THE PURSUIT OF THE PANKERA

THE PURSUIT OF THE PANKERA

A PARALLEL NOVEL ABOUT PARALLEL UNIVERSES

ROBERT A. HEINLEIN

CAEZIK
SF & FANTASY

ARC MANOR
ROCKVILLE, MARYLAND

SHAHID MAHMUD
PUBLISHER

www.caeziksf.com

Jacket art by Scott Grimando, grimstudios.com
Project Editor: Patrick LoBrutto

ISBN: 978-1-64710-001-8

First Edition. First Printing. March 2020
1 2 3 4 5 6 7 8 9 10

An imprint of Arc Manor LLC

www.caezik.com

—— For Walter and Marion Minton ——

— CONTENTS —

── PUBLISHER'S NOTE ──

Most Heinlein fans know about *The Number of the Beast*, which deals with parallel universes. What most do not realize is that *The Number of the Beast* was one of two books Heinlein wrote about these parallel universes, although it was the only one published. No one is exactly sure why the other text was never published, but many theories have been put forth.

The unpublished manuscript was largely forgotten over time and only survived in fragments. A recent examination of the manuscript (along with Heinlein's handwritten notes) made it clear that the fragments, if put together properly, would constitute the complete unpublished book. It has taken us approximately three years to put these pieces together and deal with certain other issues, but the new book is one hundred percent Heinlein. Other than regular editorial work, no additional author was asked to provide "fillers."

The two books do share a common beginning (approximately one-third of the book), but then diverge completely in Chapter XVIII, right after the characters' specially equipped car, the *Gay Deceiver*, makes its first jump to a parallel universe. We have placed a small marker [∴] in the margin on page 152 to indicate where the divergence in texts begins.

Here, then, is *The Pursuit of the Pankera*.

Shahid Mahmud
Publisher

—— INTRODUCTION ——

by David Weber

So, the question I was assigned was "How did Robert Heinlein influence you?"

That, as they say, is a leading question, and I really doubt that any honest writer of science fiction could say that he or she has *not* been influenced by Heinlein. In some cases, by opposition to his more controversial stances on things like incest, or on the whole convoluted question of how he could write such competent heroines and yet cling to such "stereotypical" concepts *about* women. In other cases, by inspiration, either stylistic or philosophical, that threads its way into the writer's work. TANSTAAFL, pay it forward, Grok—all of them, like so much else that Heinlein produced, are part of the building blocks of what we write, whether we want to call it "speculative fiction" or "science fiction." Their echoes, their repercussions, continue to reverberate and to inspire.

But if the question is how did Robert Heinlein influence *me*, part of the answer is absurdly easy: he introduced me to science fiction at a very early age and stayed with me through high school, college, and beyond. *Have Spacesuit Will Travel, Starman Jones, Rocket Ship Galileo, Space Cadet, The Star Beast, The Puppet Masters, Podkayne of Mars, Orphans of the Sky, Double Star, Citizen of the Galaxy, The Moon Is a Harsh Mistress, Glory Road, Stranger in a Strange Land* ... just that partial title list of only his *novels* is enough to explain why that was true. I always hate it when people ask me "which science fiction writer had the most influence on you," because every science fiction writer

I've ever read has influenced me, one way or another, and which one's influence was greater probably depends at any given moment on what sort of story I'm telling at that moment. Despite that, I would say that the Big Four for me were: Heinlein, H. Beam Piper, Poul Anderson, and Sprague DeCamp, with honorable mentions to at least a dozen other names, including especially Andre Norton, Annie McCaffrey, Keith Laumer, and Patricia McKillip. Not necessarily in a stylistic sense, but in the sense of what the craft is all about. And every single time I list any of the authors who influenced me, the first one up is always Heinlein.

Possibly that's because I met him at such an early age, although the first science fiction author(s) I ever read were Jack Williamson, followed by DeCamp and P. Schuyler Miller—go *Genus Homo!*—and because I was so early inculcated with both his writing voice and what he brought to the entire notion of what not just science fiction but humanity itself was about. He was an incredibly eloquent spokesman for his beliefs, he wasn't afraid to allow those beliefs to evolve (or to *refuse* to evolve), and yet he never let the story suffer. He wrote muscular prose. He chose his verbs so carefully. He was unafraid of colloquialisms. He knew how to build entire worlds by inference, out of the mosaic details built into his stories' walls. And he knew how to project both a character's competence while dealing with problems and an abiding sense of wonder about the scale and scope of the universe in which those problems resided. And he showed in his juveniles an extraordinary ability to make those concepts available to young readers.

I found greater depth in his stories as I grew older, but that was because I had become *aware* of the depth, not because it hadn't been there all along. I remember my reaction to Sam in *Starman Jones*. The first time I read the book, I recognized him as the mentor, the good adult, and I saw his death as a heroic act. But I missed the profundity of the epitaph "He ate what was set before him." That was Heinlein in a nutshell: the responsible human being, the competent human being, the human being who knows how to die gallantly when faced with the Birkenhead drill. Not because it's heroic, but because it's what responsible humans *do*. Whether it's Sam, or Podkayne, or "Kip" Russell, Pewee, and Mother Thing, or Lieutenant Dahlquist, or Lazarus Long and "Slipstick" Libby, or "Mannie" O'Kelley-Davis and Mike,

4

his protagonists are who they are and refuse to be diverted from doing what *they* believe is the right thing.

I wasn't really aware, as a preteen reader, of the more socially controversial aspects of his writing, nor of how adroitly he slipped some of it in. He was, of course, a product of his times—he was seven years younger than my grandmother—and that shows, especially in some of his tropes and, probably, in the characteristics of his female characters which strike a twenty-first-century reader as profoundly stereotypical. Given that he was seven years old when World War I began (echoes of Woodrow Wilson Smith, anyone think?), however, what's actually surprising is how often he *evaded* stereotypes. His opposition to racism was fierce yet subtle and, like Piper, he straddled the transition from women as props to women as fully realized protagonists. Sometimes they hit false notes, but Heinlein was unafraid of that. He was totally prepared to face the slings and arrows for writing stories that told details *he* thought needed telling. Indeed, he would have courted far more of those slings and arrows—and counted the wounds as honor scars—had he not so often had to deal with editorial insistence. I happen to think that the ending of *Podkayne* as originally published is a good, strong story, but the altered ending changed the story *Heinlein* wanted to tell. I think, had he been allowed to publish his original manuscript, it would have been more readily recognizable as the profoundly cautionary tale he had in mind when he wrote it.

Despite the well-deserved acclaim *Stranger in a Strange Land* and *The Moon Is a Harsh Mistress* have received, and despite my own love for the second of those titles, especially, I honestly believe that Heinlein's greatest contribution to the field lies in those juveniles of his. He refused to write "down" to kids. His readers were *young*, he would not treat them as infants, and he challenged them to deal with some pretty darned adult topics. But most of all, he instilled both a sense of wonder and the concept—the *belief*—that the future was what we chose to make it. That it was up to us, as human beings, to reach for that future, to accomplish it, to nurture it, and to defend it. Generations of astronauts, scientists, innovators—and writers—have been exposed to that wonder and that belief, and Heinlein has been their unapologetic, sometimes caustic, sometimes amusing, always entertaining guide. Often enough, their mentor.

5

And he remains in print today, thirty years after his death, because he is *still* doing that. Sure, the science is dated, societies have shifted and changed, and we've gone to places not even Robert Heinlein could have envisioned when he wrote "Life-Line" in 1939. All of that is true. But Heinlein continues to be read today because, as always, he is unapologetically *Heinlein*.

And, damn, but that man could write.

THE PURSUIT OF THE
PANKERA

Zebadiah

"He's a Mad Scientist and I'm his Beautiful Daughter."

That's what she said: the oldest cliché in pulp fiction. She wasn't old enough to remember the pulps.

The thing to do with a silly remark is to fail to hear it. I went on waltzing while taking another look down her evening formal. Nice view. Not foam rubber.

She waltzed well. Today most girls who even attempt ballroom dancing drape themselves around your neck and expect you to shove them around the floor. She kept her weight on her own feet, danced close without snuggling, and knew what I was going to do a split second before I led it. A perfect partner.

"Well?" she persisted.

My paternal grandfather—an unsavory old reactionary; the Fem-Libbers would have lynched him—used to say, "Zebadiah, the mistake we made was not in putting shoes on them or in teaching them to read—we should never have taught them to talk!"

I signaled a twirl by pressure; she floated into it and back into my arms right on the beat. I inspected her hands and the outer corners of her eyes. Yes, she really was young—minimum eighteen; Hilda Corners never permitted legal "infants" at her parties, maximum twenty-five, first approximation twenty-two. Yet she danced like her grandmother's generation.

"Well?" she repeated more firmly.

"The operative symbols were 'mad,' 'scientist,' 'beautiful,' and 'daughter.' The first has several meanings—the others denote opinions. Semantic content: zero."

She looked thoughtful rather than angry. "Pop isn't rabid ... although I did use 'mad' in ambivalent mode. 'Scientist' and 'beautiful' each contain descriptive opinions, I stipulate. But are you in doubt as to my sex? If so, are you qualified to check my twenty-third chromosome pair? With transsexual surgery so common I assume that anything less would not satisfy you."

"I prefer a field test."

"On the *dance floor*?"

"No, the bushes back of the pool. Yes, I'm qualified—laboratory or field. It was not your sex that lay in the area of opinion; that is a fact that can be established ... although the gross evidence is convincing. I—"

"Ninety-five centimeters isn't gross! Not for my height. One hundred seventy bare-footed, one eighty in these heels. It's just that I'm wasp-waisted for my mass—forty-eight centimeters versus fifty-nine kilos."

"And your teeth are your own and you don't have dandruff. Take it easy, Deedee; I didn't mean to shake your aplomb. But the symbol 'daughter' encompasses two statements, one factual—sex—and the other a matter of opinion even when stated by a forensic genetohematologist."

"Gosh, what big words you know, Mister. I mean 'Doctor.' "

" 'Mister' is correct. On this campus it is swank to assume that everyone holds a doctorate. Even I have one, Ph.D. Do you know what that stands for?"

"Doesn't everybody? I have a Ph.D., too. 'Piled Higher and Deeper.' "

I raised that maximum to twenty-six and assigned it as second approximation. "Phys. Ed.?"

"Mister Doctor, you are trying to get my goat. Won't work. I had an undergraduate double major, one being Phys. Ed. with teacher's credentials in case I needed a job. But my real major was math—which I continued in graduate school."

"And here I had been assuming that 'Deedee' meant 'Doctor of Divinity.' "

"Go wash out your mouth with soap. My nickname is my initials—Dee Tee. Or Deety. Doctor D. T. Burroughs if being formal, as I can't be 'Mister' and refuse to be 'Miz' or 'Miss.' See here, Mister; I'm supposed to be luring you with my radiant beauty, then hooking you with my feminine charm … and not getting anywhere. Let's try another tack. Tell me what you piled higher and deeper."

"Let me think. Fly casting? Or was it basketweaving? It was one of those transdisciplinary things in which the committee simply weighs the dissertation. Tell you what. I've got a copy around my digs. I'll find it and see what title the researcher who wrote it put on it."

"Don't bother. The title is 'Some Implications of a Six-Dimensional Non-Newtonian Continuum.' Pop wants to discuss it."

I stopped waltzing. "Huh? He'd better discuss that paper with the bloke who wrote it."

"Nonsense; I saw you blink—I've hooked you. Pop wants to discuss it, then offer you a job."

" 'Job!' I just slipped off the hook."

"Oh, dear! Pop will be *really* mad. Please? Please, sir!"

"You said that you had used 'mad' in ambivalent mode. How?"

"Oh. Mad-angry because his colleagues won't listen to him. Mad-psychotic in the opinions of some colleagues. They say his papers don't make sense."

"Do they make sense?"

"I'm not that good a mathematician, sir. My work is usually simplifying software. Child's play compared with n-dimensional spaces."

I wasn't required to express an opinion; the trio started *Blue Tango*. Deety melted into my arms. You don't talk if you know tango.

Deety knew. After an eternity of sensual bliss, I swung her out into position precisely on coda; she answered my bow and scrape with a deep curtsy. "Thank you, sir."

"Whew! After a tango like that the couple ought to get married."

"All right. I'll find our hostess and tell Pop. Five minutes? Front door, or side?"

She looked serenely happy. I said, "Deety, do you mean what you appear to mean? That you intend to marry *me*? A total stranger?"

Her face remained calm but the light went out. She answered steadily. "After that tango we are no longer strangers. I construed your statement as a proposal—no, a willingness—to marry me. Was I mistaken?"

My mind went into emergency, reviewing the past years the way a drowning man's life is supposed to flash before his eyes (how could anyone know that?): a rainy afternoon when my chum's older sister had initiated me into the mysteries; the curious effect caused by the first time strangers had shot back at me; a twelve-month cohabitation contract that had started with a bang and had ended without a whimper; countless events which had left me determined never to marry.

I answered instantly, "I meant what I implied—marriage, in its older meaning. I'm willing. But why are *you* willing? I'm no prize."

She took a deep breath. "Sir, you are the prize I was sent to fetch, and, when you said that we really ought to get married—hyperbole and I knew it—I suddenly realized, with a deep burst of happiness, that *this* was the means of fetching you that I wanted above all!"

She went on, "But I will not trap you through misconstruing a gallantry. If you wish, you may take me into those bushes back of the pool ... and *not* marry me." She went on firmly, "But for that ... whoring ... my fee is for you to talk with my father and to let him show you something."

"Deety, you're an idiot! You would ruin that pretty gown."

"Mussing a dress is irrelevant but I can take it off. I will. There's nothing under it."

"There's a great deal under it!"

That fetched a grin, instantly wiped away. "Thank you. Shall we head for the bushes?"

"Wait a half! I'm about to be noble and regret it the rest of my life. You've made a mistake. Your father doesn't want to talk to *me*; I don't know anything about n-dimensional geometry." (Why do I get these attacks of honesty? I've never done anything to deserve them.)

"Pop thinks you do; that is sufficient. Shall we go? I want to get Pop out of here before he busts somebody in the mouth."

"I wanted to *marry* you—but wanted to know why you were willing to marry *me*. Your answer concerned what your father wants. I'm not trying to marry your father; he's not my type. Speak for yourself, Deety. Or drop it." (Am I a masochist? There's a sunbathing couch back of those bushes.)

Solemnly she looked me over, from my formal tights to my crooked bow tie and on up to my thinning brush cut—a hundred and ninety-four centimeters of big ugly galoot. "I like your firm lead in dancing. I like the way you look. I like the way your voice rumbles. I like your hair-splitting games with words—you sound like Whorf debating Korzybski with Shannon as referee." She took another deep breath, finished almost sadly: "Most of all, I like the way you smell."

It would have taken a sharp nose to whiff me. I had been squeaky clean ninety minutes before, and it takes more than one waltz and a tango to make me sweat. But her remark had that skid in it that Deety put into almost anything. Most girls, when they want to ruin a man's judgment, squeeze his biceps and say, "Goodness, you're strong!"

I grinned down at her. "You smell good too. Your perfume could rouse a corpse."

"I'm not wearing perfume."

"Oh. Correction: your natural pheromone. Enchanting. Get your wrap. Side door. Five minutes."

"Yes, sir."

"Tell your father we're getting married. He gets that talk, free. I decided that before you started to argue. It won't take him long to decide that I'm not Lobachevski."

"That's Pop's problem," she answered, moving. "Will you let him show you this thing he's built in our basement?"

"Sure, why not? What is it?"

"A time machine."

—— II ——

Zebadiah

Tomorrow I will seven eagles see, a great comet will appear, and voices will speak from whirlwinds foretelling monstrous and fearful things—this Universe never did make sense; I suspect that it was built on government contract.

"Big basement?"

"Medium. Nine by twelve. But cluttered. Work benches and power tools."

A hundred and eight square meters—ceiling height probably two and a half— Had Pop made the mistake of the man who built a boat in his basement?

My musing was interrupted by a male voice in a high scream: "You overeducated, obstipated, pedantic ignoramus! Your mathematical intuition froze solid the day you matriculated!"

I didn't recognize the screamer but did know the stuffed shirt he addressed: Professor Neil O'Heret Brain, head of the Department of Mathematics—and God help the student who addressed a note to "Professor N. O. Brain" or even "N. O'H. Brain." "Brainy" had spent his life in search of The Truth—intending to place it under house arrest.

He was puffed up like a pouter pigeon with his professional pontifical pomposity reeling. His expression suggested that he was giving birth to a porcupine.

Deety gasped, "It's started," and dashed toward the row. Me, I stay out of rows; I'm a coward by trade and wear fake zero-prescription

14

glasses as a buffer—when some oaf snarls, "Take off your glasses!" that gives me time to retreat.

I headed straight for the row.

Deety had placed herself between the two, facing the screamer, and was saying in a low but forceful voice, "Pop, don't you dare! I won't bail you out!" She was reaching for his glasses with evident intent to put them back on his face. It was clear that he had taken them off for combat; he was holding them out of her reach.

I reached over their heads, plucked them out of his hand, gave them to Deety. She flashed me a smile and put them back on her father. He gave up and let her. She then took his arm firmly. "Aunt Hilda!"

Our hostess converged on the row. "Yes, Deety? Why did you stop them, darling? You didn't give us time to get bets down." Fights were no novelty at "Sharp" Corners' parties. Her food and liquor were lavish, the music always live; her guests were often eccentric but never dull—I had been surprised at the presence of N. O. Brain.

I now felt that I understood it: a planned hypergolic mixture.

Deety ignored her questions. "Will you excuse Pop and me and Mr. Carter? Something urgent has come up."

"You and Jake may leave if you must. But you can't drag Zebbie away. Deety, that's cheating."

Deety looked at me. "May I tell?"

"Eh? Certainly!"

That bliffy "Brainy" picked this moment to interrupt. "Mrs. Corners, Doctor Burroughs can't leave until he apologizes! I insist. My privilege!"

Our hostess looked at him with scorn. "*Merde*, Professor. I'm not one of your teaching fellows. Shout right back at Jake Burroughs if you like. If your command of invective equals his, we'll enjoy hearing it. But just *one more word* that sounds like an order to me or to one of my guests—and out you go! Then you had best go straight home; the chancellor will be trying to reach you." She turned her back on him. "Deety, you started to add something?"

"Sharp" Corners can intimidate Internal Revenue agents. She hadn't cut loose on "Brainy"—just a warning shot across his bow. But from his face one would have thought she had hulled him. However, her remark to Deety left me no time to see whether he would have a stroke.

I spoke up. "Not Deety, Hilda. Me. Zeb."

"Quiet, Zebbie. Whatever it is, the answer is No. Deety? Go ahead, dear."

Hilda Corners is related to that famous mule. I did not use a baseball bat because she comes only up to my armpits and grosses forty-odd kilos. I picked her up by her elbows and turned her around, facing me. "Hilda, we're going to get married."

"Zebbie darling! I thought you would *never* ask."

"Not you, you old harridan. Deety. I proposed, she accepted; I'm going to nail it down before the anesthetic wears off."

Hilda looked thoughtfully interested. "That's reasonable." She craned her neck to look at Deety. "Did he mention his wife in Boston, Deety? Or the twins?"

I set her back on her feet. "Pipe down, Sharpie; this is serious. Doctor Burroughs, I am unmarried, in good health, solvent, and able to support a family. I hope this meets with your approval."

"Pop says Yes," Deety answered. "I hold his power of attorney."

"You pipe down, too. My name is Carter, sir—Zeb Carter. I'm on campus; you can check my record. But I intend to marry Deety at once, if she will have me."

"I know your name and record, sir. It doesn't require my approval; Deety is of age. But you have it anyhow." He looked thoughtful. "If you two are getting married at once, you'll be too busy for shop talk. Or would you be?"

"Pop—let it be; it's all set."

"So? Thank you, Hilda, for a pleasant evening. I'll call you tomorrow."

"You'll do no such thing; you'll come straight back and give me a full report. Jake, you are not going on their honeymoon—I heard you."

"Aunt Hilda—please! I'll manage everything."

We were out the side door close on schedule. At the parking lot there was a bobble: which heap, mine or theirs. Mine is intended for two but can take four. The rear seats are okay for two for short trips. Theirs was a four-passenger family saloon, not fast but roomy—and their luggage was in it. "How much luggage?" I asked Deety, while I visualized two overnight bags strapped into one back seat with my prospective father-in-law stashed in the other.

"I don't have much, but Pop has two big bags and a fat briefcase. I had better show you."

(Damn.) "Perhaps you had better." I like my own rig, I don't like to drive other people's cars, and, while Deety probably handled controls as smoothly as she danced, I did not know that she did—and I'm chicken. I didn't figure her father into the equation; trusting my skin to his temper did not appeal. Maybe Deety would settle for letting him trail us—but my bride-to-be was going to ride with me! "Where?"

"Over in the far corner. I'll unlock it and turn on the lights."

She reached into her father's inside jacket pocket, took out a Magic Wand.

"Wait for baby!"

The shout was from our hostess. Hilda was running down the path from her house, purse clutched in one hand and about eight thousand newdollars of sunset mink flying like a flag from the other.

So the discussion started over. Seems Sharpie had decided to come along to make certain that Jake behaved himself and had taken just long enough to tell Max (her bouncer-butler-driver) when to throw the drunks out or cover them with blankets, as needed.

She listened to Deety's summary, then nodded. "Got it. I can handle yours, Deety; Jake and I will go in it. You ride with Zebbie, dear." She turned to me. "Hold down the speed, Zebbie, so that I can follow. No tricks, buster. Don't try to lose us or you'll have cops busting out of your ears."

I turned my sweet innocent eyes toward her. "Why, Sharpie darling, you know I wouldn't do anything like that."

"You'd steal city hall if you could figure a way to carry it. Who dumped that load of lime Jell-O into my swimming pool?"

"I was in Africa at that time, as you know."

"So you say. Deety darling, keep him on a short leash and don't feed him meat. But marry him—he's loaded. Now where's that radio link? And your car."

"Here," said Deety, pointed the Magic Wand and pressed the switch.

I gathered all three into my arms and dived. We hit the ground as the blast hit everything else. But not us. The blast shadow of other cars protected us.

— III —

Zebadiah

Don't ask me how. Ask a trapeze artist how he does a triple 'sault. Ask a crapshooter how he knows when he's "hot." But don't ask me how I know it's going to happen just before it hits the fan.

It doesn't tell me anything I don't need to know. I don't know what's in a letter until I open it (except the time it was a letter bomb). I have no precognition for harmless events. But this split-second knowledge when I need it has kept me alive and relatively unscarred in an era when homicide kills more people than does cancer and the favorite form of suicide is to take a rifle up some tower and keep shooting until the riot squad settles it.

I don't see the car around the curve on the wrong side; I automatically hit the ditch. When the San Andreas Fault cut loose, I jumped out a window and was in the open when the shock arrived—and didn't know why I had jumped.

Aside from this, my ESP is erratic; I bought it cheap from a war-surplus outlet.

I sprawled with three under me. I got up fast, trying to avoid crushing them. I gave a hand to each woman, then dragged Pop to his feet. No one seemed damaged. Deety stared at the fire blazing where their car had been, face impassive. Her father was looking at the ground, searching. Deety stopped him. "Here, Pop." She put his glasses back on him.

"Thank you, my dear." He started toward the fire.

I grabbed his shoulder. "*No!* Into my car—*fast!*"

"Eh? My briefcase—could have blown clear."

18

"Shut up and move! All of you!"

"Do it, Pop!" Deety grabbed Hilda's arm. We stuffed the older ones into the after-space; I shoved Deety into the front passenger seat and snapped: "Seat belts!" as I slammed the door—then was around to the left so fast that I should have caused a sonic boom. "Seat belts fastened?" I demanded as I fastened my own and locked the door.

"Jake's is fastened and so is mine, Zebbie dear," Hilda said cheerfully.

"Belt tight, door locked," Deety reported.

The heap was hot; I had left it on trickle—what use is a fast car that won't go scat? I switched from trickle to full, did not turn on lights, glanced at the board and released the brake.

It says here that duos must stay grounded inside city limits—so I was lifting her nose before she had rolled a meter and she was pointed straight up as we were clearing the parking lot.

Half a klick straight up while the gee-meter climbed—two, three, four—I let it reach five and held it, not being sure what Pop's heart would take. When the altimeter read four klicks, I cut everything—power, transponder, the works—while hitting a button that dropped chaff, and let her go ballistic. I didn't know that anyone was tracking us—I didn't want to find out.

When the altimeter showed that we had topped out, I let the wings open a trifle. When I felt them bite air, I snap-rolled onto her belly, let wings crawl out to subsonic aspect, and let her glide. "Everybody okay?"

Hilda giggled. "Whoops, dearie! Do that again! This time, somebody kiss me."

"Pipe down, you shameless old strumpet. Pop?"

"I'm okay, son."

"Deety?"

"Okay here."

"Did that fall in the parking lot hurt you?"

"No, sir. I twisted in the air and took it on one buttock while getting Pop's glasses. But next time put a bed under me, please. Or a wrestling mat."

"I'll remember." I switched on radio but not transponder, tried all police frequencies. If anyone had noticed our didoes, they weren't discussing it on the air. We were down to two klicks; I made an abrupt wingover to the right, then switched on power. "Deety, where do you and your Pop live?"

19

"Logan, Utah."

"How long does it take to get married there?"

"Zebbie," Hilda cut in, "Utah has no waiting time—"

"So we go to Logan."

"—but does require a blood test. Deety, do you know Zebbie's nickname around campus? The Wasp. For 'Wassermann Positive.' Zebbie, everybody knows that Nevada is the only state that offers twenty-four-hour service, no waiting time, no blood test. So point this bomb at Reno and sign off."

"Sharpie darling," I said gently, "would you like to walk home from two thousand meters?"

"I don't know; I've never tried it."

"That's an ejection seat ... but no parachutes."

"Oh, how romantic! Jake darling, we'll sing the *Liebestod* on the way down—you sing tenor, I'll force a soprano and we'll die in each other's arms. Zebbie, could we have more altitude? For the timing."

"Doctor Burroughs, gag that hitchhiker. Sharpie, *Liebestod* is a solo."

"Picky, picky! Isn't dead-on-arrival enough? Jealous because you can't carry a tune? I *told* Dicky Boy that should be a duet and Cosima agreed with me—"

"Sharpie, button your frimpin' lip while I explain. One: everybody at your party knows why we left and will assume that we headed for Reno. You probably called out something to that effect as you left—"

"I believe I did. Yes, I did."

"Shut up. Somebody made a professional effort to kill Doctor Burroughs. Not just kill but overkill; that combo of high explosive and Thermite was intended to leave nothing to analyze. But it is possible that no one saw us lift. We were into this go-wagon and I was goosing it less than thirty seconds after that booby trap exploded. Innocent bystanders would look at the fire, not at us. *Guilty* bystanders—there wouldn't be any. A professional who booby-traps a car either holes up or crosses a state line and gets lost. The party or parties who paid for the contract may be nearby, but if they are, Hilda, they're in your house."

"One of my *guests?*"

"Oh, shut it, Sharpie; you are never interested in the morals of your guests. If they can be depended on to throw custard pies or do impromptu strips or some other prank that will keep your party from growing dull, that qualifies them. However, I am not assuming that the boss villain was at your party; I am saying that he would not be lurking where the Man might put the arm on him. Your house would be the best place to hide and watch the plot develop.

"But, guest or not, he was someone who *knew* that Doctor Burroughs would be at your party. Hilda, who knew that key fact?"

She answered with uncustomary seriousness. "I don't know, Zebbie. I would have to think."

"Think hard."

"Mmm, not many. Several were invited because Jake was coming—you, for example—"

"I became aware of that."

"—but you weren't told that Jake would be present. Some were told—'No Brain,' for example—but I can't imagine that old fool booby-trapping a car."

"I can't either, but killers don't look like killers; they look like people. How *long* before the party did you tell 'Brainy' that Pop would be present?"

"I told him when I invited him. Mmm, eight days ago."

I sighed. "The possibles include not only the campus but the entire globe. So we must try to figure probables. Doctor Burroughs, can you think of anyone who would like to see you dead?"

"Several!"

"Let me rephrase it. Who hates your guts so bitterly that he would not hesitate to kill your daughter as long as he got *you*? And also bystanders such as Hilda and me. Not that we figure, save to show that he didn't give a hoot who caught it. A deficient personality. Amoral. *Who is he?*"

Pop Burroughs hesitated. "Doctor Carter, disagreement between mathematicians can be extremely heated … and I am not without fault." (You're telling *me*, Pop!) "But these quarrels rarely result in violence. Even the death of Archimedes was only indirectly related to his—our—profession. To encompass my daughter as well—no, even Doctor Brain, much as I despise him, does not fit the picture."

Deety said, "Zeb, could it have been *me* they were shooting at?"

"You tell *me*. Whose dolly have you busted?"

"Hmm—I can't think of anyone who dislikes me even enough to snub me. Sounds silly but it's true."

"It's the truth," put in Sharpie. "Deety is just like her mother was. When Jane—Deety's mother, and my best friend until we lost her—when Jane and I were roommates in college, I was always getting into jams and Jane was always getting me out—and never got into one herself. A peacemaker. So is Deety."

"Okay, Deety, you're out of it. So is Hilda and so am I, as whoever placed that booby trap could not predict that either Hilda or I would be in blast range. So it's Pop they're gunning for. Who we don't know, why we don't know. When we figure out why, we'll know who. Meantime we've got to keep Pop out of range. I'm going to marry you as fast as possible, not only because you smell good but to give me a legitimate interest in this fight."

"So we go first to Reno."

"Shut up, Sharpie. We've been on course for Reno since we leveled off." I flipped on the transponder, but to the left, not right. It would now answer with a registered, legal signal ... but not one registered to my name. This cost me some shekels I did not need but were appreciated by a tight-lipped family man in Indio. Sometimes it is convenient not to be identified by sky cops every time one crosses a state line.

"But we aren't going to Reno. Those cowboy maneuvers were intended to deceive the eye, radar, and heat seekers. The evasion against the heat seekers—that rough turn while we were still in glide—either worked or was not needed, as we haven't had a missile up the tail. Probably wasn't needed; people who booby-trap cars aren't likely to be prepared to shoot a duo out of the sky. But I couldn't be certain, so I ducked. We may be assumed to be dead in the blast and fire, and that assumption may stand up until the mess has cooled down and there is daylight to work by. Even later it may stand up, as the cops may not tell anyone that they were unable to find organic remains. But I must assume that Professor Moriarty isn't fooled, that he is watching by repeater scope in his secret HQ, that he knows we are headed for Reno, and that hostiles will greet us there. So we won't go there. Now quiet, please; I must tell this baby what to do."

The computer-pilot of my car can't cook but what she can do, she does well. I called for the display map, changed scale to include Utah, used the light pen to trace route—complex as it curved around Reno to the south, back north again, made easting over some very empty country, and passed north of Hill Air Force Range in approaching Logan. I fed in height-above-ground while giving her leeway to smooth out bumps, and added one change in speed-over-ground once we were clear of Reno radar. "Got it, girl?" I asked her.

"Got it, Zeb."

"Ten-minute call, please."

"Call you ten minutes before end of routing—right!"

"You're a Smart Girl, Gay."

"Boss, I bet you tell that to all the girls. Over."

"Roger and out, Gay." The display faded.

Certainly I could have programmed my autopilot to accept a plan in response to a punched "Execute." But isn't it pleasanter to be answered by a warm contralto? But the "Smart Girl" aspect lay in the fact that it took my voice to make a flight plan operative. A skilled electron pusher might find a way to override my lock, then drive her manually. But the first time he attempted to use autopilot, the car would not only not accept the program but would scream for help on all police frequencies. This causes car thieves to feel maladjusted.

I looked up and saw that Deety had been following this intently. I waited for some question. Instead Deety said, "She has a very pleasant voice, Zeb."

"*Gay Deceiver* is a very nice girl, Deety."

"And talented. Zeb, I have never before been in a Ford that can do the things this car—*Gay Deceiver?*—can do."

"After we're married I'll introduce you to her more formally. It will require reprogramming."

"I look forward to knowing her better."

"You will. Gay is not exactly all Ford. Her external appearance was made by Ford of Canada. Most of the rest of her once belonged to Australian Defense Forces. But I added a few doodads. The bowling alley. The powder room. The veranda. Little homey touches."

"I'm sure she appreciates them, Zeb. I know I do. I suspect that, had she not had them, we would all be as dead as canasta."

"You may be right. If so, it would not be the first time Gay has kept me alive. You have not seen all her talents."

"I'm beyond being surprised. So far as I could see you didn't tell her to land at Logan."

"Logan seems to be the next most likely place for a reception committee. Who in Logan knows that you and your father were going to visit Hilda?"

"No one, through me."

"Mail? Milk cartons? Newspapers?"

"No deliveries to the house, Zeb." She turned her head. "Pop, does anyone in Logan know where we went?"

"Doctor Carter, to the best of my knowledge, no one in Logan knows that we left. Having lived many years in the buzzing gossip of academe, I have learned to keep my life as private as possible."

"Then I suggest that you all ease your belts and sleep. Until ten minutes before reaching Logan there is little to do."

"Doctor Carter—"

"Better call me Zeb, Pop. Get used to it."

" 'Zeb' it is, son. On page eighty-seven of your monograph, after the equation numbered one-twenty-one in your discussion of the rotation of six-dimensional spaces of positive curvature, you said, 'From this it is evident that—' and immediately write your equation one-twenty-two. How did you do it? I'm not disagreeing, sir—on the contrary! But in an unpublished paper of my own I used a dozen pages to arrive at the same transformation. Did you have a direct intuition? Or did you simply omit publishing details? No criticism, I am impressed either way. Sheer curiosity."

"Doctor, *I* did not write that paper. I told Deety so."

"That is what he claimed, Pop."

"Oh, come now! *Two* Doctors Zebulon E. Carter on one campus?"

"No. But that's not my name. I'm Zebadiah J. Carter. Zebulon 'E'-for-Edward Carter and called 'Ed' is my cousin. While he is probably listed as being on campus, in fact he is doing an exchange year in Singapore. It's not as improbable as it sounds; *all* male members of my family have first names starting with 'Z.' It has to do with money and a will and a trust fund and the fact that my grandfather and his father were somewhat eccentric."

"Whereas *you* aren't," Hilda said sweetly.

"Quiet, dear." I turned toward Deety. "Deety, do you want to be released from our engagement? I *did* try to tell you that you had trapped the wrong bird."

"Zebadiah—"

"Yes, Deety?"

"I intend to marry you before this night is over. But you haven't kissed me. I want to be kissed."

I unfastened my seat belt, started to unfasten hers, found that she had done so.

Deety kisses even better than she tangos.

During a break for oxygen, I asked her in a whisper: "Deety, what do your initials stand for?"

"Well … please don't laugh."

"I won't. But I have to know them for the ceremony."

"I know. All right, Dee Tee stands for Dejah Thoris."

Dejah Thoris—Dejah Thoris Burroughs—Dejah Thoris *Carter*! I cracked up. I got it under control after two whoops. Too many.

Deety said sadly, "You said you wouldn't laugh."

"Deety darling, I wasn't laughing at *your* name; I was laughing at *mine*."

"I don't think 'Zebadiah' is a funny name. I like it."

"So do I. It keeps me from being mixed up with the endless Bobs and Eds and Toms. But I didn't tell my middle name. What's a funny name starting with 'J'?"

"I won't guess."

"Let me lead up to it. I was born near the campus of the university Thomas Jefferson founded. The day I graduated from college I was commissioned a second looie Aerospace Reserve. I've been promoted twice. My middle initial stands for 'John.'"

It took not quite a second for her to add it up. "Captain … John … Carter—of Virginia."

"A clean-limbed fighting man," I agreed. "Kaor, Dejah Thoris. At your service, my princess. Now and forever!"

"Kaor, Captain John Carter. Helium is proud to accept."

We fell on each other's shoulders, howling. After a bit the howling died down and turned into another kiss.

When we came up for air, Hilda tapped me on a shoulder. "Would you let us in on the joke?"

"Do we tell her, Deety?"

"I'm not sure. Aunt Hilda talks."

"Oh, nonsense! I know your full name and I've never told anyone—I held you at your christening. You were wet, too. At both ends. Now give!"

"All right. We don't have to get married—we already are. For years. More than a century."

Pop spoke up. "Eh? What's this?" I explained to him. He looked thoughtful, then nodded. "Logical." He went back to figuring he was doing in a notebook, then looked up. "Your cousin Zebulon—is he on the telephone?"

"Probably not but he lives at the New Raffles."

"Excellent. I'll try both the hotel and the university. Doctor—son—Zeb, would you be so kind as to place the call? My comcredit code is Nero Aleph eight zero one dash seven five two dash three nine three two Zed Star Zed." (Zed Star Zed credit rating—I was not going to have to support my prospective father-in-law.)

Deety cut in. "Pop, you must not call Professor Carter—Zebulon Carter—at this hour."

"But, my dear daughter, it is not late at night in—"

"Of course it isn't; I can count. You want a favor from him, so don't interrupt his after-lunch nap. 'Mad dogs and Englishmen.'"

"It isn't noon in Singapore; it's—"

"—siesta time, even hotter than noon. So wait."

"Deety is right, Pop," I interrupted, "but for the wrong reasons. It doesn't seem to be a matter of life and death to call him this minute. Whereas it might be a matter of life and death—ours, I mean—to make a call from this car ... especially with your credit code. Until we find out who the Boys in the Black Hats are, I advise that you place calls from the ground and from public phones that you can feed with newdollars instead of your code. Say a phone in Peoria. Or Paducah. Can it wait?"

"Since you put it that way, sir—yes, it can wait. Although I have trouble believing that anyone wishes to kill me."

"Available data indicate it."

"Agreed. But I have not yet grasped it emotionally."

"Takes a baseball bat," said Hilda. "I had to sit on him while Jane proposed to him."

"Why, Hilda my dear, that is utterly unfactual. I wrote my late beloved a polite note saying—"

I let them argue while I tried to add to available data. "*Gay Deceiver.*"

"Yes, Boss?"

"News, dear."

"Ready, Boss."

"Retrieval parameters. Time—since twenty-one hundred. Area—California, Nevada, Utah. Persons—your kindly boss, dear. Doctor Jacob Burroughs, Doctor D. T. Burroughs, Miz Hilda Corners—" I hesitated. "Professor Neil O'Heret Brain." I felt silly adding "Brainy"—but there had been a row between Pop and him, and years before my best teacher had said, "Never neglect the so-called trivial roots of an equation," and had pointed out that two Nobel prizes had derived from "trivial" roots.

"Parameters complete, Boss?"

Doctor Burroughs touched my shoulder. "Can your computer check the news, if any, on your cousin?"

"Mmm, maybe. She stores sixty million bytes, then wipes last-in-last-out everything not placed on permanent. But her news storage is weighted sixty-forty in favor of North America. I'll try. Smart Girl."

"Holding, Boss."

"Addendum. First retrieve by parameters given. Then retrieve by new program. Time—backward from now to wipe time. Area—Singapore. Person—Zebulon Edward Carter aka Ed Carter aka Doctor Z. E. Carter aka Professor Z. E. Carter aka Professor or Doctor Carter of Raffles University."

"Two retrieval programs in succession. Got it, Zeb."

"You're a Smart Girl, Gay."

"Boss, I bet you tell that to all the girls. Over."

"Roger, Gay. Execute!"

"AP San Francisco. A mysterious explosion disturbed the academic quiet of—" A story ending with the usual claim about an arrest being expected "momentarily" settled several points: all of us were believed dead. Our village top cop claimed to have a theory but was keeping it mum—meaning that he knew even less than we did. Since we were reported as "presumed dead" and since the news said nothing about an illegal lift-off and other capers that annoy sky cops, I assumed tentatively that police radar had not been looking at us until after we had become just one more blip behaving legally. The lack of mention of the absence of *Gay Deceiver* did not surprise me, as I had roaded in and had been last or nearly last to park—and could have arrived by taxi, public capsule, or on foot. Doctor Brain was not mentioned, nothing about the row. Guests had been questioned and released. Five cars parked near the explosion had been damaged.

"Nevada—null retrieval. Utah—UPI Salt Lake City. A fire near Utah State University campus in Logan destroyed—" Blokes in Black Hats again and Deety and her Pop were dead twice over, as they were presumed to have been overcome by smoke, unable to escape. No one else hurt or missing. Fire attributed to faulty wiring. "End of first retrieval, Zeb. Second retrieval starting." Gay shut up.

I said soberly, "Pop, somebody doesn't like you."

He groaned. "Gone! All gone!"

"No copies of your papers elsewhere? And your … gadget?"

"Eh? No, no! *Much* worse! My irreplaceable collection of pulp magazines. *Weird Tales, Argosy, All-Story,* the early *Gernsbachs, The Shadow, Black Mask*— Ooooooh!"

"Pop really does feel bad," Deety whispered, "and I could manage tears myself. I taught myself to read from that collection. *War Aces, Air Wonder*, the complete Clayton *Astoundings*—it was appraised at two hundred and thirteen thousand newdollars. Grandpop started it, Pop continued it—I grew up reading them."

"I'm sorry, Deety." I hugged her. "They should have been microfiched."

"They were. But that's not having the magazines in your hands."

"I agree. Uh, how about the … thing in the basement?"

"What 'thing in the basement?'" demanded Sharpie. "Zebbie, you sound like H. P. Lovecraft."

"Later, Sharpie. Comfort Jake; we're busy. Gay!"

"Here, Zeb. Where's the riot?"

"Display map, please." We were midway over northern Nevada. "Cancel routing and cruise random. Report nearest county seat."

"Winnemucca and Elko are equidistant to one percent. Elko closer by ETA as I am now vectored eleven degrees north of Elko bearing."

"Deety, would you like to be married in Elko?"

"Zebadiah, I would love to be married in Elko."

"Elko it is, but loving may have to wait. Gay, vector for Elko and ground us, normal private cruising speed. Report ETA in elapsed minutes."

"Roger Wilco, Elko. Nine minutes seventeen seconds."

Hilda said soothingly, "There, there, Jake darling; Mama is here"—then added in her top-sergeant voice, "Quit stalling, Zebbie! What 'Thing' in which basement?"

"Sharpie, you're nosy. It belonged to Pop and now it's destroyed and that's all you need to know."

"Oh, but it wasn't," Doctor Burroughs said. "Zeb is speaking of my continua craft, Hilda. It's safe. Not in Logan."

"What in the Name of the Dog is a 'continua craft?'"

"Pop means," Deety explained, "his time machine."

"Then why didn't he say so? Everybody savvies *Time Machine*. George Pal's *Time Machine*—a classic goodie. I've caught it on the late-late-early show more than once."

"Sharpie," I asked, "can you read?"

"Certainly I can read! 'Run, Spot, run. See Spot run.' Smarty."

"Have you ever heard of H. G. Wells?"

"Heard of him? I've *had* him."

"You are a boastful old tart, but not that old. When Mr. Wells died, you were still a virgin."

"Slanderer! Hit him, Jake—he insulted me."

"Zeb didn't mean to insult you, I feel sure. Deety won't permit me to hit people, even when they need it."

"We'll change that."

"Second retrieval complete," *Gay Deceiver* reported. "Holding."

"Report second retrieval, please."

"Reuters, Singapore. The Marston expedition in Sumatra is still unreported according to authorities at Palembang. The party is thirteen days overdue. Besides Professor Marston and native guides and assistants, the party included Doctor Z. E. Carter, Doctor Cecil Yang, and Mr. Giles Smythe-Belisha. The Minister of Tourism and Culture stated that the search will be pursued assiduously. End of retrieval."

Poor Ed. We had never been close but he had never caused me grief. I hoped that he was shacked up with something soft and sultry—rather than losing his head to a jungle machete, which seemed more likely. "Pop, a few minutes ago I said that somebody doesn't like you. I now suspect that somebody doesn't like n-dimensional geometers."

"It would seem so, Zeb. I do hope your cousin is safe—a most brilliant mind! He would be a great loss to all mankind."

(And to himself, I added mentally. And me, since family duty required that I do something about it. When what I had in mind was a honeymoon.) "Gay."

"Here, Zeb."

"Addendum. Third news retrieval program. Use all parameters second program. Add Sumatra to area. Add all proper names and titles found in second retrieval. Run until cancelled. Place retrievals in permanent memory. Report new items soonest. Start."

"Running, Boss."

"You're a good girl, Gay."

"Thank you, Zeb. Grounding Elko two minutes seven seconds."

Deety squeezed my hand harder. "Pop, as soon as I'm legally Mrs. John Carter I think we should all go to Snug Harbor."

"Eh? Obviously."

"You, too, Aunt Hilda. It might not be safe for you to go home."

"Change in plans, dear. It's going to be a double wedding. Jake. Me."

Deety looked alert but not displeased. "Pop?"

"Hilda has at last consented to marry me, dear."

"Rats," said Sharpie. "Jake has never asked me in the past and didn't this time; I simply told him. Hit him with it while he was upset over losing his comic books and unable to defend himself. It's necessary, Deety—I promised Jane I would take care of Jake and I have—through you, up to now. But from here on you'll be taking care of Zebbie, keeping him out of trouble, wiping his nose ... so I've got to hogtie Jake into marriage to keep my promise to Jane. Instead of sneaking into his bed from time to time as in the past."

"Why, Hilda dear, you have never been in my bed!"

"Don't shame me in front of the children, Jake. I gave you a test run before I let Jane marry you and you don't dare deny it."

Jake shrugged helplessly. "As you wish, dear Hilda."

"Aunt Hilda ... do you love Pop?"

"Would I marry him if I didn't? I could carry out my promise to Jane more simply by having him committed to a shrink factory. Deety, I've loved Jake longer than you have. Much! But he loved Jane ... which shows that he is basically rational despite his weird ways. I shan't try to change him, Deety; I'm simply going to see to it that he wears his overshoes and takes his vitamins—as you've been doing. I'll still be 'Aunt Hilda,' not 'Mother.' Jane was and is your mother."

"Thank you, Aunt Hilda. I thought I was happy as a woman can be, getting Zebadiah. But you've made me still happier. No worries."

(*I* had worries. Blokes with Black Hats and no faces. But I didn't say so, as Deety was snuggling closer and assuring me that it was all right because Aunt Hilda wouldn't fib about loving Pop.) "Deety, where and what is 'Snug Harbor?'"

"It's ... a nowhere place. A hideout. Land Pop leased from the government when he decided to build his time twister instead of just writing equations. But we may have to wait for daylight. Unless—can *Gay Deceiver* home in on a given latitude and longitude?"

"She certainly can! Precisely."

"Then it's all right. I can give it to you in degrees, minutes, and fractions of a second."

"Grounding," Gay warned us.

The Elko county clerk did not object to getting out of bed and seemed pleased with the century note I slipped him. The county judge was just as accommodating and pocketed her honorarium without glancing at it. I stammered but managed to say, "I, Zebadiah John, take thee, Dejah Thoris—" Deety went through it as solemnly and perfectly as if she had rehearsed it … while Hilda sniffled throughout.

A good thing that Gay can home on a pinpoint; I was in no shape to drive, even in daylight. I had her plan her route, too, a dogleg for minimum radar and no coverage at all for the last hundred-odd kilometers to this place in the Arizona Strip north of the Grand Canyon. But I had her hover before grounding—I being scared silly until I was certain there was not a third fire there.

A cabin, fireproof, with underground parking for Gay—I relaxed.

We split a bottle of Chablis. Pop seemed about to head for the basement. Sharpie tromped on it and Deety ignored it.

I carried Deety over the threshold into her bedroom, put her gently down, faced her. "Dejah Thoris—"

"Yes, John Carter?"

"I did not have time to buy you a wedding present—"

"I need no present from my captain."

"Hear me out, my princess. My Uncle Zamir did not have as fine a collection as your father had … but may I gift you with a complete set of Clayton *Astoundings*—"

She suddenly smiled.

"—and first editions of the first six Oz books, quite worn but with the original color plates? And a first in almost mint condition of *A Princess of Mars*?"

The smile became a grin and she looked nine years old. "Yes!"

"Would your father accept a complete set of *Weird Tales*?"

"Would he! Northwest Smith and Jirel of Joiry? I'm going to borrow them—or he can't look at my Oz books. I'm stubborn, I am. And selfish. And *mean!*"

" 'Stubborn' stipulated. The others denied."

Deety stuck out her tongue. "You'll find out." Suddenly her face was solemn. "But I sorrow, my prince, that I have no present for my husband."

"But you have."

"I do?"

"Yes. Beautifully wrapped and making me dizzy with heavenly fragrance."

"Oh." She looked solemn but serenely happy. "Will my husband unwrap me? Please?"

I did.

That is all anyone is ever going to know about our wedding night.

— IV —

Deety

I woke early, as I always do at Snug Harbor, wondered why I was ecstatically happy—then remembered, and turned my head. My husband—"*husband!*"—what a heart-filling word—my husband was sprawled face down beside me, snoring softly and drooling onto his pillow. I held still, thinking how beautiful he was, how gently strong and gallantly tender.

I was tempted to wake him, but I knew that my darling needed rest. So I eased out of bed and snuck noiselessly into my bath—*our* bath!—and quietly took care of this and that. I would grab that proper bath after my captain was awake.

I pulled on briefs, started to tie on a halter—stopped and looked in the mirror. I have a face-shaped face and a muscular body that I keep in top condition. I would never reach semifinals in a beauty contest.

You hear that, Deety? Don't be stubborn, don't be bossy, don't be difficult—and above all don't sulk! Mama never sulked, although Pop wasn't and isn't easy to live with. Mama told me gently that logic had little to do with keeping a husband happy and that anyone who "won" a family argument had in fact lost it. Mama never argued and Pop always did what she wanted—if she really wanted it. When, at seventeen, I had to grow up and try to replace her, I tried to emulate her—not always successfully. I inherited some of Pop's temper, some of Mama's calm. I try to suppress the former and cultivate the latter. But I'm not Jane, I'm Deety.

32

Suddenly I wondered why I was putting on a halter. The day was going to be hot. While Pop is so cubical about some things that he turns up at the corners, skin is not one of them. (Possibly he had been, then Mama had gently gotten her own way.) I like to be naked and usually am at Snug Harbor, weather permitting. Pop is almost as casual. Aunt Hilda was family-by-choice; we had often used her pool and never with suits—screened for the purpose.

So why was I putting on a bra?

Because two things equal to the same thing are never equal to each other. Basic mathematics if you select the proper sheaf of postulates. People are not abstract symbols. I could be naked with any one of them but not all three.

I felt a twinge that Pop and Aunt Hilda might be in the way on my honeymoon ... then realized that Zebadiah and I were just as much in the way on theirs—and stopped worrying; it would work out.

I started to cat-foot through our bedroom when I noticed Zebadiah's clothes—and stopped. The darling would not want to wear evening dress to breakfast. *Deety, you are not being wifely—figure this out. Are any of Pop's clothes where I can get them without waking the others?*

Yep! An old shirt that I had liberated as a house coat, khaki shorts I had been darning the last time we had been down—both in my wardrobe in my—*our!*—bathroom. I crept back, got them, laid them over my darling's evening clothes so that he could not miss them.

I went through and closed after me two soundproof doors, then no longer had to keep quiet. Pop does not tolerate anything shoddy—if it doesn't work properly, he fixes it. Pop's BS was in mechanical engineering, his MS in physics, his Ph.D. in mathematics; there isn't *anything* he can't design and build. A second Leonardo da Vinci—or a Paul Dirac.

No one in the everything room. I decided not to head for the kitchen end yet; if the others slept a bit longer, I could get in my morning tone-up. Stretch high, then palms to the floor without bending knees—ten is enough. Vertical splits, both legs, then the same to the floor with my forehead to my shin, first right, then left.

I was doing a back bend when I heard, "Ghastly. The battered bride. Deety, stop that."

I continued into a backward walkover and stood up facing Pop's bride. "Good morning, Aunt Hillbilly." I kissed and hugged her. "Not battered. Bartered, maybe."

"Battered," she repeated, yawning.

Hilda stopped to kiss me more warmly than before. "Now I'm the happiest woman in America."

"Nope. Second happiest. You're looking at the happiest."

Aunt Hilda guffawed. "I surrender. We're both the happiest woman in the world."

"And the luckiest. Aunt Nanny Goat, that robe of Pop's is too hot. I'll get something of mine. How about a tie-on fit-anybody bikini?"

"Thanks, dear, but you might wake Zebbie." Aunt Hilda opened Pop's robe and held it wide, fanning it. I looked at her with new eyes. She's had three or four term contracts, no children. At forty-two her face looks thirty-five, but from her collarbones down she could pass for eighteen. A china doll—makes me feel like a giant.

She added, "If it weren't for your husband, I would simply wear this old hide. It is hot."

"If it weren't for your husband, so would I."

"Jacob? Deety, he's changed your diapers. I know how Jane reared you. True modesty, no false modesty."

"It's not the same, Aunt Hilda. Not today."

"No, it's not. You always did have a wise head, Deety. Women are toughminded, men are not; we have to protect them … while pretending to be fragile ourselves, to build up their fragile egos. But I've never been good at it—I like to play with matches."

"Aunt Hilda, you are *very* good at it, in your own way. I'm certain Mama knows what you've done for Pop and blesses it and is happy for Pop. For all of us—all five of us."

"Don't make me cry, Deety. Let's break out the orange juice; our men will wake any time. First secret of living with a man: feed him as soon as he wakes."

"So I know."

"Yes, of course you know. Ever since we lost Jane. Does Zebbie know how lucky he is?"

"He says so. I'm going to try hard not to disillusion him."

— V —

Jake

I woke in drowsy euphoria, became aware that I was in bed in our cabin that my daughter calls "Snug Harbor"—then woke completely and looked at the other pillow—the dent in it. Not a dream! Euphoric for the best of reasons!

Hilda was not in sight. I closed my eyes and simulated sleep, as I had something to do. "Jane?" I said in my mind.

"I hear you, dearest one. It has my blessing. Now we are all happy together."

"We couldn't expect Deety to become a sour old maid, just to take care of her crotchety old father. This young man, he's okay, to the nth power. I felt it at once, and Hilda is certain of it."

"He is. Don't worry, Jacob. Our Deety can never be sour and you will never be old. This is exactly as Hilda and I planned it, more than five of your years ago. Predestined. She told you so, last night."

"Okay, darling."

"Get up and brush your teeth and take a quick shower. Don't dawdle, breakfast is waiting. Call me when you need me. Kiss."

So I got up, feeling like a boy on Christmas morning. Everything was jake with Jake; Jane had put her stamp of approval on it. Let me tell you, you nonexistent reader sitting there with a tolerant sneer: don't be smug. Jane is more real than you are.

The spirit of a good woman cannot be coded by nucleic acids arranged in a double helix, and only an overeducated fool could think so. I could prove that mathematically save that mathematics can never

35

prove anything. No mathematics has any content. All any mathematics can do is—sometimes—turn out to be useful in describing some aspects of our so-called physical universe.

That is a bonus; most forms of mathematics are as meaning-free as chess.

I don't know *any* final answers. I'm an all-around mechanic and a competent mathematician … and neither is of any use in unscrewing the inscrutable.

Some people go to church to talk to God, whoever He is. When I have something on my mind, I talk to Jane. I don't hear "voices," but the answers that come into my mind have as much claim to infallibility, it seems to me, as any handed down by any pope speaking *ex cathedra*. If this be blasphemy, make the most of it; I won't budge. Jane is, was, and ever shall be, worlds without end. I had the priceless privilege of living with her for eighteen years and I can never lose her.

Hilda was not in the bath but my toothbrush was damp. I smiled at this. Logical, as any germs I was harboring, Hilda now had—and Hilda, for all her playfulness, is no-nonsense practical. She faces danger without a qualm (had done so last night) but she would say "Gesundheit!" to an erupting volcano even as she fled from it. Jane is equally brave but would omit the quip. They are alike only in—no, not that way, either. Different but equal. Let it stand that I have been blessed in marriage by two superb women. (And blessed by a daughter whose Pop thinks she is perfect.)

I showered, shaved, and brushed my teeth in nine minutes and dressed in under nine seconds as I simply wrapped around my waist a terrycloth sarong Deety had bought for me—the day promised to be a scorcher. Even that hip wrap was a concession to propriety, i.e., I did not know my new son-in-law well enough to subject him abruptly to our casual ways; it might offend Deety.

I was last up and saw that all had made much the same decision. Deety was wearing what amounted to a bikini minimum (indecently "decent") and my bride was "dressed" in a tie-on job belonging to Deety. The tie—ties—had unusually large bows; Hilda is tiny, my daughter is not. Zeb was the only one fully dressed: an old pair of working shorts, a worn-out denim shirt Deety had confiscated, and his evening shoes. He was dressed for the street in any western town save for one thing: I'm built like a pear, Zeb is built like the Gray Lensman.

My shorts fitted him well enough—a bit loose—but his shoulders were splitting the shirt's seams. He looked uncomfortable.

I took care of amenities—a good morning to all, a kiss for my bride, one for my daughter, a handshake for my son-in-law—good hands, calloused. Then I said, "Zeb, take that shirt off. It's hot and getting hotter. Relax. This is your home."

"Thanks, Pop." Zeb peeled off my shirt.

Hilda stood up on her chair, making her about as tall as Zeb. "I'm a militant women's-rights gal," she announced, "and a wedding ring is not a ring in my nose—a ring that you have not yet given me, you old goat."

"When have I had time? You'll get one, dear—first chance."

"Excuses, excuses! Don't interrupt when I'm orating. Sauce for the gander is no excuse for goosing the goose. If you male chauvinist pigs can dress comfortably, Deety and I have the same privilege." Whereupon my lovely little bride untied that bikini top and threw it aside like a stripper.

" 'What's for breakfast?' asked Pooh," I misquoted.

I was not answered. Deety made me proud of her for the nth time. For years she had consulted me, at least with her eyes, on "policy decisions." Now she looked not at me but at her husband. Zeb was doing Old Stone Face, refusing assent or dissent. Deety stared at him, gave a tiny shrug, reached behind her and untied or unsnapped something and discarded her own top.

"I said, 'What's for breakfast?'" I repeated.

"Greedy gut," my daughter answered. "You men have had baths, while Aunt Hilda and I haven't had a chance to get clean for fear of waking you slugabeds."

" 'What's for breakfast?' "

"Aunt Hilda, in only hours Pop has lost all the training I've given him for five years. Pop, it's laid out and ready to go. How about cooking while Hilda and I grab a tub?"

Zeb stood up. "I'll cook, Deety; I've been getting my own breakfast for years."

"Hold it, buster!" my bride interrupted. "Sit down, Zebbie. Deety, never encourage a man to cook breakfast; it causes him to wonder if women are necessary. If you always get his breakfast and don't raise controversial issues until after his second cup of coffee, you can get away with murder the rest of the time. I'm going to have to coach you."

My daughter reversed the field, fast. She turned to her husband and said meekly, "What does my captain wish for breakfast?"

"My princess, whatever your lovely hands offer me."

What we were offered, as fast as Deety could pour batter and Hilda could serve, was a gourmet specialty that would enrage a *Cordon Bleu* but which, for my taste, is ambrosia: a one-eyed Texas stack—a tall stack of thin, tender buttermilk pancakes to Jane's recipe, supporting one large egg, up and easy, surrounded by hot sausage, and the edifice drowned in melting butter and hot maple syrup, with a big glass of orange juice and a big mug of coffee on the side.

Zeb ate two stacks. I concluded that my daughter would have a happy marriage.

— VI —

Hilda

Deety and I washed dishes, then soaked in her tub and talked about husbands. We giggled, and talked with the frankness of women who trust each other and are sure that no men can overhear. Do men talk that openly in parallel circumstances? From all I have been able to learn in after-midnight horizontal conversations, all passion spent, men do not. Or not men I would take to bed. Whereas a "perfect lady" (which Jane was, Deety is, and I can simulate) will talk with another "perfect lady" she trusts in a way that would cause her father, husband, or son to faint.

I had better leave out our conversation; this memoir might fall into the hands of one of the weaker sex and I would not want his death on my conscience.

Are men and women one race? I know what biologists say—but history is loaded with "scientists" jumping to conclusions from superficial evidence. It seems to me far more likely that they are symbiotes. I am not speaking from ignorance; I was one trimester short of a BS in biology (and a straight-A student) when a "biology experiment" blew up in my face and caused me to leave school abruptly.

Not that I need that degree—I've papered my private bath with honorary degrees, mostly doctorates. I hear that there are things no whore will do for money, but I have yet to find anything that a university chancellor faced with a deficit will boggle at. The secret is never to set up a permanent fund but to dole it out when need is sharpest, once every academic year. Done that way, you not only own a campus but also the town cops learn that it's a waste of time to hassle you. A univer$ity alway$ $tand$ $taunchly by it$ $olvent a$$ociate$; that'$ the ba$ic $ecret of $chola$tic $ucce$$.

Forgive my digre$$ion; we were speaking of men and women. I am strong for women's rights but was never taken in by unisex nonsense. I don't yearn to be equal; Sharpie is as unequal as possible, with all the perks and bonuses and special privileges that come from being one of the superior sex. If a man fails to hold a door for me, I fail to see him and step on his instep. I don't begrudge men one whit of their natural advantages as long as they respect mine. I am not an unhappy pseudomale; I am *female* and like it that way.

I borrowed makeup that Deety rarely uses, but I carry my own perfume in my purse and used it in the twenty-two classic places. Deety uses only the basic aphrodisiac: soap and water. Perfume on her would be gilding the lily; fresh out of a hot tub she smells like a harem. If I had her natural fragrance, I could have saved at least ten thousand newdollars over the years as well as many hours spent dabbing bait here and there.

She offered me a dress and I told her not to be silly; any dress of hers would fit me like a tent. "We've got our men gentled to nearly naked and we'll hold that gain. At first opportunity we'll get pants off all of us, too, without anything as childish as strip poker. Deety, I want us to be a solid family, and relaxed about it. So that skin doesn't mean sex, it just means we are home, *en famille*. Never tell a man anything he doesn't need to know, and lie with a straight face rather than hurt his feelings or diminish his pride."

"Aunt Nanny Goat, I just plain love you."

We quit yakking and looked for our men. Deety said that they were certain to be in the basement. "Aunt Hilda, I don't go there without invitation. It's Pop's *sanctum sanctorum*."

"You're warning me not to risk a *faux pas?*"

"I'm his daughter; you're his wife. Not the same."

"Well … he hasn't told me not to—and today he'll forgive me, if ever. Where do you hide the stairs?"

"That bookcase swings out."

"Be darned! For a so-called cabin this place is loaded with surprises. A bidet in each bath didn't startle me; Jane would have required them. Your walk-in freezer startled me only by being big enough for a restaurant. But a bookcase concealing a priest's hole—as Great-Aunt Nettie used to say, 'I do declare!'"

40

"You should see our septic tank—yours, now."

"I've seen septic tanks. Pesky things—always need pumping at the most inconvenient time."

"This one won't have to be pumped. Over three hundred meters deep. An even thousand feet."

"For the love of—*Why?*"

"It's an abandoned mine shaft below us that some optimist dug a hundred years back. Here was this big hole, so Pop used it. There is a spring farther up the mountain. Pop cleaned that out, covered it, concealed it, put pipe underground, and we have lavish pure water under pressure. The rest of Snug Harbor Pop designed mostly from prefab catalogs, fireproof and solid and heavily insulated. We have—you have, I mean—this big fireplace and the little ones in the bedrooms, but you won't need them, other than for homeyness. Radiant heat makes it skin-comfortable even in a blizzard."

"Where do you get your power? From the nearest town?"

"Oh, no! Snug Harbor is a hideout, nobody but Pop and me—and now you and Zebadiah—knows it's here. Power packs, Aunt Hilda, and an inverter in a space behind the back wall of the garage. We bring in power packs ourselves, and take them out the same way. Private. Oh, the leasehold record is buried in a computer in Washington or Denver, and the federal rangers know the leaseholds. But they don't see us if we see or hear them first. Mostly they cruise on past. Once one came by on horseback. Pop fed him beer out under the trees—and from outside this is just a prefab, a living room and two shedroof bedrooms. Nothing to show that important parts are underground."

"Deety, I'm beginning to think that this place—this cabin—cost more than my townhouse."

"Uh, probably."

"I think I'm disappointed. Sugar Pie, I married your papa because I love him and want to take care of him and promised Jane that I would. I've been thinking happily that my wedding present to my bridegroom would be his weight in bullion, so that dear man need never work again."

"Don't be disappointed, Aunt Hilda. Pop has to work; it's his nature. Me, too. Work is necessary to us. Without it, we're lost."

"Well … yes. But working because you want to is the best sort of play."

"Correct!"

"That's what I thought I could give Jacob. I don't understand it. Jane wasn't rich, she was on a scholarship. Jacob had no money—still a teaching fellow, a few months shy of his doctorate. Deety, Jacob's suit that he wore to be married in was threadbare. I know that he pulled up from that; he made full professor awfully fast. I thought it was that and Jane's good management."

"It was both."

"That doesn't account for this. Forgive me, Deety, but Utah State doesn't pay what Harvard pays."

"Pop doesn't lack offers. We like Logan. Both the town and the civilized behavior of Mormons. But—Aunt Hilda, I must tell you some things."

The child looked worried. I said, "Deety, if Jacob wants me to know something he'll tell me."

"Oh, but he won't and I must!"

"*No*, Deety!"

"Listen, please! When I said, 'I do,' I resigned as Pop's manager. When you said, 'I do,' the load landed on you. It has to be that way, Aunt Hilda. Pop won't do it; he has other things to think about, things that take genius. Mama did it for years, then I learned how, and now it's your job. Because it can't be farmed out. Do you understand accountancy?"

"Well, I *understand* it, I took a course in it. Have to understand it, or the government will skin you alive. But I don't *do* it, I have accountants for that—and smart shysters to keep it inside the law."

"Would it bother you to be outside the law? On taxes?"

"What? Heavens, no! But Sharpie wants to stay outside of jail—I detest an institutional diet."

"You'll stay out of jail. Don't worry, Aunt Hilda—I'll teach you double-entry bookkeeping they don't teach in school. *Very* double. One set for the revenooers and another set for you and Jake."

"It's that second set that worries me. That one puts you in the pokey. Fresh air alternate Wednesdays."

"Nope. The second set is not on paper; it's in the campus computer at Logan—"

"Worse!"

"Aunt Hilda, *please!* Certainly my computer address code is in the department's vault and an IRS agent could get a court order. It wouldn't do him any good. It would spill out our first set of books while wiping every trace of the second set. Inconvenient but not disastrous. Aunt Hillbilly, I'm not a champion at anything else but I'm the best software artist in the business. I'm at your elbow until you are sure of yourself.

"Now about how Pop got rich—all the time he's been teaching he's also been inventing gadgets—as automatically as a hen lays eggs. A better can opener. A lawn irrigation system that does a better job, costs less, uses less water. Lots of things. But none has his name on it and royalties trickle back in devious ways.

"But we aren't freeloaders. Every year Pop and I study the federal budget and decide what is useful and what is sheer waste by fat-arsed chairwarmers and pork-barrel raiders. Even before Mama died we were paying *more* income tax than the total of Pop's salary, and we've paid more each year while I've been running it. It *does* take a bundle to run this country. We don't begrudge money spent on roads and public health and national defense and truly useful things. But we've quit paying for parasites wherever we can identify them.

"It's your job now, Aunt Hilda. If you decide that it's dishonest or too risky, I can cause the computer to make it all open and legal so smoothly that hanky-panky would never show. It would take me maybe three years, and Pop would pay high capital gains. But *you* are in charge of Pop now."

"Deety, don't talk dirty."

"Dirty, how? I didn't even say 'spit.'"

"Suggesting that I would *willingly* pay what those clowns in Washington want to squeeze out of us. I would not be supporting so many accountants and shysters if I didn't think we were being robbed blind. Deety, how about being manager for all of us?"

"No, ma'am! I'm in charge of Zebadiah. I have my own interests to manage, too. Mama wasn't as poor as you thought. When I was a little girl, she came into a chunk from a trust her grandmother had set up. She and Pop gradually moved it over into my name and again avoided inheritance and estate taxes, all legal as Sunday school. When I was eighteen, I converted it into cash, then caused it to disappear. Besides that, I've been paying me a whopping salary as Pop's manager. I'm not as rich as you are, Aunt Hilda, and certainly not as rich as Pop. But I ain't hurtin'."

"Zebbie may be richer than all of us."

43

"You said last night that he was loaded but I didn't pay attention because I had already decided to marry him. But after experiencing what sort of car he drives I realize that you weren't kidding. Not that it matters. Yes, it *did* matter—it took both Zebadiah's courage and *Gay Deceiver*'s unusual talents to save our lives."

"You may never find out how loaded Zebbie is, dear. Some people don't let their left hands know what their right hands are doing. Zebbie doesn't let his thumb know what his fingers are doing."

Deety shrugged. "I don't care. He's kind and gentle and he's a storybook hero who saved my life and Pop's and yours …. Let's go find our men, Aunt Nanny Goat. I'll risk Pop's Holy of Holies if you'll go first."

"How do you swing back this bookcase?"

"Switch on the cove lights, then turn on the cold water at the sink. Then switch off the cove lights, then turn off the water—in that order."

" 'Curiouser and curiouser,' said Alice."

The bookcase closed behind us and was a door with a knob on the upper landing side. The staircase was wide, treads were broad and nonskid, risers gentle, guard rails on both sides—not the legbreaker most houses have as cellar stairs. Deety went down beside me, holding my hand like a child needing reassurance.

The room was beautifully lighted, well ventilated, and did not seem like a basement. Our men were at the far end, bent over a table, and did not appear to notice us. I looked around for a time machine, could not spot it—at least not anything like George Pal's or any I had ever read about. All around was machinery. A drill press looks the same anywhere and so does a lathe, but others were strange—except that they reminded me of machine shops.

My husband caught sight of us, stood up, and said, "Welcome, ladies!"

Zebbie turned his head and said sharply, "Late to class! Find seats, no whispering during the lecture, take notes; there will be a quiz at eight o'clock tomorrow morning. If you have questions, raise your hands and wait to be called on. Anyone who misbehaves will remain after class and wash the chalkboards."

Deety stuck out her tongue, sat down quietly. I rubbed his brush cut and whispered an indecency into his ear. Then I kissed my husband and sat down.

My husband resumed talking to Zebbie. "I lost more gyroscopes that way."

I held up my hand. My husband said, "Yes, Hilda dear?"

"Monkey Ward's sells gyro tops—I'll buy you a gross."

"Thank you, dearest, but these weren't that sort. They were made by Sperry Division of General Foods."

"So I'll get them from Sperry."

"Sharpie," put in Zeb, "you're honing to clean the erasers, too."

"Just a moment, son. Hilda may be the perfect case to find out whether or not what I have tried to convey to you—and which really can't be conveyed save in the equations your cousin Zebulon used, a mathematics you say is unfamiliar to you—"

"It is!"

"—but which you appear to grasp as mechanics. Would you explain the concept to Hilda? If she understands it, we may hypothesize that a continua craft can be designed to be operated by a non-technical person."

"Sure," I said scornfully, "poor little me, with a button for a head. I don't have to know where the electrons go to use television or holovision. I just twist knobs. Go ahead, Zebbie. Take a swing at it; I dare you."

"I'll try," Zebbie agreed. "But Sharpie, don't chatter, and keep your comments to the point. Or I'll ask Pop to give you a fat lip."

"He wouldn't dare—"

"So? I'm going to give him a horsewhip for a wedding present—besides the *Weird Tales*, Jake; you get those too. But you need a whip. Attention, Sharpie."

"Yes, Zebbie. And the same to you doubled."

"Do you know what 'precess' means?"

"Certainly. Precession of the equinoxes. Means that Vega will be the North Star when I'm a great-grandmother. Thirty thousand years or some such."

"Correct in essence. But you're not even a mother yet."

"You don't know what happened last night. I'm an expectant mother. Jacob doesn't dare use a whip on me."

My husband looked startled but pleased—and I felt relieved. Zebbie looked at his own bride. Deety said solemnly, "It is possible, Zebadiah. Neither of us was protected, each was on or close on ovulation. Hilda is blood type B Rhesus positive and my father is AB positive. I am A Rh positive. May I inquire yours, sir?"

"I'm an O positive. Uh … may have shot you down the first salvo."

"It would seem likely. But—does this meet with your approval?"

" 'Approval'!" Zebbie stood up, knocking over his chair. "Princess, you could not make me happier! Jake! This calls for a toast!"

My husband stopped kissing me. "Unanimous! Daughter, is there champagne chilled?"

"Yes, Pop."

"Hold it!" I said. "Let's not get excited over a normal biological function. Deety and I don't *know* that we caught; we just hope so. And—"

"So we try again," Zebbie interrupted. "What's your calendar?"

"Twenty-eight and a half days, Zebadiah. My rhythm is pendulum-steady."

"Mine's twenty-seven; Deety and I just happen to be in step. But I want that toast at dinner and a luau afterward; it might be the last for a long time. Deety, do you get morning sick?"

"I don't know; I've never been pregnant before."

"I have and I do and it's miserable. Then I lost the naked little grub after trying hard to keep it. But I'm not going to lose this one! Fresh air and proper exercise and careful diet and nothing but champagne for me tonight, then not another drop until I know. In the meantime—Professors, may I point out that class is in session? I want to know about time machines and I'm not sure I could understand with champagne buzzing my buttonhead."

"Sharpie, sometimes you astound me."

"Zebbie, sometimes I astound myself. Since my husband builds time machines, I want to know what makes them tick. Or at least which knobs to turn. He might be clawed by the Bandersnatch and I would have to pilot him home. Get on with your lecture."

"I read you loud and clear."

But we wasted ("wasted?") a few moments because everybody had to kiss everybody else—even Zebbie and my husband pounded each other on the back and kissed both cheeks Latin-style.

Class resumed. "Sharpie, can you explain precession in gyroscopes?"

"Well, maybe. Physics One was required but that was a long time ago. Push a gyroscope and it doesn't go the way you expect, but ninety degrees from that direction so that the push lines up with the spin. Like this—" I pointed a forefinger like a little boy going: *Bang! You're dead!* "My thumb is the axis, my forefinger represents the push, the other fingers show the rotation."

"Go to the head of the class. Now—think hard!—suppose we put a gyroscope in a frame, then impress equal forces at *all three* spatial coordinates at once; what would it do?"

I tried to visualize it. "I think it would either faint or drop dead."

"A good first hypothesis. According to Jake, it disappears."

"They *do* disappear, Aunt Hilda. I watched it happen several times."

"But where do they go?"

"I can't follow Jake's math; I have to accept his transformations without proof. But it is based on the notion of six space-time coordinates, three of space, the usual three that we see—marked x, y, and z—and three time coordinates: one marked 't' like this—" (t) "—and one marked 'tau,' Greek alphabet—" (τ) "—and the third from the Cyrillic alphabet, 'teh'—" ($\bar{m}$).

"Looks like an 'M' with a macron over it."

"So it does, but it's what the Russians use for 'T.'"

"No, the Russians use 'chai' for tea. In thick glasses with strawberry jam."

"Stow it, Sharpie. So we have x, y, and z; t, tau, and teh, six dimensions. It is basic to the theory that all are at right angles to each other, and that any one may be swapped for any of the others by rotation—or that a new coordinate may be found (not a seventh but replacing any of the six) by translation—say 'tau' to 'tau prime' by displacement along 'x.'"

"Zebbie, I think I fell off about four coordinates back."

My husband suggested, "Show her the caltrop, Zeb."

"Good idea." Zeb accepted a widget from my husband, placed it in front of me. It looked like jacks I used to play with as a little girl but not enough things sticking out: four instead of six. Three touched the table, a tripod; the fourth stuck straight up.

Zeb said, "This is a weapon, invented centuries ago. The points should be sharp but these have been filed down." He flipped it, let it fall to the table. "No matter how it falls, one prong is vertical. Scatter them in front of cavalry; the horses go down—discouraging. They came into use again in Wars One and Two against anything with pneumatic tires—bicycles, motorcycles, lorries, and so forth. Big enough, they disable tanks and tracked vehicles. A small sort can be whittled from thorn bushes for guerrilla warfare—usually poisoned and quite nasty.

47

"But here this lethal toy is a geometrical projection, a drawing of the coordinates of a four-dimensional space-time continuum. Each spike is exactly ninety degrees from every other spike."

"But they aren't," I objected. "Each angle is more than a right angle."

"I said it was a *projection*. Sharpie, it's an isometric projection of four-dimensional coordinates in three-dimensional space. That distorts the angles … and the human eye is even more limited. Cover one eye and hold still and you see only two dimensions. The illusion of depth is a construct of the brain."

"I'm not very good at holding still—"

"No, she isn't," agreed my bridegroom, whom I loved dearly and at that instant could have choked.

"But I can close both eyes and *feel* three dimensions with my hands."

"A good point. Close your eyes and pick this up and think of the prongs as the four directions of a four-dimensional space. Does the word tesseract mean anything to you?"

"My high school geometry teacher showed us how to construct them—projections—with modeling wax and toothpicks. Fun. I found other four-dimensional figures that were easy to project. And a number of ways to project them."

"Sharpie, you must have had an exceptional geometry teacher."

"In an exceptional geometry class. Don't faint, Zebbie, but I was grouped with what they called 'overachievers' after it became 'undemocratic' to call them 'gifted children.'"

"Be durned! Why do you always behave like a fritterhead?"

"Why don't you ever look beneath the surface, young man? I laugh because I dare not cry. This is a crazy world and the only way to enjoy it is to treat it as a joke. That doesn't mean I don't read and can't think. I read everything from Giblett to Hoyle, from Sartre to Pauling. I read in the tub, I read on the john, I read in bed, I read when I eat alone, and I would read in my sleep if I could keep my eyes open."

"OK. I apologize. Professor, we can speed up this seminar; we've been underrating our overachiever. Hilda is a brain."

"Zebbie, can we kiss and make up?"

"Class is in session."

"Zebadiah, there is always time for that. Right, Pop?"

"Kiss her, son, or she'll sulk."

"I don't sulk, I bite."

"I think you're cute, too," Zebbie answered, grabbed me by both shoulders, dragged me over the table, and kissed me hard.

He dropped me abruptly and said, "Attention, class. The two prongs of the caltrop painted blue represent our three-dimensional space of experience. The third prong painted yellow is the t-time we are used to. The red fourth prong simulates both tau-time and teh-time, the unexplored time dimensions necessary to Jake's theory. Sharpie, we have condensed six dimensions into four, then we either work by analogy into six, or we have to use math that apparently nobody but Jake and my cousin Ed understands. Unless you can think of some way to project six dimensions into three—you seem to be smart at such projections."

I closed my eyes and thought hard. "Zebbie, I don't think it can be done. Maybe Escher could have done it."

"It can be done, my dearest," answered my dearest, "but it is unsatisfactory. Even with a display computer with capacity to subtract one or more dimensions at a time. A superhypertesseract—a to the sixth power—has too many lines and corners and planes and solids and hypersolids for the eye to grasp. Cause the computer to subtract dimensions and what you have left is what you already knew. I fear it is an innate incapacity of visual conception in the human brain."

"I think Pop is right," agreed Deety. "I worked hard on that program. I don't think the late, great Dr. Marvin Minsky could have done it better in flat projection. Holovision? I don't know. I would like to try if I ever get my hands on a computer with holovideo display and the capacity to add, subtract, and rotate six coordinates."

"But why six dimensions?" I asked. "Why not five? Or even four, since you speak of rotating them interchangeably."

"Jake?" asked Zeb.

My darling looked fussed. "It bothered me that a space-time continuum seemed to require three space dimensions but only one time dimension. Granted that the universe is what it is, nevertheless nature is filled with symmetries. Even after the destruction of the parity principle, scientists kept finding new ones. Philosophers stay wedded to symmetry—but I don't count philosophers."

"Of course not," agreed Zeb. "No philosopher allows his opinions to be swayed by facts—he would be kicked out of his guild. Theologians, the lot of them."

"I concur. Hilda, my darling, after I found a way to experiment, it turned out that six dimensions existed. Possibly more—but I see no way to reach them."

"Let me see," I said. "If I understood earlier, each dimension can be swapped for any other."

"By ninety-degree rotation, yes."

"Wouldn't that be the combinations taken four at a time out of a set of six? How many is that?"

"Fifteen," Zebbie answered.

"Goodness! Fifteen whole universes? And we use only one?"

"No, no, my darling! That would be ninety-degree rotations of one Euclidean universe. But our universe, or universes, has been known to be non-Euclidean at least since 1919. Or 1886, if you prefer. I stipulate that cosmology is an imperfect discipline; nevertheless, for considerations that I cannot state in nonmathematical terms, I was forced to assume a curved space of positive radius—that is to say, a closed space. That makes the universes possibly accessible to use, either by rotation or by translation, this number." My husband rapidly wrote three sixes.

"Six sixty-six," I said wonderingly. "The Number of the Beast."

"Eh? *Oh!* The Revelation of Saint John the Divine. But I scrawled it sloppily. You took it that I wrote this: '666.' But what I intended to write was this: '$((6)^6)^6$.' Six raised to its sixth power, and the result in turn raised to its sixth power. That number is *this*: $1.03144+ \times 10^{28}$—or written in full, 10,314,424,798,490,535,546,171,949,056—or more than ten million sextillion universes in our group."

What can one say to that? Jacob went on, "Those universes are our next-door neighbors, one rotation or one translation away. But if one includes *combinations* of rotation *and* translation—think of a hyperplane slicing through superhypercontinua not at the point of here—now—the total becomes indenumerable. Not infinity—infinity has no meaning. Uncountable. Not subject to manipulation by mathematics thus far invented. Accessible to continua craft but no known way to count them."

"Pop—"

"Yes, Deety?"

"Maybe Aunt Hilda hit on something. Agnostic as you are, you nevertheless keep the Bible around as history and poetry and myth."

"Who said I was agnostic, my daughter?"

"Sorry, sir. I long ago reached that conclusion because you won't talk about it. Wrong of me. Lack of data never justifies a conclusion. But this key number—one-point-oh-three-one-four-four-plus times ten to its twenty-eighth power—perhaps that is the 'Number of the Beast.'"

"What do you mean, Deety?"

"That Revelation isn't history, it's not good poetry, and it's not myth. There must have been some reason for a large number of learned men to include it—while chucking out several dozen gospels. Why not make a first hypothesis with Occam's Razor and read it as what it purports to be? Prophecy."

"Hmm. The shelves under the stairs, next to Shakespeare. The King James version, never mind the other three."

Deety was back in a moment with a well-worn black book—which surprised me. I read the Bible for my own reasons but it never occurred to me that Jacob would. We always marry strangers.

"Here," said Deety. "Chapter thirteen, verse eighteen. 'Here is wisdom. Let him that hath understanding count the number of the beast: for it is the number of a man; and his number is Six hundred threescore and six.'"

"That can't be read as exponents, Deety."

"But this is a translation, Pop. Wasn't the original in Greek? I don't remember when exponents were invented but the Greek mathematicians of that time certainly understood powers. Suppose the original read 'Zeta, Zeta, Zeta!'—and those scholars, who weren't mathematicians, mistranslated it as six hundred and sixty-six?"

"Uh ... moondrift, daughter."

"Who taught me that the world is not only stranger than we imagine but stranger than we can imagine? Who has already taken me into two universes that are not this one ... and brought me safely home?"

"Wait a half!" Zebbie said. "You and Pop have already tried the time-space machine?"

"Didn't Pop tell you? We made one minimum translation. We didn't seem to have gone anywhere and Pop thought he had failed. Until I tried to look up a number in the phone book. No 'J' in the book. No 'J' in the Britannica. No 'J' in any dictionary. So we popped back in, and Pop returned the verniers to zero, and we got out, and the alphabet was back the way it ought to be and I stopped shaking. But our rotation was even more scary and we almost died. Out in space with blazing stars—but air was leaking out and Pop just barely put it back to zero before we passed out … and came to, back here in Snug Harbor."

"Jake," Zebbie said seriously, "that gadget has got to have more fail-safes, in series with deadman switches for homing." He frowned. "I'm going to keep my eye open for both numbers, six sixty-six and the long one. I trust Deety's hunches. Deety, where is the verse with the description of the Beast? It's somewhere in the middle of the chapter."

"Here. 'And I beheld another beast coming up out of the earth; and he had two horns like a lamb, and he spake as a dragon.'"

"Hmm—I don't know how dragons speak. But if something comes up out of the earth and has two horns … and I see or hear either number—I'm going to assume that he has a 'Black Hat' and try to do unto him before he does unto us. Deety, I'm peaceable by policy … but two near misses is too many. Next time I shoot first."

I would as lief Zebbie hadn't mentioned "Black Hats." Hard to believe that someone was trying to kill anyone as sweet and innocent and harmless as my darling Jacob. But they were—and we knew it.

I asked, "Where is this time machine? All I've seen is a claptrap."

" 'Caltrop,' Aunt Hilda. You're looking at the space-time machine."

"Huh? Where? Why aren't we in it and going somewhere fast? I don't want my husband killed; he's practically brand new. I expect to get years of wear out of him."

"Sharpie, stop the chatter," Zebbie put in. "It's on that bench, across the table from you."

"All I see is a portable sewing machine."

"That's it."

"What? How do you get inside? Or do you ride it like a broom?"

"Neither. You mount it rigidly in a vehicle—one airtight and watertight by strong preference. Pop had it mounted in his car—not quite airtight and now kaput. Pop and I are going to mount it in *Gay Deceiver*, which *is* airtight. With better fail-safes."

"*Much* better fail-safes, Zebbie," I agreed.

"They will be. I find that being married makes a difference. I used to worry about my own skin. Now I'm worried about Deety's. And yours. And Pop's. All four of us."

"Hear, hear!" I agreed. "All for one, and one for all!"

"Yup," Zebbie answered. "Us four, no more. Deety, when's lunch?"

— VII —

Deety

While Aunt Hilda and I assembled lunch, our men disappeared. They returned just in time to sit down. Zebadiah carried an intercom unit; Pop had a wire that he plugged in to a jack in the wall, then hooked to the intercom.

"Gentlemen, your timing is perfect; the work is all done," Aunt Hilda greeted them. "What is that?"

"A guest for lunch, my dearest," Pop answered. "Miss *Gay Deceiver*."

"Plenty for all," Aunt Hilda agreed. "I'll set another place." She did so; Zebadiah put the intercom on the fifth plate. "Does she take coffee or tea?"

"She's not programmed for either, Hilda," Zebadiah answered, "but I thank you on her behalf. Ladies, I got itchy about news from Singapore and Sumatra. So I asked my autopilot to report. Jake came along, then pointed out that he had spare cold circuits here and there, just in case—and this was a just-in-case. Gay is plugged to the garage end of that jack, and this is a voice-switched master-master intercom at this end. I can call Gay and she can call me if anything new comes in—and I increased her programming by reinstating the earlier programs, Logan and back home, for running retrieval of new data."

"I'll add an outlet in the basement," agreed Pop. "But, son, *this* is your home—not California."

"Well—"

"Don't fight it, Zebbie. This is *my* home since Jacob legalized me … and any step-son-in-law of mine is at home here; you heard Jacob say so. Right, Deety?"

"Of course," I agreed. "Aunt Hilda is housewife and I'm scullery maid. But Snug Harbor is my home, too, until Pop and Aunt Hilda kick me out into the snow—and that includes my husband."

"Not into snow, Deety," Aunt Hilda corrected me. "Jacob would insist on a sunny day; he's kind and gentle. But that would not leave you with no roof over your head. My California home—mine and Jacob's—has long been your home-from-home, and Zebbie has been dropping in for years, whenever he was hungry."

"I had better put my bachelor flat into the pot."

"Zebbie, you can't put Deety on your daybed. It's lumpy, Deety. Broken springs. Bruises. Zebbie, break your lease and send your furniture back to Goodwill."

"Sharpie, you're at it again. Deety, there is no daybed in my digs. An emperor-size bed big enough for three—six if they are well acquainted…. Pop, Snug Harbor continues to impress me. Did you use an architect?"

"Hrrumph! 'Architect' is a dirty word. I studied engineering. Architects copy each other's mistakes and call it 'Art.' Even Frank Lloyd Wright never understood what the Gilbreths were doing. His houses looked great from the outside—inside they were hideously inefficient. Dust collectors. Gloomy. Psych lab rat mazes. Pfui!"

"How about Neutra?"

"If he hadn't been hamstrung by building codes and union rules and zoning laws, Neutra could have been great. But people don't want efficient machines for living; they prefer to crouch in medieval hovels, as their flea-bitten forebears did. Cold, drafty, unsanitary, poor lighting, and no need for any of it."

"I respect your opinion, sir. Pop—three fireplaces … no chimneys. How? Why?"

"Zeb, I like fireplaces—and a few cords of wood can save your life in the mountains. But I see no reason to warm the outdoors or to call attention to the fact that we are in residence or to place trust in spark arresters in forest-fire country. Lighting a fire in a fireplace here automatically starts its exhaust fan. Smoke and particles are electrostatically precipitated. The precipitators are autoscrubbed when stack temperature passes twenty-five Celsius, dropping. Hot air goes through labyrinths under bathtubs and floors, then under other floors, thence into a rock heat-sink under the garage, a sink that drives the heat pump that serves the house. When flue gas finally escapes, at points distant from the house, it is so close to ambient temperature that only the most sensitive heat-seeker could sniff it. Thermal efficiency plus the security of being inconspicuous."

"But suppose you are snowed in so long that your power packs play out?"

"Franklin stoves in storage, stove pipe to match, stops in the walls removable from inside to receive thimbles for flue pipes."

"Pop," I inquired, "is this covered by Rule One? Or was Rule One abolished last night in Elko?"

"Eh? The chair must rule that it is suspended until Hilda ratifies or cancels it. Hilda my love, years back, Jane instituted Rule One—"

"I ratify it!"

"Thank you. But listen first. It applies to meals. No news broadcasts—"

"Pop," I again interrupted, "while Rule One is still in limbo—did *Gay Deceiver* have any news? I worry, I do!"

"Null retrievals, dear. With the amusing conclusion that you and I are still presumed to have died *twice*, but the news services do not appear to have noticed the discrepancy. However, Miss *Gay Deceiver* will interrupt if a bulletin comes in; Rule One is never invoked during emergencies. Zeb, do you want this rig in your bedroom at night?"

"I don't want it but should have it. Prompt notice might save our skins."

"We'll leave this here and parallel another into there, with gain stepped to wake you. Back to Rule One: no news broadcasts at meals, no newspapers. No shop talk, no business or financial matters, no discussion of ailments. No political discussion, no mention of taxes, or of foreign or domestic policy. Reading of fiction permitted *en famille*—not with guests present. Conversation limited to cheerful subjects—"

"No scandal, no gossip?" demanded Aunt Hilda.

"A matter of your judgment, dear. Cheerful gossip about friends and acquaintances, juicy scandal about people we do not like—fine! Now—do you wish to ratify, abolish, amend, or take under advisement?"

"I ratify it unchanged. Who knows some juicy scandal about someone we don't like?"

"I know an item about 'No Brain'—Doctor Neil Brain," Zebadiah offered.

"Give!"

"I got this from a reliable source but can't prove it."

"Irrelevant as long as it's juicy. Go ahead, Zebbie."

"Well, a certain zaftig coed told this on herself. She tried to give her all to 'Brainy' in exchange for a passing grade in the general math course necessary to *any* degree on our campus. It is rigged to permit prominent but stupid athletes to graduate. Miss Zaftig was flunking it, which takes exceptional talent.

"So she arranged an appointment with the department head—'Brainy'—and made her quid-pro-quo clear. He could give her horizontal tutoring then and there or in her apartment or his apartment or in a motel and she would pay for it or whenever and wherever he chose. But she *had* to pass."

"Happens on every campus, son," Pop told him.

"I haven't reached the point. She blabbed the story—not angry but puzzled. She says that she was unable to get her intention over to him (which seems impossible, I've seen this young woman). 'Brainy' didn't accept, didn't refuse, wasn't offended, didn't seem to understand. He told her that she had better talk to her instructor about getting tutoring and a re-exam. Now Miss Zaftig is circulating the story that Prof 'No Brain' must be a eunuch or a robot. Totally sexless."

"He's undoubtedly stupid," Aunt Hilda commented. "But I've never met a man I couldn't get that point across to, if I tried. Even if he was uninterested in my fair carcass. I've never tried with Professor Brain because I'm not interested in *his* carcass."

"Then, Hilda my darling, why did you invite him to your party?"

"*What?* Because of your note, Jacob. I don't refuse you favors."

"But, Hilda, I don't understand. When I talked to you by telephone, I asked you to invite Zeb—under the impression that he was his cousin Zebulon—and I did say that two or three others from the department of mathematics might make it less conspicuously an arranged meeting. But I didn't mention Doctor Brain. And I did *not* write."

"Jacob—I *have* your note. In California. On your university stationery with your name printed on it."

Professor Burroughs shook his head, looked sad. Zebadiah Carter said, "Sharpie—handwritten or typed?"

"Typed. But it was signed! Wait a moment, let me think. It has my name and address down in the lower left. Jacob's name was typed, too, but it was signed 'Jake.' Uh … 'My dear Hilda, A hasty PS to my phone call of yesterday— Would you be so kind as to include Doctor Neil O. Brain, chairman of mathematics? I don't know what possessed me that I forgot to mention him. Probably the pleasure of hearing your dear voice.

" 'Deety sends her love, as do I. Ever yours, Jacob J. Burroughs' with 'Jake' signed above the typed name."

Zebadiah said to me, " 'Watson, you know my methods.' "

"Certainly, my dear Holmes. A 'Black Hat.' In Logan."

"We knew that. What *new* data?"

"Well … Pop made that call from the house; I remember it. So somebody has a tap on our phone. Had, I mean; the fire probably destroyed it."

"A recording tap. The purpose of that fire may have been to destroy it and other evidence. For now we know that the 'Blokes in the Black Hats' knew that your father—and you, but it's Pop they are after—was in California last evening. After 'killing' him in California, they destroyed all they could in Utah. Professor, I predict that we will learn that your office was robbed last night—any papers on six-dimensional spaces."

Pop shrugged. "They wouldn't find much. I had postponed my final paper after the humiliating reception my preliminary paper received. I worked on it only at home, or here, and moved notes made in Logan to our basement here each time we came down."

"Any missing here?"

"I am certain this place has not been entered. Not that papers would matter; I have it in my head. The continua apparatus has not been touched."

"Zebadiah, is Doctor Brain a 'Black Hat?' " I asked.

"I don't know, Deety. He may be a stooge in their hire. But he's part of their plot, or they would not have risked forging a letter to put him into Hilda's house. Jake, how difficult is it to steal your professional stationery?"

"Not difficult. I don't keep a secretary; I send for a stenographer when I need one. I seldom lock my office when I'm on campus."

"Deety, can you scrounge pen and paper? I want to see how Jake signs 'Jake.' "

"Sure." I fetched them. "Pop's signature is easy; I often sign it. I hold his power of attorney."

"It's the simple signatures that are hardest to forge well enough to fool a handwriting expert. But their scheme did not require fooling an expert—phrasing the note was more difficult … since Hilda accepted it as ringing true."

"It does ring true, son; it is very like what I would have said had I written such a note to Hilda."

"The forger probably has read many of your letters and listened to many of your conversations. Jake, will you write 'Jake' four or five times, the way you sign a note to a friend?"

Pop did so; my husband studied the specimens. "Normal variations." Zebadiah then signed "Jake" about a dozen times, looked at his work, took a fresh sheet, signed "Jake" once, passed it to Aunt Hilda. "Well, Sharpie?"

Aunt Hilda studied it. "It wouldn't occur to me to question it—on Jacob's stationery under a note that sounded like his phrasing. Where do we stand now?"

"Stuck in the mud. But we have added data. At least three are involved, two 'Black Hats' and Doctor Brain, who may or may not be a 'Black Hat.' He is, at minimum, a hired hand, an unwitting stooge, or a puppet they can move around like a chessman.

"While two plus 'Brainy' is minimum, it is not the most probable number. This scheme was not whipped up overnight. It involves arson, forgery, booby-trapping a car, wiretapping, theft, and secret communications between points widely separated, with coordinated criminal actions at each end—and it may involve doing in my cousin Zebulon. We can assume that the 'Black Hats' know that I am not the Zeb Carter who is the n-dimensional geometer; I'm written off as a bystander who got himself killed.

"Which doesn't bother them. These playful darlings would swat a fly with a sledgehammer, or cure a cough with a guillotine. They are smart, organized, efficient, and vicious—and the only clue is an interest in six-dimensional non-Euclidean geometry.

"We don't have a glimmer as to 'who'—other than Doctor Brain, whose role is unclear. But, Jake, I think I know 'why'—and that will lead us to 'who.'"

"*Why*, Zebadiah?" I demanded.

"Princess, your father could have worked on endless other branches of mathematics and they would not have bothered him. But he happened—I don't mean chance; I don't believe in 'chance' in this sense—he worked on the one variety of the endless possible number of geometries—the *only* one that *correctly* describes how space-time is put together. Having found it, because he is a genius in both theory and practice, he saw that it was a means by which to build a simple craft—amazingly simple, the greatest invention since the wheel—a space-time craft that offers access to all universes to the full Number of the Beast. Plus undenumerable variations of each of those many universes.

"We have one advantage."

"I don't see any advantage! They're shooting at my Jacob!"

"One strong advantage, Sharpie. The 'Black Hats' know that Jake has worked out this mathematics. They *don't* know that he has built his space-time tail-twister; they think he has just put symbols on paper. They tried to discredit his work and were successful. They tried to kill him and barely missed. They probably think Jake is dead—and it seems likely that they have killed Ed. But they *don't* know about Snug Harbor."

"Why do you say that, Zeb? Oh, I hope they do not!— But why do you feel sure?"

"Because these blokes aren't fooling. They blew up your car and burned your flat; what would they do here—if they knew? An A-bomb?"

"Son, do you think that criminals can lay hands on atomic weapons?"

"Jake, these aren't *criminals*. A 'criminal' is a member of the subset of the larger set 'human beings.' These creatures are not human."

"*Eh?* Zeb, your reasoning escapes me."

"Deety. Run it through the computer. The one between your ears."

I did not answer; I just sat and thought. After several minutes of unpleasant thoughts I said, "Zebadiah, the 'Black Hats' don't know about the apparatus in our basement."

"Conclusive assumption," my husband agreed, "because we are still alive."

"They are determined to destroy a new work in mathematics ... and to kill the brain that produced it."

"A probability approaching unity," Zebadiah again agreed.

"Because it can be used to travel among the universes."

"Conclusive corollary," my husband noted.

"For this purpose, human beings fall into three groups. Those not interested in mathematics more complex than that needed to handle money, those who know a bit about other mathematics, and a quite small third group who could understand the possibilities."

"Yes."

"But our race does not know *anything* of other universes so far as I know."

"They don't. Necessary assumption."

"But that third group would not try to stop an attempt to travel among the universes. They would wait with intellectual interest to see how it turned out. They might believe or disbelieve or suspend judgment. But they would *not* oppose; they would be delighted if my father succeeded. The joy of intellectual discovery—the mark of a true scientist."

I sighed and added, "I see no other grouping. Save for a few sick people, psychotic, these three subsets complete the set. Our opponents are not psychotic; they are intelligent, crafty, and organized."

"As we all know too well," Zebadiah echoed.

"Therefore our opponents are not human beings. They are alien intelligences from elsewhere."

"Or elsewhen," muttered Zebadiah.

I sighed again and kept my mouth shut. Being an oracle is a no-good profession!

"Sharpie, can you kill?"

"Kill whom, Zebbie? Or what?"

"Can you kill to protect Jake?"

"You bet your frimpin' life I'll kill to protect Jacob!"

"I won't ask you, Princess; I know Dejah Thoris." Zebadiah went on, "That's the situation, ladies. We have the most valuable man on this planet to protect. We don't know from what. Jake, your bodyguard musters two Amazons, one small, one medium-large, both probably knocked up, and one Cowardly Lion. I'd hire the Dorsai if I knew their PO Box. Or the Gray Lensman and all his pals. But we are all there are and we'll try! *Avete, alieni, nos morituri vos spernimus!* Let's break out that champagne."

"My captain, do you think we should?" I asked. "I'm frightened."

"We should. I'm no good for more work today, and neither is Jake. Tomorrow we'll start installing the gadget in *Gay Deceiver*, do rewiring and reprogramming so that she will work for any of us. Meanwhile we need a couple of laughs and a night's sleep. What better time to drink life to the dregs than when we know that any hour may be our last?"

Aunt Hilda punched Zebadiah in the ribs. "Yer dern tootin', buster! I'm going to get giggle happy and make a fool of myself and then take my man and put him to sleep with Old Mother Sharpie's Time-Tested Nostrum. Deety, I prescribe the same for you."

I suddenly felt better. "Check, Aunt Hilda! Captain John Carter always wins. 'Cowardly Lion' my foot! Who is Pop? The Little Wizard?"

"I think he is."

"Could be. Pop, will you open the bubbly? I always hurt my thumbs."

"Right away, Deety. I mean 'Dejah Thoris, royal consort of the Warlord.'"

"No need to be formal, Pop. This is going to be an informal party. Very! Pop! Do I have to keep my pants on?"

"Ask your husband. You're *his* problem now."

— VIII —

Hilda

In my old age, sucking my gums in front of the fire and living over my misdeeds, I'd remembered the next few days as the happiest in my life. I'd had three honeymoons before, one with each of my term-contract husbands: two had been good, one had been okay and (eventually) very lucrative. But my honeymoon with Jacob was heavenly.

The whiff of danger sharpened the joy. Jacob seemed unworried, and Zebbie had hunches, like a horseplayer. Seeing that Zebbie was relaxed, Deety got over being jumpy—and I never was, as I hoped to end like a firecracker, not linger on, ugly, helpless, useless ....

A spice of danger adds zest to life. Even during a honeymoon—especially during a honeymoon.

An odd honeymoon. Not a group marriage but two twosomes that were one family, comfortable each with the others. I dropped most of my own sparky-bitch ways, and Zebbie sometimes called me "Hilda" rather than "Sharpie."

Jacob and I moved into marriage like ham and eggs. Jacob is not tall (one-seventy-eight centimeters) (but tall compared with my scant one-fifty-two) and his hairline recedes and he has a paunch from years at a desk—but he looks just right to me. If I wanted to look at male beauty, I could always look at Deety's giant.

I did not decide, when Zebbie came on campus, to make a pet of him for his looks but for his veering sense of humor. But if there was ever a man who could have played the role of John Carter, Warlord of Mars, it was Zebadiah Carter whose middle name just happens to be

62

"John." Indoors with clothes and wearing his fake horn-rims he looks awkward, too big, clumsy. I did not realize that he was beautiful and graceful until the first time he used my pool.

Outdoors at Snug Harbor, wearing little or no clothes, Zebbie looked at home—a mountain lion in grace and muscle. An incident one later afternoon showed me how much he was like the Warlord of Mars. Those old stories were familiar to me. My father had acquired the Ballantine Del Rey paperback reissues; they were around the house when I was a little girl. Once I learned to read, I read everything, and vastly preferred Barsoom stories to "girls'" books given to me for birthdays and Christmas. Thuvia was the heroine I identified with. I'd resolved to change my name to Thuvia when I was old enough. Then, when I was eighteen, I did not consider it. I had always been "Hilda"; a new name held no attraction.

I was responsible in part for Deety's name, one that embarrassed her until she discovered that her husband liked it. Jacob had wanted to name his daughter "Dejah Thoris" (Jacob looks like and *is* a professor, but he is incurably romantic). Jane had misgivings. I told her, "Don't be a chump, Janie. If your man wants something, and you can accommodate him with no grief, give it to him! Do you want him to love this child or to resent her?" Jane looked thoughtful and "Doris Anne" became "Dejah Thoris" at christening, then "Deety" before she could talk—which satisfied everyone.

We settled into a routine: up early every day; our men worked on instruments and wires and things and installing the time-space widget into *Gay Deceiver's* gizzard, while Deety and I gave the housework a lick and a promise (our mountain home needed little attention—more of Jacob's genius), then Deety and I got busy on a technical matter that Deety could do with some help from me.

I'm not much use for technical work, biology being the only thing I studied in depth, and never finished my degree. This was amplified by almost six thousand hours as volunteer nurse's aide in our campus medical center and I took courses that make me an uncertified nurse or medical tech or even jackleg paramedic—I don't shriek at the sight of blood and can clean up vomit without a qualm and would not hesitate to fill in as scrub nurse. Being a campus widow with too much money is fun but not soul filling. I like to feel that I've paid rent on the piece of earth I'm using.

Besides that, I have a smattering of everything from addiction to the printed page, plus attending campus lectures that sound intriguing ... then sometimes auditing a related course. I audited Descriptive Astronomy, took the final as if for credit—got an "A." I had even figured a cometary orbit correctly, to my surprise (and the professor's).

I can wire a doorbell or clean out a stopped-up soil pipe with a plumber's "snake"—but if it's really technical, I hire specialists.

So Hilda can help but usually can't do the job alone. *Gay Deceiver* had to be reprogrammed—and Deety, who does not look like a genius, is one. Jacob's daughter *should* be a genius and her mother had an IQ that startled even me, her closest friend. I ran across it while helping poor grief-stricken Jacob to decide what to save, what to burn. (I burned unflattering pictures, useless papers, and clothes. A dead person's clothes should be given away or burned; *nothing* should be kept that does not inspire happy memories. I cried a bit and that saved Jacob and Deety from having to cry later.)

We all held private duo licenses; Zebbie, as Captain Z. J. Carter, USASR, held "command" rating as well—he told us that his space rating was largely honorary, just some freefall time and one landing of a shuttle. Zebbie is mendacious, untruthful, and tells fibs; I got a chance to sneak a look at his aerospace log and shamelessly took it. He had logged more than he claimed in one exchange tour with Australia. Someday I'm going to sit on his chest and make him tell Mama Hilda the truth. Should be interesting ... if I can sort out fact from fiction. I do *not* believe his story about intimate relations with a female kangaroo.

Zebbie and Jacob decided that we all must be able to control *Gay Deceiver* all four ways: on the road, in the air, in trajectory (she's not a spaceship but can make high-trajectory jumps), and in space-time, i.e. among the universes to the Number of the Beast, plus variants impossible to count.

I had fingers crossed about being able to learn that, but both men assured me that they had worked out a fail-safe that would get me out of a crunch if I ever had to do it alone.

Part of the problem lay in the fact that *Gay Deceiver* was a one-man girl; her doors unlocked only to her master's voice or to his thumbprint, or to a tapping code if he were shy both voice and right thumb; Zeb tended to plan ahead. "Outwitting Murphy's Law," he called it, "Anything that can go wrong, will go wrong." (Grandma called it "The Butter-Side-Down Rule.")

First priority was to introduce us to *Gay Deceiver*—teach her that all four voices and right thumbprints were acceptable.

That took a couple of hours, with Deety helping Zebbie. The tapping code took even less, it being based on an old military cadence— its trickiness being that a thief would be unlikely to guess that this car would open if tapped a certain way and in guessing the correct cadence. Zebbie called the cadence "Drunken Soldier." Jacob said that it was "Bumboat." Deety claimed that its title was "Pay Day," because she had heard it from Jane's grandfather.

Our men conceded that she must be right, as she had words for it. Her words included "Drunken Sailor" instead of "Drunken Soldier"— plus both "Pay Day" and "Bumboat."

Introductions taken care of, Zeb dug out Gay's anatomy; one volume, her body, and one, her brain. He handed the latter to Deety, took the other into our basement. The next two days were easy for me, hard for Deety. I held lights and made notes on a clipboard while she studied that book and frowned and got smudged and sweaty getting herself into impossible positions and once she cursed in a fashion that would have caused Jane to scold. She added, "Aunt Nanny Goat, your step-son-in-law has done things to this mass of spaghetti that no decent computer should put up with! It's a bastard hybrid."

"You shouldn't call Gay 'it,' Deety. And she's not a bastard."

"She can't hear us; I've got her ears unhooked—except that piece that is monitoring news retrieval programs—and that goes through this wire to that jack in the wall; she can talk with Zebadiah only in the basement now. Oh, I'm sure she was a nice girl until that big ape of mine raped her. Aunt Hilda, don't worry about hurting Gay's feelings; she hasn't any. This is an idiot as computers go. Any one-horse college and most high schools own or share time in computers much more complex. This one is primarily cybernetics, an autopilot plus limited digital capacity and limited storage. But the mods Zebadiah has tacked on make it more than an autopilot but not a general-purpose computer. A misbegotten hybrid. It has far more random-number options than it needs and it has extra functions that IBM never dreamed of."

"Deety, why are you taking off cover plates? I thought you were strictly a programmer? Software. Not a mechanic."

"I *am* strictly a software mathematician. I wouldn't attempt to modify this monster even on written orders from my lovable-but-sneaky husband. But how in the name of Allah can a software hack think about simplification analysis for program if she doesn't know the circuitry? The first half of this book shows what this autopilot was manufactured to do … and the second half, the Xeroxed pages, show the follies Zebadiah has seduced her into. This bleedin' bundle of chips now speaks three logic languages, interfaced—when it was built to use only one. But it won't accept *any* of them until it has been wheedled with Zebadiah's double-talk. Even then it rarely answers a code phrase with the same answer twice in a row. What does it say in answer to: 'You're a Smart Girl, Gay.'?"

"I remember. 'Boss, I bet you tell that to all the girls. Over.'"

"Sometimes. Oftenest, as that answer is weighted to come up three times as often as any of the others. But listen to these:

" 'Zeb, I'm so smart I scare myself.'

" 'Then why did you turn me down for that raise?'

" 'Never mind the compliments! Take your hand off my knee!'

" 'Not so loud, dear. I don't want my boyfriend to hear.'

"—and there are more. There are at least four answers to any of Zebadiah's code phrases. *He* uses just one list, but the autopilot answers several ways for each of his phrases—and all any of them mean is either 'Roger' or 'Null program; rephrase.'"

"I like the idea. Fun."

"Well … I do myself. I animize a computer; I think of them as people … and this semirandom answer list makes *Gay Deceiver* feel much more alive … when she isn't. Not even versatile compared with a ground-based computer. But—" Deety gave a quick smile. "I'm going to hand my husband some surprises."

"How, Deety?"

"You know how he says, 'Good morning, Gay. How are you?' when we sit down for breakfast."

"Yes. I like it. Friendly. She usually answers, 'I'm fine, Zeb.'"

"Yes. It's a test code. It orders the autopilot to run a self-check throughout and to report any running instruction. Which takes less than a millisecond. If he didn't get that or an equivalent answer, he would rush straight here to find out what's wrong. But I'm going to add another answer. Or more."

"I thought you refused to modify anything."

"Aunt Hillbilly, this is *software*, not hardware. I'm authorized and directed to amplify the answers to include all of us, by name for each of our voices. That is programming, elementary. You say good morning to this gadget and it will—when I'm finished—answer you and call you either 'Hilda' or 'Mrs. Burroughs.'"

"Oh, let her call me 'Hilda.'"

"All right, but let her call you 'Mrs. Burroughs' now and then for variety."

"Well ... all right. Keep her a personality."

"I could even have her call you—low weighting!—'Nanny Goat.'"

I guffawed. "Do, Deety, please do. But I want to be around to see Jacob's face."

"You will be; it won't be programmed to answer that way to any voice but yours. Just don't say, 'Good morning, Gay' unless Pop *is* listening. But here's one for my husband: Zebadiah says, 'Good morning, Gay. How are you?'—and the speaker answers, 'I'm fine, Zeb. But your fly is unzipped and your eyes are bloodshot. Are you hungover *again?*'"

Deety is so solemn and yet playful. "Do it, dear! Poor Zebbie—who drinks least of any of us. But he might not be wearing anything zippered."

"Zebadiah always wears something at meals. Even his underwear shorts are zippered. He dislikes elastic."

"But he'll recognize your voice, Deety."

"Nope. Because it will be *your* voice—modified."

And it was. I'm contralto about the range of the actress—or girl-friend—who recorded *Gay Deceiver's* voice originally. I don't think my voice has her sultry, bedroom quality but I'm a natural mimic. Deety borrowed a wigglescope—oscilloscope?—from her father, my Jacob, and I practiced until my patterns for *Gay Deceiver's* original repertoire matched hers well enough—Deety said she could not tell them apart without close checking.

— IX —

Deety

Aunt Hilda and I finished reprogramming in the time it took Zebadiah and Pop to design and make the fail-safes and other mods needed to turn *Gay Deceiver*, with the time-space widget installed, into a continua traveler—which included placing the back seats twenty centimeters farther back (for legroom) after they had been pulled out to place the widget abaft the bulkhead and weld it to the shell. The precessing controls and triple verniers were remoted to the driver's instrument board—with one voice control for the widget, all others manual.

If any of our voices said, "*Gay Deceiver*, take us home!" car and passengers would instantly return to Snug Harbor.

I trust my Pop. He brought us home safe twice, doing it with *no* fail-safes and no deadman switch. The latter paralleled the "Take us home!" voice order, was normally clamped closed and covered—but could be uncovered and held in a fist, closed. There were other fail-safes for temperature, pressure, air, radar collision course, and other dangers. If we wound up inside a star or planet, none of this could save us, but it is easy to prove that the chances of falling downstairs and breaking your neck are enormously higher than the chance of co-occupying space with other matter in our native universe—space is plentiful, mass is scarce. We hoped that this would be true of other universes.

No way ahead of time to check on the Number-of-the-Beast spaces, but, "The cowards never started and the weaklings died on the way." None of us ever mentioned *not* trying to travel the universes.

Besides, our home planet had turned unfriendly. We didn't discuss "Black Hats" but we all knew that they were still there, and that we remained alive by lying doggo and letting the world think we were dead.

We ate breakfast better each morning after hearing *Gay Deceiver* offer "null report" on news retrievals. Zebadiah, I am fairly certain, had given up his cousin for dead. I feel sure Zebadiah would have gone to Sumatra to follow a lost hope, were it not that he had acquired a wife and a prospective child. I missed my next period; so did Hilda. Our men toasted our not-yet-bulging bellies; Hilda and I smugly resolved to be good girls, yes, sir!—and careful. Hilda joined my morning toning up, and the men joined us the first time they caught us at it.

Zebadiah did not need it but seemed to enjoy it. Pop brought his waistline down five centimeters in one week.

Shortly after that toast, Zebadiah pressure-tested *Gay Deceiver's* shell—four atmospheres inside her and a pressure gauge sticking out through a fitting in her shell.

There being little we could do while our space-time rover was sealed, we knocked off early. "Swim, anybody?" I asked. Snug Harbor doesn't have a city-type pool, and a mountain stream is too *cooold*. Pop had fixed that when he concealed our spring. Overflow was piped underground to a clump of bushes and thereby created a "natural" mountain rivulet that passed near the house; then Pop had made use of a huge fallen boulder, plus biggish ones, to create a pool, one that filled and spilled. He had done work with pigments in concrete to make this look like an accident of water flow.

This makes Pop sound like Paul Bunyan. Pop *could* have built Snug Harbor with his own hands. But Spanish-speaking labor from Nogales built the underground and assembled the prefab shell of the cabin. An air crane fetched parts and materials from an Albuquerque engineering company Jane had bought for Pop through a front—lawyers in Dallas. The company's manager drove the air crane himself, having had it impressed on him that this was for a rich client of the law firm, and that it would be prudent to do the job and forget it. Pop bossed the work in TexMex, with help from his secretary—me— Spanish being one language I had picked for my doctorate.

Laborers and mechanics never got a chance to pinpoint where they were, but they were well paid, well fed, comfortably housed in prefabs brought in by crane, and the backbreaking labor was done by power—who cares what "locos gringos" do? Two pilots had to know where we were building, but they homed in on a radar beacon that is no longer there.

"Blokes in Black Hats" had nothing to do with this secrecy; it was jungle caution I had learned from Mama: never let the revenooers know anything. Pay cash, keep your lips closed, put nothing through banks that does not appear later in tax returns—pay taxes greater than your apparent standard of living and declare income accordingly. We had been audited three times since Mama died; each time the government returned a small "overpayment"—I was building a reputation of being stupid and honest.

My inquiry of "Swim, anybody?" was greeted with silence. Then Pop said, "Zeb, your wife is too energetic. Deety, later the water will be warmer and the trees will give us shade. Then we can walk slowly down to the pool. Zeb?"

"I agree, Jake. I need to conserve ergs."

"Nap?"

"I don't have the energy to take one. What were you saying this morning about reengineering the system?"

Aunt Hilda looked startled. "I thought Miss *Gay Deceiver* was already engineered? Are you thinking of changing everything?"

"Take it easy, Sharpie darlin'. *Gay Deceiver* is finished. A few things to stow that have been weighed and their moment arms calculated."

I could have told her. In the course of figuring what could be stowed in every nook and cranny and what that would do to Gay's balance, I had discovered that my husband had a highly illegal laser cannon. I said nothing, merely included its mass and distance from optimum center of weight in my calculations. I sometimes wonder which of us is the outlaw: Zebadiah or me? Most males have an unhealthy tendency to obey laws. But that concealed L-cannon made me wonder.

"Why not leave well enough alone?" Aunt Hilda demanded. "Jacob and God know I'm happy here … But You All Know Why We Should Not Stay Here Longer Than We Must."

"We weren't talking about *Gay Deceiver*; Jake and I were discussing reengineering the solar system."

"The *solar system!* What's wrong with it the way it is?"

"Lots of things," Zebadiah told Aunt Hilda. "It's untidy. Real estate going to waste. This tired old planet is crowded and sort o' worn in spots. True, industry in orbit and power from orbit have helped, and both Lagrange-Four and -Five have self-supporting populations;

anybody who invested in space stations early enough made a pile." (Including Pop, Zebadiah!) "But these are minor compared with what *can* be done—and this planet is in worse shape each year. Jake's six-dimensional principle can change that."

"Move people into another universe? Would they go?"

"We weren't thinking of that, Hilda. We're trying to apply Clarke's Law."

"I don't recall it. Maybe it was while I was out with mumps."

"Arthur C. Clarke," Pop told her. "Great man—too bad he was liquidated in The Purge. Clarke defined how to make a great discovery or create a key invention. Study what the most respected authorities agree can *not* be done—then do it. My continua craft is a godchild of Clarke via his Law. His insight inspired my treatment of six-dimensional continua. But this morning Zeb added corollaries."

"Jake, don't kid the ladies. I asked a question; you grabbed the ball and ran."

"Uh, we heterodyned. Hilda, you know that the time-space traveler doesn't require power."

"I'm afraid I don't know, darling man. Why were you installing power packs in *Gay Deceiver?*"

"Auxiliary uses. So that you won't have to cook over an open fire, for example."

"But the pretzel bender doesn't use power," agreed Zebadiah. "Don't ask why. I did, and Jake started writing equations in Sanskrit and I got a headache."

"It doesn't use power, Aunt Hilda," I agreed. "Just parasitic power. A few microwatts so that the gyros never slow down, milliwatts for instrument readouts and for controls—but the widget itself uses none."

"What happened to the law of conservation of energy?"

"Sharpie," my husband answered, "as a fairish mechanic, an amateur electron pusher, and as a bloke who has herded unlikely junk through the sky, I never worry about theory as long as machinery does what it is supposed to do. I worry when a machine turns and bites me. That's why I specialize in fail-safes and backups and triple redundancy. I try *never* to get a machine sore at me. There's no theory for that but every engineer knows it."

"Hilda my beloved, the law of conservation of mass—energy is not broken by our continua craft; it is simply not relevant to it. Once Zeb understood that—"

"I didn't say I understood it."

"Well ... once Zeb stipulated that, he raised interesting questions. For example: Jupiter doesn't need Ganymede—"

"Whereas Venus does. Although Titan might be better."

"Mmm ... possible."

"Yes. Make an inhabitable base more quickly. But the urgent problem, Jake, is to seed Venus, move atmosphere to Mars, put both of them through forced aging. Then respot them. Earth-Sol Trojan points?"

"Certainly. We've had millions of years of evolution this distance from the Sun. We had best plan on living neither closer nor farther. With careful attention to stratospheric protection. But I still have doubts about anchoring in the Venerian crust. We wouldn't want to lose the planet on *tau-axis*."

"Mere R&D, Jake. Calculate pressures and temperatures; beef up the vehicle accordingly—spherical, save for exterior anchors—then apply a jigger factor of four. With automatic controls quintuply redundant. Catch it when it comes out and steady it down in Earth's orbit, sixty degrees trailing—and start selling subdivisions the size of old Spanish land grants. Jake, we should gather enough mass to create new Earths at *all* Trojan points, a hexagon around the Sun. Five brand-new Earths would give the race room enough to breed. On this maiden voyage, let's keep our eyes open."

Aunt Hilda looked at Zebadiah with horror. "Zebbie! Creating planets indeed!"

"Step-mother-in-law, these things Jake and I have been discussing are practical—once we thought about the fact that the space-time twister uses no power. Move anything anywhere—all spaces, all times. I add the plural because at first I could not see what Jake had in mind when he spoke of forced aging of a planet. Rotate Venus into the tau-axis, fetch it back along teh-axis, reinsert it centuries—or millennia—older at this point in t-axis. Perhaps translate it a year or so into the future—our future—so as to be ready for it when it returns, all sweet and green and beautiful and ready to grow children and puppies and butterflies. Terraformed but virginal."

A bit later, Zebadiah, sprawled out, looked up over the fireplace. "Pop, you were in the Navy?"

"No—Army. If you count 'chair-borne infantry.' They handed me a commission for having a doctorate in mathematics, told me they needed me for ballistics. Then I spent my whole tour as a personnel officer, signing papers."

"Standard Operating Procedure. That's a navy sword and belt up there. Thought it might be yours."

"It's Deety's—belonged to Jane's Grandfather Rodgers. I have a dress saber. Belonged to my dad, who gave it to me when the army took me. Dress blues, too. I took them with me, never had occasion to wear either." Pop got up and went into his—their—bedroom, calling back, "I'll show you the saber."

My husband said to me, "Deety, would you mind my handling your sword?"

"My captain, that sword is yours."

"Heavens, dear, I can't accept an heirloom."

"If my Warlord will not permit his princess to gift him with a sword, he can leave it where it is! I've been wanting to give you a wedding present—and did not realize that I had the perfect gift for Captain John Carter."

"My apologies, Dejah Thoris. I accept and will keep it bright. I will defend my princess with it against all enemies."

"Helium is proud to accept. If you make a cradle of your hands, I can stand in them and reach it down."

Zebadiah grasped me, a hand above each knee, and I was suddenly three meters tall. Sword and belt were on hooks; I lifted them down, and myself was placed down. My husband stood straight while I buckled it around him—then he dropped to one knee and kissed my hand.

My husband is mad north-northwest but his madness suits me. I got tears in my eyes, which Deety doesn't do much but Dejah Thoris seems prone to, since John Carter made her his.

Pop and Aunt Hilda watched—then imitated, including (I saw!) tears in Hilda's eyes after she buckled on Pop's saber, when he knelt and kissed her hand.

Zebadiah drew sword, tried its balance, sighted along its blade. "Handmade and balanced close to the hilt. Deety, your great-grandfather paid a pretty penny for this. It's an honest weapon."

"I don't think he knew what it cost. It was presented to him."

"For good reason, I feel certain." Zebadiah stood back, went into hanging guard, made fast *moulinets* vertically, left and right, then horizontally clockwise and counterclockwise—suddenly dropped into swordsman's guard—lunged and recovered, fast as a striking cat.

I said softly to Pop, "Did you notice?"

Pop answered quietly. "Know saber. Sword, too."

Hilda said loudly, "Zebbie! You never told me you went to Heidelberg."

"You never asked, Sharpie. Around the Red Ox they called me 'The Scourge of the Neckar.'"

"What happened to your scars?"

"Never got any, dear. I hung around an extra year, hoping for one. But no one got through my guard—ever. Hate to think about how many German faces I carved into checkerboards."

"Zebadiah, was that where you took your doctorate?"

My husband grinned and sat down, still wearing sword. "No, another school."

"MIT?" inquired Pop.

"Hardly. Pop, this should stay in the family. I undertook to prove that a man can get a doctorate from a major university without knowing anything and without adding anything whatever to human knowledge."

"*I* think you have a degree in aerospace engineering," Pop said flatly.

"I'll concede that I have the requisite hours. I hold two degrees—a baccalaureate in humane arts ... meaning I squeaked through ... and a doctorate from an old and prestigious school—a Ph.D. in education."

"Zebadiah! You *wouldn't!*" (I was horrified.)

"But I did, Deety. To prove that degrees, *per se*, are worthless. Often they are honorifics of true scientists or learned scholars or inspired teachers. Much more frequently they are false faces for overeducated jackasses."

Pop said, "You'll get no argument from me, Zeb. A doctorate is a union card to get a tenured job. It does not mean that the holder thereof is wise or learned."

"Yes, sir. I was taught it at my grandfather's knee—my Grandfather Zachariah, the man responsible for the initial 'Z' in the names of his male descendants. Deety, his influence on me was so strong that I must explain him—no, that's impossible; I must tell about him in order to explain me ... and how I happened to take a worthless degree."

Hilda said, "Deety, he's pulling a long bow again."

"Quiet, woman. 'Get thee to a nunnery, go!'"

"I don't take orders from my step-son-in-law. Make that a monastery and I'll consider it."

I kept my blinkin' mouf shut. My husband's fibs entertained me. (If they were fibs.)

"Grandpa Zach was as cantankerous an old coot as you'll ever meet. Hated government, hated lawyers, hated civil servants, hated preachers, hated automobiles, public schools, and telephones, was contemptuous of most editors, most writers, most professors, most of almost anything. But he overtipped waitresses and porters and would go out of his way to avoid stepping on an insect.

"Grandpa had three doctorates: biochemistry, medicine, and law—and he regarded anyone who couldn't read Latin, Greek, Hebrew, French, and German as illiterate."

"Zebbie, can you read all those?"

"Fortunately for me, my grandfather had a stroke while filling out a tax form before he could ask me that question. I don't know Hebrew. I can read Latin, puzzle out Greek, speak and read French, read technical German, understand it in some accents, swear in Russian—very useful!—and speak an ungrammatical smattering of Spanish picked up in cantinas and from horizontal dictionaries.

"Grandpa would have classed me as subliterate as I don't do any of these well—and I sometimes split infinitives, which would have infuriated him. He practiced forensic medicine, medical jurisprudence, was an expert witness in toxicology, pathology, and traumatology, bullied judges, terrorized lawyers, medical students, and law students. He once threw a tax assessor out of his office and required him to return with a search warrant setting forth in detail its constitutional limitations. He regarded the income tax and the Seventeenth Amendment and the direct primary as signs of the decay of the Republic."

"How did he feel about the Nineteenth?"

"Hilda, Grandpa Zach supported female suffrage. I remember hearing him say that if women were so dad-burned foolish as to want to assume the burden, they should be allowed to—they couldn't do the country more harm than men had. 'Votes for Women' didn't annoy him but nine thousand other things did. He lived at a slow simmer, always ready to break into a rolling boil.

"He had one hobby: collecting steel engravings."

"Steel engravings?" I repeated.

"Of dead presidents, my princess. Especially of McKinley, Cleveland, and Madison—but he didn't scorn those of Washington. He had that instinct for timing so necessary to a collector. In 1929 on Black Thursday he held not one share of common stock; instead he had sold short. When the 1933 Bank Holiday came along every old-dollar he owned, except current cash, was in Zurich in Swiss money. Eventually US citizens were forbidden by 'emergency' decree to own gold even abroad.

"Grandpa Zach ducked into Canada, applied for Swiss citizenship, got it, and thereafter split his time between Europe and America, immune to inflation and the confiscatory laws that eventually caused us to knock three zeros off the old-dollar in creating the newdollar.

"So he died rich, in Locarno—beautiful place; I stayed with him two summers as a boy. His will was probated in Switzerland and the US Revenue Service could not touch it.

"Most of it was a trust with its nature known to his offspring before his death or I would not have been named Zebadiah.

"Female descendants got pro-rata shares of income with no strings attached but males had to have first names starting with 'Z'—and even that got them not one Swiss franc; there was a 'Root, hog, or die!' clause. Zachariah believed in taking care of daughters, but sons and grandsons had to go out and scratch, with no help from their fathers, until they had earned and saved on their own—or accumulated without going to jail—assets equal to one pro-rata share of the capital sum of the trust before they shared in the trust's income."

"Sexism," said Aunt Hilda. "Raw, unadulterated sexism. Any Fem-Lib gal would sneer at his dirty old money, on those terms."

"Would you have refused it, Sharpie?"

"*Me?* Zebbie dear, are you feverish? I would have both greedy hands out. I'm strong for women's rights but no fanatic. Sharpie wants to be pampered and that's what men are best at—their natural function."

"Pop, do you need help in coping with her?"

"No, son. I like pampering Hilda. I don't see you abusing my daughter."

"I don't dare; you told me she's vicious at karate."

(I am good at karate; Pop made sure that I learned all the dirty fighting possible.)

76

"On my graduation from high school my father had a talk with me. 'Zeb,' he told me. 'The time has come. I'll put you through any school you choose. Or you can take what you have saved, strike out on your own, and try to qualify for a share in your grandfather's will. Suit yourself, I shan't influence you.'

"Folks, I had to think. My father's younger brother was past forty and *still* hadn't qualified. The size of the trust made a pro-rata of its assets amount to a requirement that a male descendant had to get rich on his own—well-to-do at least—whereupon he was suddenly twice as rich. But with over half of this country's population living on the taxes of the lesser number it is not as easy to get rich as it was in Grandpa's day.

"Turn down a paid-for education at Princeton, or MIT? Or go out and try to get rich with nothing but a high school education?—I hadn't learned much in high school; I had majored in girls.

"So I had to think hard and long. Almost ten seconds. I left home next day with one suitcase and a pitiful sum of money.

"Wound up on campus that had two things to recommend it: an Aerospace ROTC that would pick up part of my expenses, and a Phys. Ed. department willing to award me a jockstrap scholarship in exchange for daily bruises and contusions, plus all-out effort whenever we played. I took the deal."

"What did you play?" asked my father.

"Football, basketball, and track—they would have demanded more had they been able to figure a way to do it."

"I had thought you were going to mention fencing."

"No, that's another story. These did not quite close the gap. So I also waited tables for meals—food so bad the cockroaches ate out. But that closed the gap, and I added to it by tutoring in mathematics. That gave me my start toward piling up money to qualify."

I asked, "Did tutoring math pay enough to matter? I tutored math before Mama died; the hourly rate was low."

"Not *that* sort of tutoring, Princess. I taught prosperous young optimists not to draw to inside straights, and that stud poker is not a game of chance, but that craps is, controlled by mathematical laws that cannot be flouted with impunity. To quote Grandfather Zachariah, 'A man who bets on greed and dishonesty won't be wrong too often.' There is an amazingly high percentage of greedy people and it is even easier to win from a dishonest gambler than it is from an honest one … and neither is likely to know the odds at craps, especially side bets, or all of the odds in poker, in particular how odds change according to the number of players, where one is seated in relation to the dealer, and how to calculate changes as cards are exposed in stud.

"That was also how I quit drinking, my darling, except for special celebrations. In every 'friendly' game some players contribute, some take a profit; a player determined to take a profit must be neither drunk nor tired. Pop, the shadows are growing long—I don't think anybody wants to know how I got a worthless doctorate."

"I do!" I put in.

"Me, too!" echoed Aunt Hilda.

"Son, you're outvoted."

"Okay. Two years active duty after I graduated. Sky jockeys are even more optimistic than students and have more money—meanwhile I learned more math and engineering. Was sent inactive just in time to be called up again for the Spasm War. Didn't get hurt; I was safer than civilians. But that kept me on another year even though fighting was mostly over before I reported in. That made me a veteran, with benefits. I went to Manhattan and signed up for school again. Doctoral candidate. School of Education. Not serious at first, simply intending to use my veteran's benefits while enjoying the benefits of being a student—and devote most of my time to piling up cash to qualify for the trust.

"I knew that the stupidest students, the silliest professors, and the worst bull courses are concentrated in schools of education.

"By signing for large-class evening lectures and the unpopular eight a.m. classes I figured I could spend most of my time finding out how the stock market ticked. I did, by working there, before I risked a dime.

"Eventually I had to pick a research problem or give up the advantages of being a student. I was sick of a school in which the pie was all meringue and no filling, but I stuck, as I knew how to cope within which the answers are matters of opinion and the opinion that counts is that of the professor. And how to cope with those large-class evening lectures: buy the lecture notes. Read everything that professor ever published. Don't cut too often and when you do show up, get there early, sit front row center, be certain the prof catches your eye every time he looks your way—by never taking your eyes off him. Ask one question you know he can answer because you've picked it out of his published papers—and state your name in asking a question. Luckily 'Zebadiah Carter' is a name easy to remember. Family, I got straight-A's in both required courses and seminars ... because I did not study 'education,' I studied professors of education.

"But I still had to make that 'original contribution to human knowledge' without which a candidate may not be awarded a doctor's degree in most so-called disciplines ... and the few that don't require it are a tough row to hoe.

"I studied my faculty committee before letting myself be tied down to a research problem ... not only reading everything each had published but also buying their publications or paying the library to make copies of out-of-print papers."

My husband took me by my shoulders. "Dejah Thoris, here follows the title of my dissertation. You can have your divorce on your own terms."

"Zebadiah, don't talk that way!"

"Then brace yourself. *An Ad-Hoc Inquiry Concerning the Optimization of the Infrastructure of Primary Educational Institutions at the Interface Between Administration and Instruction, with Special Attention to Group Dynamics Desiderata.*"

"Zebbie! What does that mean?"

"It means nothing, Hilda."

"Zeb, quit kidding our ladies. Such a title would never be accepted."

"Jake, it seems certain that you have never taken a course in a school of education."

"Well ... no. Teaching credentials are not required at university level but—"

"But me no 'buts,' Pop. I have a copy of my dissertation; you can check its authenticity. While that paper totally lacks meaning, it is a literary gem in the sense in which a successful forging of an 'old master' is itself a work of art. It is loaded with buzz words. The average length of sentences is eighty-one words. The average word length, discounting 'of,' 'a,' 'the,' and other syntactical particles, is eleven-plus letters in slightly under four syllables. The bibliography is longer than the dissertation and cites three papers of each member of my committee and four of the chairman, and those citations are quoted in part—while avoiding any mention of matters on which I knew that members of the committee held divergent (but equally stupid) opinions.

"But the best touch was to get permission to do field work in Europe and have it count toward time on campus; half the citations were in foreign languages, ranging from Finnish to Croatian—and the translated bits invariably agreed with the prejudices of my committee. It took careful quoting out of context to achieve this, but it had the advantage that the papers were unlikely to be on campus and my committee were not likely to go to the trouble of looking them up even if they were. Most of them weren't at home in other languages, even easy ones like French, German, and Spanish.

"But I did not waste time on phony field work; I simply wanted a trip to Europe at student air fares and the use of student hostels—dirt-cheap way to travel. *And* a visit to the trustees of Grandpa's fund.

"Good news! The fund was blue chips and triple-A bonds and, at that time, speculative stocks were rising. So the current cash value of the fund was down, even though income was up. And two more of my cousins and one uncle had qualified, again reducing the pro-rata ... so, Glory Be!—I was within reaching distance. I had brought with me all that I had saved, swore before a notary that it was all mine, nothing borrowed, nothing from my father—and left it on deposit in Zurich, using the trustees as a front. And I told them about my stamp and coin collection.

"Good stamps and coins never go down, always up. I had nothing but proof sets, first-day covers, and unbroken sheets, all in perfect condition—and had a notarized inventory and appraisal with me. The trustees got me to swear that the items I had collected before I left home had come from earned money—true, the earliest items represented mowed lawns and such—and agreed to hold the pro-rata at that day's cash value—lower if the trend continued—if I would sell my collection and send a draft to Zurich, with businesslike speed as soon as I returned to the States.

"I agreed. One trustee took me to lunch, tried to get me liquored up—then offered me ten percent over appraisal if I would sell that very afternoon, then send it to him by courier at his expense (bonded couriers go back and forth between Europe and America every week).

"We shook hands on it, went back and consulted the other trustees. I signed papers transferring title, the trustee buying signed his draft to me, I endorsed it to the trustees to add to the cash I was leaving in their custody. Three weeks later I got a cable certifying that the collection matched the inventory. I had qualified.

"Five months later I was awarded the degree of Doctor of Philosophy, summa cum laude. And that, dear ones, is the shameful story of my life. Anyone have the energy to go swimming?"

"Son, if there is a word of truth in that, it is indeed a shameful story."

"Pop! That's not fair! Zebadiah used *their* rules—and outsmarted them!"

"I didn't say that *Zeb* had anything to be ashamed of. It is a commentary on American higher education. What Zeb claims to have written is no worse than trash I *know* is accepted as dissertations these days. His case is the only one I have encountered wherein an intelligent and able scholar—you, Zeb—set out to show that an 'earned' Ph.D. could be obtained from a famous institution—I know which one!—in exchange for deliberately meaningless pseudo-research. The cases I have encountered have involved button-counting by stupid and humorless young persons under the supervision of stupid and humorless old fools. I see no way to stop it; the rot is too deep. The *only* answer is to chuck the system and start over." My father shrugged. "Impossible."

"Zebbie," Aunt Hilda interjected, "what do you do on campus? I've never asked."

My husband grinned. "Oh, much what you do, Sharpie."

"I don't do anything. Enjoy myself."

"Me, too. If you look, you will find me listed as 'research professor in residence.' An examination of the university's books would show that I am paid a stipend to match my rank. Further search would show that slightly more than that amount is paid by some trustees in Zurich to the university's general fund … as long as I remain on campus, a condition not written down. I like being on campus, Sharpie; it gives me privileges not granted the barbarians outside the pale. I teach a course occasionally, as supply for someone on sabbatical or ill."

"Huh? What courses? What departments?"

"Any department but education. Engineering Mathematics. Physics One-Oh-One. Thermogoddamics. Machine Elements. Saber and Dueling Sword. Swimming, and—don't laugh—English poetry from Chaucer through the Elizabethans. I enjoy teaching something worth teaching. I don't charge for courses I teach; the chancellor and I understand each other."

"I'm not sure I understand you," I said, "but I love you anyhow. Let's go swimming."

— X —

Zebadiah

Before heading for the pool, our wives argued over how Barsoomian warriors dress—a debate complicated by the fact that I was the only one fairly sober. While I was telling my "shameful story," Jake had refreshed his Scotch-on-rocks and was genially argumentative. Our brides had stuck to one highball each but, while one jigger gave Deety a happy glow, Sharpie's mass is so slight that the same dosage made her squiffed.

Jake and I agreed to wear sidearms. Our princesses had buckled them on; we would wear them. But Deety wanted me to take off the grease-stained shorts I had worn while working. "Captain John Carter never wears clothes. He arrived on Barsoom naked, and from then on never wore anything but the leather and weapons of a fighting man. Jeweled leather for state occasions, plain leather for fighting—and sleeping silks at night. Barsoomians don't wear clothes. When John Carter first laid eyes on Dejah Thoris," Deety closed her eyes and recited: "She was as destitute of clothes as the Green Martians ... save for her highly wrought ornaments she was entirely naked ...." Deety opened her eyes, stared solemnly. "The women never wear clothes, just jewelry."

"Purty shilly," said her father, with a belch. " 'Scuse me!"

"When they were chilly, they wrapped furs around them, Pop. I mean, 'Mors Kajak, my revered father.' "

Jake answered with slow precision. "Not ... 'chilly.' *Silly!* With a clash of blades and flash of steel, man doesn't want family treasures

82

swinging in the breeze 'n' banging his knees. Distracts him. Might get 'em sliced off. Correc', Captain John Carter?"

"Logical," I agreed.

"Besides, illustrations showed men wearing breechclouts. Pro'ly steel jockstrap underneath. *I* would."

"Those pictures were painted early in the twentieth century, Pop. Censored. But the stories make it clear. Weapons for men, jewelry for women—furs for cold weather."

"I know how I should dress," put in Sharpie. "Thuvia wears jewels on bits of gauze—I remember the book cover. Not clothes. Just something to fasten jewels to. Deety—Dejah Thoris, I mean—do you have a gauze scarf I can use? Fortunately I was wearing pearls when Mors Kajak kidnapped me."

"Sharpie," I objected, "you can't be Thuvia. She married Carthoris. Mors Kajak—or Mors Ka*jake*, might be a misspelling—is your husband."

"Cer'nly Mors Jake is my husband! But I'm his *second* wife; that explains everything. But it ill becomes the Warlord to address a princess of the House of Ptarth as 'Sharpie.'" Mrs. Burroughs drew herself up to her full one hundred and fifty-two centimeters and tried to look offended.

"My humble apologies, Your Highness."

Sharpie giggled. "Can't stay mad at our Warlord. Dejah Thoris hon—green tulle? Blue? Anything but white."

"I'll go look."

"Ladies," I objected, "if we don't get moving, the pool will cool off. You can sew on pearls this evening. Anyhow, where do pearls come from on Barsoom? Dead sea bottoms—no oysters."

"From Korus, the Lost Sea of Dor," Deety explained.

"They've got you, son. But I either go swimming right now—or I have another drink … and then another, and then another. Working too hard. Too tense. Too much worry."

"Okay, Pop; we swim. Aunt H—Aunt Thuvia?"

"All right, Dejah Thoris. To save Mors Jacob from himself. But I *won't* wear Earthling clothes. You can have my mink cape; may be chilly coming back."

Jake wrapped his sarong into a breechclout, strapped it in place with his saber belt. I replaced those grimy shorts with swim briefs, which Deety conceded were "almost Barsoomian." I was no longer dependent on Jake's clothes; my travel kit, always in my car, once I got at it, supplied necessities from passport to poncho. Sharpie wore pearls and rings she had been wearing at her party, plus a scarf around her waist to which she attached all the costume jewelry Deety could dig up. Deety carried Hilda's mink cape—then wrapped it around her. "My captain, someday I want one like this."

"I'll skin the minks personally," I promised her.

"Oh, dear! I think this is synthetic."

"I don't. Ask Hilda."

"I will most carefully *not* ask her. But I'll settle for synthetic."

I said, "My beloved princess, you eat meat. Minks are vicious carnivores and the ones used for fur are raised for no other purpose—not trapped. They are well treated, then killed humanely. If your ancestors had not killed for meat and fur as the last glaciation retreated, you would not be here. Illogical sentiment leads to the sort of tragedy you find in India and Bangladesh."

Deety was silent some moments as we followed Jake and Hilda down toward the pool. "My captain—Zebadiah—"

"Yes, Deety?"

"I am proud that you made me your wife. I will try to be a good wife ... and your princess."

"You do. You have. You always will. Dejah Thoris, my princess and only love, until I met you, I was a boy playing with oversized toys. Today I am a man. With a wife to protect and cherish ... a child to plan for. I'm truly alive, at last! Hey! What are you sniffling about? Stop it!"

"I'll cry if I feel like it!"

"Well ... don't get it on Hilda's cape."

"Gimme a hanky."

"I don't even have a Kleenex." I brushed away her tears with my fingers. "Sniff hard. You can cry on me tonight. In bed."

"Let's go to bed early."

"Right after dinner. Sniffles all gone?"

"I think so. Do pregnant women always cry?"

"So I hear."

"Well ... I'm not going to do it again. No excuse for it; I'm terribly happy."

"The Polynesians do something they call 'Crying happy.' Maybe that's what you do."

"I guess so. But I'll save it for private." Deety started to shrug the cape off. "Too hot, lovely as it feels." She stopped with the cape off her shoulders, suddenly pulled it around her again. "Who's coming up the hill?"

I looked up, saw that Jake and Hilda had reached the pool—and a figure was appearing from below, beyond the boulder that dammed it.

"I don't know. Stay behind me." I hurried toward the pool.

The stranger was dressed as a federal ranger. As I closed in, I heard the stranger say to Jake, "Are you Jacob Burroughs?"

"Why do you ask?"

"Are you or aren't you? If you are, I have business with you. If you're not, you're trespassing. Federal land, restricted access."

"Jake!" I called out. "Who is he?"

The newcomer turned his head. "Who are you?"

"Wrong sequence," I told him. "You haven't identified yourself."

"Don't be funny," the stranger said. "You know this uniform. I'm Bennie Hibol, the ranger hereabouts."

I answered most carefully, "Mr. Highball, you are a man in a uniform, wearing a gun belt and a shield. That doesn't make you a federal officer. Show your credentials and state your business."

The uniformed character sighed. "I got no time to listen to smart talk." He rested his hand on the butt of his gun. "If one of you is Burroughs, speak up. I'm going to search this site and cabin. There's stuff coming up from Sonora; this sure as hell is the transfer point."

Deety suddenly came out from behind me, moved quickly and placed herself beside her father. "Where's your search warrant? Show your authority!" She had the cape clutched around her; her face quivered with indignation.

"Another joker!" This clown snapped open his holster. "Federal land—here's my authority!"

Deety suddenly dropped the cape, stood naked in front of him. I drew, lunged, and cut down in one motion—slashed the wrist, recovered, thrust upward from low line into the belly above the gun belt.

As my point entered, Jake's saber cut the side of the neck almost to decapitation. Our target collapsed like a puppet with cut strings, lay by the pool, bleeding at three wounds.

"Zebadiah, I'm sorry!"

"About what, princess?" I asked as I wiped my blade on the alleged ranger's uniform. I noticed the color of the blood with distaste.

"He didn't react! I thought my strip act would give you more time."

"You did distract him," I reassured her. "He watched you and didn't watch me. Jake, what kind of a creature has bluish-green blood?"

"I don't know."

Sharpie came forward, squatted down, dabbed a finger in the blood, sniffed it. "Hemocyanin. I think," she said calmly. "Deety, you were right. Alien. The largest terrestrial fauna with that method of oxygen transport is a lobster. But this thing is no lobster, it's a 'Black Hat.' *How did you know?*"

"I didn't. But he didn't sound right. Rangers are polite. And they never fuss about showing their IDs."

"I didn't know," I admitted. "I wasn't suspicious, just annoyed."

"You moved mighty fast," Jake approved.

"I never know why 'til it's over. You didn't waste time yourself, tovarishch. Drawing saber while he was pulling a gun—that takes guts and speed. But let's not talk now—*where are his pals?* We may be picked off getting back to the house."

"Look at his pants," Hilda suggested. "He hasn't been on horseback. Hasn't climbed far, either. Jacob, is there a Jeep trail?"

"No. This isn't accessible by Jeep—just barely by horse."

"Hasn't been anything overhead," I added. "No chopper, no air car."

"Continua craft," said Deety.

"Huh?"

"Zebadiah, the 'Black Hats' are aliens who don't want Pop to build a time-space machine. We *know* that. So it follows that *they* have continua craft. QED."

I thought about it. "Deety. I'm going to bring you breakfast in bed. Jake, how do we spot an alien continua craft? It doesn't have to look like *Gay Deceiver.*"

Jake frowned. "No. *Any* shape. But a one-passenger craft might not be much larger than a phone booth."

"If it's a one-man-one-alien job, it should be parked down in that scrub," I said, pointing. "We can find it."

"Zebadiah," protested Deety, "we don't have *time* to search. We ought to get *out* of here! *Fast!*"

Jake said, "My daughter is right but not for that reason. Its craft is not necessarily waiting. It could be parked an infinitesimal interval away along any of six axes, and either return automatically, preprogrammed, or by some method of signaling that we can postulate but not describe. The alien craft would not be here—now ... but *will* be here—later. For pickup."

"In that case, Jake, you and I and the gals should scram out of here—now to there—then. Be missing. How long has our pressure test been running? What time is it?"

"Seventeen-seventeen," Deety answered instantly.

I looked at my wife. "Naked as a frog. Where do you hide your watch, dearest? Surely, not *there*."

She stuck out her tongue. "Smarty. I have a clock in my head. I never mention it because people give me funny looks."

"Deety does have innate time-sense," agreed her father, "accurate to thirteen seconds plus or minus about four seconds; I've measured it."

"I'm sorry, Zebadiah—I don't *mean* to be a freak."

"Sorry about what, princess? I'm impressed. What do you do about time zones?"

"Same as you do. Add or subtract as necessary. Darling, *everyone* has a built-in circadian. Mine is merely more nearly exact than most people's. Like having absolute pitch—some do, some don't."

"Are you a lightning calculator?"

"Yes ... but computers are so much faster that I no longer do it much. Except one thing—I can sense a glitch—spot a wrong answer. Then I look for garbage in the program. If I don't find it, I send for a hardware specialist. Look, sweetheart, discuss my oddities later. Pop, let's dump that *thing* down the septic tank and go. I'm nervous, I am."

"Not so fast, Deety." Hilda was still squatting by the corpse. "Zebbie. Consult your hunches. Are we in danger?"

"Well ... not this instant."

"Good. I want to dissect this creature."

"Aunt Hilda!"

"Take a Miltown, Deety. Gentlemen, the Bible or somebody said, 'Know thy enemy.' This is the only 'Black Hat' we've seen ... and he's not human and not born on Earth. There is a wealth of knowledge lying here and it ought not to be shoved down a septic tank until we know more about it. Jacob, feel this."

Hilda's husband got down on his knees, let her guide his hand through the "ranger's" hair. "Feel those bumps, dearest?"

"Yes!"

87

"Much like the budding horns of a lamb, are they not?"

"Oh—'And I beheld another beast coming up out of the earth; and he had two horns like a lamb, and he spake as a dragon'!"

I squatted down, felt for horn buds. "Be damned! He did come up out of the earth—up this slope anyhow—and he spake as a dragon. Talked unfriendly, and all the dragons I've ever heard of talked mean or belched fire. Hilda, when you field-strip this critter, keep an eye out for the Number of the Beast."

"I shall! Who's going to help me get this specimen up to the house? I want three volunteers."

Deety gave a deep sigh. "I volunteer. Aunt Hilda … must you do this?"

"Deety, it ought to be done at Johns Hopkins, with X-ray and proper tools and color holovision. But I'm the best biologist for it because I'm the only biologist. Honey child, you don't have to watch. Aunt Sharpie has helped in an emergency room after a five-car crash; to me, blood is just a mess to clean up. Green blood doesn't bother me even that much."

Deety gulped. "I'll help carry. I *said* I would!"

"Dejah Thoris!"

"Sir? Yes, my captain?"

"Back away from that. Take this. And this." I unbuckled sword and belt, shoved down my swimming briefs, handed all of it to Deety. "Jake, help me get him up into fireman's carry."

"I'll help carry, son."

"No, I can tote him easier than two could. Sharpie, where do you want to work?"

"It will have to be the dining table."

"Aunt Hilda, I don't want that thing on my—! I beg your pardon; it's *your* dining table."

"You're forgiven only if you'll concede that it is our dining table. Deety, how many times must I repeat that I am *not* crowding you out of your home? We are co-housewives—my only seniority lies in being twenty years older. To my regret."

"Hilda, my dear one, what would you say to a workbench in the garage with a dropcloth on it and flood lights over it?"

"I say, 'Swell!' I don't think a dining table is the place for a dissection, either. But I couldn't think of anywhere else."

With help from Jake, I got that damned carcass draped across my shoulders in fireman's carry. Deety started up the path with me, carrying my belt and sword and my briefs in one arm so that she could hold my free hand—despite my warning that she might be splashed with alien blood. "No, Zebadiah, I got overtaken by childishness. I won't let it happen again. I must conquer all squeamishness—I'll be changing diapers soon." She was silent a moment. "That is the first time I've seen death. In a person, I mean. An alien humanoid person I should say ... but I thought he was a man. I once saw a puppy run over—I threw up. Even though it was not my puppy and I didn't go close." She added, "An adult should face up to death, should she not?"

"Face up to it, yes," I agreed. "But not grow calloused. Deety, I've seen too many men die. I've never grown inured to it. One must accept death, learn not to fear it, then never worry about it. 'Make Today Count!' as a friend whose days are numbered told me. Live in that spirit and when death comes, it will come as a welcome friend."

"You say much what my mother told me before she died."

"Your mother must have been an extraordinary woman. Deety, in the two weeks I've known you, I've heard so much about her from all three of you that I feel as if I knew her. A friend I hadn't seen lately. She sounds like a wise woman."

"I think she was, Zebadiah. Certainly she was good. Sometimes, when I have a hard choice, I ask myself, 'What would Mama do?'— and everything falls into place."

"Both good *and* wise ... and her daughter shows it. Uh, how old are you, Deety?"

"Does it matter, sir?"

"No. Curiosity."

"I wrote my birth date on our marriage license application."

"Beloved, my head was spinning so hard that I had trouble remembering my own. But I should not have asked—women have birthdays, men have ages. I want to know your birthday; I have no need to know the year."

"April twenty-second, Zebadiah—one day older than Shakespeare."

" 'Age could not wither her—' Woman, you carry your years well."

"Thank you, sir."

"That snoopy question came from having concluded in my mind that you were twenty-six ... figuring from the fact that you have a doctor's degree. Although you look younger."

"I think twenty-six is a satisfactory age."

"I wasn't asking," I said hastily. "I got confused from knowing Hilda's age ... then hearing her say that she is—or claims to be—twenty years older than you. It did not jibe with my earlier estimate, based on your probable age on graduating from high school plus your two degrees."

Jake and Hilda had lingered at the pool while Jake washed his hands and rinsed from his body smears of alien ichor. Being less burdened, they climbed the path faster than we and came up behind us just as Deety answered, "Zebadiah, I never graduated from high school."

"Oh."

"That's right," agreed her father. "Deety matriculated by taking College Boards. At fourteen. No problem since she stayed home and didn't have to live in a dorm. Got her BS in three years ... and that was a happy thing, as Jane lived to see Deety move the tassel from one side of her mortar board to the other. Jane in a wheelchair and happy as a child—her doctor said it couldn't hurt her ... meaning she was dying anyhow." He added, "Had her mother been granted only three more years she could have seen Deety's doctorate conferred, two years ago."

"Pop ... sometimes you chatter."

"Did I say something out of line?"

"No, Jake," I assured him. "But I've just learned that I robbed the cradle. I knew I had but hadn't realized how much. Deety darling, you are twenty-two."

"Is twenty-two an unsatisfactory age?"

"No, my princess. Just right."

"My captain said that women have birthdays while men have ages. Is it permitted to inquire your age, sir? I didn't pay close attention to that form we had to fill out, either."

I answered solemnly. "But Dejah Thoris knows that Captain John Carter is centuries old, cannot recall his childhood, and has always looked thirty years old."

"Zebadiah, if that is your age, you've had a busy thirty years. You said you left home when you graduated from high school, worked your way through college, spent three years on active duty, then worked your way through a doctor's degree—"

"A phony one!"

"That doesn't reduce required residence. Aunt Hilda says you've been a professor four years."

"Uh … will you settle for nine years older than you are?"

"I'll settle for whatever you say."

"He's at it again," put in Sharpie. "He was run off two other campuses. Coed scandals. Then he found that in California nobody cared, so he moved west."

I tried to look hurt. "Sharpie darling, I *always* married them. One gal turned out already to be married and in the other case the child wasn't mine; she slipped one over on me."

"The truth isn't in him, Deety. But he's brave and he bathes every day and he's rich—and we love him anyhow."

"The truth isn't in you either, Aunt Hilda. But we love you anyhow. It says in *Little Women* that a bride should be half her husband's age plus seven years. Zebadiah and I hit close to that."

"A rule that makes an old hag out of me. Jacob, I'm just Zebbie's age—thirty-one. But we've both been thirty-one for ages."

"I'll bet he does feel aged after carrying that thing uphill. Atlas, can you support your burden while I get the garage open, a bench dragged out and covered? Or shall I help you put it down?"

"I'd just have to pick it up again. But don't dally."

— XI —

Zebadiah

I felt better after I got that "ranger's" corpse dumped and the garage door closed, everyone indoors. I had told Hilda that I felt no "immediate" danger—but my wild talent does not warn me until the Moment of Truth. The "Blokes in the Black Hats" had us located. Or possibly had never lost us; what applies to human gangsters has little to do with aliens whose powers and motives and plans we had no way to guess.

We might be as naïve as a kitten who thinks he is hidden because his head is, unaware that his little rump sticks out.

They were alien, they were powerful, they were multiple (three thousand? three million?—we didn't know the Number of the Beast)—and they knew where we were. True, we had killed one—by luck, not by planning. That "ranger" would be missed; we could expect more to call in force.

Foolhardiness has never appealed to me. Given a chance to run, I run. I don't mean I'll bug out on a wingmate when the unfriendlies show up, and certainly not on a wife and unborn child. But I wanted us *all* to run—me, my wife, my blood brother who was also my father-in-law, and his wife, my chum Sharpie who was brave, practical, smart, and unsqueamish (that she would joke in the jaws of Moloch was not a fault but a source of esprit).

I wanted us to *go!*—tau-axis, teh-axis, rotate, translate, whatever—anywhere not infested by gruesomes with green gore.

I checked the gauge and felt better; Gay's inner pressure had not dropped. Too much to expect Gay to be a spaceship—not equipped

92

to scavenge and replenish air. But it was pleasant to know that she would hold pressure much longer than it would take us to scram for home if we had to—assuming that unfriendlies had not shot holes in her graceful shell.

I went by the inside passageway into the cabin, used soap and hot water, rinsed off and did it again, dried down and felt clean enough to kiss my wife, which I did. Deety held on to me and reported.

"Your kit is packed, sir. I'm finishing mine, the planned weight and space, and nothing but practical clothes—"

"Sweetheart."

"Yes, Zebadiah?"

"Take the clothes you were married in and mine too. Same for Jake and Hilda. And your father's dress uniform. Or was it burned in Logan?"

"But Zebadiah, you emphasized rugged clothes."

"So I did. To keep your mind on the fact that we can't guess the conditions we'll encounter and don't know how long we'll be gone or if we'll be back. So I listed everything that might be useful in pioneering a virgin planet—since we might be stranded and never get home. Everything from Jake's microscope and water-testing gear to technical manuals and tools. And weapons—and flea powder. But it's possible that we will have to play the roles of ambassadors for humanity at the court of His Extreme Majesty, Overlord of Galactic Empires in the thousandth-and-third continuum. We may need the gaudiest clothes we can whip up. We *don't* know, we *can't* guess."

"I'd rather pioneer."

"We may not have a choice. When you were figuring weights, do you recall spaces marked 'Assigned mass such and such—list to come'?"

"Certainly. Total exactly one hundred kilos, which seemed odd. Space slightly less than one cubic meter split into crannies."

"Those are yours, snubnose. And Pop or Hilda. Mass can be up to fifty percent over; I'll tell Gay to trim to match. Got an old doll? A security blanket? A favorite book of poems? Scrapbook? Family photographs? Bring 'em all!"

"Golly!"

(I never enjoy looking at my wife quite so much as when she lights up and is suddenly a little girl.) "Don't leave space for me. I have only what I arrived with. What about shoes for Hilda?"

"She claims she doesn't need any, Zebadiah—that her calluses are getting calluses on them. But I've worked out expedients. I got Pop some Dr. Scholl's shoe liners when we were building; I have three pairs left and can trim them. Liners and enough bobby sox make her size three-and-a-half feet fit my clodhoppers pretty well. And I have a sentimental keepsake; Keds Pop bought me when I first went to summer camp, at ten. They fit Aunt Hilda."

"Good girl!" I added, "You seem to have everything in hand. How about food? Not stores we are carrying, I mean now. Has anybody thought about dinner? Killing aliens makes me hungry."

"Buffet style, Zebadiah. Sandwiches and stuff on the kitchen counter, and I thawed and heated an apple pie. I fed one sandwich to Hilda, holding it for her; she says she's going to finish working, then scrub before she eats anything more."

"Sharpie munched a sandwich while she carved that *thing?*"

"Aunt Hilda is rugged, Zebadiah—almost as rugged as you are."

"*More* rugged than I am. I could do an autopsy if I had to—but not while eating. I think I speak for Jake, too."

"I know you speak for Pop. He saw me feeding her, turned green and went elsewhere. Go look at what she's been doing, Zebadiah; Hilda has found interesting things."

"Hmmm— Are you the little girl who had a tizzy at the idea of dissecting a dead alien?"

"No, sir, I am not. I've decided to stay grown up. It's not easy. But it's more satisfying. An adult doesn't panic at a snake; she just checks to see if it's got rattles. I'll never squeal again. I'm grown up at last … a wife instead of a pampered princess."

"You will always be my princess!"

"I hope so, my chieftain. But to merit that, I must learn to be a pioneer mother—wring the neck of a rooster, butcher a hog, load while my husband shoots, take his place and his rifle when he is wounded. I'll learn—I'm stubborn, I am. Grab a hunk of pie and go see Hilda. I know just what to do with the extra hundred kilos: books, photographs, Pop's microfilm files and portable viewer, Pop's rifle and a case of ammo that the weight schedule didn't allow for—"

"Didn't know he had it—*what caliber?*"

"Seven point six two millimeters, long cartridge."

"Glory be! Pop and I use the same ammo!"

"Didn't know you carried a rifle, Zebadiah."

"I don't advertise it, it's unlicensed. I must show all of you how to get at it."

94

"Got any use for a lady's purse gun? A needle gun, Skoda flechettes. Not much range but either they poison or they break up and expand … and it fires ninety times on one magazine."

"What are you, Deety? Honorable Hatchet Man?"

"No, sir. Pop got it for me—black market—when I started working nights. He said he would rather hire shysters to get me acquitted—or maybe probation—than to have to go down to the morgue to identify my body. Haven't had to use it; in Logan I hardly need it. Zebadiah, Pop has gone to a great deal of trouble to get me the best possible training in self-defense. He's just as highly trained—that's why I keep him out of fistfights. Because it would be a massacre. He and Mama decided this when I was a baby. Pop says cops and courts no longer protect citizens, so citizens must protect themselves."

"I'm afraid he's right."

"My husband, I can't evaluate my opinions of right and wrong because I learned them from my parents and haven't lived long enough to have formed opinions in disagreement with theirs."

"Deety, your parents did okay."

"I think so … but that's subjective. As may be, I was kept out of blackboard jungles—public schools—until we moved to Utah. And I was trained to fight—armed or unarmed. Pop and I noticed how you handled a sword. Your *moulinets* are like clockwork. And when you drop into point guard, your forearm is perfectly covered."

"Jake is no slouch. He drew so fast I never saw it, and cut precisely above the collar."

"Pop says you are better at it."

"Mmm— Longer reach. He's probably faster. Deety, the best swordmaster I ever had was your height and reach. I couldn't even cross blades with him unless he allowed me to."

"You never did say where you had taken up swordsmanship."

I grinned down at her. "YMCA in downtown Manhattan. I had foil in high school. I fiddled with saber and épée in college. But I never encountered *swordsmen* until I moved to Manhattan. Took it up because I was getting soft. Then during that so-called research trip in Europe I met swordsmen with family tradition—sons and grandsons and great-grandsons of *maîtres d'armes*. Learned that it was a way of life—and I had started too late. Deety, I fibbed to Hilda; I've never fought a student duel. But I did train in saber in Heidelberg under the *Säbelmeister* reputed to coach one underground Korps. He was the little guy I couldn't cross steel with. *Fast!* Up to then, I had thought *I* was fast. But I got faster under his tutelage. The day I was leaving he told me that he wished he had had me twenty years sooner; he might have made a swordsman of me."

"You were fast enough this afternoon!"

"No, Deety. You had his eye, I attacked from the flank. You won that fight—not me, not Pop. Although what Pop did was far more dangerous than what I did."

"My captain, I will not let you disparage yourself! I cannot hear you!"

Women, bless their warm hearts and strange minds—Deety had appointed me her hero; that settled it. I would have to try to measure up. I cut a piece of apple pie, ate it quickly while I walked slowly through the passage into the garage—didn't want to reach the "morgue" still eating.

The "ranger" was on its back with clothes cut away, open from chin to crotch, and spread. Nameless chunks of gizzard were here and there around the cadaver. It gave off a fetid odor.

Hilda was still carving, ice tongs in left hand, knife in her right, greenish goo up over her wrists. As I approached, she put down the knife, picked up a razor blade—did not look up until I spoke. "Learning things, Sharpie?"

She put down her tools, wiped her hands on a towel, pushed back her hair with her forearm. "Zebbie, you wouldn't believe it."

"Try me."

"Well … look at this." She touched the corpse's right leg and spoke to the corpse itself. "What's a nice joint like this doing in a girl like you?"

I saw what she meant: a long, gaunt leg with an extra knee lower than the human knee; it bent backward. Looking higher, I saw that its arms had similar extra articulation. "Did you say 'girl'?"

"I said 'girl.' Zebbie, this monster is either female or hermaphroditic. A fully developed uterus, two-horned like a cat, one ovary above each horn. But there appear to be testes lower down and a dingus that may be a retractable phallus. Female—but probably male as well. Bisexual but does not impregnate itself; the plumbing wouldn't hook up. I think these critters can both pitch and catch."

"Taking turns? Or simultaneously?"

"Wouldn't that be sump'n? No, for mechanical reasons I think they take turns. Whether ten minutes apart or ten years, deponent sayeth not. But I'd give a pretty to see two of 'em going to it!"

"Sharpie, you've got a one-track mind."

"It's the main track. Reproduction is the main track; the methods and mores of sexual copulation are the central feature of all higher developments of life."

"You're ignoring money and television."

"Piffle! All human activities including scientific research are either mating dances and care of the young, or the dismal sublimations of born losers in the only game in town. Don't try to kid Sharpie. Zebbie, I hate these monsters; they interfere with my plans—a rose-covered cottage, a baby in the crib, a pot roast in the oven, me in a gingham dress, and my man coming down the lane after a hard day flunking freshmen—me with his slippers and his pipe and a dry martini waiting for him. Heaven! All else is vanity and vexation. Four fully developed mammary glands but lacking the redundant fat characteristic of the human female—'cept me, damn it. A double stomach, a single intestine. A two-compartment heart that seems to pump by peristalsis rather than by beating. Cordate. I haven't examined the brain; I don't have a proper saw—but it must be as well developed as ours. Definitely humanoid, outrageously nonhuman. Don't knock over those bottles; they are specimens of body fluids."

"What are these things?"

"Splints to conceal the unhuman articulation. Plastic surgery on the face, too, I'm pretty sure, and cheaters to reshape the skull. The hair is fake; these Boojums don't have hair. Something like tattooing—or maybe masking I haven't been able to peel off—to make the face and other exposed skin look human instead of blue-green. Zeb, seven-to-two a large number of missing persons have been used as guinea pigs before they worked out methods for this masquerade. *Swoop!* A flying saucer dips down and two more guinea pigs wind up in their laboratories."

"There hasn't been a flying saucer scare in years."

"Poetic license, dear. If they have space-time twisters, they can pop up anywhere, steal what they want—or replace a real human with a convincing fake—and be gone like switching off a light."

"This one couldn't get by very long. Rangers have to take physical examinations."

"This one may be a rush job, prepared just for us. A permanent substitution might fool anything but an X-ray—and might fool even X-ray if the doctor giving the examination was one of Them ...

a theory you might think about. Zebbie, I must get to work. There is so much to learn and so little time. I can't learn a fraction of what this carcass could tell a real comparative biologist."

"Can I help?" (I was not anxious to.)

"Well—"

"I haven't much to do until Jake and Deety finish assembling the last of what they are going to take. So what can I do to help?"

"I could work twice as fast if you would take pictures. I have to stop to wipe my hands before I touch the camera."

"I'm your boy, Sharpie. Just say what angle, distance, and when."

Hilda looked relieved. "Zebbie, have I told you that I love you despite your gorilla appearance and idiot grin? Underneath you have the soul of a cherub. I want a bath so badly I can taste it—could be the last hot bath in a long time. And the bidet—the acme of civilized decadence. I've been afraid I would still be carving strange meat when Jacob said it was time to leave."

"Carve away, dear; you'll get your bath." I picked up the camera, the one Jake used for record keeping: a Polaroid Stereo-Instamatic—self-focusing, automatic irising, automatic processing, the perfect camera for engineer or scientist who needs a running record.

I took endless pictures while Hilda sweated away. "Sharpie, doesn't it worry you to work with bare hands? You might catch the Never-Get-Overs."

"Zebbie, if these critters could be killed by our bugs, they would have arrived here with no immunities and died quickly. They didn't. Therefore it seems likely that we can't by hurt by their bugs. Radically different biochemistries."

It sounded logical—but I could not forget Kettering's Law: "Logic is an organized way of going wrong with confidence."

Deety appeared, set down a loaded hamper. "That's the last." She had her hair up in a bath knot and was dressed solely in rubber gloves. "Hi, dearest. Aunt Hilda, I'm ready to help."

"Not much you can do, Deety hon—unless you want to relieve Zebbie."

Deety was staring at the corpse and did not look happy—her nipples were down flat. "Go take a bath!" I told her. "Scram."

"Do I stink that badly?"

"You stink swell, honey girl. But Sharpie pointed out that this may be our last chance at soap and hot water in quite a while. I've promised her that we won't leave for Canopus and points east until she has her bath. So get yours out of the way, then you can help me stow while she gets sanitary."

"All right." Deety backed off and her nipples showed faintly—not rigid but she was feeling better. My darling keeps her feelings out of her face, mostly—but those pretty pink spigots are barometers of her morale.

"Just a sec, Deety," Hilda added. "This afternoon you said, 'He didn't react!' What did you mean?"

"What I said. Strip in front of a man and he reacts, one way or another. Even if he tries to ignore it, his eyes give him away. But he didn't. Of course he's not a man—but I didn't know that when I tried to distract him."

I said, "But he did notice you, Deety—and that gave me my chance."

"But only the way a dog, or a horse, or any animal, will notice any movement. He noticed but ignored it. No reaction."

"Zebbie, does that remind you of anything?"

"Should it?"

"The first day we were here you told us a story about a 'zaftig coed.'"

"I did?"

"She was flunking math."

"Oh! 'Brainy.'"

"Yes, Professor N. O'Heret Brain. See any parallel?"

"But 'No Brain' has been on campus for years. Furthermore he turns red in the face. Not a tattoo job."

"I said this one might be a rush job. Would anyone be in a better position to discredit a mathematical theory than the head of the department of mathematics at a very prominent university? Especially if he was familiar with that theory and *knew* that it was correct?"

"Hey, wait a minute!" put in Deety. "Are you talking about that professor who argued with Pop? The one with the phony invitation? I thought he was just a stooge? Pop says he's a fool."

"He behaves like a pompous old fool," agreed Hilda. "I can't stand him. I plan to do an autopsy on him."

"But he's not dead."

"That can be corrected!" Sharpie said sharply.

— XII —

Hilda

By the time I was out of my bath, Jacob, Deety, and Zebbie had *Gay Deceiver* stowed and lists checked (can opener, cameras, et cetera)—even samples of fluids and tissues from the cadaver, as Zebbie's miracle car had a small refrigerator. Deety wasn't happy about my specimens being in the refrigerator but they were very well packed, layer on layer of plastic wrap, then sealed into a freezer box. Besides, that refrigerator contained mostly camera film, dynamite caps, and other noneatables. Food was mostly freeze-dried and sealed in nitrogen, except foods that wouldn't spoil.

We were dog tired. Jacob moved that we sleep, then leave. "Zeb, unless you expect a new attack in the next eight hours, we should rest. I need to be clearheaded in handling verniers. This house is almost a fortress, will be pitch black, and does not radiate any part of the spectrum. They may conclude that we ran for it right after we got their boy—hermaphrodite, I mean; the fake 'ranger'—what do you think?"

"Jake, I wouldn't have been surprised had we been clobbered at any moment. Since they didn't— Well, I don't like to handle Gay when I'm not sharp. More mistakes are made in battle through fatigue than from any other cause. Let's sack in. Anybody need a sleeping pill?"

"All I need is a bed."

"Princess, it's settled; we sleep. But I suggest that we be up before daylight. Let's not crowd our luck."

"Sensible," agreed Jacob.

I shrugged. "You men have to pilot; Deety and I are cargo. We can nap in the back seats—if we miss a few universes, what of it? If you've seen one universe, you've seen 'em all. Deety?"

"If it were up to me, I would lam out of here so fast my shoes would be left standing. But Zebadiah has to pilot and Pop has to set verniers … and both are tired and don't want to chance it. But, Zebadiah … don't fret if I rest with my eyes and ears open."

"Huh? Deety—*why?*"

"Somebody ought to be on watch. It might give us that split-second advantage—split seconds have saved us at least twice. Don't worry, darling; I often skip a night to work a long program under shared time. Doesn't hurt me; a nap next day and I'm ready to bite rattlesnakes. Tell him, Pop."

"That's correct, Zeb, but—"

Zebbie cut him off. "Maybe you gals can split watches and have breakfast ready. Right now I've got to hook up *Gay Deceiver* so that she can reach me in our bedroom. Deety, I can add a program so that she can listen around the cabin, too. Properly programmed, Gay's the best watchdog of any of us. Will that satisfy you duty-struck little broads?"

Deety said nothing so I kept quiet. Zebbie, frowning, turned back to his car, opened a door and prepared to hook Gay's voice and ears to the three house intercoms. "Want to shift the basement talky-talk to your bedroom, Jake?"

"Good idea," Jacob agreed.

"Wait a half while I ask Gay what she has. Hello, Gay."

"Howdy, Zeb. Wipe off your chin."

"Program. Running new retrievals. Report new items since last report."

"Null report, boss."

"Thank you, Gay."

"You're welcome, Zeb."

"Program, Gay. Add running news retrieval. Area, Arizona Strip north of Grand Canyon plus Utah. Persons: all persons listed in current running news retrieval programs plus rangers, federal rangers, forest rangers, park rangers, state rangers. End of added program."

"New program running, boss."

"Program. Add running acoustic report, maximum gain."

"New program running, Zeb."

"You're a Smart Girl, Gay."

"Isn't it time you married me?"

"Goodnight, Gay."

"Goodnight, Zeb. Sleep with your hands outside the covers."

"Deety, you've corrupted Gay. I'll run a lead outdoors for a microphone while Jake moves the basement intercom to the master bedroom. But maximum gain will put a coyote yapping ten miles away right into bed with you. Jake, I can tell Gay to subtract acoustic report from the news retrieval for your bedroom."

"Hilda my love, do you want the acoustic subtracted?"

I didn't but didn't say so; Gay interrupted:

"Running news retrieval, boss."

"Report!"

"Reuters, Straits Times, Singapore. Tragic News of Marston Expedition. Indonesian News Service, Palembang. Two bodies identified as Dr. Cecil Yang and Dr. Z. Edward Carter were brought by jungle buggy to National Militia Headquarters, Telukbetung. The district commandant stated that they will be transferred by air to Palembang for further transport to Singapore when the commandant-in-chief releases them to the Minister of Tourism and Culture. Professor Marston and Mr. Smythe-Belisha are still unreported. Commandants of both districts concede that hopes of finding them alive have diminished. However, a spokesman for the Minister of Tourism and Culture assured a press conference that the Indonesian government would pursue the search more assiduously than ever."

Zebbie whistled tunelessly. Finally, he said, "Opinions, anyone?"

"He was a brilliant man, son," my husband said soberly. "An irreplaceable loss. Tragic."

"Ed was a good Joe, Jake. But that's not what I mean. Our tactical situation. *Now. Here.*"

My husband paused before answering. "Zeb, whatever happened in Sumatra apparently happened about a month ago. Emotionally, I feel great turmoil. Logically, I am forced to state that I cannot see that our situation has changed."

"Hilda? Deety?"

"News retrieval report," announced Gay.

"Report!"

"AP San Francisco via satellite from Saipan, Marianas. TWA hypersonic-semiballistic liner *Winged Victory* out of San Francisco International at twenty o'clock this evening Pacific Coast Time was seen by eye and radar to implode on reentry. AP Honolulu US Navy

102

Official. USS Submersible Carrier *Flying Fish* operating near Wake Island has been ordered to proceed flank speed toward site of *Winged Victory* reentry. She will surface and launch search craft at optimum point. Navy PIO spokesman, when asked what was 'optimum,' replied 'No comment.' Associated Press' military editor noted that submerged speed of *Flying Fish* class, and type and characteristics of craft carried, are classified information. AP—UPI add San Francisco, *Winged Victory* disaster. TWA public relations released a statement—quote—if reports received concerning *Winged Victory* are correct it must be tentatively assumed that no survivors can be expected. But our engineering department denies that implosion could be cause. Collision with orbital debris decaying into atmosphere or even a strike by a meteor could—repeat could—endrep—cause disaster by mischance so unlikely that it can only be described as an Act of God—endquote. TWA spokesmen released passenger list by order of the Civil Aerospace Board. List follows: California—"

The list was longish. I did not recognize any names until Gay reached: "Doctor Neil O. Brain—"

I gasped. But no one said a word until Gay announced: "End running news retrieval."

"Thank you, Gay."

"A pleasure, Zeb."

Zebbie said, "Professor?"

"You're in command, Captain!"

"Very well, sir! All of you—lifeboat rules! I expect fast action and no back talk. Estimated departure—five minutes! First, everybody take a pee! Second, put on the clothes you'll travel in. Jake, switch off, lock up—whatever you do to secure your house for long absence. Deety—follow Jake, make sure he hasn't missed anything—then *you*, not Jake, switch out lights and close doors. Hilda, bundle what's left of that Dutch lunch and fetch it—fast, not fussy. Check the refrigerator for solid foods—no liquids—and cram what you can into Gay's refrigerator. Don't dither over choices. Questions, anyone? Move!"

I gave Jacob first crack at our bathroom because the poor dear tenses up; I used the time to slide sandwiches into a freezer sack and half a pie into another. Potato salad? Scrape it into a third and stick in one plastic picnic spoon; germs were now community property. I stuffed this and some pickles into the biggest freezer sack Deety stocked and closed it.

Jake came out of our bedroom; I threw him a kiss *en passant*, ducked into our john, turned on water in the basin, sat down, and recited mantras—that often works when I'm jumpy—then used the bidet—patted it and told it goodbye without stopping. My travel clothes were Deety's baby tennis shoes with a green-and-gold denim miniskirt dress of hers that came to my knees but wasn't too dreadful with a scarf to belt it.

I spread my cape in front of the refrigerator, dumped my purse and our picnic lunch into it, started salvaging—half a boned ham, quite a bit of cheese, a loaf and a half of bread, two pounds of butter (freezer sacks, and the same for the ham—if Deety hadn't had a lavish supply of freezer sacks I could not have salvaged much—as it was, I didn't even get spots on my cape). I decided that jams and jellies and catsup were liquid within Zebbie's meaning—except some in squeeze tubes. Half a chocolate cake, and the cupboard was bare.

By using my cape as a Santa Claus pack, I carried food into the garage and put it down by Gay—and was delighted to find that I was first.

Zebbie strode in behind me, dressed in a coverall with thigh pockets, a pilot suit. He looked at the pile on my cape. "Where's the elephant, Sharpie?"

"Cap'n Zebbie, you didn't say how *much*, you just said what. What won't go she can have." I hooked a thumb at the chopped-up corpse.

"Sorry, Hilda; you are correct." Zebbie glanced at his wrist watch, the multiple-dial sort they call a "navigator's watch."

"Cap'n, this house has loads of gimmicks and gadgets and bells and whistles. You gave them an impossible schedule."

"On purpose, dear. Let's see how much food we can stow."

Gay's cold chest is set flush in the deck of the driver's compartment. Zebbie told Gay to open up, then with his shoulders sideways, reached down and unlocked it. "Hand me stuff."

I tapped his butt. "Out of there, you overgrown midget, and let Sharpie pack. I'll let you know when it's tight as a girdle."

Space that makes Zebbie twist and grunt is roomy for me. He passed things in, I fitted them for maximum stowage. The third item he handed me was the leavings of our buffet dinner. "That's our picnic lunch," I told him, putting it on his seat.

"Can't leave it loose in the cabin."

"Cap'n, we'll eat it before it can spoil. I will be strapped down; is it okay if I clutch it to my bosom?"

"Sharpie, have I ever won an argument with you?"

"Only by brute force, dear. Can the chatter and pass the chow."

With the help of God and a shoehorn, it all went in. I was in a back seat with our lunch in my lap and my cape under me before our spouses showed up. "Cap'n Zebbie? Why did the news of Brainy's death cause your change of mind?"

"Do you disapprove, Sharpie?"

"On the contrary, skipper. Do you want my guess?"

"Yes."

"*Winged Victory* was booby-trapped. And dear Doctor Brain, who isn't the fool I thought he was, was not aboard. Those poor people were killed so that he could disappear."

"Go to the head of the class, Sharpie. Too many coincidences … and they—the 'Blokes in the Black Hats'—know where we are."

"Meaning that Professor No Brain, instead of being dead in the Pacific, might show up any second."

"He and a gang of green-blooded aliens who don't like geometers."

"Zebbie, what do you figure their plans are?"

"Can't guess. They might fumigate this planet and take it. Or conquer us as cattle or as slaves. The only data we have is that they are alien, that they are powerful—and that they have no compunction about killing us. So I have no compunction about killing them. To my regret, I don't know how. So I'm running—running scared—and taking the three I'm certain are in danger with me."

"Will we ever be able to find them and kill them?"

Zebbie didn't answer because Deety and my Jacob arrived, breathless. Father and daughter were in jumpsuits. Deety looked chesty and cute; my darling looked trim—but worried. "We're late. Sorry!"

"You're not late," Zeb told them. "But into your seats on the bounce."

"As quick as I open the garage door and switch out the lights."

"Jake, Jake—Gay is now programmed to do those things herself. In you go, Princess, and strap down. Seat belts, Sharpie. Copilot, after you lock the starboard door, check its seal all the way around by touch before you strap down."

"Wilco, Cap'n." It tickled me to hear my darling boning military. He had told me privately that he was a reserve colonel of ordnance—but that Deety had promised not to tell this to our smart young captain and that he wanted the same promise from me—because the TO was as it should be; Zeb should command while Jacob handled space-time controls—to each his own. Jacob had asked me to please take orders from Zeb with no back talk … which had miffed me a little. I was an unskilled crew member; I am not stupid, I knew this. In direst emergency I would try to get us home. But even Deety was better qualified than I.

Checkoffs completed, Gay switched off lights, opened the garage door, and backed out onto the landing flat.

"Copilot, can you read your verniers?"

"Captain, I had better loosen my chest belt."

"Do so if you wish. But your seat adjusts forward twenty centimeters—here, I'll get it." Zeb reached down, did something between their seats. "Say when."

"There—that's about right. I can read 'em and reach 'em, with chest strap in place. Orders, sir?"

"Where was your car when you and Deety went to the space-time that lacked the letter 'J'?"

"About where we are now."

"Can you send us there?"

"I think so. Minimum translation, positive—entropy increasing—along tau-axis."

My husband touched the controls. "That's it, Captain."

I couldn't see any change. Our house was still a silhouette against the sky, with the garage a black maw in front of us. The stars hadn't even flickered.

Zebbie said, "Let's check," and switched on Gay's roading lights, brightening our garage. Empty and looked normal.

Zebbie said, "*Hey!* Look at *that**/

"Look at *what?*" I demanded, and tried to see around Jacob.

"At nothing, rather. Sharpie, where's your alien?"

Then I understood. No corpse. No green-blood mess. Workbench against the wall and flood lights not rigged.

Zebbie said, "*Gay Deceiver,* take us home!"

Instantly the same scene … but with carved-up corpse. I gulped.

Zebbie switched out the lights. I felt better, but not much.

"Captain?"

"Copilot."

"Wouldn't it have been well to have checked for that letter 'J'? It would have given me a check on calibration."

"I did check, Jake."

"Eh?"

"You have bins on the back of your garage neatly stenciled. The one at left center reads 'Junk Metal.'"

"*Oh!*"

"Yes, and your analog in that space—your twin, Jake-prime, or what you will—has your neat habits. The left-corner bin read 'Iunk Metal' spelled with an 'I.' A cupboard above and to the right contained 'Iugs & Iars.' So I told Gay to take us home. I was afraid they might catch us. Embarrassing."

Deety said, "Zebadiah—I mean 'Captain'—embarrassing how, sir? Oh, that missing letter in the alphabet scared me but it no longer does. Now I'm nervous about aliens. 'Black Hats.'"

"Deety, you were lucky that first time. Because Deety-prime was not at home. But she may be, tonight. Possibly in bed with her husband, named Zebadiah-prime. Unstable cuss. Likely to shoot at a strange car shining lights into his father-in-law's garage. A violent character."

"You're teasing me."

"No, Princess; it did worry me. A parallel space, with so small a difference as the lack of one unnecessary letter, but with house and grounds you mistook for your own, seems to imply a father and daughter named 'Iacob' and 'Deiah Thoris.'" (Captain Zebbie pronounced the names "Yacob" and "Deyah Thoris.")

"Zebadiah, that scares me almost as much as aliens."

"Aliens scare me far more. Hello, Gay."

"Howdy, Zeb. Your nose is runny."

"Smart Girl, one gee vertically to one klick. Hover."

"Roger dodger, you old codger."

We rested on our backs and head rests for a few moments, then with the stomach-surging swoosh of a fast lift, we leveled off and hovered. Zebbie asked, "Deety, can the autopilot accept a change in that homing program by voice? Or does it take an offset in the verniers?"

"What do you want to do?"

"Same ell-and-ell two klicks above ground."

"I think so. Shall I? Or do you want to do it, Captain?"

"You try it, Deety."

"Yes, sir. Hello, Gay."

"Hi, Deety!"

"Program check. Define 'Home.'"

"'Home.' Cancel any-all inertials transitions translations rotations. Return to preprogrammed zero latitude-longitude, ground level."

"Report present location."

"One klick vertically above 'Home.'"

"Gay. Program revision."

"Waiting, Deety."

"Home program. Cancel 'Ground level.' Substitute 'Two klicks above ground level, hovering.'"

"Program revision recorded."

"*Gay Deceiver*, take us home!"

Instantly, with no feeling of motion, we were much higher.

Zeb said, "Two klicks on the nose! Deety, you're a Smart Girl!"

"Zebadiah, I bet you tell that to all the girls."

"No, just to some. Gay, you're a Smart Girl."

"Then why are you shacked up with that strawberry blonde?"

Zebbie craned his neck and looked at me. "Sharpie, that's your voice."

I ignored him with dignity. Zebbie drove south to the Grand Canyon, eerie in starlight. Without slowing, he said, "*Gay Deceiver*, take us home!"—and again we were hovering over our cabin. No jar, no shock, no nothing.

Zebbie said, "Jake, once I figure the angles, I'm going to quit spending money on juice. How does she do it when we haven't been anywhere?—No rotation, no translation."

"I may have given insufficient thought to a trivial root in equation ninety-seven. But it is analogous to what we were considering doing with planets. A five-dimensional transform simplified to three."

"I dunno, I just work here," Captain Zebbie admitted. "But it looks like we will be peddling gravity and transport, as well as real estate and time. Burroughs and Company, Space Warps Unlimited—'No job too large, no job too small.' Send one newdollar for our free brochure."

"Captain," suggested Jacob, "would it not be prudent to translate into another space before experimenting further? The alien danger is still with us—is it not?"

Zebbie sobered at once. "Copilot, you are right and it is your duty to advise me when I goof off. However, before we leave, we have one duty we *must* carry out."

"Something more urgent than getting our wives to safety?" my Jacob asked—and I felt humble and proud.

"Something more urgent. Jake, I've bounced her around not only to test but to make it hard to track us. Because we must break radio silence. To warn our fellow humans."

"Oh. Yes, Captain. My apologies, sir. I sometimes forget the broader picture."

"Don't we all! I've wanted to run and hide ever since this rumpus started. But that took preparation and the delay gave me time to think. Point number one: we don't know how to fight these critters so we must take cover. Point number two: we are duty-bound to tell the world what we know about aliens. While that little isn't much—we've stayed alive by the skin of our teeth—if five billion people are watching for them, they can be caught. I hope."

"Captain," asked Deety, "may I speak?"

"Of course! Anyone with ideas about how to cope with these monsters *must* speak."

"I'm sorry but I don't have such ideas. You must warn the world, sir—of course! But you won't be believed."

"I'm afraid you're right, Deety. But they don't have to believe me. That monster in the garage speaks for itself. I'm going to call rangers—real rangers!—to pick it up."

I said, "So that was why you told me just to leave it! I thought it was lack of time."

"Both, Hilda. We didn't have time to sack that cadaver and store it in the freezer room. But if I can get rangers—*real* rangers—to that garage before 'Black Hats' get there, that corpse tells its own story: an undeniable alien lying in its goo on a ranger's uniform that has been cut away from it. Not a 'close encounter' UFO that can be explained away, but a creature more startling than the duckbilled platypus ever was. But we have to hook it in with other factors to show them what to look for. Your booby-trapped car, an arson case in Logan, Professor Brain's convenient disappearance, my cousin's death in Sumatra—and your six-dimensional non-Euclidean geometry."

I said, "Excuse me, gentlemen. Can't we move somewhere away from right over our cabin before you break silence? I'm jumpy—'Black Hats' are hunting us."

"You're right, Sharpie; I'm about to move us. The story isn't long—all but the math—so I taped a summary while the rest of you were getting ready. Gay will speed-zip it, a hundred to one." Zebbie reached for the controls. "All secure?"

"Captain Zebadiah!"

"Trouble, Princess?"

"May I attempt a novel program? It may save time."

"Programming is your pidgin. Certainly."

"Hello, Gay."

"Hi, Deety!"

"Retrieve last program. Report execute-code."

"Reporting, Deety. '*Gay Deceiver*, take us home!'"

"Negative erase permanent program controlled by execute-code *Gay Deceiver* take us home. Report confirm."

"Confirmation report. Permanent program execute-coded *Gay Deceiver* take us home negative erase. I tell you three times."

"Deety," said Zeb, "a neg scrub to Gay tells her to place item in perms three places. Redundancy safety factor."

"Don't bother me, dear! She and I sling the same lingo. Hello, Gay."

"Hello, Deety!"

"Analyze latest program execute-coded '*Gay Deceiver* take us home.' Report."

"Analysis complete."

"Invert analysis."

"Null program."

Deety sighed. "Typing a program is easier. New program."

"Waiting, Deety."

"Execute-code new permanent program. *Gay Deceiver*, countermarch! At new execute-code, repeat reversed in real time latest sequence inertials transitions translations rotations before last use of program execute-code '*Gay Deceiver* take us home.'"

"New permanent program accepted."

"Gay, I tell you three times."

"Deety, I hear you three times."

"*Gay Deceiver*—countermarch!"

Instantly we were over the Grand Canyon, cruising south. I saw Zeb reach for the manual controls. "Deety, that was slick."

"I didn't save time, sir—I goofed. Gay, you're a Smart Girl."

"Deety, don't make me blush."

"You're both Smart Girls," said Captain Zebbie. "If anyone had us on radar, he must think he's getting cataracts. Vice versa, if anyone picked us up here, he's wondering how we popped up. Smart dodge, dear. You've got *Gay Deceiver* so deceptive that nobody can home on us. We'll be elsewhere."

"Yes—but I had something else in mind, too, my captain."

"Princess, I like your ideas. Spill it."

"Suppose we used that homing pre-program and went from frying pan into fire. It might be useful to have a pre-program that would take us back into the frying pan, then do something else quickly. Should I try to think up a third escape-maneuver pre-program?"

"Sure—but discuss it with the court magician, your esteemed father—not me. I'm just a sky jockey."

"Zebadiah, I will not listen to you disparage yours—"

"Deety! Lifeboat rules. Jake, are your professional papers aboard? Both theoretical and drawings?"

"Why, no, Zeb—Captain. Too bulky. Microfilms I brought. Originals are in the basement vault. Have I erred?"

"Not a bit! Is there any geometer who gave your published paper on this six-way system a friendly reception?"

"Captain, there aren't more than a handful of geometers capable of judging my postulate system without long and intensive study. It's too unorthodox. Your late cousin was one—a truly brilliant mind! Uh ... now suspect that Doctor Brain understood it and sabotaged it for his own purposes."

"Jake, is there anyone friendly to you and able to understand the stuff in your vault? I'm trying to figure out how to warn our fellow humans. A fantastic story of apparently unrelated incidents is not enough. Not even with the corpse of an extraterrestrial to back it up. You should leave mathematical theory and engineering drawings to someone able to understand them and whom you trust. We can't handle it; every time we stick our heads up, somebody takes a shot at us and we have no way to fight back. It's a job that may require our whole race. Well? Is there a man you can trust as your professional executor?"

"Well ... one, perhaps. Not my field of geometry but brilliant. He did write me a most encouraging letter when I published my first paper— the paper that was so sneered at by almost everyone except your cousin and this one other. Professor Seppo Räikannonen. Turku. Finland."

"Are you certain *he's* not an alien?"

"What? He's been on the faculty at Turku for years! Over fifteen."

I said, "Jacob ... that is about how long Professor Brain was around."

"But—" My husband looked around at me and suddenly smiled. "Hilda my love, have you ever taken sauna?"

"Once."

"Then tell our captain why I am sure that my friend Seppo is not an alien in disguise. I—Deety and I—attended a professional meeting in Helsinki last year. After the meeting we visited their summer place in the Lake Country ... and took sauna with them."

"Papa, Mama, and three kids," agreed Deety. "Unmistakably human."

" 'Brainy' was a bachelor," I added thoughtfully. "Cap'n Zebbie, wouldn't disguised aliens have to be bachelors?"

"Or single women. Or pseudo-married couples. No kids, the masquerade wouldn't hold up. Jake, let's try to phone your friend. Mmm, nearly breakfast time in Finland—or we may wake him. That's better than missing him."

"Good! My comcredit number is Nero Aleph—"

"Let's try mine. Yours might trigger something ... if 'Black Hats' are as smart as I think they are. Smart Girl."

"Yes, boss."

"Don Ameche."

"To hear is to obey, O Mighty One."

"Deety, you've been giving Gay bad habits."

Shortly, a flat male voice answered, "The communications credit number you have cited is not a valid number. Please refer to your card and try again. This is a recording."

Zebbie made a highly unlikely suggestion. "Gay *can't* send out my comcredit code incorrectly; she has it tell-me-three-times. The glitch is in their system. Pop, we have to use yours."

I said, "Try mine, Zebbie. My comcredit is good; I pre-deposit."

A female voice this time: "—not a valid number. Puh-lease refer to your card and try again. This is a recording."

Then my husband got a second female voice: "—try again. This is a recording."

Deety said, "I don't have one. Pop and I use the same number."

"It doesn't matter," Cap'n Zebbie said bitterly. "These aren't glitches. We've been scrubbed. Unpersons. We're all dead."

I didn't argue. I had suspected that we were dead since the morning two weeks before, when I woke up in bed with my cuddly new husband. But how *long* had we been dead? Since my party? Or more recently?

I didn't care. This was a better grade of heaven than a Sunday school in Terre Haute had taught me to expect. While I don't think I'd been outstandingly wicked, I hadn't been very good either. Of the Ten Commandments, I'd broken six and bent some others. But Moses apparently had not had the last Word from on High—being dead was weird and wonderful and I was enjoying every minute ... or eon, as the case may be.

— XIII —

Zebadiah

Not being able to phone from my car was my most frustrating experience since a night I spent in jail through mistake (I made the mistake). I considered grounding to phone—but the ground did not seem healthy. Even if all of us were presumed dead, nullifying our comcredit cards so quickly seemed unfriendly; all of us had high credit ratings.

Cancelling Sharpie's comcredit without proof of death was more than unfriendly; it was outrageous, as she used the pre-deposit method.

I was forced to the decision that it was my duty to make a military report; I radioed NORAD, stated name, rank, reserve commission serial number, and asked for scramble for a crash priority report.

—And ran into "correct" procedure that causes instant ulcers. What was my clearance? What led me to think that I had crash priority intelligence? By what authority did I demand a scramble code? Did you know how many screwball calls come in here every day? Get off this frequency; it's for official traffic only. *One more word out of you and I shall alert the civil sky patrol to pick you up.*

I said one more word after I chopped off. Deety and her father ignored it; Hilda said, "My sentiments exactly!"

I tried the Federal Rangers Kaibab Barracks at Jacob Lake, then the office at Littlefield—and back to Kaibab. Littlefield didn't answer; Jacob Lake answered: "This is a recording. Routine messages may be recorded during beep tone. Emergency reports should be transmitted to Flagstaff HQ. Stand by for beep tone … Beep! … Beep! … Beep!"

113

I was about to tell Gay to zip my tape—when the whole world was lighted by the brightest light imaginable.

Luckily we were cruising south with that light behind us. I goosed Gay to flank speed while telling her to tuck in her wings. Not one of my partners asked a foolish question, although I suspect that none had ever seen a fireball or mushroom cloud.

"Smart Girl."

"Here, boss."

"DR problem. Record true bearing light beacon relative bearing astern. Record radar range and bearing same beacon. Solve latitude-longitude beacon. Compare solution with fixes in perms. Confirm."

"Program confirmed."

"Execute."

"Roger Wilco, Zeb. Heard any new ones lately?" She added at once, "Solution. True bearing identical with fix execute-coded '*Gay Deceiver* take us home.' True range identical plus-minus zero point six klicks."

"You're a Smart Girl, Gay."

"Flattery will get you anywhere, Zeb. Over."

"Roger and out. Hang on to your hats, folks; we're going straight up." I had outraced the shock wave but we were close to the Mexican border; either side might send Sprint birds homing on us. "Copilot!"

"Captain."

"Move us! Out of this space!"

"Where, Captain?"

"Anywhere! *Fast!*"

"Uh, can you ease the acceleration? I can't lift my arms."

Cursing myself, I cut power, let *Gay Deceiver* climb free. Those vernier controls should have been mounted on arm rests. (Designs that look perfect on the drawing board can kill test pilots.)

"Translation complete, Captain."

"Roger, Copilot. Thank you." I glanced at the board: six-plus klicks height above ground and rising—thin but enough air to bite. "Hang on to our lunch, Sharpie!" I leaned us backward while doing an Immelman into level flight, course north, power still off. I told Gay to stretch the glide, then tell me when we had dropped to three klicks H-above-G.

What should be Phoenix was off to the right; another city—Flagstaff?—farther away, north and a bit east; we appeared to be headed home. There was no glowing cloud on the horizon. "Jake, where are we?"

"Captain, I've never been in this universe. We translated ten quanta positive tau-axis. So we should be in analogous space close to ours—ten minimum intervals or quanta."

"This looks like Arizona."

"I would expect it to, Captain. You recall that one-quantum translation on this axis was so very like our own world that Deety and I confused it with our own, until she picked up a dictionary."

"Phone book, Pop."

"Irrelevant, dear. Until she missed the letter 'J' in an alphabetical list. Ten quanta should not change geological features appreciably and placement of cities is largely controlled by geography."

"Approaching three klicks, boss."

"Thanks, Gay. Hold course and H-above-G. Correction! Hold course and absolute altitude. Confirm and execute."

"Roger Wilco, Zeb."

I had forgotten that the Grand Canyon lay ahead—or should. "Smart Girl" is smart, but she's literal-minded. She would have held height-above-ground precisely and given us the wildest roller-coaster ride in history. She is very flexible but the "garbage-in-garbage-out" law applies. She had many extra fail-safes—because *I* make mistakes. Gay *can't*; anything she does wrong is *my* mistake. Since I've been making mistakes all my life, I surrounded her with all the safeguards I could think of. But she had no program against wild rides—she was beefed up to accept them. Violent evasive tactics had saved our lives two weeks ago, and tonight as well. Being too close to a fireball can worry a man—to death.

"Gay, display map, please."

The map showed Arizona—*our* Arizona; Gay does not have in her gizzards any strange universes. I changed course to cause us to pass over our cabin site—its analog for this space-time. (Didn't dare tell her: "Gay, take us home!"—for reasons left as an exercise for the class.) "Deety, how long ago did that bomb go off?"

"Six minutes twenty-three seconds. Zebadiah, was that *really* an A-bomb?"

"Pony bomb, perhaps. Maybe two kilotons. *Gay Deceiver.*"

"I'm all ears, Zeb."

"Report time interval since radar-ranging beacon."

"Five minutes forty-four seconds, Zeb."

Deety gasped. "Was I that far off?"

"No, darling. You reported time since flash. I didn't ask Gay to range until *after* we were hypersonic."

"Oh. I feel better."

"Captain," inquired Jake, "how did Gay range an atomic explosion? I would expect radiation to make it impossible. Does she have instrumentation of which I am not aware?"

"Copilot, she has several gadgets I have not shown you. I have not been holding out—any more than you held out in not telling me about guns and ammo you—"

"My apologies, sir!"

"Oh, stuff it, Jake. Neither of us held out; we've been running under the whip. Deety, how long has it been since we killed that fake ranger?"

"That was seventeen fourteen. It is now twenty-two twenty. Five hours six minutes."

I glanced at the board; Deety's "circadian clock" apparently couldn't be jarred by anything; Gay's clock showed 0520 (Greenwich) with "ZONE PLUS SEVEN" display. "Call it five hours—feels like five weeks. We need a vacation."

"Loud cheers!" agreed Sharpie.

"Check. Jake, I didn't know that Gay could range an atomic blast. Light 'beacon' means a visible light to her just as 'radar beacon' means to her a navigational radar beacon. I told her to get a bearing on the light beacon directly aft; she selected the brightest light with that bearing. Then I told her to take radar range and bearing on it—spun my prayer wheel and prayed.

"There was 'white noise' possibly blanketing her radar frequency. But her own radar bursts are tagged; it would take a very high noise level at the same frequency to keep her from recognizing echoes with her signature. Clearly she had trouble for she reported 'plus-minus' of six hundred meters. Nevertheless range and bearing matched a fix in her permanents and told us our cabin had been bombed. Bad news. But the aliens got there too late to bomb *us*. Good news."

"Captain, I decline to grieve over material loss. We are alive."

"I agree—although I'll remember Snug Harbor as the happiest home I've ever had. But there is no point in trying to warn Earth—our Earth—about aliens. That blast destroyed the clincher: that alien's cadaver. And papers and drawings you were going to turn over to your Finnish friend. I'm not sure we *can* go home again."

"Oh, that's no problem, Captain. Two seconds to set the verniers. Not to mention the 'deadman switch' and the program in Gay's permanents."

"Jake, I wish you would knock off 'Captain' other than for command conditions."

"Zeb, I like calling you 'Captain.'"

"So do I!—my captain."

"Me, too, Cap'n Zebbie!"

"Don't overdo it. Jake, I didn't mean that you can't pilot us home; I mean we should not risk it. We've lost our last lead on the aliens. But they know who we are and have shown dismaying skill in tracking us down. I'd like to live to see two babies born and grown up."

"Amen!" said Sharpie. "This might be the place for it. Out of a million billion zillion Earths this one may be vermin-free. Highly likely."

"Hilda my dear, there are no data on which to base any assumption."

"Jacob, there is *one* datum."

"Eh? What did I miss, dear?"

"That we *do* know that our native planet is infested. So I don't want to raise kids on it. If this isn't the place we're looking for, let's keep looking."

"Mmm, logical. Yes. Cap—Zeb?"

"I agree. But we can't tell much before morning. Jake, I'm unclear on a key point. If we translated back to our own Earth now, where would we find ourselves? And *when?*"

"Pop, may I answer that?"

"Go ahead, Deety."

"The time Pop and I translated to the place with no 'J' we thought we had failed. Pop stayed in our car, trying to figure it out. I went inside, intending to fix lunch. Everything looked normal. But the phone book was on the kitchen counter and doesn't belong there. That book had a toll area map on its back cover. My eye happened to land on 'Juab County'—and it was spelled 'Iuab'—and I thought, 'What a funny misprint!' Then I looked inside and couldn't find any 'J's' and dropped the book and went running for Pop."

"I thought Deety was hysterical. But when I checked a dictionary and the *Britannica* we got out in a hurry."

"This is the point, Zebadiah. When we flipped back, I dashed into the house. The phone book was where it belonged. The alphabet was back the way it ought to be. The clock in my head said that we had been gone twenty-seven minutes. The kitchen clock confirmed it and it agreed with the clock in the car. Does that answer you, sir?"

"I think so. In a translation, duration just keeps chugging along. I wondered because I'd like to check that crater after it has had time to cool down. What about that one rotation?"

"Harder to figure, Zebadiah. We weren't in that other space-time but a few seconds and we both passed out. Indeterminate."

"I'm convinced. But Jake, what about Earth's proper motions? Rotation, revolution around the Sun, sidereal motion, and so forth."

"A theoretical answer calls for mathematics you tell me are outside your scope of study, uh—Zeb."

"Beyond my capacity, you mean."

"As you will, sir. An excursion elsewhere—and—*elsewhen* … and *return* … brings you back *to where you would have been* had you experienced that duration *on Earth*. But '*when*' requires further definition. As we were discussing, uh … earlier this afternoon but it seems longer, we can adjust the controls to reenter *any* axis at any point *with permanent change of interval*. For planetary engineering. Or other purposes. Including reentry reversed against the entropy arrow. But I suspect that would cause death."

"Why, Pop? Why wouldn't it just reverse your memory?"

"Memory is tied to entropy increase, my darling daughter. Death might be preferable to amnesia combined with prophetic knowledge. Uncertainty may be the factor that makes life tolerable. Hope is what keeps us going. Captain!"

"Copilot."

"We have just passed over North Rim."

"Thank you, Copilot." I placed my hands lightly on the controls.

"Pop, our cabin is still there. Lights in it, too."

"So I see. They've added a wing on the west."

"Yes. Where we discussed adding a library."

I said, "Family, I'm not going closer. Your analogs in this world seem to be holding a party. Flood lights show four cars on the grounding flat." I started Gay into a wide circle. "I'm not going to hover; it could draw attention. A call to their sky cops— Hell's bells, I don't even know that they speak English."

"Captain, we've seen all we need. It's not *our* cabin."

"Recommendation?"

"Sir, I suggest maximum altitude. Discuss what to do while we get there."

"*Gay Deceiver.*"

"On deck, Captain Ahab."

"One gee, vertical."

"Aye aye, sir." (How many answers had Deety taped?)

"Anybody want a sandwich?" asked Sharpie. "I do—I'm a pregnant mother."

I suddenly realized that I had had nothing but a piece of pie since noon. As we climbed we finished what was left of supper.

"Zat Marsh?"

"Don't talk with your mouth full, Sharpie."

"Zebbie you brute, I said, 'Is that Mars?' Over there."

"That's Antares. Mars is— Look left about thirty degrees. See it? Same color as Antares but brighter."

"Got it. Jacob darling, let's take that vacation on Barsoom!"

"Hilda dearest, Mars is uninhabitable. The Mars Expedition used pressure suits. We have no pressure suits."

I added, "Even if we did, they would get in the way of a honeymoon."

Hilda answered, "I read a jingle about 'A Space Suit Built for Two.' Anyhow, let's go to Barsoom! Jacob, you did tell me we could go anywhere in *zip*—nothing flat."

"Quite true."

"So let's go to Barsoom."

I decided to flank her. "Hilda, we can't go to Barsoom. Mors Kajak and John Carter don't have their swords."

"Want to bet?" Deety asked sweetly.

"Huh?"

"Sir, you left it to me to pick baggage for that unassigned space. If you'll check that long, narrow stowage under the instrument board, you'll find the sword and saber, with belts. With socks and underwear crammed in to keep them from rattling."

I said soberly, "My princess, I couldn't moan about my sword when your father took the loss of his house so calmly—but thank you, with all my heart."

"Let me add my thanks, Deety. I set much store by that old saber, unnecessary as it is."

"Father, it was *quite* necessary this afternoon."

"Hi *ho*! Hi *ho*! It's to Barsoom we go!"

"Captain, we *could* use the hours 'til dawn for a quick jaunt to Mars. Uh— Oh, dear, I have to know its present distance—I don't."

"No problem," I said. "Gay gobbles the *Aerospace Almanac* each year."

"Indeed! I'm impressed."

"*Gay Deceiver.*"

"You again? I was thinking."

"So think about this. Calculation program. Data address, Aerospace Almanac. Running calculation, line-of-sight distance to planet Mars. Report current answers on demand. Execute."

"Program running."

"Report."

"Klicks two-two-four-zero-nine-zero-eight-two-seven point plus-minus nine-eight-zero."

"Display running report."

Gay did so. "You're a Smart Girl, Gay."

"I can do card tricks, too. Program continuing."

"Jake, how do we this?"

"Align 'L' axis with your gun sight. Isn't that easiest?"

"By far!" I aimed at Mars as if to shoot her out of the sky—then got cold feet. "Jake? A little Tennessee windage? I think those figures are from center-of-gravity to center-of-gravity. Half a mil would place us a safe distance away. Over a hundred thousand klicks."

"A hundred and twelve thousand," Jake agreed, watching the display.

I offset one half mil. "Copilot."

"Captain."

"Transit when ready. Execute."

Mars in half-phase, big and round and ruddy and beautiful, was swimming off our starboard side.

— XIV —

Deety

Aunt Hilda said softly, "Barsoom. Dead sea bottoms. Green giants."
I just gulped.

"Mars, Hilda darling," Pop gently corrected her. "Barsoom is a myth."

"Barsoom," she repeated firmly. "It's not a myth; it's there. Who says its name is Mars? A bunch of long-dead Romans. Aren't the natives entitled to name it? Barsoom."

"My dearest, there are no natives. Names are assigned by an international committee sponsored by Harvard Observatory. They confirmed the traditional name."

"Pooh! They don't have any more right to name it than I have. Deety, isn't that right?"

I think Aunt Hilda had the best argument but I don't argue with Pop unless necessary; he gets emotional. My husband saved me.

"Copilot, astrogation problem. How are we going to figure distance and vector? I would like to put this wagon into orbit. But Gay is no spaceship; I don't have instruments. Not even a sextant!"

"Mmm, suppose we try it one piece at a time, Captain. We don't seem to be falling fast and—*ulp!*"

"What's the trouble, Jake!"

Pop turned pale, sweat broke out; he clenched his jaws, swallowed and re-swallowed. Then his lips barely opened. "M'sheashick."

"No, you're space sick. Deety!"

"Yessir!"

"Emergency kit, back of my seat. Unzip it, get Lomine. One pill—don't let the others get loose."

I got at the first-aid kit, found a tube marked Lomine. A second pill did get loose but I snatched it out of the air. Freefall is funny—you don't know whether you are standing on your head or floating sideways. "Here, Captain."

Pop said, "Mall righ' now. Jus' took all-over queer a moment."

"Sure, you're all right. You can take this pill—or you can have it pushed down your throat with my dirty, calloused finger. Which?"

"Uh, Captain, I'd have to have water to swallow it—and I don't think I *can*."

"Doesn't take water, pal. Chew it. Tastes good, raspberry flavor. Then keep gulping your saliva. Here." Zebadiah pinched Pop's nostrils. "Open up."

I became aware of a strangled sound beside me. Aunt Hilda had a hanky pressed to her mouth and her eyes were streaming tears—she was split seconds from adding potato salad and used sandwich to the cabin air.

Good thing I was still clutching that wayward pill. Aunt Hilda struggled but she's a little bitty. I treated her the way my husband had treated her husband, then clamped my hand over her mouth. I don't understand seasickness (or freefall nausea); I can walk on bulkheads with a sandwich in one hand and a drink in the other and enjoy it.

But the victims really are sick and somewhat out of their heads. So I held her mouth closed and whispered into her ear. "Chew it, Aunty darling, and swallow it."

Shortly I could feel her chewing. After several minutes she relaxed. I asked her, "Is it safe for me to ungag you?"

She nodded. I took my hand away. She smiled wanly and patted my hand. "Thanks, Deety. Can we kiss and make up?"

Mars—Barsoom—seemed to have grown while I was curing Aunt Hilda's space sickness. Our men were talking astrogation. My husband was saying, "Sorry, but at extreme range Gay's radar can see a thousand kilos. You tell me our distance is about a hundred times that."

"About. We're falling toward Mars. Captain, we must do it by triangulation."

"Not even a protractor where I can get at it. *How?*"

"Hmmmm— If the captain pleases, recall how you worked that 'Tennessee windage.'"

My darling looked like a schoolboy caught making a silly answer. "Jake, if you don't quit being polite when I'm stupid, I'm going to space you and put Deety in the copilot's seat. No, we need you to get us home. I'd better resign and you take over."

"Zeb, a captain *can't* resign while his ship is underway. That's universal."

"This is another universe."

"Transuniversal. As long as you are alive, you are stuck with it. Let's attempt that triangulation."

"Stand by to record." Zebadiah settled into his seat, pressed his head against its rest. "Copilot."

"Ready to record, sir."

"Damn!"

"Trouble, Captain?"

"Some. This reflectosight is scaled fifteen mils on a side, concentric circles crossed at center point horizontally and vertically. Normal to deck and parallel to deck, I mean. When I center the fifteen-mil ring on Mars, I have a border around it. I'm going to have to guesstimate. Uh, the border looks to be about eighteen mils wide. So double that and add thirty."

"Sixty-six mils."

"And a mil is one-to-one-thousand. One-to-one-thousand-and-eighteen and a whisker, actually—but one-to-a-thousand is good enough. Wait a half! I've got two sharp high lights near the meridian—if the polar caps mark the meridian. Lemme tilt this buggy and put a line crossing them—then I'll yaw and what we can't measure in one jump, we'll catch in three."

I saw the larger "upper" polar cap (north? south? Well, it *felt* north) roll gently about eighty degrees, while my husband fiddled with Gay's manual controls. "Twenty-nine point five, maybe … plus eighteen point seven … plus sixteen point three. Add."

My father answered, "Sixty-four and a half" while I said, *six four point five* in my mind and kept quiet.

"Who knows the diameter of Mars? Or shall I ask Gay?"

Hilda answered, "Six thousand seven hundred fifty kilometers, near enough."

Plenty near enough for Zebadiah's estimates. Zebadiah said, "Sharpie! How did you happen to know *that?*"

"I read comic books. You know—'Zap! Polaris is missing.'"

"I don't read comic books."

"Lots of interesting things in comic books, Zebbie. I thought the Aerospace Force used comic book instruction manuals."

My darling's ears turned red. "Some are," he admitted, "but they are edited for technical accuracy. Hmm— Maybe I had better check that figure with Gay."

I love my husband but sometimes women must stick together. "Don't bother, Zebadiah," I said in chilly tones. "Aunt Hilda is correct. The polar diameter of Mars is six seven five two point eight plus. But surely three significant figures is enough for your data."

Zebadiah did not answer ... but did *not* ask his computer. Instead he said, "Copilot, will you run it off on your pocket calculator? We can treat it as a tangent at this distance."

This time I didn't even try to keep still. Zebadiah's surprise that Hilda knew anything about astronomy caused me pique. "Our height above surface is one hundred and four thousand six hundred and seventy-two kilometers plus or minus the error of the data supplied. That assumes that Mars is spherical and ignores the edge effect or horizon bulge ... negligible for the quality of your data."

Zebadiah answered so gently that I was sorry that I had shown off: "Thank you, Deety. Would you care to calculate the time to fall to surface from rest at this point?"

"That's an unsmooth integral, sir. I can approximate it but Gay can do it faster and more accurately. Why not ask *her?* But it will be many hours."

"I had hoped to take a better look. Jake, Gay has enough juice to put us into a tight orbit, I think ... but I don't know where or when I'll be able to juice her again. If we simply fall, the air will get stale and we'll need the panic button—or *some* maneuver—without ever seeing the surface close up."

"Captain, would it suit you to read the diameter again? I don't think we've simply been falling."

Pop and Zebadiah got busy again. I let them alone, and they ran even the simplest computations through Gay. Presently, Pop said, "Over twenty-four kilometers per second! Captain, at that rate we'll be there in a little over an hour."

"Except that we'll scram before that. But ladies, you'll get your closer look. Dead sea bottoms and green giants. If any."

"Zebadiah, twenty-four kilometers per second is Mars' orbital speed."

My father answered, "Eh? Why, so it is!" He looked very puzzled, then said, "Captain—I confess to a foolish mistake."

"Not one that will keep us from getting home, I hope."

"No, sir. I'm still learning what our continua craft can do. Captain, we did not aim for Mars."

"I know. I was chicken."

"No, sir, you were properly cautious. *We aimed for a specific point in empty space.* We transited to that point ... but *not* with Mars' proper motion. With that of the solar system, yes. With Earth's motions subtracted; that is in the program. But we are a short distance ahead of Mars in its orbit ... so it is rushing toward us."

"Does that mean we can never land on any planet but Earth?"

"Not at all. Any vector can be included in the program—either before or after transition, translation or rotation. Any subsequent change in motion is taken into account by the inertial integrator. But I am learning that we still have things to learn."

"Jake, that is true even of a bicycle. Quit worrying and enjoy the ride. Brother, what a view!"

"Jake, that doesn't look like the photographs the Mars Expedition brought back."

"Of course not," said Aunt Hilda. "I *said* it was Barsoom."

I kept my mouth shut. Ever since Dr. Sagan's photographs, anyone who reads *The National Geographic*—or anything—knows what Mars looks like. But when it involves changing male minds, it is better to let men reach their own decisions; they become somewhat less pigheaded. That planet rushing toward us was not the Mars of our native sky. White clouds at the caps, big green areas that had to be forest or crops, one deep-blue area that almost certainly was water—all this against ruddy shades that dominated much of the planet.

What was lacking were the rugged mountains and craters and canyons of "our" planet Mars. There were mountains—but nothing like the Devil's Junkyard known to science.

I heard Zebadiah say, "Copilot, are you certain you took us to Mars?"

"Captain, I took us to Mars-*Ten*, via plus on tau-axis. Either that or I'm a patient in a locked ward."

"Take it easy, Jake. It doesn't resemble Mars as much as Earth-Ten resembles Earth."

"Uh, may I point out that we saw just a bit of Earth-Ten, on a moonless night?"

"Meaning we didn't see it. Conceded."

Aunt Hilda said, "I *told* you it was Barsoom. You wouldn't listen."

"Hilda, I apologize. 'Barsoom.' Copilot, log it. New planet, 'Barsoom,' named by right of discovery by Hilda Corners Burroughs, Science Officer of Continua Craft *Gay Deceiver*. We'll all witness: Z. J. Carter, Commanding—Jacob J. Burroughs, Chief Officer—D. T. B. Carter, uh, Astrogator. I'll send certified copies to Harvard Observatory as soon as possible."

"I'm not astrogator, Zebadiah!"

"Mutiny. Who reprogrammed this cloud-buster into a continua craft? I'm pilot until I can train all of you in Gay's little quirks. Jake is copilot until he can train more copilots in setting the verniers. You are astrogator because nobody else can acquire your special knowledge of programming and skill at calculation. None of your lip, young woman, and don't fight the Law of Space. Sharpie is chief of science because of her breadth of knowledge. She not only recognized a new planet as *not* being Mars quicker than anyone else but carved up that double-jointed alien with the skill of a born butcher. Right, Jake?"

"Sure thing!" agreed Pop.

"Cap'n Zebbie," Aunt Hilda drawled, "I'm science officer if you say so. But I had better be ship's cook, too. And cabin boy."

"Certainly, we all have to wear more than one hat. Log it, Copilot. 'Here's to our jolly cabin girl, the plucky little nipper—'"

"Don't finish it. Zebbie," Aunt Hilda cut in, "I don't like the way the plot develops."

> "—she carves fake ranger,
> Dubs planet stranger,
> And dazzles crew and skipper."

Aunt Hilda looked thoughtful. "That's not the classic version. I like the sentiment better ... though the scansion limps."

"Sharpie darling, you are a floccinaucinihilipilificatrix."

"Is that a compliment?"

"Certainly! Means you're so sharp you spot the slightest flaw."

I kept quiet. It was possible that Zebadiah meant it as a compliment. Just barely—

"Maybe I'd better check it in a dictionary."

126

"By all means, dear—after you are off watch." (I dismissed the matter. *Merriam Microfilm* was all we had aboard and Aunt Hilda would not find that word in anything less than the OED.)

"Copilot, got it logged?"

"Captain, I didn't know we *had* a log."

"No log? Even Vanderdecken keeps a log. Deety, the log falls in your department. Take your father's notes, get what you need from Gay, and let's have a taut ship. First time we pass a Woolworth's we'll pick up a journal and you can transcribe it—notes taken now are your rough log."

"Aye aye, sir. Tyrant."

"Tyrant, *sir*, please. Meanwhile let's share the binoculars and see if we can spot any colorful exotic natives in colorful exotic costumes singing colorful exotic songs with their colorful exotic hands out for baksheesh. First one to spot evidence of intelligent life gets to wash the dishes."

— XV —

Hilda

I was so flattered by Cap'n Zebbie's crediting me with "discovering" Barsoom that I pretended not to understand the jibe he added. It was unlikely that Deety would know such a useless word, or my beloved Jacob. It was gallant of Zeb to give in all the way, once he realized that this planet was unlike its analog in "our" universe. Zebbie is a funny one—he wears rudeness like a Hallowe'en mask, afraid that someone will discover the Galahad underneath.

I knew that "my" Barsoom was not the planet of the classic romances. But there are precedents: the first nuclear submarine was named for an imaginary undersea vessel made famous by Jules Verne; an aircraft carrier of the Second Global War had been named "*Shangri La*" for a land as nonexistent as "Erewhon"; the first space freighter had been named for a starship that existed only in the hearts of its millions of fans—the list is endless. Nature copies art.

Or as Deety put it: "Truth is more fantastic than reality."

During that hour Barsoom *rushed* at us. It began to swell and swell, so rapidly that binoculars were a nuisance—and my heart swelled with it, in childlike joy. Deety and I unstrapped so that we could see better, floating just "above" and behind our husbands while steadying ourselves on their headrests.

We were seeing it in half-phase, one half dark, the other in sunlight—ocher and umber and olive green and brown and all of it beautiful.

Our pilot and copilot did not sightsee; Zebbie kept taking sights, kept Jacob busy calculating. At last he said, "Copilot, if

128

our approximations are correct, at the height at which we will get our first radar range, we will be only a bit over half a minute from crashing. Check?"

"To the accuracy of our data, Captain."

"Too close. I don't fancy arriving like a meteor. Is it time to hit the panic button? Advise, please—but bear in mind that puts us—*should* put us—two klicks over a hot, new crater ... possibly in the middle of a radioactive cloud. Ideas?"

"Captain, we can do that just before crashing—and it either works or it doesn't. If it works, that radioactive cloud will have had more time to blow away. If it doesn't work—"

"We'll hit so hard we'll hardly notice it. *Gay Deceiver* isn't built to reenter at twenty-four klicks per second. She's beefed up—but she's still a Ford, not a reentry vehicle."

"Captain, I can try to subtract the planet's orbital speed. We've time to make the attempt."

"Fasten seat belts and report! *Move it, gals!*"

Freefall is funny stuff. I was over that deathly sickness—was enjoying weightlessness, but didn't know how to move in it. Nor did Deety. We floundered the way one does the first time on ice skates—only worse.

"Report, damn it!"

Deety got a hand on something, grabbed me. We started getting into seats—she in mine, I in hers. "Strapping down, Captain!" she called out while frantically trying to loosen my belts to fit her. (I was doing the same in reverse.)

"Speed it up!"

Deety reported, "Seat belts fastened," while still getting her chest belt buckled—by squeezing out all her breath. I reached over and helped her loosen it.

"Copilot."

"Captain!"

"Along l-axis, subtract vector twenty-four klicks per second—and for God's sake don't get the signs reversed."

"I won't!"

"Execute."

Seconds later Jacob reported, "That does it, Captain. I hope."

"Let's check. Two readings, ten seconds apart. I'll call the first, you call the end of ten seconds. *Mark!*"

Zeb added, "One point two. Record."

After what seemed a terribly long time Jacob said, "Seven seconds ... eight seconds ... nine seconds ... *mark!*"

Our men conferred, then Jacob said, "Captain, we are still falling too fast."

"Of course," said Deety. "We've been accelerating from gravity. Escape speed for Mars is five klicks per second. If Barsoom has the same mass as Mars—"

"Thank you, Astrogator. Jake, can you trim off, uh, four klicks per second?"

"Sure!"

"Do it."

"Uh ... done! How does she look?"

"Uh ... distance slowly closing. Hello, Gay."

"Howdy, Zeb."

"Program. Radar. Target dead ahead. Range."

"No reading."

"Continue ranging. Report first reading. Add program. Display running radar ranges to target."

"Program running. Who blacked your eye?"

"You're a Smart Girl, Gay."

"I'm sexy, too. Over."

"Continue program." Zeb sighed, then said, "Copilot, there's atmosphere down there. I plan to attempt to ground. Comment? Advice?"

"Captain, those are words I hoped to hear. Let's go!"

"Barsoom—here we come!"

—— XVI ——

Jake

My beloved bride was no more eager than I to visit "Barsoom." I had been afraid that our captain would do the sensible thing: establish orbit, take pictures, then return to our own space-time before our air was stale. We were not prepared to explore strange planets. *Gay Deceiver* was a bachelor's sports car. We had a little water, less food, enough air for about three hours. Our craft refreshed its air by the scoop method. If she made a "high jump," her scoop valves sealed from internal pressure just as did commercial ballistic-hypersonic intercontinental liners—but "high jump" is not space travel.

True, we could go from point to point in our own or any universe in null time, but how many heavenly bodies have breathable atmospheres? Countless billions—but a small fraction of one percent from a practical viewpoint—and no publication lists their whereabouts. We had no spectroscope, no star catalogs, no atmosphere-testing equipment, no radiation instruments, no means of detecting dangerous organisms. Columbus with his cockleshells was better equipped than we.

None of this worried me.

Reckless? Do you pause to shop for an elephant gun while an elephant is chasing you?

Three times we had escaped death by seconds. We had evaded our killers by going to earth—and that safety had not lasted. So again we fled like rabbits.

At least once every human should have to run for his life, to teach him that milk does not come from supermarkets, that safety does

131

not come from policemen, that "news" is not something that happens to other people. He might learn how his ancestors lived and that he himself is no different—in the crunch his life depends on his agility, alertness, and personal resourcefulness.

I was not distressed. I felt more alive than I had felt since the death of my first wife.

Underneath the *persona* each shows the world lies a being different from the masque. My own persona was a professorial archetype. Underneath? Would you believe a maiden knight, eager to break a lance? I could have avoided military service—married, a father, protected profession. But I spent three weeks in basic training, sweating with the rest, cursing drill instructors—and loving it! Then they took my rifle, told me I was an officer, gave me a swivel chair and a useless job. I never forgave them for that.

Hilda, until we married, I knew not at all. I had valued her as a link to my lost love but I had thought her a lightweight, a social butterfly. Then I found myself married to her and learned that I had unnecessarily suffered lonely years. Hilda was what I needed, I was what she needed—Jane had known it and blessed us when at last *we* knew it. But I *still* did not realize the diamond-hard quality of my tiny darling until I saw her dissecting that pseudo "ranger." Killing that alien was easy. But what Hilda did—I almost lost my supper.

Hilda is small and physically weak; I'll protect her with my life. But I won't underrate her again!

Zeb is the only one of us who *looks* the part of intrepid explorer—tall, broad-shouldered, strongly muscled, skilled with machines and with weapons, and (*sine qua non!*) cool-headed in crisis and gifted with the "voice of command."

One night I had been forced to reason with my darling; Hilda felt that I should lead our little band. I was oldest, I was inventor of the time-space "distorter"—it was all right for Zeb to pilot—but *I* must command. In her eyes, Zeb was somewhere between an overage adolescent and an affectionate Saint Bernard. She pointed out that Zeb claimed to be a "coward by trade" and did not *want* responsibility.

I told her that no born leader seeks command; the mantle descends on him, he wears the burden because he must. Hilda could not see it—she was willing to take orders from me but not from her pet youngster "Zebbie."

I had to be firm: either accept Zeb as commander or tomorrow Zeb and I would dismount my apparatus from Zeb's car so that Mr. and Mrs. Carter could go elsewhere. Where? *Not my business or yours, Hilda.* Hilda promised to take any orders Zeb might give—once we left.

But her capitulation was merely coerced until the gory incident at the pool. Zeb's instantaneous attack changed her attitude. From then on my darling carried out Zeb's orders without argument—and between times kidded and ragged him as always. Hilda's spirit wasn't broken; instead she placed her indomitable spirit subject to the decisions of our captain. Discipline—self-discipline; there is no other sort.

Zeb is indeed a "coward by trade"—he avoids trouble whenever possible—a most commendable trait in a leader. If a captain worries about the safety of his command, those under him need not worry.

Barsoom continued to swell. At last Gay's voice said, "Ranging, boss" as she displayed "1000 km," and flicked at once to "999 km." I started timing when Zeb made it unnecessary: "Smart Girl!"

"Here, Zeb."

"Continue range display. Show as H-above-G. Add dive rate."

"Null program."

"Correction. Add program. Display dive rate soonest."

"New program dive rate stored. Display starts H-above-G six hundred klicks."

"You're a Smart Girl, Gay."

"Smartest little girl in the county. Over."

"Continue programs."

Height-above-ground seemed to drop both quickly and with stomach-tensing slowness. No one said a word; I barely breathed. As "600 km" appeared, the figures were suddenly backed by a grid; on it was a steep curve, height-against-time, and a new figure flashed underneath the H-above-G figure: 1968 km/hr. As the figure changed, a bright abscissa lowered down on the grid.

Our captain let out a sigh. "We can handle that. But I'd give fifty cents and a double-dip ice cream cone for a parachute brake."

"What flavor?"

"Your choice, Sharpie. Don't worry, folks; I can stand her on her tail and blast. But it's an expensive way to slow up. *Gay Deceiver.*"

133

"Busy, boss."

"I keep forgetting that I can't ask her to display too many data at once. Anybody know the sea level—I mean 'surface' atmospheric pressure of Mars? Don't all speak at once."

My darling said hesitantly, "It averages about five millibars. But, Captain—this isn't Mars."

"Huh? So it isn't—and from the looks of that green stuff, Barsoom must have lots more atmosphere than Mars." Zeb took the controls, overrode the computer, cautiously waggled her elevons. "Can't feel bite. Sharpie, how come you bone astronomy? Girl Scout?"

"Never got past Tenderfoot. I audited a course, then subscribed to *Astronomy* and *Sky and Telescope*. It's sort o' fun."

"Chief of Science, you have again justified my faith in you. Copilot, as soon as I have air bite, I'm going to ease to the east. We're headed too close to the terminator. I want to ground in daylight. Keep an eye out for level ground. I'll hover at the last—but I don't want to ground in forest. Or in badlands."

"Aye aye, sir."

"Astrogator."

"Yessir!"

"Deety darling, search to port—and forward—as much as you can see around me. Jake can favor the starboard side."

"Captain—I'm on the starboard side. Behind Pop."

"Huh? How did you gals get swapped around?"

"Well ... you hurried us, sir—any old seat in a storm."

"Two demerits for wrong seat—and no syrup on the hotcakes we're going to have for breakfast as soon as we're grounded."

"Uh, I don't believe hotcakes are possible."

"I can dream, can't I? Chief Science Officer, watch my side."

"Yes, Cap'n."

"While Deety backs up Jake. Any cow pasture."

"Hey! I feel air! She bites!"

I held my breath while Zeb slowly brought the ship out of dive, easing her east. "*Gay Deceiver.*"

"How now, Brown Cow?"

"Cancel display programs. Execute."

"*Inshallâh, ya sayyid.*"

The displays faded. Zeb held her just short of stalling. We were still high, about six klicks, still hypersonic.

Zeb slowly started spreading her wings as air speed and altitude dropped. After we dropped below speed of sound, he opened her wings full for maximum lift. "Did anyone remember to bring a canary?"

"A *canary!*" said Deety. "What for, Boss Man?"

"My gentle way of reminding everyone that we have no way to test atmosphere. Copilot."

"Captain," I acknowledged.

"Uncover deadman switch. Hold it closed while you remove clamp. Hold it high where we all can see it. Once you report switch ready to operate, I'm going to crack the air scoops. If you pass out, your hand will relax and the switch will get us home. I hope. But— All hands!— If anyone feels dizzy or woozy or faint … or sees any of us start to slump, don't wait! Give the order orally. Deety, spell the order I mean. Don't say it—spell it."

"G, A, Y, D, E, C, I, E, V, E, R, T, A, K, E, U, S, H, O, M, E."

"You misspelled it."

"I did not!"

"You did so; 'i' before 'e' except after 'c.' You reversed 'em."

"Well … maybe I did. That diphthong has always given me trouble. Floccinaucinihilipilificator!"

"So you understood it? From now on, on Barsoom, 'i' comes before 'e' at all times. By order of John Carter, Warlord. I have spoken. Copilot?"

"Deadman switch ready, Captain," I answered.

"You gals hold your breaths or breathe, as you wish. Pilot and copilot will breathe. I am about to open air scoops."

I tried to breathe normally and wondered if my hand would relax if I passed out.

The cabin got suddenly chilly, then the heaters picked up. I felt normal. Cabin pressure slightly higher, I thought, under ram effect.

"Everybody feel right? Does everybody look right? Copilot?"

"I feel fine. You look okay. So does Hilda. I can't see Deety."

"Science Officer?"

"Deety looks normal. I feel fine."

"Deety. Speak up."

"Golly, I had forgotten what fresh air smells like!"

"Copilot, carefully—*most* carefully!—put the clamp back on the switch, then rack and cover it. Report completion."

A few seconds later I reported, "Deadman switch secured, Captain."

"Good. I see a golf course; we'll ground." Zeb switched to powered flight; Gay responded, felt alive. We spiraled, hovered briefly, grounded with a gentle bump. "Grounded on Barsoom. Log it, Astrogator. Time and date."

"Huh?"

"On the instrument board."

"But that says oh-eight-oh-three and it's just after dawn here."

"Log it Greenwich. With it, log estimated local time and Barsoom day one." Zeb yawned. "I wish they wouldn't hold mornings so early."

"Too sleepy for hotcakes?" my wife inquired.

"Never that sleepy."

"Aunt Hilda!"

"Deety, I stowed the pancake mix. And powdered milk. And butter. Zebbie, no syrup—sorry. But there is grape jelly in a tube. And freeze-dried coffee. If one of you will undog this bulkhead door, we'll have breakfast in a few minutes."

"Chief Science Officer, you have a duty to perform."

"I do? But— Yes, Captain?"

"Put your dainty toe to the ground. It's your planet, your privilege. Starboard side of the car, under the wing, is the ladies' powder room—portside is the men's jakes. Ladies may have armed escort on request."

I was glad Zeb remembered that. The car had a "honey bucket" under the cushion of the port rear seat, and, with it, plastic liners. I did not ever want to have to use it.

Gay Deceiver was wonderful but, as a spaceship, she left much to be desired. However, she had brought us safely to Barsoom.

Barsoom! Visions of thoats and beautiful princesses—

— XVII —

Deety

We spent our first hour on "Barsoom" getting oriented. Aunt Hilda stepped outside, then stayed out. "Isn't cold," she told us. "Going to be hot later."

"Watch where you step!" my husband warned her. "Might be snakes or anything." He hurried after her—and went head over heels.

Zebadiah was not hurt; the ground was padded, a greenish-yellow mat somewhat like "ice plant" but looking more like clover. He got up carefully, then swayed as if walking on a rubber mattress. "I don't understand it," he complained. "This gravity ought to be twice that of Luna. But I feel lighter."

Aunt Hillbilly sat down on the turf. "On the Moon, you were carrying pressure suit and tanks and equipment." She unfastened her shoes. "Here you aren't."

"Yeah, so I was," agreed my husband. "What are you doing?"

"Taking off my shoes. When were you on the Moon? Cap'n Zebbie, you're a fraud."

"Don't take off your shoes! You don't know what's in this grass."

The Hillbilly stopped, one shoe off. "If they bite me, I bite 'em back. Captain, in *Gay Deceiver* you are absolute boss. But doesn't your crew have *any* free will? I'll play it either way: free citizen ... or your thrall who dassn't even take off a shoe without permission. Just tell me."

"Uh—"

"If you try to make all decisions, all the time, you're going to get as hysterical as a hen raising ducklings. Even Deety can be notional.

137

But *I* won't even pee without permission. Shall I put this back on? Or take the other off?"

"Aunt Hilda, quit teasing my husband!" (I was annoyed!)

"Dejah Thoris, I am not teasing your husband; I am asking our captain for instructions."

Zebadiah sighed. "Sometimes I wish I'd stayed in Australia."

I said, "Is it all right for Pop and me to come out?"

"Oh. Certainly. Watch your step; it's tricky."

I jumped down, then jumped high and wide, with *entrechats* as I floated—landed *sur les pointes*. "Oh, boy! What a wonderful place for ballet!" I added, "Shouldn't do that on a full bladder. Aunt Hilda, let's see if that powder room is unoccupied."

"I was about to, dear, but I must get a ruling from our captain."

"You're teasing him."

"No, Deety; Hilda is right; doctrine has to be clear. Jake? How about taking charge on the ground?"

"No, Captain. Druther be a Balkan general, given my druthers."

Aunt Hilda stood up, shoe in hand, reached high with her other hand, patted my husband's cheek. "Zebbie, you are a dear. You worry about us all—me especially, because you think I'm a featherhead. Remember how we did at Snug Harbor? Each one did what she could do best and there was no friction. If that worked there, it ought to work here."

"Well ... all right. But will you gals *please* be careful?"

"We'll be careful. How's your ESP? Any feeling?"

Zebadiah wrinkled his forehead. "No. But I don't get advance warning. Just barely enough."

" 'Just barely' is enough. Before we had to leave, you were about to program Gay to listen at high gain. Would that change 'just barely' to 'ample'?"

"Yes! Sharpie, I'll put you in charge, on the ground."

"In your hat, buster. Zebbie, the quicker you quit dodging, the sooner you get those hotcakes. Spread my cape down and put the hot plate on the step."

We ate breakfast in basic Barsoomian dress: skin. Aunt Hilda pointed out that laundries seemed scarce, and the car's water tanks had to be saved for drinking and cooking. "Deety, I have just this dress you gave me; I'll air it and let the wrinkles hang out. An air bath is better than no bath. I know you'll divvy with me but you are no closer to a laundry than I am."

My jumpsuit joined Hilda's dress.

The same reasoning caused our men to spread their used clothing on the port wing, and caused Zebadiah to pick up Hilda's cape. "Sharpie, you can't get fur Hollanderized in this universe. Jake, you stowed some tarps?"

After dishes were "washed" (scoured with turf, placed in the sun) we were sleepy. Zebadiah wanted us to sleep inside, doors locked. Aunt Hilda and I wanted to nap on a tarpaulin in the shade of the car. I pointed out that moving rear seats aft in refitting had made it impossible to recline them.

Zebadiah offered to give up his seat to either of us women. I snapped, "Don't be silly, dear! You barely fit into a rear seat and it brings your knees so far forward that the seat in front *can't* be reclined."

Pop intervened. "Hold it! Daughter, I'm disappointed—snapping at your husband. But, Zeb, we've *got* to rest. If I sleep sitting up, I get swollen ankles, half crippled, not good for much."

"I was trying to keep us safe," Zebadiah said plaintively.

"I know, son; you've been doing so—and a smart job, or we all would be dead three times over. Deety knows it, I know it, Hilda knows it—"

"I sure do, Zebbie!"

"My captain, I'm sorry I snapped at you."

"We'll need you later. Flesh has its limits—even yours. If necessary, we would bed you down and stand guard over you—"

"No!"

"We sure would, Zebbie!"

"We *will*, my captain."

"But I doubt that it's necessary. When we sat on the ground to eat, did anyone get chigger bites or anything?"

My husband shook his head.

"Not me," Aunt Hilda agreed.

I added, "I saw some little beasties but they didn't bother me."

"Apparently," Pop went on, "they don't like our taste. A ferocious-looking dingus sniffed at my ankle—but it scurried away. Zeb, Gay can hear better than we can?"

"Oh, *much* better!"

"Can her radar be programmed to warn us?"

Zebadiah looked thoughtful. "Uh ... anti-collision alarm would wake the dead. If I pulled it in to minimum range, then— No, the display would be cluttered with 'grass.' We're on the ground. False returns."

I said, "Subtract static display, Zebadiah."

"Eh? How, Deety?"

"Gay can do it. Shall I try?"

"Deety, if you switch on radar, we have to sleep inside. Microwaves cook your brains."

"I know, sir. Gay has sidelookers, eyes fore and aft, belly, and umbrella—has she not?"

"Yes. That's why—"

"Switch off her belly eye. Can sidelookers hurt us if we sleep *under* her?"

His eyes widened. "Astrogator, you know more about my car than I do. I'd better sign her over to you."

"My captain, you have already endowed me with all your worldly goods. I don't know more about Gay; I know more about *programming*."

We made a bed under the car by opening Zebadiah's sleeping bag out flat, a tarpaulin on each side. Aunt Hilda dug out sheets: "In case anyone gets chilly."

"Unlikely," Pop told her. "Hot now, not a cloud and no breeze."

"Keep it by you, dearest. Here's one for Zebbie." She dropped two more on the sleeping bag, lay down on it. "Down flat, gentlemen"—waited for them to comply, then called to me: "Deety! Everybody's down."

From inside I called back, "*Right with you!*"—then said, "Hello, Gay."

"Hi, Deety!"

"Retrieve newest program. Execute."

Five scopes lighted, faded to dimness; the belly eye remained blank. I told her, "You're a good girl, Gay."

"I like you, too, Deety. Over."

"Roger and out, sister." I scrunched down, got at the stowage under the instrument board, pulled out padding and removed saber and sword, each with belt. These I placed at the door by a pie tin used at breakfast. I slithered head-first out the door, turned without rising, got swords and pie plate, and crawled toward the pallet, left arm cluttered with hardware.

I stopped. "Your sword, Captain."

"Deety! Do I need a sword to nap?"

"No, sir. *I* shall sleep soundly knowing that my captain has his sword."

140

"Hmm—" Zebadiah withdrew it a span, returned it with a click. "Silly ... but *I* feel comforted by it, too."

"I see nothing silly, sir. Ten hours ago you killed a *thing* with it that would have killed me."

"I stand—sprawl—corrected, my princess. Dejah Thoris is always correct."

"I hope my chieftain will always think so."

"He will. Give me a big kiss. What's the pie pan for?"

"Radar alarm test."

Having delivered the kiss, I crawled past Hilda and handed Pop his saber. He grinned at me. "Deety hon, you're a one! Just the security blanket I need. How did you know?"

"Because Aunt Hilda and I need it. With our warriors armed, we will sleep soundly." I kissed Pop, crawled out from under. "Cover your ears!"

I got to my knees, sailed that pan far and high, dropped flat and covered my ears. As the pan sailed into the zone of microwave radiation, a horrid clamor sounded inside the car, kept up until the pan struck the ground and stopped rolling—chopped off. "Somebody remind me to recover that. Goodnight, all!"

I crawled back, stretched out by Hilda, kissed her goodnight, set the clock in my head for six hours, went to sleep.

The sun was saying that it was fourteen instead of fourteen-fifteen and I decided that my circadian did not fit Barsoom. Would the clock in my head "slow" to match a day forty minutes longer? Would it give me trouble? Not likely—I've always been able to sleep anytime. I felt grand and ready for anything.

I crept off the pallet, snaked up into the car's cabin, and stretched. Felt good!

I crawled through the bulkhead door back of the rear seats, got some scarves and my jewelry case, went forward into the space between seats and instrument board.

I tried tying a filmy green scarf as a bikini bottom, but it looked like a diaper. I took it off, folded it corner to corner, pinned it at my left hip with a jeweled brooch. Lots better! "Indecently decent," Pop would say.

I looped a rope of imitation pearls around my hips, arranged strands to drape with the cloth, fastened them at the brooch. I hung around my neck a pendant of pearls and cabochon emeralds—from my father the day I received the title Doctor of Philosophy.

I was adding bracelets and rings when I heard "*Psst!*"—looked down and saw the Hillbilly's head and hands at the doorsill. Hilda put a finger to her lips. I nodded, gave her a hand up, whispered, "Still asleep?"

"Like babies."

"Let's get you dressed ... 'Princess Thuvia.'"

Aunt Hilda giggled. "Thank you ... 'Princess' Dejah Thoris."

"Want anything but jewelry?"

"Just something to anchor it. That old-gold scarf if you can spare it."

"'Course I can! Nothing's too good for my Aunt Thuvia and that scarf is durn near nothing. Baby doll, we're going to deck you out for the auction block. Will you do my hair?"

"And you mine. Deety—I mean 'Dejah Thoris'—I miss a three-way mirror."

"We'll be mirrors for each other," I told her. "I don't mind camping out. My great-great-great-grandmother had two babies in a sod house. Hold still. Or shall I pin it through your skin?"

"Either way, dear. We'll find water—all this ground cover."

"Ground cover doesn't prove running water. This place may be a 'dead sea bottom of Barsoom.'"

"Doesn't look dead," Aunt Hilda countered. "It's pretty."

"Yes, but this looks like a dead sea bottom. Which gave me an idea. Hold up your hair; I want to arrange your necklaces."

"What idea?" Aunt Hilda demanded.

"Zebadiah told me to figure a third escape program. The first two—I'll paraphrase, Gay is awake. One tells her to take us back to a height over Snug Harbor; the other tells her to scoot back to where she was before she was last given the first order."

"I thought that one told her to place us over the Grand Canyon?"

"It does, at present. But if she got the first order *now*, that would change the second order. Instead of over the Grand Canyon, we would be back here quicker'n a frog could wink its eye."

"Okay if you say so."

"She's programmed that way. Hit the panic button and we are over our cabin site. Suppose we arrive there and find trouble, then use the 'C' order. She takes us *back to wherever she last got the 'T' order*. Dangerous, or we would not have left in a rush. So we need a *third* escape program, to take us to a safe place. This looks safe."

"It's peaceful."

"Seems so. There!—more doodads than a Christmas tree and you look nakeder than ever."

"That's the effect we want, isn't it? Sit down in the copilot's seat; I'll do your hair."

"Want shoes?" I asked.

"On *Barsoom?* Dejah Thoris, thank you for your little-girl shoes. But they pinch my toes. You're going to wear *shoes?*"

"Not bleedin' likely, Aunt Nanny Goat. I toughened my feet for karate—I can break a four-by-nine with my feet and get nary a bruise. Or run on sharp gravel. What's a good escape phrase? I plan to store in Gay an emergency signal for every spot we visit that looks like a safe hidey-hole. So give me a phrase."

"Your mudder chaws terbacker!"

"Nanny Goat! A code phrase should have a built-in mnemonic."

" 'Bug Out'?"

"A horrid expression and just what we need. 'Bug Out' will mean to take us to this exact spot. I'll program it. And post it and others on the instrument board so that, if anyone forgets, she can read it."

"And so could any outsider, if she got in."

"Fat lot of good it would do her! Gay ignores an order not in our voices. Hello, Gay."

"Hello, Deety!"

"Retrieve present location. Report."

"Null program."

"Are we *lost?*"

"Not at all, Aunt Hilda. I was sloppy. Gay, program check. Define 'Home.' "

"Cancel any-all transitions translations rotations inertials. Return to zero-designated latitude-longitude two klicks above ground level hovering."

"Search memory reversed—real-time for last order execute-coded *Gay Deceiver* take us home."

"Retrieved."

"From time of retrieved order integrate to time-present all transitions translations rotations inertials."

"Integrated."

143

"Test check. Report summary of integration."

"Origin 'Home.' Countermarch program executed. Complex maneuver inertials. Translation tau-axis ten minimals positive. Complex maneuver inertials. Translation Ell axis two-two-four-zero-nine-zero-eight-two-seven point zero klicks. Negative vector Ell axis twenty-four klicks per sec. Negative vector Ell axis four klicks per sec. Complex maneuver inertials. Grounded here—then oh-eight-oh-two-forty-nine. Grounded inertials continuing eight hours three minutes nineteen seconds *mark!* Grounded inertials continue running real-time."

"New program. Here-now grounded inertial location real-time running to real-time new execute order equals code phrase bug-out. Report new program."

Gay answered, "New program code phrase bug-out. Definition: here-now grounded inertials running real-time to future-time execute order code phrase bug-out."

"Gay, I tell you three times."

"Deety, I hear you three times."

"New program. Execute-coded *Gay Deceiver* Bug Out. At execute-code move to location coded 'bug-out.' I tell you three times."

"I hear you three times."

"*Gay Deceiver*, you're a Smart Girl."

"Deety, why don't you leave that big ape and live with me? Over."

"Goodnight, Gay. Roger and out. Hillbilly, I didn't give you that answer." I tried to look fierce.

"Why, Deety, how could you say such a thing?"

"I know I didn't. Well?"

"I 'fess up, Deetikins. A few days ago while you and I were working, you were called away. While I waited, I stuck that in. Want it erased?"

I don't know how to look fierce; I snickered. "No. Maybe Zebadiah will be around the next time it pops up. I wish our men would wake, I do."

"They need rest, dear."

"I know. But I want to check that new program."

"It sounded complex."

"Can be, by voice. I'd rather work on paper. A computer doesn't accept excuses. A mistake can be anything from 'null program' to disaster. This one has features I've never tried. I don't really *understand* what Pop does. Non-Euclidean n-dimensional geometry is way out in left field."

"To me it's not in the ball park."

"So I'm itchy."

"Let's talk about something else."

"Did I show you our micro walkie-talkies?"

"Jacob gave me one."

"There's one for each. Tiny but amazingly long-ranged. Uses less power than a hand calculator and weighs less—under two hundred grams. Mass, I mean—weight—here is much less. Today I thought of a new use. Gay can accept their frequency."

"That's nice. How do you plan to use this?"

"This car can be remote-controlled."

"Deety, who would you want to do *that?*"

I admitted that I did not know. "But Gay can be preprogrammed to do almost anything. For example, we could go outside and tell Gay, via walkie-talkie, to carry out two programs in succession: H,O,M,E, followed by B,U,G,O,U,T. Imagine Zebadiah's face when he wakes up from sun in his eyes—because his car has vanished—then his expression two hours later when it pops back into existence."

"Deety, go stand in the corner for *thinking* such an unfunny joke!" Then Aunt Hilda looked thoughtful. "Why would it take two hours? I thought Gay could go anywhere in *no* time."

"Depends on your postulates, Princess Thuvia. We took a couple of hours to get here because we fiddled. Gay would have to follow that route in reverse because it's the only one she knows. Then—" I stopped, suddenly confused. "Or would it be *four* hours? No, vectors would cancel and— But that would make it instantaneous; we would never know that she had left. Or would we? Aunt Hilda, I don't *know!* Oh, I wish our men would wake up, I do!" The world wobbled and I felt scared.

"I'm awake," Pop answered, his head just showing above the doorsill.

"Pop," I asked, "is Zebadiah asleep?"

"Just woke up."

I spoke to Gay, then to Pop: "Will you tell Zebadiah radar is off? He can stand up without getting his ears fried."

"Sure." Pop ducked down and yelled, "Zeb, it's safe."

"Coming!" Zebadiah's voice rumbled back. "Tell Deety to put the steaks on." My darling appeared wearing sword, carrying pie pan and sheets. "Are the steaks ready?" he asked, then kissed me.

"Not quite, sir," I told him. "First, go shoot a thoat. Or will you settle for peanut butter sandwiches?"

"Don't talk dirty. Did you say 'thoat'?"

"Yes. This is Barsoom."

"I thoat that was what you said."

"If that's a pun, you can eat it for supper. With peanut butter."

Zebadiah shuddered. "I'd rather cut my thoat."

Pop said, "Don't do it, Zeb. A man can't eat with his thoat cut. He can't even talk clearly."

Aunt Hilda said mildly, "If you three will cease those atrocities, I'll see what I can scrape up for dinner."

"I'll help," I told her, "but can we run my test first? I'm itchy."

"Certainly, Deety. It will be a scratch meal."

Pop looked at Aunt Hilda reproachfully. "And you told us to stop."

"What test?" demanded my husband.

I explained the Bug Out program. "I *think* I programmed it correctly. But here is a test. Road the car a hundred meters. If my program works—fine! If it tests null, no harm done but you and Pop will have to teach me more about the twister before I'll risk new programming."

"I don't want to road the car, Deety; I'm stingy with every erg until I know when and where I can juice Gay. However—Jake, what's your minimum transition?"

"Ten kilometers. Can't use spatial quanta for transitions—too small. But the scale goes up fast—logarithmic. That's short range. Middle range is in light years—logarithmic again."

"What's long range, Jake?"

"Gravitic radiation versus time. We won't use *that* one."

"Why not, Jacob?" asked Aunt Hilda.

Pop looked sheepish. "I'm scared of it, dearest. There are three major theories concerning gravitic propagation. At the time I machined those controls, one theory seemed proved. Since then other physicists have reported not being able to reproduce the data. So I blocked off long-range." Pop smiled sourly. "I know the gun is loaded but not what it will do. So I spiked it."

"Sensible," agreed my husband. "Russian roulette lacks appeal. Jake, do you have any guess as to what options you shut off?"

"Better than a guess, Zeb. It reduces the number of universes accessible to us on this axis from the sixth power of six to the sixth power to a mere six to the sixth power. Forty-six thousand six hundred fifty-six."

"Gee, that's tough!"

"I didn't mean it as a joke, Zeb."

"Jake, I was laughing at *me*. I've been looking forward to a lifetime exploring universes—and now I learn that I'm limited to a fiddlin' forty-six thousand and some. Suppose I have a half century of exploration left in me. Assume that I take off no time for eating, sleeping, or teasing the cat, how much time can I spend in each universe?"

"About nine hours twenty minutes per universe," I told him. "Nine hours, twenty-three minutes, thirty-eight point seven-two-two seconds, plus, to be more nearly accurate."

"Deety, let's do be accurate," Zebadiah said solemnly. "If we stayed a minute too long in each universe, we would miss nearly a hundred universes."

I was getting into the spirit. "Let's hurry instead. If we work at it, we can do three universes a day for fifty years—one of us on watch, one on standby, two off duty—and still squeeze in maintenance, plus a few hours on the ground, once a year. If we hurry."

"We haven't a second to lose!" Zebadiah answered. "All hands!—Places! Stand by to lift! *Move!*"

I was startled but hurried to my seat. Pop's chin dropped but he took his place. Aunt Hilda hesitated a split second before diving for her seat, but, as she strapped herself in, wailed, "Captain? Are we *really* leaving Barsoom?"

"Quiet, please. *Gay Deceiver*, close doors! Report seat belts. Copilot, check starboard door seal."

"Seat belt fastened," I reported with no expression.

"Mine's fastened. *Oh, dear!*"

"Copilot, by low range, 'H' axis upward, minimum transition."

"Set, Captain."

"Execute."

Sky outside was dark, the ground far below. "Ten klicks exactly," my husband approved. "Astrogator, take the conn, test your new program. Science Officer, observe."

"Yessir. *Gay Deceiver—Bug Out!*"

We were parked on the ground.

"Science Officer—report," Zebadiah ordered.

"Report what?" Aunt Hilda demanded.

"We tested a new program. Did it pass test?"

"Uh, we seem to be back where we were. We were weightless maybe ten seconds. I guess the test was okay, except—"

"Except what?"

"Captain Zebbie, you're the worst tease on Earth! And Barsoom! You did so put lime Jell-O in my pool!"

"I was in Africa."

"Then you arranged it!"

"Hilda—please! I *never* said we were leaving Barsoom. I said that we hadn't a second to waste. We don't, with so much to explore."

"Excuses. *What about my clothes?* All on the starboard wing. Where are they now? Floating up in the stratosphere? Coming down *where?* I'll *never* find them."

"I thought you preferred to dress Barsoomian style?"

"Doesn't mean I want to be *forced* to! Besides, Deety lent them to me. I'm sorry, Deety."

I patted her hand. "S'all right, Aunt Hilda. I'll lend you more. Give them, I mean." I hesitated, then said firmly, "Zebadiah, you should apologize to Aunt Hilda."

"Oh, for the love of— Sharpie? Sharpie darling."

"Yes, Zebbie?"

"I'm sorry I let you think that we were leaving Barsoom. I'll buy you clothes that fit. We'll make a quick trip back to Earth—"

"Don't want to go back to Earth! *Aliens!* They scare me."

"They scare me, too. I started to say: 'Earth-without-a-J.' It's so much like our own that I can probably use US money. If not, I have gold. Or I can barter. For you, Sharpie, I'll *steal* clothes. We'll go to Phoenix-without-a-J tomorrow—today we take a walk and see some of this planet—*your* planet—and we'll stay on your planet until you get tired of it. Is that enough? Or must I confess putting Jell-O into your pool when I *didn't?*"

"You really didn't?"

"Cross my heart."

"Be darned. Actually I thought it was funny. I wonder who did it? Aliens, maybe?"

"They play rougher than that. Sharpie darling, I'm not the only weirdo in your stable—not by dozens."

"Guess maybe. Zebbie? Will you kiss Sharpie and make up?"

On the ground, under the starboard wing, we found our travel clothes, and under the port wing, those of our husbands. Zebadiah looked bemused. "Jake? I thought Hilda was right. It had slipped my mind that we had clothing on the wings."

"Use your head, son."

"I'm not sure I have one."

"I don't understand it either, darling," Aunt Hilda added.

"Daughter?" Pop asked.

"Pop, I *think* I know. But—I pass!"

"Zeb, the car never moved. Instead—"

Aunt Hilda interrupted, "Jacob, are you saying that we did not go straight up? We were *there*—five minutes ago."

"Yes, my darling. But we didn't *move* there. Motion has a definable meaning: a duration of changing locations. But no duration was involved. We did not successively occupy loci between here-then and there-then."

Aunt Hilda shook her head. "I don't understand. We went *whoosh!* up into the sky ... then *whoosh!* back where we started."

"My darling, we didn't *whoosh!* Deety! Don't be reticent."

I sighed. "Pop, I'm not sure there exists a symbol for the referent. Aunt Hilda. Zebadiah. A discontinuity. The car—"

"Got it!" said Zebadiah.

"*I* didn't," Aunt Hilda persisted.

"Like this, Sharpie," my husband went on. "My car is *here. Spung!*—it vanishes. Our clothes fall to the ground. Ten seconds later—*flip!*—we're back where we started. But our clothes are on the ground. Get it now?"

"I—I guess so. Yes."

"I'm glad you do ... because *I* don't. To me, it's magic." Zebadiah shrugged. " 'Magic.' "

"Magic," I stated, "is a symbol for any process not understood."

"That's what I said, Deety. 'Magic.' Jake, would it have mattered if the car had been indoors?"

"Well ... that fretted me the first time Deety and I translated to Earth-without-the-letter-J. So I moved our car outdoors. But now I think that only the destination matters. It should be empty—I *think*. But I'm too timid to experiment."

"Might be interesting. Unmanned vehicle. Worthless target. A small asteroid. A baby Sun?"

"I don't *know*, Zeb. Nor do I have apparatus to spare. It took me three years to build this one."

"So we wait a few years. Jake? Air has mass."

"That worried me also. But any mass, other than degenerate mass, is mostly empty space. Air—Earth sea-level air—has about a thousandth the density of the human body. The body is mostly water and water accepts air readily. I can't say that it has no effect—twice I've thought that my temperature went up a trifle at transition or translation in atmosphere but it could have been excitement. I've never experienced caisson disease from it. Has any of us felt discomfort?"

"Not me, Jake."

"I've felt all right, Pop," I agreed.

"I got space sick. 'Til Deety cured it," Aunt Hilda added.

"So did I, my darling. But that was into vacuo and could not involve the phenomenon."

"Pop," I said earnestly, "we weren't hurt; we don't have to know *why*. A basic proposition of epistemology, bedrock both for the three basic statements of semantics and for information theory, is that an observed fact requires no proof. It simply *is*, self-demonstrating. Let philosophers worry about it; they haven't anything better to do."

"Suits me!" agreed Hilda. "You big-brains had Sharpie panting. I thought we were going to take a walk?"

"We are, dear," agreed my husband. "Right after those steaks."

─ XVIII ─

Zebadiah

Four Dagwoods later we were ready to start walkabout. Deety delayed by wanting to repeat her test by remote control. I put my foot down. "No!"

"Why not, my captain? I've taught Gay a program to take her straight up ten klicks. It's G, A, Y, B, O, U, N, C, E—a new fast-escape with no execution word necessary. Then I'll recall her by B, U, G, O, U, T. If one works via walkie-talkie, so will the second. It can save our lives, it can!"

"Uh—" I went on folding tarps and stowing my sleeping bag. The female mind is too fast for me. I often can reach the same conclusion; a woman gets there first and *never* by the route I have to follow. Besides that, Deety is a genius.

"You were saying, my captain?"

"I was thinking. Deety, do it with me aboard. I won't touch the controls. Check pilot, nothing more."

"Then it won't be a test."

"Yes, it will. I promise, Cub Scout honor, to let it fall sixty seconds. Or to three klicks H-above-G, whichever comes first."

"These walkie-talkies have more range than ten kilometers even between themselves. Gay's reception is *much* better."

"Deety, you trust machinery; I don't. If Gay doesn't pick up your second command—sunspots, interference, open circuit, anything— I'll keep her from crashing."

151

"But if something else goes wrong and you *did* crash, I would have *killed* you!"

So we compromised. Her way. The exact test she had originally proposed.

I wasted juice by roading *Gay Deceiver* a hundred meters, got out, and we all backed off. Deety said into her walkie-talkie, "*Gay Deceiver ... Bug Out!*"

Not even an implosion *Splat!* Perhaps her non-spherical shape caused acoustic cancel-out by interference. Perhaps I would have heard something if I had been standing right by her. Or perhaps not. Magic.

So we started out. The sun was still high despite two engineering tests, considerable yak-yak, and making and eating Dagwoods. We headed for the nearest point of the old shoreline (if that was what it was), a hill that stuck out from the rest, perhaps two kilometers away and half a kilometer above the "sea bottom," judging by eye.

We were armed and in open patrol, and I was back in command. Not my idea—Sharpie's. She had asked, "Lifeboat rules, Captain?"

I had answered, "Uh ..." Jake had said, "Certainly!" and Deety had echoed, "Of course!" So I shrugged and accepted it.

"I'll head for that nearest hill. When I've gone two hundred paces, I'll raise my arm, and you, Hilda, start after me. Try to hold that interval; I won't hurry. Jake and Deety, start at the same time, but angle off to right and left and drop back. Try to form an equilateral triangle, with me at point, Deety and Jake right and left drag, and Hilda spang in middle. Talk only via walkie-talkie and keep it low; the range is short. Don't chatter, but report anything you see. Address the person you are talking to *before* you say what you have to say—keep it brief and always use 'Over' and 'Roger and Out!' This is a drill as well as sightseeing; we may do this on many planets ... and this looks like an easy place to practice. Questions?"

"Captain," asked Jake, "how long are we going to stay out?"

"I intend to have us back inside while the sun is still an hour high. I hope that we will reach the top of that hill and look around from there. But if I've misjudged the distance—or how fast the sun moves through the sky—I'll head back without reaching the hill. At a trot, if necessary. Or a dead run. However fast Hilda can move. But we're going to be inside the car and buttoned up before sunset. Uh, Deety, got the time figured out here?"

"No, sir, not yet. I could make a guess by assuming that it matches Mars. But I don't *know* that it does."

"So don't assume that it does. Look back over your shoulder occasionally, and also watch your own shadow, and don't hesitate to tell me to turn back—you have, by far, the best time-sense of any of us."

"Yessir."

"Any more questions? Hilda, watch for my signal." I started off, feeling like both Lewis and Clark—the comedy team, not the explorers. I was dressed in a pair of Jake's boxing shorts because they were more comfortable and cooler than the swim briefs I had worn as my first "Martian" costume. The rest was mostly sword belt and that wonderful sword. But the belt also supported walkie-talkie and gun, a police special of the caliber still called "thirty-eight." It did not have the punching power of the still older army automatic Jake carried on his Sam Browne opposite his saber—but I had hand-loaded the ammo and had converted the bullets into illegal (and highly effective) dumdums.

So Jake and I were equipped effectively alike. Hilda was in the center because she was armed solely with a hunting knife mounted on one of Deety's belts. Hilda had never learned to shoot, but we (and a dead alien) knew how well she handled a knife.

Deety was armed three ways: a knife at her belt, her Skoda fléchette pistol on the other side, and her own shotgun, a 12-gauge pump gun, with spare cartridges in her belt. Jake assured me she was a "natural" with it.

However, she had nothing but bird shot, so her range was less than that of Jake's pistol, and her striking power much less. I had placed her as right flank drag, but being the point farthest from the hills.

In putting on belts, weapons, and walkie-talkies, our ladies had *not* removed one bauble of their barbaric jewelry. They delighted in being dressed "Barsoomian style," and there seemed to be no reason not to go along with their whim. Jewelry did not interfere with weapons—so why not? Bare skin seemed appropriate, too. This place might be cold at night, but it was warm once the sun was up and rather too warm now, mid-afternoon.

I had fretted about shoes. Hilda's total choice lay between tennis shoes that had already started a blister, and dancing slippers with high heels. Deety did have stout country shoes—but she had said, "Zebadiah, I don't *need* shoes. If you give me orders as our commander, I'll wear them. But you'll make me less able to defend myself."

(For an absolute monarch, I win very few arguments.)

Jake and I each had field boots. I got as far as putting mine on and lacing one up. But my feet seemed to have spread during two weeks barefooted. And they were hot. I thought about the horrid case of jungle rot I had gotten wearing them in Kenya—no doubt fungus was still infecting them. I took them off. Jake re-stowed them—and his own.

Besides, I had found it difficult to stay balanced in them. We hadn't had the time to jury-rig a way to measure local gravity (easy with a spring scale—we had no spring scale), but Barsoom's gravity was certainly low, surprisingly low for its air pressure (about that of Snug Harbor, according to my pressure altimeter). But low gravity is both an advantage ... and a snare. All our reflexes, all our walking, running, and jumping habits, are based on "mass equals weight." When one kilogram mass weighs only three or four grams (my guesstimate), one can jump quite high—but it is safer to crawl like a baby.

Ten days on Luna with the Aussies had given me practice in one-sixth gee—but only old Moon-hands lope in Lunar gravity: new chums use a clumsy two-footed hop. (That time on Luna is not part of my "official" record. There was a spare seat; my ADF CO gave me two weeks' leave and looked the other way—Aussies are born non-reg; they enjoy breaking rules.)

I had mastered the art of walking on Barsoom—barefooted. But I suspected that those stiff field boots would trip me.

Our midget-sized walkie-talkies were so small and light that they could be carried in-hand, strapped to an arm, placed in a pocket, hung on a belt, or slung around the neck. Short range, they could be hand-held; for long range, an ear button and a throat mic gave them around ten times the reach. Jake hung his on his Sam Browne and ran the wire up the digital strap, taped it at his shoulder. Seeing what her father had done, Deety placed hers on its shoulder strap, then belted over it; Hilda and I imitated her. It left us all equipped for long range, both hands free, at what was, in fact, short range—okay with the gain down to minimum, but we could still hear each other swallow. It did show that our party could spread out, long distance if need be, yet still be "together."

We needed water canteens. The only suppliers were millions of kilometers and ten universes away.

I almost got cross-eyed trying to scan terrain ahead while watching where I put my feet—not only because low gravity and bouncy ground cover made me unsteady, but also through watching for the local equivalents of sidewinders or Gila monsters—which might look like rocks or lox. Sure, we had gotten nary an insect bite at breakfast—which proved that we had gotten nary an insect bite at breakfast. We were totally unsophisticated in *terra*, utterly *incognito*; some "pretty little flower" might be more deadly than a bushmaster.

Not that I let it worry me; worry itself is a killer. But I was supercautious by intent. We needed an armored Land Rover, or a tank. What we had were shanks' ponies and scratch weapons. We did have a fast, armed-and-armored vehicle—*Gay Deceiver*—but with no way to juice her, her power must be conserved for emergency maneuvers.

In romances about interstellar exploration there is always a giant mother ship with inexhaustible power, plus long-range and versatile landing craft.

Somehow we weren't doing this "by the book." We should go back and re-equip. But home base was destroyed and we were "dead" and "the book" thrown away. We had no choice but to face the unknown with what we had. I trudged ahead.

While trying to scan that hill ahead, I tangled my feet in ground cover, tripped, and did a short, brilliant *pas-à-seul* that would have fetched applause to a clown in an ice show. Instead, I applauded myself.

Hilda's voice answered, "Why, Cap'n Zebbie! Such *language.*"

"Pipe down," I answered grumpily. Thereafter I watched each step for fifty paces, stopped, searched ahead a second—and repeat. Endlessly.

During one such eyes-down interval I felt the ground tremble, felt it despite the spongy turf. Earthquake? Marsquake? Barsoomquake? I stopped to look.

Around the shoulder of that hill was charging at me a many-legged monster midway between a dinosaur and a rhinoceros that had had too many vitamins; astride this nightmare was a green giant twice as tall as I was and much uglier. His face had a built-in unfriendly look, not improved by eyeteeth that were tusks curling up almost to his eyebrows.

Couched at the ready in his two *right* hands was a telephone pole, sharp at one end—that end was aimed at my belly button. He was brandishing a big rifle in his upper left hand, but his attention was fixed on making shish kebab of *me*.

This takes many words to describe, but it was burned instantly into my brain in living holocolor—while my rudely awakened subconscious was tearing around inside my skull, beating on the bone, and screaming, "Le' me out o' here! Le' me out o' here! Look, it's all a mistake! I'm not a hero; I don't belong here—you got the wrong guy! Zeb! *Zeb!* Wake up! *We're in the wrong dream!*"

I said bitterly to myself, "Sharpie, this is the last time I'll let *you* name a planet—and this looks like the last time."—while another part of my much-split personality was considering: "How did the other Captain John Carter—the one without the 'Z'—handle this type of situation? Keep cool, boy, don't panic—use the tested tactic. Charge straight toward it and jump! Jump high—this is Barsoom—remember? You jump right over it. *High!* Stab his gun arm and, as you twist in the air to withdraw, slash at his upper lance arm—try to! You'll land beyond him and that beast is too big to turn fast—so jump again and slash again at his lance arms. Take *him*—then worry about his mount; it's big, but stupid."

So the red haze of battle veiled my steel gray eyes and I charged, sword at port and shouting my war cry: "*Kartago delenda est! Smerts y Rosroushen yah! Illegitimi Nihil Carborundum!*"—and leapt.

And caught my toe in that damned crabgrass, went arse over teacup, and barely managed to roll aside as the pads of that preposterous pachyderm pounded past.

Breath was knocked out of me; I fought to get it back as I got to my feet—and saw a sight tragic and heroic: little Sharpie swarming up a giant green leg like a kitten up a tree and attempting to take that giant apart with her knife.

Nothing else for it—the clean-limbed fighting man charged again. "*Allah il Allah Akbar!*"

If I thrust right under that beast's tail, would it confuse the situation enough for me to do something about Sharpie? The giant had let go his lance with his upper right hand, had her by the wrist and was keeping her from poking his eyes, while he held her waist with his lower left hand, almost spanning it.

He turned his head to look at me, and lisped around his tusks: "Oh, I say, old chap, do speak English. If you know it."

I stopped charging the quick way—tripped again and picked myself up. "Certainly, I do! Put her down!"

"But I *cahn't*, you know. She's trying to blind me. And do please tell your friends to cease firing. It makes the thoats quite nervous. Quite."

A bullet kicked up leaves and dust between me and the giant, followed a split second by the *crack!* of an old-style automatic. I flinched—when you hear the bullet before you hear the gun, you are on the wrong end of the firing.

Jake was about a hundred meters away, on one knee, steadying his weapon with two hands. "*Cease firing!*" The very different *Bang!* of a shotgun sounded. I looked under the snout of the thoat, saw Deety standing, gun pointed toward us.

"Don't blast the mic," Jake answered, blasting the mic. "Did you give 'cease firing'?"

I lowered my voice. "Yes. Cease firing, both of you. You might hit Hilda. Both of you, stay where you are. I'll try to negotiate."

"Aye aye, Captain."

I heard a neighing squeal behind me, looked around—and almost fainted. I was staring up into the red, piggish eyes of another thoat. This was a bad angle to appreciate one. It was pawing the ground and rocking, apparently anxious to trample me. Then I became aware that there were three of them—three thoats, three green giants, each one uglier than both of the others. Apparently they had attacked in Vee formation, and I had been too occupied to see the wing men. A fighter pilot can get his tail shot off making that mistake.

I didn't cringe—professional heroes can't afford to show fear. I simply moved around to the front, rather quickly, of the giant who had Hilda—but did *not* stand directly in front of this thoat. Hilda was struggling, still trying to fit him out with tin cup and white cane.

"Sharpie!"

"Yes, Cap'n! Give me a hand!"

"Sharpie, I've got to negotiate this. Flag of truce and so forth."

"Half a second while I poke his eyes out and *he'll* have to negotiate!"

"Sharpie, there are *three* of them!"

"You knock 'em down, I'll knife 'em!"

"Hilda! Hilda, my darling," came Jake's voice by walkie-talkie. "Do what the captain says! *Please!*"

Hilda stopped struggling. "Zebbie, did you say *three?*"

"Look around. Count 'em. But they aren't trying to hurt us."

Hilda looked around, counted. "Tell this smelly ape to take his dirty paws off me."

"What a rude remark from a lady." (It sounded more like "wude wemark.") "Apes are a dirty white. And utterly beastly. Not human."

"She didn't mean to insult you, sir. She's quite upset. Hilda, if this gentleman lets you—*slowly!*—lower your arm, will you sheath your knife and let him place you on the ground?"

"Cap'n Zebbie, are you sure that's what you want me to do?"

"Sharpie, it's the *only* thing to do. He doesn't want to hurt you— but he doesn't want his eyes put out, either."

"Well ... will he say 'King's X'?"

"I'm sure he will. Sir, 'King's X' means 'flag of truce.' No more hostilities."

"But there were no hothtilitieth until *you* attacked *uth*. We were thimply twying to give you the formal theremony of welcome when you yelled at me and she attacked me while I wath dithtracted!" (His lisp had become worse under grievance—but *you* try saying the letter "s" with both thumbs in the corners of your mouth. Go ahead—try it. When not excited, he compensated rather well. I won't spell it out again.)

He added, "Will *she* say 'King's X'?"

"Say it, Hilda—and cross your heart."

They both said it, but the green giant could not cross his heart; all four of his hands were busy. He lowered her wrist, holding it well away from him, until she could reach her belt. She sheathed her hunting knife. He started to lift her gently down; she shrugged loose and jumped, landed lightly. I put an arm around her, she started to tremble. I said, "There, there, honey—it's over. You were magnificent!"

"I was scared silly," she whispered.

"It's all right now, dear." I went on to him, "I think explanations are in order. This is the Princess Hilda."

"Kaor, Princess Hilda. Tawm Takus, at your service."

"Kaor, Tawm Takus. Thank you."

"And over there is Princess Deety. Princess *Deety*," I emphasized, hoping that Deety would twig that I judged "Dejah Thoris" to be a name she should not use in this neighborhood. "To your right is Doctor Jacob Burroughs. The *famous* Doctor Burroughs," I added. "Jeddak of Logan, Master of Time and Space, Explorer of Universes, Master

Galactic Engineer, Veteran of the Pentagon, Emperor of Ruritania, Supreme Pontiff of the Nine Mysteries and privy to the Number of the Beast, First Commander of—but why go on? Everyone is familiar with his unparalleled distinctions."

"Yes, of course," the giant agreed slowly. "But I never *dreamt* that I would have the privilege of actually *seeing* him."

"You see him now and may talk with him—he's quite democratic. And modest. A word to the wise, old chap—address him simply as 'Doctor Burroughs.' He prefers not to be reminded of his many honors. Detests formality."

"Is he here incognito?"

"Let's say semi-incognito. Prefers to pursue his scientific researches undisturbed by protocol. For example, I am in nominal command of his party ... so that the famous doctor need not waste time on trivial details. But I haven't given you my own name. Captain Zebadiah Carter, of Virginia."

Tawm Takus' eyes widened; he started to say something, checked himself—then said, "The famous doctor dislikes formality, you say ... Captain Zebadiah Carter?"

"As little as possible. He tolerates it when necessary."

"Do you suppose .... Is it possible .... In your opinion ... would he permit us to offer the ceremony of welcome? Start over, I mean, since it was broken off through a *most* unfortunate misunderstanding." He sounded wistful.

I pretended to consider it, frowning. "How long does it take?" My guess put sundown two hours away—and it was a long walk back.

Deety's voice spoke in my right ear: "My captain, must we stand out here? We get your half of the powwow but only snatches of Tommy Tucker's remarks. But he seems friendly."

"Wait a half, Princess. Doctor Burroughs—*igpay atinlay, el verde hombre—ci is antsy-pantsy à faire* Royal Canadian Mounted Police drill *avec vous* cast as Hail Caesar. Copacetic? Or Box Cars?"

"I heard those bald-faced lies. 'Veteran of the Pentagon!' You'll pay for that, son. Now about this Maypole dance— Recommendation?"

"Authentic *Golden Bough* stuff, *je pense*, Herr Doktor-Professor."

"Hmm— Da solid, man. *Mais schnell*. Dig?"

"*Pronto, amigo*. Rally 'round the flag, *ici*. Execute." I looked up at the Jolly Green Giant. "The learned doctor will grant your request if you can do it quickly. His time is extremely valuable."

"At once, Captain Zebadiah Carter!" With no spoken command, the three thoats executed 'Troopers left about!' and headed at ground-shaking speed for the shoulder of the hill where they had appeared. Deety and Jake closed in quickly. Deety hugged me, banging me on the back of my noggin with the barrel of her shotgun in doing so.

"Oh, my captain, I'm so proud of you!"

I kissed her. "Hilda is the hero, not me."

"I'm proud of Hilda, too. Aunt Hilda, are you all right, honey?"

Hilda stopped nuzzling her man long enough to answer. "That big lunk bruised my ribs. But he couldn't help it. He's rather sweet, actually. Handsome, too."

" 'Handsome'!"

"Deety baby, you don't expect a Great Dane to be pretty by the same rules as a butterfly."

Deety looked thoughtful. "That's logical. I must look at him again, with unprejudiced eye."

"Postpone the debate, girls, and listen. Jake, can you manage a sword salute?"

"Eh? Certainly!"

"Okay, here's the drill. We line up, Jake on the right, Hilda next, Deety next, me beside Deety—Deety, you can 'Present arms' with a gun?"

"I've seen it. I can fake it."

"Good. Hilda, all you have to do is a Girl Scout salute. I give 'Draw—*Swords!*' You gals do nothing; Jake and I draw and come to order arms in three counts. Then I give 'Present—*Arms!*' Jake and I do it, two counts, one for each word—but Deety, don't move until I say 'Arms!' "

"I'll be out of step," Deety objected.

"They won't be critical. When I 'Return … *swords!*' you come back to order arms—and I'll say, "Fall out" and Doctor Burroughs—you're Doctor Burroughs in public from now on and you two are always 'Princess' and I'm always 'Captain.' Protocol. Any questions? I hear them coming."

We lined up. The thundering herd rounded the shoulder and came straight at us, lances at charge, only this time it was the starboard wing man who was about to skewer me. They didn't slow and I was ready to beat the Barsoomian record for backward broad jump—but couldn't because both women remained rock steady.

When it seemed impossible that they could stop, the thoats slammed on brakes with all twenty-four legs, and stopped dead as three lances swung up vertically into perfect salutes. My boy almost brushed the tip of my nose with his, but upright his lance was four meters away.

"Draw!—*Swords!*" (Grab—Draw—Down! Hup! two! three!)—and Sharpie tossed in her own variations. No Girl Scout salute for her—she followed our motions, right on the beat, with her hunting knife.

" 'Present'!"—hilts to three chins—"Harmp!" Blades flashed down while Deety chucked her gun into the air, caught it with both hands. I've seen it done more by the book, but never with more snap.

The three giants let out wild yells, which I chose to interpret as cheers. I waited a long beat, then dismissed my "troops."

But the big boys weren't through. Tawm Takus glanced right and left, and suddenly bunting bloomed from those upright lances, joined together into one big banner (magnets? magic?), spelling:

WELCOME TO BARSOOM!
Greater Helium Chamber of Commerce

— XIX —

Hilda

I started to clap, Deety joined me; our men joined in. Tommy Tucker grinned like a happy warthog and so did the other two. They were pleased as puppies, so I suddenly sang out:

"Hip hip!"

"Hoo*ray!*" my gang answered.

"Hip hip!"

"Hoo*ray!*"

"Hip hip!"

"Hooray! Barsoom! Barsoom! Barsoom!"

We were ragged on the first "Barsoom" but the third bounced off the horizon. That wrapped up protocol, honor was satisfied; Sohrab and Rustum had no need to fight. At a glance from Tawm Takus, all three dismounted and dropped to one knee, which made them only two heads taller than Zebbie. This (I learned later) is the polite way for a green man to converse with a red man (we were "honorary" red men) in friendly informality.

If it's not friendly, a green man doesn't palaver; he charges— lance, sword, gun—whatever is at hand, and Barsoomians always have weapons at hand. But he doesn't finish with a salute. He rams it on through until he or his opponent is dead. Their ceremony of welcome is similar to that of the Maori, an item I picked up on campus at a Kreuber Memorial lecture—and confirmed by Zebbie, who had experienced it in New Zealand. Maori use war dances to welcome honored visitors.

(But there ought to be some way to tell a ceremonial charge from intent to massacre. This time it almost cost Tawm Takus his pretty pop-eyes. I would have managed it if my foot hadn't slipped on his sweaty thigh. Wouldn't that have been dreadful?)

We were introduced. "These are my employees," said Tawm Takus.

"Partners," the one on his right corrected.

"Assistants," Tawm Takus conceded. "On my left is Kach Kachkan, mighty warrior, survivor of fifteen games in the arena of the War-hoons, now in the service of Helium, the holder of the Order of Merit of the Warlord, Third Class."

Kach Kachkan jumped into the air and yelled, waving his ten-me-ter toothpick and brandishing his rifle—managed to land precisely as he had been, one knee to the moss, the other up, two hands holding his lance erect, face as impassive as Deety's 'cept his eyes showed pleasure.

"The other, the one who rudely interrupted me, is my brood-neph-ew Kad. He is a stripling of eighty cycles, barely out of the shell, and has not won a second name ...."

"No wars," objected Kad.

"... and has no record to recount. But he is my responsibility, for I pledged to my brood-uncle that I would see to his education when he was allowed to go to the Capital of the Warlord. Perhaps I made a mistake ...."

"You did."

"... in thinking I could train him. But he is going to learn the trade of Greeter and Courier even if I am forced to break off his other tusk—the missing one not being lost in combat, but in stum-bling over his own feet."

"Slander. It was a private duel. Don't want to herd tourists! Want to fight!"

Then Zebbie did a foolish thing. I love our Zebbie and obey him willingly as our captain. But he can be childish. I think the dear boy was still smarting over having stumbled when attempting to save us by killing Tawm Takus (and wouldn't that have been tragic?). Doesn't Zebbie know that it is the spirit that counts? He had unhesitatingly tackled a giant twice his height (eight times his size if the biologi-cal cube-square law applies to Barsoom's lower surface gravity—I'm not certain) and armed to the teeth, and mounted on a tremenjus, ill-tempered thoat. I'm sure none of us laughed when he fell—I was simply possessed by terror that we were about to lose our Zebbie, and raced toward him with no plan in mind, just needing to help.

Not that I did help. Tawm Takus handled me as easily as a kitten, and as gently. Tommy is sweet.

Zeb half-drew his sword, "Tawm Takus, if your nephew wants to fight, I can accommodate him."

Tommy turned a very pale green. "No, no, no! Most noble captain! Know you that all visitors to Barsoom are under the protection of the Warlord. Were I to countenance such an unthinkable, even though you won—as I am certain you would, fighting dismounted and only with blade—nevertheless I would be dishonored and disgraced, made homeless; my goods all be confiscated, my wives' eggs be broken, and they themselves given to others. Please, sir!"

The click of Zebbie's sword being invaginated answered him. Tommy relaxed with a sigh and his skin took on a more healthy color. "My deepest thanks, most noble captain. Thank him, Kad."

When the "stripling" (a century and a half old, if I had understood Tawm's words) failed to obey at once, Tawm Takus hit him with a rapid-fire Barsoomian, every syllable a lash. I understood none of it—and all of it. A chewing-out by an expert is the same in any language; only the sounds differ. Kad flinched, stood up and bowed deeply to Zebbie. "I thank you, most gracious warrior. You are too kind."

"*De nada*, son. No offense meant, none taken."

"Although," Tommy went on, "were the captain dismounted and armed only with blade while my ignoble brood-nephew were mounted and fully armed, I would refrain from wagering on my brood-kin. All Barsoom knows what mighty warriors Earthlings are. Issus! Our Warlord is himself an Earthling—from Virginia." He waited, then added, "Only treacherous footing leaves me alive this moment. I know."

"Possibly," Zebbie answered. "Tawm Takus, there must be halls for sword-masters in the capital."

"Yes, certainly—the finest sword-masters in Barsoom. You wish to practice, noble captain?"

"No, I need no practice—I made my last kill less than a day ago." (My Soul, had it been only yesterday? I had lived ten years in a day.) "I was thinking that, if he wishes—when I have the time—I could show your nephew some of the finer points of the art of the sword."

This time Kad did not wait to be told. He jumped to his feet, bowed, and blurted out, "This humble student most happily accepts the great swordsman's generous offer!"

"Sure thing, son. First morning I have free. Duties, you know. The doctor's wishes come first." Zebbie stuck out a hand, shook Kad's lower right hand. "A good workout, then a glass of something cool together."

(*Sharpie*, I said to myself, *Deety and Jacob and I were going to keep you so busy that you won't ever have a free morning. If those classic romances are true—and they seemed to be, essentially, in this universe— Barsoomians had never heard of foils and plastrons and masks. A "practice workout" meant that the loser needed a surgeon. Or an undertaker. Zebbie, you are like hell going to fight for fun! We need you all in one piece.*)

Kad was so overcome that all he could do was to grin like a gargoyle and nod. His uncle thanked Zebbie for him ... then got around to the question he had been quivering to ask—but had to work up his courage.

"Captain Zebadiah Carter ... of Virginia." Tawm Takus hesitated. "You know, I am sure, the hatching name of our Warlord?"

"Surely. Captain John Carter of Virginia—now Jeddak of Jeddaks, Warlord of Barsoom."

"Yes, yes!" Tommy paused. "Carter is an unusual name."

"Not in Virginia. You're asking are we related? Yes, but distant cousins. Had I the Carter family archives at hand I could show you the concatenation. Let it stand that we both are descended from John Carter the Great, founder of Virginia. But your John Carter is from a cadet line and family legend has it that this was why he left Virginia to seek fame and fortune elsewhere. As may be, he was gone a long time before we heard of him again. How is the old boy these days? Spry and restless as ever?"

"I am sure he is, most royal captain—but he is away from Helium on one of his many scientific and exploratory expeditions. The prince regent and his consort, Princess Thuvia, attend to state affairs in his absence."

"Has something happened Dejah Thoris? Oh, I hope not!"

"Your imperial cousin is well, sire. But she is pleased to delegate affairs of state to her son. On only formal state occasions does she appear in person. She has dispensed with most protocol until the return of her husband. That is her custom."

"Well, I am sorry that Cousin John is away ... but that last is pleasing. I dislike stuffy protocol almost as much as the distinguished doctor. Standing for hours watching processions—parties and balls and receptions that bore a fighting man—you know. But I promised my mother that I could bring her any news of Dejah Thoris ... and now I can do so without pother and folderol."

"I fancy a private audience can be arranged."

"Well, I should think so! Or Mother will send Cousin John a message that will make his ears burn! You know how it is with senior dowagers of a great house. They expect their wishes to be met."

Tawm Takus nodded ruefully. "I know how it is among Tharks. It's the same as Helium."

" 'Tharks?' You are from the lands of the Tharks?"

"I was hatched there, sire."

"Hmm ... 'Takus'—any connection with Tars Tarkas?"

Tommy looked like a happy golliwog. "My brood-uncle of whom I spoke. That's why I *must* see to the discipline and training of Kad."

"I see. I look forward to meeting Tars Tarkas."

"Tars Tarkas is general-in-chief of all Imperial Forces, Red, Green, Yellow, and Black, stationed at the capital. But, alas, he is with the Warlord. They are well-nigh inseparable," he added proudly.

Zebbie sighed. "That's the story of my life. Tawm Takus. When the elephants go past, I'm always out for a short beer."

"I do not understand ... sire."

"Just meaning that I am sorry not to be able to meet your uncle and to gossip with my cousin. I've rattled on too long; we must return. First, however, I must add to the introductions. Did I say that my full name is Captain Zebadiah John Carter?"

"Zebadiah *John* Carter?"

"Yes, both my cousin and I are named for our illustrious ancestor. I conjecture that my cousin dropped his first name when he left home— many of us do. I did not because that would make too many 'John Carters' in Virginia. And one is enough for Barsoom so I'll continue to be known as 'Zebadiah'—a word to the wise, friend. But it gives me great pleasure to say that Princess Deety made me her consort ... so she is known in Virginia as Milady Zebadiah John Carter. And Princess Hilda is Frau Herr-Doktor-Professor Burroughs, consort of the famous doctor. And Milady Carter, Princess Deety, is daughter of Doctor Burroughs. A family party."

Tommy's eyes were growing so round I thought they would pop out of his sleek head. "A *royal* family party!"

"No, no, Tawm Takus, don't think of us that way. A group of scientists traveling together who happened to be related. No protocol! None."

Deety interrupted this horrendous string of lies and half-truths with: "Zebadiah … the sun is dropping. We must leave."

"Right away, dear. The Princess Deety keeps track of priorities for her illustrious father. Tell me how to find you in Helium."

"Just leave word at American Express."

Zebbie didn't blink. "Fine. See you, Kad, in the sword-masters' halls. Kaor, Kach Kachkan. Tawm Takus my friend, get word to the Empress that I will send in my card soon and await her conveniences … subject only to the doctor's researches. Kaor!"

"But mighty Captain!" Tommy almost wailed.

We were interrupted by a crackling voice from the pommel—no, not 'pommel' as those thoats were ridden bareback. A girth, like those on Brahma bulls ridden at rodeos, but far more ornate and with several items mounted where a pommel should be. "Businessman to Laughing Boy. Come in."

Tommy looked torn. "Excuse me, a short moment, gentle sirs and ladies." He rushed to his thoat, grazing nearby, reached up. "Laughing Boy to Businessman, I read you,"—then muttered, "confound these cheap portable wirelesses! Never work except when you don't want them."

"Can't you find those tourists? You've been gone long enough."

"I found them. In the Bay of Blood, southwest of the Greater Helium."

"The Observatory told you that. You *haven't* found them."

"But I *have*. Their sky chariot is three haads west of the Promontory of Tears. Businessman—*listen carefully!* They are *here. In earshot.*"

"Why didn't you say so? Have you signed them up?"

"No."

"Why not? Don't tell me that Thomas Cook beat you to it *again*. If so, don't bother to come back—and your lazy nephew. Let me talk to Kach Kachkan."

"You don't *understand!*" Tommy's lisp was giving him fits. I felt sorry for him.

"I understand you've muffed an easy sale."

Tommy broke into Barsoomian. All I caught was "John Carter," "Dejah Thoris," and "Zebadiah John Carter."

"Talk English, you overgrown derrick. You know I can't understand Barsoomian over the wireless."

Tommy sighed. "*Bolless, lillisellen tulu meelee. Thellese nollet Mallarallakalless. Rollayallal Pallarrallattee. Kullussillynn ulloff Wallarallallawllarralladd.*"

Deety whispered to me, "Dig it, doll baby?"

"Not a bit. English. Not even substitution. Nonsense syllables stuck between letters. The Jolly Green Giant told him who we are. Warning his boss to 'Handle with care.'"

"Have you gone crazy?" the wireless sputtered.

"Businessman! Official. *Urgent!* I am not *crazy*. If I am, you can feed me to banths. If *you* are silly enough to muff this one, I'll wager seven to one that the Empress will have *you* fed to banths. By the sacred dugs of Issus, I swear it."

(A tense, waiting silence—) "Businessman to Laughing Boy, put Kach Kachkan on the wireless."

The two giants shifted places. Tommy's thoat rocked and squealed, but let Kach Kachkan stand by him. "Catcher's Mitt to Businessman. Over."

"Kach, what the devil is going on? Has Tawm lost his mind?"

"Boss, you had better believe him. It's true."

I heard a sigh right through the horrible static of that Barsoomian walkie-talkie. "Kach, tell me who's in this party. Who and how many? Exactly."

"Four. Two chieftains, two princesses. The sky chariot is a private yacht, belongs to the head chieftain, the distinguished Doctor Burroughs, greatest scientist in all the starry voids. Commanding his yacht is Captain Zedubiyuh John Carter—of Virginia. His princess—"

"'Captain Zebadiah *John* Carter?'"

"That's what I said. Captain Zebah Diyuh *John* Carter—Cousin of the Warlord ... and Jeddak of Virginia. His consort is the Princess Dee Dee, daughter of the great Doctor Burroughs. And *his* consort is the Princess Hilda ... who almost killed Laughing Boy when she thought he was mistreating Captain Zebber Dyer John Carter."

"What did that idiot do? Oh, I'll feed him to banths myself!"

I'm a sweet even-tempered person, mostly—but I won't see my friends pushed around. I rushed up to Tommy's thoat, swarmed up its leather girth, got astride its withers to reach that wireless. The thoat tossed its head, tried to throw me, but I hung on. Tommy moved fast, put his hand on it and quieted it.

The wireless said, "Kach, answer me!"

"Businessman, *SHUT UP!* This is the Princess Hilda! It was a natural mistake ... and Tawm Takus was a perfect gentleman—which you are *not!* One more silly word out of you and I'll tell Dejah Thoris all about your misbehavior! Is *this* the way you treat guests? Tawm Takus is under my *personal* protection! Do you understand *that*, Businessman? Or would you rather be out of business and on the streets, begging for a crust of bread?"

"My princess, I ..."

"I am *not* 'your princess'—have you no manners at all? I am Her Highness, the Princess Hilda, consort of Doctor Burroughs."

"I most humbly crave your pardon, Your Highness. I simply ..."

"You simply made another loutish mistake. We will overlook it. But I am warning you—once, and only once—that if I hear that you have tried to blame *any* of this silly foofooraw on Tawm Takus, it will be not your license that you lose, but your life! The Princess Thuvia's pet banths are always hungry, I hear."

"Your Highness, what can I do to make amends?"

"You can listen to Tawm Takus!—and take his advice! I have spoken."

Tommy lifted me down with both hands, and I went straight into my husband's arms, shaking uncontrollably. Jacob petted me. "There, there, my darling; it's all right." He smiled at me, tilting my face up with a finger under my chin. "Zeb tells me that you intimidate IRS agents. I believe it."

"Why can't I be a lady, like Deety? I don't like fights, they scare me."

"You *are* a lady like Deety, my only love. She doesn't like to fight, either. She's bigger than you are, that's all and uses different methods. I recall once in Chicago ... professional meeting and Deety was coming back to our hotel, alone. Two men. The cops had to send stretchers for them. But you do all right, your way."

Dear Jacob is such a comfort. I've always felt like a midget in a world of giants. But Jacob makes me feel as big as anyone.

Zebbie and Deety patted me and congratulated me on what Zebbie called "a star performance—even for Sharpie." Then he looked at the sun and added, "Deety, if we don't start at once, we may have to get Hilda to persuade our friends to give us a hitchhike home. I don't fancy being out in this wasteland after dark."

Tommy stopped talking with his boss and turned to us, rubbing all four hands together and grinning. "All arranged. No protocol. No inspections—courtesy of the port and keys to the city. Your apartments will be waiting. In the palace, probably—certainly tomorrow. If that, then tonight the finest suite in Hilton Interplanetary, compliments of American Express. I was asked if you each preferred separate quarters. I said that I was sure you would prefer to stay together, one large apartment. Did I do right?"

"Yes," agreed my husband, "except that tonight we return to our sky chariot. The captain was wondering whether or not your thoats could carry extra passengers. If so, you could favor us with a ride to our chariot? Our ladies are weary."

Poor Tommy was upset again. "But you are expected in the city! Sir. Distinguished doctor."

"Impossible, I'm afraid. We have nothing with us for overnight. No fresh clothing, no toilet articles, no ..."

"Believe me, Doctor Burroughs, all has been anticipated, all will be provided."

"But our chariot ..."

"Can it be hurt by night weather? Or by animals?"

"Captain?" my husband asked.

"No, not by weather, not by animals. But, Tawm Takus, how long will it take to reach the city?"

This caused a huddle between my husband, Tommy, and Deety; they had trouble matching units—Tommy did not know what a kilometer was, we didn't know what a haad was, and Deety was still uncertain about Barsoom's rotation, the local day.

But Deety had Zebbie stand by Tommy, then (using Zebbie's height, one hundred ninety-four centimeters) she was able to mark two meters (using her shotgun to point the height; Deety has trouble stretching that high). Half that gave a meter, then defining a kilometer was no problem; Tommy knew the decimal system. It turned out that the gates of Greater Helium were about a hundred kilometers away. The thoats could reach there long before local midnight.

Zebbie shook his head. "Even if the princesses could endure the ride, it will be cold once the sun sets. Far too cold for ladies, I'm certain. They don't have their furs with them."

My Tommy was undaunted. All was provided—*all*. Furs in saddlebags (never mind that there were no saddles), even an emergency tent. But soon a flier would be leaving from a city platform; the pilot would know our route and find us—before sundown—and whisk us to Helium. So Zebbie gave in.

Doctor Burroughs, how many doors does your sky chariot have?"

"Two," Zebbie answered. "Why?"

"We will protect it." Tawm Takus opened a belt pouch, took out a package, broke the seal. "The Warlord's personal sigil. American Express is, by special appointment, permitted to use it in emergencies to protect the peace of the realm. I deem this to be such an emergency. With this seal on your doors, no Barsoomian, red, green, yellow, white, black, or piebald, will enter or even touch your chariot. Kad!"

(Zebbie didn't tell him that *Gay Deceiver* could protect herself against any ordinary intruder; he gravely thanked Tommy.)

The "Stripling" hurried to us. "Yes, Uncle?"

"Tear out there and stick the Warlord's sign on each door. Then mind you catch up before dark. We're leaving now."

I suspect that Tawm Takus, as senior and straw boss, expected to carry Captain Zebadiah *John* Carter and his princess. But I expressed my wishes at once, knowing that Deety would not care—and I *did* care. Tommy's my pet; I wanted to ride with him, partly to let him know that I wanted to ride with *him*, but also because I really did. Less than an hour before, he could have broken me in two with one hand, and no one could have blamed him as I had been doing my best to blind him.

But the dear, sweet thing had handled me as gently as possible, while patiently avoiding my attempts to poke out his eyes. Sharpie does not forget such knightly gallantry (and doesn't forget injuries done her, either).

"Jacob, I would feel safest if I rode between you and Tawm Takus."

"Certainly, my dear one … if our host permits. Tawm Takus?"

"I am deeply honored, Doctor Burroughs."

Tommy put his rifle into a big scabbard on the nigh hind quarter of his thoat, racked his lance on the other side—outrigger gadgets that snapped out of the way if he grabbed for them—mounted his steed, scooted back a little, reached down with four hands and seated me gently in front of him, held me with his lower hands, reached past me with his upper hands and helped Jacob.

Once up, he held me with his lower hands, held Jacob under his armpits with his upper hands, and Jacob grabbed the leather girth, making all three of us practically married to the beast. I felt safe.

Tommy's solid, muscly tummy made a fine backrest; his hands were better than a seat belt, stronger, but gentler. From a man I might have felt that his hands were a touch too intimate. But to a Green Barsoomian giant I would be just sort of a talking doll, or cat; he wouldn't take any interest in me that way.

Or would he? There was that horrid story about Tal Hajus.

But my Tommy wasn't like that. We wheeled and then we walked and then we trotted and then we fairly flew, the thoat's pads making no sound on the turf.

"Feels swell, doesn't it?" Jacob yelled back over his shoulder.

"Surely does, dearest!"

—— XX ——

Zebadiah

Deety and I rode with Kach Kachkan while Jake and Hilda were mounted with "Laughing Boy," Tawm Takus, our worried host. Hilda was sandwiched between Jake and Tawm, unable to fall off. I suggested the arrangement to Deety, who vetoed it. "Zebadiah, only if you insist. I'd like to sit in front so that I can see the sights. I couldn't see around your shoulders but you can see over my head ... can't you?"

"Well enough—and I'm not driving. Kach Kachkan can certainly see over mine. You won't fall off? No stirrups."

"My captain, I promise to hang on to this belly band with at least one hand every second. But if you're afraid I'll fall off, you can hold me around the waist."

"Any excuse to hold my princess around the waist is a good one. And hanging on to your waist will keep *me* from falling off; I can't reach the girth strap."

"Oh. I wasn't being considerate. I can't fall off if I hang on to your belt. Let's swap places."

Deety has never learned how to be inconsiderate; she automatically gives the other fellow the biggest piece of pie. "Nosiree, ma'am! You picked it; I won't swap."

Turned out I was in no danger of falling; Kach Kachkan held me gently but firmly with his lower hands. I feel certain that he felt responsible for "valuable" cargo—if we had taken a tumble, he would have joined the Foreign Legion or its Barsoomian opposite number.

I had examined all three giants to be sure that I could call them by name later—might want to run for alderman someday. Not easy with green men—like peas in a pod or sheep in a mob. But forget species resemblance, concentrate on details, and each is as distinctly individual as you or I. Kad was no problem; just call any "youngster" with his left tusk broken off three centimeters above the lip "Kad!"— then see if he answers.

Tawm Takus was already a distinct personality; I wouldn't forget him. Kach Kachkan had had little to say—no time to get acquainted. I could feel his washboard belly against my back, could not see him. I concentrated on visualizing him. Five meters tall, I thought—a head taller than Tawm Takus. Broad-shouldered, heavily muscled, moved like a cat—and "Heidelberg face" all over his body. I doubt that I could have placed the flat of my hand on him anywhere without touching scar tissue. Tawm Takus had half a dozen scars; Kach Kachkan had ten times as many.

That and a world-weary aura made me guess that he was much older than Tawm Takus—yet Tawm Takus had been in charge. Why? Let's find out … indirectly.

Thoats have a smooth gait. They are so massive that they are slow to get underway; for the same reason, they can't turn quickly. But once they reach cruising speed (thirty knots, I would say) they are almost billiard-table steady and can keep it up for hours. I think their many legs smooth out chuckholes; all a rider feels is a pleasant surge, more a vibration than a tiring motion.

Their gait is noiseless on turf; almost so (I learned later) on pavement. A thirty-knot wind does not prevent conversation—or residents of Wyoming would have been forced into sign language generations ago. Deety wanted to "see the scenery"—but when you've seen one dead sea bottom, you've seen 'em all: endless stretches of yellow-orange turf—not even a jackrabbit. Once we rounded that promontory, the bay opened out. In twenty minutes the hills—or "shoreline"—were almost too distant to see.

"Kach Kachkan, may I ask a question about yourself?"

"Captain Zed-Zeb-uh-die-uh John Carter may ask whatever he pleases."

Kach Kachkan spoke English slowly and with care, with occasional errors in syntax and usage; it seemed to me that he was still translating, other than with phrases he used often. So I spoke slowly and tried to avoid unusual idiom. "Kach Kachkan, I heard Tawm Takus say that you are 'survivor of fifteen games in arena at Warhoons.' I thought that my cousin, John, the Warlord, had put a stop to arena games?"

"Captain Zed-Zeb—"

"'Captain' is enough," I cut in. "My name is too long to repeat with each remark."

"Thank you, Captain. My answer to your question be both 'yes' and 'no.' The Red men never followed arena custom. Or not for many cycles of cycles. Yellow men I know little about. Green men—our customs vary from horde to horde. general-in-chief Tars Tarkus abolished games among Tharks. The Warlord's order, given from the throne and sealed with his hand, forbade everywhere in use of the games of prisoners captured in battle; he did not abolish the games.

"Men convicted of crimes and sentenced to die could choose the arena or choose to have their cases placed on the Pedestal of Truth before the Throne of Righteousness in the Temple of Reward in Greater Helium. Some prisoners choose arena for quick death fighting or the small hope of eventually winning freedom. Some choose to wait in the dungeons until the Warlord's Judges of Truth review their cases ... then die dishonorably or live on in the dungeons for a number of cycles set by the judges ... or—seldom!—be set free with honor restored.

"But, by your cousin's decree, no woman, green, red, or other color, could be sent to the arena. The ignoble practice of staining the sand with blood of women to amuse the crowd has ended throughout Barsoom. Or so I believe."

Kach Kachkan's slow speech stopped. I thought the subject was ended and was wondering what horrendous crime the big fellow could have committed that had forced him to fight fifteen times in the arena rather than trust this case to the Appellate Court.

No, he was gathering his thoughts and arranging them in English. "Convicted criminals willing to roll dice with Issus in the arena were few. The crowds grew bored and royal revenues decreased. But we have a saying, 'Where there is a market willing to buy, there are sellers willing to sell.' Do Earthlings have that saying ... may I ask?"

"Some say that. Or something very like it." (I thought about endless governmental attempts to deny this truism ... and the black markets that always resulted. But I had no wish to advertise, in Barsoom, the follies of my native planet.)

"I became a seller. I was hatched ..." The big fellow stopped. "I regret. I am not making hospitality to bore the captain and his princess. My life has been a dullness."

"Go on!" said Deety. "You aren't boring us. We are strangers in a strange land. What is dull to you is new and exciting to us."

"The princess speaks truth, Kach Kachkan."

"I do, Kach Kachkan. If you don't tell us how you got from your hatching to the arena—and from there to American Express—I'm going to get off this thoat and walk! By the way, what's his name? Or her name? Is this thoat a mare or a stallion?"

Deety had gone outside Kach Kachkan's English vocabulary; he fumbled and tried to apologize. I explained that Deety wanted to know the sex of the beast, male or female—and had to find ways to force our limited mutual vocabulary to fit even this simple question.

"She is she," answered Kach Kachkan.

"What is her name?" I continued.

"Thoats cannot have names. They have no speech. I send thoughts to her. She is—(blank)."

I got nothing but the beast squealed like a canary, an oddly musical sound to come from such a mass. But Deety leaned back, twisted her face to mine and whispered, "If I were a lady, I would blush. What *powerful* emotion."

"Come again?"

"The sentiment, fully expressed, sometimes ends, 'If she could only cook!' Don't misunderstand me; it's platonic—as well as mechanically impossible. But *warmly* platonic ... and *strong*. And mutual. Great empathy between them."

"Deety, do you hear thoughts? Telepathic?" (Since I am not, I wasn't sure whether to be worried or pleased at the notion.)

"Huh? Heavens, no! But I sometimes feel emotions. This time I did and it warmed me clear to my belly button. Such beautiful rapport. They can't be lonely; they have each other." Deety raised her voice to buck the wind and said, "Kach Kachkan, since we Earthlings cannot send thoughts to her, may I suggest a name for her? 'Cannot Cook.'"

"But, Princess, a female does not have two names."

"My cousin-in-law Dejah Thoris has two names."

176

"But she is Empress. (blank) is a thoat."

"Animals may have names, and *should* have names. Our cousin the Warlord has a calot named Woola. Do I speak truth?"

"I proposed but *one* name, suggested to me by your name. Kanakook. Kach Kachkan and Kanakook—do they not sound well together?"

Our big friend answered with obvious pleasure, "Kach Kachkan and Kanakook." (Again, that canary-clear squeal.) "Princess, this has your blessing? May I call her that?"

"Would you like Dejah Thoris to publish a proclamation?"

"No, no, no! I could not presume. But your blessing would make it lawful."

"The Princess Deety blesses your thoat with the name 'Kanakook.'" The thoat repeated the canary song. "I have spoken."

Deety added, "She already knows her name! You try it, darling."

I doubted, but tried it. "Kanakook!" Our mount again uttered the shrill song.

"Goody!" Deety started clapping.

"Damn it, hang on!"

"Sorry, dearest; I got excited." She grabbed the girth strap and added, "Kach Kachkan, you try it. Call her by name."

"Kanakook." The thoat gave out the same three notes.

Our big friend yelled in excitement and repeated it. "Kanakook!"—and was answered. The green giant could hardly contain himself. "Thank you, thank you, Princess! Kanakook!" Kanakook echoed him.

Deety can make friends with anyone, man or beast. But now she muttered, "I'm being bombarded by both their emotions … and getting *too* excited myself—and this is neither the time nor the place. Help me change the subject."

"Sure thing. I'm too tired, anyhow."

"Husband, the conventional ploy is 'I have a headache, dear.' But I don't have headaches."

"Get the leer out of your voice, wench. Kach Kachkan, you started a sentence, 'I was hatched'—and broke off."

"Yes, Captain. I was hatched many cycles ago, in a small horde that lay between land of Tharks and land of Warhoons. This was long before the Warlord put an end to senseless wars and fruitless battles. We were ground as between millstones, until our city was destroyed, our incubator wrecked, our Jed killed, our people dead or scattered—many times more dead than scattered, for we were fierce in battle and never surrendered, knowing what miserable fate awaited prisoners of Thark or Warhoon. Our own women killed our badly wounded and killed themselves rather than become prisoners. So our very name is forgotten, we are no more.

"That final battle was not the first time that Kanakook saved my life, nor the last time. I was sore wounded and Kanakook ... sensing that I could not defend myself, fled the field of battle at her greatest speed, much faster than we are now going. I managed, I know not how, to cling to the leather. She took me to a small oasis, not on traveled routes. A plant is, sap is drink, pulp is food. I lived. I grew strong. Time passed, I searched for my brood-horde, found never. Kanakook ..."

("Kiss me.")

("I'll pinch you instead.")

("Ouch! Brute. I mean 'Captain Brute, sir.'")

"... hatched the very day I was hatched and given to me by my brood-father to raise and train, we now had only each other. I became—the word is 'panthan' and means a warrior without a chief, seeking work wherever he finds it. For many cycles I fought for Jed after Jed, always moving on after winning one duel and avoiding duels when possible."

"Why?" asked Deety. "I mean, 'Why did you move on?' You must have won every duel—you are here, you are alive. Wouldn't it have saved trouble to stay with one horde?"

Kach Kachkan was silent so long that I thought Deety had offended him—I should have known better. It was no longer possible for Deety to offend this giant no matter what she said or did ... and her immunity had nothing to do with her status as "princess" deriving from the most brassy lies I have ever told. Deety had named Kanakook and made it "official" with a harmless fib that matched my lies. Our friend now owned (or was owned by; the relationship was reciprocal) the *only* thoat in Barsoom having a name. Deety could do no wrong.

"Not easy to explain; ancient custom, Princess. Winner of duel always challenged again. And again. Until day comes when Jed fights winner to stop losing warriors and to ... get rid of ... rival. I had no wish to be Jed. I moved on, I moved on, I moved on.

"Times change. Your cousin, the Warlord, makes profession of panthan have little use. I speak no treason, I speak history. My lance and my sword are pledged to Warlord until Issus takes me. No longer panthan—citizen! Helium is my city, the Warlord's banner, my banner. My skin is green … but by imperial decree I am *Red*. Am I understood?"

" 'Better red than dead.' "

"If the captain says so," Kach Kachkan said dubiously. "But I did not pledge to the Warlord to escape death. First, was not needful. Second, my life is of little value. I would have made the pilgrimage before Captain John Carter of Virginia came to teach us new customs were not Kanakook my responsibility. Once, many cycles ago, I tried to get her to join a herd of wild thoats. I removed her leathers and ordered her to leave me and join her own kind. She would *not* obey … the only time she has ever refused in both our lives. So I am not free to die while she needs me. Am I making a true understanding?" he added anxiously.

I answered soberly, "Be certain of it, our friend. We of Earth have a similar custom followed by all honorable men and women. Often, a man or woman forces himself to stay alive when his body needs to die … because a debt remains unpaid. Is that what you are saying?"

"The captain speaks truth."

"You could not die with honor while Kanakook lived and needed you. We understand it … and beings who do not live by this rule are less than animals. Trash. So Kanakook and Kach Kachkan both lived by this rule. Then hard times came knocking at the door. What then?"

"Captain … my English are few. Your pardon?"

"No, I beg your pardon, our friend. I think you said that there were no jobs for your profession. Panthan."

"Is truth, Captain. No Jed willing to hire my lance. But arena of Warhoons needed blood. We went there, Kanakook and I, and I apprenticed to a free gamesman, a veteran warrior, paying fee to join their guild by indentures. Do I make understanding? I sold me. I did not sell Kanakook."

("Golly Moses! Would you sell *me*, Zebadiah?")

("Not cheaply; I have too much invested in you. Wait 'til the price is right." Then I added, "Don't stick out your tongue; you'll get it wind-burned.")

"We understand you, Kach Kachkan. What does an apprentice do?"

"Serves his master. Attends his thoat. Cares for his weapons and his leather. Massages him before games, dresses his wounds after. Keeps master in practice between games, taking care not to wound him. Sleeps in the stables and eats what his master gives him. And waits."

"Waits for what?" Deety asked.

"Whatever comes, Princess. His master may die on the sand, thus ending indenture. A freed apprentice may sell himself again ... or may choose the arena when next his dead master will—would—would have foughten. But in my case, the games master watched me at practice, bought my indenture from my master and entered me in the lists ... and in my first game pitted me against my former master." Kach Kachkan paused. "I killed him. I gained no joy in the killing; I knew his weak points, he did not know mine—since it is not proper for apprentice to wound master.

"So I won his weapons and his thoat, kept what I needed, sold his thoat—and my name was posted for games thereafter. I fought."

Pushed by curiosity, I asked a snoopy question. "Kach Kachkan, what's it like, being a professional gladiator?"

I felt him shrug. "It's a living."

Shut my mouth! But apparently the question was not offensive, for he continued: "A dull living most time, but comfortable. One eats well. Too well, perhaps; time between games is long, and a warrior can grow fat and soft and slow if he eats too much and trains not enough. Thus end most gladiators, and none but Mother Issus knows whether they sought to sleep in her arms or arrived there through carelessness and sloth."

He shrugged again. "I was not careless."

"Clearly you were not," I answered, with no sarcasm. "You won fifteen bouts." I added quietly to Deety: "What are the odds?"

("Thirty-two thousand seven hundred sixty-eight *against*, assuming that each bout was evenly matched. Clearly not true—I think.")

Kach Kachkan again took time to arrange his thoughts. "Pardon me, noble Captain—not easy for me to speak true in your tongue. Games four times each cycle. Or more. Or less. Ten days mark one game."

Deety whispered, "A hundred and fifty days of fighting—I can't even guess at the odds. Men are not dice."

"Kach Kachkan, you fought every day? Fifteen games, each ten days long?"

"No, no, Captain. At first—yes. And many ways. Against men, on foot. Against mounted men, Kanakook and I. Against wild calots.

Against banths. But the games master is ordered by the Jed to weight each bout evenly, for the crowds will not wager on a known outcome. A man on foot is not pitted against a banth. The banth would win and Jed would order the games master himself to fight the banth next—on foot.

"A warrior who wins many times will be pitted only against other seasoned warriors—not against wild animals, not against beginning warriors. At first I fought daily each ten-day game. Then I fought fewer times for higher stakes. During my last cycle in the games, I fought only seven bouts, all against other seasoned survivors."

"So once again you ran out of work?"

"No, Captain. I wearied. I grew tired of useless killing. My ancestors would have thought me mad, disowned me. But each new bout became simply a chore to finish quickly, so that I could feed Kanakook, bathe myself, curl up in my silks against her, and sleep. I removed my name from the lists, paying the games master his due, and enrolled in the Berlitz School for English."

— XXI —

Jake

Both Hilda and I enjoyed that thoatback ride with Tawm Takus. The scenery was monotonous, but the ride had the carefree feeling of Sunday-afternoon drives of my childhood, when people were content to drive on the ground—instead of zipping across several states without time for scenery, monotonous or otherwise.

Best of all, here was no smog, no fumes, no "Sunday drivers," no traffic cops—and no need for them. The motion of a thoat is remarkably smooth, no danger of being jounced off. No danger of any sort that I could see. Once, when hills closed in near the end of the ride, Tawm Takus pointed out what he said was a wild banth on the skyline. But that gave only the tiniest thrill of danger, as the speck he pointed out could have been anything. I think the Green Barsoomians have better distance vision than we have—reasonable, since they live in vast vistas like the Plains Amerindians of our history. My distance vision is 20/20 (I wear bifocals, but the upper lenses are zero prescription); I think Tawm Takus must have 40/20 for distance—eagle's eye.

He assured us that banths never came close to mounted thoats in daylight—although they preyed on wild thoats. They had learned to be wary of rifles.

Tawm Takus was a cultured gentleman—and a soldier, and a courier for tourists, both from Earth and from distant parts of Barsoom. I wondered aloud how he combined the professions. Simple—*all* Barsoomians were soldiers, from Warlord to simplest peasant. But save for the few staff and "housekeeping" jobs and certain technicians of their air navy, being in the armed forces was not a livelihood. It is much like the Swiss citizen-soldiery, a civic duty but not usually a trade.

Exception: slaves are not soldiers. But the Warlord had abolished hereditary serfdom and the Barsoomian word translated as "slave." I am sure that my daughter, Deety, a nitpicker in such matters, would construe "indentured servant" as the maximum legal contract wherever the writ of the Warlord was twenty cycles. However—if I understood what I was told—twenty cycles is thirty-eight years, Earth time, and that amounts to slavery in my eyes. It may not seem so to Barsoomians with natural lifespans so long that death by violence or accident is enormously more frequent than death by old age. Tawm Takus assured me that daughters of peasant families swarmed into the capital, eager to list themselves for the auction block at maximum indenture—so numerous that they are a public nuisance. Men were less a problem; commerce needed muscles in this society.

Tawm Takus held rank equivalent to captain on the staff of the Thark regiment stationed at the capital. He described Kach Kachkan as best (Barsoomian obscenity) "sergeant major" and hand-weapons instructor in the whole (obscenity-profanity) planet Barsoom—then apologized abjectly for having let his enthusiasm cause him to lapse into barracks language in Princess Hilda's presence.

We both assured him that idioms in a language not known to us could not possibly offend Hilda's refined feelings. Then my playful little bride offered to teach him the full gamut of lurid English improprieties ... if "Tommy Tucker" would tutor her in Barsoomian gutter idioms, barracks talk, et cetera.

Tawm Takus was shocked—and tried not to show it while also trying gracefully to refuse without actually saying no to a request from a "princess."

"Tell him, Doctor," Hilda urged, while pinching me out of our courier's sight. "Reassure him as to my scientific interest."

I attempted one of Zeb's flights of fancy, helped by the fact that our giant friend could not see my face. "Tawm Takus, my friend, the princess is a linguistic scientist, widely known as the top authority on comparative vulgar and improper idiom among nine representative terrestrial languages. She was awarded the Medal of Mark Twain with diamond cluster for this, as well as the Order of Sir Richard Burton. You would greatly assist my anthropological researches on this planet, were you to grant her request. Whether you wish to learn what she can teach you of this science is, of course, your choice. Is English your principal interest? Or do you know other terrestrial language?"

Once convinced that Hilda's interest was "scientific," Tawm Takus eagerly agreed, and accepted the offer of a chance to learn "improper" English (English being the only non-Barsoomian tongue he knew)— it appears that tourists had already left him in doubt as to how well he knew English. His tutor had been an Englishman, sent down from Oxford, and (I surmise) shipped to Barsoom to get him out of sight. Tawm Takus knew some British idioms and words not meant for the parlor—but had *not* been warned by his tutor.

Hilda agreed to set him straight; they solemnly shook hands on the bargain—a terrestrial custom he knew.

The reddened sun was touching the horizon when the flier found us—I had worried, toward the end, and tried not to show it. Banths did not worry me, but the temperature was dropping. Despite reassurances about furs and about the certainty of the flier finding us, I thought it likely that we would at least have frostbitten hands and feet if anything went wrong.

But this time we escaped Murphy's Law; the flier settled beside us while it was still light, but getting dark.

Both women were distressed at leaving our new friends to ride home in the dark and cold. But Tawm Takus assured us that riding all night was no hardship to them or their mounts—and this was no all-night march, but an easy jaunt about twice the distance we had covered.

We had to accept their assurances; it was Hobson's choice, as the flier was too small to carry the three giants (Kad had joined up in mid-march) even if the thoats had been turned loose to go home alone. (Thoats can do this, just as dogs and horses can.)

After Tawm Takus lifted me down, Hilda stood up on our thoat, turned, reached high and grabbed Tawm Takus by his tusks. "Tommy Tucker, you go straight home! You hear me? And *be careful!*" Then she jumped (floated) down. My daughter was saying good-night to Kach Kachkan while standing at the head of his thoat as she did so and scratching the ugly beast's snout. Far from resenting it, the monster was uttering squeals that seemed to suggest pleasure.

Deety called out, "Thanks, Kach Kachkan! We'll see you soon!"—turned to leave. The beast stretched its neck, bumped her shoulder, almost knocking her down.

Deety was not hurt, did not mind it. She caught her balance, turned again, petted it, saying "Kanakook, not so hard, dear! Deety will come see you. I promise."

The beast trilled like a bird. My son-in-law and I are most fortunate. I have little talent with people. Zeb is better at it; nevertheless he keeps most people at arm's length by his easy banter. But my daughter and my beloved wife can make friends with anyone, anywhere, anytime, man or beast. (Hilda has the added talent of being able to spank anyone who annoys her—Deety is more inclined to walk away.)

The Barsoomian flier looked more like a boat than an aircraft. No apparent means of propulsion or control. Bow and stern looked alike and the top was decked over. This deck was covered by a transparent canopy that lifted as the hull touched down; the pilot got out—a handsome young-looking Red man dressed in military harness, sword at side, and the Sigil of the Warlord on his chest ornament.

He smiled at us, said, "Kaor!"—then spoke to Tawm Takus in rapid-fire Barsoomian.

Tawm Takus listened, then spoke. "This officer is personal pilot to the Princess Thuvia, consort of the Regent. His name is Jopar Falum ...."

The pilot grinned. "Call me Joe!"

"... and he does not speak your language other than that one phrase, one you may take literally. His rank is "padwar" but, he having invited you to use his English nickname, I am sure that he would feel reprimanded if you addressed him by rank. Of course you may if you wish; it is correct protocol, I am not advising you not to do so. He knows who you are and where to take you—to the palace, not to the Hilton, I am happy to learn. Doctor Burroughs, you ordered 'no protocol.' May I introduce your pilot to you? Or is that against your wishes?"

"Eh? Introduce us all. Certainly." I began to wonder just how far 'no protocol' went. A modicum of ritual smooths relations ... but one *must* know the ritual.

"Thank you, Doctor; you are gracious. The Princess Hilda, allow me to present your servant, Jopar Falum."

"Kaor, Joe!" My darling gave him her sunniest smile.

185

Joe answered, "Kaor, (Barsoomian title) Hilda!" while bowing deeply. The honorific I did not catch then—but it is one used for a Barsoomian woman royal by birth or marriage, so "Princess" will do. The same word with possessive inflection has a different meaning and must be used with great care. The nuances of the Barsoomian language are so complex that it is safer to speak English. *None* of the couriers employed by American Express or Thomas Cook is ter-restrial human.

Joe added a sentence as he straightened up. "What did he say?" demanded Hilda.

"A compliment to you, Princess. It does not translate easily."

"You can try, can't you?"

"Princess Hilda, a literal translation would distort the true mean-ing deplorably." Tawm Takus' lisp had taken over strongly, a sure sign that he was embarrassed.

I told Hilda to drop it.

She seemed about to balk, then shrugged and smiled. "Okay, Tommy Tucker—but remember it for our first language session."

He agreed, then Deety got the same routine. She said, "Tommy, if that's another you don't want to translate, just save it up and tell Hilda later." It was.

For me and for Zeb the routine was simpler. Joe answered us with "Kaor, Doctor Burroughs," and "Kaor, Captain Zebadiah John Carter," each with a Barsoomian open-handed salute, which we imitated.

We boarded then, found that we were expected (by Joe showing us) to lie down and each hang on to a looped strap, two of us forward (Deety and Zeb) and my wife and I aft. The deck was padded; we were comfortable.

Joe went forward, lay down on his belly; we took off with a surge. Twenty minutes later we landed on the roof of the palace.

The canopy swung up; Joe jumped out and offered his forearm to our ladies. We were boxed by a hollow square of swordsmen, each with sword at point and their commander with his held high. Their leather was crusted with sparkling ornaments. No protocol?

No protocol—a man not of the guard and armed only with a sword was standing where we debarked. "Doctor Burroughs?"

"I am he. Kaor."

"Kaor, learned doctor. I am Navok, (Barsoomian word), Mayor of the Palace, Majordomo to the Regent. The Regent sends greetings to you and to his senior cousin Captain Zebadiah John Carter and his respects to your consorts, the Princess Hilda and the Princess Deety. It is his understanding that you prefer no formality—but if such be not the case, he directs me to call out the Guard and to inform him post haste so that the Regent and his consort may hurry here to greet you."

(So this was not "the guard"!)

Zeb moved in quickly, spoke for me. "Please tell my young cousin that our message reached him correctly. The doctor wishes no fuss to be made over his visit. He is here to pursue his researches, not to have his time taken up with ceremonies. Tonight we are weary; tomorrow will be soon enough for informal greetings ... or so it seems to me."

"Certainly, Captain Zebadiah John Carter of Virginia." Navok spoke more slowly now—I think his opening speech had been memorized. His grammar remained perfect and his accent precise, with a flavor of the Old Dominion. "The doctor's wishes will be met and your suggestion will be conveyed to the Regent."

"Good. It seems to me these watchmen could return to their posts. We appreciate the salute but there is no need to continue it."

"Yes, Captain." The palace boss tossed a word over his shoulder; the (officer of the watch? sergeant of the guard?) brought his blade down smartly, the hollow square broke and they trotted away in all directions—it was a *very* big roof. But a squad remained and stationed themselves around us. No protocol? Navok continued, "I bring greetings also from Tardos Mors, Jeddak of Helium, Mors Kajak, Jed of Lesser Helium—but by wireless; they are not in residence. Dejah Thoris, granddaughter of Tardos Mors, daughter of Mors Kajak, Princess of Helium, consort of the Warlord, Mother of the Regent, Empress, sends her warmest greetings to Hilda, Princess of Logan, and to Deety, Princess of Virginia, and looks forward to greeting them in person. Meanwhile, she has sent a surrogate to ensure that your slightest wish be met. I am under the same orders. Tell any servant, any watchman, and I will come at once, night or day. I have spoken. *Tira!*"

From out of the shadows a woman appeared, almost running, and prostrated herself in front of Hilda and Deety, forehead and hands to the landing platform, knees tucked under her. She moved so quickly that I did not get a good look at her, just a glimpse that told me that she was shapely and bare as an egg. No ornaments. Not even a dagger at belt or a ring on her fingers.

Hilda squatted down, touched her arm. "Dear, don't do that. Stand up!"

Tira flowed to her feet (yes, she was shapely—but in Helium, as in Charleston, South Carolina, an unsightly female is hard to find ... with the difference that the Red women of Barsoom look as young as coeds for so very long that some violent death usually catches up with them before entropy does. A blessing? Or a curse?).

Tira said softly, "The princess is most gracious." She stopped, then added, "May I guide you to your apartments?" Her English had a lilt to it, as if she had come from middle Sweden, near Uppsala.

"The sooner the better, dear. 'Tira,' is it? Chilly up here at night."

(Chilly indeed, but not as cold as I had expected. The landing platform felt warm to my bare feet. Radiant heating?)

"Come this way, please."

The remaining squad formed around us. I turned to say goodnight to Joe and to Navok; both had vanished. We moved off, halted at a spot that seemed not to be marked—it dropped under us.

Zeb steadied my elbow. Just a lift, and one that immediately acquired high guard sides. The palace, and all of Barsoom that we saw, was not difficult to cope with ... *if* you were used to it. (Imagine a Barsoomian in Manhattan's subways and you'll have the idea.)

A "sophisticate" is a person who knows where the light switch is. In Helium we rarely knew "where the light switch is"—or anything else.

So Tira realized (or had been told). That palace contained hundreds of people, five of them fluent in English. Three of the five were royal. One was the boss' flunky, Navok. One was a slave, Tira.

Okay, "indentured"—but I insist that an indenture of almost forty Earth years is slavery. Tira, who spoke English so well that she could think in it and knew quite a bit of slang, referred to herself as a slave. Anyone in the palace who wore no ornaments and no weapons was a slave.

I might as well spend the ten minutes it took us to reach our apartments in trying to explain Tira, as the trip was monotonous—but we could not have made it alone; every archway, every door, had armed guards. We were challenged throughout our passage—but never slowed down as the petty officer in charge of our escort sang out to each challenge, whereupon the guards we passed shifted instantly to sword salute, Barsoomian style.

Tira called herself a slave as cheerfully as my daughter might answer, "I'm a computer software specialist." Tira did not feel oppressed; she was a success and proud of it. Her parents were minor shopkeepers in Lesser Helium. She was still learning to read and write Barsoomian, although she had spoken it almost from hatching.

But she spoke fluent, grammatical English, read it as easily, and wrote it in penmanship far better than mine. How? A planned and successful strategy.

Her prospects had been negligible—no education and she worked without pay for her parents. But she saved her coins ... and don't ask me how she got them; I refrained from asking. She used her savings to learn English at Berlitz night school in Lesser Helium, studying under an expatriate couple from Minneapolis—and studied hard. Learning a language does not mean passing examinations (although most students and instructors seem to think so); *learning* a language means being possessed by a drive to *master* that language until one uses it as easily as one's native tongue. I've never had that drive, although I read the languages useful to mathematicians (five) and can get by orally in three (macerating accent and syntax).

Tira had the drive; she mastered English. She could then have picked from many good jobs—travel bureau, Hilton Interplanetary, export-import firms—but she had set her sights higher. She got word (bribery, probably) to the palace that a Red woman who spoke excellent English offered herself for sale—but not on the auction block. Private sale. Then she waited.

Navok interviewed her, offered her a good price. She thanked him and turned it down. A ten-day later a palace guard was sent to fetch her; the Princess Thuvia wanted to inspect this oddity. Thuvia bought her as a present for her mother-in-law, Dejah Thoris.

We came to large doors flanked by guards. They saluted; we went through and our escort remained outside while Tira came in. The great doors closed. We went on through a large foyer into a comfy "living room" about four times as big as Hilda's ballroom and lavish enough for Mad King Ludwig.

Eight—count 'em, eight—Red females were lined upon the padded floor, in that same full submission Tira had offered us. Our slaves-on-loan—two for each of us.

Hilda and Deety at once tried to put a stop to it—without success. Tira said, "Miladies Princesses, they know no English. That is why I am here."

"Then you tell them!" said Deety.

Tira spoke; the eight stood up, waited. Deety added, "Now tell them they are not to do that again. Not with us. Not with any of us."

"I will tell them" Tira agreed, "but I am not sure they will understand. They have been carefully trained. They will think that you are displeased with them."

Deety looked frustrated. My darling took over. "Tira, do you know what a curtsy is?"

"I think I know, Princess Hilda—but doesn't it require those floor-length ornaments worn by Earthling ladies?"

(No one told her that long skirts had become scarce on Earth. Then I recalled that I had no notion of what women were wearing on Earth-Ten.)

"Not at all!" Deety answered. "Like *this*." She dropped her right foot behind her, bobbed down with her left knee, spine erect. "Try it."

Tira tried it. "No," Deety corrected, "not quite. Your right toe barely touches, with all your weight on your left leg." She did it slowly. "Like that, but quicker. Now try again."

Tira curtsied, correctly. "That's it. There is another sort, for long skirts, but it is used in dancing. This curtsy is the correct way for a domestic servant to salute her mistress, or master, or guest, on Earth. Prostration all the way to the floor may be correct for Helium, but never for Virginia or for Logan. Never! It offends us. Please explain this to them. Then teach them proper manners for serving Earthlings. Go ahead—you did it beautifully."

Tira dimples when she smiles.

Her talk to the eight slave girls ("girls"?—the one who looked sixteen may have been a century old)—Tira's explanation drew surprise, doubt, beginning comprehension, acceptance, in that order. Then we had a chorus line, by the numbers—One! Two! Three!—Down! Hold! Up!

A beautiful sight! All had red skins, black hair on their heads, no body hair worth mentioning, and any of them would have placed in the finals in any beauty contest on Earth. But their skin colors ran from copper to mahogany, they ranged in height from as short as my beloved to slightly taller than my daughter, from willowy slender to pleasantly plump.

One little girl stumbled, her lip trembled; Deety quickly moved in beside her, placed a firm arm around her waist, did it with her, smiling at her. Hilda moved in on another one, then moved on to a third—then watched. "That's enough, Tira," she decided. "They all have it perfectly, stop them."

Deety squeezed little Tremble-Lip (smiling now), kissed her quickly. "Good girl! You've got it, Tira! Tell her what 'Good girl!' means."

Tremble-Chin dimples, too, but also blushes, from warm copper to deep red.

"Tira," said my daughter, "we don't know their names. Or what they do."

"They do whatever you wish, Princess. But I must tell them ... at first. I think that you will find that they learn quickly. Now these three, and that one"—Tira pointed—"are especially skilled as ladies' maids. The other four are experienced in serving gentlemen. However, any of them can do either. If I may suggest it, each of you could pick two as your personal slaves ... but you all can expect service from whichever one is nearest. And from me, always. I am not here just to translate; the Empress has given me to you for however many cycles you choose to live in the palace. Or to travel with you if such be your pleasure."

"Travel on Barsoom, you mean," I said, "as we will be traveling elsewhere, to other planets, when I have completed my scientific investigations here."

Tira looked interested, but not daunted. "The jeddara placed no restriction, Doctor Burroughs. I am your slave until such time as it pleases your fancy to give me back." She looked at me thoughtfully. "Travel is broadening, I have heard. I have never been outside the gates of the twin cities of Helium."

We had to make choices; Tira had strongly implied that we were expected to do so. But no one was willing to risk hurting the feelings of any of them. One of the saddest things in childhood is being picked last in choosing up sides—and these grown women felt childlike to me in their vulnerability ... even though the youngest might be older than I.

My daughter solved it by lottery with no hurt feelings: two maids to Hilda, two to her, with the "vallettes" split between me and Zeb. My two were Kissa and Teeka, the latter being "Tremble-Chin" whose chin never trembled again (impossible to be stern with such willingness to please) even when mistakes were made through lack of common language and background.

At Hilda's suggestion, Tira took us on a tour of our apartment, a parade of threes, as Teeka and Kissa placed themselves one on each side of me, as did the other six with my wife, my daughter, and Zeb. But it was not a column of three as no passage was so narrow as not to allow nine people abreast had we wished. Instead, we milled around. Deety was prone to dart off to the side to look at something (pursued by two wood nymphs), then call to Hilda or all of us to "Come see, too!"

In addition to a large foyer and that enormous living room (about six meters to the ornate ceiling, and broad and wide in proportion) there were four large sleeping rooms—no beds; the floors were pleasantly soft-firm, with sleeping silks, cushions, and furs in colorful heaps. The corridors of the palace had appeared to be paved in marble, but all floors in our apartment were soft to the feet; sleeping rooms were more deeply padded.

There was a banquet hall with a long, low table—no chairs but many cushions. I saw no chairs anywhere but there were many places suitable for sitting: alcoves, benches that were integral with walls, and something like love seats.

The apartment had only one bath—but the "tub" was an oval pool flush with the floor and twenty meters long. It was not a "bathroom" in the American idiomatic sense; instead every room had at least one "powder room" but with fixtures so unlike ours that I had to puzzle them out, being (I confess) too shy to ask Tira. But I was not left in ignorance; Deety poked into everything, asked questions, and the word filtered to us males.

I was pleased to see, also, a small dining room. It opened on a balcony, as did all major rooms. The balcony hung over an inner garden but we could see little, it being night—and too chilly to be outdoors. Of greater interest was the lavish buffet in that refectory.

My daughter said, "Golly, that looks good! I had been intending to bathe before asking about food—but now I'm torn. Pop, what do you think?"

"You're married now. Ask your husband."

"Zeb just tells me to make up my own mind."

Tira said, "If I may suggest, Princess Deety, there is no need to make a choice."

"Explain yourself, Tira hon."

"Yes, Princess. I have heard and I have read that on Earth it is the custom to eat at certain times, sleep at certain times, bathe at certain times. In Helium, and especially in the palace, there are no customs in such matters save on formal occasions. One eats when one is hungry, sleeps when one is sleepy, bathes when one feels the wish. Not infrequently hunger and a wish to bathe can occur at the same time ... especially, I have noticed, after traveling. So one does both."

"How?" Deety challenged.

"It is the happy duty of Larlo and Fig to bathe and feed the princess whenever she wishes. Shall I tell them to do so now?"

"Zebadiah, this is the best hotel I've ever been in! Want to join me? Get soap suds in your soup?"

We all joined her, all having the same dilemma. Me, I felt that I should stink of thoat—ridiculous, as thoats do not carry an odor.

Tira gave an order; all eight slave girls got very busy while we four and Tira started back toward the bathing room, about a hundred meters away. Zeb muttered something about " 'All this joint lacks is bicycles.' "

Tira caught it and said, "Captain and Prince, I have seen, I think, pictures of bicycles. Two-wheeled chariots, are they not? It is probable that our artisans can build bicycles from pictures ... but not tonight, not that quickly. I can send for a small chariot which you could ride and Wogi and Ajal could pull."

"Zebadiah," said my daughter, "if you accept that offer, I am going to take a picture, even though I'll have to run all the way back to *Gay Deceiver* to pick up the camera."

"Sweetheart, you'll have time to run all the way to Snug Harbor. I refused to try a rickshaw even though the rickshaw man was huskier than I am. I outweigh Ajal and Wogi combined. Tira, my remark about bicycles was a figure of speech, an inverted compliment."

" 'An inverted compliment?' I am forced to say that this appears to be an idiom I have yet to learn."

"Well ... what would you say if I told my wife that she was an ugly, little monkey?"

Tira looked startled. "But the princess is taller than I and beautiful. I have never seen a monkey, but pictures of them look not at all like the princess."

"He called me that just a couple of days ago, Tira. It pleased me. Meant that, in his opinion, I was the exact opposite. An inverted compliment."

"Oh, I must think about this."

When we arrived at the bathing room, the eight wood nymphs were there ahead of us, with supper set up by the pool. I was forced to assume that either a) there was a shortcut passageway and that I had incorrectly visualized the complex layout of that huge apartment, or b) Barsoomians had solved the problem of instantaneous transitions by my method or some other. Then I thought of conveyor belts and forgot the matter; Kissa started undressing me while Teeka starting popping goodies into my mouth.

Kissa hesitated with her hands on the buckle of my Sam Brown, looked at Tira. She said, "Doctor Burroughs, she cannot remove your sword without specific permission. Just place your hand on her head, Doctor. That grants a slave permission to do anything she's unsure about."

I did so, Kissa studied the buckle, then opened it. I remembered to take out my automatic, remove the clip, and jack the cartridge out of the chamber—couldn't have the child shooting her foot off by accident. While I did this, she removed my shorts—and I made an involuntary start of surprise.

From behind me Zeb drawled, "Jake, were you ever in a bathhouse in Japan?"

"No."

"But you mentioned taking Finnish sauna. Relax and enjoy it. Or think about Gödel's proof or Fermat's last theorem."

I did all of those things—especially when they combined forces to lather me all over. Yes, I relaxed and enjoyed it.

Deety gets her own way. She asked when the girls ate, was told that slaves ate after their masters, whatever was left. So Deety started shoving bites into Larlo and Fig, who squealed and tried to avoid it—and gave in when Deety got Tira to order them to permit it.

The same thing happened after we were rinsed and got into the pool (just under body temperature, just deep enough that Hilda's head was above water—luxurious!); our servants lay by the pool and continued to feed us. Deety insisted that they come in, too. Tira looked startled; Deety made it a flat order.

I have never seen nine women lather and rinse each other so fast—in fact, I have never seen nine women do it slowly either.

Sharing that pool with eleven beautiful women is something out of Muslim Paradise. I relaxed and enjoyed it.

Our apartment was two wings with that "living room" great hall at its center, two sleeping rooms in each wing. Tira took it for granted that we would each select a sleeping room. I kept quiet, knowing that Hilda and I would wind up in the same room, Zeb and Deety in another—goodness, you could have bedded down a platoon in one of them.

Deety is not one to let matters be. "Where do you and the girls sleep?"

"Wherever we are told to sleep, Princess. Unless you tell them to do otherwise, Larlo and Fig will sleep outside your door—with one ear open should you call. Or, if you wish them nearer, they will sleep at your feet so that a whisper will suffice should you wake and wish to be massaged back to sleep—at which they are skillful. Or to fetch you food or drink. They are here to carry out your wishes, whatever they may be. If they do not understand, I will appear at once to translate. I will be in the foyer, close to all four rooms."

Deety looked thoughtful. My wife said, "Let me get this straight. Two each. Laba and Kona with me, outside my door or at my feet. And the same for our chieftains—to carry out their wishes, whatever they may be. Just how far does that go? Spell it out, Tira."

Tira looked perplexed. "I do not understand, Princess Hilda. Each slave will do whatever her lord or lady requires. If she does not understand, she will call me; I will explain—or do it myself if it is beyond her skills. If it is a wish unanticipated that I cannot solve, I will send a swift message by a watchman-of-the-night and Navok will solve it. Does the princess have some special wish in mind?"

"No, just asking." Hilda looked at me, looked at Kissa and Teeka, looked back at me. "Jacob, is your insurance paid up?"

I said, "Why, Hilda my love! Tira meant nothing of the sort, I'm certain."

"Zebbie? Are you going to risk *your* life, too?"

"Sharpie, knock it off! I'm sleeping with Deety."

Tira looked puzzled and distressed. "I do not understand. Have I, in my ignorance, offended my masters and mistresses?"

Deety put an arm around Tira's waist. "Not a bit, Tira; you've been grand. My Aunt Hilda loves to tease."

It wound up as I knew it would: Hilda and me in one room, Zeb and my daughter in the other sleeping room in that wing, and our Girl Scout Troop bedded down in a sleeping room beyond the big parlor, along with their Troop Mistress. We had trouble getting Tira to accept this arrangement. It took I-tell-you-three-times to make it stick.

Once the eight giggleheimers were chased off to bed and out of earshot, we all gathered in Hilda's-and-my room for a nightcap: five—we included Tira.

Each sleeping room held a low, round chow bench loaded with wines and midnight snacks—and I'm blessed if I know when the girls found time to place this, as these benches had been bare when we took the grand tour. Sent in from outside, certainly, and I admit I did not muster them every ten minutes. Tira, maybe—she seemed to be triplets in her ability to handle many things at once.

Hilda at once exercised her prime talent. "Tira, knock off this slave nonsense; the girls are out of earshot. You can pick it up again whenever someone else is around; we don't want to put any strain on you. But you're our substitute hostess and we are your guests and friends—'friends' if you will let us be."

"Yes, Princess. Thank you."

"Try that again. Just say, 'Sure, Hilda. Why. Not?'"

"Sure ... Hilda ... why ... not."

"Better, but your heart isn't it in yet. My husband, Doctor Burroughs, is called 'Jake' by his friends. Not 'Jacob,' that's *my* name for him. Say 'Howdy, Jake!'"

"Howdy, Jake."

"Just fine, Tira—if you'll smile and show those dimples," I answered.

Tira can blush too ... but I got those dimples.

"And I'm Deety, Tira darling, and I want you to love me."

"No one could fail to love the Princess Dee .... Sorry! Deety, you're awfully easy to love. You're friendly and warm. All the girls felt it. They told me so. Larlo and Fig were disappointed not to be allowed to sleep at your feet."

"Well ... I'll try to soothe their feelings tomorrow."

— XXII —

Zebadiah

When I woke, Deety was missing—the last I remember she was clinging like a koala bear and sound asleep.

The room was dark, but as I yawned and stretched, tall drapes were silently swept aside and I was looking out into bright sunshine. The door opposite the tall windows opened; Ajal and Wogi entered silently, bearing trays. They curtsied in unison. I said, "Kaor, kids. Wogi, Ajal."

"Kaor Kap Tan Zeb Uh Die Uh John Carter," they sang in chorus.

"Good girls! Thank you." Someone has been training them. Tira? They smiled happily, rushed toward me, dropped to their knees, started assaulting me with hot, perfumed towels.

I relaxed to the inevitable; they gave me a bed bath with gentle efficiency and dried me. Wogi then poured a few cc. of amber liquid into a tumbler, raised it to her lips, and waited, eyes on mine.

I placed a hand on her head. She smiled, poured it into her mouth, gargled gently, closed her lips and worked her mouth and jaw around, forcing the liquid through her teeth. She spat it daintily into a small basin. Then she poured a larger amount and offered it to me.

I did everything she had done. Fresh, spicy, nonalcoholic—and beat the hell out of Listerine, Lavoris, or Cepacol—finished swishing it through my teeth and spat it into the basin.

It not only freshened my mouth, but also those slimy little sweaters were gone from my teeth. This planet didn't need toothbrushes.

I had to restrain them to keep them from following me into the jakes. When I came out, Ajal was holding my sword and belt; Wogi

197

had my police special in one hand, cartridges in the other (I had ejected them before letting them bathe me the night before) and my walkie-talkie hanging from the crook of that elbow.

I took the walkie-talkie, flipped it on, said "Deety? Come in, Deety."

No answer—I put the button in my ear, stepped it up to full gain, held the mic to my throat. "Come in, Deety. Come in anybody."

"*DEETY ISN'T HERE*"—I hastily turned down the gain. "Both the gals are gone. I'm on the balcony outside the ballroom, Zeb. How do you like your eggs?"

"Kaor, Jake. Up and easy."

"You aren't going to get any; eggs are taboo on this planet. But you won't starve. Come on out."

"Okay. Over and out."

I placed the walkie-talkie, gun, and ammo on the chow bench. It had been cleared off—pixies again. Ajal was holding my sword belt open and looking expectant. I touched the top of her head. She smiled and buckled it around me, hooked up my sword wrong way. I rehooked it, but assured her that she was a "Good girl!"—told Wogi the same. Looked around for my shorts ….

No pants—well, the girls were wearing none; I was getting used to it. I went out, my "staff" in formation with me.

No, I wasn't going to starve. Jake had finished eating; what was left would make a Thanksgiving dinner for a dozen. My girls started feeding me—hot bites, cold bites, a hot drink that wasn't coffee but was bracing, a cold one that looked like milk but had a vanilla flavor. Every time I started to speak, something wound up in my mouth.

I caught Wogi by the wrist. "Jake, how do you avoid too much service?"

He spoke one word; my girls poised for flight, waited. I patted each on the head. "Good girls!" They left—went outside, sat down on the floor tailor fashion—or was it "lotus?"—where they could see me. Clearly they had understood Jake's order, but their "master" had to confirm it.

"I see you're learning the lingo, Doc."

"Six words. I had Tira's help. When you are through eating, call your kids and let them take it away. Tira and her Campfire Girls won't eat until you are through."

"I thought we had settled that nonsense?"

"Only in private. I'm not sure Deety and Hilda should have crowded it, even in private. People always prefer their own time-tried customs. Were you ever an enlisted man?"

"No."

"I was. Only weeks—but long enough to get the flavor. Enlisted men don't like officers who insist on getting chummy. Tira is a slave, but an *important* slave, one who takes pride in her status and her perfect service. Didn't you notice last night that she got upset in trying to play the role of 'member of the family'?"

Yes, I had—but I had confidence in Deety's ability to make it work. Give it a day or two. "Jake, you worry too much."

"I do worry. I'm worried now, three ways. No, four."

"Pop, you'll burn out your bearings. Here you are, looking down at the most beautiful garden this side of Vancouver Island, belching over a Sybaritic breakfast, living in luxury with nine beautiful servants waiting breathlessly for your least whim—and you worry. Man, even if they are planning to hang you at sunset, you should enjoy this day."

"They might. Hang us at sunset."

"All the more reason to enjoy your last day."

"Maybe you're right, Zeb."

"I *am* right. But what's this about 'hanging at sunset'?"

"Zeb, how long will our lies stand up?"

"*My* lies, you mean. They've stood us in good stead so far. Would you rather be out in the middle of … 'The Bay of Blood,' I think Tawm Takus called it, eating peanut butter sandwiches and trying to make up your mind between sleeping sitting up with your ankles swelling … or risking frostbite and hungry banths outside? Look, Doctor, with your get-there-zip gadget we can leave this planet later today, if you like. I think I can fast-talk our friends out of some fast thoats. Or Joe and his flier."

"Might be smart."

"Why this attack of nerves? They've got power here. Whether it's AC, DC, or Simon-says-wiggle-waggle, I can figure a way to juice *Gay Deceiver*. And, while the evidence indicates that women's dress shops are scarce, they have cloth from which Deety and Hilda can whip up clothes for Hilda. You can't expect her to explore umpteen universes with one cotton dress and a borrowed pair of panties. Count your blessings, man! This is that fitting-out base we were too rushed to use, back home. Give me time to look over the facilities. They have technicians—it's just not our technology."

Damn it, I get annoyed at cold feet—and never expected Jake to fall ill with them. "Where did the girls go?"

"I don't know … Princess Thuvia …"

" 'Princess Thuvia!' "

"Oh, shut up and listen, son. I slept late; they were gone. Tira told me that the Princess Thuvia, consort of the Regent, had come and taken them away. That's all she seemed to know. But Tira seemed to think everything was jolly, so I tried not to show any misgivings. But we can't tell what danger they might run into. Zeb, was that string of lies necessary?"

"What lies? Think it over, Doc."

"You aren't related to the Warlord."

"Who says I'm not? Jake, I gave my correct name, rank, and serial number. They can check it in my flight log. My passport shows—in *Gay Deceiver*, now!—where I was born. Virginia. I never said that we were *close* relatives—I distinctly said *distant*. What relations are you to Edgar Rice Burroughs?"

"Why, none, that I know of."

"Do you *know* that you are not? If he were alive and claimed to be your fifth cousin, twice removed, could you disprove it?"

"No, but ..."

"A simple 'no' will do. It is statistically probable that you are more closely related than that. However, most American family records are neither complete nor assembled. But I am certain of one thing: *my* name isn't phony and I have proof. If the Warlord is using a phony name, he won't be anxious to throw doubt on *my* credentials. He'll accept me as his distant cousin, treat me as such, and never open his peeper. Contrari-wise, if John Carter *is* his right name—I have no reason to doubt it—the odds that we are cousins of some sort are so high that he'll accept it. He has no reason to make an issue of it—not after we've been accepted as guests in his palace."

"Zeb, in those books the Warlord says time and again that he doesn't remember when or where he was born."

"Jake, we're not in a book. We're in a balcony, overlooking a beautiful garden, in a palace on the fourth planet from the Sun in Universe-Ten. The palace belongs to a bloke with my surname and we were born in the same state. Fact. Any discrepancies result from an excited green man who doesn't speak English too well making a garbled report to his boss who is a blithering idiot—and who then relayed that report, with more garbling you can be certain, to the palace. The essentials got through—my name, rank, and place of birth. All else is irrelevant."

"What about that garbage you told about me?"

"What garbage? You *are* a veteran of the Pentagon."

"Well ... you don't have to rub it in. 'Emperor of Ruritanis!' My god."

"Jake, you've got the twitches over nothing. None of that got on the air—think back. Three green men heard it, no one else—and not one of them knows Ruritania from rural Pennsylvania. Not that it would matter; Deety has Kach Kachkan eating out of her hand; he would kill anyone who said a word against her, Sharpie seems to have done as good a job on Tawm Takus ...."

"She did. I don't know how she does it."

"There are no flies on Hilda; we won't slip up through her. Wherever she is, right now she's taking someone into camp. Jake, your lovable little wife can fast-talk a touchy situation better than I can. You hear her yesterday. You got yourself a prize, Jake."

"I know it."

"And so did I—and I know it. Our wives are our major assets. But before you moan about a little fast talk, mine or Hilda's, you might try thinking about *why* we were fast-talking it. You did some shooting. Why?"

"Because ..." Jake shut up.

"Because Hilda appeared to be in danger. But an old-style automatic is no good at that range; just luck you didn't kill your wife. I'm not blaming you, we were all doing our best in a sticky situation. I wasn't effective either—until it penetrated my panic that it was time to talk, not fight. Then I talked. Some was garbage, I admit. Let me rehearse it next time and I won't mention the Pentagon—hadn't realized you feel touchy about it. But I was *extemporizing*—trying to save our necks. I wasn't calm. Nervous isn't too strong a word."

"Captain ... I apologize."

"Oh, dreck! We're too close for apologies; we've shared too many dangers. Blood brothers. Jake, what are you *really* worried about?"

"Uh ... Zeb, this isn't Barsoom."

"So? Have they changed its name since yesterday?"

"But Barsoom isn't a real place! It's just in a story. Like Oz."

I ate a Barsoomian grape—no seeds and big as a plum. "So it's in a story and it turned out to be real. You want to sue?"

"No. I want a hypothesis to account for it."

"You sound like a philosopher! Jake, theories are a dime a dozen and causation is a myth. But if you want a theory, slip this one on for size. Edgar Rice Burroughs—or maybe John Carter, since Burroughs insisted that he simply recorded what was handed to him—somebody, call him 'X,' found a way to reach, not Mars, but Barsoom on Universe-Ten, tau-axis. We *know* it's possible, but *we* did ... but someone else did too and beat us to it. Shucks, we *know* American Express beat us to it, but John Carter got here even sooner. Does that theory fit?"

"Uh ... this Barsoom isn't quite like the one in those classic romances. Similar ... but not the same."

"What of it? It wouldn't be the first time that a reporter slanted his story. My theory covers all data, I think. Got a better one?"

"Well ... no."

"My theory is pure hogwash, Jake, whipped up as fast as the stuff I was shoveling yesterday. Why don't you stick to what you are best at?"

"Eh?"

"You've told me—and I believe it—that you are one of the new breed of mathematical physicists who doesn't worry about what *ought* to be—a meaningless concept, you said, and I agree—but instead attempts to invent mathematics to describe the real world, as you see it. This is a *real* world we are in—our bellies are full ... and we've got nine girls getting hungry while we've been yakking; we should be ashamed. Hey! Wogi! Ajal!"

My little shadows came zipping out; sign language sufficed; they cleared things off like a prairie fire, leaving us each a cup of uncoffee. "Good girls!" I called after them. "Jake, your genius for inventing new math gave us the key to the universes, an unthinkable number of them—the Number of the Beast. Now we find that one of them matches, or almost, what we had both thought of as a fictional universe. If this planet had been utterly unfamiliar, neither of us would have boggled. Instead, you are moaning because it's *too* familiar. Can't you devise a sheaf of postulates to include this Barsoom?" If you can, will your description also fit *other* universes we've always thought of as fiction? Some might turn out to be as real as this Barsoom. I don't say *all* of them; that's too much to ask. But *some*. Atlantis. Doc Smith's Gray Lensman. Can you write equations for a few?"

Jake said slowly, "I can write equations for *all* of them."

"Hey! I didn't ask to buy the store. I'll settle for a few."

"Zeb, I've been sitting here thinking about three theories. One, I was killed in that explosion in the parking lot and this is where I wound up. A dying dream, or possibly another life."

"Huh *uh!* No, Doc. That may fit you, it doesn't fit *me*."

"I anticipated your objection. The second theory is solipsism."

"Solipsism is a cop-out, Jake. It explains everything and nothing. Nor can I buy *your* solipsism; it's got to be *mine*."

"Yes, that's the weakness of solipsism. Ever hear the theory that in endless time and space, not only everything *can* happen but *has* happened and *will* happen? Mathematically, it is equivalent to Cantor's Alephs, or higher infinities—and contains the same fallacy. But a brilliant writer named Brown wrote a fine story about it."

"Fredric Brown's *What Mad Universe*—Yes, I know that book, Jake. A classic. You say it contains a fallacy? I was impressed by its logic."

"I didn't say the *story* contained a fallacy; I said that the mathematical theory contained a fallacy. Mr. Brown's story may be utterly real. *Is real* ... if the formulation I've been thinking about has any merit."

"Go ahead."

"Zeb, the most powerful concept in modern physics is the quantum. The longer it is studied, the more we find out about how nature ticks. Discrete units, everywhere we look. World has texture; that texture is quantum mechanics. All I did was to extend that notion of smallest units and applied it to closed space ... and we started making quantum jumps. Suppose human thought exists in discrete and smallest—not divisible—units?"

"I'm not sure I follow you."

" 'Tisn't necessary yet; I haven't tried writing it down. Or ever necessary, as you tell me you don't follow the math we used to come here."

"I don't. It *works*. I'm not a worrier as to *why* it works."

"Well ... if human thought, or imagination, exists in quants, then *every conceivable universe* lies somewhere in the Number of the Beast. A very large number ... so large as not to be physically countable—just written. But still a number. Not infinity. Zeb, if *thought* is quantized, *every story ever told*—or to be told—same idea in closed continua— is *real*. *Gulliver's Travels*. Travis McGee. *The Wizard of Oz*. Barsoom. Wagner's *Ring Cycle*. Doesn't matter. Room for all of them. And we may find ourselves in *any* of them. Although it is a high improbability that we will—in one lifetime—happen to hit another that we recognize as being a fiction story in the universe we were born in. Although we might. A basic law of statistics is that the extremely unlikely is as real as the humdrum almost-certain."

"Hmm ... I'd better stick to the left seat while you twist the verniers. You said you were worried about a fourth thing."

"Yes. Pregnant women ... on a planet that doesn't use obstetrics!"

—— XXIII ——

Jake

Zeb and I were still lazing on the balcony when a gong sounded. Zeb's talk, and, even more, his presence, had done me a world of good. I'm a worrier; Zeb is not. I don't mean that Zeb is happy-go-lucky; he's not. There is an old prayer that goes something like this: "God grant me the strength to cope with troubles I can solve, the serenity to endure those I cannot solve—and the wisdom to know the one from the other."

The wording is not exact, and I don't know who first said it. Zeb Carter seems to have been born knowing it. But he wouldn't phrase it that way. Zeb would be more likely to say, "Don't bang your head against a stone wall." He might add: "Climb over, go around, tunnel under, knock a hole in it—and if nothing works, forget it! Change your plans. Or take a nap. But don't get ulcers."

I had gotten up fretful because I've come to expect Hilda to be within arm's reach—or not too far away to call. But I woke in a strange place and she was gone—and I got up so suddenly that I omitted my morning ritual of "talking" with Jane. A mistake.

So I fretted—instead of savoring the most lavish breakfast I have ever seen. Solipsism, for heaven's sake! God invented people to amuse Him because He didn't have television—that makes just as much sense! The world of experience is the only "reality" (undefined term) I know, so that was the one to cope with.

Zeb reduced our problems to two practical ones: 1) how best to outfit for more travel, and b) find a friendly planet with skilled obstetricians, if possible, during the first trimester of our darlings.

All else was either irrelevant or must be tabled for later. Including "Blokes in Black Hats" with double-hinged legs and green blood.

Meanwhile, whenever I had time, I could think about the elegant notion of trying to apply quantum mechanics to human imagination. Is there somewhere—when—a Seacoast Bohemia? Is Dorothy walking the Yellow Brick Road with companions as grotesque and as friendly as Kach Kachkan and Kanakook? Does Huck Finn float down an end-less Mississippi with imposters as preposterous as we? Is Allan Quar-termain exploring the Mountains of the Moon? The Gray Lensman righting Galactic wrongs? Is the Mad Tea Party going strong—with, of course, "the best butter"? When—where—will Wotan sell one eye that the human race may flourish? What verniers must I touch, what translations, what rotations, to find the Once-and-Future King seated opposite Siege Perilous with his knights in circle around him?

What of 221B Baker Street and the house on West 35th? Did Ma-jor Edgar Allan Poe "Go South" in '61 or did his West Point indoc-trination cause him to die fighting for "damn Yankees"? Either way, did he find time to write the loveliest lyrics since Shakespeare? Does Kuka Shan dream of her restless barbarian in company with Dido and Poor Butterfly in some land no farther away than a twist of my dials?

My mind was buzzing happily with new symbols and an urge to manipulate them as equations when that gong broke my recovery.

Tira hurried in out onto the balcony—started to drop into full pros-tration, caught herself, curtsied, started a rush of worlds: "The prince regent commands ..." stopped, stuttered, and started over, saying most carefully, while staring straight ahead: "Prince Carthoris sends this inquiry to Captain Zebadiah John Carter of Virginia: is this a convenient time for him to call on his senior cousin? Or should he try again some later time?"

Zeb said, "Take it easy, Tira, nobody's going to bite you. Certainly, this is as good a time as any."

I interrupted before she could back away. "Did the prince want to see *me*? Or does he want to speak to the captain alone?"

"The prince regent did not mention the distinguished doctor. I cannot answer your question; I do not know."

Zeb said, "Stick around, Jake; he'll see us both. I'll do the talk-ing—unless you feel like chucking in something. I mean, I'm willing to carry the ball. Tira, send word to my cousin that he's welcome. How soon can we expect him?"

"Captain, he's right outside your doors!"

"Oh! Go let him in! Come on, Jake; we'll meet our guest at the door."

Instead of taking off like an arrow, Tira stammered again. "C-C-Captain, *must* I c-c-curtsy?"

"Oh. Honey chill, do whatever makes you feel easiest. Now scoot!"

She scooted. As we reached the foyer, the big doors started to open, and a voice boomed: "The Prince Regent!"

A handsome, well-built young Red man came in. He was wearing plain leather, no ornaments, but his belt buckle was shaped in the sigil of the Warlord. He was wearing a sword, no other weapons. "Sorry about that," he said, grinning. "I told them 'no protocol.' I'm Cartho-ris." He glanced at each of us. "Senior Cousin?"

Zeb stepped forward, stuck out his hand. "I'm Zeb Carter."

The prince shook hands. "I'm happy to meet you, Senior Cousin. Our home is yours."

"Thanks, Prince. In the family I'm called 'Zeb.' This is my father-in-law, Doctor Burroughs."

Carthoris bowed to me. "I am honored, distinguished doctor."

I stuck out my hand instead of bowing back. "My name inside our family is 'Jake,' Your Imperial Highness."

"Doctor, I'd be most pleased to be treated as a member of your family, as well as Zeb's and mine—and call you 'Jake'—if you'll knock off the fancy titles with me. I'm called 'Cart' at home ... except that my mother uses my full name. However, she named me." He grinned again, a most engaging grin. He was smooth-shaven—if Red men had beards; I wasn't sure.

"'Cart,' it is," I agreed, as Zeb urged us all inside. Tira was still face down, knees drawn under her, motionless. Carthoris glanced at her.

"Zeb, she won't stir until you tell her to. *I* can't tell her; she belonged to my mother until Mother gave her to you."

Zeb leaned down, patted Tira's head. "Get up, Tira, and say hello to the prince."

Tira got to her feet like an opening flower, stood with downcast eyes. "This humble one is deeply honored to be permitted to greet the prince regent."

"Tira," Carthoris said mildly, "that wasn't what your master told you to say. He said for you to say hello to the prince."

She raised her eyes, said solemnly, "Hello … Prince."

"Howdy, Tira. Zeb, servants are deucedly conservative. You and I—and Jake—can dispense with protocol. But *they* won't. Tira has known me many cycles; she is a member of our family in all but rank. But she insists on doing that full salute dozens of times each day—as if the ink were still wet on her contract. No way to stop her. Won't get up without permission."

"We stopped her, Cart," said Zeb.

"What? *How?* Tell me your secret."

"Tira had special permission from me to prostrate herself to you. But with us—we substituted a simpler salute used in Virginia. Tira, please curtsy to the prince."

Her eyes widened, but she bobbed up and down at once.

"See?" Zeb went on. "It's like giving a hand salute instead of bothering to draw sword. Means the same but quicker and more convenient. Saves time, both for you and your servant. Since your servant's time is yours, it doubly saves your time."

"By Issus, that's clever! I must tell Mother. Mother is always looking for better ways to do things. You say this is common in Virginia?"

"Yes." (Zeb didn't tell him that servants were no longer common.)

"Then my father is familiar with the custom. We can have every servant in the palace trained in it before he gets back. Using it. Except for visiting jeds and jeddaks, I think."

"May I make a suggestion, Cart?" I put in.

"The distinguished Doct—Jake, your words of wisdom are welcome always."

"This isn't wisdom, but it may be common sense. How many servants are there in the palace?"

"Tira?"

"Two thousand one hundred and eighty-eight last ten-day muster, Highness. The free citizens employ …"

"Never mind those. So many? No wonder Mother mutters over the grocery bills."

"Cart, how many are habitually in contact with royalty? Or with nobility or any others to whom they prostrate themselves?"

"There aren't any others besides family and a few resident nobility. Servants must be respectful to officers of the guard and to upper servants, but not by dropping to the floor. Wouldn't get any work done. Tira, in answer to the distinguished doctor—how many?"

"Imperial Highness, I can but estimate."

"Come off it, dear. You know the palace better than I do. Make a guess."

Tira couldn't come out with an instant answer the way my daughter can. I could see her lips move. "Highness and Doctor, approximately one hundred and twenty slaves come in contact with royalty and nobility one or more times each day. The number varies because some—personal servants—are close at hand day and night. And some several times a day. And some may live in the palace a full cycle and never see royalty or nobility ... but the very next day might be sent on an errand that would take her clear into the inner chambers of the jeddara."

I said, "Simple enough, Cart. Limit the curtsy to upper servants, and to any habitually in close contact with your family and resident nobles. I assume that servants serving your family are your best."

"Oh, certainly!"

"So make it a mark of distinction limited to those few—inner servants and supervisor servants. You'll accomplish the same time-saving ... and yet those few are the very ones smart enough to shift to the old way when serving visiting royalty. In addition to making it a privilege, you can use it another way. Minor punishment. If a curtsy-privileged servant slacks off or does something she knows she should not do, you can assign loss of privilege—back to prostrations for a day or a ten-day or whatever the offense merits."

Carthoris grinned. "Wouldn't have to whip them so often. Tira, how many times have you been whipped?"

Her eyes widened. "Highness, not once."

"About how many whippings in the palace each ten-day?"

She hesitated. "Highness, none ... that I know of."

"She's right, gentle friends. Since my father became Jeddak of Jeddaks, no servant's been whipped in this household. It is still lawful in Helium ... but rare, so strong is the example of my parents. You see .... Well, perhaps you don't; I don't know how much of our history you know. But I, my wife, my mother, and even my father have been slaves one time or another. Complete slaves, not servants under indenture. So we know what the lash means and are too proud to use it on the helpless. Flogging for crimes not meriting death, yes. But not for peccadillos of servants. Tira, what do you think of the proposal? Speak truth, speak my name, look me in the eye. I have spoken."

Tira took a deep breath. "Carthoris, I think it a good proposal. It would be a source of pride ... and its mirror use as a means of discipline would cause such shame that rarely it would be needed. Service would never be slack, I think, but I do not recommend it without reservations."

"How so, woman? You just did recommend all of it."

"I recommend that it be *tried* ... for two ten-days. If it does not work well, you can return to the old way before your grandfather and your great-grandfather return from Okar."

Zeb chortled. "She knows Murphy's Law!"

Tira looked startled. The prince cocked a brow. "Perhaps Tira does, but I don't."

" 'What can go wrong, will go wrong.' So always test a process or a machine or whatever as thoroughly as possible—then *still* be careful. It may turn and bite you."

"Oh. We have a similar saying. But this is a shrewd one, is Tira. She should have been born a princess—and some smart Jed may make her his princess yet. Lay his sword at her feet and marry her in full state."

"Highness ... that could never happen."

"That's what the pilot said just before he crashed. Remember Murphy's Law, dear. But you won't be sold; you must love him or Mother would never consent." Carthoris patted her cheek, kissed her quickly, a mere peck. "Now tell me: have you been taking good care of our guests?"

"Highness, I have tried."

"Just 'tried'? What untrained apprentices have you been using? Let me see them. With your permission, Zeb?" he added.

"Certainly, Cart."

Tira clapped twice; our girls came bursting out their side corridor as if for fire drill, lined upon the bounce, dropped in full prostration in unison. Zeb and I started patting heads, they stood up and waited.

"Tira," I said, "Have them show a curtsy."

"At once, Doctor." Perhaps she used a hand signal—they bobbled down and up perfectly in step.

Carthoris cheered. "Again, Tira!" Tira had them do it six times, like clockwork. My daughter could have made a chorus line of those beauties in a fortnight. Carthoris called a halt. "Yes," he said, "I see that Tira provided 'raw recruits.' Teeka there has been my grandfather's favorite masseuse for many cycles. Kissa and Wogi belong to Tardos Mors, and Ajal is at least nominally mine. Larlo and Laba serve my grandmother; Kona and Fig belong to my wife. Tira, have they behaved themselves?"

I interrupted. "They've *all* been good girls, Cart. Very."

They caught the phrase "good girls" and looked pleased. Teeka held my eye and dimpled. I said to Zeb, "I think we can let them go back to whatever they do when they aren't being super-helpful." Zeb agreed; Tira sent them away. Some of them looked disappointed. But I wanted to get acquainted with this young prince and I think Zeb did, too—Carthoris was the key to whatever we needed. What *did* we need? Power … food that would keep … a carbon dioxide scavenger and air bottles if their technology went that way … clothes for Hilda. Shoes for her? I wasn't certain women here ever wore shoes. Could their leather workers measure Hilda's dainty feet and get her properly shod? What else?

We went out onto the balcony where we had breakfasted; Tira remained in the foyer. The table where we had eaten, clear, except for two mugs of uncoffee minutes before, now held several sorts of wine and bowls of munching food. That balcony could not be reached from other balconies, yet those girls had not gone past us through the great hall. I became certain that the apartment held concealed passageways. Occam's Razor. Then I changed it from "certainty" to "working hypothesis"—Occam's Razor was not always sharp.

The prince wanted to discuss politics and economics. His father, he told us, had instituted many reforms. But each reform seemed to create a new problem knottier than the one it corrected. "Cousin Zeb, Doctor, don't think I'm criticizing my father; I am not. He is many, many cycles wiser than I. But the truth is, and he is the first to admit it, that the Warlord is bored by administrative detail. And my beloved mother refuses to rule; she simply reigns. So I must mind the shop. I'm not complaining—but both of you have experience with a larger planet with a far larger population. You must know things I do not."

The problems of Barsoom and the Helium hegemony (less than half the planet, but the richest and most civilized part) were painfully easy to state. No coal. No petroleum. Almost no remaining ore. No water power whatever. Some radium (uranium and rhodium, I suspect, but Carthoris called it "radium" in translating a Barsoomian jawbreaker) but most "radium" resources were hoarded to keep the planet alive: pumping its precious water and running an air plant that renewed the planet's thin atmosphere—whether this involved transmutation, or breaking down of oxides, wasn't discussed; the air plant was the sole thing on the planet held sacred by civilized nations and barbarians alike.

In the meantime, John Carter's humane reforms had resulted in more and more people. Helium was on the edge of starvation.

I thought about the food that had been lavished on us—and then thought again. That food had not been thrown away—"slaves ate after their masters." Now I knew why a small royal family had over two thousand slaves—plus Issus knew (I didn't) how many employees, guards, et cetera. The palace was one huge make-work "welfare" project.

"Gentlemen, our old ways, rough as they were, kept the population down to what we could feed. Now we no longer have even the River Iss as a partial solution; my father exposed it for what it was: a slaughterhouse chute of a fake religion. So now we are trying from the other end—"birth control," the English phrase is, I believe—but we call it "egg breaking." We've tried to make it popular. My dear mother is Patroness of the Greater Helium Egg Breaking Festivals, and my wife Thuvia and I lead off every celebration by publicly breaking one of her eggs. We don't cheat; it is indeed one that she has laid—not one from a slave woman. I tell you in confidence that we have several fertile eggs in stasis, hidden in diverse places inside and outside the city—a royal family has a duty to continue its line, not leave the realm open to a power struggle.

"But despite the thousands of eggs destroyed every quarter cycle, our population grows—and more and more peasants swarm into the city. I wish you could see—no, I hope you *never* see—this city at night. Homeless people huddled in every hole or alcove that offers any shelter, like wild thoats at night, and covered with any fur or silk they can lay hands on. Yet every morning the black chariots remove bodies frozen at the outside of each huddle or suffocated at its core. Yet *still* the city grows. How do you handle such problems in Virginia?"

Zeb was blunt. "We don't."

"Eh?"

Zeb explained that Earth faced similar problems on a larger scale ... and had tried and was still trying analogous "solutions"— none of which worked.

"Cart, so far as I know, all you can be sure of is that an ecology always balances. *Always*. But the *way* it balances may be a disaster. Earth rebalances blindly. Every few cycles we have a senseless war ... and its only good effect—if one can call it "good" without vomiting— is that it thins the herd. But our wars have reached a point where many people feel that the next one may sterilize the planet. Balance

211

its ecology at zero. I don't know, I'm not that wise. But for the past century and a half our wars have grown steadily more deadly. The only advice I can offer—stupid advice, as I don't know your planet—is to step up the egg breaking. But how, I don't know."

"Nor do I," I agreed. "Zeb has painted a time picture. We aren't solving our own problems." (I considered telling him about a new one—invading aliens with green blood. Ask him if they had ever been seen on Barsoom. It would be hard for them to hide on a planet where naked bodies were as common as naked faces. The disguise Zeb had penetrated with a sword would not work on Barsoom. But probably those aliens wouldn't bother with an almost worn-out planet. I decided to wait.)

Carthoris looked glum. "Well ... I thought I must ask. But each must ride his own thoat. Please don't mention this talk to my father; it might displease him, my dumping our problems in the laps of honored guests instead of entertaining them." Suddenly he grinned. "Let's forget that I opened my big mouth. We still live! And while we live, let's enjoy it! Will you take a walk with me?"

"Certainly," I agreed. "But are we dressed for it?"

The prince looked puzzled. "You are dressed as I am—leather and sword. What more does a man need? Are there other weapons you wish to carry? You won't need them, I promise. Ornaments? If you wish. I don't bother with them at home. But you may have different tastes."

Zeb said, "No. I'm ready."

"Me, too," I agreed.

"Then let's go. It isn't far."

We went farther down the corridor, perhaps a hundred and fifty meters, while Carthoris returned salutes and answered with a word that seemed to mean "at ease!" I found myself saluting US style, then trying to imitate Barsoomian salute—then gave up. Carthoris paid no attention and the guards couldn't seem to see Zeb and me at all. We turned into a side door, through an empty apartment, out onto a balcony overlooking another enclosed garden.

"My mother's apartments are directly across from us," Carthoris said.

I'm certain Carthoris did not intend us to look across—I looked down. Zeb let out a grunt of surprise.

Occupying the middle of the garden was *Gay Deceiver*.

We both stared. Then Zeb asked, "*How?*"

Carthoris grinned and looked very pleased. "Not difficult, with enough help. You assured American Express that your sky chariot would be safe. But I knew, being a pilot myself, that if it were *my* flier, I would not wish to leave it unguarded in the Bay of Blood. So our fastest class of destroyer left from Lesser Helium at the same time my wife's little yacht left here to pick you up. Your craft was under guard long before the sun went down."

"Thanks," Zeb answered. "I didn't want to leave her out there, unguarded. But by 'How?' I meant 'How did you put her *here?*' I'm reasonably certain that even a skilled technician would have trouble opening her doors."

"Issus! Zeb, no one—*no one*—touched her doors. I would bust an officer down to recruit for that, and have him flogged to boot. We simply picked her up and deposited her gently. Quite gently; I supervised it."

"I still don't see how. There doesn't seem to be a mark on her."

"I'm certain there isn't; I inspected before and after. First, gardeners spent part of the night removing plants to make room once her overall size was wirelessed back. Then she was carefully measured in all dimensions, a scale model constructed on the spot by a master sculptor, correctness checked optically, and model and all measurements flown back to the city. From these the sling was constructed—triple silk; a swarm of tailors worked the last half of the night. Fortunately many grommets were sewed into the sling; she turned out to be far heavier than we expected—we haven't figured out yet how she gets off the ground. Then thirty-two fliers, piloted as one from a thirty-third—by me"—he grinned again, boyishly pleased with himself—"took strains on lines of various lengths—to keep the fliers clear of each other, you know—and we lifted. My best pilots were in the lifting craft; we kept the strains balanced, and lifts and turns were made as precisely as in battle.

"By mid-morning we were over the palace—and Tira sent word to me that you two were still asleep ... which pleased me, as you could have seen her being lowered had you been on a balcony. I do love a surprise. She was lowered below roof level—you could still have seen my fliers but she was out of your sight—then we placed her most cautiously on the ground, detached the lines, removed the sling ... and saved it, as we will lift her out and place her on an open, level field whenever you say."

"Thanks," said Zeb, "but it won't be necessary."

"But …. Aren't those wings?"

"Yes."

"You must be a master pilot, Cousin!"

"Adequate. My captaincy is in aerospace."

Our host looked momentarily glum. "I wish I could say the same. But we haven't the metal to build even one spaceship. If I am ever to visit Earth—a prime ambition if I ever have time—it must be as a passenger, buying a ticket through Thomas Cook of American Express." Suddenly he brightened. "But I was thinking of the Earthling liners. Perhaps we *could* build—*one*—the size of yours. Or could we?"

"Jake?"

My brain raced. Give continua-craft secrets to another planet? When I had not turned them over to my own government—as yet? But what about two pregnant women and our need for the favor of this prince?

Call me turncoat. Or take it up with one "Colonel Duggins." Or wrap it in Form 1040! When we left Earth, we had done so under duress, unprotected from booby traps and atomic bombs and other deadly hazards, thrown solely on our own resources. I opted to protect our wives.

"I can supply plans, Highness. By rigging a projector for microfilm. Up to you how the projections could be copied; we don't have equipment here for that. It's also up to you to work from those plans; I haven't the slightest idea whether or not your technicians can duplicate my apparatus." (Cart, old man, I can give you specs on those gyros—but can your people do as well as Sperry Division? *I* can't.) "Zeb, how about the car manual? It's not microfilmed. Or is it?"

"No, but it's not a problem. Project the pages. Camera Obscure, in reverse. The sort of picture-postcard projector that was once popular. I could jury-rig one. With any sort of magnifying glass."

I turned back to Carthoris. "Cart, I won't kid you. We will turn over to you full plans, with full explanations. But if you don't have the technology to use them—and at present I can't guess—you might spend a cycle of cycles on it and still be disappointed. That little ship represents the combined talent of hundreds of thousands—I don't *know* how many—specialized experts in many, many fields. There are items in it, many of them, that neither Zeb nor I could build. We bought them. We can explain them, give you pictures and plans for them. But we did not make them. Only the overall design is mine. I built on the shoulders of other men."

Prince Carthoris smiled and for a moment looked the way I feel that royalty—*true* royalty, not exiles in Estoril—*should* look. "I couldn't ask for more, Doctor. If we fail, it's our failure. But Helium understands teamwork, too."

—— XXIV ——

Zebadiah

I didn't say much as Jake and Cart and I walked back to our apartment. We had told Cart the truth—but he didn't grasp it. We *tried* to tell him that duplicating *Gay Deceiver* on Barsoom was a nearly zero possibility. Like asking the Wright brothers to build the first Moonship. I knew they had high technology; some of it looked like magic to me. But it wasn't *our* technology.

Take a simple pocket pen, so cheap that they are given away as advertising. Back of it lie several sorts of chemists, metallurgists, synthetic polymer experts, mechanical engineers, extrusion presses, computer programmers, computers, computer technicians, toolmakers, electrical engineers, a planet-wide petroleum industry, five or more sorts of mines with mining engineers, geologists, miners, railroads, steamships, production engineers, management specialists, merchandizing psychologists—et cetera to a splitting headache. It is impossible even to list the myriad special skills that underlie even the most trivial trade item of our enormously complex and interdependent industrial web. Hell, I didn't even mention power grids.

Or accountants, banking systems, financiers—I left those out on purpose. I assumed that the prince could handle the money end. If not, we could not help him.

Could we help him at all? Well, we could *try* all-out and suppress our misgivings. Mmm, maybe the approach was not a monkey-copy *Gay Deceiver*, but to find out whether or not even *one* Barsoomian mathematician could understand Jake's math—and go from there.

They might wind up with an inter-universes space-time craft shaped like an egg and a third the size of the *Gay Deceiver*—mostly life-support and gyros. Must talk to Jake—as twinning *Gay Deceiver* could *not* be done off her home planet. Nor was it necessary. Continua craft didn't need wings. With accurate radar, or even precise optical range finders, I could have grounded *Gay Deceiver* without unfolding her wings. She had never been intended to be a spaceship; she was a bastard (forgive me, Smart Girl!), outfitted for space-time travel because she was what we had.

But Carthoris could start from scratch and stick to essentials. Maybe it would work. It might even solve his population problem. Or fill those dead sea bottoms with water. Or fetch metal to Barsoom. Cheap transportation is the key to almost any economic problem— and what could be cheaper than a freighter that goes *any* distance in *no* time (or even switches universes) at less than the price of paper clip?—once you get it operating.

I reached our digs feeling better; maybe we could help our friend yet.

Tira met us, curtsied. "Highness, Captain, Doctor, the princesses have returned."

"Out here, Cart!"

"Coming, Thuv! Thanks, Tira."

Standing in the archway at the far end of the big room was a figure silhouetted by bright sunlight. I called out, "Deety, honey, I missed you!"

"I am flattered, Senior Cousin," the silhouetted figure answered, "but I am not your princess. I am Thuvia." And durn if she didn't curtsy to me!

I hurried toward Princess Thuvia while Deety called out, "I'm out here, Tarzan. And I'm flattered, too."

"Coming." Thuvia had her hand stuck out to shake mine. I took it, bowed deeply over it while turning it ninety degrees and kissing it, giving it a semi-Polish treatment—i.e., not the all-out Warsaw invitation to better things, but not a stage actor's fake, nuther. Just strong enough so that she was certain her hand had been kissed.

Thuvia giggled. "Cart, Mother Dejah is right. He not only looks like the Warlord—he acts like him, too."

When did Dejah Thoris get a look at me? Was this joint bugged like a Moscow hotel? Spy eyes? Spy cameras—if they had photography; I had seen no photographs. Wait a half! I had been on a balcony where Cart had said, "My mother's apartments are directly across from here." But "across" was at least a hundred meters—binoculars? No, the timing wasn't right; our wives and Thuvia must have left there by then, as the jeddara's quarters were three times as far from our apartment as that balcony we had been on—and they beat us home. I dropped it—no data. But that palace had the privacy of a zoo.

I straightened up and took a better look at the princess ... and saw why the silhouette had fooled me. Aside from pigmentation, Cart's wife and mine could have passed for twin sisters. Use body makeup on Deety and spray her pretty hair black and anyone would believe it. I had plenty of chance to make certain, as Princess Thuvia's costume was a jeweled belt around her wasp-waist and a dagger in a matching sheath.

I said, "Cart, come on. Want you to meet our owners."

"Wives," Jake corrected.

"Is there a difference?" I asked.

Cart answered, "Well ... now that you put it that way ...."

"Careful what you say, dear," Thuvia cautioned. "I'll tell Mother Dejah. Be a gentleman, Cart; I want you to meet some ladies."

Neither Deety nor Sharpie stood up to meet the prince regent— I was proud of them. The drooling eagerness of most of my female compatriots on being exposed to royalty, I do not like. We fought to get rid of kings; we insist that our presidents kiss babies and mingle with the peepul ... then slobber over the worn-out royalty of Europe.

The royal house of Helium (and other Barsoomian royalty, at least in those classic romances that appear to be more history than fiction) are the sort of royalty of our Middle Ages; they fought their way up and hold tenure by ruling wisely (or they lose, both tenure and life). Jungle Law—but the Law of the Jungle has outlasted all written law.

Thuvia and Carthoris were just plain fun to have around. They accepted us as equals, slightly senior to them, but "family," and that let them relax.

Cart did one thing that was definitely protocol before he relaxed: after being introduced to our wives—and bending over and kissing their hands, somewhat awkwardly, he then unbuckled his sword and placed it at their feet, midway between them.

This is, I understand, between a single man and a maid, is or can be a proposal of marriage. It did not mean that now; we all were most visibly married. So it had its other meaning; "I will defend you with my life, now and forever." It is *never* a polite gesture; it is a blood oath, to the death.

I'm proud of our women. Deety was at once solemn, but she does that easily. Hilda dropped the jester's mask she wears most of the time—and showed the lady (and heroine) underneath.

Neither smiled, both had tears in their eyes. Working together, they buckled his sword back on. Then Hilda spoke for both of them: "We thank you, Prince Carthoris. You have honored us. We will try always to justify your faith in us."

Jake caught my eye; he started fumbling at his Sam Browne as I unhooked my Navy belt. Together, we laid our weapons at the feet of Princess Thuvia.

She'd had more experience at this than our girls had, probably by a factor of several hundred. She stood very straight and sang: "Gentle sirs, senior cousin, learned doctor, I pray that I will ever deport myself to bring honor to your blades. I feel warmly safe knowing that they protect me. I accept their shelter and thank you for it."

"And Helium thanks you," Cart rumbled. "I have spoken."

Thuvia picked up our weapons, let the Sam Browne hang on her forearm while she hooked up my sword belt, then turned to Jake, figured out how it had to go, put the shoulder strap over his head and onto his shoulder, then buckled the belt. His saber had come unhooked; she fumbled a bit, while Jake quietly helped her. Then she went into his arms and gave him an all-out Deety kiss.

Then it was my turn.

That ended all ceremony. By then all three women were dripping tears, and Deety and Sharpie were streaking their makeup. For they were indeed made up from their toes to maybe fifteen centimeters above their heads, complex hairdos studded with jewelry.

Each was wearing a dagger and a jeweled belt, like Thuvia. That was just a starter. Wrist bracelets, upper arm bracelets, rings, pendants, necklaces, anklets, and things I have no names for—all crusty with gems. Deety had an emerald in her navel that should have been in the forehead of an image in some jungle temple. I don't know what held it there. A corkscrew? Self-confidence?

A horseback guess says that each of our wives was wearing a couple of hundred thousand newdollars in colorful doodads—plus their inestimable value (on Earth) as anthropological items. Maybe I underestimated.

But I was a perfect little gentleman. I didn't ask why Deety and Hilda were dressed like birds of paradise; I just joined Jake in shooing everyone back onto the balcony, where the ladies had been lounging when we returned. The table out there had been replenished with wines and snacks, but not the assortment we three men had shared half an hour before. I saw why mealtimes were vague in the palace; lavish food was always in reach. Now and then a pixie—Ajal, Kissa, somebody—would glance out, remove anything partly emptied and replace it with fresh. With masterly deduction I figured out that the Campfire Girls were holding a picnic in the room assigned to them.

Cart and Thuvia are easy company. Old-shoe comfortable. Cart is sober-sided except for his infectious grin—but he had heavy burdens. Thuvia had Deety's three major expressions: thoughtfully impassive, big grin, and little-girl startled. But balanced differently; Thuvia grinned most of the time, talked a lot without committing herself over much, and had an easy bawdiness. While she looked Deety's age, she was older than Deety (*much* older) and far more experienced.

She kidded her husband much as Sharpie did Jake. Deety made unexpected remarks that sounded like kidding but were not; Deety herself was most unexpected. But Sharpie's remarks were serious only when needful.

Thuvia sat on a balustrade, one knee up high with her inner leg dragging, while Deety faced her in the same pose, mirror image. I sat on a cushion where I could hand food and wine to each of them, and tried not to stare too overtly at Thuvia, although she clearly didn't give a hoot. (There was *no* "body modesty" on Barsoom; they didn't have the concept any more than a kitten has. They wore ornaments, they wore furs for warmth—and I understood that in the far north furs were fashioned into full clothes, for warmth. They wore weapons and sometimes body armor. But they didn't wear clothes for "decency"— that indecent Garden-of-Eden myth that corrupts our culture never took hold there.)

Cart stretched on his back and stared openly at Deety. I knew that Deety didn't mind; she's been a lifetime rebel against that taboo ...

and I didn't mind; it enriched Cart without impoverishing me—staring is the most harmless of recreations and should be encouraged. Sharpie was stretched on her belly near Cart and fed him the way our pixies fed us, when we let them.

Thuvia asked me, "Is it really true that Earth's incredible oceans are several meters deep?"

Deety answered for me. "Thu, several meters deep would just be a pond. Or a small lake. Oceans are much more than a kilometer deep. Often many kilometers deep."

"Issus! I have trouble visualizing it. I've heard it before … but it sounded like travelers' tall tales."

"I must think about it in haads. A haad is …."

"… about half a kilometer, Thu. I had to estimate just yesterday."

"A haad is six-tenths of a kilometer, Deety," Cart put in.

"Near enough. I didn't have anything to measure with. I just stood my husband up by a green friend of mine and pointed to a place on his tummy that would mark about two meters, knowing how tall Zebadiah is. Goodness! I promised both Tommy Tucker and Kach I would get in touch today. And I haven't."

Sharpie suddenly sat up. "And so did I! Thu! How do we get in touch with American Express?"

Cart answered, "You ask Tira. But Deety, what do you need from American Express? Perhaps we have it in the palace."

"Not this, you don't. Our green friends, Cart. Tommy Tucker—Tawm Takus. And another one. Kach Kachkan."

"Tawm Takus I know; he's a brood-nephew to my godfather General-in-Chief Tars Tarkus. A good man, Tawm Takus. Conscientious—but no sense of humor."

"Look who's talking," Thuvia drawled.

"Peace, my princess—had one once; I'll find it again … once I get some worries cleared up. 'Kach Kachkan?' Unusually tall, even for a green man? Heavily muscled? Scars all over him?"

Sharpie answered, "I don't know how tall green giants usually are but that's a perfect description of Kach. He's taller than Tawm Takus, quite a bit."

"It has to be the same man. Senior Underofficer of the Thark regiment of the Allied Forces stationed here. And, except for my father, the deadliest warrior on Barsoom. Deadly even without weapons."

I said, "Tawm Takus referred to Kach as 'sergeant major.'"

"Same rank, different use of English idiom. If Tawm Takus is with American Express, he probably knows more English than I do. Thuv is the only member of our family who speaks it as well as my father does." Cart smiled ruefully. "She learned it first, from my father. They used to joke in it ... until Mother and I learned it in self-defense. But Thu uses idioms and words my mother and I haven't learned."

"Yes," agreed Thuvia comfortably, "including some your father says I should not use. Although I learned them from hearing him use them when he was vexed. Deety, after the revolution I'm going to work for Thomas Cook. So I'm always trying to enrich my English vocabulary. You and Hilda have enriched it today."

"After the revolution you'll be a slave, Thuv," her husband said.

"Thu," put in Sharpie, "I made a deal with Tommy Tucker—Tawm Takus—to teach him impolite English in exchange for his teaching me the swear words and barracks language of soldiers here. You could join the class—if it won't make you blush."

"A woman who has spent many cycles as a slave of the Holy Therns forgets how to blush, Hilda."

"If she ever knew," added Thuvia's husband.

"Ignore my husband, Sharpie. He's a ... what was that very long word?"

"Floccinaucinihilipilificator."

"Zeb, has my honor been maligned?" Cart asked me.

"Comrade, you'll probably die from it. But not for many cycles."

"Then I won't worry. Flocksy nasty— Oh, to Iss with it!"

"Cart," Deety said plaintively, "how do I get to American Express?"

"It's about three haads straight down the Avenue of Heroes. But Deety, you don't go there; you require American Express to come *here*."

"But I don't want American Express. I just want to see Kach. And Sharpie wants to see Tommy."

"Now?"

"Well ... as soon as possible."

"Very well. Tira!"

Tira materialized as if Cart had rubbed the Magic Lamp. "Highness, you called?"

"With your permission, Zeb? Tira ...." Cart shifted to Barsoomian; I caught only "American Express" and the names of our green friends. Cart turned back as Tira vanished. "They will be here in ... perhaps twenty of your minutes. Unless they are farther away than

222

the office of American Express. Deety, what are you looking upset about? Are my arrangements not satisfactory?"

"Yes, but ... I promised Kanakook ... that Kach Kachkan's thoat ... that I would see *her*, too."

"You promised a *thoat?*"

"Why not? She's a friend of mine. One doesn't break promises to children or animals, ever."

"She did promise the thoat," I agreed. "I heard Deety. And the thoat understood her."

The prince regent looked impressed. "Cousin, you have been blessed with a most remarkable wife."

"I know it, Cart. But so have *you*."

"The central fact of my existence, Zeb."

"I got dealt a pretty good hand, too," Jake said smugly. "Five aces."

"Five? But there are only .... Sorry! 'Five.'"

Sharpie said, "If anyone mentions the joker, I'm leaving the room. Balcony." She reached out and gently tickled her husband's thigh with her toes.

"Now," Thuvia said softly, "that you gentlemen have finished building up our morale—for which we thank you—let's put Deety's mind at rest. Deety dear, Cart told Tira 'all possible speed.' Since our green allies can't fit into our tubes or ground fliers, they must either walk, or ride their giant thoats. Since the order came from the Regent and included 'all possible speed,' now or very quickly a Navy flier is clearing the Avenue of Heroes ahead of two giant thoats running their fastest. Unless your friends are far from American Express. If so, Tira will report it in a moment or two. But they will *still* come with all possible speed, even if they are a hundred haads away. The Regent's orders are not questioned."

"But suppose they are working? They are couriers."

"If so, they are not working for the Regent. Deety, there are disadvantages to being royal—some days I would almost welcome being a slave again. But there are advantages, too. Cart exercised a minor advantage for a guest we are very anxious to please. You, dear."

My darling got her little-girl look. "I didn't *mean* to be a nuisance—but thank you, Cart; Sharpie and I do want to see our friends. How do we go down to see them?"

"Oh, they'll come up here," our host assured her, "with an escort to clear the way. Deety, when my father made allies of the largest Green Hordes, apartments in this guest wing were modified to accommodate our giant friends. This hall behind us has a ceiling high enough even for Kach Kachkan. So, I think, does your dining hall. There is at least one retreat room with washing trays and other fixtures designed for the somewhat different needs of green men. Tira knows where it is—I don't. Will your guests be staying overnight?"

"Why ... I hadn't thought about it."

"Either way, no need to tell anyone but Tira. Your guests are our guests as long as you wish them to stay. For one night I think they would be comfortable in this hall behind us; they are used to sleeping anywhere. For longer than overnight, tell Tira; a nearby apartment will be provided."

"I ... I'm overwhelmed. But how do I see Kanakook? A thoat can't come up here."

Cart gave a wry grin. "True. But you will be able to see her from here and go down to where she is; just tell Tira—escort is at hand. See that fenced-off area in this courtyard? All large houses are built somewhat like this one and provide for thoats ... so that no thief can reach them in the night. Tira! Dear, tell the Watch that the thoats of the green guests of our guests are to graze in this courtyard, not with the other thoats."

"Yes, Highness. I have already told them."

"Tira, if I could persuade my mother to part with you, I would return your indenture and appoint you Secretary of State for Domestic Affairs—and load half the work of the realm on you."

"Don't let him do it to you!" Thuvia cut in. "You'd never have a moment's peace."

"Highness, I have no political ambitions."

"Nor do I, Issus take it! But I can't avoid it. Are all your problems solved, Deety? I should get back to work. This has been a delightful rest, for which I thank you."

Thuvia stretched and yawned. "Duty calls me, too. Girls, don't ever marry a politician. Sirs, ladies, may we be excused?"

"Just a moment!" said Jake. "Cart, will you answer one question for me; directly, no dodging?"

Cart said quietly, "As my father's deputy, I can do no other. Speak, distinguished Doctor."

"My daughter, without intending to, is bringing two green men into your home. Is it possible that this is why the prince regent and his royal consort now have duties elsewhere?"

"No, distinguished Doctor, it is *not* possible. But I must clarify it. Tawm Takus is my relative through Tars Tarkus ... in all but egg. Kach Kachkan is not; I have seen him only on parade. I regret to say that we have never fought side by side—although we have shared blood of Helium's enemies in the same battle. But tomorrow or ten cycles from now we may fight side by side, or back to back. Do you think me such a ... a 'popinjay,' I think I have the right word—such a snob that I would not share wine and sleeping silk with a warrior such as he?"

"Your Highness, I offer my apologies."

"I can't accept them, Jake, for no offense was intended, and I intended none. My princess, I think we should wait and meet the guests of our guests, who are thereby *our* guests."

"My chieftain, you speak with your father's wisdom. I agree."

"Hey!" said Deety, almost in tears, "Pop, Thu, Cart, you're all making too much of this! You've got work to do; go do it! You're certain to meet our friends another time—you'll like 'em. But it doesn't have to be *today!* Oh, *dear!*"

The prince relaxed, no longer ramrod straight. He grinned that grin that made him look younger than I was. "Okay, Deety dear."

Thuvia and that man she lives with should have left then, but Sharpie interrupted. "Deety, we forgot to give back the pretties! Tira! We need help. And someone to carry them back." She was shucking off "pretties," a thousand newdollars a shuck. Deety looked startled, moved quickly to catch up.

Thuvia grabbed each by an arm. "Darlings! What in the world are you doing?"

"Handing back the jewelry you loaned us. I'll send Laba and Kona along with you to carry them."

"But those are *not* loans. They are gifts."

"Thuvia, if you think we'll accept gifts this lavish, you don't know me very well. Or Deety, either."

Yes, Thuvia was capable of the helpless-little-girl-with-too-big-a-problem look, too. Had she and Deety been twins in some other time-space? Or would be—pick the tense you like. "If you send them back, I'll be forced to store them until you want them. And those from Mother Dejah, too. Returned gifts are terribly bad fortune—they mean a broken friendship."

Carthoris confirmed it. "But perhaps this will help. On Barsoom most jewelry is very old. Most of it winds up, eventually, with royal houses. But jewels can't be eaten, they are useless as weapons—and usually can't be sold as jewelry, usually comes into one's possession as a gift. Mother must have at least a chest of jewelry she has never worn. What *can* be done with jewelry is to give it to some dear friend who will wear it. But if you two won't keep these trinkets, they simply become burdens, never to be touched."

So our two darlings, willy-nilly, came into a fortune of priceless jewelry. The only outcome was that they put back on what they hastily stripped off ... and insisted on being kissed again, this time by *both* Cart and Thuvia. So Jake and I kissed Thuvia's hand and shook Cart's hand. They left, a bit late.

Deety, as always, had a problem. "Aunt Hilda, should we wear these jewels for Kach and Tommy Tucker? Or take off all but dagger and belt, as Thu did?"

"We'll ask Tira, of course. How about it, Tira hon?"

"The Princess Thuvia was correct both times. When she sent these for you and then came to escort you, the occasion was formal even though the jeddara's invitation did not so describe it. But when she returned with you, it was no longer formal, so she changed."

I finally got it straight. Our dears had been allowed to sleep until they woke, then had been undisturbed while they broke fast. Then they had been set upon by all eight pixies under Tira's supervision—bathed, made up from head to toe, hair arranged in splendor, and adorned with more jewelry than I had ever seen on a woman.

Right on the dot of the completion of Tira's masterpieces, Thuvia had arrived, decked out just as ornately, escorted by a guard in dress leathers, and they had been taken to call on the jeddara, Dejah Thoris.

"What sort of a person is she?" I asked.

"Sweet, very gracious."

"But what does she look like?" asked Jake. "Pretty as she is supposed to be?"

"Uh, not exactly. I don't think you two should try to see her."

"Correct," agreed Sharpie. "She's an old woman, you know. One walleye, sort of hunched, hair stringy and mostly white. Wrinkles ...."

"Sharpie!"

"Just backing your play, kiddo."

"Zebadiah, have you ever been an actor?"

"Tried it once, went up on my lines. Why?"

"Do you understand the term 'upstaged'?"

"Certainly."

"Who was the most beautiful woman in history?"

"Helen of Troy."

"Try again. Do better."

"Venus? Paris didn't think so."

"Keep trying."

"Cleopatra?"

Hilda said, "That's three strikes and you're out. Dejah Thoris."

"And if you two ever see her," Deety added, "Neither of you will be satisfied with us common broads again. You'll leave us. I'm not sure that what she did is 'upstaging'—maybe 'underplaying' is the word. But we three were, Thuvia wearing more hunks of gorgeous rocks than we were. Even though most of what Sharpie wore came from Dejah Thoris, Thuv told us—mine are Thuv's excess, out-of-style geegaws. But guess what Dejah Thoris wore?"

"A diamond overcoat? Maybe with rubies and sapphires to set it off?"

"Better than that."

"I know," said Jake. "A dagger on a belt. Like Thuvia when she came back here."

"Wrong. But she did wear something."

"Quit stalling, Deety," I told her firmly. "What did Dejah Thoris wear?"

"A smile. Just a smile. Not even makeup or perfume. Hair just brushed down her back. And she was the most gorgeously dressed of any of us. I think she knew it."

"I'm *sure* she knew it," said Sharpie. "But she never let on. Treated us as her favorite big sisters. And told us how beautiful *we* were. Darn her big, lovely liquid eyes! If she returns the call—she threatened to— *I'm* going to wear just skin. Mine's not much, compared with hers. But it's my own and I'm going to flaunt it. With a hip wiggle."

— XXV —

Zebadiah

We refugees from Earth-Zero kept very busy the next ten-day; Doctor Burroughs tackled the problem of how to convey the methods of "moving" by quanta jumps via six-dimensional space to Prince Carthoris. I spent my time trying to modify *Gay Deceiver* from a sports car jury-rigged with a Burroughs' time-space twister into something more like a spaceship—a life-support capsule in space that would also be a strong, safe, and tolerable igloo in any weather on any planet we risked grounding on. It was a knotty problem, primarily through shortage of space inside *Gay Deceiver*.

I had already learned that our prime need was space for four to stretch out horizontally. How to do it was a jigsaw puzzle, and one that had to be solved within limits set by the shell of *Gay Deceiver's* body, a space cluttered with seats, controls, instrument board, computer, L-gun, Burroughs 6-space distorter, wiring, tubing, supplies, clothing, power packs, water tank, gadgets, gear, and a big main thrust motor never intended to fit inside the monocoque of a Ford duo.

I never considered altering the shell. The strength of Gay's skin was our protection against the buffeting of weather (What weather? What sorts of planets?), gut-wrenching maneuvers, radiation, attacks from outside. She had weak points enough in her doors, in the mounting of the transparent quintuple sandwich of her "windshield," the L-guns' "eye," the dissimilar "eyes" of ranging radar and anti-collision radars, and other points (such as air scoops) where for one reason or another, her shell had been penetrated, then beefed up to offset the stress-raisers thus formed, and sealed against loss of air.

228

Her wheel wells, and her wing-root recesses that let her fold wings for hypersonic flight or spread them for subsonic, were outside her gas-tight shell. Those cavities blemished her lovely shape by creating weirdly varying concentrations of stress—again offset by beefing up ... parasitic weight, but such trade-offs had to be accepted.

I hoped that her chief designer, materials engineer, aerodynamicist, and chief inspector had all been pessimists soaked in the bitter wisdom of Murphy's Law. I *thought* they all had been such—the old girl had never let me down. But there was always that first time ... that could be a last time. I shrugged and said, "Goodnight, Gay. Over."

"Sleep tight, Zeb. Over."

"Thank you, Gay. Over and out."

Besides sleeping space, I wanted to add air bottles (if Barsoom technology had such), a CO_2 scavenger (I thought I could manage one if Barsoom chemistry was as advanced as it appeared to be). I rejected the notion of pure O_2, even if available—many organic polymer items aboard, all potentially explosive in straight oxygen—odd that human beings breathed the most dangerous element of all.

The simplest—and hardest—problem was sleeping space.

I wasn't getting anywhere crawling around inside Gay—all knees and elbows, getting in my own way every time I tried to take a measurement. What had Cart said about a "master sculptor?" A model that could be opened up, with manikins exactly to scale, might make a solution evident.

I got out of the car, telling Gay to button up. The sergeant of the guard around the car called the guard to attention, saluted. "At ease!" I called out in Barsoomian and returned the salute. My escort fell into step around me.

"It's not that I'm the better mathematician, Zeb," Burroughs explained. "Mobyas Toras might be superior to any mathematician on Earth. He's not the narrow specialist that I and most of my colleagues are." Burroughs looked wistful. "What ... I mean 'how much' ... could a man learn if he had a thousand years in which to poke into the fascinating byways of mathematics? Gracious!"

"Is Mobyas Toras actually that old?"

"I don't know and shan't ask. I've gathered an impression that age is not a polite subject. I don't know how old Mobyas Toras is, but he is the only man I've met who has gray hair, wrinkles, and other signs of old age."

"Probably means he has only century or two left in him."

"How can you say 'probably' when you have no data? I *do* know that he is skilled in many abstruse branches of mathematics, many more than I am, and some I've never heard of. But I've had less success in trying to explain my postulates for n-dimensional closed continua to him than I had with you."

"You had zero success with me; you're …"

"Pig's tripe! You have the engineering approach, Zeb. Certain transformations were Greek to you—and would be to anyone without proper foundation. You accepted my abstract work without worrying about it, just as it doesn't bother an electronics engineer to accept the square root of minus one. Zeb, you *do* understand the *practical* equations I wound up with. You could build another continua craft without my help."

"Well … maybe."

"Certainly you could! And your second-stage article would have better design. Mine is a breadboard job, patched together with off-the-shelf items. Does a designer today repeat the work of the Wright brothers or of Goddard? Mine is a Model T Ford; yours might be a Rolls Royce. Or might not—but yours would surpass my Model T; that's an elementary fact of development engineering. But back to the learned Mobyas Toras; the obstacle is *language*."

"I suppose so. Thuvia's English isn't up to the job? Not a mathematician?—no reason why she should be, of course."

"No, no! As near as I can judge, Thuvia knows quite a lot of what I would describe as practical engineering mathematics—"

"Like me, huh?"

"Possibly. Although she wouldn't be able to read your reference books—even though she reads English—much more easily than you could read hers. The trouble is *basic*. Zeb, mathematics is *language*—and that's all it is."

"So what is new? I learned that as an undergraduate."

"Maybe you don't have it deep in your bones—the way Deety has, being a symbologist by profession. Zeb, can you use an abacus?"

"I've tried it. Learned simple multiplication—slowly. But I use a hand calculator for routine problems. For something lengthy or complex I turn it over to someone like Deety to shove through a computer." Zeb grinned happily. "Got my own software artist now."

"I'm proud of that girl, if I do say so as shouldn't."

"Jake, I wouldn't even like you if you weren't proud of your daughter."

"Zeb, let's get back to Mobyas Toras. Speaking by analogy, I'm using an abacus while he uses a slide rule. Our symbols don't match, even by substitution. Took us most of one day and wore Thuv to a frazzle to get across this one idea: two plus two equals four. Mobyas finally agreed that it sometimes was true ... but not often."

"Well ... he's right."

"So I told him, through Thuvia. He answered, in effect, 'Then *why* didn't you say so?' He ended the session soon after; he was tired and visibly restraining his irritation at my stupidity. Zeb, it may be necessary to *show* him, physically, how *Gay Deceiver* works, before I can get anywhere with him."

"Let him tinker with it? No!"

"Your reasons, sir?"

"Doctor, you might try asking your wife. Sharpie will tell you, I think, that the simplest and usual way to demonstrate elementary physiology is to dissect a living frog. But the frog isn't much use afterward. Jake, the working parts of your apparatus that make *Gay Deceiver* more than just a duo are hermetically sealed. Do you want to unseal them? If so, you had better plan on homesteading here. A planet with no obstetricians. Even if *you* want to risk your apparatus—*I* don't—but if you want to, I think you should first clear it with your wife. And your daughter."

"Zeb, Zeb! Of course I don't want to open the gyro housings. But we could demonstrate what *Gay Deceiver* can do."

"Jake, I'm not anxious to demonstrate our car until we are ready to leave. Call it a hunch, but I can rationalize it if you wish. But, aside from hunch, I don't think you would convince Mobyas Toras of *anything* merely by physical demonstration. Have you ever seen fire walking?"

"No. I've heard the usual tales."

"I've seen it. It's not fake. Barefooted people totally unharmed by intensely hot fire."

"Some preparation that insulates their feet. And probably thick calluses."

"Deety has thick calluses. Do you think *she* can walk, unharmed, through a fire pit ten meters long and so hot that I could feel my face start to blister when I tried to move close to the edge of the pit?"

"Some sort of preparation ... even if you could not see it."

"You're saying that I'm not a competent observer. For the record, I had not been drinking, I was not hypnotized, it was bright sunlight, and I had an unobstructed view from as close as I could approach without unendurable discomfort. About a meter from the edge for a few moments during the fire walking, then I backed off a couple of meters—but still with a clear view. However, there *was* preparation."

"What sort?"

"An old priestess stepped down into the fire pit and *stood* in it, not walking, while she prayed. She also sprinkled a few grains of something on the fire. She didn't sprinkle it all over, just in the spot where she stood. That was the preparation—an old woman's prayers."

"Oh, for heaven's sake! You missed something."

"If I did, you would have missed it, too. I have normal eyesight. Jake, you refuse to believe that I saw what I *did* see because it runs contrary to your beliefs. But there is a classic explanation of what I saw. Standard 'least hypothesis.' Occam's Razor."

"Hmm. State of hypothesis."

"Magic."

Burroughs sighed. "Zeb, do be serious."

"I'm dead serious, Jake. 'Magic' is the classic—and correct—word—symbol—for any phenomenon totally unfamiliar to a culture. Not explainable by the concepts of that culture. You can't teach new mathematics to an old, learned mathematician by showing him magical tricks. He will either reject it as fakery—which is what *you* did—or he will call it by whatever Barsoomian word translates as 'magic' ... and dismiss it as having nothing to do with mathematics. But you *won't* convince him that you have learned a six-dimensional closed-space geometry and how to apply it as engineering. He will resent your attempt to make a fool of him by magical trickery. You will make an enemy unnecessarily—apparently an influential one. You say Thuvia treats him with deference?"

"Oh, quite! She doesn't prostrate herself, but she treats him with extreme respect. I wish that coeds I have taught treated me with a tenth the respect she shows Mobyas Toras."

"Consort of the Prince Regent. Even money Cart is just as respectful."

"Oh, he is! Both he and Dejah Thoris made a try at translating for me—didn't I say? Both of them treated him the way a ... well, the way a Catholic king might treat the Pope. Not cringing, but most carefully respectful."

"Hmm … Jake, if you have any respect for my opinion, you'll either learn his mathematical terminology and symbols, or find some way to teach him yours. Or give it up. But you won't risk anything so crass as an engineering demonstration to this savant without his *first* understanding this math I couldn't follow."

Burroughs sighed again. "I'll try. But it is hard to teach a student who feels that he knows more than you do. Worse yet, in this case my student is right. Overall, I mean. Just not in my narrow specialty."

"Deety to Zebadiah. Come in, Zebadiah."

"Zeb to Deety, I read you loud and clear. How far away are you?"

"I'll ask Kach. Kach Kachkan, how far have we gone? He says we are about halfway to the spot where we'll picnic. Let me test directly to Gay, dear."

"Okay, I'll shut up. Over and out."

"Hello, Gay!"

"Howdy, Deety!"

"You're a Smart Girl, Gay."

"Not so loud, Deety. You keep my secrets, I'll keep yours."

"Goodnight, Gay. Over."

"Hurry back, Deety. Over."

"Over and out, Gay. Deety to Zebadiah, come in."

"Zeb to Deety. I could hear both ends. Your voice in my ear plug, Gay's voice here in the cabin. Both loud and clear."

"Pretty tight hookup, huh? Sounds good."

"Maybe. Inverse Square Law may lick us. And we may be enjoying a lucky bounce. This building doesn't seem to have much metal in it; attrition may be low. But you must be over the horizon, and I'm in a hole, so to speak."

"Look at the hole, not the doughnut."

"You mean, 'Look at the dough ….'"

"I meant what I said, sweet innocent darling. Zebadiah, quit being pessimistic. Eight months from now I'm going to say, '*Ouch!*' in some nice, bright, horribly antiseptic hospital and you'll be the father of a four-kilo bouncing boy. I have confidence in you."

"A three-kilo girl."

"Anything but a hermaphrodite with green blood. A human baby. One who will throw up all over your necktie, Papa."

"I'm not wearing a necktie and don't ever plan to again. Deety, any baby of yours is welcome to throw up on me anytime."

233

"Three cheers for Zebbie! Deety, our Zebbie talks good, as a husband should."

"Sharpie"—Zeb's voice sounded stern—"have you been eavesdropping *again?*"

"I always do when possible, dear—I learn so many interesting things. Want to make something of it?"

"Not with a gal who fights giants for me. Your babies are welcome to throw up on me, too, Sharpie."

"Why, thank you, Zebbie! You can change their diapers, too."

"Hey, wait a half …. Okay, I guess I can learn."

"I'll supply a clothes pin, dear. Tawm Takus sends his respects to Captain Zebadiah John Carter of Virginia. Official."

"Oh. Our green friends are getting only half of this—right?"

"Natch. Deety and I are using ear plugs. And they ignore the half they do hear. But Tommy heard me say your name."

"Please tell him that I return his sentiments with thanks—but add that I think that's purty durn formal from a man who got drunk with me just last night."

"I didn't hear that second part, Zebbie, so I can't relay it. They *are* formal here, dear—and especially *los hombres verdes*."

"Do it your way, Sharpie; you always do. Over to Deety. No need to test again, until you reach the spot. I'll stay hooked in, I've work to do in the cabin. Cart sends word not to wonder about a flier circling you about a klick up and a klick out. It's there to protect you. Over."

"Why, Kach and Tommy can protect us from anything! Over."

"Or die trying; I'm certain of that. Deety, Cart is a suspenders-and-belt man, just as I am. If that burns out a bearing or ten thousand maddened banths come charging out of the foothills, half the Helium Navy will swoop down and save you before you can say, 'The Marines have landed!' Besides that, if you get tired, you can come home by air. Just holler. Over."

"Zebadiah, if you think we would leave Kach and Tommy out here to come home alone when it's not necessary, then you have misjudged both Hilda and me. Over."

"I don't think I've misjudged either of you. You've both got hearts too big for your size and courage to match your hearts. But I have in mind that you two are knocked-up frails. Combining this test with a picnic is a worthy ploy; our Sharpie is sharp. But if either of you miscarry as a result of too long a thoat ride, I'll give you long odds that both Tommy and Kach will fall on their swords to regain lost honor. Think about it. Over."

"Sharpie to Zeb! I can assure you, from years of volunteer hospital experience and quite a bit of study, we aren't even close to a critical date. Hell's bells, buster, we're not a full month gone. Over."

"Zeb to Sharpie. Hilda, I love and respect you. And while you show a reckless tendency to fight out of your weight, you sometimes can keep Deety straight when she won't listen to me or to her father. If *you* feel the least bit tired, will you ask for that flier? If you are beyond range for walkie-talkie even for Gay's ears, Tawm Takus can relay through Western Union. Deety won't listen to me; I'm just her husband. But if her Aunt Hilda wants to fly home, she'll come with you ... I think. So, please? Pretty please with sugar on it? Promise?"

"Zebbie, you could sell cornflakes to cannibals. I promise. If I get tired, I'll holler."

"My captain?"

"Yes, Deety?"

"My captain, we will fly home. It is now ten-thirty-one local sun time. Since we are halfway there, we should arrive very close to local noon. Say two hours for a picnic lunch, or fourteen o'clock. I'll convert that to their time, so will you please request the prince regent to have us picked up at ..."

"My princess!"

"Yessir."

"No need to hurry. Since you are flying home, make it one hour or five—suit yourselves. Have a leisurely picnic. Stretch out and take a nap. Wake up and have tea and a snack. Pet Kanakook and tell her I said she's a good girl. Have a holiday and enjoy yourselves. If you haven't called for a flier by about sixteen-thirty, the patrol flier will land and ask your pleasure."

"Yes, my captain. Thank you. And please convey our thanks to the prince regent. Over."

"Cart will be relieved, so will Jake. Over and out."

Hilda and Deety hardly needed a holiday; they had been having one. Neither could be of use to Jake as an interpreter; I neither needed nor wanted help in deciding how to rearrange and resupply *Gay Deceiver*. So they were free to poke around the city—safely, as Tawm

Takus and Kach Kachkan were their personal guards, on detached duty from their regiment, assigned as military aides to the prince regent and reassigned by him as bodyguards to the Princesses Hilda and Deety. The giants were quartered across the corridor from the Burroughs-Carter ménage, always wore regimental full-dress leathers with insignia, military awards, helmets, and all weapons but their lances: long sword, short sword, rifle, and pistol. The banquet hall turned out to be useful as they often ate with the family, and when they did, foods preferred by green men showed up at once, under Tira's management, as well as huge goblets shaped to fit giant mouths with tusks.

Hilda tried to get them to leave their weapons in the foyer during meals. Kach Kachkan said nothing; his superior officer, Tawm Takus, fell into so strong a lisp as to be unintelligible in a frantic attempt to do the impossible: agree to *anything* the Princess Hilda wished while simultaneously refusing her suggestion.

Of course I had to intervene. "Wait a half, Sharpie. What you are doing is equivalent to asking a teaching fellow back home to come to dinner at your house without his trousers. Let me handle this. Tawm, note that Jake is wearing just his saber, no pistol. All I'm wearing is my sword. This is family—and you two *are* family, by adoption; you're our oldest friends on this planet and you rescued us from the wilderness. Wouldn't a belt and a short sword be suitable at home?"

Tawm Takus got over his lisp. Helmets, trappings, ornaments, long swords, pistols, rifles, and nameless gear were placed on the floor of the foyer, laid out for quick retrieval. The giants lost their military stiffness and behaved as friends in the company of friends.

This wasn't a shot in the dark; I had gauged the situation better than Hilda had, being a touch more chameleon than she. But our family had quickly adjusted to Barsoomian customs in dress. Save for bathing and sleeping, Hilda and Deety *always* wore daggers and seldom anything else; Jake and I did the same with sword and saber.

One more mix-up occurred over dress. One afternoon when we men were away, as the story was related to me, Dejah Thoris sent word that she would call—if convenient. Both women understood that the jeddara's wish was a command, but Deety felt that they must have Tira and her eight helpers make them up and deck them out in every item of gifted finery ... while Mrs. Burroughs insisted shrilly that Dejah Thoris had set the precedent and she was damn well going to receive the jeddara in her hide! She knew it wasn't much of a hide compared with Dejah's but, by yumpin' yiminy, it was *hers* and she would wear it!

They compromised; each wore dagger and sword and fresh baths—no makeup—and received Dejah Thoris in the foyer, Deety nervous, Hilda miffed. Tira had blandly refused to advise them.

The jeddara and Princess Thuvia arrived, Thuvia decked out as ornately as she had been when she had come to escort them to meet her mother-in-law. But the jeddara's jewels and ornaments made Thuvia look as if she had grabbed a few knickknacks at the last minute—and both women from Earth felt their hearts sink. *Faux pas!*

The feeling lasted only seconds, according to Deety. Dejah Thoris clapped her slender hands together under her chin and exclaimed, "Oh, how lovely you two are! I had not fully realized, the other day; there was too much hiding your beauty." Then she had glided forward, slipped an arm around Deety's waist, the other around Hilda's shoulders, kissed Hilda, kissed Deety.

They went on into the great hall. On the right wall, the divan stretched some four meters long and a meter deep on elevation of the floor thirty centimeters high, padded as softly as a sleeping room and heaped with cushions. Hilda had draped across it her mink cape to make the borrowed apartment a touch their own. The jeddara went straight for this divan, lounged on it like a cat—thereby letting her hostesses and daughter-in-law sit or lounge. Tira's troop got busy with wines and bits of food.

Dejah Thoris accepted a tidbit, touched a cup of wine to her lips, made polite conversation—then squirmed uncomfortably. "Dears," she asked, "could I have your gentle consent to be as comfortable as you are?"

In eleven seconds flat, I was told, Tira, Fig, Kona, and Larlo had Jeddara and Prince's Consort bare to their daggers. Dejah Thoris stretched, starfished, slumped into a round heap, then rubbed her cheek against the mink cape—seemed to notice it for the first time. "Deety, this is not from Barsoom?"

Hilda answered, "From Earth, Imperial Majesty."

"Why, Hilda! I thought we were friends? Must I be formal here?"

"Sorry, Dej'. It's a cape of mutated mink. This shade is called 'sunset.' Try it on—I think the shade goes well with your hair and complexion."

Dejah Thoris floated to her feet; Hilda slipped it on her, showed her how to wear it. "It fastens at the throat. Or you can hold it tight around you by the inside pockets. Or let it drop off one shoulder. Or both."

The jeddara tried it all four ways. "Feels *lush!* Does Tira have a mirror?"

Four of Tira's squad appeared at once, with a thin, highly polished metal mirror, almost a meter wide, almost as tall as the slaves. (Deety later told me that she'd wondered, "Where has Tira been hiding *that*?"—could've used it several times.)

Dejah Thoris tried the cape all four ways again, then found endless variations, from wrapped tightly, to half a dozen sweetly provocative striptease effects, save that she was not teasing but unselfconsciously seeing what could be done with a beautiful garment.

At last she slipped it off, let Tira return it to the divan. "Thank you for letting me try it, Hilda."

"It's yours, Dej'." As Hilda explained to Jake—it just looked like it was made for her.

The jeddara looked troubled. "Hilda, I feel *certain* that this is a gift to you from your learned doctor."

"No such thing, Dej'. I bought it with my own money long, long before I was married."

"That's right," agreed Deety. "I know Hilda owned it at least two cycles before she married Pop. I remember seeing her wear it."

Dejah Thoris curtsied (and startled Deety again). "I shall wear it often, Hilda—thinking of you. I can barely wait for my husband to see it."

She stayed another half hour, then said, "To my regret, I must appear with my son at a dullness. Don't you hurry, child," she added to Thuvia. "Carthoris and I will handle it and send them on their way. No, Tira, I won't put those on 'til I must." She left, wearing the cape, followed by Laba and Teeka carrying her formal ornaments, and surrounded by armed men.

Thuvia came back from the doors with her hostesses, dropped to the floor, scratched her ribs, and said, "Chums, tell me your secret."

"What secret, Thu?" asked Deety.

"How did you know that Mama Dej' hates to dress up? I didn't tell you; I was told not to. Tira? Not Tira; she won't admit what day it is. Besides, Tira *likes* to dress up ... while she enjoys the comfort of never having to wear even a dagger belt. Tira, you're a tyrant! So who spilled it? Cart?"

"Pure logic," explained Hilda; she had to do it a second time for me. "Since Dej' has had to dress formally thousands of times …."

"Tens of thousands of times, Hillbilly. Me, not as often—but far too many."

"… and since she received us informally, not even her dagger belt, and asked us to treat her as a friend, naturally we knew how to dress. But we assumed that omitting the dagger belt would be overstepping the line." (Deety used her impassive face.)

"Yes, Mother Dejah is the only one who can receive guests without that formality—I don't dare, even with chums. And I don't have many chums—can't have; my job doesn't permit it. Which makes you folks so precious to Cart and me—gosh, we'll miss you when you leave! *If* you leave—we hope you don't."

"We must, Thuv."

"I know, Deety. You want to have them at home. Must be a strange feeling—to keep a fertile egg inside you. It's a loving thought—but I'm not sure I'd want the responsibility." She suddenly reached for her belt. "I don't even want to wear this. Invite me to take a bath with you. My answer is 'yes.'"

"Thuv, I'm sweaty. Come take a bath with me."

"Why, *thank* you, Deety! Tira—here, catch!"

"Wait for baby!" demanded Mrs. Burroughs.

It was a wonderful story that proved how resourceful our brides were.

— XXVI —

Zebadiah

A situation can be so desperate that it is necessary to tell the truth. I don't recommend it for daily use. I've yet to meet a man who prided himself on "always telling the truth" who had any friends. "The truth, the whole truth, and nothing but the truth" should be reserved for courtrooms; it is poison in social relations. Some people (my wife Deety, for example) have no talent for creative distortion and must take refuge in clamming up ... which Deety does beautifully. This serves her as well as does the razzle-dazzle Sharpie uses to conceal her thoughts.

But a *reputation* for truth is a great asset. However, one does not acquire that reputation by blurting out everything one knows. It comes from telling the truth selectively, keeping one's lip zipped much of the time, and by telling no unnecessary lies ... especially ones that can turn and sink their fangs in you.

Barsoom stretched my talent for creative soothsaying to the limit. Until ... I'd better lay a foundation.

The trouble started from a most innocent source: the warm-heartedness of Deety and Sharpie, and Cart's generosity. His calling Tawm Takus and Kach Kachkan to active duty, attaching them to the royal household and assigning them as bodyguards to our ladies was a kingly thing to do. It pleased our wives, it pleased our giant friends, it pleased Jake and me—and it pleased Cart because he was the sort who gained great pleasure from doing something nice for his friends.

240

But, in addition to being a pleasure, it was a great help to Jake, to me, and to Cart himself. I had work to do—fiddling, but lots of it—trying to modify *Gay Deceiver* to make her a tolerable home in freefall or on the ground (anywhere!) and for longer, unpredictable periods. (The translation and transition to Barsoom had scared me more than I had admitted. I had no reason to expect the air of Barsoom to be breathable; the atmosphere of her analog, Mars, is *not*. It is possible to choose between certain suffocation and taking chances over a fresh, radioactive crater—but it is not a happy choice. This next time I planned to be better prepared.)

Jake had still more difficult work: trying to carry out our promise to give Cart space-time travel—a gift that might solve the politico-economic problems of his realm and, at least, put Barsoom in a more nearly even footing with Earth-Ten in export-import. How important that was we did not learn at once; all we knew was that Earth sent tourist ships about twice a month. That told me that Earth-Ten had solved the problem of constant-boost ships, a conclusion confirmed by seeing one ground: nothing as clumsy as rockets; that spaceship simply floated down from zenith, first a speck, then a disc, then at last a huge cylinder a kilometer away on a broad stretch of dead sea bottom.

The spaceport was under extraterritorial agreement; citizens of Barsoom did not board spaceships. Cart and other royalty had been taken on a red-carpet tour, and Cart admitted sheepishly that the tour had not included control room or engineering spaces—and questions about them had been answered with vague ambiguity. But even the Warlord had not pressed the matter because that one tour showed that a planet terribly impoverished in energy and in metal could not build such a ship even if its people knew how. (John Carter must have understood far more than his subjects did about the enormous in-dustrial complex that lay behind even an ocean freighter; I wondered whether or not his long absences from the capital were caused by dis-taste for lopsided interplanetary trade—even though Helium needed the "invisible export" of tourism. I do not envy kings … or jeddaks. I recalled what had happened to the once-great nations of Polynesia and decided that the only thing that saved Barsoom from the same sorry fate was that Barsoom was an interesting place for Earthlings to visit—but not to live.)

Once I had *Gay Deceiver's* needs figured out and Barsoomian arti-sans fashioning from my sketches some fittings we needed, I tried to help with Jake's problem. Even compressed air in spheres and an odd sort of CO_2 scavenger turned out to be possible, as a planet that had as its greatest engineering achievement a plant for replenishing its atmosphere did have gas technology even though it lacked printing presses and myriad other sorts of machinery.

I was not foolish enough to attempt to teach mathematics I did not comprehend—I leapfrogged it. I took an engineering approach with Cart. Engineers do not insist on knowing *why* as long as they know *how*.

I told Cart that I did *not* understand the mathematics behind Doctor Burroughs' continua manipulator ... *but, Cart, I can tell you how to move space chariots with it, and these films show its gizzards—do you want to see whether or not your technologies can duplicate its gizzards?*

Projecting microfilm turned out to be easy. They had been making lenses so far back that their history recorded no beginning. The projector they built overnight did not look like anything from Eastman Kodak, but it blew those films up to any size without distortion and with cold light. Photograph and projections? No, project them on translucent screens and careful artists painted those blowups on the backs of screens. Two days later twenty artists were painting from twenty projectors.

Cart knew spherical geometry—which I should have guessed, as his race had been navigating their planet in the air when my race thought the Earth was flat.

From there it was an easy jump to the notion of a closed, curved space. I spent one morning with Cart making thread models of tesseracts and hypertetrahedrons and such, using clay and "toothpicks" (slivers of a Barsoomian bamboo)—when Cart suddenly got the idea. "Zeb, if that thing is a sketch of a cube with an extra dimension—a hypercube, a 'tesseract' you called it—and I understand now that it is, then there could be a hypersphere, just as a sphere is a hypercircle, and a cube is a hypersquare! By the Eggs of Issus, Yes! Though I can't visualize what a hypersphere would look like."

"Neither can I, Cart. I doubt that Jake can. But it isn't necessary to visualize it; it's enough to realize that one could exist."

It was another easy step to the caltrop analogy. Before we stopped to eat, Cart was *thinking* in terms of six dimensions—and very excited. So we drank more than we ate, and talked still more, and both of us got tipsy.

Thuvia found us in that state, started to kid us about it—got fascinated by what could be done with little balls of clay and slender sticks, built a tesseract projection under her husband's direction—and started drinking with us.

The least halfway coherent remark I recall from that session was Thuvia saying, while we were being steamed out in their bathing room (like our own, but larger): "Tell me, Zeb—a hypercircle is a sphere, and a hypersphere is one more dimension—what does a hyperteat look like?"

At that moment she seemed to have four. I managed to get my eyes to track and said very carefully: "Princess Suvia—Princess *Thuvia*—let's not even *think* about it! Some things are perfect the way they are. I have spoken!"

"Hear, hear!" agreed her husband, and ducked her. Whereupon she ducked me. Then we both ducked him. It was a highly successful seminar in higher geometry.

Cart concluded, some days later, that the only things needed that could not be built, on Barsoom by Barsoomian artisans, were the gyros. "I guess that whips us, Zeb."

"Does it? Can you buy things from Earth?"

"Yes. But we rarely do. Expensive."

"Let's find out just how expensive. We have the specifications for the gyroscopes. Can't the Trade Commissioner at the Terrestrial Embassy get a price for you, delivered in Helium?"

"I suppose he could. But I think it would be a jeddara's ransom."

"Hmm ... maybe we can get competition for a lower price. Don't ask for *Sperry* gyroscopes—just ask for bids to meet the specifications. I'll phrase the specifications; you translate them into Barsoomian. Get Thuv to translate them back into English and Earth units. I'll check to see that her translation means exactly what we want it to say. Then you submit the Barsoomian version along with Thuv's English version ... and they'll never guess why you want them or that I had a hand in it. They'll laugh at how easy it is ... and overcharge you. But not nearly as much as they would have had you not said 'lowest bidder.' Let 'em think that you are trying to decide whether it's cheaper to buy them or cheaper to make them. I'll write to make it sound that way. Then we'll see how Thuvia's sounds. She must *not* see my version until *after* she translates your version. You'll be robbed … but not as outrageously as you would be if the commissioner thought you were helpless."

"Then this Earthling Sperry is not the only one who can make these?"

"Sperry isn't a man; it's a division of a big manufacturing company. Cart, there are at least a dozen companies on Earth that can make gyros to those specs. The idea is to get them to bid against each other, hoping for a bigger order later. I'll imply that you want them for gyro navigators for your air boats—this is a trial order."

"What is a gyro navigator?"

"Something like the automatic navigators you use now—but yours are better. I don't know how yours work … but I do know they are accurate at any latitude, more so than ours."

Having Tawm Takus and Kach Kachkan as squires to our ladies was a big help. Neither Jake nor I needed extra hands often—but we had them on call. Their prime job was to outfit Hilda with protective clothing, any climate—and clothing for *protection* was not new to Helium; the tailors who had built the sling for *Gay Deceiver* could duplicate everything in Deety's wardrobe in Hilda's size—but better … so much better that Deety discarded several items so that she could have clothes like Hilda's.

So did Jake and I, once we caught on. The fanciest was an all-fur coverall called "Apt-hunter's costume" that had built-in antiglare goggles and integral mukluks with nonskid soles. Furthermore, it "breathed"—sweat is dangerous in the Arctic: see your neighborhood Eskimo. Yet all four stowed in space gained by discarding my parka.

Shoes for Hilda came from showing Deety's shoes to leather-workers, who then made casts of Hilda's tiny feet and created shoes to match—improved: more durable, more comfortable, better design. So Deety got new shoes, too. I was forced to rule that Deety must discard one pair for each new pair acquired and that Hilda could have as many pairs as Deety, but no more. Shoes are bulky; space was precious as gold.

Gold—the services of Tawm Takus and Kach Kachkan set free Hilda and Deety to do the sightseeing Jake and I wanted to do but lacked time. So we did it through their eyes, their ears, their reports (dictated to *Gay Deceiver*, zipcoded by Gay and stored, then tape wiped for their next day's adventures), plus rationed stereo Polaroid films (irreplaceable, and no telling how many worlds we would visit). Tawm Takus and Kach Kachkan set Jake and me free to work without worrying about our darlings. Even a luxury apartment can be a prison. We did not have to try to persuade them to stay home for their own safety—Helium, for all its beauty, is more dangerous than the jungles of New York City. But with giant warriors and giant thoats to insulate them from crowds (and from tourists), they could go anywhere.

A platoon of Red warriors could not have guarded them as well.

So Jake and I were beholden to Tommy Tucker and Kach, as much, or more, than were our darlings. Besides that, both were good company for Jake and me the evenings we did not work—friends we would miss.

I gave no thought to how we had acquired them, save to thank Cart. If the acting commander-in-chief saw fit to assign warriors as aides to honored guests—well, the practice was common on Earth. I once spent two weeks dancing attendance on a visiting US senator's wife while on duty with the Aussie DF.

Then Deety discovered that all was not copacetic—Deety pokes into things. One evening she came to me quite upset.

"Zebadiah, did you know that *every day* that Tommy and Kach are with us costs these poor dears money?"

I had not known. I asked Cart about it. He seemed puzzled. "Zeb, every able-bodied male citizen is subject to call for military duty. On duty each one receives one ration, in food or in cash, quarters when not in the field, an allowance for uniform leathers and weapons, forage for his thoat as necessary. What else does a soldier need? Your friends are quartered in the palace, fed from the palace's kitchens, and their thoats are tended by slaves. Their duties aren't onerous, and I doubt that they've ever had to draw a weapon. What's the problem?"

"Cart, both were working for American Express."

"Yes. Their jobs will be waiting when I release them; you can be certain. This Earthling that manages American Express is a pimple, I have heard ... but he doesn't buck the Regent."

"But in the meantime they aren't making money. That's what bothers Deety."

Cart looked annoyed. "I'm sorry the Princess Deety is troubled. But I don't hire warriors from American Express. They fight for me— or perform other duties—as needed. I have spoken."

If I hadn't been a rude, crude American, I would have accepted that sign-off. "Wait a half, Cart! Don't be so durned official. I've got to solve this or Deety and Hilda won't accept squiring around by our giant friends. Which would be inconvenient for them—and for Jake and for me—and for you, too; I wouldn't spend nearly as much time trying to work out with you a way to build for Helium a space-time ship. I'm not welching; I mean that I would have to devote more time to Deety, and Jake to Hilda. We can't lock them up—and you yourself warned against their going outside unescorted. I am *not* suggesting that you hire warriors from American Express; that would be bad precedent. So Jake and I must pay them what they are losing. Gold is money here, is it not?"

"Gold is money anywhere, isn't it? We use it, and I assume that Earthling money is gold, as tourists pay in gold, and we pay gold for the few items we import form Earth. A tanpi is a dollar, more or less—the exchange varies."

I didn't know how much gold a tanpi was; I hadn't used money since we had fled Snug Harbor. Nor did I know what an Earth-Ten dollar came to in gold—it could be a fraction of a newdollar or many times as much. No matter, I could find out what a tanpi was in grams of gold. I had bullion and a store of Aussie gold money—Aussies will bet on *anything*—plus newdollars in gold, stashed in *Gay Deceiver.* Emergency cash, getaway money, bribe money, cash that clinks can buy you out of a jam when a million in a Boston Bank is useless. Jake evidently thought so, too; he had taken along, as coins and bullion, more gold than I had.

"So I'll ask Tawm and Kach how much American Express paid them, then Jake and I will pay them. We aren't broke. You won't be involved, Cart—no bad precedents. Just forget this conversation."

"I can forget it." Cart smiled lopsidedly. "But your problem isn't solved. My problem, too, as I *can't* permit the Princesses Deety and Hilda to go unguarded—and I seem trapped between Deety's stubbornness and yours."

"Not stubbornness, Highness. Honor. Our concept justice."

" 'Highness,' is it! Now who's being 'official' with a friend?"

"Sorry, Cart. Why won't my answer work?"

"Zeb, if you think your honor is touchy, do something that offends a green warrior. I would rather tease a banth, barehanded. If you ask Tawm Takus what he is paid at American Express, he'll excuse your

246

crudeness because you are a stranger. But he *won't* tell you; he will carefully misunderstand—so pointedly that you won't rephrase your questions. If you attempt to *give* him money—I can't guess the outcome. He would not accept it; I am certain. He would be offended clear back to his egg. He would not kill you; you are my guest and he has been ordered to guard you and yours. But he might suddenly forget every word of English—speaking English is not part of a warrior's duties. He would never again eat with you, drink with you, or relax in your presence. Do you want that? It would not solve Deety's problem."

I shook my head. "Cart, I'm confused. About a triple ten-day ago, the jeddara and Thuvia gave Deety and Hilda jewelry so valuable that I can't estimate it—and they *had* to accept it. No choice. Later, Hilda gave your mother a cape—one quite expensive on Earth; I don't know what it is worth here. The jeddara simply made sure that the cape was not a gift from Jake to Hilda—it was not; I am certain—then the jeddara accepted it readily. Yet I can't seem to find a way to reimburse two friends for money lost on my account. Why is one gift proper but not the other? I suspect that the cape cost more than what Tawm Takus earns in a full cycle."

"Your conjecture is a certainty, although ten cycles is more likely. You say that cape was expensive on Earth ...?"

"Quite. Hilda is independently wealthy."

"I am unsurprised. That fur would be expensive if it were from this planet; since it was imported from Earth it is a gift lavish even to make to the Warlord's jeddara—Mother hardly lets it out of her sight. Zeb, your confusion comes from adding unlike things—impossible, I think, in any mathematics. Tawm Takus is not poor; he comes from a prosperous horde and is brood-nephew to its Jed. But he is not wealthy. Kach Kachkan, I suspect, is poor in money—wealthy only in unblemished honor. He will *not* accept our smallest coin from you, his friend; honor would not permit it. But had the Princess Hilda elected to give him that magnificent cape, he would have accepted it with grace, courtesy—and cherished it to his death."

"Cart—I'm walled in. How am I going to satisfy Deety? And Hilda? Hilda might possibly understand ... but Deety is *stubborn*."

Cart grinned. "I know! Zeb, have you noticed a resemblance in our lady wives?"

"Do you recall the first time I saw Thuv? Silhouetted against bright sunlight—I called her 'Deety.'"

"So you did! Were they both bleached white as a Thern, or dyed black as a First Born, one would swear they hatched from the same egg. But it goes deeper. Twin spirits—both ... *stubborn!*"

"Can I tell Deety what you said ... with your permission?"

"Sure, sure! Meanwhile I'll think about your problem—and it *is* a problem."

"You could ask Thuv to think about it. She understands Deety ... and she understands your customs, which Deety does not."

"Hey, that may be the answer!"

"Meantime, I'll try to stave off Deety. How much in grams of gold is one tanpi? You and I were working in centimeters and grams just the other day. Can you figure it for me?"

"One moment." Cart dipped a stylus in ink, started figuring in Barsoomian figures as confusing to me as the Persian alphabet. "Slightly over one gram of gold. Call it a gram."

"How much does a mechanic earn in a day? A skilled carpenter. Ten tanpi?"

"Issus, no! One tanpi, if he's good."

"Does a courier make more? Or less?"

"A bodyguard makes less than a skilled mechanic—and that's all a courier is ... unless he speaks English. Zeb, any job requiring English commands better wages than would be paid for the same work if knowledge of both languages was not needed. At a thoatback guess, an English-speaking bodyguard might get a tanpi and a half per day, or even two tanpi if he could read it, too. But, even if we knew exactly, it wouldn't solve your problem, as money *can't* solve it. So explain it to Deety and tell her to wait."

Whereupon I did something foolish, although it did not seem so at the time. That evening, with servants out of earshot, I tried to explain the situation to Deety, Hilda, and Jake. Deety said, "Ridiculous! Hilda, we can't put up with this—can we?"

Hilda looked unhappy. Jake said soothingly, "My darling daughter, we've got to assume that Cart knows what he is talking about."

"But he doesn't see it from *our* viewpoint! I'm going right straight to Dejah Thoris! She'll know what to do."

Hilda said, "Deetykins. No."

"Aunt Hilda! Don't tell me *you* are against me? Why, you were as indignant as I am."

"I still am. But let's save our Dej' for our Sunday punch. Zebbie, we can't give them *money* ... but we can give them presents that are *not* money—is that right?"

"As I understand it— Yes."

"Then it can be solved. Deety, calm down. It has to be a present— presents, one for each—worth at least as much as they are losing."

"But we don't even know how much that is! And we can't find out! Zebadiah, Cart gave you the straight word about that ... because I *did* ask, and both Tommy and Kach acted as if they didn't understand the question. But Tommy started to lisp in dodging me ... so I shied off."

"Yes," agreed Hilda, "Deety did manage not to burn the barn after it was stolen. Never mind, Deety hon; we'll find out. And we'll pick lavish presents."

"The presents should be something useful," put in Jake.

"Why?" demanded Deety. "Remember what Mama used to say: 'Presents should be something a person wouldn't buy for himself. A luxury. Or at least frivolous.'"

"Deety," Hilda said, "Jane was right ...."

"Hear that, Pop?"

"... usually. But she was never on Barsoom and she doesn't know Tommy and Kach. Jacob is right, I think. And Jane, too. We must find presents that they wouldn't and possibly couldn't buy. Luxuries. But luxuries useful to Tommy and to Kach—where they are and what they are."

"That's a tall order!"

"Thuv will help us."

Residents of Helium got used to the sight of two Earthling women, dressed as Red ladies, perched in front of green giants on the giant breed of thoat used only by green warriors. Tourists did not. Jake and I didn't care and Hilda and Deety ignored their stares and were careful not to speak English where a tourist might hear—even though their command of Barsoomian extended only to a few dozen words and phrases useful in dealing with their maids. So far as they knew, Earth-Ten knew nothing of their presence on Barsoom, and I felt that it was best to keep it that way. Jake, of course, agreed.

A visit to what Deety described to us as a "museum" and Tawm Takus translated as "Palace of Memories" seemed to confirm this.

They spent a day looking at room after room of ancient relics of dead cities, lost arts, strange artifacts, other rooms of more recent exhibits. They lingered especially in halls that displayed the green giants in miniature; on the march, camped, in battle, in their cities. Tawm Takus did almost all explaining while Kach Kachkan watched in all directions, a hand on his pistol butt, another at his short sword, two others ready for anything.

Once Kach Kachkan pointed, while still rotating an eye before and behind. "Arena of Warhoons," he said. "Much blood. Some mine."

Hilda told me she'd shivered when she saw it. A green warrior on foot was facing a calot with his long sword while trying to hold off another behind him by short sword. The miniatures were distressingly lifelike—and it looked as if the green warrior's chances were poor.

Deety had touched her elbow. "Stop making yourself ill, Hillbilly. Let's go home. My feet are tired of marble floors, and three times we've had to duck to avoid gaggles of tourists."

We'd learned that tourists from Earth-Ten were not usually a problem, as they were not permitted to leave the enclave of Hilton Interplanetary without armed escorts, at least one per tourist, while the tourists themselves were unarmed—precautionary practices that derived from unfortunate incidents when tourism had started. Packaged tours included group excursions surrounded by guards, or a wealthy tourist could hire armed couriers through Thomas Cook or American Express, not fewer than two for each tourist, one of whom had to be able to translate.

Even Earthlings who were not tourists—residents of the Terrestrial Embassy and a few businessmen—never ventured out without armed Barsoomian guards. The cultures were not miscible and any attempt to mix them could result in sudden death all too easily—*had* so resulted before these rules had been made law by edict of the Warlord.

"*Tourists!*" Hilda agreed, making the word an obscenity. Deety enjoyed relating the tale. "The next fat female who points a camera at me is going to get a spitball between her eyes! No, I'll have Tommy scoop her up and shake her—bust her camera and scare her silly."

"Aunt Hilda!"

"No, Jacob wouldn't like it and it would cause headaches for Cart. But I agree; we've been educated enough for one day. Tommy, what's the shortest cut to where we parked Kokkid and Kanakook?"

Tawm Takus led them through that hall of green men displays. And this was why both our ladies were so anxious to tell us about what happened. Hilda spotted something and stopped suddenly. "What's *that?*"

"It's horrid," said Deety. "I won't look. Come on."

"Wait, Deety. Tommy?"

"Extinct vermin, Princess. Not important."

"Come on, Hilda—please!"

"Deety, stop being childish and *look*. I know a 'Bloke in a Black Hat' when I see one. Tommy Tucker, you say these things—these *vermin*—are extinct? What happened to them?"

"We ate 'em." Hilda and Deety told us they'd gasped. "Considered to be quite tasty, prepared properly. Drained and braised in zitadar fat over a slow fire. Then dipped in thoat oil with a sprinkling of cheevil. Some say tansery ... but my brood-mother's brood-mother used cheevil. Tansery is for people with no taste buds. Gourmands. Not gourmets." The giant added, "They could be eaten raw if thoroughly drained—but their blood is odd; it angered the stomachs."

"Hilda," Deety had said, "I'm getting sick. Anyways, that's not a 'Black Hat.'"

"Clench your jaw. Or throw up in a corner; this is important. It *is* a 'Black Hat.' You stick to computers and leave biology to me. I dissected one; you didn't. Same weird articulation, same external genitalia, same horn buds above where its forehead ought to be. The details that don't match are in the places where I suspected plastic surgery. We'll come back tomorrow with my photos—you'll see. Zebbie will confirm it—he didn't go sissy-pants and refuse to look."

Deety braced herself and looked squarely at the exhibit—gulped once, and said, "You could be right."

"I *am* right. Tommy. How long have these been extinct?"

"I don't know, Princess Hilda. Kach Kachkan?"

"Nor do I." The larger giant added, "My horde used tansery. Cheevil was hard to find."

"Kach!" Deety exploded. "You have eaten them?"

"No, Princess Deety. They were gone before I was hatched."

"I feel better."

"I don't," said Hilda. "I don't care who ate them or how they were cooked. I want to know how long ago this was—and where they came

251

from. Tommy, say your brood-mother's brood-mother cooked them. How many cycles ago would that be?"

Tawm Takus looked helpless. "Princess Hilda, how can this one tell? My people keep no records; we had no written language. Stories were handed down around campfires ... and, I feel certain, sometimes changed in the telling. The expression 'brood-mother's brood-mother' does not mean 'grandmother'—it means"—the giant hesitated— " 'Once upon a time!' Or 'Many cycles ago.' Where they came from? Issus alone knows. They are not like any other creature in Barsoom. Legend has it that they appeared in great numbers ... then they were gone. Eaten. Or back to whatever lair they were hatched in. But they are no longer seen on Barsoom." He pointed to an inscription. "That reads, 'Gone where the oceans went.' I translated it as 'extinct.'"

"I wish they were," said Hilda. "But they are not. Come, we must hurry home."

— XXVII —

Zebadiah

The next day I decided to help our gals by finding out the going price on couriers. But I decided to be "cute" about it. A haystack is no place to hide a needle—hide it in a stack of other needles. I got hold of Tira, explained what I wanted to find out, and my notion of how to conceal it. She listened, then said, "Captain, may I offer one suggestion?"

"Tira, your suggestions are always valuable."

"Captain, I thank you and pray that I will continue to merit your good opinion."

"Don't be humble, Tira; you're smarter than I am—and you know it."

Tira managed not to hear the comparison. "I suggest that the captain send identical messages to American Express and to Thomas Cook. That might conceal even more thoroughly the point you wish to know."

I thought so, too. Tira turned out to have access to palace stationery—scrolls that looked like parchment; each had the sigil of the Warlord on it.

Here's what she wrote, one to each agency:

To the Manager of American Express in Helium—

Greetings—

In anticipation of the pleasure of entertaining honored guests, I desire to learn what services of all sorts you are prepared to supply for the edification and amusement of strangers to this great city. I trust that your reply will include full details concerning each diversion offered with tariff schedules both for parties of several guests and for escorted single guests or couples. Please quote fees for refreshments separately and state them both for service in the Hilton Interplanetary and for service elsewhere, with all details.

For this courtesy, I thank you. My messenger will wait for your reply—which, I trust, will be prompt.

Captain Zebadiah John Carter of Virginia,
Senior Cousin of the Jeddak of Jeddaks,
Warlord of Barsoom
Given at the Palace—My Hand

At the bottom on each was space for my handprint—nothing as messy as ink; the parchment, when a hand was pressed to it, produced a sharp print—impregnated somehow.

I read each letter while thinking about the relative merits of being hanged as a sheep rather than as a lamb. However, my claim of cousinship to a "fictional" character who had turned out to be real was known to the manager of American Express from the day we arrived (and soon after, I suspected, to Thomas Cook Agency)—and known and accepted by the royal family ... and, no doubt common gossip throughout the city; I hadn't dared try to keep my claim quiet. Still, I hoped that my "cousin" would not return until after we were gone. I pressed my hand to each sheet, handed them to Tira, thanked her—turned to other matters and put it out of my mind.

Service was good—in less than two hours answers were handed in by our door guards.

The packages were mostly brochures of guided tours. I had barely time to find one item on the American Express schedule of tariffs when Deety and Hilda returned—the item being:

"Personal Courier (English-speaking), by the day—Tanpi 50"

"Personal Courier (no English), by the day—Tanpi 25"

I got no further because Hilda and Deety had seen a 'Bloke in a Black Hat,' a double-jointed alien with green blood. It took a number of questions to tell, first, that it was a *dead* alien. Second, that it was a museum exhibit. Third, it was possible that it was a "Madame

Tussaud" job, a realistic simulacrum—although Deety did not think so and Hilda felt certain that it was not ... some sort of perfect embalming.

Tawm and Kach had assured them that the "vermin" were "extinct" on Barsoom (I hoped so!) and had been for longer than either of them knew.

Nevertheless, I sent across the corridor for them and questioned them myself—while I was doing so, Jake returned and went over the same ground.

Tawm stated that it was an actual body, preserved; then conceded that it could have been a reproduction, but he knew of no reason why a substitution would be necessary or why the sign would not have mentioned it. (I couldn't see that it mattered—mummy or wax image—if Hilda was correct ... and she was mostly firmly certain.) Stipulating that she was right, the nasties *did* have continua craft (but we had deduced that before we fled from the attacks on us).

The major new datum was that the nasties seemed to make a habit of invading wherever they could get a toehold ... even on a dying planet. It made traveling among the universes less attractive. How widespread were they? What was the Number of the Beast?

There was one somewhat comforting corollary: they had been driven off Barsoom with primitive weapons (I doubted that *all* had been eaten; they had fled). I began to think longingly of a planet of civilized human nudists—where double-jointed aliens could never disguise themselves. Had there been even *one* obstetrician on Barsoom I would have favored staying right there—banths and all.

I called in Tira and questioned her. She had never been to the museum, almost never left the palace. But Hilda can sketch and knew that anatomy. Yes, Tira had heard of them. It was long ago, she was certain, but she knew what they were. She suggested that the captain ask the prince regent; there might be records—she didn't know.

It was next morning before I got a chance to examine those two packages. Deety is courageous—recall who gave Jake and me our chance to kill that armed fake "ranger" and how she did it—but courage is the complement of fear and those double-jointed "Black Hats" gave Deety the willies. Once we were alone in our sleeping room she got taken by the shakes—fear she had kept bottled up since afternoon. So I had no time for brochures; I had to comfort her. Eventually, she got to sleep and clung like a limpet all night.

The next day our gals spent with Thuvia. I had nothing urgent to do aside from minor items. *Gay Deceiver* was ready to travel. The space-for-sleeping problem had been worked out. A double bed that was nothing but a sleeping silk stretched taut by a light frame (dural, it seemed to be, but more rigid) was suspended *over* all four seats and the instrument board, and secured port and starboard, fore and aft. This offered a springy surface over two meters long, nearly two meters wide, and more than half a meter high—a bed comfortable for two, even with one of them a lout my size.

The space abaft the bulkhead had been greatly revised. The decking was now clear except for the space-time twister. We had packed in great haste; by re-stowing at leisure, discarding wrappings and packaging plus unnecessaries fetched through hasty judgment, we now carried *more* in less space—especially food, water, and compressed air.

One item discarded was my bulky, oversized sleeping bag. We now had *four* sleeping bags that took less space than my old one—thin but warm fur lined with silk. Cart claimed that you could sleep on ice in that fur and never notice it.

I didn't risk moving the Burroughs continua apparatus; it worked fine where it was, at *Gay Deceiver's* center of mass (Jake assured me that this was not necessary, but that was how I had positioned it to balance the car more easily)—since it worked, I left it undisturbed.

Despite that small apparatus, the cleared deck space was ample for two persons of ordinary size. Even I could scrunch into it, in some positions.

Our sleeping bags stowed back there and could be used as bags or blankets as they "unzipped"—not zippers but more like Velcro; the edges clung together under finger pressure, or peeled apart as easily. The bed frame stowed there, too—snapped together and the silk rolled around the frame, like a two-meter flagpole.

Even with garage doors closed, we could rig for sleeping in ten minutes, unrig in five—we proved it one night by sleeping in *Gay Deceiver*.

So we were almost ready to leave—except that we owed Cart our best efforts concerning a Burroughs-type craft. I was hoping that bids on gyroscopes would show up soon (and was holding back a notion on how to pay for them, if the bids staggered Cart). And, while I had explained that the Burroughs gear did *not* require *Gay Deceiver*, that any airtight craft would serve (such as one of his air boats, modified by sealing), nevertheless, I had promised him copies of *Gay Deceiver's* manuals. (Never mind that they could not build a solid-state computer, or Gay's power plant, or an L-gun; a promise is a promise. Cart had gone all-out for us; we would not short-change him. So Gay's anatomy was being copied, page by page, but this time by painting on translucent overlays with a master artist checking each page.

My efforts to teach Cart the engineering motions behind Jake's continua twister *without* resorting to abstruse math resulted in a change in attitude by Mobyas Toras; he now treated Jake with respect instead of brushing him off as a nuisance. Like this—

Cart and Thuvia, without Jake, had a session with the ancient savant. Mobyas Toras would not be so uncouth as to fail to listen to Prince Regent and Consort even though he esteemed himself (correctly) as being their mental superior. So, speaking their own language, writing in their own mathematical symbols, and illustrating what they were saying with sketches and thread-model projections done in bamboo slivers and clay pellets, Cart and Thuv passed on to Mobyas Toras my kindergarten version of n-dimensional, curved, and closed space.

Thuvia told me that the old mathematician had listened, bored, but attentive—then had suddenly brightened: "*Oh! That* branch of metronomy! Why hadn't the Earthling doctor *said* so?"

Thuvia had answered, "Because, Learned Elder, he had no language in common with you. He was attempting to build one, starting with basic elements."

"Mmmph! That must be corrected. His field of mathematics is a most amusing one—even if of no possible use. I shall enjoy discussing it with him."

Cart then asserted that the Earthling doctor's knowledge of this branch of mathematics was *very* useful ... and essential to the welfare of Helium.

"Zeb," Thuvia told me later, "Mobyas Toras agreed with Cart's opinion—but with the sort of politeness that means he didn't agree at all. Understand me?" I said I did. "Nevertheless, he is now eager to talk with Jake. Mobyas Toras doesn't care whether mathematics is useful or not."

"Very few mathematicians do."

I was present at one of these later sessions between Mobyas Toras and Jake (with Thuvia as an animate dictionary) because of Jake's belief (mistaken) that I could add something. I listened for a half hour while these two yakked at each other, drew sketches, and wrote symbols. I left as soon as I could—sentences, from each of them, that were weird mixtures of English words, Barsoomian words, and mathematicians' argot, caused me to need aspirin. So I blew Thuv a kiss, she smiled, and I left. Neither of the Big Brains noticed my departure.

So it looked as if we could leave Cart, not only a wealth of engineering new to him, but also mathematics to back it up. It would be up to Cart to get his stiff-necked savant to admit that there could be a connection—if Jake couldn't swing it.

I later asked Jake whether or not Mobyas Toras was beginning to understand six-dimensional, quantized, closed-space geometry. Jake had looked startled. "Why, we're way past *that*. I'm learning concepts I never dreamed of. Zeb, I could spend a century here."

"Pop, we don't *have* a century. Two bombs, ticking away—and timed to explode in less than seven months. Remember?"

"Yes, of course—that comes first. But I want to come back later." He got that faraway look in his eyes that told me that the monkey was on his back. Oh, well, when the day came—soon—I would take him by the hand and lead him to the starboard control seat. With verniers in front of him, Jake would wake up—meanwhile I would catch last-minute details.

Even the puzzle of how to reimburse our giant friends was clearing up. I had not been wearing my navigator's watch since arrival, as it did not match the local day by about a half hour. I did not adjust it to match this planet; that was a job for a factory horologist. It is accurate to twenty seconds a year and its principal dial shows Greenwich time with a display for Greenwich date—perfect for navigation ... and perfect for pregnant wombs. It had an outer ring that could be moved to show zone time (I never use it; a pilot finds it simpler to do that in his head), and all the usual bells and whistles of a good, versatile watch. Costly, of course—and not essential, as *Gay Deceiver* kept time as accurately.

I usually kept it in *Gay Deceiver*, as I did not want to leave it behind by accident. Deety's clock-in-her-head had adjusted in about a ten-day to the local circadian; she could answer with correct local time either in hours and minutes (stretched by two and a half percent to match Barsoom's rotation), or in Barsoomian time units—which never meant much to me.

One day when Deety was helping me re-stow *Gay Deceiver*, I asked her what time it was in Snug Harbor. She hesitated a minute, then said, "Sixteen-thirty-two—time to go swimming." Then she giggled and added, "That piece of me was asleep. I had to wake it."

I didn't remind her that her swimming pool was destroyed in the blast—no use making the kid homesick; I simply showed her my watch. She was dead on. She nodded and took it for granted.

Cart stopped by soon after, making a friendly check on our progress. I had Deety repeat the trick for him, three ways: Helium time, Helium time converted to hours and minutes—then asked for Greenwich time. She clicked them all off, and I showed him on my watch that she had correctly called Greenwich time. He was only mildly impressed by her knowing local time—said that her talent was fairly common on Barsoom, especially among farmers ... although he did not have the talent himself. "But Deety, you may be the only person *anywhere* who knows the time on *two* planets."

Deety grinned and wrinkled her nose. Cart then added, "That's a piloting timepiece, isn't it, Zeb?" I had agreed that it was. "Thought so. I have one—different shape and different markings and I don't wear it on my wrist. But I felt sure that it had the same purpose."

"Cart, what do portable timekeepers—watches—cost here?"

"Why, whatever one wishes to spend. A cheap one might cost ten tanpi. A good one might be ten times that price. But one could easily spend a thousand tanpi. No limit for one intended as a gift for a princess, as you would be paying for gems as well. But ..." that charming grin! ... "*Your* princess doesn't need a watch ... and her eyes are gems beyond price."

"No argument out of me. Deety, do Tommy and Kach have watches?"

"Why ... I don't think so. I've never seen either of them look at anything that looked like a timepiece to me. I don't know what all they carry in their pouches ... but I think I would have noticed."

"Cart, wouldn't a watch be useful to a courier? If so, would it be a present a green warrior could accept without wounding his honor?"

"Certainly he could. If I were a courier, I feel sure that I would need one."

Deety became alert. "Cart, where does one buy watches?"

"Here, of course. Princess, you don't go to tradesmen; you send for them. But if you are as smart as I know you are, you'll ask Thuv to help you. Or you'll be charged ten times what you should pay."

So things were shaping up and I had time that morning to look over those brochures and price schedules from American Express and Thomas Cook. The American Express charge by the day for an English-speaking courier had surprised me. Apparently, Cart had grossly underestimated what a tourist courier was paid—but there was no reason why Cart should know; a reigning prince would never be a tourist in his own capital. True, he might have guests who would need guides and guards ... but they would come from his own household.

I checked Thomas Cook's tariff schedule: non-English-speaking courier, 22 tanpi—but an English-speaking one cost 28 tanpi more, or 50 tanpi, the same price quoted by their competitor. On checking other items, I found mild variations: If one charged a few tanpi more for a tour, the other charged a bit higher for some other tour—it balanced out. I smelled a "gentlemen's agreement" and wondered how the much-abused word "gentleman" was ever assigned to price-fixing conniving ....

I tried to guess what couriers were paid. An applied overhead of one hundred percent seemed possible. I did not know what taxes they paid, what office expenses they had, what "squeeze" might be customary—but one hundred percent overhead was a good working figure until I knew more. In that case, both Tommy and Kach should earn about twenty-five tanpi ($25 Earth-Ten) in wages per day—possibly more for Tommy (better English and a straw boss at times), possibly less for Kach. Were they on salary, or were they called as needed?—it could make a difference. Overtime? Again, I did not know—I simply knew that they had worked to around the middle of the night the day we met them. And they supplied their own thoats. No clue about that in tariffs. But "excursions by thoatback" appeared in each agency's offerings ... and those excursions were far more expensive than any in Greater or Lesser Helium.

I did not know enough about the economy here to have opinions—analogies from another planet ten universes away could only mislead me. Wait a half, old son—get your data first.

The brochures were as glowing as I expected—I have yet to see one for a tourist trip that was not. Sometimes they are truthful; there is no way to exaggerate the Taj Mahal, or Glacier Bay, or the glow worm caves in New Zealand. And Helium was indeed a city of wondrous beauty and beautiful wonders.

But I found myself feeling itchy at our Red hosts being described as "barbarians" and the green giants as "savages." Tawm Takus was no savage; he was a gentleman of meticulous honor and fine courtesy. Kach Kachkan had a less civilized background ... but the way he had lifted himself by his bootstraps was utterly admirable. Kach had not been "born a gentleman"—he simply *was* a gentleman, "*sans peur et sans reproche.*"

As for "bloodthirsty hordes," Earth-Zero humans have a history as "bloodthirsty" as that of the green giants, and its last century had not been one whit better than earlier ones—worse, if anything. I knew nothing about Earth-Ten, as yet. Must find out ....

I sat in thought for a longish time ... then repackaged everything, put the packages under my arm, picked up an escort at the door, and went looking for Cart. Whatever Earth-Ten was, it was *not* my planet, I owed it no loyalty—and did owe loyalty to Cart. I felt certain that he had never seen these brochures. If he had seen them, no harm done—if he had not, surely he was entitled to know how his realm was advertised to tourists.

He met me at the inner door of his apartments. "Zeb! I just sent a messenger to find you. Got news for you!"

"Good, I hope."

"Some of both. First, please tell Deety that my spies dug out one thing she wanted to know ... without troubling the minds of your green friends. Tawm Takus earns by the day tanpi two, Kach Kachkan's daily wage is one and a half—that should let her judge how much to spend on presents for them."

"Is *that* all they earn?"

" 'Is that *all?*' Kach Kachkan commands twice the wage of a skilled stonecarver, Tawm Takus even more. Being a courier can't be too difficult—it's knowledge of English that puts them into a higher bracket."

"What is the other news?"

"Oh. Bad news. The bids for those gyroscopes."

He sent for them. We sat and I accepted wine and a tidbit while I checked them. Three bids had been forwarded—lowest from Japan, one slightly higher from Skoda, highest from Sperry.

"Cart, I recommend that you buy from Sperry."

"Why Sperry? Not that it matters, I can't afford even the low bid."

"Because there is less than a five percent spread between lowest and highest. These other companies might do as well—they are both good firms—but we *know* that Sperry gyroscopes to these specs will do the job; *Gay Deceiver* is equipped with them."

The prince looked sad. "I see your logic. I might as well pick the best—since I can't have any of them."

"Cart, how strongly do you want to make Helium—and Barsoom—independent of Earth in space travel? Never mind that *Gay Deceiver* can do other things: let's speak just of trade. In the history of my own planet, any nation that became totally dependent on merchant ships of other nations was courting disaster. Different planets, different conditions—granted. But I doubt that the principle changes. I suspect that, in the long run, you can't afford to allow Earthling ships to ground here … unless you can send ships of your own to Earth. These bids—you can bet that they have been greatly increased to cover shipping charges … yet gyroscopes aren't all that heavy … and travel from Earth can't be so terribly expensive or you wouldn't have so many tourists. You're paying through the nose because you are helpless. So pay—once! Buy two sets—one for your first ship, one for your most skilled technologists to study and duplicate. Then you can build ships that can move goods—or anything!—*much* faster and *much* cheaper than the ships that come here now."

"Zeb, can't you understand that I can't buy even *one* set?"

"No, because I don't believe it. The jewelry that your wife and your mother lavished on Deety and on Hilda would, if sold on Earth, buy a dozen sets of gyros. More likely a hundred."

"Out of the question, Captain!"

"Let me talk. You said something about your mother having a trunkful of such jewelry that she never uses. Are there *no* circumstances under which such wealth can be used? I understand that Thuvia was once a captive, a slave—would your mother use those jewels to ransom her daughter-in-law, if that was what it took?"

The prince chewed his lip. "We'd go to war."

"Cart, I meant 'if paying that jewelry for ransom was *the only possible* way to free your wife!' Don't tell me that the men of Helium would die for the princess; I *know* that. My *own* sword is at Thuvia's feet—and you know it. Answer the question the way I put it: no other choices."

"*Issus!* Mother would pay ransoms."

"How many bodies did the black chariots clear out of your streets this dawn?"

"I don't know. If you have reason for wanting to know, I will find out."

"The exact number I don't need to know. What I do wonder is this: how long can the prince regent of a great city-state allow his people to freeze or starve before it penetrates his skull that it might be better to change an age-old custom than to let them go on dying?"

"Captain, you go too far!"

I stood up. "I have no wish to offend the prince regent. I stated a question, but the prince owes me no answer. He owes the answer to *himself.* My family and I will leave your roof as quickly as I can locate them. Within the hour, if possible. Please extend my apologies to the jeddara and to the Princess Thuvia for not saying farewell in person ... and please tell my cousin John, the Warlord, that I regret that my unseemly words have made it impossible for me to remain to see him."

"Damn it, Zeb! *Sit down!*"

I remained standing. "Highness, I can't be 'Zeb' one moment and 'Captain' the next, then 'Zeb' again ... then 'Captain.' It makes me dizzy and I don't know where I stand. I am not your subject, I am not a citizen of Helium. I can no longer be your guest. Will His Imperial Highness either allow me to leave in peace—or make me his prisoner?"

Cart looked as if I had slapped him. I *had*—verbally. He got himself under control, then said slowly and in lower tones: "Zeb ... would you have my mother refusing to see me? My wife closing her door to me? My father—your cousin—black angry with me? Would you do that to me? Zeb, Zeb—I was wrong! Forgive me—if you can." Suddenly he was reaching for his sword—I started to reach for mine.

His hand never touched the grip. He unhooked it with his leather and it lay at my feet, hilt toward me.

It was quicker for me to unhook my belt. My sword lay by his, hilt toward him.

Then we were pounding each other on the back in a tight embrace. Cart was almost sobbing and I think I felt a tear against my neck— and I didn't feel any too steady myself. Shock treatment can hurt the

263

one who gives it almost as much as the one on the receiving end. I was shaking.

We both sat down again, sprawled; Cart made a slight gesture, goblets of wine were in our hands at once. It occurred to me that at least as many guards must be watching as female slaves. If I had touched the hilt of my sword, how long would I have lived?

We didn't toast each other; we simply had a drink as medicine while our nerves stopped twanging. Presently, Cart sighed. "Zeb, I was never cut out to be a monarch. I do the best I can because I must. I'll have to talk this over with Mother ... and with her grandfather when he returns ... and with my father, your cousin—if possible. Damn! I wish I knew where he is; I'd send my fastest flier. For this won't be easy; I'll need his backing. But Helium *must* have spaceships."

I thought of other angles without mentioning them aloud. I could buy those damn gyros ... if I dared to return to my home planet. As a bachelor, I would have risked it—I thought. But a married man and prospective father finds himself with a brand-new set of values. I was still breaking them in, like a new pair of shoes—they pinched a bit, but I must wear them. Helium was not my responsibility—Deety *was*.

Cart was having "new shoes" trouble, too. But we each had to break in our own pair. Did we dare go to Earth-Ten? Plenty of obstetricians there, that seemed certain, and apparently Earth-Ten's analog of Sperry Division could sell me gyroscopes—without horrendous delivery charges tacked on—and I could *give* Cart those gyros; he would accept a gift. But not money. But would something so silly as a missing letter from the alphabet trip me up? It need not be a missing letter; it could be *anything*. Or many things. Mars-Ten, known as Barsoom, was very different from Mars-Zero of my universe—Earth-Ten might be just as different ... and I might wind up in the calaboose when Deety needed me most through something as silly as stepping on a taboo crack. Must talk it over with Jake.

(I knew of one important difference: Earth-Ten had space travel far in advance of the primitive aerospace vehicles I was familiar with. Its tourists dressed oddly, but tourists always dress oddly, everywhere. Those brochures didn't indicate any difference—but they described Barsoom, not Earth-Ten. All they showed was a tendency toward legal larceny, "all the traffic will bear"—a trait commonplace on Earth-Zero.) "Cart?"

"Eh? Sorry, I was thinking. What, Zeb?"

"I was thinking, too. Helium is very short on gold—gold as money, I mean."

"Quite. So short that most transactions are by draft, with settlements made at intervals."

"I had that figured from two things. Three. A very low wage scale. Lots of jewelry based on gold. And most of the jewelry quite old. Cart, Helium—and Barsoom in general—has been tying up its gold in jewelry, freezing it, for thousands of cycles. Hasn't it?"

"Longer than that, Zeb. Yes, there are no longer rich gold mines—there hasn't been a rich lode discovered since I was hatched. We've quit making gold coins—just copper and some silver. I don't recall ever seeing a one—tanpi gold coin—too small; they've disappeared. Fifty or a hundred tanpi coins are more convenient for making settlements—but most business is done by personal draft. Checks?—I think that might be the idiomatic word."

" 'Checks,' yes. Cart, this planet reminds me of India—a very poor country with nobody-knows-how-many billions of dollars in coins or jewelry hidden away, buried, or otherwise out of circulation. Very little gold for use in trade with other countries."

The prince gave a wry, one-sided smile. "It does not parallel. It didn't seem to matter until we started trading with Earth. I thought tourists would bring in gold, make it possible to buy form Earth. And they *do*—but not what I expected."

"Take a look at these." I handed him the packages I had fetched.

He thumbed through them, said, "These are things for tourists. Why should I look at them?"

"Read them. Read all of them."

"Must I, Zeb? My mind is on other things."

"Cart, *I* think they are important. I ask it as a favor."

"Very well." Reluctantly, he started reading. The tariffs I had placed on top. Shortly, he looked up. "This can't be right. Some clerk has miscopied. Tanpi fifty per day must be tanpi five. Or do I misread your conventional way of expressing money?"

"Go ahead reading. Then we'll discuss it."

"Zeb, you're as stubborn as Thuv." He went on reading, stopped, reread—thumbed through, read other bits—while his face turned very dark, deep mahogany, and his features set in grim lines. He looked up. "Guard!"

"Wait a half!" I said urgently. "If I tell you why you've called the guard, will you listen?"

A dozen guards were already in the chamber, their officer waiting at salute. "Speak," he conceded.

"You were about to send for the managers of Thomas Cook and American Express."

"Essentially correct. I was about to have them arrested and fetched here."

"I don't question your decision, I do question its timing. Finish reading, then let's discuss it. Cart, you need more data."

Cart hesitated, then said, "Return to your posts." They vanished.

I asked, "Any chance that they will talk? When you do act, it should be a surprise."

"Zeb, those are my most trusted men—they keep me from being assassinated. However … Office of the Guard."

"Highness."

"Rog Retnor, keep all men who were in here on duty until I send for you—a special job later. And be *certain* they talk with no one. *No* one. Servants, other guardsmen, even members of my own family. Until I send for you. I have spoken."

The officer saluted and left.

"Now finish reading, Cart."

"I will. But this word 'barbarian' …. My father uses it in a derogatory sense."

"My cousin uses it correctly."

"And 'savage'?"

"Even worse."

"Hmm …. It would be well were the general-in-chief, Tars Tarkas, never to see this. Perhaps it is well that he speaks little English, reads it not at all."

"Cart, from his reputation, if Tars Tarkas understood that piece of paper, there would be bloodshed."

"Hmm … I can't imagine Tawm Takus reading it without anger … yet Tawm Takus is slow to anger."

"Cart, I doubt that couriers ever see this garbage. They are probably given their orders orally. As for tourists, anyone who has ever herded tourists learns to ignore their silly chatter. Regards them as children, to be protected, but not taken seriously."

"Hmm …." He went on reading. At last he said, "Very well, I have read all of it. You have something to say?—before I put those two into the dungeons while I decide what the charges are?"

"I wouldn't mind seeing one of them spend a night in jail; I've heard how he talks to my friend Tawm Takus. But if you jail those two, you won't get at the source. Cart, what landing fee do you charge Earthling ships? And how much per head do you charge tourists to come here?"

"Landing fee? Do you mean payment for grounding here? Why should I charge anything? That spaceport land has no value, it can't be irrigated. Strictly speaking, it is not part of Helium—although all worthless land near us is under my control, when necessary. I mean that I would not let an unfriendly army or a Green Horde not allied with us to approach that closely. What's this about charging tourists? We want tourists; we need gold."

"But you aren't getting it. Cart, Deety and Hilda were in the museum recently. 'Palace of Memories' I think it is called. I feel sure they did not pay to get in; they carry no money. What do tourists pay?"

"Zeb, the Palace of Memories is open to everyone; it is a cultural treasure."

"What payments do you receive from Hilton and American Express and Thomas Cook for their franchises?"

"Fran-chise-ess? That phrase is new to me?"

"Those three have a monopoly on your tourist trade—only it's not *your* tourist trade; it's *theirs*. Cart, all those tourists are wealthy, or they could not afford a trip to Barsoom. Look at those schedules of prices! Wealthy, or they would not come here. But, while they bring much gold to Barsoom, that gold does not *stay* on Barsoom. All but a dribble goes back to Earth. *You* have been supplying the attractions—great and wonderful attractions! Tourists are willing to pay to see the beauties and the strange—strange to them—wonders of your world. I am sure they go home and boast about it the rest of their lives. But while Helium supplies the attractions, the profits—all but a tiny dribble—return to Earth."

"Zeb, you never talk idly ...."

"The devil I don't."

"... on serious matters. You have some solution in mind?"

"The prime solution is to own your own ships. But there are things to do in the meantime. Why should two companies from Earth—or one, as I suspect that, on Barsoom, American Express and Thomas Cook are two sides of the same coin—why give them a monopoly? Why can't the people of Helium, say under the sign of your Greater Helium Chamber of Commerce, open their *own* tourist bureau?

Charge less for tours, pay more to couriers, use advertising that doesn't insult your citizens and your green allies—and *still* make a fat profit and keep *all* of the gold on Barsoom?"

Cart looked pleased at the thought … then shook his head. "The tourists wouldn't come to us, Zeb. The ships and that inn of theirs, the Hilton Interplanetary, arrange everything. You see, we had some trouble at first. The tourists don't understand our ways and some of my citizens are hot-tempered. So now all tourists are taken under guard from ship to inn. These tourist companies sell their tours at the inn … and their couriers pick them up there and return them there."

"Cart, do you play cards?"

" 'Cards.' Earthling games played with colored squares of parchment?"

"Yes."

"Your cousin, my father, knows card games and taught some to my mother and my sister and to Thuv. They tried to teach me but it seemed a waste of time; I dropped it. Why?"

"Do you understand the idiom 'To hold all the trumps'?"

" 'Trumps ….' Doesn't that mean the tactical situation in which one player has all the winning squares of parchment? Or is it the reverse?"

"You had it right the first time. Cart, you hold all the trumps. All but one: they own the ships. But you hold *all* the others. Never mind that you will have ships, too, someday; you can win *now*. They have to hire local guards or they are not in business. In effect, they must hire guards from *you*."

"Issus! That's true … but we agreed to let them hire guards from us, after that initial trouble. Zeb, we don't go back on our word."

"Agreed. But did you give them your word not to set up your own tourist bureau?"

Cart looked startled. "The subject was never mentioned."

"Then keeping your word doesn't enter into it. It won't be necessary to arrest those hirelings who manage the Earthling tourist bureaus to make them behave. To put a stop to their larcenous prices, their stingy wages, their insulting brochures. The compound of the Hilton is inside the city gates … and it's not under diplomatic immunity the way their embassy is; it is a private business, no more, no less. Or pretends to be—I don't know, but it doesn't matter. The Greater Helium Chamber of Commerce Hospitality Bureau can sell tours inside that compound just as legally as those other two bureaus. But at lower prices and paying higher wages and giving better service—better service because the best couriers—most experienced, best guards, best command of English—will go where wages are higher. Tawm Takus would jump at the chance and so would Kach Kachkan; their present boss is an oaf. Hell's bells, Cart, Tawm and Kach and Tira *alone* could set up a better service than these bunglers—Tira selling tours in the inn's compound, Tawm and Kach each leading groups of warrior couriers and doing the interpreting."

"My mother holds Tira's indentures ... and I don't think Tira wants to leave the palace."

"Just an illustration of how easy it is. Your Lady Mother might be amused to allow one of her slaves to make fools of greedy Earthling businessmen. Do you know a noble of high honor, not greedy, and yet a shrewd head for business?"

"That's a tall order. But .... Yes, I can think of three."

"Put one of them in charge. Or use all three, with the senior as chairman of the board—Earthling idiom—and the most able as president and chief executive. I'll help set it up—but I'll keep out of sight and so will you. But you supply some initial capital—it won't take much—and hang on to fifty-one percent of the stock through a trusted friend. Cart, if you do this, it might not be necessary to sell unused jewelry to buy gyros. If you are patient, tourists will buy those gyros for you."

"How long would it take?"

"I won't guess; I lack data. But it must not be hurried; you must not be greedy just to get gyros. Did my cousin ever tell you the story of the goose that laid the golden eggs?"

"No, I don't .... Yes, he did! Many cycles ago. A 'goose' is an Earthling animal that lays eggs, which, so I hear, most do not. This one laid golden eggs and the peasant killed it to get at the gold inside—only there wasn't any inside. Right?"

"Correct. So treat this goose with tender loving care and it will produce gold for you for endless cycles. Be greedy and you'll kill it."

"I see your point. But I think I would rather command an army in battle than run a business."

"Pick the right man and you won't have to run it. Just don't let him get greedy. I'll help. I can start by rewriting these brochures so that they will be still more attractive but not insulting."

Cart pounded a table. "Yes! That must stop. *Today!* Zeb, if you are through advising me—I value your advice and thank you for it and plan to use it—I'll send the guard for those two knaves!"

"Fine. But may I suggest something more to do to them?"

"Flog them? I may yet … but they must have a trial for that."

"Flogging them might cause a stink with the Earthling Embassy. But this will hurt them worse in the long run. How many clerks do you have who can read English? Especially business records in English, mostly figures?"

"Eh? None. I can do it, Thuv can do it, Tira possibly. No clerks."

"Hmm …. There are about twenty artists copying *Gay Deceiver's* manuals—in English and lots of figures. Cart, send for those two managers. But send a large-enough guard to fetch back every business record in each office. And be sure to get all those brochures—confiscate them as insulting to your realm. While you are skinning them alive for the libelous language in their advertising, artists can start copying their business records."

"What excuse do I give for seizing their records? In Helium, a common tradesman would draw sword rather than submit to such indignity."

"Use a search warrant to—"

"What is a search warrant?"

"In this case it's a farce. But Earthlings are used to obeying them. A document signed by Joe Doakes—anybody—with the title under his name of 'Chief Tax Inspector of Helium.' It orders them to produce forthwith all their records for official inspection and verification. You endorse under it: 'Approved, Carthoris, Regent.' Better send a zitadar's freight chariot; the papers may be bulky. Meanwhile, enjoy yourself making those two wish they had never been hatched. Born. While your artists start copying, I'll stay out of sight, but you send copies to me as fast as they are made. Once I've read them I'll be able to write a manual on how to run a tourist bureau in Helium—and do it right; not the way they've been doing it. And I'll be able, with Deety's help, to tell you exactly how much gold has been going back to Earth when it was earned here by *your* citizens—and should have stayed here."

Cart grinned. "I'm going to enjoy this. *Dola!* Send in my secretary. Uh … Zeb, could you spare Tira for a bit? She writes the prettiest hand in English I've ever seen."

"Of course. Send a runner for her. I'll be on my way."

"Kaor. Zeb? No more misunderstandings between us, ever."

"I hope not, Cart. Kaor."

— XXVIII —

Zebadiah

It took five days for twenty-one artists to copy the records of the tourist bureaus. I read the copies as quickly as each file came in, still had time to put the finishing touches on *Gay Deceiver*. That fifth evening, after sending the servants to bed, I gathered the others in the Carter sleeping room.

"Family, aside from having Hilda edit my rough drafts of advertising copy for the Greater Helium Hospitality Company, we are, as far as I know, ready to travel. Comment? Suggestions? Motions? Jake?"

"I'm ready, son. I hate to stop studying under Mobyas Toras. God willing, I'll come back someday."

"We will. We could spend our tenth wedding anniversary here. Bring all the kids and let 'em ride thoats." I added, "Doc, was Mobyas Toras able to throw any more light on Hilda's pet 'Black Hat'?"

"It is *not* my 'pet Black Hat'!"

"He's mine, Sharpie, because he's dead. That's the way I like my green-blooded aliens: dead as long as possible."

"Zebadiah, don't tease Aunt Hilda. This awake she was a bit morning sick."

"I was not, either! Just something I ate. I feel fine, just fine."

"How about you, Deety? Have you had any 'something you ate'?"

"*Me?* Healthy as a thoat ... and twice as hungry."

"Just wondered, darling. You've been up earlier than me three mornings running."

271

"Because you've stayed up late reading bookkeeping. You can stop wondering. I'm going to have this hungry little monster as easy as Thu lays an egg."

"Jake, I asked you a question … but the conversation got as confused as it usually does. We ought to use Robert's Rules of Order."

"If we did, Zebbie, you'd always be making points of order."

"Pipe down, Sharpie, and let your henpecked husband have the floor."

"Jacob, do you feel henpecked?"

"Fifth Amendment. Zeb, nothing more about aliens than I already reported. Mobyas knew what I meant, said that it was long before he was hatched, then took me and introduced me to the custodian or chief historian—translates either way, I think—of the Palace of Memories. Language trouble, I should have taken Tira along. But the date is uncertain. However, it was indeed a major infestation and *not* from this planet. The only new item, I got just today, from Cart. He says that if the boss of the Palace of Memories doesn't know, nobody knows—at least in Helium. He added that Helium's written records go back more than ten thousand cycles."

"Did he mean ten thousand Barsoomian years? Or was that his translation of the idiom equivalent to our 'Since the mind of man runneth not to the contrary'—that is to say, a period too long to reckon historically?"

"*You* ask him. I didn't take it as an idiom."

"Guess it doesn't matter—the vermin are dead."

"Zebadiah, if you don't shut up about aliens, it *will* be 'something I ate.' In your lap."

"Sorry, dear. Want to sit in my lap, instead?"

"Yes."

"Then do so. Here you weigh only twenty-two kilos—less than four-tenths gee. But the surface gravity might be much more than one gee on whatever planet we are on two days from now."

" '*Two days!*' Zebbie, you don't mean it. You're teasing."

"I'm sorry to say I'm *not* teasing, Hilda dear. We've been here longer than we had planned. Ask your husband."

"We didn't plan anything. We just got out of town fast as we could scram—with aliens snapping at our tails."

"Hilda my beloved, Zeb means 'planned after we got here.' But we've got to get you two to a civilized planet …."

"Helium is civilized!"

"… with human beings who don't lay eggs. Because neither Zeb nor I is an MD, much less one specializing in obstetrics. We aren't going to take chances with you two … and we may have to check many planets. If we don't find one fairly soon, I would favor sneaking back to Earth-Zero."

"*No!*"

"My darling daughter, your husband could put us down at night in someplace such as New Zealand. Or Tasmania. Use phony names and claim to be distressed travelers, say, from Canada. We've lost our IDs …."

"Jake, with the gold we have in *Gay Deceiver*—just a tiny fraction of it—I guarantee to buy convincing IDs *anywhere*. Give me an hour in the wrong end of town in *any* big city and I can smell out the right black market."

"Zebadiah, you don't know that New Zealand, or Tasmania, is any safer than Snug Harbor was—and we *felt* safe there. They got your cousin Ed in *Sumatra*—of all places! We *know* too much—they want us *dead*. I don't want to be dead, with a baby inside me! I don't *ever* want to go home! I'd rather take my chances here. Women had babies long before there were obstetricians."

"Yes, and a lot of them died, too. Deety, I don't want to lose you. I don't intend to."

"I was just going to say," Doc Burroughs said mildly, "that Earth-Zero is a last resort. Zeb, it seems to me that we should translate outwards along both 'tau' and 'teh', both positive and negative, looking for a satisfactory Earth-Zero analog. It appears likely, albeit from meager data, that one-quantum translations have universes—thus analogs of Earth—very similar each to its nearest neighbor."

"That may be the best search routine, Jake—but I have a suggestion we might use first."

"Do you mean Earth-Ten?" asked Hilda. "Its people are humans just like us. And advanced, too, or they wouldn't have spaceships. Noticed, while I was helping you to decipher that bookkeeping, that several tourists signed themselves 'MD.'"

"How do you *know* they're human like us?" demanded Deety. "They may lay eggs."

"Belly buttons."

"Thuv has a belly button. So does Dej', so does Tira and all our girls. *All* Red women have belly buttons."

"They all have lovely navels," agreed Hilda. "All you named. But it's not a scar from tying off the cord. The egg's umbilicus goes to the nutriment. It's absorbed, just before hatching—no scar, just a deep dimple. I've been learning about local biology; it's fascinating."

"Maybe these Earth-Ten tourists are like that, too."

"Deety girl, many tourists go around with their bellies showing, as we've both noticed. I've seen too many hospital cases not to know a Caesarean scar when I see one—and I've seen several on tourist families. Viviparous. Jacob, it might be possible to hire one of those MD. tourists to stay over to take care of us."

"A lottery, dearest. If we use an Earth-Ten MD, we will *go* to Earth-Ten, and get the best. Zeb, you said you had a suggestion for something we might try first?"

"Rotation. Now that I have, thanks to Cart, a small spectroscope custom-made by the optical experts of Helium Observatory, I can spot a Sol-type star in seconds. Check to see, I mean. No need to check white giants or red giants or red dwarfs—just any nearby star that looks promising. We can check the sheaf of ninety-degree rotations almost as fast as you can twist the dials."

"Stipulated, Zeb—but what is the advantage? We know that Earth—our native Earth—has analogs strung out like beads. Suppose you find a star of matching spectral type of Sol. You're assuming that it will have an Earth-like planet. Stipulating that you may be right—even probably right; it's an appealing hypothesis—it may not have humans on it. Or perhaps it has ... but they are in the Stone Age. Highly unlikely that they will match or surpass us. No, I retract that. No data, so I must refrain from assigning even a vague probability."

"It *might* be an advantage, Jake. Something Mobyas told you, and you repeated to me. You were almost boyishly pleased—a great compliment, coming from him, so you told me."

"*Oh!* That I had achieved theory for quantized rotation at the same time as theory for quantized translation. He said that the two had been worked out—as theory, since he still doesn't believe that we use it—that it was learned two steps, a thousand cycles apart. The simpler—translation—coming first. It was at that point that he decided that I was a mathematician, even though a narrowly specialized one. That's why I was, yes, boyishly gleeful. He's hard to impress. Very!"

"Jake, if a race as intelligent and as long-lived as the race in which Mobyas Torus is a member, took nearly two thousand Earth years to go from one step to the second ... possibly the queer-jointed aliens have never made that second step."

Deety looked bright-eyed. "Pop! We would get away from them *forever*. I vote to rotate."

"Deety ...."

"Yes, Zebadiah?"

"It will not be decided by vote. The only one who understands this mode of travel—your father—will decide. I'm captain, underway. But I will take *Gay Deceiver* where Doctor Burroughs tells me to take her."

"Yessir."

"Your tongue looks coated ...."

"Is not!"

"... in glory. Let's bring this meeting to order. Unless someone else has a comment, Doctor, I think we can get underway the day after tomorrow, early. Does that suit you, sir?"

"Yes, Captain. We'll do it that way."

"Jacob, I don't want to leave *so soon*."

Burroughs patted his wife's hand. "Dearest one, not one of us *wants* to leave this pleasant place ... and our friends. But we must."

Deety straightened up. "Aunt Hilda ... I don't want to leave Thu, and Dej', and Cart ... and Tira and all our sweet girls ... and Tommy Tucker and Kach—and especially Kanakook because I can't tell her *why* I must leave or that I will come back to see her!" Deety brushed at a tear. "But it wouldn't be easier a month from now; it would be *harder*. If I were deciding—I'm not—I would rather leave tomorrow, not the day after. Say goodbye quickly and *go!* Oh, whoever thought up that nonsense about 'parting is such sweet sorrow!'"

"Chap by the name of Shakespeare," I said. "But he was writing for money. Anything for a tear. Or a laugh. Either way, he got paid. He killed 'em off, at the end—and got paid for that, too."

"I know he did. Made me cry. What a *shameful* way for a grown man to make a living! I wish Kanakook could talk, I wish!"

Late the following afternoon I took the last of his new advertising copy to the prince regent—glumly; I'd put off as long as possible telling Cart that we were leaving. I was admitted, plumped it down on a table near the prince, and said, "There it is, Cart. The new come-ons for the tourists, and the last of my notes on how to run a tourist business. Good luck with it." I took a deep breath and blurted out, "We're leaving tomorrow."

The Regent did not answer. Embarrassed, I said, "Well? What are you looking grim about? You knew we planned to leave as soon as we could refit; you know, too, that I've stuck around longer than we had planned to help you with this job." I indicated the new copy. "So why cloud up? We've enjoyed your lavish hospitality; we've tried to repay it by being helpful. Wish us luck and send us on our way—but *smile!*"

Carthoris did not smile. "Zeb, what is the meaning of the English word 'extradition'? It's new to me."

That raised my eyebrows. "It's a legal process, used on Earth, by which one nation requests another to return a fugitive from justice to the nation from which the fugitive fled. It's more complicated than that, but that's the gist of it. Why?"

"I thought from the context that the meaning was something of that sort ... but I'm sorry to hear you confirm it."

"Why 'sorry'? Has some tourist been a bad boy back home? Has he asked you for sanctuary? Or has one of your own people taken refuge in the Earthling Embassy? It can happen both ways ... and can get very complicated. I'm no lawyer—not on Earth and certainly not on Barsoom. But I've had a couple of courses in law and I was attached to an embassy once—I've seen extradition. What's the situation? If I can throw light on it, I will."

The prince was very slow in answering. "Zeb, you've never had to rule a nation. Or have you?"

"*Me?* Hell, no!"

"But you are a military officer."

"Yes. But that's nothing like ruling a country."

"There is some similarity. As an officer, did you ever have to perform in your public and official capacity some duty which, in your private and personal self, you deplored?"

I thought hard and grimly. "Yes. Sometimes a duty can be very unpleasant—to put it mildly. But inescapable."

"Zeb, less than a ten-day ago I said to you 'No more misunderstandings between us, ever'—you remember?"

"How could I forget it? You placed your sword at my feet, I placed mine at yours. Cart, what is all this?"

"Zeb, I'm caught between honor and duty! My sword is at your feet—now! But I must surrender my claim to the throne of Helium ... and that takes time! There is not another male member of my family here; I *can't* abdicate today ... I must wait. Zeb, you must not leave tomorrow; I need *time*. Will you give me your word that you will *not* leave until someone senior to me comes home? Tardos Mors, or Mors Kajak, or—if the Gods smile on us—your cousin, my father?"

"No."

"Oh, damn your stubbornness! I *knew* you would say 'No.' Excuse me a moment; I'll be right back." The prince left the grand chamber that was his "private office." He was back within seconds. He sprawled out, sighed, and relaxed—looked not happy, but calm. "That solves it. Both duty and honor. Zeb, my beloved friend, when the time comes we will fight side by side. Back to back. They will kill us—but they will not take either of us alive. I have spoken. Some wine? To toast our deaths—together!" He smiled.

"Some wine, yes. But I won't toast our deaths. As my cousin often said, 'We still live!' Cart, what is this?"

"Nothing, really. I will postpone your extradition until I can surrender all claim to power to one of my elders and seniors. Then if the ruling goes against you, I will be at your side. We will die together, honorably."

"*My* extradition? Who wants to extradite *me* and why? What are the charges?"

"Does it matter? You will not be surrendered; I pledge you that. We will die together."

"Damn it, Cart, quiet down. I'm not ready to die; *I* have duties I *can't* abdicate, whether your elders show up or not. So that's out. Now give me details. Who wants me and what excuses do they offer? Whatever they are, excuses are all they are. False charges—for I'm not guilty of any crime, anywhere. *None*. I have spoken."

"Zeb, it warms my heart to know that. But believe me, I would fight with you and for you and die with you if you were guilty of the blackest crimes. I have spoken."

"I believe you with all my heart, Cart. But, while you have spoken, you haven't answered. Details, man! Extradition isn't a simple request, filled automatically." Zeb thought back to a course in international law he had taken. "One, the fugitive must be positively identified. Two, he must have fled from the country in which the alleged crime took place. Three, the alleged crime must be a crime both in the country of origin and in the county to which he has fled for sanctuary. Four, there must be an extradition treaty between the two nations, defining the conditions for extradition. I think that's all the essentials. No, I left out the most important one. The nation asking extradition must present convincing evidence of the alleged crime and evidence that the fugitive committed it. I can't see how any of that fits me. I didn't commit any crimes back home and I haven't been outside Helium here. So who's snapping at my heels, and why?"

The prince reached for a scroll. "Here is the demand for extradition. It comes from the United Nations of Earth through their ambassador here. It demands that we deliver to their embassy for return to Earth one Zebadiah John Carter also known as Captain Zebadiah J. Carter, United States Aerospace Forces Reserve, also known as Professor Z. J. Carter, BA, Ph.D. ...."

"That's me, no argument. Go on."

"You are charged with murder, arson, abduction, criminal bombing, resisting a federal officer of the United States of America when he attempted to arrest you, fleeing the scenes of your crimes to evade justice—that's the gist of it. What's 'arson'?"

"Setting fire to something illegally. 'Not guilty,' to all of them. What evidence do they offer? Whom am I supposed to have killed and where and when? And 'abduction'—that baffles me. Who? When? Where?"

"Mrs. Hannah H. Corners."

Zeb looked startled, then guffawed.

The prince said, "I don't see anything to laugh about."

"Cart, that's the Princess *Hilda!*"

"I don't understand."

" 'Hannah Hilda Corners' is Hilda's unmarried name. She never liked her first name and very few know it ... but 'Hannah Hilda Corners' is the way she signed her marriage license; I witnessed it. Jake has it in his papers in *Gay Deceiver*, he can show it to you. Where did I commit this arson?"

"In a place called 'Logan, Utah ....'"

"Never been in Logan in my life."

"... and that is connected with two of the murders."

"Only *two?* I must be slipping."

"Please, Zeb, this is serious. No, there was a third one—the federal officer you resisted."

"Now we're getting somewhere. I stuck this sword right in his belly when he tried to shoot Deety—and Jake, and Hilda. Only he wasn't an officer; he was a phony. The other two murders? I don't recall killing anyone else lately. Just this phony, a deadly dangerous alien, not human. The same type of alien that we've been asking about—that extinct vermin on exhibit in the Palace of Memories."

"Really? I had wondered at your interest in that exhibit."

"Really truly, Cart. Now those other two murders?"

"Both in Logan, where you tell me you have never been. One described as Professor J. H. Burroughs—that couldn't be Jake?"

"It could indeed be Jake, in the flesh. But he is alive and well and under your roof, not dead in Logan."

"The other is also named Burroughs—Assistant Professor Dejah T. Burroughs. A relative of Jake?"

"A close relative. His daughter, my wife, the Princess Deety. Cart, you'll have to decide whether or not to tell this to your mother—but my wife was named for her: Dejah Thoris Burroughs. Deety is a nickname, her initials: 'D' and 'T.' When we got there, we decided an extra 'Dejah Thoris' was one too many ... so we went on calling her by her nickname. But, again, our wedding license will show it. So I killed Deety, did I? She'll be surprised."

"She can't be half as surprised as I am. Or as confused. Since I know that you are a man of honor, *this* stuff"—the prince gestured angrily at the scroll—"is preposterous nonsense. Yet they ask for you by name and you agree that you are the one they seek to arrest. Along with this demand they supply sworn statements from various Earthling officials as to your alleged crimes—I suppose that is the substantiating evidence you spoke of. But ...."

"I said '*convincing* evidence.' Do sworn statements by someone on Earth convince you that I killed Deety and Jake? Does Hilda behave as if I had kidnapped her?" I reached for the scroll, said, "May I?"—then took consent for granted. "Hey, they've even got my fingerprints! Or what they say are my fingerprints; I'm no expert."

"They are your fingerprints, Zeb."

"Huh?"

"The first goblet you touched this morning was fetched to me. Comparisons have been made; they matched."

"Well, well! Cart, that's the first sneaky thing I've known you to do. Which of our little darlings did this for you? I don't want her around me any longer."

The prince's jaw muscles clenched. "Zeb, one does not explain to a slave and a slave does not question orders. You are not being fair to the girl."

"Mmm, no, I'm not … since her first loyalty must be to you. The poor kid probably did not have the slightest idea what it was all about."

"No, she didn't. In fact she was led to believe that your prints were wanted in order to read your tastes for a surprise gift to you—as here the superstitious believe that a person's tastes, personality, even his future, can be read from the lines on his hand and fingers."

"A belief not limited to Barsoom. And you certainly did hand me a surprise gift. Why didn't you *ask* me for my prints, to my face? You could have had them at once. Instead, you had an innocent slave girl get them behind my back. I thought better of you, Cart."

"Zeb, Zeb, I didn't *expect* the prints to match! I expected to return this scroll with a scornful rejection—one so sharp that a man of honor would ask the Regent to lay aside his immunity and cross swords. I took delight in drafting a rejection, loading it with vitriol. Then my experts reported that the prints were yours!—and I required them to *show* me, print by print, with a strong enlarging lens. I was forced to admit it … and I've been moping here ever since, hoping you would show up—and dreading it, too! Because I wouldn't send a guard to fetch you, Zeb; I couldn't do that to *you*. So I waited. And waited."

"I see. I'm sorry I failed to guess your motives."

"If the prints had *not* matched, this sorry mess would never have been brought to your attention … my brother. My senior cousin but brother in sword."

" 'Blood brother,' we sometimes call it. Yes, Cart, we are blood brothers just as Jake and I are blood brothers, even though he is my wife's father. But I wonder how they—no, I don't! Cart! See anything odd about those prints?"

"What should I see?"

"The thumb print. It's from the side—not the ball of the thumb."

"But when you place your hand down flat the thumb always prints on the side. Unless your hand is very different from mine."

"It isn't. I was wondering how they got my prints here so quickly. I knew their ships were fast, but from what I had heard they weren't *that* fast. But now I know. These prints weren't sent from Earth or any of this so-called evidence. All that came from Earth was a wireless message. The prints and the evidence were faked, in their embassy."

"They do have better wireless than we have, much better. But how did you deduce the rest?"

"To obtain those tariff schedules I had Tira write letters for me. I signed them each with my sword-hand print."

"Yes, of course."

"On Earth it's not 'of course.' Palm prints aren't used. For some purposes—licenses, pocket identification—either the ball of the thumb or of the forefinger is enough. But for *full* identification, ten prints are used—both thumbs, all eight fingers, each taken separately, and the face-on ball of each thumb is recorded. *Never* the side of the thumb. My own ten prints are on record that way several places on Earth. So these are *not* my prints from Earth. All this junk was faked right here, using my right palm-and-fingerprint and a wireless message from Earth."

"But *why*, Zeb? Surely not because your inquiry resulted in my confiscating those insulting brochures? I kept your name out of it."

"But my letters started it and brought my name to their attention. Cart, we four—Hilda, Jake, Deety, and I—are indeed fugitives from Earth. But not criminals. We were fleeing for our lives."

"Zeb, the more I hear about this, the less I understand it."

I took a deep breath and decided that one of those rare times had come when nothing less than great chunks of raw truth would serve—preposterous as it would sound. "Cart, the sun is about to set. Can we step out on your western balcony? I want to show you something."

"If you wish it, certainly."

The two friends went outside into the dusk. "Cart, see that big, bright planet with the bluish-green cast to it?"

"Of course. Earth. 'Jasoom' we call it ... but my father taught me to call it 'Earth.' Your home planet ... and his."

"Not *my* home planet, Cart—and I don't think it is your father's home planet."

"I don't understand you."

"There is much about it that I don't understand myself. But I've tried to teach you how *Gay Deceiver* works so that you can build spaceships—and Mobyas Toras has confirmed that Jake's—Doctor Burroughs'—mathematics are indeed correct ... even though the old gentleman still doesn't seem convinced that we use it for practical engineering. But I did tell you about the many universes opened up by this mathematics, each only a quantum jump from its nearest neighbor—but still so far apart that they don't touch at all."

"You did. Agreed."

"This is not our universe. Privately, we four—Hilda, Jake, Deety, and I—call that planet 'Earth-Ten' and we call our home planet 'Earth-Zero.' In our own universe there is a planet—Mars-Zero, I would have to call it, which would make Barsoom 'Mars-Ten.' Mars-Zero, or simply 'Mars' is a planet this size, in this position—but long dead. Her air is so thin as be unbreathable even if it were pure oxygen—which it is not. Her water is a merest trace, frozen at her poles. There is nothing alive on her surface. Bare rock, nothing more. There are signs that there were once mighty rivers, basins that could once have held oceans. Nothing now. If a race of Red men once lived on Mars-Zero, then they either never succeeded in building an oxygen plant—or it failed, cycles and cycles ago. I don't know.

"This is not guesswork I'm telling. My race, on Earth-Zero, has visited Mars-Zero and photographed it from all sides."

The prince regent stared at the bright evening star in the west. "Then you are not from Jasoom."

"If you mean Earth-Ten up there, no, I'm not."

"Then you are not my father's senior cousin?"

"I'm not certain that I should be called 'senior.' He and I would have to compare family records. 'Cousins,' yes—but the Carter family is a large one, and it would take family records and the help of the genealogist of the Carter Family Association to establish the exact degree of relationship. My guess, without records at hand, is first cousin thrice removed. As may be, I am Captain Zebadiah John Carter of Virginia."

"But Virginia is *there*." The prince pointed.

"There may be a place called 'Virginia' on Jasoom, I do not know. But I don't think your father was ever there. His letters and his own accounts of his life on Barsoom have so many, many details that match in all respects Earth-Zero that I feel certain that your father came from Earth-Zero—my planet—to Barsoom, ten universes away."

"I'm confused again. *How?*"

"According to his own stories about his career, he never knew how he did it. One instant he was in the mountains of Arizona, the next instant he was on Barsoom, near the incubator of the Thark Horde. The next time, about twenty years later, he grounded in Thern country, near the south of the River Iss."

"You *do* know his history!"

"Not as well as Doctor Burroughs knows it. I told you that he named his daughter, my wife, for your mother. However, the exploits of your father are widely known on Earth-Zero. He is a heroic character to many, many millions."

The prince kept silent several moments, then said, "Let's go inside. The sun has set, it's growing chilly."

"Okay. No, wait a half! They are about to change guard around *Gay Deceiver*; I like to watch it. No smarter soldiers anywhere, Cart."

"Oh, come on in, Zeb!"

"You go in—I won't get to see this after tomorrow."

Cart looked grim, but waited. I watched the changing of the guard with delight—noted a variation with no surprise. "Smart troops," I said as the two men went back inside. "I do love to watch troops who take pride in drill. Aerospace has so little of it that it's always a treat to me. I see that you've tripled the guard."

"Yes."

"With a senior officer commanding where there was just a sergeant yesterday. I'm feeling telepathic, Cart. That officer and every man under him has orders from you not to let *anyone* touch *Gay Deceiver*. With special emphasis on *me*. All four of us by name, but with my name underlined. And you are feeling very, very bad about it. It hurts you inside."

"Issus! You read minds as well as my father does. And I *can't* read yours."

"Stop hurting inside, Cart. You did what you *had* to do. What I forced you to do. When I refused to give my parole not to leave, you stepped outside and gave the orders, and I knew it. But believe me, it doesn't matter. So quit hurting. I also prophesy. Shall I prophesy for you now?—so that you can quit feeling sick over an unpleasant duty?"

"Uh .... Damn it. I *had* to!"

"Of course you had to, Cart. You aren't the boss; you're the unhappy youngster who tends the shop while the boss is away ... and you've suddenly found yourself with a nasty mess on your hands and no policy to guide you. But it doesn't *matter*, Cart, truly it doesn't! Shall I prophesy for you?"

"Zeb, if you can tell me anything that will let me stop hating myself, please speak!"

"Very well. A little background first. There is no extradition treaty between Helium and Earth. Earth-Ten, I mean, that embassy that sent you that scroll of lies."

"I don't *know!* That's one thing that has my hands tied."

"There is no such treaty—but I'm not asking you to remove that tripled guard. Had there been such a treaty, your father—or Tardos Mors—or both, more likely both—would never have left you unaware of its existence. So it's a bluff, just as their evidence is fake. But it doesn't matter, because you will make no objection to our leaving on schedule. Prophecy."

"But I *can't* let you leave yet. You know why."

" 'Prophecy,' I said. Authentic prophecy. You will have compelling reasons to change your mind. You'll do it and Dejah Thoris—the jeddara, I mean; not my Dejah Thoris, Deety—the jeddara will back you up. But even without the authority of your mother, you would still change your mind. Because, no matter what *I* have done—and I have committed no crimes, here or on Earth-Zero, or on Earth-Ten where I have never been—and no matter what lies they tell about me—and no matter how helpless you feel in the absence of your father and your maternal grandfather and great-grandfather—you don't have it in you to condemn Hilda and Deety to death."

"What!"

"Define the English word 'obstetrics.'"

"It's not a word I know."

"How about 'eclampsia'? 'Fallopian pregnancy'?"

"I don't know any of those words. Should I?"

"You don't know them for the same reason you didn't know the word 'extradition.' Because your father never expected you to need to know such words. It's possible that the jeddara or the Princess Thuvia knows one or more of them; babies are very interesting to women, and your father may have told your mother something about the differences between the way your women have babies and the way our women do."

"Well, I do know that much. Our women lay eggs; yours have live birth. There is one life form on Barsoom that does that. But what's the difference? Laying eggs requires tending an incubator for a rather long time. Possibly it is better to incubate the egg inside where there is no worry about always keeping the right temperature."

284

"Cart, it's roughly the difference between being annoyed by a hangnail and being clawed by a wild banth. 'Obstetrics' is the name of a highly difficult specialty practiced by learned physicians to make the extremely dangerous process of live birth less dangerous. Did you know that both Deety and Hilda are pregnant? Have fertilized eggs inside them, I mean; you may not know the usual word. I think they told Princess Thuvia; she may not have told you."

"Thuvia did tell me; she said they were both happy about it."

"Yes, Cart, they are; Hilda and Deety are brave. But if you want to have innocent blood on your hands and the deaths of two women on your conscience—women at whose feet you placed your sword—go ahead with your plans to keep us here against our will."

The prince chewed his lip and looked agonized. "Zeb, are you still my blood brother?"

"Now and forever, Cart. My sword was at your feet. Shall I place it there again?"

"It *is* at my feet and mine is at yours. I think I must abdicate to my mother. But first I will remove that guard around your space chariot. I will seek out my mother ... tomorrow morning, when she is ready to receive people. But I will remove the guard *now!*"

"Cart, you're telling me to take *Gay Deceiver* and escape. While you turn your back. I see that you remember that I told you that I could pilot out of the courtyard garden without help. Yes, I can. But I am still prophesying. You will leave that guard where it is. You will *not* abdicate. You will *not* close your eyes to something that would blemish your honor. I will *not* enter that courtyard garden like a thief in the night. Instead, tomorrow we will all have a farewell picnic. All of us. These be firm prophecies."

"A picnic!"

"Certainly. Friends often say farewell with a party, do they not? But I want this one outdoors at a particular spot because I have something to do there. Two things, besides the farewell picnic. Thuvia helped Deety and Hilda to choose good timepieces for Tawm Takus and Kach Kachkan. Then Thuv insisted on lending them her credit by writing a draft in payment. But Deety and Hilda are both proud—conscientious—and insisted on Thuvia keeping the timepieces until they could redeem her draft. We brought a supply of gold to Barsoom with us ... but, not knowing what we would run into, I left it in the Bay of Blood."

"The Bay of Blood? Why didn't you tell me earlier? I would have sent you out in a flier with an armed escort. That gold may be gone now. Issus!"

"It will be there, when we go for it—tomorrow. I hid it most carefully and know exactly how to find it. Cart, quit worrying; I prophesy that all will be happy. Tomorrow will be a jolly picnic—the next day we will be gone. But I need your help with tomorrow's picnic. I want all our friends there. You, Thuvia, your gracious mother—yes, and by all means Mobyas Toras; Jake would be disappointed if Mobyas were not there. Will you offer me the use of a flier big enough for all our party? More than the number I mentioned because, if I may, I think it would be a gracious gesture for us to take along Tira and her eight pixies. They can serve the picnic—they wouldn't be happy not serving—and they will picnic, too. Cart, how can I arrange catering for a large picnic?"

" 'Catering?' Another word I do not know."

"The wine, the food—including food for our two green giant friends—and how early must they start to arrive at a reasonable hour when they aren't hampered by passengers—as they were when they picked us up there. A sentimental reason for making it the Bay of Blood, too; it was where we met our giant friends."

"Their thoats are very fast; just tell them when to meet you and where. But this 'catering' thing—this is your home; the palace kitchens will provide everything."

"Cart, I want to give this party, not have it given to me."

"You will be giving it. Tell Tira what you require. I have spoken."

Carter shrugged. "You have me blocked in—I can't possibly work out how to cater it outside the palace without your help. Is it permitted to make presents of money to slaves? Indentured servants? Or does that touch honor, too?"

"Quite proper, even expected. Not lavish, please."

"Would small gold coins from Earth—Earth-Zero—be acceptable?"

"Yes. But they will keep such coins as keepsakes, not change them into tanpi. Now I'm prophesying!"

"It takes a brave prophet to predict what women will do. Oh, I forgot one point. Will you please ask Thuvia to fetch along those timepieces? I think Hilda and Deety will want to present them at the picnic. Cart, could we meet at the Promontory of Tears in the Bay of

Blood? Say at midday tomorrow? Would that timing suit your ladies, do you think?"

"I see no obstacle. How will your princesses dress? Dagger and belt?"

"I think they would enjoy a last chance to dress up as ladies of Helium. But would that annoy the jeddara and Thuv?"

"No. Or rather, they, too, must dress up anyhow. For this will be a public occasion, Zeb. I must provide guards. Will your honor be offended if there are fliers overhead?"

"Meaning I might think they were there to keep me from leaving suddenly?"

"Oh, you wouldn't be leaving from *there*. But that's wild country; I must protect Mother and Thu—and Deety and Hilda."

"Cart, you know I refused to promise not to leave. I still won't promise—I might leave very suddenly. So put the whole Helium Navy overhead if you wish. But let's all enjoy a happy time and not worry about the ambassador and his knavish lies. After the picnic is over is soon enough for this nonsense—let's have a jolly time! Feel better?"

"Much better. Zeb, you're a strange one—I would never have guessed that you could prophesy."

— XXIX —

Hilda

I still think our Zebbie boy had something to do with that lime Jell-O in my swimming pool. I don't mean he lied to me; Zebbie is too smart for that. But if I had tape recordings of every word Zebbie has ever said to me about lime Jell-O, then got a trained semanticist (like Deety, only Deety wouldn't do it) to analyze it, I'll bet there would be a loophole you could drive a lorry through.

But I don't want to catch Zebbie out. He's the perfect skipper for our pirate crew. My Jacob is too candid for the job; he doesn't even have Deety's ability to go deadpan.

Zebbie got back the night before, told us all that we were going on a picnic, then sent Tira to consult with the executive chef of the palace. He chased our eight wood nymphs into their rooms, then called a conference, *tête à tête à tête.*

"Pipe down and listen. Hold all questions." Zebbie spoke very quietly for a quarter of an hour. "Do you all understand your assignments?"

"Yes," agreed Deety, "but I don't understand why I must ...."

"Deety. Lifeboat rules."

She looked startled. "Yessir!"

"Zeb," Jacob said, "wouldn't it be better to tell ...."

"Lifeboat rules for you, too—unless you want to boss the operation. I'm willing—want the job?"

Jacob blinked. "No, Captain. Aye aye, sir."

(I decided not to ask the question that had been niggling at me.)

"Now each repeat back to me your precise instructions. Copilot."

"I am to get word to Mobyas Toras—if I can reach him ...."

"Precise! Start over."

"Uh, I will *find* Mobyas Toras and invite him to a feast excursion in honor of the jeddara and the prince regent. He is expected at the regent's apartments half a zode—call it an hour and fifteen minutes—before midday, local noon. I will not tell him how to dress, but will make clear that all our family and all the royal family will be in full formal leathers and decorations."

"Correct. Hilda?"

Call-me-Joe piloted us. I called him "Joe"; he grinned and saluted. But he was not in command. It was a *big* flying ship, the flagship (I think) of the Helium Navy. The captain (or maybe the admiral—anyhow the one in front at the gangway when Dej'—the jeddara—came aboard and all the bugles sounded)—the captain—admiral—was so covered with fancy leather and decorations that I had to look twice to see that he was almost as scarred as Kach.

But it wasn't like a warship aboard; it was more like an excursion steamer, gay with banners, and with silks and furs and cushions 'most everywhere. I didn't see anything that I recognized as weapons 'cept the swords and personal weapons of the swarm of warriors we had with us—but the L-gun in Gay doesn't look like a weapon either; that airship may have been armed to the teeth.

I stayed at the gangway while Tira shooed her brood aboard, each with a curtsy to me. "Tira, our darlings don't look happy. What's the matter, dear? Didn't you tell them that this is a picnic, for fun?"

"Yes, Princess. But they are frightened. None of us has ever flown before."

"Are *you* scared?"

She managed a dimple. "Not as frightened as I was, Princess Hilda. I'll be all right."

"Sure you will be. So calm them down and have them start serving."

We cruised slowly, so slowly that the windscreens protected our hairdos. I understand that our big ship could have reached the Promontory of Tears in only minutes, but we went the long way around, circling both Greater and Lesser Helium, sightseeing, as we had more than an hour to kill. I sought out Thuv and Dej', seated on big cushions back aft, and got on with my assignment—listened as they pointed out palaces and places of interest, while I worked the talk around to babies—not difficult; Dej' and Thuv both are grandmothers. Of course, they were intensely interested in how *we* do it. Soon I had them listening with horrified fascination to every grisly delivery-room story I had on tap, some that I had actually seen, some that I had simply heard about—but I told all of it as if I myself had been present … and embellished the horror, made them more horrid.

After one, Dej' said, "Oh, that poor girl! Why did they let her suffer so long? Why didn't her surgeons grant her the grace of a quick death?"

"But, Dej' darling, she lived through it—didn't I make that clear? And so did her baby—a fine, healthy, young lad now, tall as Zebbie's shoulder. And she had two more babies after that, both healthy, and no more than normal pain and blood." (Two lies and a damned lie in that one; her OB tied off her tubes.)

Thuvia shivered. "I'm glad we lay eggs. Hillbilly—aren't you *scared?*"

I managed a wan smile. "All of the women of my race go through this. I will be proud to endure it to give my beloved Jacob an heir." Then I swallowed air on purpose and belched. "Excuse me—a touch of morning sickness." (They already knew, from me, what I meant by that.)

"Thuvia! Send for our physician!"

I put my hand on her arm. "Dej', I'm all right—and your physician won't know what to do for me—he *can't* know." I added, "But I'm worried about Deety."

"The Princess Deety is 'morning sick'?"

"No. A much graver worry than that. You see …. No, I must explain. I'm not very muscular and I'm very limber—and I have good measurements. But Deety is an athlete, as strong as a man and somewhat muscle-bound by it. And despite her size, her pelvic measurements are less than mine"—two lies in that; Deety is limber as a worm and seems to have been specially designed to have babies—"so when she goes into labor, her baby could get its skull stuck in her pelvis … and both would die"—still another lie; while that should not be allowed to happen, it's usually possible to save either the baby or the mother—a horrid choice—"so you can bet everything you own that Sharpie will be standing by … and at the first suggestion of trouble, I'm going to insist on a caesarean at once!"

Thuvia said, "But Hilda, didn't you tell me that you two were egg-fertilized at the same time? Won't you be—'in labor,' you called it—at the same time?"

I grudgingly admitted that it could happen … but probably one of us would reach the finish line first, by a day or two. (Mild fibs, no, flat lies—but useful.) "But there is really nothing to worry about. As soon as the prince regent permits us to leave, our husbands will take us to the finest obstetricians to be found." Then I looked thoughtfully worried. "But I do hope the prince regent will grant permission soon. It should be soon—for Deety's sake."

Dejah Thoris jumped at the bait. "What's this about my son not permitting you to leave? What do you mean, dear child? You are not prisoners—you are my guests!"

I looked helpless—I can look very helpless when I try. "Uh …. Oh, dear! Jacob always did say I talk too much. Imperial Majesty—forgive me!"

"Forgive you for *what*, dear? Explain yourself."

I didn't answer. I just shrank up and made myself still smaller and looked frightened and miserable—I've had that down pat most of my life though I haven't needed it much the past twenty-odd years.

Dej' put her arm around me and called out, "*Guard!*" An officer resplendent was suddenly in front of her. She spoke to him very rapidly in Barsoomian and I caught not a word. He saluted and was gone so fast he might as well have jumped overboard.

Cart showed up quickly, noticed that I was with his mother, spoke in English—the dear boy is always polite. "The jeddara commands my presence?"

Dej' spoke to her son in their own language. Cart was standing as she started in—standing but relaxed. Then he snapped to attention like a United States Marine on parade—and stayed that way throughout the exchange. Dej' spoke softly; her words couldn't have carried very far, and Cart answered the same way—but his face got redder and redder until he was almost purple, while his features never moved. They both did a lot of talking—but Dej' interrupted Cart more than once while he never interrupted her. I felt sorry for him; Cart is a truly sweet man. No sense of humor, but men so seldom do.

At last he said two words, ones I had learned from Tira; they translated as three words: "At once, Jeddara!"

"Wait!" Dej' said in English. "Tell the Princess Hilda the gist of it. Then find Captain Zebadiah John Carter of Virginia. Tell *him* all of it."

"Yes, milady Mother. Princess Hilda, I purposed telling Zeb this publicly at your picnic, but my mother has ruled otherwise. I summoned to my apartments early this morning the ambassador from Earth and directed that he bring with him his official copy of the extradition treaty between Helium and Earth. He showed up but he had no treaty with him—just some notes, which he said were a summary—claimed that the treaty itself was on Earth. I … Zeb has told you about this matter? A demand on Helium that we surrender Zeb to him, I mean? Do you know the word 'extradition'?"

"Certainly, Cart."

"It's more than I knew—until yesterday."

"Zeb told us the essentials, I think. Silly business, isn't it? Do *I* look kidnapped?"

Dej' tightened her arm around me. "The Princess Hilda is kidnapped by *me*, at the moment. Thuvia, do you think your pet banths would enjoy a meal of raw ambassador?"

"Mama, it might poison them. Bad meat."

"Joking, dear daughter. We are not barbarians; an emissary even from an enemy is inviolate in his person. But I propose restricting him and all his diplomatic party to his embassy until my grandfather or my husband returns—at which time he will be sent home, I firmly predict. Restricted, save for one appearance before me—*tomorrow!* Tell her, my son."

"Yes, Mother. Princess Hilda, I think you know that my authority is merely delegated; I have none of my own. During the absence of the jeddak, and the jeddak of jeddaks—and the jed of Lesser Helium—all authority is in the person of the jeddara. But it pleases my mother to have me practice ruling so that I may—"

"Don't make excuses for me, Carthoris. Ruling bores me. I'm lazy, Hilda; I let men do the work."

"So do I, Dej'—when possible."

" 'When possible.' But sometimes it is not. Go on, son."

"Yesterday I found myself in an impossible position. I tried to work it out and I thought I had—mostly. But now my mother has taken over the problem by assuming the authority vested in her—to my great relief, I should add."

"Skip the comments, Carthoris."

"Yes, Mother. Tomorrow, the ambassador will be summoned by the jeddara; she will receive him from the throne—I received him in my chambers." Cart grinned for the first time. "I would not wish to be in his shoes!"

I suddenly straightened up. "Cart, does he wear shoes? Or does he dress as we do?"

Dej' said, "What does it matter what he wears, Hilda? Not only are the charges against our dear cousin Zebadiah ridiculous, but also I *know* that there was no so-called extradition treaty. Little as I care for the weary business of statecraft, I attended every session with the men of Jasoom when first they came here; it was my husband's wish. My son missed some of them ...."

"We were in Ptarth, Mother," put in Thuvia. "You know why."

"My son and Princess Thuvia were representing my husband and me at the capital of our closest ally, Hilda. I was not imputing lack of diligence to Carthoris. Hilda, I have heard that treaties on Jasoom are often long and complex; here they are not. If a jeddak's word is not to be trusted, of what use is a long and complex document? In the agreement by which we permitted Earthling ships to land here and agreed to their embassy and to treat Earthling visitors as guests, there was no word about arresting fugitives for them. The idea is foreign to us and I do not see its usefulness. We have a saying, 'The banths make good judges'—meaning that an evil-doer cannot escape forever the fate he makes for himself. Not only do I know by my own ears that there was no such agreement, but also, had there been, my husband and my grandfather would have instructed my son before leaving him as Regent."

"Mother, I *thought* that must be the case ...."

"Place more faith in your elders, my dear."

"Yes, Mother. I did not know that you had attended those conferences—all of them, I mean. I did not wish to trouble you with it ... I was troubled enough myself!"

Dej' reached out, took Cart's hand, pulled his face down to hers and kissed him. "You have always treated ladies with gallant thoughtfulness, my son; your father and I are proud of you. But this need trouble you no more. This one bit of statecraft I shall *enjoy*—I'll sweat him 'til his collar wilts! Carthoris, see to it that the chamber in which he waits my pleasure is much too warm for clothing; I intend to keep him waiting at least half a zode."

Cart grinned. "Jeddara, your wish is my pleasure!"

I suddenly blurted out, "Dej', does this creature *always* wear full Earthling dress? Long trousers? Long sleeves?"

"Hilda that's twice you've asked about his mode of dressing. Why, dear?"

I had already completed my assigned duties ... but Cap'n Zebbie hadn't placed me under "lifeboat rules" about *this*—and who was the "expert" on aliens? The "science officer" (me—what a giggle!)—but I had taken one apart to see what made it tick ... and I felt certain that no amount of plastic surgery could make one look human if its arms and legs were bare. Besides, while I'm not the brain Jacob is, or Deety, or even Zebbie, I don't need a map to tell me it's raining. If the ambassador from Earth-Ten knew things that had happened on Earth-Zero that only those weird aliens knew—with the facts mixed up in a fashion they might mix them up to confuse things—then Earth-Ten was at least as infested as our own Earth. If it was even worse infested, that ambassador himself might be an alien. At the very least he was carrying out their dirty work.

I found myself telling what I knew about strangely articulated hermaphrodites with hemocyanin (or something like it) instead of hemoglobin.

Dej' and Thuv listened quietly—no ohs or ahs or "I can't believe it!" Once Dej' glanced up at Cart; he said quietly, "Cousin Zebadiah confirms this." I didn't try to explain higher geometry, I didn't mention it. "That's why we *can't* go home—and also why our husbands haven't any time to waste in finding us a safe planet." "A safe planet *with obstetricians*," Dej' corrected. (No flies on that gal!—maybe there's something to this "royalty" notion ... at least on Barsoom.)

"Yes. Our space chariot can go anywhere ... but it may take some time to find one. I'm worried about Deety."

"I'm worried about both of you, dear Hilda. Carthoris, has anyone ever seen the ambassador dressed as gentlemen dress? Or does he always wear those strange ugly garments?"

"I've never seen him in anything else. Bundled up as if he planned to hunt apts on ice."

"Dej', the tourists—or most of them at least—are human. I know."

"How, dear?"

"Two tourist ships have grounded while we've been here. The first day a tourist is here he or she is usually covered up pretty thoroughly. Then they see how comfortable we are. They gradually wear less and less—both men and women in shorts, men in short-sleeved shirts or no shirts at all. Even some of the women, especially the younger ones, start being bare to the waist. An alien can't possibly get away with that; it couldn't disguise its weirdness."

"Prince Regent."

"Jeddara?"

"Require their ambassador to present himself before me in formal court harness. Send leather and sword to him and be certain that it is ornate to befit his rank. Be very sure that he understands that he *cannot* enter the throne room improperly attired. Be sure that he realizes that any other costume is a deadly insult to Helium."

"Jeddara, again your wish is my great pleasure!"

"Dej', if he's a—*Pankera*, that thing in the Palace of Memories—if he's the sort of alien he won't wear it. He'll be taken suddenly ill and have to send a substitute. Or something."

Dej' patted my shoulder. "I realize that, dear Hilda. Carthoris, send enough court harnesses for a party of proper protocol. Hilda, we know how many are in their embassy and the ranks of each. If he does send a substitute, we will know by how junior he is the number of aliens there are here. If the ambassador dare not appear himself, we shall see what we shall see."

"Dej' ... you might be in danger. They may have weapons that don't look like weapons."

"My son will protect me."

"Princess Hilda, the Guard will be alert. And the jeddara will not enter the throne room until I personally, as deputy to the Warlord, have made sure that each harness carries nothing more deadly than a sword. Not altered, nothing added. And the swordsman who can fight his way to the throne past my Guard has yet to be hatched."

We grounded soon after, almost on the spot by the Promontory of Tears where Tommy Tucker and I had had our unfortunate misunderstanding. Or "fortunate" since it had gained us our first friends. Where I had tried to poke out his pretty pop-eyes. As we grounded they charged again—just two of them this time—full speed and yelling bloodcurdling war cries, and came to a skidding stop just short of the flagship, with their lances swept up in perfect salute.

I almost didn't recognize our friends. Tommy was looking fierce and military behind his finery and Kach was so covered with decorations that his scars hardly showed. They were utterly immobile, waiting (I suppose) for some sign from the jeddara—even their mounts were frozen "at attention," which thoats seldom are. But Deety doesn't bother with protocol; she called out, "Hi, Kanakook dear!"—and Kanakook tossed her head and answered with her three-note canary call that she uses only with Deety and Kach and (sometimes) me. But she loves Deety and tolerates me simply because I'm Deety's friend.

I suppose Dej' acknowledged the salute, for our friends wheeled about, trotted away maybe fifty meters, wheeled again and waited, lances *couchant*. Warriors (sailors? airmen?) started rigging out the gangway. I heard Zebbie say, "Just a moment, Cart; this isn't where we will picnic. This is just the rendezvous to meet our giant friends."

"Very well, Cousin; where shall I tell the skipper to place the ship?"

Cap'n Zebbie had to be a smarty-pants about it. He pointed and said, "If you look off that way, I'll be able to show you, in a moment, the exact spot where I hid what I told you about."

When I heard Zebbie say that, I stuffed my ear button into place. I had been wearing my walkie-talkie all along and it didn't go very well with the load of jewelry I was wearing. But jewels and my ornate harness covered the shoulder strap and my dagger belt held the little radio against my hip. A diamond-and-ruby choker covered my throat mic; all I had to do was reach up, pull the button out from under the choker, and stuff it into my ear. Zebbie had told us that, if we were asked, to tell the truth: a portable wireless to talk to each other if we were far enough apart to need them. But no one asked me.

Deety had slipped away to the fantail; everyone else in our party was forward, looking where Zebbie was pointing. Cart said, "I don't see anything out there, Zeb."

"You'll spot it in a moment. Your air cover may see it first. What is it—the whole Helium Navy? One could almost walk across the sky, stepping from ship to ship."

"Considerably less than half of it, Zeb. I still don't see anything."

"You'll spot it … just … about—*now!*"

I glanced back at Deety; she had her face turned away from everyone. "Hello, Gay."

"Hi, Deety!"

"*Gay Deceiver—Bug Out!*"

I turned my head quickly, just as everyone (but us) gasped. There, over a kilometer away, beautiful and sleek and shiny, was the fifth member of our family, *Gay Deceiver*, in person.

I was back of the crowd, where I could see Deety, and thus not too close to Jacob and Captain Zebbie and the royal family and

Mobyas Toras and the captain-admiral. But the range was so short that I could pick up every word, almost too loud, via Jacob's and Zebbie's throat mics.

Cart said very slowly, "Interesting. Very interesting. How, Zeb?"

"I told you I could pilot it out of that hole without help. You'll find it still more interesting when you have built your own. It is necessary to warn your air cover not to attack?"

"No. But I'll do so, to set your mind at rest." Cart called out something in Barsoomian, *much* too loudly; it hurt my ear. Someone answered with two words that meant: "At once, Highness!" I could see why Zebbie had asked; fliers were diving on Gay. They always straightened out without touching her but some came mighty close.

Cart said something to Mobyas Toras—all I caught was his name. The old man answered in a high, excited voice. Cart said, "Mobyas Toras says that he must refrain from comment until he has had time to study this."

"Mobyas Toras is a wise man, Cart. It took Jake time to teach me the little I know about it. Wouldn't it be well to send word back to the palace? I suspect that your officer of the guard is having fits."

"Should have thought of that myself." Cart gave another order. "Zeb, how about trading jobs with me?"

Zeb laughed at him. "And take on *your* headaches? Go lay an egg!" Said in Barsoomian (I know the phrase, but Zebbie said it in English), this is a *very* rude remark for one man to make to another. Of course most of the ones there knew no English—but Thuv guffawed, then suppressed it. Dej' pretended not to notice.

Cart said sadly, "I knew you would say that, you ape's offspring."

"Cousin Zebadiah, may we go closer?"

"Certainly, Cousin Dejah Thoris, if you will tell your captain. As close as you wish. Would you like to take a ride in our sky chariot?"

"What a tempting offer! Carthoris?"

"Your Imperial Majesty, as deputy for my father the Warlord, I am forced to advise against it."

"I suppose you must. Oh, dear!"

"But, Mother, if I were you, I would tell my son to go ride a banth and do exactly as I pleased!"

"You're as naughty as your father. Now I'll have to decide for my-self. Oh, dear! *Men!*"

—— XXX ——

Zebadiah

Not since the year with the Aussies have I had so much fun; that picnic was a luau!

The "Bug Out" pre-program worked like magic—and made me Head Magician. I had not been sure it would work until it *did*. An earlier test, same range but in another direction, showed that it was extreme range for Gay to receive orders by walkie-talkie—borderline of failure. If it did fail (so *many* things can go wrong), the only backup I had was to whop up some lie to get one of us into the air as a passenger on one of their fliers, then go halfway to Helium if necessary until signal was strong enough. Fishy.

But variables that affect radio reception hit the jackpot for me. When Gay's signal read loud and clear: "Hi, Deety!" I re-swallowed my stomach; a second later at "Bug Out!" I resumed breathing—there she lay, instantaneously, shining bright.

I couldn't have done it so spectacularly without the Sorcerer's Apprentice, my gal Deety. While everyone else was forward and I kept up a running chatter while pointing the general direction, Deety went aft. I hadn't dared get any closer than this promontory—Gay knew exactly where she had been parked but *I* didn't, not within two hundred meters. Make that *three* hundred. I had never dreamed that twenty-odd ships would pick her up and move her, like Lilliputians move Gulliver.

The best I could do was to make rendezvous at my only landmark, well back from where we had once been parked, search that field to make sure there was *nothing* in it, not even a wild animal, while pointing at nothing and urging everybody to spot what I was (*not!*) pointing at.

When Deety's voice in my ear button said quietly, "Okay," I tacked her "Execute" signal onto the end of a sentence: "... *now!*"

How many gals (or males) could have refrained from claiming some of the applause? I didn't caution Deety not boast about her role, warn her not to kill the "magic" by explaining it. That was not in her "Lifeboat" instructions; she was free to boast if she wished.

Not Deety! She mingled with the crowd while everyone was still staring. When I glanced at her, the button was no longer in her ear. I noticed later that Hilda had tucked hers away, too. A walkie-talkie can fail; Hilda was first backup if Deety's picked that moment to quit. Jake was nominal second backup (he can be absent-minded), and I was last—if utterly necessary.

But I wanted simply to *point*—and have it happen—and, while Gay will accept any program from any of us four, if worded correctly and clearly enunciated, I wanted Deety to give this order because her voice had been used to pre-program; this might help if signal were faint and noise level high.

It turned out that all my worrying and fallback positions weren't needed—but, damn it, if you *don't* worry ahead of time, you'll regret it later.

So, it stayed "magic."

Except to Mobyas Toras.

That old boy fooled me by doing a full flip-flop. Opsimathic ability, the capacity to grasp new ideas in old age, varies from individual to individual. Some minds freeze solid at eighteen, never have a new thought. Some geniuses remain creative almost 'til death—e.g., Paul Dirac, Leonardo da Vinci. But most scientists do their best work before thirty-five and Earth humans capable of grasping a completely new concept after fifty are exceptional.

Mobyas Toras was almost a thousand years old and reputed to be their greatest mathematician. Jake had found him decidedly set in his opinions (apparently with good reason) and I had warned Jake against offering engineering demonstrations to Mobyas Toras, as I believed the old man would brush it off as trickery.

But Mobyas Toras was an even greater genius than I had thought. He had seen a "miracle"—and at once made the difficult jump from his firm opinion of "abstract mathematics with no relation to the real world" to "this is *engineering* based on that mathematics; no other explanation covers the facts—I was *wrong*"—made this intellectual jump almost as quickly as *Gay Deceiver* had made her instantaneous jump from Palace to Bay of Blood.

Most surprising of all, he bore no resentment; he was delighted and wanted to know *how?*—the nuts—and—bolts of it please; *how* is this mathematics applied in practice?

He was already discussing it with Jake in that mishmash of English, Barsoomian, and mathematics that they used as pidgin talk while others were still staring. They went on jabbering while the fleet admiral (near enough; their ranks don't match ours) had the ship lifted and moved to a grounding a few meters from *Gay Deceiver*. They still talked while our picnic was set up; we almost had to drag them to lunch.

There were two picnics, our family party under the spread starboard wing of Gay and a larger party of warriors and officers about fifty meters away. Hilda and Deety, as hostesses, played hob with Helium protocol. Our "table" (a long silk placed on the ground and surrounded by cushions) had our own four, the royal family, Mobyas Toras, Fleet Admiral Hal Halsa (Hilda invited him, with Dejah Thoris translating), Call-Me-Joe (Deety simply took him by the hand, led him over), Tawm Takus, Kach Kachkan—and Tira.

Tira did her utmost to refuse without flatly disobeying … until a word from Dejah Thoris caused her to curtsy, then sit down and behave as if eating with royalty in public were something she had done all her life. Larlo took over as straw boss.

Call-Me-Joe Jovial was possibly more embarrassed, even after Cart said something which I guessed at as being "Lieutenant, do as your hostess wishes." He sat down, but was still stiff until the fleet admiral spoke to him. Again, I did not ask for translation; I didn't need to—it was something equivalent to "Relax, son, and *smile*—you're putting a damper on the party."

Tawm Takus seemed ill at ease only at first; Kach Kachkan did not—if the lords of creation wanted him to eat with them, the old sergeant accepted it.

How do you arrange two green giants and eleven others when three don't speak English and four don't speak the local language—and two giants, reclining, would use up all of one side of your "table"?

Hilda's solution: ignore protocol, both that of Helium and of Earth. Cluster those who want to talk about mathematics/*Gay Deceiver*/military and economic potentials thereto (Jake, Cart, Mobyas, the admiral) together. Put the giants diagonally off the corners. Place those who would rather talk babies together. Make sure that the three who lacked English were placed with at least one who spoke both languages.

This worked out so that Tira had Call-Me-Joe on her right and the admiral on her left—and neither man seemed displeased—and I suddenly realized Tira looked better dressed in her graceful self than did any of our "ladies" in their excessively lavish jewelry ... even the incomparable Dejah Thoris. I noticed because Call-Me-Joe was getting cross-eyed through trying to give all attention to his jeddara on his right while staring at jeddara's slave on his left.

Then I saw that the admiral was all ears to the discussion of mathematics and engineering (with Cart translating for him), but managing to look at Tira by cupping one ear to the technical talk and thereby half-turning his head to his right—at Tira.

I deduced a minor truth: gems make fine accents for female beauty—but *only* as accents; beauty is fundamental. Better no jewelry than to deck a lovely woman like a Christmas tree.

The party milled around some. Thuvia was called by Cart to help explain some point to the admiral that both Jake and Mobyas took as obvious but the admiral wanted clarified (I knew how he felt; applied relativistic ballistics is about my limit ... and now Jake comes along and kicks the tar out of relativism while retaining curved space). Wogi and Ajal were dead set on getting me drunk; I hollered for help to Tira, asking whether or not we had fetched *anything* nonalcoholic? Even water.

Tira looked as surprised as she ever does (not very), whereupon she called Larlo to her and from then on the pixies let me have fruit juices. I drank juice and got food into me, then got up and took care of a couple of errands. I went inside my car, got at my gold, took eight 1929 Half Eagles and one 1926 Eagle—worth quite a lot as collector's items on Earth-Zero ... but nothing but bullion to me since I planned never to go back there. Figured by mass as tanpi they were suitable tips—but I thought our girls would rather have pretty coins than the same mass as plain bullion. I put them into my belt pouch.

I counted out a pre-calculated number of coins, figuring them as bullion, tied them into a handkerchief, went outside, got Thuvia's ear, said quietly, "I have a package for you. Do you have one for me?"

"Two," she answered just as quietly.

"Both the same? Or do I deliver one to Deety, one to Hilda?"

"Exactly alike." We made the exchange unobtrusively—although by then almost anything would be unobtrusive; it was beginning to resemble one of Sharpie's parties on Earth-Zero.

I slipped one package to Hilda; it disappeared. I took the other around to Deety, who had shifted around to the jeddara's place when Dej' had moved down to hear something the admiral was saying—about military potential of the Burroughs Drive, I guess—it wasn't English. Deety was sitting on Kach's chest, dropping food into his mouth and talking to Call-Me-Joe through Tira. I slipped her the package; she slid it somewhere into that ornate harness without breaking her chatter.

I said to Kach in a low voice, "The baggage items—which thoat? Or both?"

"Kanakook," he answered even more quietly. "Shall I call her here? Or does the captain wish to ...?"

Deety jumped up. "I'll call her! *Kanakook!* Come here, dear!"

I swore silently. The thoats were grazing off the port side of the car, away from both picnics—I having asked their owners to tell them to stay there. But my silent swearing was not at Deety; it was my goof— I had neglected to tell her what I had in mind.

The thoat answered at once, her three-note squeal very loud—and around the tail of my car came this misshapen mastodon at flank speed.

As she skidded to a stop, her ferocious face ten centimeters from Deety's face, what had been the larger picnic fifty meters away was now a line of warriors charging pell-mell to save the royal family.

I figure it was the fact that the Princess Deety had her arms around as much of the thoat's head as she could stretch saved Kanakook's life that day; at least half of those warriors had drawn pistols rather than swords.

Cart snapped something at the admiral; he let out a bellow that bounced off that charge; it suddenly halted. He added another order, not quite so loudly; they returned to their rather-trampled feast.

Deety looked around, still petting Kanakook. "What's the trouble? Hey, Cart! What's going on?"

"Nothing, Princess. Everything's all right."

"When did I stop being 'Deety' to you? Why were those men running? Don't fib to me, Cart—know I missed something."

"Pri ... Deety, everything's all right now. It's just that my guardsmen aren't used to seeing a thoat charging at their jeddara."

"But she wasn't charging at *anybody*. She just came to me when I called her. Kanakook wouldn't hurt anyone; she's gentle as a lamb. As a sorak." (Kanakook answered her name again.) "Dej'! Come meet my friend."

The jeddara at once stood up; Cart said hastily, "Mother! Do be cautious!"

"*You* be cautious, Carthoris."

The jeddara went straight to my wife. Kach Kachkan stepped closer to the thoat, placed his hand on her neck.

"Dej', this is my friend Kanakook; she's sweet and gentle. Kanakook, greet your jeddara, Dejah Thoris."

The thoat sounded her birdcall, then added to it a longer flourish. Deety clapped. "Why, she said hello to you! That's how she says it—she *likes* you, Dej'!"

"I said Kaor directly to her mind, dear. She is indeed a sweet creature. Kach Kachkan, you are fortunate."

"Your Imperial Majesty, I have long thought so. Thank you."

Cart came up, followed by Thuvia and the admiral; they all discussed thoats-we-have-known, with Thuvia and Dej' translating for Deety and for the admiral. I waited, then looked up at Kach, his face three meters higher than mine. "Kach, where is the stuff?" I asked, trying to make it a stage whisper.

"In my rifle boot and in the bag behind it. I'll get it, sir—but I had best stay here now."

(Should have kept my mouth shut. I couldn't reach either one without a ladder. And Kanakook was rocking just a touch, no doubt made nervous by too many strangers.)

Eventually they stopped and all went back to the "table." Kach got out what he had carried for us: a silk-wrapped package containing two pairs of laundered boxer shorts, two laundered scarves, a smaller included package of jewelry, both real and costume, and a separate package containing shotgun shells, a loaded clip for an automatic, and ammo for my revolver—Jake and I were wearing firearms but decided against wearing them loaded—someone might want to look at strange firearms and it might be impolite to refuse.

Kach then removed his big rifle from its boot scabbard, reached far down with his upper right arm, hauled out Deety's shotgun. He insisted on carrying everything for me—well, he had four hands. Feeling foolish, I walked with him to *Gay Deceiver's* starboard door, placed the gear inside. If I had had the foresight to tell Deety my intention, the stuff would have been loaded in from the *port* side, out of sight of guests.

I returned to the picnic, accepted more fruit juice from Wogi while dreaming of a dry martini. A few minutes later Cart moved over and joined me. "You are leaving today," he said quietly.

"Yes."

"No criticism, I realized it before you loaded your baggage. Let me know when you want the air cover pulled back."

"Cart, you saw how I moved our chariot here. Was your air cover on station? Did I tear a hole in your palace?"

He got a wry look. "Perhaps I don't yet believe it in my belly."

"I know, I went through that stage."

"We'll miss you." He was silent a moment, then added, "I noticed the transaction with Thuv. Zeb, it wasn't necessary to tell me you had buried your gold out here. The picnic would have been held anyhow."

"Cart, I never said I had *buried* the gold out here. I said that I had *left* it out here. *You* took it to the palace—not me." I added, "When you groused that it wasn't safe, I told you that it was quite safe—and it *was*; you had a triple guard around it. I did not lie to you. But I *had* to get our space chariot out here—and you were trying to stop me. I wasn't going to beg you to let me move my own property ... not when your sole reason was a bunch of trumped-up charges. I know that you felt duty-bound to hold us here—to hold us in Helium, I mean. But, if I understood you a few days ago, this wasteland is *not* Helium—and we are neither a Green Horde not allied to you nor an unfriendly army."

"No. But I could still stop you ... and would, if duty required."

"*Could* you, Cart? Are you *certain* that all your fliers overhead are as powerful as this one chariot? I offered you a harmless demonstration—do you insist on a more convincing one? It would give me no pleasure to destroy even one of your ships ... and I certainly would not wish to kill those warriors behind us."

"I know your ship is armored, Zeb. But you aren't in it."

I raised my voice just enough to be sure that the skin mic over the starboard door would pick it up. "*Gay Deceiver*—open up."

The doors swung wide. I added, "*Gay Deceiver*—close up." She closed again. "Anything more you want to see, Cart? I noticed that Hal Halsa was startled. But perhaps *you* noticed that Hilda was *not*. Cart, are you still bound by duty? You made every reasonable effort to hold me in Helium in answer to that phony extradition. But *I* am bound by duty, too—to protect my wife, to protect Hilda. I tried to make it easy for you by coming here, outside Helium. But we could have left last night … and *nothing* could have stopped us. I *told* you that guards did not matter. Nor do these guards matter. How much proof does it take?"

I thought he was changing the subject. "Milady Mother really chewed me out today. I have no further duty in the matter, as you know. You are free to leave anytime, as I also told you."

"Yes, you told me. I was most happy to learn that we could leave freely. We would have left *without* permission. But it would have sorrowed us to be forced to do it that way. That's why I waited and gave you an easy way out. But I'm glad that the jeddara *knew* that there was no duty involved over that silly extradition scroll. If you had still felt yourself bound by it, we would have left three hours ago—without bloodshed. We still can—even if your Lady Mother were to change her mind and order us held."

"*Hunh!*" It was a more than a laugh. "Mother does not change her mind."

"You still seem to be wrestling with your soul rather than thinking with your brain. I've asked you the same question again and again; you haven't answered. Do you think that all the power of Helium can hold us? Those weird aliens tried to stop us with far stronger weapons; they failed. I would happily have killed them all. But they were disguised, too well hidden among our own people. Had we fought, many of our people would have died. So we fled—four innocent people in a private chariot. Someday we will find some way to dig them out, tear off their disguises. If we do— No, *when* we do"—I hammered the ground with clenched fist—"we'll kill them all!"

"I wish you luck, blood brother. When the time comes, my sword fights with yours!"

"I know it, Cart. We'll kill as many as possible personally, you and I. Cart, these aren't honorable enemies; they are vermin. Intelligent and dangerous—but *vermin*, to be killed on sight." I added, "You aren't safe—Helium is not safe from them."

"We figured that out—or Hilda did. Tomorrow we will know more."

"Take no chances with them. Hmm …. Does Helium require health inspection?"

"Eh?"

"Incoming strangers. We were cleared without inspection. What inspections are routine?"

"Why, freight inspections are made at the gates. Certain imports are not permitted, others may be taxed—or may not; it varies. Each stranger must identify himself." He smiled. "Sometimes we make mistakes—but not for long."

"No, no!" I explained to him the idea of health inspection at immigration. "Each nation has its own law on this. Not even diplomatic immunity can exempt a newcomer from whatever health inspection that nation finds necessary to protect the health of its citizens. You can require them to strip naked. But simply examining arms and legs would unmask these vermin—I think. Let me call our expert. *Hilda!* Can you spare a moment?"

We were ready to leave when a hitch developed. Presents had been made—fancy watches to Kach and to Tommy Tucker, gold pieces to our borrowed domestic staff … and to Cart from Hilda, three spares of her record shots, stereo Polaroid, of the corpse of that fake "ranger"—how it had looked in uniform, stretched out dead on a workbench, how it had looked naked with extra joints and stub horns showing, and a stomach-retching view of it opened, greenish-blue blood everywhere. She showed these with a portable viewer.

Cart asked her to show them to Hal Halsa and to Mobyas Toras—did not want his mother and his wife to look at them. One word from the jeddara changed his mind.

Dej' looked at all three, long and carefully, and, so far as her face showed, no emotion. Thuv looked at the first with interest, the second with fascination, the third with horrified disgust—but she examined them as carefully as her mother-in-law.

Hilda told Cart that she was sorry that there was no spare viewer. He asked, "May I see it a moment?"—looked at it again, called Hal Halsa and Mobyas Toras into conference.

Cart handed it back. "We'll have one later tonight. Mobyas Toras asked me to tell you that the vermin pictured is beyond doubt a

Pankera—of the *Panki* that once invaded Barsoom. Hal Halsa adds that we shall kill them again ... to the last monster."

"Good!" (Gentle little Hilda is bloodthirsty—when blood has the wrong color.)

I was forced to add, "Tell him not to be overconfident, Cart. Swords aren't much use against these things."

"You did well with a sword, blood brother. That was a nice belly thrust—I could see."

"But Cart, they operate by stealth, in hiding. And now they have weapons that can destroy whole cities." (I didn't know that Earth-Ten had H-bombs, N-bombs, et cetera—but I knew that the vermin on Earth-Zero were in cahoots with vermin on Earth-Ten. Proof: that phony extradition.)

"Cousin Zebadiah ...?"

"Cousin Dejah Thoris?"

"Any that are here now will be unmasked and destroyed. Any that come here will be destroyed at once. I have spoken."

"Jeddara, *don't* underrate the enemy. They are powerful. *I* have spoken!"

"Captain, your words will be taken most seriously."

Deety had kissed goodbye nineteen people and one thoat. I had kissed eleven myself, clapped shoulders and shaken hands with men, and petted Kanakook—when a hitch developed: Hal Halsa, Mobyas Toras, Cart, Thuv, and Dej' all wanted a ride in our sky carriage—Jake had already promised a ride to Mobyas Toras.

"But we have seats for only four."

"I know, Zeb. But Hilda and Deety are willing to wait while ...."

"Lifeboat rules, Copilot. Our party will not be separated."

"But ...."

"Pipe down. Remember Murphy's Law."

"Aye aye, Captain."

Hilda came up with a solution. "Captain, I don't know why you installed safety belts in those sleeping spaces back behind ...."

"Murphy's Law. One of us might be hurt, or ill."

"... but now we can use them. Deety and I can ride back there. I don't want to be separated from Jacob. I agreed just because they've been so nice to us."

Robert A. Heinlein

That solved everything but whom. The jeddara forbade the heir apparent to risk it. Cart, speaking for his father, forbade his mother to risk it. I welcomed the head-on collision; I didn't want to be responsible for either jeddara or heir apparent—and neither would budge.

But Cart appealed to me. "Zeb, please explain to Mother that I need to know the military possibilities of this type of craft."

I may be a fool—but not an idiot. I'd rather argue with a cop than be drawn into a family argument. My brain whizzed. "Cart, speak frankly. Which of you, you or Hal Halsa, is more skilled in strategy and tactics? I'm not speaking of skill as a warrior—you are probably second only to your father in that. I mean skilled in art of warfare."

"Damn it, Zeb, that's most unfair. Hal Halsa puts his whole time on it; he's chief of staff and deputy to Tars Tarkus. But I have to spend my time on the grimy details of government. If I had the ti—"

"You've answered me. Now go give your mother your frank opinion."

"Oh, go lay an egg!" He stormed off, told his mother that Hal Halsa should go.

Still a problem—Hal Halsa knew no English. Mobyas Toras and Jake could talk that horrible pidgin ... but my copilot must *not* be distracted—or I would cancel the ride. I *ordered* Jake on that point ... and got Dej' to give Mobyas Toras the same order—explain to him that I would not allow him to board unless he gave his word of honor not to speak to captain and copilot once we were aboard.

"He understands it, Cousin Zebadiah. He did not like the order—but the supreme authority of a ship's commander underway is the same with us as it seems to be with you. The learned one is a man of honor; he will speak only with Hal Halsa."

But that left us with no interpreter, even a half-arsed one such as Jake. No skin off my nose, but it could be inconvenient.

I'm glad I'm not royal; they operate by different rules. The jeddara and the prince had stymied each other; neither could leave the ground. Thuvia herself could not inherit the throne; she was a princess of Ptarth. She was princess consort to the prince and might be jeddara someday, if and when Cart became jeddak. Her daughter Tara, Jeddara of Gathol, was hatched Princess of Helium and thus was in the direct line of succession—if her older brother, her father, her mother's grandfather and great-grandfather, and her grandmother Dejah Thoris (hatched Princess of Helium) were all dead (unlikely).

But Thuvia was not in the line of succession in Helium; her prime duty as consort was to provide fertilized eggs, potential heirs; this she had done—Thuvia was expendable.

Logical? The wild logic of *Alice in Wonderland*.

Space—those back seats weren't narrow, never had been. It was fore-and-aft space that had made them inaccessible to me, until I refitted *Gay Deceiver* at the palace. "Thuv, everybody straps down, including me. *Everybody*—or we don't lift off. Only two sets of straps in the back seat. The belts are long enough—but would you rather cuddle up to Hal Halsa, or to Mobyas Toras? Has to be one or the other."

She wrinkled her nose like Deety, and grinned. "I suspect that Hal Halsa would be a better cuddle—but it would embarrass the poor man; he can't forget who I am."

"Neither could I. And I don't mean 'Princess.'"

She giggled. "Thank you, Zeb—it's mutual. Mobyas is so old and skinny his bones will probably cut me. But he and I together won't take up much more space that Hal Halsa. And, as you may have noticed, our great savant is not impressed by royalty. And he is so old that he would as lief cuddle a thoat as me."

"I hope I never get that old."

"You won't, Zeb. Like my father, like my husband, you will die fighting."

I changed the subject to camera, explained Jake's stereo Polaroid to her. "Got it? Practically everything automatic. Don't touch the focus; I'll leave it locked on infinity. It's loaded; all you have to do is to point it and push the button whenever I yell, '*Picture.*' But only then; film is scarce and I can't get more. These pictures Hal Halsa and Cart will need to prove to the Warlord how useful craft like *Gay Deceiver* can be. The strap goes around your neck—but *at all times* hold the camera firmly by at least one hand."

One minor bobble—Hal Halsa was indignant at the idea of removing his sword. Cart intervened. "Zeb, you can't expect a gentleman to give up his sword."

"No room for it, Cart. Jake and I are about to stow our swords and pistols. I want him to remove all that dress junk he's wearing too; we can't have *anything* that might get loose in the cabin and bounce around. You, too, Thuv. Leave your pretties behind. Deety, Hilda— time to stow all your jewelry."

Thuv made no fuss; she summoned Larlo, and quickly was only in dagger and belt. "That, too, Thuv."

Her eyes widened, but she unbuckled it, handed it to Larlo. I added, "Deety has a spare coverall, a flying suit, if you want it."

"Will I be cold without it?"

"Not at all, Thuv," Deety called out. She was standing in the door of the car, naked as an oyster on the half shell, and as untroubled by it as Tira.

I said, "Astrogator, you and the science officer get back in there and strap down! We're wasting time." I turned back to the others. "Suit yourself, Thuv. Cart, Hal Halsa need not remove his sword ...."

"Good!"

"... but if he won't, he doesn't go. I obeyed his regulations in his ship; I expect obedience to *my* orders and *my* regulations in *my* ship. He can wear plain leather and one closed pouch, nothing else—or he stays behind. I regret that I have no way to stow his weapons securely. But don't tell him that. Tell him what else I said and don't soften it. No apologies, no explanations. I run a taut ship and require instant, unquestioning obedience. Tell him so."

Cart must have let him have it straight; he was brief. The old warrior straightened himself to full attention, barked one phrase I recognized. It was equivalent to "Aye aye, sir." Or "Roger Wilco." He then barked a longer phrase toward his guardsmen: an officer answered and a soldier came running over. In twenty seconds, Hal Halsa was wearing plain leather, no weapons.

Mobyas Toras didn't give a hoot, he was simply impatient to go. His leather was plain anyhow and he wore nothing but a short sword; he unbuckled it and put it on the ground. Cart picked it up, said something—promised to care for it, I suppose.

"One last instruction, Cart. Surround this ship with your guard. Nothing and no one is to go inside that ring of soldiers until return. That means you and the jeddara—no exceptions, no excuses, not even for one instant. I saw a sorak aboard your flagship; it should be locked up. Cart, if you value the life of your wife, you will do this *exactly*."

"It will be done. May I ask why?"

"It would cause a tremendous explosion. I can't take time to explain why, but it would kill everyone in my chariot, destroy the chariot, and kill or badly wound anyone nearby. But if nothing enters that locus, I'll deliver your princess back to you safe and sound." (*Or I'll be dead, too, pal—but let's not talk about that.*)

"Nothing will enter it. I have spoken."

"All hands, man the ship! Thuvia, get your charges inside."

"Zeb." Cart's voice sounded plaintive.

"Yeah, Cart? I'm busy. Better get your guard in place."

"I will at once—but how *did* you summon your ship?"

"Oh. I didn't. Deety did."

"*Deety!* But she was with us."

"Station your guard, man. I'll give it to you in ten words, just before I close the doors and leave." I went around to the port side, found Jake waiting, saw that while Hal Halsa had figured out the safety belts, Thuv was having heavy weather getting the old man and herself adjusted. They were strapped in but the diagonal belt was across her left breast—obviously uncomfortable, could be painful if I had to wrassle Gay. I worked at readjusting it, felt a touch on my arm. Hal Halsa had removed one shoulder strap from borrowed harness, was offering it. "Tell him 'thank you,' Thuv—we can use it. And, Thuv, once those doors are closed, you are no longer a princess; you are the lowest-ranking crew member, in charge of passengers and photography."

"Yes, Captain."

"You forgot to stick out your tongue, dear."

"Like Deety?" She giggled, and stuck out her tongue at me.

"That's just like Deety. She obeys me—when she must. But she reminds me that things will be different, later. And so they will be. When those doors open, you'll be a princess again."

"I think I like being a crew member. Being a princess can be dull."

"Less chatter, please." I got them comfortable, Mobyas Toras with an arm around Thuv and she with both hands free for photography. I checked Hal Halsa, found that his waist strap was too tight; I loosened it until it was firm but safe, got into my own seat, started strapping down. Shoes? Hadn't worn 'em lately; they were stowed. But my feet were cold. "Copilot, where are your specs?"

"Eh? Captain, I haven't worn them lately." He opened the glove compartment, got out his bifocals case. "I don't think I need them."

"Check and see. If you don't read those verniers correctly, we can all be mighty sorry—or worse."

"Yes, Captain. Uh, I see better *without* them. Dear me!"

311

"So re-stow them but keep them handy." I saw that Cart had the guard positioned. "Oh, Cart! Here a moment, please!" I added, "All hands check all around you for loose gear of any sort. Astrogator, get out five Bonine pills, one for science officer, three for Thuv and passengers, one for copilot. Thuv, these pills are to be chewed and swallowed, no argument permitted or that passenger gets out. Would have done it earlier if Hal Halsa hadn't yakked. Hi, Cart. Stick your head in. Hello, Gay."

"Zeb, dear—I've *missed* you, darling." (Hilda had put her best bedroom tones into that one—but why did the durn thing have to pop up now? Could the gals have rigged it on me? No, impossible! Or was it?)

I ignored it. "That's how Deety summoned the ship, Cart."

He looked startled. "You have a woman hidden in there?"

"An automatic pilot, different from the sort you use. Go back and study the copies of the manual I left with you. Machinery, Cart, remotely controlled by wireless. Deety was waiting back aft and wearing a wireless concealed in her ornaments. When I signaled Deety—I did, with one word, intended not to be noticed—when I said, '*Now*,' Deety ordered this sky chariot to move to this spot. Think about it; your technologists can do the same, if they study it. Useful for killing aliens—or other enemies. Thuv, make sure that both passengers get full translations. Cart, if you're ready, get back of your guard line and *stay* there—we're leaving."

Cart muttered, "*Wireless!*" and trotted toward his encircling warriors.

"*Gay Deceiver*, close your doors. All hands, report safety belts fastened and pills chewed and swallowed. Science Officer."

"Strapped down, Cap'n Zebbie, and I took my medicine."

"Astrogator."

"Strapped down, Captain. I wasn't told to take one."

"Photographic Officer, report passengers and self."

"Captain, you checked our straps; we haven't changed them. All three of us chewed and swallowed our pills. Hal Halsa says they taste good—I think so, too—and asks what they are for."

"They prevent sickness from motions in flying."

"I told him I thought that might be it. He and I don't need them. Perhaps Mobyas Toras does."

"I couldn't be sure. They're harmless. No more unnecessary chatter to captain or copilot. You may talk with anyone else. Copilot, report."

"Belts fastened, door seal checked, Captain."

I handed Jake a schedule I had been writing while we ran through the checklist. "Read this. Any questions must not use words that might trigger automatic pilot. Then post it above verniers." I checked the portside door seal. "Left door sealed, check-off complete. Photography Officer, be ready to photograph on command."

Jake said, "The schedule is clear, Captain. It is more than I expected."

"Might as well go the scenic route, Jake. Any questions?"

"Do I do numbers three and five?"

"No, I give the oral ones. Corrections; if I am disabled, or you see danger, order number five without hesitation. And be sure that you are set up to do number four *before* I order number three. But don't execute number four until I order it. Unless you spot danger—in which case, order number five *at once*. Understood?"

"Follow routine except to escape danger, Captain."

"Set first transition and report ready."

"H-axis, upward, fifty times minimum transition, or five hundred kilometers—set. Ready."

"Execute."

I ignored the gasps—sunlight to starry sky does that. "Thuvia, you'll shoot—photograph—between our heads when I order it." I was tilting my baby's nose down by her space controls. The planet under us swung into view—more gasps—and I aimed her nose down to Helium, easy to spot and beautiful. "Picture!"

"I think I got it. I hope I got it." Her voice trembled.

"You probably did. Have Hal Halsa hold it, by the edges. Tell him to watch for pictures to appear." I was leveling off. "Ready, Copilot?"

"H-axis, upward, one thousand minimum, or three by vernier. Ten thousand kilometers, set. Ready."

"Execute!" I turned her nose down again; the whole planet swung into view. "Thuvia, can you get all of Barsoom into your view finder?" I held *Gay Deceiver* steady for her.

Her voice was very shaky. "I think so, Captain."

"Shall I go higher?"

"I can see it all—but my hands tremble!"

"Can you stretch forward enough to steady it on the head rest? I'll duck my head out of the way."

"I think so. Yes, I can."

"Picture!" At ten thousand klicks, plenty of time— "Copilot, the next one is mine ... but get number four set up. We'll try for one picture. Thuvia, is your first one beginning to show a picture? Ask Hal Halsa."

"One moment .... Yes, it is! Captain, it's *beautiful!*"

"It'll be sharper soon."

"Captain," said Deety, "can we loosen these straps? Even though the door is dogged open and by twisting our necks all we can, we can't see much."

"Permission denied. You've seen all this before; this trip is for our passengers. Don't twist your necks, lie flat. That is not a request, it's an order. I may have to take evasive tactics; I don't want broken necks. Thuvia, warn the passengers. Astrogator, what time is it in Snug Harbor?"

" 'Snug Harbor'?"

"Or Greenwich, if you prefer. I'm using you to check G. D.'s chronometer; my watch is still put away. Reminds me—did Kach like his watch? I can't read his expression—and he would have thanked you just as much for a burnt match."

"I didn't know green giants could shed tears. They can."

"Number four ready, Captain," Jake reported quietly.

"Keep your thumb near the button. Deety, can't you give me a time check?"

"Snug Harbor is sixteen-sixteen in the afternoon. Greenwich is twenty-three sixteen."

"Good time to hunt rangers. G. D. says you're thirty seconds slow."

"You tell her that I say she's thirty seconds fast!"

"Tell her yourself, later. Right now she's on duty. Thuvia, is the second picture coming out?"

"Yes, 'Captain.' Uh, I ... I'm glad I ate that little pink sweet—I'm almost too excited."

"Almost hit me in the tummy, the first time, dear," I lied. "And I've been flying all my life. Let me know whether or not the second picture is sharp. I'll use one more film if it isn't—but I'll take it myself. Ask your passengers whether or not they've seen enough. I'm in no hurry, but we've got a lot of people waiting—including your undoubtedly worried husband."

I paused during a few moments of words I didn't know.

"They both admit—reluctantly—that they've seen all they can see. The second picture is quite sharp ... to my surprise."

314

"Not to mine, I've got a good photography officer. *Gay Deceiver, take us home!*"

Instantly, we were two klicks over Snug Harbor. I got her under control, dead-stick, and pointed her nose down. "Picture!"

Thuvia gasped, but her camera clicked.

"Jake! As I come level"—I tried to pull her wings off—but *Gay Deceiver* is sturdy—"*Execute!*"

We were a hundred thousand kilometers above Earth—and I was nervous. "Thuvia, be ready—you'll get just one chance. Jake, watch the board for missiles; I'll watch outside."

"Ready for picture! *Where are we*, Captain?"

"That's Earth—Jasoom. Tell them. *Picture!*"

"Got it!"

"Let me know when it shows." I carefully kept my voice steady. I was scared silly, but not rationally. Even a Sprint missile can't go a hundred thousand kilometers fast enough to reach us—plus reaction time to decide that we were a target. Probably we were on some screen at NORAD ... but merely as an unidentified flying object, not in an attack trajectory—so forget it! An armed satellite might be close—but not inside Gay's extreme radar range—no hazard. It was those damned aliens that made me jittery—continua craft of some sort and *I* didn't know what sort or what they could do ... and those ugly monsters reacted fast and unexpectedly.

"Picture is showing, Captain. Your passengers want to know: is that *really* Jasoom? Earth."

"Tell 'em to show it to the Warlord; he'll identify it. Thuvia, I can see Virginia—it's an unusually clear day."

Jake said quickly but quietly, "Captain, something just showed on radar. Bottom display."

"*Gay Deceiver—Bug Out!*"

We were parked in the Bay of Blood. I re-swallowed *all* my guts and said, "You're a Smart Girl, Gay."

"Boss, I'll bet you tell that to all the girls. Over."

"Over and out, Gay. Copilot, open your door manually." I opened the portside door. "All passengers disembark. Princess Thuvia, I have been greatly honored to have you as such an efficient crew member; tell your husband so—and here he comes. All hands, prepare for space. Secure everything aft, take your usual seats and strap down."

"Captain," Deety said heart-brokenly, "Can't we have just a *few* minutes? We've been gone only sixteen minutes."

"G. D.'s chronometer says seventeen minutes."

"I *told* you she was slow!"

"Deety, if you get out, you'll be kissing everybody goodbye again."

"What's wrong with that?"

"Takes time. No."

Hilda said sweetly, "Cap'n Zebbie, may I call you 'Captain Bligh'?"

"Go ahead, Science Officer—but I feel more like 'Kapitan Vander-decken'—I repeat: all hands, prepare to lift!"

I don't have much authority on the ground with the doors open. Not one of my ill-sorted crew flatly refused, and Jake said nothing. But Cart was so excited he could hardly speak English and wanted to talk to me—and so did the jeddara.

So I unstrapped, told the others they could get out—but to stay close; this was only for five minutes!

"Zeb!" blurted out Cart. "Hal Halsa says you've been all the way to Jasoom! Earth, I mean. Earth-Ten, I mean ...."

"No. Earth-Zero. Ten universes away. Where your father came from. And all of us four."

"You never said you were going that far."

"You didn't ask. You wanted Hal Halsa and Mobyas Toras to see what a continua craft could do; I showed them. What are you complaining about, blood brother? I told you I would bring your princess back safely; I did. We weren't gone long."

"I know you weren't; that's why it's so hard to believe."

"Cart, if you're going to use continua craft, you'll have to practice believing seven impossible things before breakfast. Hilda, honey, can you lay hands on your stereo viewer? We've got an unbeliever on our hands."

Thuv had done a good job; every picture was sharp and properly framed—in spite of buck fever, which can hit anyone—you should see the blurry shots I got camera-hunting lion in Africa.

Jake's viewer not only turns paired frames into stereo; it enlarges 4x. "That one, Cart, is the crater of a small atomic bomb—where Jake's mountain home in Arizona used to be. The *Panki* did it, only a little over a zode after Jake and I killed that *Pankera* Hilda dissected. That bomb missed us only by moments. See this one—North and South America. North America spang in the middle. A clear day and Thuv is a natural artist with a camera. If you look closely you'll make out a big bay on the east coast. Chesapeake Bay. From there west runs Virginia, my birthplace and where your father comes from."

"I recognize it. My father, your cousin, painted a map; it matches. I *have* to believe."

Thuv was nearby, talking with Hal Halsa, Mobyas Toras, and her mother-in-law, confirming their excited report. She had resumed belt and dagger, hadn't yet bothered with more. Hal Halsa was again wearing sword, but still wore the leather of a common warrior—Mobyas Toras had not yet put on even that propriety.

Thuv said smugly, "My chieftain, you had *better* believe! Zeb, Mobyas Toras asks me to tell you that, now that he understands it, he is sure that there is a simpler method without gyroscopes. But, so he claims, gyroscopes of proper quality are no problem, either. He intends to put our best scientists to work on *both* methods."

"Thuv, I wouldn't understand either one. I'm just the pilot."

"You are more than 'just a pilot,' Senior Cousin and Captain."

Thuvia's report made it almost impossible to drag Jake away—he started spouting pidgin to Mobyas Toras.

Nevertheless, in a half hour I managed to herd my motley gang aboard. "All hands, report readiness." My mouth still tasted of Thuv, Dej', and Tira—the flavors blended nicely. Deety may have kissed everyone again—she tried. So did Hilda. My sword hand was crushed and my shoulder bruised from Hal Halsa's farewell, with a translated word to me that he and I, together, would destroy all *Panki* vermin everywhere. I agreed, not believing it—but certain now that every *Pankera* on Barsoom (if any) was in for a rough time. All in all, I felt that we had repaid our hosts.

"Belts fastened, Captain."

"All tight, Cap'n Bligh, honey."

"Belt fastened, door seal checked, Captain."

"Portside door seal checked. Copilot, by plan—rotate. *Execute!*"

Gay Deceiver rotated—somewhere.

— XXXI —

Zebadiah

Nowhere ....
          Freefall and utter blackness ....

The cabin of *Gay Deceiver* held only the faint light of the instrument board, barely enough to count one's fingers *if* a hand were passed between eyes and board, not enough light to see each other's faces.

My wife broke the silence with hushed tones; "Zebadiah ... uh, Captain, could we hlave the inside lights on? This is spooky."

"No. Copilot?"

Dr. Burroughs was slow in answering. "No opinion ... yet. I would like to see in all directions."

"Skewed? Or a tumbling pigeon?"

"The latter, I think, Captain. A hundred and eighty degrees should suffice."

"Jake, do you object to three sixty?"

"Not if you wish it, Captain."

"I prefer it because I can do it by pre-program. Change attitude around l-axis, clockwise as seen from starboard, one full turn and back to zero, and stop. Done that way, I can switch off the instrument board lighting."

"Oh, no!"

"Pipe down, Deety. We'll all be trying to see things much fainter than lighted instruments. The full tumble will take twenty seconds. How's the clock in your head?"

"I think it's stopped."

"No matter, I'll be counting seconds. And we'll all be able to feel both the start and the stop, as well as a slight pressure against your seat belts since we are all forward of the center of mass. Science Officer, watch the sky to starboard; Astrogator, the same to port."

"Yessir."

"Aye aye, Cap'n Bligh. I'm scared."

"That makes four of us. Pilot and copilot will scan forward. Hello, Gay."

"Howdy, Zeb."

"Tumbling pigeon, Gay."

"Forward somersault, Zeb."

I switched off instrument lighting. "Execute!" I started counting locomotives in my mind and felt pressure against my safety belts. I reached 'nineteen locomotives' as Deety announced "Twenty seconds!" and Gay reported "Tumble completed." We were again in freefall, no pressure against our belts. I switched back on the board lights. "You're a Smart Girl, Gay."

"If I were smart, I wouldn't be pushing this baby carriage. Over."

"Over and out, Gay. Jake, did you see anything? I didn't."

"Nothing, Captain."

"Astrogator?"

"Just blankness. Please, can we have the lights on?"

I flipped on the overhead lights. "Science Officer?"

"USS *Enterprise* being chased by a Klingon cruiser."

"Sharpie, that's a false report. The *Enterprise* doesn't run from just one Klingon cruiser."

"It was going boldly where no man has gone before. Aside from that, I didn't see a thing. Let's try another universe; this one stinks."

"That stink is me, Sharpie; your captain is chicken. Jake, of what use is an empty universe?"

"Captain, 'empty universe' is a meaningless expression. Space-time implies mass-energy, and vice versa."

"It looked awfully empty to me, Jake."

"And to me. Captain, I'm troubled by a dilemma in theory. Is the mass in this space-time so far away that we can't see it with bare eyes? Or is it in a state of 'cold death,' level entropy? Or … did we create it by rotating?"

"Create it? *Huh?*"

"A theoretical possibility. If we are the only mass in this universe, then it had no existence until we created it by rotation. But it will not collapse when we rotate out of it … because we will be leaving behind quanta radiated."

"Hmm … Jake, I'm not even going to attempt to understand that; I'm just a sky jockey. But I'm bothered by something else. We started from Universe-Ten and made one normal or ninety-degree rotation—correct?"

"Yes. We rotated as planned around axis h and thereby moved each of the other five ninety degrees. We are now experiencing duration along the axis, while our former axis of duration, t, replaces h as a spatial axis—and so on."

"Hmm …. Deety, what Greenwich time is it?" I watched my autopilot clock.

"Huh? Uh …. Zero-zero-thirteen."

"Gay says you're still about twenty seconds slow." I opened the glove compartment, got out my navigation watch, strapped it on. "But my watch splits the difference, just about. How many minutes since we left the Bay of Blood?"

"Nine minutes thirteen seconds. Ask me a hard one."

"I'm going to ask your father a hard one, instead. Jake, if I now tell G. D. to use the B, U, G, O, U, T program, would we bump into anything?"

"Why, I suppose we might, Captain. Ten minutes isn't very long to tidy up after our picnic. If you have some reason to go back, why not wait a half hour? Or longer."

"Would it make a difference? You just told me that we were experiencing duration along the axis."

"But …. *Oh!* I'm stupid. I'm stupid! *No* time has elapsed on t-axis; we would return at the exact instant we left. Oh, how Mobyas Toras will laugh at me!"

"Deety, hon? Do you agree with your father?"

She opened her mouth, closed it—suddenly looked very upset. "I … *I don't know!* Pop! That first trip to the world without the letter "J"—time did pass, it did!"

I said gently, "But that was translation, Deety. You were still experiencing duration along t-axis."

"But Gay agrees with me. And so does your watch. And …. But …. Oh, I'm confused! Zebadiah, I don't know *what* time it is—I'm sorry."

I reached behind, found my wife's hand, squeezed it. "You have nothing to be sorry about, my darling. All three of you—you and the two mechaniwockles—are continuing to measure duration. We just made a right-angle turn from Main Street onto Broadway, that's all. If we make a U-turn and go back, we arrive at the same intersection. Jake wouldn't describe it that way, but he's a mathematician and I'm not. I just skip over the hard parts and look up the answer in the back of the book."

"Captain, you are an intuitive geometer."

"The hell I am, Jake! I've simply tried to memorize all the things you told me this buggy would do. Are you certain that we would return at that exact instant?"

Burroughs did not hesitate. "I'm certain."

"Deety?"

She let out a deep sigh. "Pop is right, Zebadiah. I wasn't thinking straight. I can't experience duration on two axes at once, any more than Gay can. But will I ever get the clock in my head set right again?"

"Sure you will. Just like crossing a time zone. But I agree with Hilda; this universe stinks. I want to get out of it … but I don't want to get lost doing so. Copilot, I still think we ought to try one schedule of normal rotations—but not from here. So I propose this sequence. Back to the Bay of Blood. You present your verniers for a hundred thousand klicks, straight us up. The instant you see the Bay of Blood—execute!"

"One hundred thousand kilometers, ten thousand minimums of transition, or four by vernier. Captain, may I ask why?"

"You not only may ask but I won't do it at all without your approval, Jake. I want to put us back into Universe-Zero … but I don't want to do it on the ground; I want plenty of empty space around us. Then …."

"Cap'n Bligh, I don't *want* to go back to Universe-Zero! *Monsters!* Just let me off at the Bay of Blood; I'll hitch a ride back to Helium."

"Sharpie dear, let me finish explaining to your husband the schedule of transitions, translations, and rotations I'd like to impose—one simple enough that I think I can follow it without getting lost among the universes and without tangling with something big and heavy such as a planet. We *can't* check all the accessible universes; there are too many of them—we settled that the day we arrived at the Bay of Blood. But the schedule I have in mind may give us a representative sample fast enough to get you two bulging bellies to an obstetrician before our power, air, and supplies run out."

"I'm sorry, Cap'n Zebbie. I'll keep quiet."

"No, I don't want you to keep quiet. I want opinions from everybody, *after* I finish and after Jake decides on feasibility. First step, back to Bay of Blood. Second step, preset for transition straight up one hundred thousand kilometers executed at once—and don't bother to stick your tongue out, Deety; you are *not* going to kiss everybody goodbye a third time—they won't even know we've been gone. Third step, translation to Universe-Zero, near Mars but with elbow room. Fourth step, run straight through six rotations—and, Jake, in each case you preset the next rotation so that we can duck out fast if we run into something sticky …."

"Excuse me, Captain, but I can't preset the next one until the preceding one is made."

"Uh, Deety, can you preset six rotations into G. D.?"

My wife answered slowly, "I would rather not attempt to do it orally, Captain; it's awfully easy to bollix up an oral program. I would want to write them down and try to debug them on paper … and even then I might make a mistake. I do think rotating by vernier is safer, I do. But I'll try if you tell me to."

"Mmm, no, we'll have Jake do that. Jake, is the sequence in its simplest order? Easiest to set up?"

"Easiest, yes. Simplest, no. Because I plan on using twenty rotations to sample fifteen universes normal to this one. I planned to do it in five groups, returning to zero at the end of each group—six, then five, then four, then three, then two. The last rotation in each group simply brings us back to home base—but it keeps me from getting mixed up and doesn't take any time, really, ten seconds or less wasted, all told."

"We'll do it your way, Jake. Fifth step, after running through those twenty rotations—and we will run through them quite fast—Science Officer."

"Still aboard, Cap'n honey."

"Hilda, please keep a written record, in order, of all twenty rotations—brief notes, so that Jake can take us back to one that looks promising without searching for it. The fifth step, one that assumes that we do *not* find what we want by rotation, is to start searching by translation along the axis from Earth-Zero. Comment?"

"Why teh-axis, Captain?"

"Jake, we know that tau-axis is infested by *Panki* at Earth-Zero and Earth-Ten. To me that suggests that any or all analogs of Earth-Zero are open to *Panki* and may be infested. You remember how tickled you were when Mobyas Toras told you that he was impressed by your invention of math to cover both rotation and translation ... when there had been a lapse of a couple of thousand years between steps in Barsoomian math?"

"Yes, certainly."

"We don't know what mathematical theory the *Panki* use—but the oldest and simplest theory of multiple universes is the one that uses the analogy of pages of a book ... parallel universes separated by infinitesimals. That one doesn't even require curved space to describe it. Nor does it require quantum mechanics. Merely the notion of one additional spatial dimension. Like Newtonian mechanics, it would be an early approximation. Jake, it seems to me possible that the *Panki* are not nearly as sophisticated in mathematical physics as you are; they may have discovered the sheaf of universes along the tau-axis ... without ever suspecting that there is another sheaf along the teh-axis."

"Possible. I can't assign a probability to it."

"Neither can I, Jake. But Sharpie pointed out about a week ago that tau-axis was *not* the place to look. Which leaves teh-axis as a better bet ... if we miss by rotation. Shucks, tau-axis could keep them busy for millions of years. Comments, anybody?"

"I go along with your reasoning, Captain. No certainty, of course—but I see no better approach."

"Hilda? Deety?"

"Suits me, Cap'n Zebbie. Let's get cracking."

"Zebadiah, I like it, too. But may I offer a definition—my notion of a definition—of what we are looking for?"

"Certainly, sweetheart."

"An analog of Earth with an advanced civilization of viviparous human beings living on it. Maybe a touch more tropical than Earth is now ... because we will want to be able to tell just by looking without landing that they go naked or nearly naked much of the time. I don't think I could ever feel safe again on a planet where those monsters can hide just by disguising themselves. If our own planet didn't have such stupid notions about 'modesty,' those *things* could never have invaded."

Hilda started clapping. "Passed by acclamation!"

"Copilot."

"Captain."

"Preset the transition."

"Ten thousand minimums—set, Captain!"

"Execute without orders on arrival Bay of Blood. Hello, Gay."

"Howdy, Zeb."

"*Gay Deceiver—Bug Out!*"

For a split second we were again on Barsoom, then at once were a hundred thousand kilometers above it. Hilda said, "Thuvia was still waving!"

"I didn't even have time to spot Kanakook."

"Knock it off, gals. Copilot, set for first rotation, by your schedule. Family, we can spare a few moments to look at Mars—Mars-Zero. No photographs—Carl Sagan's boys have done a far better job of photographing this Mars than we can possibly do with one Polaroid." I was tilting the nose down as I spoke. "Hilda, you got the binox?"

"Getting them, Cap'n!"

"Verniers set for first rotation, Captain."

"Thank you, Copilot." I steadied *Gay Deceiver* so that Mars centered the windscreen. "Jake, feed me some makee-learnee. Do you care what attitude this craft is in at rotation?"

"Only for transitions, Zeb. For translations and for rotations, attitude does not matter."

"Hmm ... then it follows as the night from day thou canst not then predict what attitude we'll be in whenever we arrive in a new universe."

"Only with respect to the built-in arbitrary zero reference frame. Does it matter?"

"Not as long as we always have plenty of space around us. But I don't want to risk any more translations or rotations parked on the surface of a planet. You've lucked through twice, I've lucked through twice—the fifth time might come up snake-eyes. Sharpie, give Deety a crack at the binoculars, too, then pass 'em forward."

"Deety has them now, Cap'n Zebbie; I saw all I wanted to see. A most inferior planet. I prefer Barsoom."

"Me, too. Here're the glasses, Zebadiah."

"Here, Jake; give it a gander. Don't be snooty, you two in the peanut gallery; you wouldn't look any better than that if you'd had all your breath knocked out some millions of years back. Wait 'til Jake and I get through terraforming it—it'll sell like beach frontage in Florida."

"Zebbie, are you and Jacob serious about terraforming other planets?"

"Dead serious ... once we clear up some minor problems. *Panki.* Pregnancy. Provisions, power, et cetera. How does she look, Jake?"

"Much like the NASA photographs." Jake passed me the binoculars. "But I consider it as an empirical confirmation of our methodology. That planet is the Mars of our home universe. It checks—does it not?"

"It does for me—but I'm no expert. Here, Hilda, hang on to 'em. All hands, prepare for rotation. At each rotation I'll do one tumbling pigeon, with all four of us scanning as before—unless we spot danger. If we do, Jake will make the next rotation with all possible speed. Jake, at each completion of rotation please set up your next rotation *at once*, before even glancing outside, and announce '*Set!*'—because I may yell '*Execute!*' so fast I'll step on your heels."

"Aye aye, Captain."

"If you ever sniff danger, don't wait for my orders; rotate at once. And, all hands, the standing order that permits any one of us to use G, A, Y, D, E, C, I, V, E, R, T, A, K, E, U, S, H, O, M, E, still applies at all times. In case of doubt, *use it at once!* We used it an hour ago; we know we can handle it. Jake, if one of us uses it, take us straight up to a hundred thousand kilometers without waiting for orders, just as you did ten minutes ago at the Bay of Blood. That will give us time to decide what to do next—since we can't really go home. But—*Hear This!*—do *not* use B, U, G, O, U, T, again. Some time has passed on t-axis; we don't know that our landing spot is clear—and I don't ever want to find out by personal experience what happens when two masses occupy the same space. Someday by remote control, maybe, from a million kilometers away—but not in person. Astrogator, we could use a scram program that would take us back to about this point instead of Bay of Blood."

"I'll work on one, Zebadiah."

"Any questions? We are about to rotate. Copilot ... *execute!*"

Utter blackness ....

"Set!" Jake reported.

"Tumbling pigeon, coming up." I switched off the instrument board lights, then ordered the autopilot to carry out the maneuver.

Half a minute later, having shut down the autopilot, I asked, "Anybody see anything?"

"Not me."

"Nor me, Zebadiah."

"Nothing, Captain."

"That makes four of us. Record it, Hilda. Stand by to rotate. Co-pilot … execute."

Again, utter blackness ….

Again I went through tumbling pigeon routine. "Anybody see anything?"

Hilda answered, "I'm not certain. I think I did … but it was faint. Could we do that tumble again?"

"Certainly. Deety? Report."

"Nothing on my side … that I could see."

"Copilot?"

"Nothing, Captain."

"Sharpie, call out when you see it." By autopilot I started the maneuver again.

"There!"

"*Gay Deceiver—stop!* Hilda, do you still see it?"

"Yes. A fuzzy star. Jacob, let me turn your head toward it." Mrs. Burroughs leaned forward, took her husband's head between her hands, gently turned it to the right and up. "See it, dear one?"

"Uh … yes, I do! Hilda, the binoculars, please!"

I waited. Shortly my copilot said slowly, "Captain, it looks to me like a lenticular or spiral galaxy seen not quite on edge. Or it might be an entire family of galaxies still more distant. Whatever it is, it is a long, long way off. Millions of light years … but how many millions I have no way of guessing."

"Can you reach it by transition?"

"I think so. I would set middle range on six, then keep punching until I could see some change in angular width. Then either increase or decrease scale to let me sneak up on it. It might take an hour. Do you want to look at it, Captain? I think you'll have to unstrap to do so."

"No, I wouldn't learn anything that you haven't already reported. You say it's at least a million light years away?"

"Several millions of light years, at least—if this universe is at all similar to ours. But on that I lack sufficient data for an opinion."

"In any case, that is fossil light … isn't it?"

"Eh? Oh! Yes, the light we are seeing it by has been traveling for some millions of years."

"That's my point. We're seeing something that happened a long, long time ago. If we did try to sneak up on it, we might find that all those millions of stars had burned out. Maybe some neutron stars, maybe some black holes. Or maybe not. But fossil light doesn't tell us anything that we can use. Hilda, designate that galaxy as 'Last Chance.' All hands, stand by to rotate."

"Zebadiah, can't I look at it?"

"No, Deety. We are not sightseeing; we are looking for a good obstetrician on an Earth-like planet with no *Panki* vermin."

"Yessir."

"Did you stick your tongue out?"

"No, Zebadiah. That's childish behavior; I shan't do it again."

"Oh, honey! Don't change—I love you just as you are. Mature adult whenever the chips are down—delightful little girl when there is time to relax. Deety darling, I've laughed more since I met you than I had in many years before I met you. You're an entire harem in one. I wouldn't trade you for Dej', Thuv, and Tira, combined."

"How about Hilda?"

"I have no hesitation in saying that I have no comment—and you can quote me that that is strictly off the record. Copilot ... *execute!*"

Blinding light .... "Jake! Rotate! Execute!"

Suddenly we were in a starry void, almost homelike but with more and brighter stars. I heaved a sigh of relief. "Jake, what in hell did we fall into?"

"I don't know, Captain. Fortunately I had my head down over the verniers; I didn't get dazzled—or I might not have been able to set the escape rotation."

"Well ... we could have gotten out by the T, U, H, scram. Or by the deadman switch. But I *did* get dazzled ... and wouldn't have been able to wrassle this heap manually. New standing order: at each time of "execute," both pilot and copilot will close their eyes and duck their heads ... and stay that way until each is certain that he is safe from dazzle. I goofed again ... but I won't pull *that* goof again. Sorry, folks."

"Next rotation is set, Captain."

"Thank you. But we're going to sit right here until I get my eyes back. This looks like a pretty nice universe—what I can see of it around the purple spots floating in front of my eyes. Hilda, Deety, either of you have any notion of what we fell into?"

"Not me, Zebadiah."

"Cap'n Zebbie, I have three hypotheses, not one of them worth much."

"Modesty ill becomes you, Sharpie. Give."

"Interior of a global star cluster, or near the nucleus of a galaxy, or—just possibly—the early part of an expanding universe when the new stars are almost rubbing shoulders with each other."

"Hmm ... all of them jolly places to be. Jake, do you suppose we could have picked up an unhealthy dose of radiation?"

"I've no way to guess, Captain."

"Well ... the shell of this buggy is opaque to most radiation, and that sandwich windshield has one layer that is heavily leaded glass—but no way to tell, so I'll quit worrying."

"Zebadiah, there may be one way to tell. If the film in the camera is ruined, some fairly heavy stuff got through. But if the next picture is okay, we're probably okay."

Hilda said, "I'm glad you thought of that, Deety. I wasn't going to mention it—but I don't like the idea of penetrating radiation while I'm pregnant. And you, too, hon."

Zebadiah said, "I'm sorry I opened the subject, since there is nothing we can do about it. Hilda, do you want to shoot one film to check?"

"No, Zebbie, it's a waste of film."

"As you wish. My eyes are coming back; I'll start the pigeon tumble. Jake, do you want to try for spectral readings?"

"Captain, I think that it is almost certain that there are G-type stars out there and that some of them have Earth-type planets. But the search could take a long, long time. Unless the tumble maneuver shows that we are quite close to a star resembling Sol, I think we should mark this down for later exploration ... unless we find exactly what we need on teh-axis."

"Okay." I put us through one pigeon tumble. "Report, Hilda?"

"Just lots of big beautiful stars, Zebbie, but I didn't see a one close enough to show a disc."

"Me, too, Zebadiah. But what a beautiful sky!"

"Null report, Captain."

"Nothing new from the tumble, then. Hilda, mark it down as 'promising.' All hands, stand by for fifth rotation. Pilot and copilot will keep eyes closed and heads down. Astrogator and science officer are advised but not ordered to do so. Here goes. *Execute!*"

I gasped. "Where in hell are we?"

"In Hell, I think, Zebbie."

"Copilot?"

"Hilda wasn't too far off, Captain. It's something I could not have believed three months ago, before we discovered that the fantastic romances about Barsoom are essentially factual. This is some sort of inside-out universe."

"Pellucidar!" said Deety.

"No, my dear daughter. One: we are not inside our home planet; we are in another universe entirely. Two: this universe has physical laws that differ from those of our own universe. The inside of a spherical shell does not and cannot have a gravitational field *by the physical laws of our universe.* Yet I see a large river flowing below us ... and we seem to be falling toward it. Captain, are we in air or in vacuuo?"

I wiggled the manual controls. "Got a little bit of air. Probably could get some support with the wings fully extended."

"Then I would advise the captain to do so—unless you want us to rotate out of here at once."

I brought my car, manually, into a dead-stick glide just short of stalling. "Does anyone want to homestead here? I don't, because this place gives me simultaneously both agoraphobia and claustrophobia. It's so damn *big*—ten thousand kilometers in diameter, at a guess. Nevertheless it's completely enclosed. No sky. No horizons. Never again to see a night sky sprinkled with stars. I don't know what that light at the center is, but it's not a star even though it looks like the Sun. Too small—much too small. But if and when we do leave, we aren't coming back—because the god who takes care of fools and explorers let us arrive in empty space ... instead of maybe ten thousand kilometers underground."

"It may not have been luck, Captain, but logical necessity."

"Huh? You've lost me, Jake."

"You're thinking of this place as a spherical shell. But there is no basis for assuming that it has no outside. It may not have an outside of any sort."

"What? Endless millions of light years of solid rock?"

"No, no! *Nothing* outside. And by nothing I do not mean space; I mean a total absence of existence of *any sort*. Different physical laws and a different topology. We may be seeing the totality of this universe. A small universe with a different sort of closed space."

"I can't visualize it, Jake."

"Deety, my dear, rephrase for the captain."

"I'll try, Pop. Zebadiah, I'm not a geometer ... but Pop is right. Depends on what postulates you select ... and the geometry of this place may require a different set of postulates from those that work back home. I'm sure you have played with Möbius strips ...."

"Certainly. A surface with only one side. But this is a sphere."

"Pop is saying that it may be a hollow sphere with only side, the inside. Have you ever tried to figure out a Klein bottle?"

"I got cross-eyed and a headache."

"This could be sort of a Klein-bottle thing. It might turn out that if you tunneled down in a straight line anywhere down there on the ground, you might emerge at the top opposite point, still inside. And that straight line might be—would be, I think—shorter than the distance across. Maybe much shorter."

"Point three one eight zero nine is the ratio by the simplest postulates," agreed Doctor Burroughs. "The reciprocal of *pi*—if *pi* is the same here as it is at home, a point on which I have no opinion. But the geometry of this place may not be that simple. However, Captain, assuming that this is a total universe—and I think it is—our chances of arriving in open space were far greater than the chance of conflicting with a mass. But to answer your first question: no, I would not wish to homestead here—pretty as it is—unless Hilda wants to. Nevertheless, we might check it out for obstetricians."

"No obstetricians," I answered firmly.

"Why so, Captain?"

"If there are human beings here, they do *not* have an advanced culture. I've been following a curved glide path that approximates that big river below us. Did you notice where the other largish river joined it? Also look dead ahead where it meets the sea. No city either place. No warehouses. No traffic on the river. No air traffic and no signs of roads. That means to me no hospitals and no medical schools. We don't need to check elsewhere, as this is choice real estate by human standards. Ergo, no advanced culture anywhere and a small population, if any. If anyone wants to refute me, please do so in the next five minutes; I can't hold this heap in the air much longer than that without using power—power more precious than fine gold."

"I check you, Cap'n Zebbie. They *might* be so advanced that they can make the whole joint look like a national park. But I wouldn't bet on it. Let's continue shopping."

"Deety?"

"The Hillbilly is right, Zebadiah. But it's *so* pretty!"

"That makes it unanimous; we scram. Hilda, expend one film on it, as a souvenir. Then we rotate." I nosed the car down a bit to permit a better picture.

A click .... "Got it, Zebbie."

"Stand by to rotate! Execute!"

Mars of Universe-Zero lay to starboard.

I sighed. "Pretty as it was, I'm glad to be out of there. It upsets me to see rivers run uphill. Sharpie, did you get a picture?"

"Hold the phone," she drawled. "Hmm ... yuup, picture coming up!"

"Good!"

"Zebbie, I thought you didn't like that inside-out world?"

"I don't. But I wanted to check the film. If that picture is sharp—not fogged—you two knocked-up broads weren't hit by radiation where it counts. No fogging?"

"Not a bit, Cap'n Honey ... and brighter color every second. Here ... look."

"I don't need to see it. I've been there. My sole interest was in radiation. Jake, I'm beginning to have misgivings about this rotation schedule. The sampling called for fifteen. We've tried five, and only one—number four—was even vaguely homelike. One of the five had a serious radiation hazard to our wives and unborn kids. While we seem to have lucked through on that one—how about the next ten? So far, the pickings have been slim and the dangers seem excessive; rotations take us into some very weird universes. But we already know that Earth-analogs along tau- and teh-axis are quite Earth-like ...."

"With monsters," put in Hilda. "*Panki.*"

"On tau-axis, probably. Or almost certainly. But we haven't explored teh-axis. Jake, are we justified in exposing our wives to conditions we can't even imagine?

"Pop and Zebadiah, may I say something first?"

—— XXXII ——

Hilda

If Zebbie and my husband, Jacob, have a fault in common, it is over-protectiveness toward Deety and me. Me, I don't find this a fault. Having always been the runt of the litter, I have always been quite willing to accept protection from anyone larger than I am. But Deety sometimes rebels.

When Captain Zebbie asked Jacob whether or not they were justified in exposing us to unknown dangers of ten more universes, Deety stuck her oar in—and Zebbie tried to hush her.

Zebbie should have known better!

But he is just her husband and barely getting acquainted with her, whereas I've known her since her diaper days. Once, when I was taking care of her for Jane and Deety was, oh, possibly four, I started to tie her shoes for her. She pulled away from me. "Deety do!" she announced indignantly—and Deety did: a loose half-bow on one shoe that came apart almost at once, and a Gordian knot on the other that no Boy Scout ever heard of, but which required the Alexandrian solution; come her bedtime, I cut that shoestring with scissors.

It's been "Deety do!" ever since, backed by native genius and indomitable will.

Deety answered him, "Zebadiah, I realize that you're commanding this craft ... but you have asked the opinions of the rest of us up 'til now. Is there some reason to exclude Hilda and me from discussions of this decision?"

"Damn it, Deety, this is one that husbands *have* to decide!"

"Damn it, Zebadiah, this is one time when wives *must* be consulted!"

Our Zebbie was shocked. I feel certain that she had never before spoken to him that way. But he could not possibly show anger even if he felt it; Deety had simply matched him in manner and rhetoric.

Zebbie is no fool; he backed down from his impossible position at once. "I'm sorry, hon," he said soberly. "I shouldn't have spoken to you that way. I will make the final decision—I must; I can't avoid it. But I should get opinions from everyone. Go ahead, you have the floor."

"Yessir. I do have something to say, for Hilda and me—and Hilda will want to add her opinion, too. I know I speak for both of us when I say that we both appreciate that both you and Pop would each die bravely for either one of us ... and that you both feel this more intensely now that we are pregnant.

"But we have not been pregnant long enough to be physically handicapped by it. Our 'bulging bellies' do not, in fact, bulge, not yet. They *will* bulge, I know, and that gives us a deadline that we must meet. But for that very reason we will either sample those other ten rotation universes *today* ... or we will never sample them. Never!"

"Why do you say 'never,' Deety?"

"Because of timing and the deadline of our bellies. We've sampled five in less than an hour and, scary as some of it has been, I wouldn't have missed it for anything. We can take at least a quick look at the other ten in the next couple of hours or so. But if we break off at this point and start searching the axis for a suitable analog of Earth, there is no predicting how long it will take. We may check hundreds before we find what we are looking for—I don't know. But I offered that definition of the sort of world we must find in an attempt to make it possible to eliminate unsatisfactory worlds quickly.

"Let's say we find it. What then? We'll be strangers; we may not—probably not—even speak the local language. But we'll settle down somehow and Hilda and I will have our babies with skilled medical attention. Then what? Zebadiah, my beloved, are you going to be more willing to take two women and two babies into ten strange universes than you are to take us today *without* babies?"

"Uh ... I don't think that's quite the way to put it, Deety."

"How would *you* put it, sir? Are you possibly thinking that you and Pop might check out those ten while Hilda and I stay home and take care of the kids?"

"Well ... yes, I suppose I was. Something of that sort."

"Zebadiah, I married you for better, for worse, for richer, for poorer, in sickness and in health ... but I did not marry you to walk the widow's walk! I can't speak for Hilda on this point—but where you go, I go!—'til death do us part."

"Deety speaks for me," I said and shut up. I wasn't as dead set on seeing ten more universes as she seemed to be—but Sharpie durn well wasn't going to walk a widow's walk, nuther! And Deety had it figured out exactly. If Jacob and Zebbie didn't finish that schedule of rotations today, then they would both have that "far horizons" look in their eyes the rest of their lives, no matter how utopian a planet we found—and they wouldn't want to take us along. Not with kids. But Sharpie wasn't going to hold still for that. No, Sir!

"Deety, are you through?"

"Not quite, sir. I know that I sound like a spoiled brat. But I'm not and I don't want to leave that impression. All humans are created unequal, and anyone who can count above ten with his shoes on can see it. You are bigger and stronger than Pop; I am bigger and stronger than Hilda. I have the least number of years of experience; Pop has the most. Pop is a super-genius ... but he concentrates so hard and so long when he tackles a problem that he forgets to eat—unless he has a nursemaid to watch over him, as Mama did, as I did, and as Hilda now does. You, sir, are the most all-around practical man I've ever met, whether you are handling a duo, or dancing, or telling outrageous half-truths to get us all out of jams. Three of us have eight or nine earned degrees ... but Aunt Hilda is a walking encyclopedia just from having an insatiable curiosity and an extraordinary memory. Two of us are baby factories, two of us are not—but one man can impregnate fifty women ... or five hundred. I could go on listing the many ways that we are *un*-equal, no two of us are alike. But in one supremely important way all four of us are *equals*.

"We are all pioneers.

"Pioneer women go where their men go. Men by themselves are not pioneers; they can't be. Pioneer mothers share exactly the same dangers that pioneer fathers do ... and go on having babies while they do it. Babies were born on the *Mayflower*, lots of babies were born in covered wagons, and a lot of them died, too—men, women, and children. But those women didn't stay home where it was safe; they went along.

"Zebadiah, I am not asking to be taken to those next ten universes ...."

"You're not? It certainly sounds like it."

"Then you didn't listen to me, sir. Yes, certainly, I would *like* to finish sampling those rotation universes ... and I'm not scared off by the possible dangers. But I never asked for that and I don't ask now. It's my preference but not a demand. What I do demand I have already stated. *Where you go, I go.* Today ... and to the end of our lives. Unless you tell me to get out, you don't want me anymore. I have spoken."

"You certainly have, dear. Hilda?"

Fish or cut bait. Sharpie—what do you want to do? I didn't really care which way it fell; *any* universe was going to be strange. Deety had laid down the party line; I didn't want to fuzz things up by trying to amend it—so I answered instantly, "Deety speaks for me in every word she said. *I* have spoken."

"Jake? Back to my original question: 'Are we justified in exposing our wives to conditions we can't even imagine?' I'm asking my copilot for advice."

"Captain, you were the one who convinced me that it would be prudent to sample the universes accessible through rotation before searching for a satisfactory analog of Earth by translation."

"True. But that was before we sampled five of them."

"But Captain, I don't see how the situation has changed. We are going to be exposing our wives—and ourselves and our unborn children—to strange conditions no matter what we do. But an imaginable danger is not necessarily better than unimaginable one; it may be much worse. The planet we were forced to flee from has grave shortcomings and known dangers even before we accidentally tangled with *Panki*. No need to list them because we all know that the Four Horsemen of the Apocalypse were ready to ride again. But I can think of a *very* close analog of our home planet that would be *far* worse than Earth—one even if it didn't have a single *Pankera* on it."

"Go on."

"The analog in which Hitler got atomic weapons but we did not. It seems probable to me that there are several such analogs because I can think of several very small changes any one of which would have produced that result. Despite an aversion to their inhuman shape and odd color of blood, I can't see that *Panki* are more to be feared than

Hitler's SS Corps. In fact, the cold sadism of some human beings—not just stormtroopers; you can find it in any nation including the United States—is more frightening to me than *Panki*."

"Not to me!" (Deety and I blurted it out together.)

"But, my dears, we have no data whatever that the *Panki* are cruel. We got in their way; they tried to kill us. They did *not* try to torture us. There is a world of difference."

"Maybe there is, Pop, but I don't see it. Those things give me the creeps. I'll bet they'd torture us if they could."

"My very dear daughter, that's muddy thinking. How old are you?"

"Huh? Pop, you should know if anybody does."

"I do know. I was reminding you that you said that you have the fewest years of experience of any of us—and I have the most. I was years older than you are before I was cured of that sort of muddy thinking—and not by myself. By Jane, your mother. Hilda?"

"Jacob is telling you not to judge a book by its cover," I said crisply. "I learned it from Jane, too—as Jacob knows. A *Pankera's* external appearance tells us nothing about its capacity for the human vice of sadism. Jacob, I am not going to try to bring up your daughter; please don't ask me to again. It's Zebbie's job. If she needs it. Which she doesn't."

"Sorry, dear."

Captain Zebbie said, "I'm not bringing Deety up; she's playing Wendy to my Peter Pan—and I like it that way. Does anyone have anything *new* to add to the discussion? Speak up … very well; I've reached a decision. We will finish the scheduled rotations before exploring the axis. However … is anyone tired or hungry? Jake and I can put *Gay Deceiver* into a stable orbit around Mars with one small transition vector; we can call it a day anytime."

"Cap'n Zebbie, I'm still full of picnic."

"Me, too."

"Captain, I suggest that we continue. We may find a place to spend the night safely on the ground. If not, we can return here in nothing flat! (I silently applauded my husband. Zebbie had done a marvelous job of refitting *Gay Deceiver*, but lack of space made her freefall powder room barely "adequate" rather than satisfactory. With a Bonine pill in, I now enjoyed freefall. But gravity has its advantages.)

"Copilot, by your schedule, set to rotate."

"Set, sir!"

"All hands, stand by to rotate. Execute!"

We were no longer in a starry sky with a dead planet nearby: we were in sunlight and upside down. Then for a few seconds we were thrown around a bit, then we leveled off and my rump settled into the seat cushion, full weight. I heard Zebbie say, "Hello, Gay."

"Howdy, Zeb."

"Hold course, speed, and height-above-ground."

"Got it, Zeb."

"You're a Smart Girl, Gay."

"But we can't go on meeting like this. Over."

"Over and out, Gay. *Whew!* Time out while your skipper has a small nervous breakdown. Jake, what does that altimeter say? My eyes won't focus."

"Eleven klicks H-above-G. Pressure eight oh three millibars."

"Deety, what's the statistical probability of winding up this close to a planet without getting killed?"

"Impossible to calculate, Captain. Vanishingly small, I think. No data."

"Maybe you're dead and don't know it. Copilot, deadman switch routine; I'm going to check the air."

"Right away, Captain." Jacob got at the switch, unclamped it, held it high. "Ready, sir."

"Oh. Just a moment." Jacob still held up the deadman switch while he reset his dials. "One hundred thousand klicks straight up—set!"

"All hands but the captain will hold their breaths during air check. Jake, if I pass out, do the double scram at once. Then you'll have to go on holding your breath while you flush out the cabin. Damn it all, I should have rigged at least one oxygen mask—too many details, too little time."

I asked, "Captain?"

"What is it, Hilda? I'm busy."

"May I suggest, Cap'n Zebbie, that *I* be the canary? Not you."

"No."

"But it's part of my duties, sir! I am science officer—and most expendable. You are least expendable—and you know it."

There was a long, long silence—felt like hours but was probably not over a minute—while we cruised slowly over a beautiful countryside. Truly, I didn't feel particularly heroic about it; it looked far more like Earth than Barsoom had looked. I could see woods and a lake, and in the distance, what surely must be a village. But if it wasn't safe— truly, I would rather pass out with Zebbie and Jacob alert and at the controls than *not* pass out while Zebbie slumped in his seat. Certainly my husband would try to do it all … but we needed both pilot and copilot if there were danger … and we didn't need *me*.

Zebbie gave sort of a groan. "Copilot, I am not consulting you in this. Very well, you midget-sized pioneer mother, you are the guinea pig. Jake, Deety—and me—deep breaths, hyperventilate. Deety, you keep your eyes on Hilda. I'll count to three and open the air scoop. One … two … *three!*"

I felt my ears pop, so I took another breath. Smelled sweet—"I feel fine, Cap'n Zebbie. But I'll go on talking and breathing. The fresh air smells good. I don't feel the least bit woozy. Deety is beginning to turn red in the face; I don't know how much longer she can hold her breath. If this air has anything in it we aren't used to breathing, it must not be anything poisonous. I'm running out of things to chatter about; am I still making sense? I feel fine but Deety is about to pop. I think that—"

"Test completed. Copilot, clamp and stow deadman switch."

"Aye aye, sir." Jacob carefully replaced the clamp and tightened it, put it back into its hidey-hole. He sounded grumpy.

"Jake," said Zebbie, "if you feel like chewing me out, get on with it. We're on autopilot and you may consider yourself off duty. Get it off your chest."

"Captain, I have no criticism." That was what Jacob said but that wasn't what his tone or voice said—it was icy.

I decided that it was better for Jacob to be sore at me than at Zebbie. Deety and I are passengers, mostly; the true safety of all of us lay in Zebbie and Jacob getting along like ham and eggs. "Jacob!"

"Yes, Hilda?"

"Don't you dare get shirty with Zebbie! He made exactly the right decision … and it cost him a lot, I know! Zebbie would *always* rather take on all the dangers himself. That's his one weakness … because it could get all of us killed. I'm the littlest but that does not make me a child. I'm just as much a pioneer as any of us. When a job comes along that I can do best, I must be permitted to do it."

"I *said* I had no criticism."

"It was the way you said it. If you were captain, you would not have permitted me to do it. But I have to pull my weight in the boat, *too*—or I shouldn't be along. Zebbie realizes this—when he has his nose rubbed in it. But you don't. Not yet. Deety and I have to protect both of you as much as we can ... or you two won't be able to protect us when we need it. Now tell him you're sorry."

"Keep all seat belts fastened," Zebbie ordered. "I'm going to override on manual a bit so that we can see better. Jake, I won't use Hilda as our canary again; it upsets you too much."

"Now wait a minute, Captain! You made the correct decision. Hilda is right and I'm aware of it. It's just that my judgment isn't much good where Hilda is concerned. But she's right. It's all for one, and one for all—or it isn't anything."

"Pop, I'll be canary next time."

"No, daughter. You can come closer to replacing either Zeb or me than Hilda can—she knows it, I know it. And since she has the least body mass she's probably the most sensitive to bad atmosphere. Shorter reaction time."

"Let's all pipe down about it," growled Cap'n Zebbie, "and look this place over. We might want to stay here; it looks good from the air. But we won't be coming back if we leave ... unless Deety can debug a perfect program to get us back here safely. Jake, I must be losing my touch; I didn't get that split-second warning of danger."

I said, "Then maybe we weren't really in danger. Cap'n Zebbie, could we transit about thirty klicks straight up?"

"I suppose so. Any special reason, Science Officer?"

"I'm not sure, Cap'n Zebbie. But I want us to see more of this country as a whole. Which way is north? I can't see Gay's compass."

"North is off to our left."

"Is that sun rising or setting?"

"It's setting," said Deety. "I know."

Zebbie thought about it. "Then this planet has a retrograde motion. That can't hurt us."

"No, it can't. But it fits. Can we have that better look?"

"Copilot."

"Captain."

"Set thirty klicks straight up."

"Uh ... set, Captain."

"Execute."

Zebbie turned Gay's nose down; we all had a beautiful view out the front. Zebbie said, "Be durned. A big rectangular oasis completely surrounded by desert. Populated, too. That's a fair-sized town or small city right in the middle."

"Doesn't anyone recognize it? I do. From a map."

My Jacob said, "But Hilda dearest, this is an unexplored universe."

"Pop! It's the Land of Oz!"

"It certainly is," I agreed, and passed the binoculars to Deety. "The Yellow Brick Road, dear—running into Emerald City from the left."

"But, Hilda, that's ...."

"Don't say it's impossible, Jacob. Unless you want to say that Barsoom is impossible—and Cart and Thuv and Tommy Tucker. My own theory is that we've all been dead quite a piece now—killed in the parking lot back of my home. If so, I'm not dissatisfied. But Deety and I may be the first female ghosts in search of an obstetrician. Deety, how would you like to raise kids in the Land of Oz?"

"I'd love it!"

"Are you certain, hon? As I recall it, nobody ever dies in the Land of Oz ... yet the population doesn't get any bigger. I don't recall any babies being born in any of the Oz stories—I don't recall any babies. Or MDs—or hospitals. Jacob, you said that the inside-out universe had different physical laws. If Zebbie grounds *Gay Deceiver*, will we ever be able to leave? Oz works by magic. Not engineering."

"Deety, can Jake and I have a crack at those binox?"

"Right away, Zebadiah. Look at the Emerald City first; it really is loaded with emeralds. Or lots of green glass."

"Keep an eye on the altimeter, Jake."

Zebbie stared through the glasses until Jacob said, "Approaching fifteen klicks, Captain, and dropping fast."

"Your turn at the glasses, Jake. But let me put her into level flight, then you take her back up again."

Again we *whooshed* up high and Jacob studied the land below while we fell. Presently Zebbie leveled us out again and passed control back to Gay with instructions to cruise in a wide circle, one that carried us to the Great Sandy Waste in the south and the Impassable

Desert in the north and cut across the Yellow Brick Road in the east and over the Castle of the Tin Woodman in the west.

"Copilot. Your opinions, please?"

"Captain, Hilda's theory about us all being killed in the parking lot is probably least hypothesis by Occam's Razor. However, I don't feel dead and I decline to assume that I am dead. That leaves me forced to believe that this *is* the Land of Oz ... just as I was forced to believe in Barsoom. Everything fits. Even to the predominantly yellow vegetation on the east—I mean 'west,' as the compass rose is reversed, as Hilda noted. We now appear to be passing over the palace of Glinda the Good."

"Why are we passing over it?" asked Deety. "Why not ground Gay and pay a call on her? If we grounded at the Emerald City we might upset a lot of people. But I'm certain we can't upset Glinda."

"Copilot. Advice, please."

"I have no objection to grounding. Since Gay functions at this altitude, I assume that she will function on the ground. We can rotate from the ground as easily as from here. However, if I meet a living scarecrow I may go stark, raving mad. Besides ... that palace must have a bathroom in it."

"A good point. Although I would settle for a bush. Deety, dig out our flying suits. Or something. In Oz we must be fully dressed. No weapons. Shoes are optional."

— XXXIII —

Deety

Zebadiah didn't put us down right by the palace of Glinda the Good. He circled around and found a meadow clearing in woods around it, maybe a hundred kilometers from the palace and screened from it by tall elms and walnut trees.

I unstrapped, opened the bulkhead door, and crawled through to get our flying suits—and thought better of it. Aunt Hilda had followed me and headed straight for her own locker. I rolled into lotus (can't quite stand up back in there) and asked, "Aunt Hilda, what are you going to wear?"

"My best. The dress I got married in and the wedding ring Jacob had made for me in Helium."

"Jewelry?"

"Nothing from Barsoom. Probably what I wore that night but not as much."

Mama told me years ago that Aunt Hilda's instinct for clothes was unbeatable. I got the long dress I wore to hook Zebadiah, a pendant Pop had given me, my own wedding ring, my dancing slippers. Put my darling in mess jacket? No, but in formal tights topped off with a white silk bolero-shirt thing Tira and I had made for him when we were getting Aunt Hilda outfitted. Red sash, dancing pumps, socks to match, jockey shorts—yes, that was all he needed.

I slipped my dress over my head and wiggle-wormed forward, clutching the plunder to me. Our men were still in their seats, Gay's doors still closed. I asked, "Why the closed doors? It's warm and getting stuffy."

"Look out to the left and you'll see why. Hand me my flying suit."

I looked out to the left. A pretty little storybook cottage with a sign over the door: "WELCOME." It had not been there when we grounded. "I see," I agreed. "So pull on your shorts and your tights. Pop, Hilda has your trousers. Then we can open up."

"Deety, is that all you have to say?"

"Should I say more, sir? You have taken me to some very strange places. But in Oz I am not a stranger in a strange land; I've been thoroughly at home in Oz since I was a baby. I know what to expect."

"But damn it all …."

"Shush, Zebadiah. One does not say 'damn' in Oz. Not all sort of profanity or vulgarity. Vocabulary limited to that of the Mauve Decade. Mildest euphemisms or, better yet, no mention."

"Deety, I'm durned if I'll be anything but myself."

"You can be yourself, sir; you can never be anything else. But I am speaking professionally. One does not use FORTRAN to a computer that knows only Loglan. Can we open up now? Pop has his trousers on."

It was a pretty little cottage with a broad stoop and a pink climbing rose over the door—but it wasn't a house to live in, just one small room with a table and no other furniture. The table held a bowl of fruit, a pitcher of milk, and four tumblers. There was a door to the right and a door to the left; the one on the left had painted on it, quite small, a little girl in a poke bonnet, the other had a boy in a Buster Brown suit.

So Hilda and I headed for the poke bonnet. But I snatched a glass of milk and a bunch of Thompson seedless grapes on the way, and put on a milk moustache at once; I hadn't tasted milk, real milk, in ages. Delicious!

Hilda was drawing us a tub and had peeled off her dress. The window was open but it was up high, so I peeled off mine. Hilda didn't want milk but accepted some grapes. Then we made ourselves clean and "beautiful," i.e., we restored our Barsoomian hairdos but without the jewelry. Whatever it was we needed, that combination bath-and-dressing room had, right at hand, from a loofa sponge to a lipstick just Aunt Hilda's shade.

We could have spent three hours in there and enjoyed every minute, but we hurried and did it in forty-two minutes. Zebadiah looked beautiful (I knew he would; I'd picked that combo with care) and Pop looked just as smart in dark trousers and a richly simple Aloha shirt worn outside his trousers (I'd given him that shirt for his birthday and it was intended to hide a paunch that he no longer had).

There was a path from that meadow leading through the woods toward the palace. Pop, with Aunt Hilda on his arm, led off; we followed. Aunt Hilda was carrying her high-heeled shoes, so I stopped and took mine off, and glanced back toward the clearing. *Gay Deceiver* was there but the little cottage was missing, just as I expected. Zebadiah noticed it, too, but didn't say anything. His face was an interesting study in total lack of expression. "I'll put my slippers back on as we come out of the woods," I said. "They aren't tight, because I've always been used to going barefooted. But I can't walk on high heels until I reach a hard surface."

The grassy path debouched into the garden in front of the palace; the patch through it was hard, so Hilda and I put our shoes on. I didn't know much about architecture but Glinda's palace was more like a Norman château or a "Stately Home of England" than it was like the dreary castles on the Rhine—but it all had a fairyland perfection and grace, like the Taj. It would, of course.

As we started up the broad, sweeping, marble steps to the great doorway, Zebadiah stumbled. "What the hell?"

"Sssh!" I said. "Mind your language, dear. A magical staircase of course. Glinda would not make her guests have to climb to reach here. Just pretend that Escher designed these steps—he may have. Just look proud and walk as if they were level."

As we reached the broad landing two tall trumpeters stepped out of the great doorway, one on each side, raised their long trumpets, and sounded four flourishes. An old man with a merry grin, a fringe of whiskers, a shiny bald head, a wooden left leg, and wearing a sailor's oilskins, came out as the flourishes ended. I recognized him but wondered why he was here and not at Emerald City.

He took a pipe from his mouth and said, "Welcome to the palace of Glinda the Good! I'm Cap'n Bill. You, sir, are Doctor Burroughs the Wizard, with your wonderful wife the Princess Hilda. You must be Cap'n Zeb—howdy, Cap'n!—and everybody knows the Princess Deety; she's spent so much of her life in Oz. Howdy, Deety! Last time I seen you, you weren't more'n knee high to a tall duck. And now look at you! Almost up to my shoulder and *married!* Congratulations, Cap'n! Yer a lucky man!"

"I think so, Captain."

"I know so. Deety, Oz sends her best wishes and sez to tell you that you and your family are welcome to stay in the Royal Kingdom of Oz as long as you like."

"Please thank Her Royal Majesty for me, Cap'n Bill." (Actually I'm taller than Cap'n Bill now—but of course I'll always be a little girl to him. It's nice.)

"Oh, I will, I will! Come on inside, folks; we ain't formal here. Or I'm not. This ain't my reg'lar job; I'm standing this watch for a friend o' mine off on a little holiday." He took my hand; it was horny and felt like Zeb's—and just as gentle.

He led us inside, still holding my hand. "Where's Trot?" I asked.

"Around somewhere; you'll see her. Prob'ly picking out her best hair ribbon in your honor. Or maybe helping Betsy with Hank—little Betsy Curtis ain't happy unless she's workin' ... although Neptune knows that mule gets more attention than all the mules that ever came out of Missoura. This way to the library, friends."

How does one describe Glinda the Good? Everyone knows that she is tall and stately and blond and beautiful and never frowns and wears all day long what I would think of as beautiful evening gowns with sweeping trains. But those are just words. Perhaps it's enough to say that, just as Dejah Thoris is the most beautiful woman in the universe, the Sorceress is the most beautiful in hers.

She was surrounded by her bevy of all the most beautiful girls from all over Oz, any one of them a beauty contest winner. But Glinda outshone them all without trying. The name of the Egyptian Queen Nefertiti means both "beautiful" and "good," all in one word; I think that explains Glinda.

She got up from her Great Book of Records, where she spends most of her time, and glided toward us—kissed Hilda first, kissed me and said, "Welcome home, Deety!" and I was so choked up I couldn't talk; I just curtsied. She offered a hand each to Zebadiah and Pop while greeting them; they bowed simultaneously and kissed her hands.

She waved at chairs (that hadn't been there a moment before) and invited us to sit down. Zebadiah whispered to me out of the side of his mouth, "You seem to own this place."

"Not really," I whispered back. "But I guess I've lived in Oz longer than anywhere else"—which was true; Mama and Pop lived at several campuses while I was growing up ... but I always took Oz along with me wherever we moved, so I was never lonely.

"Well ... I'm glad you made me dress up."

We were introduced to each of Glinda's girls and each one curtsied; it felt like being home in Helium—except that these girls weren't slaves in any sense, no indentures. When I stopped to think about it, I couldn't recall that money was ever used in Oz; it didn't have an "economy."

The girls were beautifully dressed, each differently but each dress was predominately the color of her own country, Munchkin blue, Gillikin purple, Winkie yellow or gold, a few in green. One girl waiting to be introduced was in red—Quadling, of course, where we were—looked familiar. That glossy black hair and dark skin with rosy cheeks—I said to her, "Is your name Fig?"

She was startled. "Why, yes, Your Highness—how did you know?" She dropped a curtsy quickly.

"I've been here before; ask Captain Bill. I'm not 'Your Highness,' I'm just Deety. Do you have a friend named Larlo?"

"Yes, Your ... yes, Deety. But she's not here now; she's at the College of Professor Wogglebug." Then she had to hurry to get back to her place in line. I made a mental note to tell Tira about it ... someday.

I can't tell all about everyone we met at Glinda's palace; there were too many and more kept arriving. Everyone seemed to expect us and seemed pleased to see us. Pop did not go stark, raving mad when he met the Scarecrow because he was already deep in conversation with Professor Wogglebug and with Oz the Great, Royal Wizard to Queen Ozma—in fact, Pop was just barely polite about it, shook hands and said, "Howd'you do, Mr. Scarecrow," and went right on talking to H. M. Wogglebug T. E. and the Wizard. I'm not sure he even looked at the Scarecrow. He was saying, "You put it very neatly, Professor. I wish my friend Professor Mobyas Toras were here to hear your formulation of it. If we set alpha equal to zero, it is obvious that ...."

I wandered off then, because when Pop says, "It is obvious that ..." what is really obvious is that Deety should leave. Once I pointed out to him that he had filled up five pages proving that zero equals zero. He sulked for days. Since then I've avoided his field of mathematics, and he's not interested in the simple field I'm in ... other than to shove calculations at me sometimes and ask me to program them and push them through a computer.

Dinner was in the banquet hall and the crowd of guests exactly filled it ... which of course it would because Glinda's banquet hall is always just the right size for the number of persons eating there—or there and not eating, as the case may be, for Jack Pumpkinhead, Tik-Tok, the Tin Woodman, the Sawhorse, the Scarecrow, and other people who didn't eat were seated there, too, and also people who weren't people people but were animal people; the Cowardly Lion, the Hungry Tiger, the Woozy, the King of the Flying Monkeys, Hank, Toto, and a beautiful long-haired cat with supercilious manners.

Glinda the Good was seated at the head of the table at one end and Queen Ozma of Oz was at the head of the table at the other end. Pop was on Glinda's right and Zebadiah was on Ozma's right. The Wizard of Oz was on Glinda's left, and Professor Wogglebug was on Ozma's left. Aunt Hilda and I were opposite each other at the middle of the long table. She had the Tin Woodman on one side and the Scarecrow on the other and was doing her best to charm both of them and both were trying to charm her and all three were succeeding.

I had three dinner companions. I had started out with two, the Cowardly Lion and the Hungry Tiger. The Lion ate what the others who ate did but the Tiger had a bowl of cornflakes the size of a small washtub and ate from it very daintily with a spoon to match the bowl. The Cowardly Lion and I had just started on our seafood cocktails when this cat brushed against my leg to get my attention, looked up and said, "You smell like a cat person. Make me a lap, I'm coming up"—and jumped.

I asked, "Eureka, do you have Dorothy's permission?"

"What a silly way to talk. Dorothy has to get *my* permission. Feed me the lobster first, then the shrimp. You may have the last piece of shrimp for yourself."

The Hungry Tiger put down his big spoon and said, "Highness, may I abate this Nuisance for you?"

"Don't trouble yourself, Old Boy," the Lion said, "I'll abite it instead, in one bite. But do please pass the tabasco sauce; cats have so little taste."

"Pay no attention to those peasants, wench, and get on with the lobster. Animals should not be allowed to eat at the table."

"Look who is calling whom an animal," growled the Cowardly Lion.

"It's not an animal, Leo," the Hungry Tiger objected. "It's an insect. Highness, I'm a vegetarian, usually—but I would be happy to break over this one and slice it into my cornflakes. Shall I?"

"Dorothy wouldn't like it, Rajah."

"You have a point, ma'am. Shall I ask Toto to chase it out?"

"Eureka may stay. I don't mind."

"Wench, the correct answer is 'I am honored.' Ignore these jungle beasts; they are not cats. Be it known *Felis domesticus* has been civilized more generations than all you lesser breeds combined. As my serene ancestress, Bubastis, Goddess of the Nile, was wont to say: 'Where Cat is, *is* civilization.' Hurry up with that lobster."

So I hurried. Eureka accepted each bit daintily, barely flicking my fingertips with her scratchy tongue. At last she averted her mouth. "Don't overdo it; I'll tell you when I require more. Scratch behind my left ear—gently. I shall sing, then I shall sleep. Maintain a respectful silence."

I did as ordered. Eureka purred very loudly. As the buzzing gave way to soft snores I slowly stopped scratching. I had to eat with one hand then, as the other was needed to keep her from falling.

As Aunt Hilda has placed a full record of that evening in Gay by interviewing all of us and combining it, I will stick to parts that mattered. After the rest had gone home or retired to their rooms, we four were invited into the library. It was smaller than it had been, cozy, as Glinda's girls had gone to their rooms. Glinda was at her Great Book of Records as we were ushered in; she smiled and bowed without getting up as we sat down.

"Friends," she said, "Doctor, Captain, Princess Hilda, and Deety, I will save time by telling you that, during the dancing, I conferred with Ozma, the Wizard, and Professor Wogglebug. I had already studied the Records of your strange adventures and read a resume to them before we discussed your problems. First, let me say that Ozma repeats her invitation. All of you are welcome to stay here forever; you will find hospitality wherever you go. Deety of course knows this, and Princess Hilda knows it, too, although she is not quite as sure of it as Deety is.

"But to reassure you gentlemen, the Wizard and I have made the Land of Oz one quarter of an inch wider in all directions, a change too small to be noticed. But you, Doctor, as a geometer, will recognize that this provides ample *lebensraum* for four more good people, as well as for your sky chariot Miss *Gay Deceiver*. A quarter of an inch, Captain, is six and thirty-five hundredths millimeters.

"While we were about it, on the advice of Professor Wogglebug, we made one small change in Miss *Gay Deceiver* ...."

Zebadiah gave a start and looked very upset. Of course Gay was his sweetheart long before I was; he took care of her just as carefully as he took care of me. But he should have trusted Glinda.

Glinda smiled warmly at him. "Don't be alarmed, Captain; no harm has been done to the structural integrity or the functioning of your beloved craft. When you notice it—you *will* notice it—if you do not like the change, all you need to do is to say aloud, 'Glinda, change Miss *Gay Deceiver* back the way she was.' I will read your wish here in my Book and will carry out your wish. But I do not think that you will ask me to do this. That is not a prophecy; a good witch does not prophesy. But it is my firm opinion.

"Now to major matters— There are no *Panki* in Oz. Should one ever be so foolish as to come here, I would know it at once from my Book, and it would be ejected into the Deadly Desert. Concerning what would happen to it there, the less said, the better—but evil is not tolerated in Oz.

"As to the problem of *Panki* in your home world, it does not lie in Ozma's jurisdiction. My own powers are very limited there. While my Great Book of Records tells me what happens there, it does not distinguish between *Panki* disguised as human beings and human beings who, by their own nature, are evil. I could cast a spell over all four of you, which would keep you away from them. Do you wish that?"

Pop glanced at Zebadiah; my husband said, "Just a moment, Glinda the Good. I don't know much about spells. Just what does that mean?"

"Spells are always literal, Captain; that's why they can cause so much trouble. I rarely use them. This one means what I said: you would be kept away from any *Pankera*."

"In that case we couldn't recognize one, could we? Or get close enough to destroy it."

"I think you would have to devise a way to do both at a distance. Spells do not reason, Captain. Like computers, they operate literally."

"Could they recognize *us*? Booby-trap us? Bomb us?"

"I do not know, Captain. My Book records only what they have done, not what they may do. Even then, as I have said, the Records do not unmask a disguised *Pankera*. Therefore I know very little about them. Do you wish the spell? You need not decide at once. If you remain in Oz, you won't need it."

I blurted out, "We ought to stay here!"

Glinda smiled at me, but it was not a happy smile. "Deer Deety—you have decided not to have your baby?"

"Huh? I mean, 'Excuse me, Glinda?'"

"You have been in Fairyland more than the others. You know that your little girl will not be born here … just as no one ever dies here."

Aunt Hilda spoke up so quickly I couldn't get a word in. "Glinda, thank you very much but I will not be staying."

I gulped. "I won't be staying either, Aunt Glinda." I didn't look at Zebadiah.

"So I strongly suspected. Do you want my advice, dear?"

"Yes. Certainly!"

"Having decided to be a woman and not a little girl like Dorothy or Trot, leave here quickly … lest you be tempted to stay in Fairyland forever."

Pop glanced at Zebadiah, then said, "Madame Glinda, we'll be leaving in the morning. We are grateful for your lavish hospitality … but I think that is best."

"I think so, too, Doctor. But remember: Ozma's invitation stands. When you are weary of the outside world, come here for a holiday … and by all means bring your children. Children are happy here and never get hurt. Oz was designed for children."

"We will, we certainly will!"

"Is there anything more to discuss? If not …."

"Just a second!" put in Aunt Hilda. "You told Deety—will you tell *me?*"

Glinda smiled. "My Book states that you are growing a boy."

—— XXXIV ——

Zebadiah

I didn't sleep with Deety that night. I didn't plan it that way; it just happened. A footman showed me to a room; Deety and Hilda were still standing at the top of the stairs (more magical stairs—okay as long as you don't look down) and talking excitedly, with Jake nearby.

When I saw that the room had only a single bed, not even twin beds, the footman had vanished. When I stepped outside, so had Deety and Hilda and Jake, and the upper hall was dark. So I said a word one mustn't use in Oz and went back into my assigned room. Even a single bed looked inviting; it had been a long day. I went to sleep at once.

Glinda had breakfast with us, in what seemed to be the banquet hall, considerably shrunken. The food in Helium was wonderful but I had almost forgotten how good ham and eggs and toast and fresh orange juice can be. I drank three cups of coffee and felt ready to wrassle alligators.

Glinda kissed Deety and Hilda goodbye at the top of those Escher steps, and Jake and I bent over her hands. She wished us good luck ... which probably counted for more from her. Oz may not be a place to live but it was a wonderful place to visit. Once we entered the woods, the gals took off their shoes.

Gay Deceiver looked good in the morning sunlight. Tik-Tok was standing at her nose. "Good mor-ning," he said. "I have been con-ver-sing with Miss Gay De-cei-ver all night. She is a ve-ry Smart Girl."

"Howdy, Zeb."

"Howdy, Gay. What have I told you about picking up strange men?"

"You've told me nothing, Zeb. And Tik-Tok is not a strange man. He is a gentleman, which is more than I can say for some people."

"Tru-ly, Cap-tain, I meant no im-propri-e-ty."

"Just kidding, folks. Thanks for keeping Gay company, Tik-Tok."

"It was a plea-sure and a pri-vi-lege. I ar-ranged with the night watch-man to wind me up each hour on the hour in or-der that our con-ver-sa-tion be not a-brupt-ly ter-mi-na-ted."

"Smart of you. Thanks again and we'll see you again. We'll be back for a visit, first chance. Gay, open up."

"You didn't say 'Please,'" my autopilot answered, but she opened her doors.

"I am de-ligh-ted to hear that you are re-tur-ning. Miss Gay De-cei-ver and I have much in com-mon."

"So I see. All hands, man the car and prepare for space. Jake, I think we had better wear flight suits this time; we don't know where we'll pop out next."

"Captain, I agree."

Sharpie said goodbye to Tik-Tok, went inside. Deety not only said goodbye but kissed his copper cheek—I'm sure Deety would kiss a pig if the pig would hold still for it (and if he didn't, I would turn him into sausage; kissing Deety is a treat not to be scorned).

Hilda reappeared, still in evening gown. "Deety, come in here. Hurry!"

I shook hands with Tik-Tok (odd!) and suggested that he back off a little. Then I went inside. No sign of our wives—I called to them, "Shake it up in there. I want my jumpsuit."

Deety called out, "Zebadiah, wiggle your way through the bulkhead."

"I can't change my clothes back there."

"Please, dear. I need you."

When Deety says she needs me, I go. But I got out of that fancy white shirt and scarlet sash first—cramped back there. So I wiggled through, and the space didn't seem as cramped as it had been when I was working on it in the jeddara's garden. I could almost stand up. "Where are you?"

"In here. Port side," came Deety's somewhat muffled voice. I turned around, banging my head on the overhead, and found a door where a door shouldn't be. I had to stoop quite a lot to get through it, but once through it I could stand up. A small room, slightly bigger than a telephone booth—a door aft, a door forward, Sunbonnet Sue to the left, Buster Brown to the right. Deety opened the door on the left. "Come look!"

A luxurious dressing room and bathroom for ladies—"It's the same one as in the 'Welcome' cottage," said Deety, "except that the window is closed and frosted. It doesn't open. But the air is fresh."

I said, "Hmmm ...." Then I added, "Well, well!" I was just filled with witty comments. But I didn't have anything for an encore, so I checked out Buster Brown. Yes, the same bathroom that Jake and I had used the day before. Not as fancy as the ladies' room and a shower instead of a tub. Well, maybe the gals would let me use their tub occasionally; when you're tired, a hot soak beats a shower.

Jake stuck his head in. I said, "Well, Perfesser, give me the benefit of your wisdom."

"Zeb, I'm fresh out."

"Copilot—your advice, please. Is this craft ready for space?"

"Captain, I don't know."

"Let's check the outside. Carefully."

We did. We went over the monoque shell with eyes on figures, both port and starboard. That car was absolutely unblemished—outside. But from the opened doors I heard the sound, somewhat muffled, of a toilet flushing.

Nevertheless, ten minutes later, we were settling into our seats. I asked, "Did anyone leave anything in our new annex?"

"Both Hilda and I hung up our dresses. There's plenty of hanging space."

"Deety, do you realize that that confounded magical space warp will probably go back wherever it came from the instant we leave here?"

"Want to bet? Glinda the Good wouldn't pull that sort of a trick on us."

"It's your dress, dear. But don't *anyone* leave anything essential in there during maneuvers. Standing order, now and forever. Gay, are you going to go on being talkative on your own?"

"Zeb, once I'm back on watch, I'll be strictly business. But a girl is entitled to a night out once in a while."

"You're a Smart Girl, Gay."

"So Tik-Tok told me, Zeb. Over."

"Over and out, Gay. All hands, report readiness for space."

"I took a pill, Cap'n. Seat belt tight."

"Seat belt fastened, Zebadiah. And I fastened all three bathroom doors."

"Belt fastened, starboard door seal checked."

"Port door seal checked. Copilot, set transition, h-axis, One hundred thousand klicks upward."

"A hundred thousand kilometers straight up, minimum-range scale vernier setting four. Set."

"Execute!"

I tilted her nose down right after transit. Out the screen was a very Earth-like planet but I couldn't recognize any continental shapes—sort of murky all over. "Science Officer, hand the copilot the binox, then unstrap and find out whether or not our new wing is still attached."

"Aye aye, Cap'n Zebbie."

Jake inspected carefully by binoculars. "Captain, I can make out Oz very easily. But it's hazy everywhere else." He handed me the glasses.

"Jake, as soon as your eyes adjust, take a look at the stars." I inspected the planet myself. I thought I could make out polar caps but there was haze everywhere but Oz. By focusing carefully I could see Emerald City.

Jake said, "Captain, it's our own universe."

"It is, eh? On which side of Orion is the Bull?"

"Why, on … Jesus, Allah, and Zoroaster! It's turned inside out!"

"Yeah, but not the way that other inside-out place was. Like Oz itself. East for west. Deety, is there anything odd about duration here?"

"Doesn't *feel* odd. But I'm going to have to reset my head sometime. Or someplace. I realize we are on a different time axis. But it's been over a century since those three little girls moved to Oz. I don't know what it feels like to them, and I carefully didn't ask. Did anybody else notice that there were no clocks and no calendars?"

"Cap'n Zebbie!"

"Yes, Hilda."

"Our new plumbing works just dandy, though I can't see how. But be careful going in there during freefall … because it's not freefall beyond the first door; the floor is *down*. One-gravity, it feels like. I did a spectacular somersault."

"Hilda my love, are you hurt?"

"Not a bit, Jacob. But next time I'll hang on to something and pull myself down even with the deck, and slither in."

"Science Officer, secure those doors, return to your seat, and strap down. Copilot, once Hilda reports, set your next rotation by your schedule."

"I fastened the doors as I came out. Or back in, maybe. And now I'm dogging the bulkhead door. Okay, I'm strapping down. But where are the binoculars?"

"Deety stowed them. All hands, stand by to rotate."

"Rotation set, Captain."

"Execute."

Another totally black one … I said, "Deety, I'm going to tumble first. Then it's your turn to check the new plumbing."

"It is not Deety's turn! I'm science officer and that includes hygiene, plumbing, and space warps."

"Jake, do you have any influence over her?"

"Not much, Captain."

I switched out the instrument lights. We went through one full tumbling pigeon—null report from everyone. So I switched back on the instrument lights and added the cabin lights. "Science Officer, check our time-space warp. But do be careful, Sharpie. Set up the next rotation, Jake. It's universe number eight coming up, isn't it? Third of the second group."

"Correct, Skipper. One more after that and we return to home base. Near Mars, I mean. Rotation set. Ready to go once Hilda is in her seat and strapped down."

Sharpie was back fairly promptly. "I stopped to brush my teeth. Didn't have a chance to after breakfast. Cap'n Zebbie, it's awful dark outside but there is sunlight coming in through both bathroom windows. Riddle me that." She added, "Seat belt fastened, all three doors fastened."

"You riddle it; you're the science officer. Stand by to rotate. Execute."

I got her leveled out rather hastily. "Copilot, H-above-G and pressure!"

"Thirteen hundred klicks, nine hundred nineteen millibars."

"Too close! Jake, any more of those hair-breadth misses and I'm going to retire and take up tatting. Where are we? I can't see a damn thing. I'm on instruments."

"We're over water, Captain, with a light fog. Not very thick, I can see a shoreline to starboard."

I turned Gay to the right, picked out the shoreline myself, was able to shift to visual. I've held IFR rating for years but I'm always easier with a horizon I can see. Gay's wings were already spread; I held her on an easy hundred knots and placed her on automatic. "We leave this kite sealed for now; I won't check the air without going up pretty high."

"Sail ho!"

"Where away, Sharpie?"

"On the starboard bow and down on the water, of course. A real sail—a sailing ship."

Durn if it wasn't. A square rigger right out of the eighteenth century, with a high forecastle and sterncastle. I dipped down for a better look. I wasn't afraid of it; people who sailed ships like that didn't use guided missiles—or so I kept telling myself.

It was a pretty sight. I dropped the starboard wing so that we could have a good look. But we must have been a "pretty sight" to them, for there were sailors rushing around and the helmsman apparently lost his senses completely. He let her get away from him and she fell into irons, with her canvas flapping foolishly. Not wanting to get the poor fellow keelhauled, I leveled off and got out of there, headed for land.

Jake said, "Good god, Captain, you scared me silly."

"Why, Jake? They were scared, sure—but surely you aren't scared of black powder cannon?"

"No, I'm not. But you almost put the wing on this side into the water."

"Don't be silly, Jake; I was above two hundred meters. Well, maybe a hundred and fifty when I did that steep turn to let us see better. But plenty of room."

"Take a look at your altimeter. And pressure."

I looked. The radar altimeter stated that we were nineteen meters above the water; I had to change scales to read it closely. Pressure showed slightly over a thousand millibars—a sea-level high. So I promptly took us up to a thousand meters.

"Copilot, how did I make that error? I sure don't want to make it again."

"I don't know, Captain. I can see that wing tip; you can't from your seat. When it looked to me as if you might cut the water, I looked at the instruments. I was about to yell when you straightened out."

"Jake, I was flying seat of my pants by the ship's masts. I would swear I never got within three hundred meters of that ship, on the slant. That would put me plenty high up for a calm day. That water barely had whitecaps."

Sharpie asked, "Don't you recognize the place, Cap'n Zebbie?"

"Sharpie, don't tell me you've been here before?"

"Only in books, Zebbie. But several times in books. A child's version in about third grade. Then a more detailed version in junior high. Then I finally laid hands on the complete unexpurgated eighteenth century version, which was pretty racy for the age I was then. I still find it pleasantly bawdy."

"Sharpie, whatever are you talking about?"

Jake answered me. "Captain, what sort of ship could cause you to think you were high in the air when in fact you were about to polevault into the sea on your starboard wing?"

"I give up."

"One manned by sailors fifteen centimeters high."

I thought about it. We were approaching land now; I carefully climbed to a thousand klicks by instrument and told Gay to hold us there—although it seemed much higher. "If any of you run across Dean Swift, will you please give him a swift kick in the rump for me?"

Deety asked, "Zebadiah, do you suppose the land of the giants—Brobdingnag—is on this same continent?"

"I hope not."

"Why not, dear? It should be fun."

"Because we don't have time to waste on either Lilliputians or giants. Neither would have obstetricians able to take care of you two … and the level of medical art would be eighteenth-century. Jake, get ready to take us up a hundred thousand klicks. Get set to rotate immediately thereafter. Does anyone have any rational theory about what has been happening to us? Or am I simply struggling with my straitjacket in our friendly neighborhood shrink factory?"

"I have a theory of sorts, Zebbie."

"Give, Sharpie."

"Don't laugh—because, as I recall, you yourself told me that you and Jacob had discussed the heart of it, the idea that human thought existed as quanta. I don't know quanta from Qantas Air Lines, but I've been told that a quantum is an indivisible unit. You told me that you and Jacob discussed the possibility that imagination had its own sort of indivisible units or quanta—you called them 'fictions'—or was it ficta? Either way, the notion was that every story ever told—or to be told, if there is a difference—existed in reality somewhere in the Number of the Beast."

"But Hilda my love, that was merely abstract mathematics!"

"Jacob, Mobyas Toras regarded this car as abstract mathematics ... until he rode in it. And didn't you tell me that the human body itself is merely complex equations of wave forms? That was when I bit you—I don't mind being a wave format; waves are pretty; I bit you for using the adverb 'merely.'"

"Zebadiah, there is a city over on the left, not very far. Can't we look at it before we leave here?"

"Deety, I'm going to make you decide that yourself. You saw what a panic we caused in that toy-sized ship. Imagine yourself to be not more than fourteen centimeters tall and living in that city. Along comes a great sky monster and dives on your city. Would you like it? How many will faint? How many will die of heart failure? How many of those little people are you willing to kill to satisfy your curiosity?" I added, "To those little people we are monsters worse than *Panki*."

"Oh, dear! You're right, Zebadiah—dismally right. Let's get out of here."

"Copilot, set to transit straight up one hundred thousand klicks."

"Transition h-axis, positive, vernier four-set."

"Execute." I continued, "We can sit here for a while; we're too far away to frighten them or even be seen. Sharpie, you have the floor. We aren't going anywhere until we've heard your theory and discussed it. Jake, I'm not sure I'm willing to risk another rotation anyhow. I've been scared silly four times by narrow escapes in rotations. I know how to translate safely from one Earth-analog to the next; just use plenty of elbow room. But these rotations are making me white-haired—I can't *plan* for elbow room and I'm not getting it. The laws of chance are going to catch up with me ... when I thought the odds were stacked strongly in our favor."

"Zebbie, I don't think the laws of chance have anything to do with it. I don't think we have been in any danger in any rotation."

"So? Sharpie, you know how to drive a duo. I'm about to swap seats with you ... as quickly as I can move this seat forward its maximum so that you can reach all its controls."

"No, no! I—"

"Chicken!"

"Zebbie, I don't have your ESP for danger. I'll take a watch at the controls if you tell me to ... although I certainly don't have your skill at flying. But I'll just be the pilot on watch; you must be captain—because your hunches are part of why I say that I don't think the so-called laws of chance are relevant."

"Sharpie, statistical laws are the most firmly established of all natural laws."

"Do they apply in the Land of Oz?"

"Uh .... Damned if I know! *Touché!*"

"Captain, Hilda has not expressed it as a mathematician would; nevertheless, I agree with her. To call the equations used in statistics in our home universe 'laws of nature' is a grave misnomer. Those equations measure the degree of our ignorance. When I flip a coin and say that the chance of heads or tails is fifty-fifty, I am simply declaring total ignorance as to the outcome. But if I knew all the conditions—I don't—the outcome could be precalculated by macromechanics. But we have already experienced at least two universes having physical laws quite unlike those of our home universe."

"Three, Jacob. Lilliput makes three."

"I don't quite follow you, my dear."

"The cube-square law that runs all through biology does not apply here; it has its own. I can state flatly that a human brain can't be placed in a space the size of a thimble by our laws. But we're getting away from the theory Zebbie told me to expound. Shall I go on?"

"Yes," I ruled. "Everybody shut up but Sharpie. I've been the worst offender; I'm zipping my lip. Sharpie—proceed."

"All right. It's not chance that we have been in three universes—Barsoom, the Land of Oz, and Lilliput—in ... less than twenty-four hours, isn't it, Deety?"

"Less than sixteen, Aunt Hilda, from leaving the Bay of Blood to arriving here."

"Thanks, hon. And that those three all are 'fictional' universes—I have to call them that for lack of a better word—well-known to each of us. By chance—and again I don't have a good word but it's not 'chance'—all four of us are addicted to fanciful stories: fantasy. Science fiction. Call it what you wish. But we all like the same sort of stories. How many of us like detective stories?"

"Some of 'em—not all of 'em," said Deety.

"My sole loyalty is to Sherlock Holmes," said Hilda's husband.

"Waste of time. The puzzles are too simple, the writing is usually atrocious. I prefer mathematics."

"I'd like to try an experiment," Hilda went on. "All of us write down the twenty stories you have enjoyed the most, as nearly as you can think of them. Or groups of related stories—the Oz books would count as one, so would the Edgar Rice Burroughs Mars series, and so would the four voyages of *Gulliver's Travels*. But don't list those three; we've been there. And don't discuss it or compare notes. Make them stories you've read and re-read 'til you wore out the books. And if anybody puts down *War and Peace*, I'll know he's cheated; some people read that one once, hardly anyone reads it twice—and most people bog down unless it's a much-cut version. Put down things you re-read for pleasure when you are too tired to tackle a new book." She added, "Anybody need pencil and paper?"

"Sharpie, is it cheating to ask how you mean to use this?"

"No, Cap'n Zebbie. If my theory is right, the next time we rotate and find ourselves close to a planet, it will turn out to be the scene of a story or group of stories that appears on all four lists. And we'll be high enough that you will have plenty of time to level off *Gay Deceiver* ... but close enough that we can ground if we want to. But we will never rotate into a mass or into any other danger that you and Jacob can't handle by some sort of scram. This isn't chance; we haven't been dealing with chance. Barsoom startled me. The Land of Oz surprised me a little. But Lilliput didn't surprise me at all; I expected it. Or at least some place that all of us knew through stories."

"How about the empty universes?"

"I don't know. Maybe they are places about which stories will be written or maybe the stories have already been told but they aren't stories that are favorites of us four, so we don't emerge close to their scenes. But those are just guesses—no data. So far as my theory is concerned such universes are 'null'—they don't count one way or the other. We'll find *our* universes."

"Sharpie, you have just invented multiperson solipsism. I didn't think it was mathematically possible."

"Captain, *everything* is mathematically possible. Mathematics has no content."

"Thanks, Jacob. Zebbie, 'solipsism' is a buzz word. I'm simply saying that we've stumbled onto *The Door in the Wall*, the one that leads to the land of heart's desire. I don't know how we did it and my buttonhead can't use fancy philosophical rationalizations. I see a pattern, that's all—I'm not trying to explain it. It just *is*."

"How does that hollow world fit your theory?"

"Well, Deety called it Pellucidar ...."

"It was!"

"... but I've read dozens of stories about worlds underground, and I'll bet everyone else here has, too. Jules Verne, S. Fowler Wright, H. G. Wells, C. L. Moore, Lovecraft—all the great masters of fantasy have taken a crack at it one or more times. Please, can we stop talking and work on those lists? I realize that we don't fall very fast way out here—but I would like to have all four lists before we rotate again."

We all got silently to work. I changed attitude so that Lilliput's planet was dead ahead and told Gay to hold it there so I'd notice any gross change in distance. The planet looked very small, as if we were a million kilometers out from it rather than one hundred thousand—which was only reasonable. I wrote down "the Dorsai yarns."

At last Deety announced, "I'm through, Aunt Hillbilly." She passed over her list, kept quiet.

Soon after, her father passed back his list. "Don't count those I've lined out, dear—I had trouble holding it down to twenty."

"Twenty is arbitrary, Jacob. I can leave the extras in."

"No, dear, after careful thought I'm sure that the four I eliminated, much as I like them, do not stand as high in my favor as the twenty I retained."

After a short wait I announced, "Sharpie, I'm stuck at seventeen. Got a baker's dozen more in mind, but no real choice among them."

"Seventeen will do ... if they are your prime favorites."

"They are."

Hilda accepted my list, ran her gaze down it. "A psychoanalyst would have a wonderful time with these four lists."

"Wait a half! Sharpie, I told the *truth*. If you're going to let a shrink see those lists, I want mine back. Now."

"Zebbie darling, I wouldn't do that to you or any of us. I'm all three of the Three Little Monkeys. But doesn't anyone mind if I copy off the ones I haven't read? I apparently missed some goodies."

No one objected; she added, "I need a few minutes to tally the score."

"Take as long as you like," I said. "Need help?"

"No, and it won't take long. I've tallied a 'one' after all on my list. I've checked Deety's against mine and tallied a 'two' wherever they matched, and added to the bottom of my list, with one vote tallied against each, those she picked but I didn't. Not very many, Deety;

your taste and mine almost match. Now I'm doing the same with Jacob's list, and tallying threes and twos and ones. Then Zebbie and we'll wind up with a four-vote list—unanimous!—and a list of stories or related stories with three votes each—and a list with two, and a list with one."

Hilda kept very busy for some minutes, then took a fresh sheet, listed the stories or story groups that had been picked by all of them, folded it three times. "This should be in a sealed envelope. To establish my reputation as a fortune-teller. Captain Zebbie, there are nine *soi-disant* fictional universes listed. Any close approach we make by rotation should be near one of five of them—because I have lined out the four we have already visited."

" 'Four?' You included Pellucidar? I didn't vote for it."

"No, Cap'n. Pellucidar got only two votes. I stick to my theory that the inside-out world is a composite scene of all underground fantasies. But our vote identified that third universe—the blinding lights, the one that worried you about radiation."

"The hell you say!"

"Or I think it did. Doctor Isaac Asimov's *Nightfall*. Only he wasn't a doctor then; he wrote it in his teens. I rather expected his Foundation stories to make it but got only three votes. Too bad, because his library planet might have been able to tell us what the *Panki* are, where they come from—and how to beat them."

"My fault, Aunt Hillbilly. Pop told us I should read that series ... but I got caught up in the pressure of work and never did. I'm sorry."

"Sharpie dear, better hand that list to Deety; she won't peek ... whereas I might. Copilot, shall I rotate? The science officer has me half-convinced that we can get away with it ... so let's do it before I lose my nerve. Fourth and last universe in the second group, isn't it?"

"Yes, Captain. Verniers set to rotate."

"Anybody as chicken as I am, speak now or forever hold your peace! ... Isn't *anybody* going to get me out of this? ... *Execute!*"

—— XXXV ——

Zebadiah

G*ay Deceiver* was right-side-up and no more than five hundred meters above a sunlit, gentle countryside. I moved quickly, set her to cruise slowly in a circle. "Are we back on Oz? Looks like it to me. Jake—check your setting."

"Not Oz, Captain. Impossible. Different universe. I've stuck to the schedule."

"Sharpie?"

"If it's one of the five—and it ought to be—then it's—" Hilda broke off, wrote a word on the bottom of a fresh sheet, tore it off, folded it, and handed it to me. "Stick this in your pocket, look at it later. This place is safe."

I tucked it away. "Well … I'll ground us in that meadow ahead. We'll check the air while we're down. Safer."

The field was small; I covered, then squatted her in. "Deety …."

"Yessir."

"Worked out that new scram program?"

"I think so. One to do just what you've been doing: take G. D. straight up a hundred thousand klicks, but do it in two words, instead of setting dials. Do it in total darkness, if you wish. Or with eyes dazzled, or anything. As long as any of the four of us is able to get out two syllables we'll be able to get far enough away from trouble that we'll have time to work out what to do next."

"Can you program it orally before I open a door?"

"I think so, Zebadiah. But in cutting it to two syllables I've cut out all preliminaries. If she's asleep, G. D. will wake up and do it at

363

once. We'll all have to be careful not to say those two syllables unless we mean it."

"Bad deal if her doors are open. Can you program not to let that happen?"

"Uh ... yessir."

"Okay, program it. Jake, set up the same thing on your dials as a backup. Meanwhile, I'm going to give the plumbing a field test. Don't touch the doors 'til I get back. Squeeze past me, honey, and take my seat."

I returned in a few minutes. "Our magic space warp is still with us and functioning—and don't ask me why or I'll scream. New program inserted?"

"Yessir. On tell-me-three-times memory and protected against execution without the doors being closed and locked. I've written down the magic words; Pop and Aunt Hilda know them. Don't read them aloud. Here." Deety handed her husband a scrap of paper.

On it was: Gay—*Bounce!*

"Just that?"

"It's the shortest program I can work out for an emergency. I think. The only hazard is never to use those two syllables casually. But I can wipe it and make it more complex if you wish."

"As long as it can't work with the doors open, it should be okay. Its shortness may save our necks sometime. Sharpie, it's my turn to be pioneer-mother and canary; we're on the ground. Everybody, hold your breath; I'm going to sniff the outside air."

"Cap'n Zebbie. This planet is Earth-like to nine decimal places."

"Which gives me a cheap chance to play hero. Pipe down and hold your breath." I cautiously opened the door a crack by hand, sniffed.

"I feel okay—I think. Anybody woozy?"

"Open the door wide, Zebbie, this place is *safe*."

I did so and stepped out into a field of daisies; the others followed me through the portside door. It certainly seemed safe—quiet, warm, peaceful, a meadow bounded by a hedgerow.

Suddenly a white rabbit came running past, headed for the hedge. He barely paused, pulled a watch from his waistcoat pocket, glanced at it, then moaned. "Oh dear! Oh dear! I shall be too late!" and ran even faster. Deety started after him.

"*Deety!*" I yelled.

She stopped short. "But I must find the hole."

"Then keep your eye on *her*. But you're not going down the rabbit hole."

"On whom?" Deety turned back toward the hedgerow. A little girl in a pinafore was hurrying toward the spot where the rabbit had disappeared. "Oh. But it didn't hurt her to go down the hole, Zebadiah; you know it didn't."

"No, but Alice got in lots of difficulties before she got out. We haven't time for that; this is not a place where we can stay."

"Why not?"

"Because England in mid-nineteenth century did *not* have advanced medicine."

"Zebbie," put in Hilda, "this isn't England. Look in your pocket. The scrap of paper I handed you."

I unfolded the bit of paper, read: *Wonderland.* "Just so," I agreed, and handed it to my wife. "But the background is modeled on England sometime in the eighteen-sixties. It either has no medicine at all, like Oz, or it has pre-Pasteur medicine. Possibly even pre-Semmelweiss practices, since England tended to be cautious about adopting newfangled notions from the Continent. Deety, do you want to die from childbed fever?"

"No, I want to go to the Mad Tea Party."

"We can have a mad tea party right here; I went mad several universes back—and it's time for lunch anyhow. Sharpie, you win the Order of Nostradamus with diamond cluster; it will be awarded as soon as possible. May I ask you two questions?"

"One may always ask."

"Is H. P. Lovecraft on that list?"

"He got only one vote, Zebbie. Yours."

"Cthulhu be thanked! Sharpie, his stories fascinate me the way snakes are said to fascinate birds. But I would rather be trapped with the "King in Yellow" than be caught up in any of the worlds in *Necronomicon.* Uh ... did any horrids get four votes?"

"No, dear, the rest of us all prefer happy endings."

"So do I, so do I! Especially when I'm in it. Did Heinlein get his name in the hat?"

"Four votes, but split. Two for his *Future History*, two for *Stranger in a Strange Land.* So he didn't make it."

"Well *I* didn't vote for *Stranger* and I'll refrain from embarrassing anyone by asking who did. My god, the things some writers will do for money."

"Samuel Johnson said that anyone who wrote for any other reason was a fool."

"Johnson was a fat, pompous, gluttonous dirty old fool who would have faded into the obscurity he so richly deserved had he not been followed around by a spit-licking sycophant. Better spell that 'psycho.' " I added, "Did Poul Anderson get in? Or Niven?"

"Zebbie, that's far more than two questions."

"I haven't even reached the second question ... which is; what do we have for lunch? Or a mad tea party?"

"Surprise! Glinda had a packed picnic basket placed in our dressing room."

"I didn't see it."

"You didn't look in the wardrobe. It was the first thing I checked on after we left Oz." Hilda grinned. "Can sandwiches from Oz be eaten in Wonderland? Or will they 'softly and silently vanish away'?"

" 'Be off, or I'll kick you downstairs!' "

Several hundred calories later, Deety noticed a young man hovering nearby. He seemed to want to speak to them but was too diffident to do so. She promptly jumped up, trotted toward him. "The Reverend Mister Dodgson, is it not? I'm Mrs. Zebadiah Carter."

He quickly removed his straw boater—his only concession to the weather. "Mr. Dodgson, yes, uh, Mrs. Carter. Have we met?"

"A long time ago, before I was married. But it doesn't matter. You were looking for Alice, were you not?"

"Dear me! Why, yes, I am. But how ...."

"I saw her. She went down the rabbit hole."

Dodgson looked relieved. "Then she is perfectly safe, and she will be back soon enough. I promised to return her and her sisters to Christ Church before dark."

"You did. I mean, you will. Same thing, depending on the coordinates selected. Come meet my family. Have you had luncheon?"

"Oh, I say, I don't mean to intrude."

"You aren't intruding. There's plenty left." Deety took him by the hand, firmly. Since she was stronger than he was, he had no choice other than by struggling. So he came along, rather awkwardly and blushing ... and let go her hand hastily as soon as she loosened her grip. Jake and I got to our feet; Hilda remained in lotus.

"Aunt Hilda, this is Mr. Dodgson, lecturer in mathematics at Christ Church College, Oxford. My stepmother, Mrs. Burroughs."

"How do you do, Mrs. Burroughs. Oh dear, I am intruding!"

"Not at all, Mr. Dodgson. Do sit down."

"And this is my father, Dr. Burroughs, professor of mathematics. And, Mr. Dodgson, my dear husband Captain Carter. Aunt Hilda, will you find a clean plate for Mr. Dodgson? He's been searching for Alice; he must be hungry."

The young don visibly relaxed once formal introductions had been made but he was still far more formal than Deety intended to permit. He sat down on the turf, placed his hat carefully beside him, and said, "Truly, Mrs. Burroughs, I've just finished tea with three little girls, sisters. One of them wandered off and that is how I chanced by."

Deety ignored his protests while she piled his plate with little sandwiches and cakes. Hilda poured tea from a thermos jug. Thus they nailed him down with cup and plate. Jake advised, "Don't fight it, son, unless you really must leave this instant. Are Alice's sisters safe?"

"Why, yes, Professor: they are napping in the shade of a hayrick nearby. But ...."

"Then relax and be at home. You must wait until Alice returns, in any case. What branch of mathematics do you pursue?"

"Algebraic logic, usually, sir, with some attention to its applications in geometry." The Reverend Mr. Dodgson was seated so that he faced *Gay Deceiver* and sat in the shade of her port wing but nothing in his manner showed that he had even noticed the anachronism.

"Have your studies led you into multidimensional non-Euclidean geometries?"

Dodgson blinked. "I fear that I tend to be conservative in geometry, rathuh."

"Father, Mr. Dodgson doesn't work in your field; he works in mine."

Dodgson raised his eyebrows slightly but remained silent. Jake said, "I suspect that my daughter did not introduce herself fully. She is Mrs. Carter but her maiden name is Doctor D. T. Burroughs. Her field is mathematical logic."

"And that is why I am so pleased that you are here, Mr. Dodgson. Your book *Symbolic Logic* is a milestone in our field."

"But, my dear lady, I have not written a work titled *Symbolic Logic*."

"I've confused things again. I'm sorry. Again, it is matter of selection of the proper coordinates. At the end of the reign of

Queen Victoria you will have published it five years earlier. Is that clear?"

He answered very solemnly. "Quite clear. Then all I need do is to ask Her Majesty how much longer she is going to reign, and subtract five years."

"That should do it. Do you like to play with sorites?"

For the first time, he smiled. "Oh, very much!"

"Shall we make up some? Then trade and solve them?"

"Well ... not too lengthy. I really must get back to my young charges."

"We can't stay long, either. Anyone else want to play?"

No one else elected to play. Jake and Hilda went for a walk, Jake promising that they would stay in sight and Hilda cautioning Deety not to bother with tidy-up until later. I stretched out on the grass with a handkerchief over my face.

"Shall we hold the incomplete statements down to groups of six?" Dodgson suggested.

"All right. But the conclusion must be true. Not nonsense. Agreed?"

Both of them kept quiet while I "rested." I peeked a lot—who wouldn't? Deety was a "lady" for a while; then she sprawled on her belly and chewed her pencil, having learned most of her life ago that this position facilitated thought.

First she selected the conclusion to be proved, then covered several pages with scratch work in developing statements, incomplete in themselves, which would arrive at that and only that conclusion. Having done so, then tested them by symbolic logic, she wrote out her list of six statements, mixing them randomly—then looked up.

The young mathematician was looking at her solemnly, his notepad in hand. "Finished?" she asked.

"Just finished. Mrs. Carter, you remind me of my little friend Alice Liddell."

"I know," she said. "That's how I recognized her. Shall we trade?"

Dodgson tore out a sheet from his pad. "This is to be solved in the first person; the conclusion applies to you."

"All right, I'll try it." Deety read:

1. Every idea of mine, that cannot be expressed as a syllogism, is really ridiculous;

2. None of my ideas about bath-buns are worth writing down;

3. No idea of mine, that fails to come true, can be expressed as a syllogism;
4. I never have any really ridiculous ideas that I do not at once refer to my solicitor;
5. My dreams are all about bath-buns;
6. I never refer any idea of mine to my solicitor, unless it is worth writing down.

Deety read it and chortled. "How very sweet of you! It *is* true, you know, all my dreams *do* come true!"

"You solved it so quickly?"

"But it's only six statements. Have you solved mine?"

"I haven't read it yet. I will now." He read:

1. Everything, not absolutely ugly, may be kept in a drawing room;
2. Nothing, that is encrusted with salt, is ever quite dry;
3. Nothing should be kept in a drawing room, unless it is free from damp;
4. Time-traveling machines are always kept near the sea;
5. Nothing, that is what you expect it to be, can be absolutely ugly;
6. Whatever is kept near the sea gets encrusted with salt.

He blinked at the list. "The conclusion is true?" he asked.

"Yes."

For the first time he stared openly at *Gay Deceiver*. "That, then—I infer—is a 'time-traveling machine.'"

"Yes ... although it does several other things as well."

"It is certainly not what I expected it to be ... although I am not sure what I expected a time-traveling machine to be. I haven't given it much thought before today."

I pulled the handkerchief off my face. "Do you want to take a ride in it, Mr. Dodgson?"

The young don looked wistful. "I am sorely tempted, Captain. But I am responsible for three little girls and cannot leave them. So I must thank you for your hospitality and bid you goodbye. Will you offer my apologies to Professor and Mrs. Burroughs and explain that duty calls me?"

— XXXVI —

Jake

Our captain said, "Deety, how does it feel to say goodbye without getting kissed?"

"Zebadiah, I didn't even make it possible. The record shows that Lewis Carroll was terrified by females over the age of puberty."

"If not terrified," my dear wife Hilda added, "at least he did not pick them to chum with. Tended to avoid them."

"That's why I stayed close by. Deety hon, if I had gone with Jake and Hilda, he would have left at once."

"I can't figure out how he got there in the first place," Hilda went on. "Lewis Carroll was never *in* Wonderland; he simply wrote about it. But this is Wonderland—unless rabbits in England wear waistcoats and watches."

"You aren't being logical, Aunt Hilda. Who can possibly be as deeply inside a story as the person who writes it?"

"Hmm ... I think I'll have to study that one."

"Study it later. All hands, stand by to rotate. Set it up, by your schedule, Copilot. Deety, we're going to try your new scram. In my voice, just for drill. Copilot, if it works, rotate at once. That's for drill, too. Mars, isn't it? End of group."

"Right, Captain," I agreed. "Next stop off: Mars, Universe-One."

"Gay ... *Bounce!*"

At once we were high. I pushed the "execute" button—and at once Mars-Zero was swimming ahead of us, in half-phase and looking the proper distance.

"Copilot, set rotation, by schedule."

"First rotation of third group, to tenth rotation universe—set!"

"All hands, stand by to rotate! Execute!"

A quite homelike starry void ....But I saw no recognizable constellations.

"Copilot, set your next rotation, then turn out the instrument lights. All hands; pigeon tumble coming up. Stand by."

We went through a full somersault; no one reported anything near us—and I still saw no familiar constellations. The captain said, "Science Officer, mark this one as promising." He turned on the instrument lights. "Ready to rotate, Jake?"

"Set, Captain."

"All hands, stand by to rotate. Execute."

Still another star-filled universe— But to my considerable surprise, these constellations were indeed familiar; I was looking right at the Big Dipper, Ursa Major, and the Little Dipper, Ursa Minor, was in its correct place, with Polaris at the end of its handle. I hastily checked the dials. No, we couldn't possibly be in Universe-Zero. Besides, Mars was missing.

"All hands, stand by for tumbling pigeon routine."

I kept quiet while the captain took us through the familiar scanning procedure, expecting each moment to disclose at least our familiar Sun. Not only did I fail to see it but also, no other celestial body was near enough to show, other than as a bright point of light. However, all constellations that I observed seemed familiar—save that I confess that the sky as seen from Earth's Southern Hemisphere is not too familiar to me. I spotted, I thought, Crux, the Southern Cross, and both the Magellanic Clouds; I was less sure of others.

But there could be no doubt about Leo and Cygnus and the square of Pegasus and others that decorate the night sky of Arizona and anywhere in northern latitudes.

"Copilot? Where are we?"

"Apparently in our home universe, Captain. And this time Taurus is on the correct side of Orion. I noticed."

"Yes, but where in hell is *Sol?* Deety, Hilda—we seem to have mislaid the Sun. Either of you see it?"

"No, sir."

"No, Cap'n Zebbie."

"Jake, I don't like this a little bit. Is your next rotation set?"

"Yes, Captain," I acknowledged. "I set it up at once, pursuant to standing orders."

371

"Good. Keep your finger near the button. Science Officer, how does this fit your theory? I don't recall listing a fictional universe that doesn't have the solar system in it."

"Cap'n Zebbie, it could fit two of the four still left ... or any one of a dozen that got three votes—especially any of that half a dozen that you might have listed. If you hadn't had a 'baker's dozen,' I think you said, tied in your mind. Were any of that baker's dozen space-travel stories? Or groups of stories?"

"Almost all of them."

"In that case we could be in any of several *soi-disant* fictional universes that take our own universe as a frame of reference ... but far enough from the sun so that it appears as second- or third-magnitude. That wouldn't have to be very far for the constellations to look familiar; our Sun is pretty faint as stars go. So this could be the Darkover universe, or Niven's Known Space, or Dr. Williamson's Legion of Space Universe, or the *Star Trek* universe, or Anderson's world of the Polesotechnic League, or Dr. Smith's Galactic Patrol World. Or several more. Did you have any of those in mind?"

"All of them, I think—including some that I voted for. As you know."

"As you know, yes."

"Sharpie, you mentioned that there were two that this could not be? Care to name them? Or is that cheating?"

"No, it can't hurt to name them. The world of King Arthur and the Knights of the Round Table, and the world of the Hobbits—*The Fellowship of the Ring.*"

"Well ... if we find ourselves in either of those, we leave quickly. No obstetricians. We'll just mark them down as nice places to visit once our kids are big enough for travel. Jake, is there any point in staying here any longer?"

"None that I see, Captain," I answered.

"I can see good reason to scram. Several of those space-opera universes can be pretty sticky. I don't care to catch a photon torpedo or a vortex bomb or a negative-matter projectile or anything else, just through a failure to identify ourselves promptly. All hands, stand by to rotate. Execute!"

This time we weren't merely close; we were on the ground—and maybe I ... perhaps Captain Zeb shouldn't have asked Hilda what those other two were—possibly it affected the outcome. I found very persuasive her theory that we were not going places at random; these were all dream universes mutually shared ... but in the too, too solid flesh.

Charging straight at us was a knight in full armor, his lance couched in attack. I think it unlikely that a lance could damage *Gay Deceiver*. As may be, this "gentle knight" was unfriendly; I did not wait for orders but shouted, "Gay! *Bounce!*"

Sighed with relief at sudden darkness and set the next rotation at once—and hoped that the captain would not notice that I had not done so before raising my head (as his standing order required).

Either he had not or chose not to mention it; the captain's next words were: "Thanks, Copilot. You were on your toes."

"Thank *you*, sir. Next rotation set. End of group three. Back to the neighborhood of Mars."

"I suppose we might as well get on with it. All hands ...."

"Zebadiah!" my daughter interrupted. "Captain, I mean. Is *that* all that we are going to see of the Round Table? And King Arthur and his knights?"

"Deety, that wasn't one of King Arthur's knights. He was wearing full-plated mail. Didn't anyone else notice?"

"That's my impression," my beloved wife agreed. "But I gave more attention to his shield. Field sable, argent bend sinister, in chief sun proper with crown, both or."

"Sir Mordred," my daughter decided. "I just knew he was a baddie. Dear, you should have hit him with your L-gun. Burned him down."

"And killed that beautiful beer-wagon horse? A Percheron. Or maybe a Clydesdale. Deety, I do know something of the history of arms and armor. That sort of armor wasn't made earlier than the fifteenth century, five hundred years or more after the days of King Arthur. If he ever lived."

"Then why was he carrying Sir Mordred's shield?"

"Heraldry is not a subject I know. Sharpie, was that Sir Mordred's coat of arms?"

"I don't know, Cap'n Zebbie. I simply blazoned what I saw. But aren't you nit-picking in objecting to plate armor merely because it's anachronistic?"

"But history shows clearly that—"

"That's the point, Zebbie. Camelot isn't history; it's *fiction*."

Our captain was silent a moment, then said, "Shut my big mouth."

"Barsoom was loaded with anachronisms; so was Oz. Zebbie, I venture to guess that the version of Camelot we blundered into is a patchwork of all of our concepts of King Arthur and the Round Table. I picked up most of mine from Tennyson, then revised them from end to end when I laid hands on *Le Morte d'Arthur.* Where did you get yours? There is a great variety, much of it contradictory, to choose from."

"I haven't read either of the two you named. Um, I guess Mark Twain gave me most of mine—at least—*A Connecticut Yankee at King Arthur's Court* was my major introduction. Add on some Prince Valiant, too. I don't know. I read some kids' stories, too—but the *Connecticut Yankee* stands out. Jake?"

I said, "Captain, there seems little doubt that there was indeed a king or a general named Arthur or Arturius or some such. But I think most people think of King Arthur from fiction having little or no connection with the historical person, if indeed there ever was one. *The Sword in the Stone* and *The Once and Future King* are my favorites. Although I've dabbled in others."

My daughter persisted, "I do believe in the Round Table, I do! We were just there—why don't we go back and *look?* Instead of guessing."

"Deety," our Captain said gently, "first, because you and Hilda are not going to be subjected to fifth- or ninth-century midwifery, or whatever it is. Second, because the jolly, murderous ways of that gang of roughnecks called the Knights of the Round Table are fun to read about but not to know socially. That bloke would have killed us if we hadn't been safe inside this car. Nor are people the only dangers. There would be honest-to-god dragons, and wyverns, and malevolent magic—not the Glinda-the-Good variety. We've learned—so far—the easy way that these alternate worlds are just as real as the one we came from. I don't want to learn it the hard way by getting suddenly dead."

"Jacob," said my wife, "suppose this party were made up of people who don't like fanciful stories and never read them. What sort of rotation worlds would they find?"

"I don't know, Hilda. I venture to speculate that they would visit only humdrum slice-of-life universes indistinguishable from the real world. Correction: substitute 'Universe-Zero' for 'real world'—because, as the captain pointed out, all these worlds are equally real."

"Jacob, why do you call our universe 'Universe-Zero'?"

"Eh ... for convenience, I suppose."

"That's what I'm trying to find out. Didn't you tell me once that no frame of reference is preferred over any other? In other words, each of one of the Number of the Beast is equally zero-zero in six axes?"

"Well ... theory requires it."

"Then *we* are simply fiction in all those other myriad universes. Or have I reasoned incorrectly?"

I was slow in answering. "That would seem to be a necessary corollary. But I would want to give it much thought. It's a disturbing idea. The notion that we ourselves are merely figments of imagination."

"I'm nobody's figment!" my daughter protested. "I'm real, I am! Pinch me! .... *Ouch!* Hey, Hillbilly, not so hard!"

"You asked for it, hon," said the captain.

"My husband is a brute. And I've got a cruel stepmother just like Snow White. I mean, Cinderella. And my Pop thinks I'm imaginary. But I love you all anyway because you're all I've got."

"If you fictional characters will all pipe down, we'll get this show back on the road. All hands, stand by to rotate. *Execute!*"

Mars was where it should be. I felt more real.

── XXXVII ──

Zebadiah

"Next rotation set, Captain. Starting fourth group. Thirteenth rotation universe. Correct, Hilda?"

"That's what I have, Jacob. Camelot was number twelve."

"Check. Say when, Captain."

"Let's catch our breaths first." I stared out at the ruddy, barren, rugged face of Mars-Zero. "That piece of rock looks downright homelike. At least we're back in our own universe. I feel like the sort of tourist who tries to cover thirty countries in a two-week vacation—then can't remember anything but the hotel rooms. Shock. Not 'future shock' but something like it. Continue shock?"

"Homesickness," said Hilda. "Knowing that we can't ever go back to Snug Harbor. Zebbie, it just doesn't do to think about it ... or you'll find yourself crying in your pillow. But somewhere, somewhen, somehow, we'll build another Snug Harbor. Won't we, Jacob?"

Jake reached back and patted his wife's knee. "We will, dearest."

Deety said wistfully, "I'd like to see Kanakook."

"Deety, are you over that pioneer-mother jag?"

"No, Zebadiah. I know what we have to do. But I can get homesick, too. Like you. Like Hilda. Like everybody but Pop."

"Correction, daughter. Count me in. I don't miss Logan especially, but I don't think Hilda misses California ...."

"Not a bit!"

"Me, neither," I agreed. "I just had a rented flat there. Didn't count, no sentimental attachment. But Snug Harbor was home to all of us."

"True. I didn't really *hate* the Panki—just feared them—until they bombed our home into a radioactive crater. Now I want to exterminate them. Utterly." Burroughs added, "But we've got to find a new home first. Comfortable as this car is, we can't live in it indefinitely."

"Check. Science Officer, your theory about rotation universes seems to be checking out on the nose. You have the list. Is there any reason to finish this schedule of rotations? Should we go directly to the axis?"

"Cap'n Zebbie, I don't know. But we haven't been wasting our time. Granted that most rotations didn't amount to more than sightseeing, if we *hadn't* followed Jacob's schedule, this car would not be nearly so comfortable. Do you know of another Ford duo that has two bathrooms?"

"Hilda, I don't know of one that has *one* bathroom. Yes, our space-warp special is not only a comfort—beats the hell out of a honey bucket!—but also it enables us to stay in space as long as our air holds out. And food. But air is the critical factor now."

"I thought that recharger widget Cart's people made for us would pump up those air spheres?"

"It will, but we have to be in the atmosphere of a planet with breathable air. Could be risky."

"It need not be," Burroughs pointed out. "I can place us in Oz, or in Wonderland, in seconds. Sweet air, no danger."

"Gentlemen, Deety and I haven't mentioned one more asset we have. Cap'n Zebbie, would you like a banana?"

"There aren't any more, Hilda. I ate the last one just before I buried our garbage. While you and Deety were washing dishes, just before we left Wonderland."

"Tell him, Deety."

"Zebadiah, Hilda and I salvaged all the picnic that was left, and washed the dishes, and put everything back in the basket. Hilda started to put it into the bottom of our wardrobe—and found that it was heavy. So we uncovered it and looked. Packed tight as it was when we left Oz. Six bananas—and everything else. Cross my heart. Go look for yourself."

"Hmm …. No, I'll accept the report of my department heads. Jake, can you write equations covering a picnic basket that refills itself? Will it go on doing so?"

"Yes to the first, Captain; equations can be written to describe anything. To the second, I have no data; we'll have to wait and see.

But the mathematical description would be simpler for a picnic basket that replenishes itself indefinitely then for one that does it once and then stops—I would have to describe the discontinuity. But I am no longer troubled by natural—or 'unnatural'—laws that don't apply here in Universe-Zero."

"Sharpie, your earlier answer recommended that we complete the rotations."

"No, Cap'n Bligh. I simply pointed out that the first twelve had not been unprofitable. I might add that we could have completed the last three by now, had we not spent time debating it."

"Hilda honey, your cowardly captain needed that time to get his nerve back. My yumpin' Yiminy, once we settle down, all three of you are going to practice handling this craft. Then we'll elect a new skipper."

"We would simply re-elect you, Zeb. Each of us will go on doing what he or she can do best."

" 'Time is out of joint. O cursèd spite, that I was ever picked to set it right.' "

"You misquoted."

"I always do. What sort of universe do we wind up in next, Hilda?"

"Cap'n, we have three more to complete Jacob's schedule, and I have four more on the list of highest probability. One of them is utterly useless to us—we couldn't stay—but amusing and safe. The other three are possible places to live but each has its own dangers. If I tell you and Jacob—or even Deety, it might affect the outcome and we might miss the one we need most. As the chief of surgery back on campus used to say: 'I dunno, let's operate and find out.' "

I sighed. "All hands, stand by to rotate. Report."

"Strapped down, Cap'n Bligh honey."

"Copilot."

"Rotation still set. This group is around t-axis with the usual ninety-degree displacements. h and w are null; teh, tau, and l are spatial axes this time, but the group is only two, as the remaining three rotations duplicate earlier ones, one for each earlier group."

"Jacob, how do you keep track of that?"

"A check-off list."

"No, dear; how do you *understand* it?"

"I don't. But this is what our six-dimensional equations call for. So far, it has worked. Hilda, my love, once a scientist thinks he *understands* a process, his mind begins to ossify."

"Stand by; *execute!*"

Green fire—"Rotate! Execute!"

A formless red fog—"Rotate! Execute!"

We came out in a starry universe.

"Captain, these constellations look familiar—don't you think?"

"I think so."

"They *are* familiar," Hilda asserted. "Except that there is one bright star near the Gemini that doesn't belong there. So that ought to be our own Sun. We're way out past Pluto, where the comets spend the winter. Let's move in closer and find Earth."

"Don't be in such a hurry, Science Officer. What was that first rotation? Green fire?"

"Would you settle for the deadly green nebula in *The Legion of Space*? It was on the way to the Runaway Star where Aladoree had been taken after she was kidnapped."

"That was on your list?"

"All four of us voted for it. Three of us voted for the three stories as a group; you voted specifically for the first story."

"Sharpie, I never had a chance to read the other two. How about that red fog we rotated into?"

"That one is a little harder to figure. It could be any space-opera universe, especially one by any writer that pays respectful attention to astronomy—Clement, Anderson, and so forth. But there were two votes for Niven's 'Known Space' and two for *The Mote in God's Eye*. I lumped them together as four. But whether the old gentleman had anything to do with it or not, I think we blundered into a red giant star ... and got out again before it mattered. After all, a red giant isn't mass, exactly—it's closer to what we call vacuum. Anyhow, we weren't hurt; we were there about two seconds."

"Less than that, beloved; I set it with one click, and barely had my thumb off the 'execute' button. Captain, do you wish to transit toward that bright star? Or shall I check its spectral signature first?"

"Let's chop off thirty or forty AUs—with some careful 'Tennessee windage'—and get a rough cross-fix. Maybe that will give us a disc I can measure. If not, we'll narrow it down until it does show a disc. I'll measure it and you can place us one AU from the Sun—not necessarily in the ecliptic but anywhere on the sphere from which the Sun subtends half a degree. From there we'll be able to see Earth easily. After which we play by ear. Copilot? Advice."

"No problem, Captain. But I suggest that you make that offset *wide*. Say fifteen degrees. When we did it to reach Mars, it was sufficient simply to miss it. With the Sun, I would want to be sure that we were more than one AU."

"Jake, you are *so* right! I don't want to fry my eyeballs. All hands, when I measure the Sun's angular width, everybody duck down out of direct sunlight and *don't* look."

"Zebadiah, you'll blind yourself!"

"Deety darling, the gunsight has a built-in polarizer. Didn't I show it to you?"

"Nossir, you did *not*. You be careful."

"Hon, I'll start with the polarizer fully crossed, then open it carefully. Promise."

"Spacecraft! Identify yourself."

That made me jerk with surprise. "Who said that?"

"Lensman Ted Smith, Lieutenant Galactic Patrol, Entity, commanding Patrol Vessel *Nighthawk*. I regret being forced to enter your mind, but you have been ignoring sub-ether radio for seven minutes thirty-two seconds. Switch it on and I will get out of your mind. Do not maneuver: we have weapons trained on you."

"Captain," Jake whispered, "I've set to rotate."

"Don't do it, Jake. Lensman, we don't *have* sub-ether radio. This is Continua Craft *Gay Deceiver*, Captain Zeb Carter speaking. Do you read me?"

"I read you loud and clear. What happened to your sub-ether radio? Do you need help?"

"Captain Smith, I don't know what sub-ether radio is. No, I don't think we need help … but we could use some astrogational advice. Where are we?"

"For the moment, the important point is that you are in my patrol sector. You are an unscheduled ship insufficiently identified. I repeat: DO NOT MANEUVER. By order of the Galactic Patrol. Do you understand?"

"Roger Wilco, Lensman. I regret having intruded into your patrol space. This is a private ship engaged in peaceful exploration."

"That is what I am about to determine, Captain. Stay where you are and make no hostile moves and you will be safe."

"Uh, Lensman, can you see through my eyes?"

"Are you inviting me to do so?"

"Certainly. Use my eyes, use my ears. But don't try to take over my mind or this ship will disappear." I squeezed my copilot's knee; Jake kept his thumb on the 'execute' button.

"I warned you not to maneuver. Ah ... interesting."

Hilda snapped, "Lieutenant, quit threatening us! A Lensman is supposed to be an officer and a gentleman! I intend to report you to Prime Base! To the Port Admiral himself. You're an oaf!"

"Sorry, madam. I do not wish to offend but I have duty to perform. Captain, will you please turn your head so that I can see who is speaking?"

"Certainly. But let me introduce all of them. On my right"—I looked at Jake—"is Dr. Jacob Burroughs." (I intentionally omitted "copilot.") "Behind him"—I then looked at Hilda—"is his wife, Dr. Hilda Burroughs, xenobiologist and chief of science ... and let me offer you this advice, Lensman: it is *never* safe to offend Dr. Hilda."

"I gathered that impression, Captain. Madam, I would not willingly offend—but I have duties. Shall I get out of your mind entirely? If you speak to me, I will hear with Captain Carter's ears. He can, if he will, repeat to you any thought in answer."

"Oh, I suppose it's all right just in conversation. But don't go any deeper into my mind! Mentor would not like it—as you know quite well!"

"Dr. Hilda, your mention of ... a certain entity ... surprises me—from one who is not a Lensman."

"I don't *need* a Lens. You can check that with Arisia."

I said hastily, "Shall we get on with the introductions? Directly behind me:"—I loosened my belt and twisted to look at Deety—"is my wife, Dr. D. T. Carter, general symbologist and astrogator. Lensman, are you now satisfied that we are a peaceful party of scientists? Or is there something more that you wish to know?"

"Captain, I can see that this ship is not a pirate vessel—unarmed and unarmored. Oh, I noted the controls for a coherent light gun but that wouldn't be much use to a pirate. Nor can I visualize two men and two women attempting to attack a space liner. But that is just one of my responsibilities. This ship, small as it is, could be carrying millions of credits in contraband."

"Say what you mean, Lensman," snapped Hilda. "Drugs. But don't use the word *zwilnik*."

They could all hear his sigh, mentally. "Yes, Dr. Hilda—drugs. But I did not introduce that offensive word into the discussion."

"I heard you thinking it. Don't do it again."

"Lensman," I intervened, "we have a few medical drugs aboard. The only one you could be interested in is a few milligrams of morphine in our medical kit, for emergencies. Dr. Hilda is also our medical officer and is qualified to administer it prudently—and so am I. As a command pilot I am a qualified paramedic. But we carry no *thionite*, no *bentlam*, no *hadive*, no *nitrolabe*. You are using your Lens; you know that I am telling the truth."

"Captain, it's not that easy. Before I first hailed you I did try a slight probe—please, Dr. Burroughs; it was in line of duty! I don't think I've ever encountered four minds so fully blocked. And this is a most curious craft. It is obviously designed for aerodynamic use rather than for space. Yet here you are, where you have no business to be—and I can't see how you got here. I'm afraid I have no choice but to detain you ... and examine this ship thoroughly. Take it apart piece by piece, if necessary."

"Lensman," I said earnestly, "don't be hasty. Use your Lens. You can search this vessel much more thoroughly by Lens than any other way. Go ahead. We've nothing to hide ... and we have a great deal to offer the Galactic Patrol. But you won't get it by pushing us around."

"You certainly won't! Cap'n, let us leave! I'm tired of stupidity!"

"Wait a half, Dr. Hilda—please! Use your Lens, Captain Smith. Search us with it."

"I am forced to say that I can't."

"You don't know *how?* Klono's brass whiskers! What are you doing on patrol? Get in touch with someone who *can* use a Lens properly. Kinnison, Worsel, Tregonsee. Someone competent."

The Lensman's thought was as stiff as if he had spoken aloud. "I am not a Second Stage Lensman, I am not even unattached. An officer of my rank does not disturb Second Stage Lensmen with minor patrol problems. Remain where you are, do not maneuver. We will match your intrinsic and take you into our cargo hold. It will be necessary to sweep back your wings; please do that now. Nothing else."

"Wait a half! In the first place, you *can't*. Not unless I choose to let you. How do you *think* we got here? Mull that over, Lensman! I want to show our means to Sir Austin Cardynge ... and give it to the Patrol. If you won't help, we'll go to Prime Base *without* your permission. While Dr. Hilda is giving a full report of this encounter with you to the Port Admiral, Dr. Burroughs and I will show Sir Austin what we have that can benefit the Patrol enormously. But we aren't going *anywhere* as your prisoners, Lensman—put that in your pipe and smoke it!"

"I have placed a tractor beam on you. Don't fight it."

"GayBounce GayBounce GayBounce GayBounce GayBounce GayBounce! Lensman, have you found us again? Come in, Lensman Ted Smith; come in Lensman Ted Smith ...."

"I've located you again. What did you do?"

"I'll tell Sir Austin; you wouldn't understand it. I purposely did not go far, so that you *could* find me again. But touch us once more with one of your damned beams and I'll go so far and fast that you'll *never* find me! Until Prime Base calls you in to find out why you botched this contact. Will you agree not to use beams or weapons while we talk like civilized people? Or do you want another game of tiddly-winks? Make up your mind!"

The Lensman appeared to take a moment to think it over. "I suggest that we each take no action while we confer."

"No weapons? No beams?"

"No weapons, no beams, no mental reservations."

"And no mental reservations on my part, Lensman. Flag of truce while we powwow. Agreed?"

"I agree, Captain Carter."

"Thank you, sir. You have Bergenholms for inertialess drive; that makes the *Nighthawk* very fast. Correct?"

"Quite fast—correct."

"Limited only by the power of your drive and the amount of mass in so-called empty space, I believe."

"I can't discuss the capabilities of my ship, Captain. Classified information."

"That's okay because I *can* discuss the capabilities of mine. They aren't classified but I prefer to give them to the Galactic Patrol rather than let them become public knowledge—for Boskone to use, for example."

I felt the Lensman's emotional reaction, instantly quenched and followed up at once. "I hulled you with that—sorry. I simply want you to know that we must be taken seriously. The *Nighthawk* is fast; *Gay Deceiver* is enormously faster. *Unthinkably* faster. You saw how quickly I broke your tractor beam and went elsewhere. Is a second demonstration necessary?"

"Not at the moment. Perhaps later."

"As you wish, Lensman. We are going to Prime Base. We can do it any of three ways. With your friendly advice in astrogation and with your sub-ether or Lens message to the Port Admiral that we are coming. Or we can end this powwow, leaving you free to capture us or blow us out of space—doesn't matter which because you can't do either—and we will go to Prime Base unassisted. But a third way is what I recommend. Take us and our car into your ship *as guests*. With your word as a Lensman that we and our car may leave freely at any time and that you will not resume hostilities—correction: police action, with respect to us—until we are out of your ship. Do it that way and I will let you inspect our vessel. You yourself, I mean—not thumb-fingered mechanics who might damage equipment they don't understand. You will see that we have techniques useful to the Patrol … and it will be to your credit that you recognized their value and brought them in."

"A Lensman does not seek credit, Captain; he carries out his duty."

"True. But when the Port Admiral pats you on the back, I don't think you'll spit in his face."

I could feel Ted Smith's wry amusement. "No, I don't think I would."

"I would like to see you get that pat on the back; you strike me as a man doing your best in unique circumstances. I would rather not have Dr. Hilda reporting you to the Port Admiral; she eats cateagles for breakfast. Well? Shall we do it the friendly way? Or shall we leave while you try to stop us? Take plenty of time to make up your mind. Ten seconds isn't too long; I'm patient."

Smith took three seconds. "Let's do it the friendly way."

"Good. Spell it out, please."

"Captain Carter, on behalf of the Galactic Patrol and by authority vested in me as a Patrol ship's master in space, I invite you and your companions—especially Dr. Hilda who eats cateagles—with your ship, into my ship *as guests*. You and your ship may leave at any time and no Patrol action will be taken with respect to your ship until you are clear of my ship. At least as far apart as we are now. Is that fair?"

"Sounds fair to me. How far apart are we?"

"Slightly over a billion miles. Do you want that in kilometers? I note that your instruments are scaled in kilometers."

"Immaterial, we understand both scales. Are you free or inert? And what is your orientation, Lensman?"

"We are inert but will approach free, then I will inert again and we will match your intrinsic and take you inside. The three maneuvers will take less than an hour."

"Wait a half, Lensman! That takes you off station, wastes an hour, and wastes power. As the *Nighthawk* must be huge compared with us. I can do it much faster and without wasting power—if you will supply astrogational data."

"What data do you need, Captain?"

"Your intrinsic and your …. No, I have a suggestion. You are using my eyes; would you like to conn my ship? Then you would gain some feeling for what *Gay Deceiver* can do. We're giving the techniques to the Patrol in any case; you can, if you wish, be the first Patrol officer to handle this type of ship. Does that appeal to you?"

I saw that we all felt the Lensman's burst of pleasure and professional eagerness. "Yes, Captain! I've turned the conn over to my astrogator. How do we do this?"

"Which do you want to do first, Lensman Smith? Match intrinsic? Or approach your ship?"

"Ordinarily we approach, then match. But if you can reverse that order, the vector problem is simpler. Can you?"

"Certainly. Use my eyes to coach my hands. Don't try to control my hands."

"I can't control your hands, Captain, and would not if I could. I have only recently learned to see through another entity's eyes via the Lens—a special tutoring class under a Gray Lensman."

"*The* Gray Lensman?"

"No, no! Not a Second Stage. Dr. Jerry Doheny, a psychologist. Shall we begin?"

"Yes. Tell me when to point this bucket. I want to line my gunsight along your intrinsic vector, positive."

"Very well, sir. Please change attitude so that I can see Rigel. There! Can you bring Sirius into view at the same time? Good! Imagine a point midway and go south of it about nine degrees. Beta Lepi. Only third-magnitude but there's not much out that way."

"That one, Lensman?"

"Right! Now take her left slowly—*mark!* Raise your bow just a hair … *mark!* Steady on, keep it so. I think that's the best we can do by gunsight, Captain."

"Is it good enough?"

"Yes. *Nighthawk* can make fine adjustments after approach. Our intrinsic along that line is, in kilometers per second relative to you, ninety-seven thousand three hundred sixty-two point six—but I'll settle for anything close to one hundred thousand."

"Positive per second nine seven three six two point six—set, Captain."

"Change velocity. Execute. Thank you, Dr. Burroughs."

"Let me get a report … great balls of fire! My astrogator says you are dead in space with respect to us."

"That was what you asked for, Lensman. Now coach me so that we line up with your ship, then tell us how far to move."

"One second …. Will you get Deneb in your gunsight first? There we are! Now—easy!—toward the Coal Sack—*mark*! Dead on, Captain. Our distance from you in kilometers is one billion six hundred nine million fourteen thousand three hundred twenty."

"Transit positive, 1-axis, short range, one six oh nine oh one four three two oh point oh—set, Captain."

"Do not execute, Dr. Burroughs. Lensman, is that distance correct?"

"I listened to the doctor read it back, Captain. It is correct."

"And you said that we were 'dead on.' Captain, I want to *miss* your ship both in distance and direction." I moved my point of sight slightly toward Deneb. "Doctor, please chop ten thousand kilometers off that setting."

"Minus ten thousand. Reset, Captain."

"Really, Captain Carter, there is no danger, as the *Nighthawk* will now go free. In the extremely unlikely event of a direct hit in over a billion miles, my ship will bounce ever so lightly that it won't even put a scratch on yours."

"Lensman, do you know how my ship works?"

"No, but …."

"But me no buts, sir. Take my word for it that a direct hit even with your ship free of inertia would produce the most amazing explosion either of us has ever seen. But we would never see it. Both ships would be an expanding cloud of plasma, and all hands would be fitted either with halos or coal scoops. I agree that the chance of a hit is small … but I'm a cautious skipper; I take no chances I can avoid."

"Neither do I, Captain—so the *Nighthawk* now goes free."

"Reasonable. All hands, prepare to transit. Execute! Lensman, where are we now?"

"Klono's claws! You're dead in space to us, sixty-eight hundred miles—make that ten thousand nine hundred and forty kilometers. We see you near Canopus, so we are in Draco to you."

"Can you give us a bright beacon? Blinking, by preference."

"Certainly, Captain. Do you see it?"

"Uh ... got you. Please set for transit, Doctor. I'm going to miss that beacon by half a mil."

"Set, Captain."

"Execute."

Off to port, five kilometers away, swam a giant spaceship. As it appeared, its dazzling beacon shut down but milder lighting from the distant sun let us see it.

"Captain, that's the most amazing display of piloting I've ever seen—and thank you for letting me take part in it."

"I couldn't have done it without your coaching, Lensman. Do you now think that we have something the Patrol can use?"

"I know you have! I can't wait to see your ship with my own eyes instead of yours. Captain, if you will permit me to place a tractor beam on you, we will take you inboard. It will be quite gentle; we are still free of inertia."

"Lensman Smith, you know your ship just as I know mine. I don't want you to put *anything* on me, even a light line, until you can assure me that we have zero relative motion to about nineteen decimals. I don't have instrumentation for that. As you noted, this vessel started life as an atmosphere craft. But I assume that *you* have."

"We have. My astrogator is making fine adjustment to meet your safety requirements. There—relative motion zero to a tenth of an inch per hour. Is that satisfactory?"

"Yes. Do you have internal artificial gravity?"

"Yes, Captain. But it won't be switched on in the cargo hold until your ship is clamped in place.

"Good. Just a moment. Hello, Gay."

"Howdy, Zeb."

"*Gay Deceiver*, fold your wings, put down your wheels."

"Sure thing, Zeb. Heard any new ones lately?"

"You're a Smart Girl, Gay."

"Why won't you marry me, Zeb? Philanderer! Over."

"Over and out, Gay. Lensman, you can take us inboard now."

"Captain, I assume that that was a recording. I hope it was."

"I hope so, too. We're ready."

Deety squeaked when the huge ship flashed up to us. Then it backed off slightly, opened clamshell doors, gently took us inside. Armored crewmen clamped us to a large, flat surface as the doors closed. Shortly, we heard hissing that gradually faded. The voice in my head said, "Normal Tellurian atmosphere at nine hundred millibars, Captain. Welcome aboard! I hope that you and your companions will do us the honor of dining with me and my officers at eighteen hours, ship's time."

"Thank you, Lensman; we accept. What is ship's time now?"

"Fourteen oh two ten. That's Tellurian units, not Galactic Standard. The Inner Patrol stays matched with Prime Base."

I adjusted the outer ring on my watch, checked *Gay Deceiver's* time, wrote down the difference. "Got it, Deety?"

"Yessir. Feels good to have my head set right again."

"Captain, I'm about to withdraw from your mind and come down to greet you in person. Side honors?"

"Please dispense with honors, Lensman. Before we leave our ship, I want to show you one more thing it can do. You are welcome to stay in my mind and watch. Do you have a piloting officer who would enjoy a short ride in our ship?"

"I'm certain they all would, so I'll send the most junior of the top watch list, Lieutenant Nganagana."

"We'll expect him. Deety, please open the bulkhead door and strap down, as you did for Thuv and Hal and Mobyas. Hilda, will you dog it open? You won't miss anything, Deety—promise. All hands stay strapped or get strapped."

By the time Deety's seat was vacant, a young lieutenant arrived breathlessly. I opened the door and said, "Come in, Lieutenant. Slide past me and strap down—introductions later. Hilda, help him, please."

As I checked the door seal, Hilda reported, "He's belted down, Cap'n." Deety echoed her. I instantly said, "Gay—Bounce!"

Lieutenant Nganagana gasped. The voice in my head said, "Captain Carter, what did you *do?*"

"Just a demonstration. Have you noted our position? Got us on your screens?"

"Uh … yes, you are sixty-two thousand one hundred and fifty miles away."

"And four tenths," corrected Deety. "Lensman, you're four tenths of a mile wrong."

"My apologies, Dr. Carter; you are right. That's around … one hundred thousand kilometers. But we didn't even open the cargo hold!"

"Explanations later, Lensman, and please keep quiet; I'm piloting. Expect us in your immediate vicinity at once. Dr. Burroughs, I've set just a hair of Tennessee windage; you can make the return exact."

"Axis *l*, vernier setting four—set, Captain."

"Execute."

We popped out within a kilometer of the *Nighthawk*. I swallowed my stomach and said nothing … and was glad that my slaphappy crew treated it as routine—I had intended to miss by at least ten kilometers. "Lensman, please take us inboard again. I will not maneuver."

"Very well, Captain."

Zeb introduced their guest while they were being taken into the ship. The young officer seemed to be suppressing shock and made a brave effort to be formally polite.

Deety said, "What's your first name, Lieutenant? Call me 'Deety' if you like; we aren't very formal."

"Uh, ma'am, around the wardroom they usually call me 'goo' or 'goop.' That's short for 'Agú'—means 'Leopard.'"

While we were waiting for pressure I said, "Lieutenant, please tell Captain Smith not to expect us at once. We need to bathe and change clothes before we see anyone."

"Aye aye, sir."

"Captain," Smith lensed, "Mr. Nganagana can take you directly to guest quarters. Quite comfortable, and roomier than your vessel, I'm certain."

"Thank you, Captain Smith—but I'm sure you know that ladies dislike to be seen until they've had time to dress properly. Dr. Hilda, how much time will be needed?"

"Deety?"

"Aunt Hilda, I can make it in forty-five minutes if you can."

"Suits."

"Lensman, please make that fifty minutes—seventeen hours, ship's time. Now, if we may have privacy?"

"Certainly, Captain. I will not enter your mind or any of your party again, other than by direct invitation."

—— XXXVIII ——

Deety

Zebadiah had us all gather in Hilda's—my—dressing room after Agú left us and the doors were locked again. Pop asked, "What are the plans, Skipper?"

"Jake, the Lensman knows how cramped our cabin is and Goop knows—"

I broke in with: "Zebadiah, don't call him 'Goop!' It's Ah-*goo*."

"... that the after compartment is so low that Deety had to lie down to make room for him. But they don't know about our Land-of-Oz space warp—and won't, until if and when we show it off. So we'll surprise 'em. They will expect us to show up washed a bit and, possibly, in fresh flight suits. So we give 'em the works. Hilda, can you put Deety's hair up Barsoomian style?"

"Certainly. And she can do mine just as well."

"Okay. High heels and your prettiest formals—the ones you were married in, if that suits you, but it's your choice. High style with jewelry in your hair. Not all-out Barsoomian but more rocks than you wore last night at Glinda's party."

"Good heavens, was that only last night!"

"Sure was, Aunt Nanny Goat. Despite all the ducking in and out we've done, we've wound up with ship's time only thirteen minutes later than Oz time. Is that chance? Or necessity? How does it fit your theory?"

"Discuss it later, darlings. Jake, do you have black tie along?"

390

"He does," said Aunt Hilda. "Both white mess jacket and black coat. I fetched everything Jacob had when I learned that there was extra mass allowance. Then I got them cleaned and pressed in Helium."

" 'Cleaned and pressed?' *How?*"

"Tira can solve any problem. Deety had your clothes cleaned, too. Poor little boys—you both need nursemaids."

"We married 'em. Good work, dears."

"Zeb," Pop said worriedly, "aren't you overdoing it?"

"Jake, I intend to. They have no idea what correct dress is where we come from, so we'll set our own styles and knock their eyes out. Wear the white mess jacket; it's short enough that you can put it over your Sam Browne without fouling your saber."

" 'Saber?' "

"Saber. I'll lend you miniature ribbons for your lapel. I'm going to wear the medals themselves on my only suit of aerospace dress blues—and before you ask, I've always carried it on *Gay Deceiver* because the only times I needed to wear it involved trips away from campus. I'll wear navy sword and belt over it ... and not mention that they don't belong together."

"Zebadiah," I asked, "can you dance wearing sword?"

"Try me, just try me."

"I will if there's a chance. They have artificial gravity, I'm sure they must have music. If I get a chance to dance, I'll grab it."

"As may be. Forty minutes; let's get cracking. I've got to shave."

"Forty-three minutes, Zebadiah. We'll be on time."

Boy oh boy, did I have fun! I think everybody did and I'm *certain* Aunt Hilda did. Did you ever go to a party where you could legitimately split three dozen men with only one other woman?—all of them young and healthy and handsome (at least nice-looking) and all of them terribly anxious to please? Even the Lensman wasn't much older than Zebadiah, although he did have gray in his hair and some worry wrinkles. Understandable.

I don't want to be a Lensman; I just want to be Deety—and married to Zebadiah, who would be a Lensman (*I* think!) had he been born where-when they have Lensmen. But that wouldn't suit me, as Lensmen lead a tough life and are hardly ever at home and rarely marry as young as Zebadiah is. As Lewis Carroll told me, all my dreams *do* come true.

Pop needn't have worried; Zebadiah wasn't overdoing it because the Patrol's everyday uniform, all black and silver and gold, is fancy as can be. Add medals (they wore them that night, but don't when working) and it's downright gaudy.

A Lens makes even Barsoomian jewelry look plain. I don't know what I expected but whatever it was, a Lens is *more*. The nearest I can think of is an enormous fire opal with a light behind it—but take that and cube it. It's all colors and the colors keep changing and the lights come from the Lens itself and dance like a color organ but brighter and more alive—and I still haven't described it.

I got a chance to ask the Lensman about it at the "cocktail" party from seventeen to eighteen. I put "cocktail" in quotes because my husband had warned us not to get spiffed. Fat chance: there wasn't a cup of alcohol in the *Nighthawk,* outside of sick bay. The drinks were soft drinks, including tea and coffee, hot and cold. I took Coca-Cola because I had never expected to see a Coke again.

Later at dinner they drank toasts in a red wine called *fayalin* but it's a stimulant not a depressant and tastes better (to me) than any of the alcoholic red wines.

But about the Lens ... I asked Lensman Smith (or "Captain" as his officers called him) if it was true that touching a Lens would kill anyone but the wearer?

He said, "Oh, no, no, no!—that was a common misconception. The Lens will kill anyone who tried to wear it except the person it was fitted to, but it is perfectly safe to touch it while it is being worn—go ahead, Doctor; touch it."

So I did—and snatched my finger back. Not a hurt but a thrill so intense that I can compare it only to orgasm but entirely different. And I suddenly knew that he was in my mind.

"Sorry, Doctor," he said soberly. "I should have warned you. I didn't go deep and I didn't learn anything that I didn't already know."

"Please don't call me 'Doctor.' Oh, I am one, but I'm not called by it, not even on campus. I'm not called 'Professor' often, either, and anyhow I'm not a full professor like my father; I'm just an assistant professor. Call me 'Deety,' that's my usual name."

"If you will call me 'Ted,' dear lady."

"But I *can't*, sir. In your own ship you're 'Captain'; you can't be anything else. Why, I rarely call my husband anything but 'Captain' when we're in *Gay Deceiver*, and my father *always* calls Zebadiah 'Captain' when we are underway. Even though Pop—my father—is older and they are more than friends. Blood brothers."

"What do you mean by 'blood brothers'?"

"Meaning that they have fought and killed side by side, sir. What else could it mean?"

"Only that, to me. But some use that idiom loosely."

I suddenly realized that now was the time to ask him something. "Lensman, come into my mind." I turned my thoughts to a panic-stricken time by our lost-forever swimming hole.

"Goodness!" he said. "You really do mean it. The swords they are wearing?"

"Yessir."

"They handle them as well as Major van Vogt handles a space ax. Against firearms, that takes courage. A nasty customer."

"Keep looking, Lensman." I showed him that "ranger" with its clothes cut away, then opened up by Hilda—then the *Pankera* in the Palace of Memories. Then I blanked out and he withdrew. "Captain, have you ever seen one of those vermin?"

"No, and I hope I never do." He gave a shudder, just like ordinary people.

"I should not have brought it up at a party. But my husband and my father and Dr. Hilda will want to ask your advice, later."

"They shall have it, if I'm asked. I'm not sure what it's worth." He frowned. "I wonder …. But later, later."

At dinner, Aunt Hilda was on the captain's right and Zebadiah was on his left—and my husband got very little attention because the Hillbilly was taking the Lensman into camp. I've studied her in action but it's not something I can duplicate, so I don't try. He may have started out thinking Hildy ate cateagles for breakfast but before he finished the soup, I'm sure he was convinced that she was sugar and spice and everything nice. Hilda is like a kitten—paws as gentle as snowflakes … until she shows her claws.

I was on the chief engineer's right at the far end of the wardroom table, with Pop on his left. Chief engineers are always Scots in stories, but Chief Lee was from Mauritius and was Chinese and Tamil and looked Amerindian to me. He was pleasant but I spent most of my time talking to Major van Vogt on my right because Pop and the chief got involved in equations and almost didn't eat—I had to catch Pop's attention and signal "No!" when he started to write on a napkin. The chief produced paper and the table linen was saved.

Major van Vogt commanded the ship's boarding party, he admitted. "But we don't get much of that sort of fun. From day to day we're the ship's guard, so I guess you could call me the chief of police. My top sergeant does the work. What I specialize in is sleeping. I'm very good at that."

He was so big that I had to look up to talk to him, even sitting down. Seven feet tall, I learned later—that was two hundred thirteen and a third centimeters, forty-three centimeters taller than I am, almost twenty centimeters taller than Zebadiah … and massing about twice what my husband masses. He wasn't a freak; all the ship's guard came from Valeria, where they grow 'em that size.

"Then these medals are for sleeping?"

"Not all of them, Deety. This one is for doing a good deed every day, and this one is for spelling, and this one is for whistling."

"But anyone can whistle."

"I do it under water. Can you?"

"I don't know. I haven't tried. But porpoises can; I guess I can learn. I'll try it in the bathtub tonight."

"Deety, I'm sorry but there isn't a bathtub in this ship. If we had known you were coming, the boys would have built one just for you."

"Oh, there's one bathtub, I know—I took a bath in it eighty-seven minutes ago."

"Really?"

"Really truly, Major. It's in this ship because our ship is in this ship." He had been pulling my leg; now he was certain I was pulling his. I tried to estimate how wide and how thick he was. "Can you wiggle through a bulkhead door"—I paused to convert—"twenty inches wide and forty inches high?"

"A bit snug but, if I tackle it sideways and let out all my breath, I can make it."

"That's the tight spot; the bathrooms are abaft the transverse bulkhead. But both bathroom ceilings are a bit higher than you are tall. It's a date but I must check first. Father. Excuse me, Chief—*Pop!*"

Pop looked up. "Yes, Deety? What's the fifth root of nine hundred thirty-two point two?"

"Three point nine two five five six plus."

"Thanks, dear. Now, Chief, if we—"

"Pop!"

"What is it, Deety?"

"Has Captain Zebadiah okayed taking visitors into *Gay Deceiver*?"

Pop blinked like an owl. "The Captain intends to take the Lensman through our craft after dinner. The chief engineer and I will go then, whenever that is. You may check with the captain if you wish … but I assume that there is no objection. Mmm …. Protocol. Perhaps it would be polite to wait until after Captain Smith has seen it."

"But Agú—Mr. Nganagana—has been aboard."

"Ordered aboard as the Lensman's surrogate, dear. Different."

Protocol! I've never had any use for it. "Major, we'll sneak down fast as soon as dinner is over. Our ship isn't big enough for six people at once."

He answered quietly: "I had better wait, Dr. Carter."

"When did I stop being 'Deety?'"

"When you extracted a fifth root in your head."

"But that's just mental arithmetic. Anybody can do it, with practice."

"So? My space ax masses sixty kilos. Could you learn to swing it—with practice?"

"What? Why, that's a kilo more than *I* mass. No … but I could learn to swing one proportionate to my mass. I'm quite muscular, for my size."

"That's just it, Doctor. You don't have the muscles I do; your skeleton could not accept them. I don't have the mental muscles you have; I lack the capacity."

"Major, if you don't stop calling me 'Doctor,' I'll—I'll—I'll sic Dr. Hilda on you. She eats cateagles for breakfast!"

"So I hear." He glanced down the table at Aunt Hilda, looking tiny and doll-like and fragile. "Can she do your sort of mental arithmetic?"

"She does something much more difficult. Or it is to me. She knows everything.

"Not everything here of course; we've never been in a ship of the Galactic Patrol before. But she remembers everything that she has ever seen, read, or heard. By the way, you didn't fool me a bit; I know combat medals when I see them, even though ours are different. Do I sic Dr. Hilda on you?"

"Deety, I surrender. But *you* fooled *me*. You told me that you did 'programming on campus.' I thought you meant assist students in arranging their study programs. Administration."

"Oh. No, I'm not in administration. My degree is in computer science. The mathematical end, not the hardware—although a programmer must understand the hardware or she can't write an optimum program for the computer she is using. I'm designated 'Astrogator' for our vessel, but I don't do much astrogation. Mostly I devise special piloting programs for our autopilot."

"Did you devise the program that put the whole ship in an uproar?"

"Did we cause an uproar?"

"You certainly did. That maneuver when you had young Nganagana as a passenger. If I hadn't been watching a screen in the control room, I wouldn't have believed it. I might not have believed my own eyes if I hadn't glanced at the old man right after you disappeared. Deety, it takes a lot to shock a Lensman; Lensmen have the most stable minds in the galaxy. But I think you folks managed it; he looked as bewildered as I felt. How *did* you get out of that hold? Those doors are gas-tight."

"Major, I'm willing to answer that question but I *can't*. It involves mathematics outside my field. My father invented the continua machine; my husband engineered the adaptation of it to our ship; I simply program its maneuvers—or some of them."

"Did you program the one that scared Goo almost blond?"

"He didn't act scared. Yes, I did. I'm rather pleased with that program—only two syllables, and we left the cargo hold and were a hundred thousand kilometers away. But it's perfectly safe because I've programmed the autopilot not to accept any voices but those of us four. If *you* said those two syllables in *Gay Deceiver*, she wouldn't hear you. She can't hear them with the doors open, either; she has to be ready for space. Yes, it's a nice program; I like it. I enjoy writing a truly economical program."

The major sighed—like a walrus sighing but I didn't say so. "Deety, you've told me everything but how you got out."

"Uh, do you understand parallel universes?"

"I know of them; I don't understand them."

"I'm not sure a three-dimensional brain *can* understand them. But they can be manipulated. We didn't go *out* of that cargo hold; Pop's continua machine pinned that locus, through other dimensions, to a second locus a hundred thousand kilometers away. My program simply told *Gay Deceiver* to do it. So we did. One gets used to it, though it's spooky at first." I reviewed in my mind whether or not I was under

396

orders not to discuss certain matters. No, neither my husband nor my father had placed "classified" on anything ... and I couldn't give away the "secrets" of the continua drive even if I tried. "Major, we are not from this universe."

He answered slowly, "I've been dodging that conclusion for the past two hours. I'm glad you dragged it out on the deck."

"In the past twenty-nine hours, subjective time for us, we have been in seventeen universes. Some were very much like our own; some were very strange indeed. This one is the most like our native universe of any we've been in—so close an analog that we both speak English. Almost the same English—different accent, somewhat different vocabulary—but near enough."

Major van Vogt said thoughtfully, "English is not the ship's working language."

"It isn't?"

"No. It's being spoken because you folks speak it and almost everyone in the ship understands English—except some of my Dutchmen and some other crew members. But this table has been arranged so that those who speak English the most fluently are seated with you four."

"That was thoughtful of the captain. But I can always manage to talk. If I don't know the language, I wave my hands and point ... and presently, I *do* know the language. But I enjoy sitting by you, Major."

"Me too, Deety."

After toasts, dinner was over but the party went on—with music one could dance to. I looked around for Zebadiah but he and the captain had disappeared, so I conscripted Agú and asked him to dance with me. Praise Klono! He had a firm lead, and that was all I asked. He started out easy, discovered that I could follow—and started to embroider. I didn't fall down, I stayed in step. Fun! Shortly all chairs were back against bulkheads and the table had already disappeared, somehow, and Hilda was dancing with an officer I had barely met. When the music stopped, an officer with the same stripes as the captain but no Lens put his hand on Agú's shoulder and said, "RHIP, son"—then said to me: "May I have this dance, Doctor?"

"Yes, if you'll call me 'Deety.' Thanks, Agú, that was fun!"

He thanked me with a big, toothy grin. I said to my new partner, "You're the astrogator."

"Yes, and you are astrogator of your ship. I need some coaching from you."

"All right, we'll trade. But now let's dance." He couldn't dance the way Agú could, but he knew all the classic steps and some I was pleased to learn—and he had a firm lead. I could tell a real man from a namby-pamby just by his lead. Some officers in *Nighthawk* could dance better than others but all had firm leads.

Thirty-odd men can keep two women awfully busy; they almost danced our shoes off—we loved it! The major asked Hilda to dance; it didn't work too well as she came up about to his medals even in high heels. They *did* dance, in step, with the major holding down his strides and the Hillbilly really stretching—then the major picked her up, set her on his left shoulder, held her there with one huge hand, and waltzed solemnly with himself. Everybody applauded and Aunt Hilda laughed and threw kisses at them and kicked up her heels, and a slipper came off.

Somebody caught it and they started drinking *fayalin* from it, almost-not-quite fighting for the privilege and RHIP got lost in the rush. Major van Vogt went right on waltzing. The tape of whatever they used segued into another waltz, a familiar one. Aunt Hilda had a nice mezzo and a big voice for her size; she started singing:

"Waaay down in Missoooori where I learnnned this melody ...."

... and everybody joined in, those who didn't know the words faking it.

A soggy slipper isn't much good for dancing but the Galactic Patrol can meet any emergency. Hilda told me later that it was bone dry (blown dry, I suppose, as with a hair dryer) and had talcum or some such dusted into it; the officer who claimed the privilege had no trouble slipping it onto her tiny foot. She went on dancing.

Aunt Hilda was the belle of the ball—but there was plenty for me. I forgot all about time until I spotted my husband and suddenly realized that I had hardly thought about my husband for three hours and seven minutes.

He came up and claimed me. Yes, Zebadiah can dance while wearing a sword. The music shifted to "The Merry Widow" and we danced it as a pattern, which I didn't know he knew (I'm still learning things about my husband). He finished it with an exaggerated bow while "making a knee" and I curtsied almost to the deck, knowing that Zebadiah's strong hand would lift me out of it. We got wave after wave of applause.

Hilda had been dancing with the captain; we swapped—and I almost got stage fright; I was dancing with a *Lensman*. But Captain Ted Smith was as easy as an old shoe; he didn't try anything fancy, apologized for being rusty, said he was sorry to have missed most of the party but hoped his officers had kept me entertained.

I assured him that they had.

"Your husband Captain Carter and your father Doctor Burroughs have been showing me so many stupendously fascinating things that I could hardly tear myself away. Then I had to send a rather long message." He added, "Part of what I saw were holopix—correction: stereopictures—of what you showed me in your mind earlier. That vermin."

"We weren't equipped to shoot holograms; we were taken by surprise."

"Not so taken by surprise that two heroes—and two heroines—couldn't handle it. Your husband and your father let me see into their minds to supplement the still pictures. I'm much impressed by both you and Dr. Hilda."

I suddenly remembered parts of it and wondered if I could still blush. Apparently not. Then I recalled that Lensmen learned to accept *any* cultural mores no matter how prudish the ones of their childhoods.

"Your father also showed me a stereo of the crater where your home had been, and a mental picture of its destruction. All pictures, all data, are now at Prime Base and are being sent throughout civilization. We don't know that this universe is infested but we are grateful for the warning—forewarned is forearmed."

I didn't want to think about *Panki*. "Did my husband show you our bathroom?"

The Lensman managed to frown and laugh at the same time. "Yes. I don't understand it and wish I could see Sr. Austin Cardynge's face when *he* sees it. The only explanation your father offered was 'magic.'"

"Captain, what other word is appropriate for engineering one cannot explain?"

"Clarke's Theorem. Yes. But I would like to see Sir Austin's face."

The party was over at the end of that dance. The invisible orchestra gave way to a military band, playing "Our Patrol." Nobody told us to stand at attention but all four of us did. Then a young officer escorted us to our quarters. They were roomier than I expected them to be in a warship: a common room flanked by two staterooms, each with a small but complete bath—showers, no tubs. I expected double bunks, probably stacked—but each stateroom held a double bed.

I asked, "Zebadiah, what is this? Admiral's quarters? Or does the *Gray Lensman* use this suite?"

"I don't think so, to both. Jake, look at this."

Pop and Zebadiah studied something at one of the doorways. "Well?" said my husband.

"They don't do things by halves, do they?"

"What are you two talking about?" Aunt Hilda demanded.

"My dear, this suite was constructed *after* we came aboard. It probably started right after we insisted on dressing in *Gay Deceiver*. But I think that the beds were built during the last two hours. Eh, Holmes?"

" 'You know my methods, Watson.' " (My husband loves to show off.) "Gals, we showed the captain and the chief engineer how quickly we could rig two double beds in Gay—the big one forward for you and me, the smaller one after for Sharpie and Jake. The captain glanced at the chief—Lensed him, maybe—and as soon as we had the forward one unrigged, the chief 'remembered' that he had to phone the power room. He stepped outside Gay for about five minutes, then came back. But I'm not going to look a gift horse in the mouth; I'm going to sleep in it."

"Suppose he bites down while you're asleep, Zebbie?"

"That's the horse's problem. Sharpie, if it worries you, you can doss in *Gay Deceiver*. You can't get lost; the passageway outside this suite, if you turn left, leads directly to the cargo hold where she is nested, with all side doors locked off—for our convenience and privacy, the chief said ... although probably also to keep us from wandering into spaces where we should not be. But we aren't prisoners; turn right and you are back in the wardroom and the pantry is manned all night. And that thing over there is a telephone; you can phone the pantry, or anywhere else. Even the captain's cabin."

Next morning we were at Prime Base.

— XXXIX —

Zebadiah

I woke up when we went inertialess; Deety didn't. It's a queasy feeling, unlike freefall. It didn't nauseate me, quite—but it didn't seem to affect Deety's cast-iron stomach at all; she still clung like a koala while we bounced feather-light off the overhead. I managed to grab something, pulled us down, found the glowing light I had been told to look for, tapped it, and a net snapped over us—went back to sleep.

I woke once more when we acquired weight, rearranged my pet koala—went back to sleep; it had been a long day.

When we woke and stayed awake, it was about eight and we were hungry. Jake and Hilda were already awake, in the common room, and eating. "Lazybones," she said, "Nothing left, we ate it all."

"Sharpie, how do I order what you are eating? And where did you find those dressing gowns?"

"Look in your wardrobe, dear. As for ordering, you don't—because when I heard your shower, I ordered for you. Hotcakes, sausage, poached eggs, melon, and milk for Deety, she's eating for two. Dry toast and coffee for you, Zebbie; you're getting paunchy. It'll be here in a moment; that little cupboard is sort of a dumbwaiter."

It arrived before I could tell Sharpie what she could do with her dry toast—same order for both of us, plus milk for Deety.

At nine, the captain phoned me. "Captain, how soon would it suit you and your party to leave the ship?"

I was startled but answered quickly, "We can leave at once if you wish, sir. I may ask for astrogational advice. Am I to assume that

401

Prime Base is expecting us?" (I didn't want us burned out of space; these boys had weapons that made Sprint missiles seem like BB guns).

"Sorry, Captain, first I should have said that we are now *at* Prime Base."

"I slept through it," I told him, trying to sound matter-of-fact. "We can leave as quickly as we can man our ship. Say ten minutes. Or twice that if *Gay Deceiver's* attitude is not horizontal with respect to ground level. I'll take her straight up to any designated altitude if you will alert your ground defenses to expect us at that locus but I do need to know true horizontal since I will be flying blind in taking her out of your hold. Then I'll need a beacon to show me where to land."

"Again, Captain Carter, I have expressed myself poorly. If you are willing to do so, we will leave by gangway ... and I hope you will accept side honors this time; the Port Admiral expressed his intention of meeting you at the foot of the gangway."

"Captain, give it to me by Lens. What do *you* prefer?"

"Zeb, my new friend, both Port Admiral Haynes and I will be disappointed if you do not accept full honors. But we do not insist."

"Very well, sir—full honors. In that case we will need at least an hour; we must get clothes from *Gay Deceiver*—and dress in her if she's right-side-up ...."

"She is."

"Good. I'll take her out of your ship later. Unless you intend to leave Prime Base as soon as we disembark."

"No, we were relieved on station by Patrol Vessel *Horned Owl* and my crew will be granted a few days groundside. Captain Carter, if you will trust me, your ship will be moved with utmost care, inertia-free, to a safe and convenient hangar. She already has the intrinsic of Prime Base and to make doubly sure of not disturbing your instruments and apparatus, she will be placed in the exact attitude and orientation she is now in. By 'safe hangar,' I mean one where she could not be hurt short of Prime Base itself being reduced to molten rock and metal. This is the most heavily defended spot in this galaxy. Believe me, sir, after what you have shown me, the Patrol is as anxious to protect your ship as you are."

"You reassure me. By the way, what happens to open water surfaces in a state free of inertia? Our water closets are not like yours." (Indeed they weren't; theirs weren't truly "water" closets at all. Better. Clever engineering I planned to investigate. But a few liters of water loose in our magic bathrooms would be merely a sloppy mess, not a catastrophe.)

The Lensman took an inordinately long time—for him—to answer. Possibly five seconds. "If there could be damage of that sort, it has already been done during the night. If so, I regret it and will make every possible effort to rectify it."

"Take it easy, Captain; I'm certain that no real harm could be done. Just curiosity." I added, "Suppose we go to our ship now, then call you when we return here. An hour, at a guess."

"Thank you, Captain Carter. It is now nine oh four oh seven. Is it likely that we could all make rendezvous in the wardroom shortly before eleven?"

"I see no difficulty. If one develops, I will call you."

"Zebadiah, I'm scared. I haven't the slightest idea what is meant by 'full honors.' How do we act? How do we *dress?* Neither Hilda nor I have any smart daytime clothes."

"Deety hon, quit worrying. The honors will be rendered to *us.* So we don't have to do a durn thing but stand in line and receive them. Once they're over, I'll salute and you three will barely bow—like *this*—hardly more than inclining your heads. No, Jake and I salute; we've established a precedent; Jake and I wear sidearms at all times. Sharpie, you said you fetched all of Jake's clothes. That wouldn't include an army uniform, would it?"

"It would. Dress blues."

"I wish I had known that last night."

"I don't. Pop looked just perfect."

"I think so, too, Zebbie."

" 'Jake's folly,' I call it. Zeb, when they sent me to the Pentagon, I consoled myself with a silly hope that I might someday be invited to the White House. Or even sent there on an errand. After I had paid for it, dress uniforms were cancelled for the duration. So I've worn it *once.* To an Army Day Ball. But now I can't get into it. I'm too big in the waist."

"Jacob, I have later data. It fits."

"Huh? But, Hilda my dear ...."

"Shush, my modest darling. Tira was prepared to alter it but we checked your waistline from the notch you use on your Sam Browne. My slender hero, that uniform fits you. All Tira did was have it cleaned and that magic no-wrinkle stuff put on it that they use on silks."

"I'll believe it fits me when I try it on. Did you fetch the dress belt? A Sam Browne is a World War I anachronism."

"Doesn't matter whether she did or not, Jake ...."

"I did."

"... because we are setting our own styles and can't be wrong. While this universe seems to be based on Doctor E. E. Smith's colossal space operas—maybe vice versa ...."

"It's the same either way, Zebbie. You're still hung up on causation. Forget it."

"... it's at least two or three centuries in our future ... if we were on the same time axis, which we aren't. So we *can't* be wrong. Wear the belt you prefer. But you and I *always* wear sidearms."

"Zebbie, any reason Deety and I can't wear our pretty daggers?"

"Not if you want to. Why?"

"Just thinking, dear, just thinking."

We spent more time working out how to dress than we did dressing. I had kept my academic regalia in my car for the same reason I had uniforms there; more likely to need the stuff at some other campus than on my own—and still at hand if I joined the academic procession where I was nominally a professor. Deety and Jake had no reason to keep gowns and hoods and such at Snug Harbor, but three months earlier they had packed their car to go to Snug Harbor before they attended commencement at Logan—then had headed for Snug Harbor, just chucking their robes into the back seat. The stuff had never been returned to Logan.

So we put Dr. Hilda into Deety's academic gown through the gals' shortening the hemline in a hurry. Deety is broad-shouldered and, in high heels, almost as tall as Jake. So with high heels, his gown fitted her well enough. Jake's hood was large for Hilda but those things don't really have to fit—and it had a magnificent gold and scarlet lining. They tacked it up a bit and made sure that the lining showed well. It set off the sky blue lining of Deety's hood.

But Jake's mortarboard could not fit Hilda short of thumbtacks. No matter, that degree factory I went to uses a soft hat for doctorates resembling a four-cornered tam o'shanter—right out of the Middle Ages, which that school is *not*. Its gold tassel tied in with her hood. Needle and thread and some hairpins and Hilda looked good in it.

"Hillbilly, what are we going to wear *under* these?"

"Those fancy lightweight flying suits Tira had made for us. And our daggers."

"But, Aunt Hilda, those things are leotards, tights. And translucent."

"Not all that translucent. And the swirly colors worked into them confuse the issue. We showed lots more skin last night. Cap'n Zebbie said we could set our own styles. I'm going to wear the flesh-colored stick-on cheaters I wore last night … so that if I'm invited to take off this nightgown, I'll still be smartly dressed. Tell her, Zebbie."

I was about to back up Deety but I suddenly switched sides. Deety didn't want to wear a gingham dress or slacks or jeans (such being the sort of clothes she had had at Snug Harbor); she just wanted to be assured that what amounted to a paint job put on with an airbrush was all right. "Deety girl, are you running a fever? A couple of days ago I saw you standing in the starboard door of *Gay Deceiver* dressed in a happy smile, in full view of at least five hundred men and a dozen women."

"But … but that was Barsoom!"

"And this is Prime Base in another universe—and they know we come from still another universe. Sharpie is right; we set our own styles and can't be wrong."

We were dressed and back in our suite in the *Nighthawk* before ten-thirty. We hadn't been slowed by water slopping around; either being inertia-free doesn't bother a surface of water or our bathrooms are in another universe—I favor the latter theory. I had time to renew my shave while the gals were busy with hasty sewing. I called Captain Smith, told him that *Gay Deceiver* was not in his tender care, then Jake and I practiced sword salutes, by the numbers, counting cadence silently, holding each position for two counts—just "Draw … *swords!*" and the rest of it silent drill. We got it down pat.

We tried it with our wives between us. Yes, with Deety on my left, I could handle the return to scabbard without poking out one of her eyes—she needs both of them.

At five minutes before eleven we showed up in the wardroom.

Captain Smith bowed to our ladies, said good morning, shook hands. "Thanks for being so prompt, Captain."

"There was nothing to slow us up; water in our bathrooms had not spilled."

"Really? I'm relieved to hear it … and would like to look into the phenomenon … later. The Port Admiral is ready … if you are."

"We're ready. What's the drill, Captain?"

"Quite simple. You four will leave the ship first; I will follow you. The Port Admiral and his party will be facing the gangway about thirty feet from its foot. There is a gold line on the floor about midway between the gangway and the Port Admiral's party. If you and your companions will stop at that line and wait, honors will be rendered. Immediately following honors, the Port Admiral requests that you accompany him to his lounge for lunch—if that suits your convenience. If not …."

"It does. Please tell him so."

"I have so told him." (Lenses have their minor uses, too! No messenger ….) "I was about to say that you could be taken to your guest quarters, and let me add that the hangar for *Gay Deceiver* is reached by a short private passageway from your quarters."

"Most convenient and thoughtful. Shall we get on with it, sir?"

"This way, please."

When we reached the "quarterdeck"—a big compartment with a door leading out—I could see that Lensman Ted Smith had gone all out … as I had suspected when I saw how he was dressed: a black and silver and gold uniform dressier than that he had worn the night before—and polished DeLameters at his hips.

I had expected him to dress up; he had said "full honors" but I had not expected some touches hoary with tradition. The Officer of the Watch at the gangway was the astrogator (reasonable) but he carried, tucked under his left arm, an ancient spyglass—reasonable! I wondered if it functioned, then decided that the Patrol would not use a fake.

After seeing that, I was not surprised at eight sideboys and still not surprised but much flattered that they were junior officers rather than enlisted spacemen.

The ship's guard took up most of the deck space; fifty-odd Valerian Dutchmen all about the size of their commander use a lot of cubage. As we appeared, Major van Vogt gave "Pr'*sent!* … *Harmp!*" and fifty space axes flashed high and came abruptly down.

I twice asked permission to leave the ship, first of the captain since he was present, then of the astrogator since he had the deck, with a hand salute to each, then headed out between the double rank of sideboys.

Trust Deety to toss a curve into anything— One of our sideboys was Lieutenant Nganagana. Deety, right behind me, said, "Hi, Agú!" Nganagana kept silent, stayed rigidly at attention, eyes front, frozen ebony. Deety stopped dead, said to the Lensman, "Captain, my friend won't speak to me."

This would not have mattered had I not at that instant stepped over the nonexistent "waterway," and saluted their colors (I assumed they had colors; I never saw them) in the direction I thought of as "aft," thereby formally leaving the ship—and the shrill whistle of the boatswain's pipe sounded. Hell's bells, I don't think the Galactic Patrol *had* boatswains! (But they did have "boats"—small spaceships carried aboard—and there must be some officer responsible for their upkeep, so he may be known as "Boats'n" regardless of rank.) As may be, somebody had a boatswain's pipe, knew how to play it, and *had* to get us all across that gangway on one lungful of air.

Meanwhile, Deety held up the procession.

I heard Smith say sharply, "Nganagana, answer the lady!"

"Hi, Deety!"

"Take care of yourself, Agú—I'll see you!" Deety consented to resume the march; I waited until she was beside me, then hurried a little. The gangway was a horizontal footbridge about four meters wide and forty long; I wanted to get us to the far end before that lilting skirl stopped, both for the player's lungs and for his face.

We made it but it was a dead heat—I hope he didn't rupture a blood vessel.

We stopped at that gold line: me, Deety, Hilda, Jake at far left, spaced out to let Jake and me handle swords. Captain Smith stopped short of the line, on my right. Facing us was more gold lace than I had ever seen, even at the Embassy in Melbourne.

We were somewhere underground but in a gargantuan hall or cavern so wide, high, and long, and so brilliantly lighted, that it felt like outdoors. To our left was a huge military band in uniforms more colorful—*gaudy!*—than the display of gold lace and medals facing us. Facing the band, on our right, was rank after rank of Patrolmen; the far end of this guard I could not see but it was at least a regiment.

As we stopped, loudspeakers everywhere boomed: "Present! *Arms!*" Captain Smith saluted; the Port Admiral and his party saluted; I did not, Jake did not—but my hand quivered in restrained reflex.

A line of trumpeters, front rank of the band, lifted their gleaming, bannered, bell-flared instruments and started flourishes, while drummers behind them matched them with ruffles:

"Tah titti tah tah *taaaah!*" ("Boom titti boom boom *booooom!*")

I expected them to stop with four, enough for any skipper, but they continued with a fifth ... and a *sixth!*—and I knew we were in for it. (*Zeb, you four-flusher, can you swing this?* I wished I were back in my teens again, mowing lawns and throwing papers—I even felt homesick for Jockstrap U, where the cockroaches ate out.)

But I recognized the music that followed ruffles and flourishes; this brought me into focus—I knew the role I was expected to play. It was the "Viceroy March," also called the "Ambassador." (The Patrol calls it something else—no matter; it's as high as you can go: sovereignty saluting sovereignty, equals acknowledging equals.)

When it reached its crashing coda, I expected honors to end, since they couldn't play our national anthem, not knowing where we were from. I waited for the command to order arms, ready to signal Jake.

Nope! From the rear of that mighty hall, over half a kilometer away, came a line of flashes—then, about two seconds later: "Ka-*boom!*" The sound reached us both directly and echoing endlessly off ceiling, walls, and floor, so that it was still rumbling out when the next line of flashes appeared. Traditional black powder? I didn't know but it looked and sounded like it. If so, they must have enormous scavengers to suck the smoke away. On the other hand, it may have been done by exact simulation—no powder, no cannon. (I never did ask.)

I counted four-second intervals between flashes, while wondering where they would stop. Twenty-one? Fifty? More? The Port Admiral and party stayed frozen at salute, the guard of honor at present arms. When I saw the twenty-first flash, then counted six seconds past it, I knew they were through—so, as the rumbling roar died out, I signaled Jake: "Draw ... *swords!*" We went through it like clockwork, a twelve-second silent drill. Out of the corner of my eye I saw Deety give a slight but distinct bow as we came to present arms, then straightened and stood tall as we returned swords. Hilda was right with her. Our pipsqueak salute was nothing compared with their full honors—but we did it correctly and in step. I felt relieved.

The loudspeakers boomed, "Order ... *Harmp!*"

The Port Admiral's party broke and moved toward us, as we moved toward them. As introductions were made, I heard the troops ordered to parade rest. All the reception party wore Lenses; two of them were in plain gray leather uniforms—but neither was *the* Gray Lensman, Kinnison. Port Admiral Haynes was entitled to wear Gray but chooses to accept the burden of commander in chief, and wore black, with rank insignia. However his chest was not covered with medals; he wore just one, around his neck.

Shortly, a car glided out from behind the band. I should say "vehicle," as it was a very low platform with a long bench on it—no wheels, no noise, no apparent source of propulsion or guidance, no driver. It stopped by us; the Port Admiral handed up Hilda and seated her, his flag lieutenant Captain Fernandez seated Deety, and Jake and I wound up between Dr. Lacy and Commander Ted Smith (still dressed as "Captain" even though groundside). The dozen-odd others melted away (I didn't see where); once we eight were seated, this vehicle started down the long line of troops at about three knots.

As we approached each unit—company, battery, troop, combat team, whatever—its commander brought it to attention and saluted. Haynes returned salutes but the other officers did not, so Jake and I refrained. We were "inspecting" the honor guard, but pro-forma, not de-facto. But I'll take any odds that, had we stopped and put on white gloves, we could not have soiled them.

This moving platform delivered us into the Port Admiral's lounge, paused while we stepped off, then backed out, and the doors closed behind it. I made mental note to ask later how it was guided (I thought of three possibilities, one of which required a Lens)—but never asked.

Haynes and his flag lieutenant seated us in a circle of nine chairs, then Haynes started in without inanities. "That empty chair is for Sir Austin Cardynge. With luck he'll be with us before lunch at thirteen-thirty. He was at a conference some distance away, about eight hundred light years, and, when I called him, he told me to go soak my head." Haynes grinned and suddenly looked younger. "He's been telling me that for thirty years. But I managed to convince him that there was something here beyond my capacity—which did not surprise him; he has a low opinion of most mentalities—and that the problem was worthy of his attention." Haynes looked at me. "Captain Carter, Sir Austin says that your alleged space drive is 'poppycock.'"

I've met high brass before; I don't expect them to be diplomatic other than when it suits them. I made my answer low-key. "Admiral, I don't recall alleging that I had a 'space drive.' I did not allege anything that I did not follow with demonstration. Ask Captain Smith."

"Correction accepted. Captain Smith has just reminded me that his report did not use the phrase 'space drive.' 'Continua craft' is the phrase you used. He also has now reminded me of other phenomena that he reported, including something you called a 'time-space warp.' But your unsupported allegations referred to 'continua travel'—travel in universes parallel to this one."

Jake grabbed that one. "No, no, Admiral! We have traveled in several universes but not one of them is parallel to this one. I did not say they were."

"Again Captain Smith has corrected me. You said 'other universes.' I acknowledge the correction but fail to see the difference."

"That's because you're not a mathematician!" Jake's voice was getting high. One more use of "alleged" or "allegation" was likely to set him off.

Hilda spotted it and tossed in a diversion. She was across from Haynes in the circle and not in my line of sight, as I was closer to the admiral—only Captain Smith between us—and I had turned my chair to face him. She said, "Admiral, you two are discussing us via your Lenses! Do you consider that polite treatment of guests?" She used her best top-sergeant voice.

I turned to look at her. She had laid back her academic gown— the room was rather warm, at least for four people who had gone naked or nearly so most of eight or nine subjective weeks. She was sitting on her feet with her spine straight. She looked very female, and extremely haughty. "Well? Answer me! Is that the way the Patrol's Port Admiral treats guests?"

"Madam, your exact status is still to be determined."

"Please address me correctly!"

"Dr. Hilda Burroughs, your party was apprehended in our space …."

"*Your* space? What arrogance! Show me your deed to it! Did Klono sign it? I'm sure Mentor did not. Admiral Haynes, to speak of empty space a billion kilometers from nowhere as 'yours' is nonsense. We …."

"Space we patrol, Doctor. Correction accepted."

"Hold your tongue, sir; I am not through. We were *not* apprehended. To 'apprehend' is to arrest. Captain Smith, did you tell Port Admiral Haynes that you had arrested us?"

"No, Dr. Hilda, I did not."

"Thank you, Captain. Port Admiral, we came freely, as invited guests. You received us as *honored* guests. Now you say that our 'status is still to be determined'—what do you mean by *that*, sir?"

Haynes looked embarrassed, but dogged. "Doctor, I meant just what I said. Captain Smith reported what he saw ... or thought he saw. But I have been unable to confirm it by examining your minds ...."

Sharpie gave a gasp of outrage. "*Oh!* So those prods were *not* just clumsy accidents? I had excused them as I would forgive a dog for trying to lick my face. What sort of a little boy were you, Admiral? A peeping Tom? A keyhole snooper? *Shame* on you, you dirty little boy!"

I was alert but did not interrupt. Sharpie has her own weapons and knows how to use them ... and I didn't have any delusions about the usefulness of one sword and one saber against a heavily fortified military base. We had been hornswoggled; perhaps Sharpie could get us out of it.

The admiral's face became as impassive as Deety's. "Doctor, whether you like it or I like it—and I often do not—it is my duty to protect this galaxy as best I can. Some entities are enormously skilled at creating hallucinations. According to Sir Austin Cardynge, Captain Smith's report is most readily explained as a skillfully contrived mass hallucination. On this point I thought I could test you four ... but I have been unable to reach first check-station. So I must wait for help. I am sorry that you do not like my methods."

"I don't!"

"In the meantime you are guests. Within limits."

I said quickly, "Hilda, I'll answer that!"—and stood up. "Port Admiral Haynes, we will not be having lunch with you."

"Eh? Sit down, Captain."

"No, Admiral. You met us with ambassadorial honors. I see now that those honors are phony. We do not accept phony hospitality, even that of a comfortable chair." Deety stood up at once, so did Jake and Hilda—Jake helped her back into her academic gown. "I ask for escort back to our ship—armed, of course, and thought-screened against 'hallucinations.' We have no further business here." I looked at Captain Smith. "Sorry, Ted—I thought we could give it to the Patrol. Not your fault."

"I'm sorry, too, Zeb." He took a deep breath and stood up. "Port Admiral, I don't like your methods, either."

411

"Smith, sit down!"

"No, sir. I made a complete report to you, including the promises I made to them—Lensman's Word. On behalf of the Galactic Patrol and by authority vested in me as a Patrol ship's master in space, I invited them into the *Nighthawk* as *guests*. They were not 'apprehended'; Dr. Hilda is correct. All the power at my command was not enough to arrest them; they came voluntarily by my invitation. I guaranteed that they and their ship could leave at any time … and that no Patrol action would be taken against them and their ship until it was at least as far away as it was at that time—that is to say, slightly over a billion miles from the nearest Patrol ship. I made these guarantees without mental reservations—and also promised to stay out of their minds with my Lens.

"You know all this, Port Admiral, and so do they. By accepting my report and telling me to bring them to Prime Base, you implicitly confirmed my promises to them—including, in my opinion, a promise not to Lens them other than by direct invitation.

"You have stripped me of Lensman's honor, sir." Ted Smith slowly, solemnly removed his Lens; it turned dark. He placed it on a side table by the admiral. He unbuckled his belt, placed his DeLameters on the rug—ran a forefinger down the front of his tunic; it opened. He took it off, dropped it on the rug. Shocked as I was, I still had room for surprise to find that he wore nothing under it. He was bare to the waist—and utterly without insignia.

Smith looked up and met the admiral's eyes. "That completes it. I will confirm in writing at this moment."

"Smith, I'll take care of you later!"

"No, sir. To take care of me now or later, you must prefer charges before the Galactic Council. Charges would lack merit as I have obeyed your orders and Patrol regulations both in letter and in spirit up to the moment you forced me to resign. I am now a civilian. I intend to show my friends to their ship, then leave Prime Base."

"Young man, don't you realize that these entities may be enemies of civilization?"

For the first time, the surgeon-marshal joined in. "Take it easy, Haynes!"

— XL —

Deety

When Dr. Lacy spoke up, I was feeling sick. Poor Captain Ted! Aunt Hilda had done what she had to do—and beautifully; I wasn't criticizing *her*. Zebadiah had said what had to be said—and Captain Ted did what he felt honor-bound to do. But when his Lens turned dark, my heart sank—I wanted to tell Mama Jane about it.

Admiral Haynes had seemed such a nice person ... but I *knew* Captain Ted was—and now he had thrown away his career for us. I wished that I could turn back time twenty hours—we'd been nothing but bad luck for him.

Admiral Haynes said. "Eh? Lacy, what do you mean?"

"You've been clacking your tongue without hooking it into your brain—expressing opinions before collecting data. Now you've forced a Lensman into an intolerable position." Dr. Lacy turned to Captain Ted. "Son, put that Lens back on, please."

"No, sir."

"Um. If you find yourself before the Galactic Council, I'll be witness for you. I'm proud of you."

"Lacy, this isn't your jurisdiction," Haynes interjected.

"Isn't it? If you don't want my opinions, why did you invite me to the party? Never mind; you're going to get 'em anyhow. First place, don't call them 'entities.' They're human to the last decimal place—more human than you are, you regenerated old retread."

"How do you know? You're guessing."

"Hrrmph! Did you notice what I called you? Who operated on you? While you've been guessing, I've been finding out. From Phillips.

413

I've been close-linked with our Posenian friend and learning things while you've been exercising your lingual muscles. Phillips has examined each of them in detail, every organ. *Human.* He took me along; it's *my* professional report, too. Dr. Hilda, the examination did not penetrate your minds; both Phillips and I found you four to have amazingly strong mind blocks. But we wouldn't have tried to touch your minds, had we known of Ted Smith's promise. Let me add that Phillips is *not* human; he's a Posenian Lensman with a sense of perception in place of sight and hearing—greatest neural surgeon in this galaxy. If he says a mind is blocked, it's *blocked*."

Aunt Hilda answered, "I know who Dr. Phillips is. He regenerated Admiral Haynes and Commandant von Hohendorff—and then *the* Gray Lensman, Kimball Kinnison. Doctor, I don't mind examinations by medical men; it was the uninvited attempt by *him*"—Aunt Hilda pointed and managed to suggest that Admiral Haynes was something nasty in the soup—"to invade our privacy that I resented."

Admiral Haynes looked startled when Aunt Hilda mentioned his regeneration operation—then shut down his face. We had the advantage that we knew quite a bit about them but they didn't know anything about us … and for a moment I wondered whether or not *we* could be storybook characters to some other universe the way Aunt Hilda's theory suggested, and then decided that we couldn't be because we were just people sort of people, not romantic ones like *the* Gray Lensman.

"Doctor Hilda, I'm pleased to hear that," Dr. Lacy answered. "I doubt that even Worsel could penetrate your block—but that old snake wouldn't try unless you asked him to. By the way, Phillips says, and I agree, that all of you are in excellent health. But I would have that appendix out, if I were you, before your second trimester. It's healthy but could cause trouble later. Have it out here at Base Hospital if you like. With Phillips as co-operator you'll be back on your feet and feeling fine in forty-eight hours. It's amazing what a sense of perception can do for diagnosis and surgery."

"Thank you, Dr. Lacy—but our captain has decided that we leave at once."

"I was hoping to entice you to stay—repair some of the damage that old martinet did. Haynes, the only possible excuse you have even to suspect that these four might be enemies of civilization— and it's not a *reason*—is that *your* mind isn't strong enough even

414

with a Lens to get past their mind blocks. If you really had cause to suspect them, you should never have let them into Prime Base. But you *don't* have cause."

"All right, all right," growled Admiral Haynes. "I let my mouth run ahead of my brain. Getting old—senile, perhaps. Ladies and gentlemen, I apologize to all of you. To you, too, Smith."

Zebadiah answered for us: "Admiral, before we can accept apologies, I must know something. Will we be permitted to leave freely and at any time as was guaranteed to us yesterday?"

"Of course, of course!"

"Dr. Hilda, is he carrying any mental reservations? Scan his mind." (Was my darling pulling a bluff? So far as I know, Aunt Hilda didn't read minds. But would I know?)

"He has one mental reservation, Captain Zebbie. If he decides later that we *are* enemies of civilization—all bets are off."

"Well, Admiral?"

I didn't think the expression "turned purple" was literal. Well, perhaps it isn't; Admiral Haynes' shade was more of a delicate mauve. "Captain, in that unlikely event, flag of truce will protect you, and your ship will be placed where it was when it was detected and any and all Patrol vessels will withdraw at least as far as *Nighthawk* was at that time."

"That isn't necessary, Admiral. Simply assure me that we will be freely allowed to man our ship; it is much faster than any of yours. We can go to Lundmark's nebula and back while your best speedster is getting clear of Tellus' atmosphere."

"I find that hard to believe."

Pop spoke up. "You'd better believe it! We've offered you the greatest advantage over Boskone you could ever hope for ... and you've treated us like *dirt*. I resent that, sir! And your 'Sir Austin' is a fool. 'Poppycock' indeed! Captain, let's leave at once and find a universe that has competent mathematicians."

"Just a moment, Dr. Burroughs. I think the admiral is trying to make amends. Dr. Hilda, can we trust him this time? Go deep."

Aunt Hilda answered at once. "He means it, Cap'n. He's very much upset ... but he has placed 'Lensman's Word' on this agreement."

"Thank you, Dr. Hilda. Very well, sir, we accept the agreement and your apology. When Dr. Hilda goes deep, it's impossible to lie to her."

"Thank you, Captain; thank you, Dr. Hilda. Will you now stay for lunch?"

"We will," Aunt Hilda answered for us, "but Dr. Deety and I wish to go to our ship first. Get rid of these hot gowns and change into something else. Possibly a quick tub. And, Admiral ... I'm sorry I called you a 'dirty little boy.' You are not. You are simply a man with too heavy a burden who sometimes makes mistakes."

The admiral sighed. "I can't disagree with a word of that. Thank you, Dr. Hilda. Smith, will you put your Lens back on and join us?"

"No, sir."

"Why not, sir?"

"You've let me down once. I no longer wish to serve under you."

That was a sad note to finish on ... but as Mama told me long ago, I must not try to run other people's lives. Ted was a grown man—but it made me feel awful to see his Lens lying there, all dark and forlorn. But I couldn't stop it. Captain Fernandez took us to our quarters and showed us that *Gay Deceiver* was only a short distance, less than fifty meters, away. Our quarters were lovely—not as big as ours in Helium but more than ample. But I wanted us to climb right into *Gay Deceiver* and rotate out of there. Poor Ted!

Aunt Hilda reminded me that we had promised to stay for lunch. "And quit worrying about Ted, Deety; I'm not leaving this joint until I get that straightened out—you'll see. Now let's see what we can whip up in a hurry out of Barsoomian silk that will look good and be even more a scandal to the jaybirds than these tights. I don't need a bath."

"I do. You decide and I'll wear it."

Zebadiah said, "You two snap it up! It's thirteen o'clock and lunch is half past."

"The admiral will have to wait," Aunt Hilda said tranquilly. "He caused the delay. Unless you two dears want something, go back to our suite and wait."

"Uh ... this dress uniform is too hot. I think I'll cut back to summer khaki and a shirt, no blouse. Insignia but no medals. No necktie. How about you, Jake?"

"Wearing your sword?"

"Always. Wear your saber but wear anything else you like."

"Then it won't be uniform; these blues are an oven. Mmm ... slacks and a sport shirt. And saber."

"Grab 'em and git," Aunt Hilda urged, "unless you want to talk secrets. A Lens can't reach in here."

"Why not, Sharpie?"

"Because this dressing room is in Oz."

"I thought that was what you meant. Sharpie, that was an *ichiban* job you did on Haynes. Congratulations."

"He wasn't difficult. On the whole, he's rather nice. I hated to spank him."

Aunt Hilda's notion of what to do with scraps of silk would get us arrested some places. We could have hired out as advertisements for White Rock. Except that I'm too husky to be a water sprite. A hamadryad, maybe ... or an oak tree.

I was hoping she would say bare feet but she put us in Cinderella slippers—white thoat skin—and decreed that our hair must be up high instead of the low coiffures we had to wear for mortarboards. With jeweled pins in our hair, and a jeweled clasp to pull in the silk that went over one shoulder, and our jeweled belts and daggers—me in wavily green, Hilda in light blue—we looked dressy but not overdressed. Underdressed, maybe, in one sense, but they wouldn't know what we wore to luncheons at home—and Hilda looked as if she might grow gauzy wings and fly away.

We went back through the passage to our suite, only nine minutes late, and found the flag lieutenant, Captain Fernandez, waiting with our husbands. The captain—Carlos, his name was—didn't say a word about us being late; he just clapped his hands together and told us we looked beautiful. Then we went on another of those little scooter cars to the admiral's dining room.

A Gray Lensman was there, talking to the admiral. His back was toward us and I was wondering if it could possibly be *the* Gray Lensman, when he turned around. If I had false teeth, I would have swallowed them. "*Ted!*"

"Hi Deety!" He looked sheepish. "Funny, isn't it? The admiral trumped my ace. So now I've got to start thinking for myself."

The admiral said, "Dr. Deety, my lunch has turned into a celebration. I hadn't intended to do this until the end of Ted's tour as a skipper ... but what can I do when a man is too valuable to lose and won't take orders? Turn him loose and stop giving him orders, that's all. Ted claims he isn't ready for it ... but they all say that ... said it myself about thirty years ago. Or centuries, it feels like. Hrrmph!"

"Admiral, I'm *so* happy! Ted, you look *magnificent!*" He did, too. That gray leather was so plain, and nearly skin tight, that if a man had the physique to wear it, you found out how handsome he was. Ted looked taller and his shoulders broader and waist trimmer than he had looked when gold and silver and medals and things were cluttering the view. All that set off his uniform now were his shiny DeLameters and his Lens, which seemed even brighter.

"Deety, *you* are the one who looks magnificent."

"She certainly does. Dr. Deety, look me straight in the eye and tell me how you ladies knew that this would be an occasion to dress so prettily. Did Dr. Hilda Lens it—I mean not-Lens it; Ted tells me she doesn't need a Lens and I know he's right—did Dr. Hilda pick this intention out of my mind when she went deep?"

"It's true that Aunt Hilda doesn't need a Lens. Could it be the other way around? That she placed the thought in there? Dr. Hilda would not read your mind other than for the specific purpose that my husband, our captain, told her to read you—with your knowing that she was about to do so. But she might have left a thought of her own for you to chew on. She didn't *like* what you forced Ted to do—and neither did I and I was fretting and she told me to stop because she was fixing it." (Almost true! Just shaded a bit.)

"Oh, No! Ted, read me my Lens. I *did* intend to release you—I just hadn't planned to do it today."

I said, "Perhaps that is all she dropped in, Admiral—the date. Why don't you ask her? If you dare."

Port Admiral Haynes looked across the room at the Hillbilly, scratched his head, and grinned. "You're right. I don't dare."

— XLI —

Zebadiah

When we started our Odyssey, I would have rated us in this order: Jake, me, Deety, Sharpie. A good thing I'm not a real CO who makes out efficiency reports; I would have been tearing them up and doing them over again and again. If a table has four legs, which one can you afford to throw away?

Each of us is very different from the other three—equals only in each being dependent on the others, we could not have made it if any of us had stayed behind.

But it took endless time to get it through my skull that Sharpie was the most unusual of the three geniuses I had for crew. I had known her for four years as a campus widow, a playgirl, a Sybarite. I revised my opinion again and again, especially one fine day in the Bay of Blood.

But long-held opinions die hard. I continued subconsciously to think of her as the lightweight in our team merely because she was physically a light weight and looked like a kitten.

Could Sharpie read minds? Possibly Sharpie's "mind reading" was like that of a carny mentalist who picked up minor clues, put them together, then went ahead on sheer brass.

As may be, when I told her to "go deep" into the mind of a Gray Lensman, I knew she would not let me down.

Nor did she. If I need "mind reading" again, I'll call on "Doctor" Hilda—I won't pretend I can do it myself; I don't have the gall

419

to put it over. Whether her talent is cold nerve or true telepathy, Sharpie will deliver.

Ted Smith in Gray with his Lens back where it belonged was a heart-warming sight. I hadn't been surprised when he kicked over his career to stand up for what he felt was right. Real officers did that. I felt no urge to interfere; Ted had not done it for us, he had obeyed his sense of honor and duty. But I *had* felt *sick!* Sometimes a man forced to that drastic action gets away with it; more often he does not—while the bootlickers, the brown-noses, the eager ones with their fingers on their numbers, got promoted. In peacetime, that was standard.

But this was wartime and the Galactic Patrol was no ordinary outfit. Ted got promoted.

A promotion party was a happy occasion, but I'm glad the Patrol did it with *fayalin* rather than Aussie beer—I needed to hang on to what judgment I had. Sir Austin Cardynge arrived shortly before we sat down to eat—and as soon as I met him I resolved to insulate him from Jake even if I had to crowd it, with me on one side and Deety or Hilda on the other, and Jake at the far side of the table.

I've met Sir-Austins on a dozen campuses. They acted as if your presence was an intrusion on their valuable time, one they tolerated only under duress—and wouldn't put up with much longer. But they expected *you* to tolerate their boorish rudeness ... because *they* were so important.

This Sir Austin was a tall, thin, elderly chap, with a hatchet face and a chronic expression, as if he had just whiffed a bad odor—probably *you*. He managed to dismiss me as being beneath notice even as he was (barely) shaking hands and saying, "Howjuh do, Captain Cartwright." I didn't mind, I'd been insulted by experts. But I resolved not to put him in the same cage with Jake without me there to stop biting in the clinches.

But I wasn't host and couldn't swing it; there were place cards and Haynes (or his flag lieutenant) had arranged an unbalanced table (nine) with exact protocol for the luncheon's triple purpose: 1) hospitality to distinguished guests (the Port Admiral was bound by the ambassadorial honors we had received); 2) wetting-down of Ted's promotion; and 3) a social meeting between mathematicians before they got down to work.

Following protocol was usually sensible. But protocol is as automatic as a computer and can be just as stupid—this was how it worked out:

Haynes
Hilda, Sir Austin
Dr. Lacy, Jake
Capt. Fernandez
Me, Deety
Ted Smith

Most faced the guest of honor, newly Released Gray Lensman Smith; senior female guest on host's right; junior female guest on the right of the guest of honor; senior male guest (Sir Austin) on host's left; senior male guest of our party on the left of the guest of honor ("senior" being me, not Jake, because I "commanded"); Jake placed next to the big-brain he was to meet; and the two officers Haynes had picked to help him entertain guests opposite each other.

An embassy's chief of protocol could not have done it more neatly. And it was all wrong!

Jake was mild and sensible, unless someone pushed his "mad" button. While we were dressing, I had suggested that mathematical theory be postponed until socializing was over, and Jake had agreed. He told me he tried to avoid the subject.

But Sir Austin didn't give a hoot for social amenities.

I was keeping fingers crossed and talking shop with Ted Smith while Deety was chatting with Carlos Fernandez. Hilda was keeping Surgeon-Marshal Lacy busy. This left Jake on his own with Sir Austin, with Haynes on the other side of Sir Austin. Maybe the Port Admiral tried to keep the ship steady—Jake said he did—but was unsuccessful.

We hadn't reached the entrée when I heard: "Utter bilge, sir! Childish nonsense! Any schoolboy knows that normal space is rectilinear."

Jake answered (his voice not high yet); "How did you measure it, Sir Austin?"

"*Measure* it? I'm a mathematician, not a surveyor! I *proved* it."

"So? Perhaps—after lunch—you will show me your proof."

"*What?* It's not my business to prove anything to *you!*" Sir Austin turned his head away from Jake. "Haynes, I told you you were wasting my time. I told you!"

Hilda had her ear cocked; she cut in: "Sir Austin ...."

"What? What, madam?"

Hilda used her schoolmistress manner, one notch milder than her top-sergeant act: "I am Doctor Hilda Burroughs, Chief Science Officer of our exploration party—you called me 'Burns' when we were introduced."

"What? What, what? Perhaps I did. High noise level and so forth. No offense intended. What do you want, Doctor ... Burrow?"

"I had no trouble hearing your name, Sir Austin Cardynge. I find that in social life, as in science, attention to detail is essential. You still do not have my name right. Dr. Hilda *Burroughs*. That is Dr. Jacob Burroughs by you. I suggest you address me as Dr. Hilda."

That got his attention; he turned from pink to red—and the heat was off Jake and on him. " 'Dr. Hilda *Burroughs*,' " he repeated stiffly. "Very well, Dr. Hilda, what is it you wish to ask me?"

"I have no wish to ask you anything, Sir Austin; I intend to *tell* you something ... if you can keep quiet long enough to listen."

Apparently he had no heart trouble; he didn't conk out. He paused about two beats, then said tensely, "Ma ... Dr. Hilda—I am listening."

"If you are a scientist, sir, as well as a mathematician, you know that in science—true science—one verifiable fact can destroy the most elegant mathematical theory ... if that theory is mistaken."

"Eh? Stipulated. What are you getting at?"

"If you are truly a scientist, sir, I suggest that you stop bickering with my husband and ask the Port Admiral where our ship was found, then ask Gray Lensman Smith what sort of ship it is. If you do that, then follow up by seeking other facts instead of plonking your theories at us, you may learn something ... even at your age."

Maybe Sharpie didn't need to twist the dagger. But maybe she did—nothing gravels an old man like being told that he was too old to learn.

Sir Austin still hadn't realized that he was fighting out of his weight. Obviously he was in the habit of bullying others ... but Sharpie has raised bullying to a high art. She had used that sharp blade; she was now offering him the pinch of snuff. Would he take it?

He took it. "I've heard that preposterous story! Poppycock! Hallucinations!"

Sharpie didn't answer, she didn't need to—she now had him flanked with her heavy artillery. Her mouth twitched in the fashion that suggested suppression of a snicker; she looked at Admiral Haynes and kept her gaze on him, ignoring Sir Austin.

Haynes saw that she had tossed the play to him; he must either back her up or surrender. He couldn't surrender; he had already declared for us, indirectly but unmistakably, in putting Gray on Ted Smith—a Lensman wasn't awarded Gray for "hallucinating." But Sir Austin didn't know all the circumstances. He arrived late and was too self-centered.

Haynes came out slugging, as he had at us. That time, it had annoyed me and angered Jake—this time we could enjoy the carnage. "Cardynge, don't be silly. Even the Overlords of Delgon can't hallucinate a ship into space. Last night I didn't argue with you ... but today that ship has been fetched here from beyond Neptune and Pluto by one of my own vessels. It's here *now*, in Prime Base. Go look at it. Touch it, bite it. Then tell me *you* are hallucinating, too. Otherwise, stop talking about 'hallucinations.' Either way, stop using such words as 'poppycock,' 'nonsense,' and 'bilge' to my guests."

Cardynge fumed a moment; I think he felt tongue-tied by being deprived of billingsgate. "What's so wonderful about a ship being out there?"

Ted Smith answered him. "It's not a spaceship, Sir Austin. It's a very small atmosphere craft, aerodynamic."

"What's that got to do with it? Silly business, taking an atmosphere craft into space. But simple Bergenholms. We've been building them small enough for a spacesuit for years. No trick to install one in an atmosphere vehicle."

"No Bergenholms, Sir Austin. This ship doesn't use them, doesn't need them. Yet it's faster than anything we have. Much. It can do things we can't do. Sealed into the cargo hold of *Nighthawk*, she left *without* opening cargo doors, and was a hundred thousand kilometers away before you could say 'scat.' Then returned just as quickly."

"Lensman—what's your name? Schmidt? Haynes has seen fit to deprive me of an appropriate technical term but it is well-known that an entire ship's company can see—or think they see—impossibility. That doesn't make it true. I stipulate that this atmosphere craft exists, since Haynes assures me that it is here. As for its alleged performance"—Cardynge shrugged—"contrary to well-established physical laws. I'm enjoined from using a one-word description."

Ted kept his temper—still euphoric over his Grays, perhaps, but I'm not sure Ted ever lost his temper. Even when he bucked the Port Admiral and stripped off his Lens and rank, he had not raised his voice or shown the slightest discourtesy. "Sir Austin, stipulating that such mental control is possible, do you think that recording equipment can be hypnotized? As regulations require, all aspects of that contact were automatically photographed off the screens and automatically recorded in all routine ways. In particular, now that we use recording meters on all doors, the door meter and the automatic photorecords show that the ship entered the cargo hold *twice*—but never left in the usual way until after *Nighthawk* docked here. It simply vanished from the hold, did a flit, returned as quickly, was taken inside a second time. You can examine the records; it's not necessary to depend on my memory or that of my ship's company."

"*Your* ship? What's a Gray Lensman doing commanding a ship of the Inner Patrol?"

Haynes said quickly, "Besides the point, Cardynge. Smith was there. I've had those records and instruments checked by Base personnel. There's no way to tamper with automatic recorders—Thorndyke saw to that."

"Mmmph." Cardynge looked back at Ted. "Well, sir? How do *you* explain it?"

"I can't. We were hoping that you could."

"So you're stumped. Much as I dislike to waste time, I'll inspect those recording instruments. Thorndyke is an engineer, not a mathematician. There is some simple point he's missed."

There was no need for me to stick in my oar—but Jake had frowned when Sir Austin had used that snide word "alleged" ... and his last supercilious comment had annoyed even me. I decided that it was my pidgin—and my turn to keep the heat off Jake. "Admiral, your mention of Master Technician LaVerne Thorndyke gives me a solution to this."

"Yes, Captain Carter? I'm glad to hear it—go ahead, please!"

"We can demonstrate our vessel to Thorndyke and to anyone you select. We will supply full working drawings of Dr. Burroughs' invention to Thorndyke. He can build duplicates, probably with improvements. With the facilities you have here, he could breadboard his first one in a few days. The engineering isn't hard; it's the *concept* that is difficult. But Dr. Burroughs' genius has already solved the mathematical concept. We want the Patrol to have this; you need it. Dr. Burroughs will supply full mathematical treatment for others to study. You have mathematicians who are willing to learn. Sir

Austin is no help—he's certain he knows it all and won't look. Consequently, he *can't* learn."

Sir Austin stood up, threw down his napkin, shouted: "Haynes, I will not remain at your table to be insulted!" He started for the door ....

And found himself blocked. By a dragon.

But no one was frightened as a sweet voice rang in our minds:

"Hold it! Get back, Sir Austin; you're off course and about to crash. New friends, I'm Worsel. I've been coming with speed at the request of Kimball Kinnison ... and I see I've barely arrived in time. Oh, no, you don't, Sir Austin; this job you must finish." Cardynge had tried to get past Worsel, but no frail human being goes through a door blocked by solid loops of Velantian dragon. "I've been following this fascinating discussion via the surgeon-marshal's Lens; I'm happy to join it in person. Hi, Deety!"

"Hi, Worsel! Golly, I'm glad you're here!"

"Greetings, Dr. Hilda. Be assured, dear lady, that I am not in your mind; I am merely projecting human speech to you because I lack speech organs. But I must ask you to speak aloud to me—or project your thoughts if you prefer. I find I *can't* read your thoughts. *Most* interesting! May I ask where you trained? Or is that an invasion of privacy?"

I said, "Worsel, we weren't trained; we were born this way."

"Still more interesting! Kinnison will be fascinated. Captain Carter, perhaps we can discuss it later. Admiral, what's for lunch? I haven't eaten lately."

"Nothing you would enjoy, old snake. But I'll see what the galley can rustle up. Will you have it in ton lots, or just in hogsheads?"

"Neither at the moment, thank you; there is too much to think about. In a day or two, perhaps. Deety, that old fraud spreads slander about me that I eat pretty girls. Isn't that rude of him?"

Sharpie answered, "Worsel, that isn't what the admiral said at all. He said you were fond of pretty girls. Different meaning."

"Is it? English is so complex. In your case I could mean it both ways. I'm sure you would be tasty, without mustard."

"Worsel, you're an old fraud."

The dragon sighed, almost blowing over goblets. "Nobody ever takes me seriously. Deety, will you take me seriously?"

"I do, I do! I've always wanted to meet you!"

"I feel better."

— XLII —

Hilda

Worsel solved the trouble between my husband, Jacob, and Sir Austin Cardynge. Arguing with a ten-meter dragon who is also a Second Stage Lensman would be futile, I think. Sir Austin returned to the table, kept quiet, and toyed with his food. He wouldn't meet my eye.

Our side of the table had one less place on it; Dr. Lacy and Cap'n Zebbie shoved down while I moved closer to Admiral Haynes, and Worsel joined us at the table on the right. He did this by bringing much of himself into the dining room and placing his head on a level with my shoulders. But he left a loop of himself blocking the door, with his scimitar tail waving gently—*no* one was going to use that door until he unblocked it. Admiral Haynes didn't seem to mind. He became quite jovial—he had not been, before.

I have never had a more charming luncheon companion. Worsel was so incredibly grotesque that he is beautiful. His eyes were on stalks and he has enough of them that he kept one trained on each of us. He also gave each of us full attention; he had enough tracks in his mind to do this—don't ask me to explain it; I can't think about more than three things at a time.

I became aware of this because Deety was talking to him, and I had something I wanted to say and had placed it on "hold" waiting for her to finish—when Worsel answered me while Deety was still talking. From then on I didn't speak out loud to Worsel unless it was a matter of general interest. Worsel didn't hear sounds; he "hears"

426

telepathically. When he had asked us to "speak aloud" to him, he was simply ensuring that our thoughts intended as speech would reach him. But it was easy to do it the other way, and much faster.

It occurred to me that there were now five Lensmen at the table: Worsel, Admiral Haynes, Captain Carlos, Gray Lensman Ted, and Dr. Lacy. So I thought at Worsel: *Are you and the other Lensmen talking with each other via your Lenses?*

Yes dear new friend Hilda. But be assured that we are not discussing you or Deety or Cap'n Zebbie or your Jacob; Admiral Haynes has forbidden that other than by spoke-up words ... or its equivalent in my case, a thought projected to everyone. To Admiral Haynes I have been projecting a report from Kimball Kinnison. I have been telling young Ted Smith how delighted I am to see him in Gray and he has been telling me about his experience with your wonderful ship. Sawbones and Carlos are old friends of mine; we are chatting, getting caught up, as friends do. Let me add that I am pleasured that you have learned to dispense with spoken words so quickly. Some phonic races find it awkward—but it does save time.

Worsel's speeches were usually long, but I "heard" each one as a gestalt once I dropped speaking aloud to him. *Just as a telephone call is faster than writing a letter.*

Excellent analogy, pretty little girl who doesn't need mustard. I cannot write letters or use telephones, but I know their characteristics from others.

Worsel, why do you call me 'a pretty little girl'? To you I must be a soft white grub, hardly worth noticing.

Not at all, beautiful Doctor Hilda. Having learned to know human beauty through the minds of my human friends, it is delicious to me as it is to them. Carlos can hardly keep his eyes off you and is getting cross-eyed trying to look at Deety at the same time. Carlos needs eyestalks like mine. (Gentle chuckle.) *There, I've lent him one so that he can look at Deety from this side while looking at you with his own eyes. He has asked me to tell you that he means no harm by it; he simply enjoys beauty.*

Please tell him that Deety and I are shameless exhibitionists who enjoy being stared at.

Carlos thanks you for letting him know this. He will stare at every opportunity, pretty no-mustard.

Why no-mustard, Worsel?

Each person has his—her unique flavor. Your tang is delicious. Your soul—spirit—life-force is enchantingly beautiful.

It's not mechanically possible to be seduced by a Velantian drag-on—but if it were, Worsel could be an always-successful wolf. *Oh, fiddlesticks! I'm selfish and I bully people.*

Every person is selfish, beautiful Hilda. But you have no malice. You bully only as needed. As I do. As you saw me do with Sir Austin. He is a bad-tempered child with a brilliant mind. Sometimes he must be disciplined. Few humans can handle his tantrums. But I have the jets to do it and he knows it. I do it without malice and without hesitation. I neither pleasure in it nor dislike doing it. It needed doing; I did it. Kinnison visualized that my force might be needed; I came with speed.

When lunch was over, Worsel said "aloud" to everyone: "Let's get to work, Sir Austin; I must report to Kimball Kinnison with least delay. Professor Burroughs, will you help us now?"

Sir Austin still looked grumpy but went along without arguing. One of those slide-away platforms came for Jacob and Sir Austin; Worsel slithered after them, his leathery wings folded and the Lens riveted to his neck shining like a Christmas tree. Admiral Haynes smoothly turned us over to Carlos and Ted; he and Dr. Lacy disappeared. Another platform appeared and we were taken sightseeing. My main impression of Prime Base is that it is *huge*. Yet I don't know whether we saw five percent or ninety-five; it just went on and on. Once we appeared to be outdoors, a beautiful park. But Zebbie glanced up and said:

"That's not the Sun and that's no sky."

"No, certainly not," Ted agreed. "Carlos, how far underground are we?"

"Oh, three-quarters of a mile, more or less, at the sky ceiling. Do you want it exact?"

"Close enough. Zeb, most Base personnel, civilians especially, prefer to live on the surface. But they can be evacuated quickly to quarters below the Base. When that is necessary, this park and others give them room to work off claustrophobia—it's especially nice for kids. Between alerts, it's a favorite place for lunch; there are a dozen open-air restaurants here and there. Shifts are staggered and restaurants are busy twenty-four hours a day." Ted suddenly looked thoughtful. "Did you get that, Carlos?"

"Yes, Gray Lensman. Captain Carter, could you spare Master Technician Thorndyke some time?"

"Certainly."

"The admiral says that Thorndyke would like to see your ship. Shall I send word for him to go to your hangar?"

"Fine. But inspecting *Gay Deceiver* will take about seven minutes. Most of what I can show him are Kodachrome slides and stereo Polaroid. Is it possible to project them? A hand viewer isn't too satisfactory in explaining engineering details."

"Can you describe these slides? I don't know them by those names."

"The transparencies are about five centimeters square. The stereos are larger, double frames spaced eye distance apart."

"No difficulty. Any holographs?"

"Some. I don't think we'll need 'em today."

"Zeb," said Ted, "may I come along, please?"

His wistful question made the oddness of our situation hit me. Up to that sightseeing ride, everything had been under pressure, and I had been scheming and conniving, trying to help keep our heads above water. Then I heard a *Gray* Lensman ask my lazy campus chum Zebbie for permission to do something at Galactic Patrol Prime Base ... and I suddenly realized that this charming Latin and this shy Midwestern farm boy were *Lensmen* ... and I had had lunch with a Velantian dragon, the famous Worsel himself. It hit me hard.

Carlos asked, "Something troubling you, Dr. Hilda?"

"No. Just swallowed the wrong way. Carlos, will you drop the 'Doctor' and call me Hilda?"

"Certainly, Hilda. Thank you."

Deety and I didn't wait to be invited; we went along. Worsel was in our hangar, filling a good chunk of it. Gay had her doors open; Jacob was in the passenger compartment. Sir Austin was not in sight. But I heard his voice: "I say, Burroughs, ask Worsel to try to reach me now."

"Certainly, Cardynge. Worsel, can you reach him?"

Worsel broadcast, "It seems to cut off precisely at the skin of the ship. I can neither see him nor talk to him. Ask him to come slowly back into *Gay Deceiver*. Hello, pretty little Hilda. Hi, Deety!"

"Hi, Worsel! What's cooking?"

"I'm trying to check your space discontinuity. Regrettably I am too big to go inside your ship. My perception doesn't see your washroom wing and I can't hear thoughts from it or project thoughts into it. *Most* fascinating!"

"Of course you can't," said Deety. "It's in the Land of Oz. Another universe."

Sir Austin was coming back out. "What, what? What were you saying, Dr. Deety?"

"I said our bathrooms are in another universe. I don't remember the axes but my father has it on his schedule. Pop, how many axes do we share with Oz?"

"Two. Different time axis, however."

"Burroughs, it obviously has to be in another continuum. I can see a fact when it's shoved under my nose. But what's this about a different duration axis?"

"Deety?"

"Pop, I think you had better check your schedule. Duration in our bathrooms matches duration here. It didn't matter out in space. But here we would notice it. Can we rig a periscope so that Worsel can see, too?"

The ensuing days were as delightful as Helium and utterly different. Jacob spent his time with Sir Austin, who became quite pleasant in a cold-fish way. He and Jacob became cronies, with mutual respect, and spent endless hours talking mathematics far over my head—but I wasn't expected to join in and I let them be, happy as two Boy Scouts working on a merit badge together. Sir Austin often stayed for dinner, then the two would talk far into the night.

When Sir Austin ate with us, he made a brave effort to be sociable, but the poor dear had no talent for it. He was meticulously polite to me, always addressing me as "Dr. Hilda," holding my chair for me, standing whenever I entered a room. Deety he treated with abrupt friendliness—she became a junior colleague, one he respected in a minor way because she could do something he could not: lightning calculation. At first he just used her talent as Jacob did ... until one day (I happened to be present) when Deety corrected him on some point—"entropy" and "Shannon's Law" were mentioned.

Sir Austin started to swell up; Jacob interrupted, "Cardynge, dear chap, I suggest that you be very careful in disputing with my daughter about information theory. You'll come a cropper."

Sir Austin deflated at once, actually *listened* to Deety—and from then on treated her with more respect. Mental arithmetic was merely a convenience that avoided the nuisance of calculation … but Deety had turned out to be more skilled than he was in one branch of mathematical theory. He stopped calling her "Doctor" and quit treating her as a "lady"—an inverted compliment, his way of acknowledging that she was a mathematician, entitled to the same warm rudeness that Jacob and he used to each other.

But this followed his capitulation to Jacob. Sir Austin had implicitly agreed to an armistice the day he saw our magic bathrooms. He was still puzzling over them when Zebbie said to Jacob, "Doctor, both Thorndyke and Ted want to ride in Gay. How about it? Advice, please."

"What does Admiral Haynes say?"

Ted answered seriously, "I no longer require his permission … and I'm not going to consult him; he might object."

"My sentiments exactly," LaVerne Thorndyke agreed. "Hey, Worsel, you overfed crocodile, we're going to play hooky. Keep it under your hat—QX?"

"QX, LaVerne … if I'm offered the proper bribe"

"What do you want? The pound of flesh nearest my heart?"

"Old friend, you don't have flesh there, just transistors. I looked. As you noted, I am much too overfed to ride in *Gay Deceiver*. So I require that you install your first model in a ship large enough to hold me … and take me along on your test flight."

Ted laughed. "He's got you cornered, Thorndyke."

"He's got us both cornered … because you'll have to see to it that I get a ship that size … instead of the little speedster the admiral would assign to me."

"It's a deal."

Zebbie said, "Deety, will you whop up a 'B, U, G, O, U, T,' program for this spot? Jake, how about a short schedule, one we can do in an hour? Leave out the four we classed as dangerous, especially that hollow world. We won't ground anywhere."

Deety had Gay wipe "B, U, G, O, U, T," and substitute "Prime Base," using wording that had already been debugged, when a hitch ensured ….

Sir Austin demanded to go along. "Gray Lensman Smith, on this project I am chief of theory, just as Thorndyke is chief of technology. There being only two seats it is obvious that you should withdraw."

I could see Ted struggling with his conscience and about to be noble, so I butted in. "Cap'n Zebbie, all three are trim in the waist—whereas Hal Halsa and Thuvia are both a bit broad in the beam. Huh?"

Cushions from our apartment and straps LaVerne Thorndyke supplied and our back seat held all three—crowded! LaVerne brought along a tiny motion picture camera when he got the straps.

I was much relieved when Cap'n Zebbie cited standing order number one: we four must never be separated—and ordered Deety and me to get in back and strap down. He reminded me to get out Bonine pills and asked who, if anyone, was unaccustomed to freefall?

Jacob, LaVerne, Sir Austin, and I took pills. Worsel placed his mighty body against the hangar doors, his head against the passageway door, and assured Zebbie that our parking spot would be undisturbed. "Friends, I will not move until you return. I will think. Clear ether!"

Then it was the homey sound of: "Copilot,"—"Captain!"—"set to transit h-axis, positive, one billion kilometers." "Short range, h-axis positive, one hundred million minimums, vernier setting eight—set, Captain!"

"Immediately after transit, set first rotation by schedule."

"Aye aye, Captain!"

"Execute!"

I heard them gasp, then I took a nap. We weren't going to ground, I had been all those places before, and we couldn't see out without violating Cap'n Zebbie's rules ... and if Deety cheated a little, Aunt Sharpie didn't want to know it. It had been a short night and a wearing day; it was restful to be back home in *Gay Deceiver*.

The next I knew Deety was poking me in the ribs and we were back. Zebbie was saying, "You're a Smart Girl, Gay."

"I take after my old man, Zeb. Wait 'til you see his shotgun. Over."

"Over and out, Gay."

Worsel was broadcasting: "Welcome back, friends! Your departure and return were spectacular. But you are back sooner than I had anticipated."

LaVerne glanced at his watch. "Fifty-seven minutes. About what Captain Carter said it would be."

"May I suggest that you check time with Base Observatory?"

"Eight minutes thirteen seconds," said Deety. "Right, Worsel? Pop, I said that Oz was on this time axis, I said. Fifty-seven minutes four seconds by ship's time; Prime Base duration equals seven minutes forty-one seconds spent touring the Land of Oz, plus two short maneuvers in this universe."

"Imposs—" Sir Austin said, and choked it off. The poor man was sluggy.

"My astrogator does not make mistakes," Cap'n Zebbie said firmly. "In traveling the universes, we can't afford mistakes."

Ted Smith said, "Klono's claws! She's precisely right. I've just checked with the Observatory."

"Gray Lensman Ted, no doubt you noticed that I was able to stay with you?"

"I wasn't sure, Worsel. I thought I had lost you on the first rotation."

"Not quite. I had a dazzling impression of superimposed spaces, then a delightful ride over a lovely countryside—Oz, I know it to be. But I didn't distract you, for I experienced something else. Dr. Burroughs, your washroom annex suddenly was open to me. It still is. Having located that universe, I will not lose it. Deety, your friend Glinda the Wise and Beautiful and Good sends you her love."

"Zebadiah, we should have grounded!"

"Glinda understands why it was not prudent. She says to tell Captain Zebadiah that it would be well not to linger here too long. This saddens me but Glinda is right. This is not your final resting place. *Hilda no-mustard, if you step into your dressing room, I think I will be able to receive your thoughts.*"

"*At once, Worsel!*" I hurried back into the car while telling Jacob, "Be right back, dear!"

"Worsel, are you there?"

"Yes, Pretty Hilda. Thank you. I have much to think about."

Sir Austin was a true scientist. After that demonstration, he surrendered horse and foot; chucked his assumptions, and studied carefully what Jacob could teach him. But LaVerne Thorndyke was better company at the table and with us about as often, as he was not only learning how to build Burroughs continua apparatus for the Patrol; he was designing and building, or having built, many improvements for Gay. Zebbie wouldn't let her shell be touched but there were instruments she needed: much more accurate aiming than was possible by gunsight, truly long range and accurate measurement of distance—such things the Galactic Patrol had and gave us happily for what we could give them. For many of these new instruments Deety wrote new voice programs so that Gay could help Zebbie and Jacob.

But I, the perennial butterfly, didn't have much to do. No cooking—we could have a dozen to dinner and the delivery cubby in our suite would provide. House cleaning? Fussbudgety little automatons took care of our suite, never got in the way, never asked for "Maid's Day off."

I spent much time with Worsel.

He could barely get his head inside our apartment, so I went to his—a large austere place that supplied his needs though I was never sure what they were. He always seemed to have time for me. His current duty, he told me, was liaison for Kimball Kinnison; he could follow everything that LaVerne was doing and assist him through Worsel's own sense of perception, keep in touch with Admiral Haynes, and report to the Gray Lensman, without leaving his quarters, and still have more mind than most people to share with me.

He was studying me—with my permission; I let him go as deeply into my mind as was possible for me. But he told me, not sadly, but with deep interest, that unlike other minds, even with my cooperation, he could perceive only what I thought about and consciously remembered.

I opened to him as widely as possible, sitting quietly in lotus and trying for total recall. I hadn't lived a very useful life and I've done many things frowned upon by the church I was reared in but I did not think I had done anything I would mind a wingety dragon knowing. I invited him in and relived in my mind as much experience as possible, all forty-two years. I tried especially hard to let Worsel experience what it means to be a woman and in love—mentally, emotionally, spiritually, physically.

But first I told Jacob that I wanted to do this. He kissed me and told me to go ahead—he valued privacy but he saw no reason not to admit a Velantian into our lives. Jacob had talked with Worsel enough to know that he was a friend who could be trusted … and our races were so unlike that it would be silly to feel shy with Worsel.

Was it possible for a woman to fall in love with a dragon? It was … but it did not diminish my love for Jacob; it enhanced it. This old nanny goat tried so hard to relive for her dragon her most intense experiences that more than once I flashed back into *total* recall with Worsel as deep into my mind as I could hold him. If my beloved dragon does not now know the inner truths of being a woman—*this* woman—then it's not possible to convey them.

Those sessions left me feeling wrung out, refreshed, and spiritually cleansed.

He *told* me that he shared my experiences. We discussed them, mind-to-mind, and it was like musing to myself—but joyful.

I *think* Worsel lived my life, all the important parts, good and bad, and filed it away for meditation in that great brain of his.

But I will never truly know.

He took me flying. *Real* flying, up in the air, riding his back, with his great wings beating. Jacob fretted more over this than over my opening to Worsel—I don't think that fretted him at all or I wouldn't have done it. But Dr. Lacy assured Jacob that Worsel was so fast that I could jump off Worsel in the air—and Worsel would be under me at once and catch me like a juggler catching an egg on a plate. Dr. Lacy said "jump off" because, as he told Jacob, I could *not* fall off because Worsel would guard me every second unless I intentionally shut my mind. But then, shutting my mind to Worsel was the last thing I wanted; I kept trying to open it wider.

But that block always remained; I had to *try* every time to let him in at all.

— XLIII —

Jake

Hilda is the perfect mate for me—always there when I needed her, didn't bother me when I was working, didn't fuss when I worked long hours, didn't attempt to "share" mathematics beyond her training, didn't expect me to "share" interests of hers that were not mine. We were complements, not twins.

So great is her empathy that she consulted me before trying a daring experiment with Worsel. I said, "My love, *quo animo?* If you wanted to climb on the confession couch to Carlos, I might wonder about the other uses of couches. I would not try to stop you and I trust that I am mature enough that it would not dismay me. But with Worsel the question '*Quo animo?*' answers itself; Worsel's spirit is benign. He won't hurt you, you can't hurt him—and you both may learn. I'm terribly tied up with work and neglecting you; I'm delighted that you aren't bored. Go ahead!"

My only regret was that I could not borrow that enormous brain myself. But Worsel and his race are psychologists rather than mathematicians. They were able enough in any mathematics they needed, but their driving interest was in the mind. Hilda would be enriched by Worsel—and I suspected, with private amusement, that Worsel was in for surprises, too. I didn't pretend to understand Hilda; I simply basked in her love.

I was busy as a mother cat with nine kittens. I could spend twenty-four hours a day learning from Cardynge; he was almost in a class with Mobyas Toras—with no language barrier. Once he realized that

436

I did indeed have something new to him, he tackled it with the tenacity of a pit bull ... simplifying my formulations, deriving corollaries unsuspected by me, inventing notation easier to handle, making the treatment more elegant.

He built such a grand edifice on my foundation that I started referring to it as the "Burroughs-Cardynge transformations." He protested: "Oh, no, dear chap! Can't have that. All I've done is donkey work." Nevertheless, he was pleased. When our final draft for the Base's Library of Science was complete, without consulting him I titled it: *Burroughs-Cardynge Transformations: Quantum Mechanics of n-Space Continua.*

He protested feebly and let me overrule him—and almost purred. It suited me. I wasn't beset by publish-perish; reputation meant nothing to me here. As soon as Zeb and LaVerne finished the mods on *Gay Deceiver*, I expected to leave. Adding a second author to that paper tied down superb mathematical staffing and let me turn my attention to engineering.

Zeb and Thorndyke did not need my help but I needed to understand what they were doing—and Deety and Hilda, too. We didn't expect them to take the front seats; we were too pushed by their biological calendars for them to practice. But they *did* need to know all controls so that they could replace one or both of us in emergency. Both could handle a duo in the air or on the ground, although neither was used to a car as hot as *Gay Deceiver*. (Nor am I!) Deety already knew the vernier controls; I taught them to Hilda ... and taught them both the new mods as I learned them.

Deus volent, they would use none of this until their bellies were flat again, in some peaceful land having advanced obstetrics.

We considered remaining at Prime Base a year—Dr. Lacy urged us to; Admiral Haynes notified us that, on advice of Gray Lensman Smith, Master Technologist Thorndyke, Sir Austin Cardynge, and Second Stage Lensman Worsel, he had assigned us lifetime class-ten drawing accounts and quarters—i.e., we were rich as long as we remained on Tellus or anywhere in that galaxy, or whenever we returned. Sir Austin was class ten, so was LaVerne; the Patrol was paying handsomely for the continua device.

We four discussed it late one night. It was tempting—wealth greater than that we had abandoned when we became refugees, not only advanced obstetrics but medical science so high that it included controlled regeneration, a culture more advanced than our own, which seemed to be derived from ours. (We knew it was not).

We discussed pros and cons for hours, then took a vote, after agreeing that only a unanimous vote would be decisive. We used secret ballot so that no one would have to declare first.

Four to nothing to leave as soon as mods were complete.

"That settles it," said Zeb. "We leave and explore teh-axis. Anybody want to say why? Why leave paradise and hit the road again? If anyone wants to hear, I'll state my reasons."

"Zebadiah, tell us."

"Deety hon, there is war here. We know—although they don't and we can't tell them—that it will be going on a long, long time. About another generation if those romances we've all read are correct—I assume they must be, or this universe would not match so closely Dr. Smith's stories. Possibly the device we've been able to give them may shorten that period ... or it may have no effect. They don't lack weapons, their ships have plenty of legs—this war is supposed to depend on detective work more than weapons and we can't help with that. And on deeds to be done by children not yet born—shucks, their parents aren't married yet: Clarissa MacDougall is on duty at Base Hospital.

"It's not *our* war. If we stayed, it would *be* our war. I couldn't stay out of it. God knows I'm not the hero type ... but I'd get itchy and join up—probably as a boot spaceman; that's all I'm good for *here*. Deety, I'd be enlisting almost at once and I'd still be on active duty when that baby in you is old enough to vote—if I wasn't killed first. So I want to scram before it starts feeling like *my* war."

Deety said, "Zebadiah, just before we leave, we could tell them about Eddorians and Eddore."

"Deety, you never want anybody hurt—and I love you. But one thing those stories made emphatically clear: civilization *must* go through this ordeal to become strong enough for whatever comes next. No easy way, no shortcuts. If we tried to tell them, we either would not be believed ... or Mentor would stop us. His way of stopping us might be rough ... but stop us he would."

I said, "Zeb, your mention of Mentor reminds me of something. Hilda my love, when *Nighthawk* first spotted us, you mentioned Mentor in talking with Ted. Remember?"

"Of course I do, Jacob. I told him not to try to go deeper into my mind than necessary for talking—that Mentor would not like it."

"What did he answer?"

"He said that he was surprised at my mention of—he didn't say 'Mentor,' he said 'a certain entity'—from one who is not a Lensman. I told him I didn't need a Lens and he could check that with Arisia."

"Zeb, that accounts for those ambassadorial honors. Not because we had something they wanted."

"Do you mean that Ted did check with Arisia? I don't think he can."

"No, no! Ted reported it to *Haynes*, every word, a complete report. Haynes passed it to Kinnison, Kinnison to Worsel. I doubt that a single word was left out. Possibly Kinnison checked with Arisia; it doesn't matter either way. That report causes us to be treated like ambassadors from another universe."

"Jacob, Admiral Haynes didn't treat us that way at first. I had to spank him."

"So you did. And you mentioned Mentor again. Family, has anyone mentioned 'Mentor' or 'Arisia' to anyone not a Lensman? I haven't."

"Of course not, Pop. We all know that those are Lensmen secrets."

Zeb said, "Wait a half, Deety. Jake, how about first contact? The whole control room."

"Zeb, better run that through again, you punched the wrong key."

"Uh …. Goofed again. Contact by Lens. So only Ted heard it … and repeated it to no one but Haynes. Hilda my dearest, the admiral invited that spanking."

"I know he did, Jacob. Darn him, I like him! Why did he do it?"

"On purpose."

"But *why?*"

Zeb looked at me; I answered, "Probably because Kinnison asked him to. Not through forgetting one word of Ted's report, you can bet on that. The admiral intentionally set out to get us sore."

"I wasn't angry, Jacob; you know I don't get angry. I butted in because I had to. Before someone *did* get angry."

"But why would Admiral Haynes do it, Pop? Poor Ted! I felt so sorry for him."

Zeb said, "Deety—you too, Sharpie. It's penetrated my skull what Jake is driving at. The old whipsaw, Jake? The Hard Man, Haynes … then the Soft Man, Dr. Lacy."

"Yes," I agreed. "I'm not sure Ted was in on the frame-up; I don't think he's much of an actor. But Worsel was."

"Pop! Worsel is nice."

"Deety hon," my daughter's husband said gravely, "Worsel *is* nice. And he would blast us right out of space if it served his purpose. So would Haynes. They wouldn't enjoy it but they would do it. Worsel's arrival was too pat. He starts from half a galaxy away, maybe, and arrives at the exact instant that Sir Austin blows his top ... and saves the bacon. Act two, huh, Jake?"

"Act three. Act one was receiving us with top honors."

"Got it, Jake. Has anyone noticed that, despite the fact that we know far too much about this universe for freshly arrived visitors— and have shown it more than once—Ted is the only one who has shown any surprise? And he, only at first?"

"I've noticed," I agreed.

"I guess I didn't," said my daughter. "People treat me nice, I treat them nice. If they don't, I walk away. I don't worry much."

"That's my Deety. Jake, in Barsoom we had a cover story and managed to make it stick. Just barely. Here we have none. When does the other shoe drop?"

"Zebbie," said my wife, "I don't think it does. You remember the theory you called 'multiperson solipsism'?"

"I wish I could forget it, Sharpie. Spooky."

"Spooky, yes. Because the essence of it requires *all* fictional characters to be as real as we are—somewhere. Conversely, since we are in it, too, *we* are fictional characters when we are out of our own universe."

"That's the part I'd like to forget."

"It doesn't mean that we are unreal, Zebbie; it simply means that *they* too are real. Thuvia. Jack Pumpkinhead. Ted Smith, Worsel. They're comfortable with it; why shouldn't we be? I've been talking with Worsel; he takes it more seriously than you and Jacob ever have. Worsel says that it's a tenable hypothesis and offers to check it for us."

"Check it *how*, Sharpie?"

"Find the story *we* are in. Search not only here but on every planet of civilization that has the literary form, fiction. He says that some don't."

"Klono be thanked for that! I was afraid that was what you meant by 'check it for us.' Sharpie, tell him not to bother! If we're characters in a story, I don't want to read it—I might be tempted to peek at the ending."

"But Zebadiah, it might tell us where our Snug Harbor is. We could go straight there!"

"Yes, Deety, but it might tell us that we never find it. No, honey, if we're in a book, I want to live it chapter by chapter and not know the end 'til I reach it."

"Zebbie, I thought you would say that. But I don't think Worsel could ever find our book … or perhaps we could never read it. Because when Worsel and I discussed quantizing of thought and, by corollary, of all fiction, I found that I didn't remember anything about the Boskone War beyond today. Yet I *know* I've read *Children of the Lens*; it was in Grandfather Rodgers' library. I remember it now; civilization finally wins and the Arisians depart, their work finished. But if Worsel and I discuss it again, I feel sure I'll pull another blank. Zebbie, I don't think it's *possible* to tell a character in a story how it ends; I think that's implicit in the theory."

"I hope so!"

"Worsel won't order a search unless I ask for it … and I won't. But I did learn one thing today. Worsel and I were discussing the fact that Tellus is as much like Earth as we knew it … yet so different in details. Zebbie, how well do you know history?"

"Just middlin'. Why?"

"Who was president after Truman?"

"Eisenhower. Why?"

"Who comes next?"

"The first Kennedy. He died in office and his vice president finished his term, then ran on his own. Nineteen sixty-four, I think that would be. He didn't finish his term, either; Humphrey moved up late in sixty-five. The …."

"Not on Tellus. Not by the histories here at the Base."

"What happened in this universe?"

"History was just as I remember it up to nineteen sixty-five; the split seems to be that year. Humphrey never was president. Johnson finished that term and was followed by somebody I've never heard of. Goldwater."

"Another general."

"No, Zeb," I interrupted. "Senator. I remember because he was from Arizona; the name is well-known there. But he was never president."

"Not in our world, Jacob, of course. But *here* he was elected for the same full term that we associate with President Humphrey. I won't try to list them any further; I didn't recognize the presidents after 'sixty-five. Johnson was *not* killed in a car crash that year, so Humphrey didn't move up. From there on, all is confusion. This Goldwater—senator or general or whatever. What party did he belong to?"

"Union."

"I don't think so, Zeb."

"Does it matter, Jake? He was never president in our world; Humphrey served that term. And in this world he is about three centuries in the past. Let's forget it. Wherever we end up, we're going to have to learn new history."

"Just a moment, sirs. While I didn't recognize the presidents after the split in 'sixty-five, I did note the name of the president at the date—here—that we left home. A former college professor."

"Jake Burroughs?"

"No, Zebbie. Jacob would never do a thing like *that*. J. Worthington Jones."

"Huh? *Infested!* Let's get out of here!"

"Formerly infested. Worsel says that Tellus is *not* infested now. There was an interregnum after Jones, then a period of disorders. Worsel knows what *Panki* are, doesn't know where they came from. Says they aren't important, because such minor vermin never last against any advanced culture. But he's working on ways for us to spot them if we run across them again. But he says that mimics—his category term for vermin that simulate true men such as Velantians or humans—aren't really dangerous unless they are hallucigenerators. He seems certain that we four are immune to that sort, because of our built-in mind blocks. I wish I was as certain as he is: the Overlords of Delgon would be even worse than *Panki*."

— XLIV —

Zebadiah

"All hands, prepare for space. Astrogator."

"Range-and-direction ready. Washrooms and bulkhead doors secured. Belt fastened."

"Science Officer."

"Perceptron manned, belt fastened. I took my pill, Cap'n Zebbie."

"Copilot."

"Verniers manned, auxiliaries green. Pill taken. Starboard door seal checked, Captain. Belt fastened."

"Pilot's belt is fastened, port door seal is checked. Six seconds to say goodbye, then we maneuver. Goodbye, friends! Thanks for everything! Keep slugging!"

Admiral Haynes' voice reached us by speaker: "Clear ether, Captain!"

"Goodbye, Cardynge."—"Cheerio, Burroughs."—"Bye, Ted! LaVerne! Carlos!"

Worsel's sweet voice sang in our heads: "Clear ether, dear friends! Lovely and lovable No-Mustard, call and I will come with speed."

"*My dragon, I must not weep. Aloha 'til then.* Goodbye, Worsel, Teddy, Admiral, Carlos, Surgeon—and tell Dr. Phillips thanks!"

"Goodbye, everybody! Oh, I love you all!"

"And everybody loves Deety! Tell her, old snake."

"I shall, Carlos. Sweet daughter Deety, you remain in the hearts of all of us."

"Stand by to maneuver. Hello, Gay."

"Howdy Zeb. You look hung-over."

"I am. *Gay Deceiver ... take us home!*"

Arizona was almost cloudless. "Crater verified, Cap'n Zebbie."

"L-axis, plus-one by schedule—set, Captain!"

"Execute!"

"No crater, Cap'n. No house, either. Just mountains."

"The two plus—set, Captain."

"Roger, Jake. Routine check first? Advice?"

"No data either way, Captain. Voice routine, short schedule, maybe?"

"Suits. *Gay Deceiver* ... sightseeing trip. Ten klicks, H-over-G."

"Ogle the yokels at ten thousand meters. Let's go!"

"Jake, keep your thumb on the button. Gay—Miami Beach."

Below lay a fantastic but familiar strip city. "Sharpie, what do you see?"

"What I *don't* see. Flip on your repeater, Cap'n."

"Switch it on, Jake. Well, Hilda?"

"Zebbie, the streets are crowded. Sunny day. Beaches empty. Why?"

"Bogie six o'clock low, Captain!"

"Gay *Bounce!*"

Earth-Teh-One-Plus swam warm and huge below us. Almost directly under, a hurricane approached Texas. I asked, "Anyone want to see any more of that one?"

"Zebadiah, how can I see more when I haven't seen any yet?"

"But Sharpie has, Deety, and Jake. Folks, I find myself unenthusiastic about a world where they shoot at me without challenging first. Jake, your bogie *was* a missile, wasn't it?"

"I think so, Captain. Collision course with a Doppler signature over a thousand knots and increasing."

"That's a missile—out of Homestead—analog, probably. Folks, the blokes are too quick on the trigger and I'm chicken. Comment?"

"Cap'n Zebbie, I don't disagree but I find those empty beaches more disturbing. I can think of several reasons why the beach at Miami would be empty on a nice day—all of them unpleasant."

"Want to check San Diego or Long Beach? I can get more scram time by increasing height above ground to your extreme preceptor range."

"Captain, I don't advise that. One down check was supposed to be enough ... and we have over twenty thousand analogs on this axis."

"Deety?"

"Pop said it, Zebadiah."

"Very well, folks. Just wanted to be sure how you all felt. We'll stick fast to the doctrine. Shop each world just long enough to find something wrong with it. Can be anything—*Panki*, war, low technology, no human population, bad climate, overpopulated, or factor X. If we don't find our Snug Harbor in the next two weeks, we'll consider returning to Prime Base and Dr. Lacy's baby-cotchin-experts."

"Zebadiah, if we wait at Prime Base to have our babies, then wait again until they are big enough to travel, I don't think we'll *ever* find Snug Harbor. It was hard enough to leave just now."

"I said 'consider.' We may find an attractive way station where we can shack up for five months or so, then slam back to Base Hospital for the Grand Openings. Might be an empty world—no people, I mean, but pleasant otherwise. Food is no problem now and we get our water from Oz. All we'll lack is television ...."

"Sharpie, I thought you liked *Star Trek?*"

"I do. But I've seen five years of it and we've got our own *Star Trek* now."

"Yes, but that's what the surgeon-marshal warned me not to let you two pregnant pretties have too much of our real *Star Trek* or for too long. A stern Dutch-uncle talk. Or especially in freefall, as he gave me a set of printed instructions that included daily exercise and so forth. Detailed."

"Zebbie dear, Deety and I both have exactly the same instruction pamphlet. Betcha."

"No doubt. And so had Jake. Dr. Lacy was covering all angles. We'll cover as many worlds as possible each day, but bulging-belly routines will be strictly followed."

"Then let's get cracking, Cap'n Zebbie."

"Copilot."

"Captain."

"Execute."

Earth-Teh-One-Minus replaced Teh-One-Plus. "Jake, it doesn't look right. Astrogator, I want us a hundred kilometers up, over—not Florida, make it the Mississippi valley about St. Louis or anywhere in that area. Give Jake a setting. Want me to change attitude?"

"Not necessary, Zebadiah, but quicker if you'll point Gay at your target—it will let me skip setting angle."

"How's that?"

445

"Fine. Pop, set l-axis plus transition nine thousand eight hundred forty minimums."

"Set, Captain."

"Execute."

"Zebbie, that's what I call a hard winter."

"I don't. It's a *long* winter. Actually it's summer, I think. Earth-analog should be in the same place in orbit as Earth. Jake?"

"By theory, yes—but we're dealing with fact. But it doesn't matter either way, Captain; that's glaciations. Teh-Two-Plus set."

"We can't homestead on an ice sheet. Execute."

"Jake, how many ice ages have we hit so far?"

"Five, I think. Deety?"

"Five is right, Zebadiah. Plus two worlds with war going on, one where they shot at us, and one in the Stone Age even in Europe."

"So we're hitting more ice than not."

"Five to four has little or no statistical significance, Zebadiah. At least Aunt Hilda hasn't perceived even one *Pankera*."

"Sharpie, how good is your magic dingus?"

"Zebbie, if I can't get 'em on screen at all, I'll spot 'em, no matter how they're disguised. In the simulation drills Worsel and LaVerne cooked up for us, I spotted the gait by preceptor every time Deety identified it by computer and Fourier analysis."

"I know that. How much confidence do you yourself have in it? In the field, not in sims."

"Make that 'How much confidence do I have in Worsel's training?' Plenty. The machine doesn't do it all; it just lets me see. LaVerne told me to think of it as an electronic telescope."

"Yes, yes, the spy-ray gizmo is electronic—a gadget I hope to understand once I get time to study the specs. You feel confident, that's enough?"

"Zebbie, I don't have a real sense of perception; Worsel didn't have time to train me and I'm not sure I could learn. But for this one purpose—I think I could spot one at a hundred meters without the preceptor and with a blindfold over my eyes. Worsel got me very highly tuned to that awkward gait, both with and without splints. But I wanted to mention something else. According to geologists, when we were home—Earth where we were born, I mean—we were in a brief period of warm climate between two glaciations."

"So I've heard."

"If their theories are right, we'll usually hit glaciations."

"Probably. 'If …'"

"Yes, 'if'…. But you know what they look like now. If you and Jacob can make it a drill, you can flip past ice ages as fast as you spot one."

"We'll try to speed it up. Copilot—*execute!*"

"Captain, *wait!*"

"Why, Deety? We're about to translate."

"Because I don't think we're going about it the right way. Pop is set for Teh-Five-Plus, is he not?"

"Jake?"

"That's right, Captain."

"Then what's the trouble, Astrogator? We're set to go."

"Yes, but … Zebadiah, I said that five-to-four had little statistical significance. That's true. But I see a pattern—I think."

"Spill it dear, spill it!"

"All glaciations, so far, have been on teh-minus. That still could be random chance but …."

"… but it doesn't look like it. You mean you want us to explore axis teh-plus first? Okay, I guess. Copilot?"

"No, no, Zebadiah! Captain. I mean I would like us to see enough of teh-minus to have a statistically significant sample. At least a hundred."

"Jake?"

"Captain, if we check in one pseudodirection only—say teh-minus—it'll be four or five times as fast as hunting back and forth between plus and minus. Alternating is slow; I have to be so very careful. But if I don't have to alternate, I can set with one click and you can call out 'Execute!' as soon as you are satisfied."

"Jake, alternation was based on our assumption—pure assumption save for that one datum, the world without the letter 'J'—that worlds nearest our own in hyperspace would be most like our native world. That assumption turns out to be cockeyed. So we'll get Deety her statistical sample. But faster. Set Teh-Six-Minus."

"Uh … set, Captain."

"When I say 'Start,' I want you to start flipping them past as fast as you can *without* waiting for orders. Like slides in a projector. Since all I'll be looking for is ice ages, I can spot one in a split second. If I see a warm world, I'll yell 'Stop!' Deety, can you count them?"

"Yes, Captain."

"Okay. If Deety or I yell 'Stop,' you stop. You, too, Hilda; give your perception a rest—we're looking for glaciers versus green worlds. Got it, Jake?"

"Run out teh-minus axis as fast as I can set and translate. Stop when anyone yells. Aye aye, sir."

"Start!"

"STOP!" yelped Deety.

"Jake, I've *never* seen so much ice! Deety, how many martinis would that make?"

"On the rocks or straight up? I must estimate the amount of ...."

"Never mind; we don't have any vermouth. Did you get your sample?"

"Yes, Captain. One hundred ice ages, no warm worlds. That's statistically significant; I'm satisfied."

"I'm not. Jake, I want to extrapolate Deety's sample logarithmically—go to a world teh-minus-one-thousand, then ten thousand, a hundred thousand, and so on. How long will it take? Getting Deety her sample took less than two minutes, I think."

"One minute forty-nine seconds," said Deety.

Jake looked worried. "Captain, I can set my scales for translation by vernier setting five, or one hundred thousand. But that last translation would take us more than twice around a superhyper great circle—I think."

"Elucidate, please. I'm a sky jockey, not a geometer."

"And I'm a geometer, not a philosopher—I don't want to get us lost. The Burroughs-Cardynge transformation appear to be a sufficient description of six-dimensional space of positive curvature; they've worked—so far. But Euclidean geometry and Newtonian mechanics worked just fine as long as the human race stayed on Earth-Zero and didn't monkey with velocities approaching the speed of light. From there on, the approximations weren't close enough. I don't *know* that the final plenum can be described with only six space-time coordinates. It might be more than six—possibly *far* more. Cardynge and I discussed this at length—but never reached a conclusion, because abstract mathematics has no content. Mathematics can be used for prediction only *after* experimentation to test it against the real world."

"But we've been doing that, Jake—transition, translation, and rotation."

"But never very far from our point origin, the world we call Earth-Zero. I *think* the extrapolation you propose would take us more than twice around a superhyper great circle to .... What world, Deety?"

"World seventeen thousand seven hundred seventy-eight on teh-minus axis, Pop."

"Thanks, Deety. Captain, if we arrived there, we could return to Earth-Zero by one positive setting of that many quants. But I said, '*If* ... Instead of a recursive superhyper great circle we might follow a helix or some other curve through dimensions we know not of."

"Wouldn't Gay return us simply to T, A, K, E, U, S, H, O, M, E?"

"Possibly. But those voice programs instruct a machine that has built into it only six dimensions. Perhaps she would ... but to our native universe so far from Earth-Zero that we would be hopelessly lost. Captain, if you and I were bachelors, I would say, 'Let's go!' But we aren't bachelor explorers, we're married pioneers."

"With a deadline to meet. Copilot, set the next one. Teh-Five-Plus, isn't it?"

"Right, Captain."

"Cap'n Zebbie, I'm game! The *long* trip!"

"Me, too!"

"Quiet in the peanut gallery! Those babies are ours as much as they are yours—and Jake and I are taking no unnecessary risks. So pipe down or be fined three Brownie points each. Copilot?"

"Set, Captain."

"Execute!"

"Looks like a nice place ... to stop for lunch at least. Hilda, start sniffing for Panki."

"Take me down lower, Captain Bligh honey. Even set for extreme range my magic eye can't see much from this altitude. How about ten thousand klicks above ground?"

"Will you settle for twenty?"

"Sissy pants. Yes, if you'll zip us around the nightside to check for city lights. If they don't have lighted cities, it's no place for us."

"Except a lunch stop ... on some lonely tropical island. I don't care to lunch with dinosaurs or lions—I might *be* the lunch. Give her what she wants, Jake, but do it by transiting; an orbit at twenty

449

thousand takes too long. 'Give me operations … way out on some lonely atoll! For … I am too young to diiiie! I just wanta grow old!'"

"You're off key, Zebbie."

"Mutiny. Anybody spot any city lights? I haven't."

No lighted cities were found. A quick spot check of the daylight side at half a dozen places where cities should be—mouths of major rivers primarily—on any inhabited, civilized planet disclosed none. So I put us down for lunch out on a lonely atoll, first making certain that it had nothing on it but a few palm trees. It was so warm that Deety stripped off her flying suit at once, started her prescribed ration of exercises.

Hilda joined her; Jake and I set out a picnic lunch, also dressed in stylish tropical skin. The only less than idyllic note came when I flatly refused to permit Deety to swim in the lovely clear lagoon. But Hilda backed by me by pointing out to Deety that a coral lagoon could harbor unsuspected dangers.

"Deety, that's not a swimming pool despite how clear it is. Anything living in it has defense of some sort or the breed wouldn't have survived. The first law of biology is eat or be eaten. We didn't make that law but we live or die by it. The only thing that keeps us from being eaten is being smarter and more careful. A shark could have been washed over the reef years back, eaten all the fish—and now delighted to have us for lunch."

"Ugh!"

"Exactly. But even coral can be dangerous."

— XLV —

Jake

My dear wife Hilda (or all of us, properly) found us a satisfactory planet just barely inside our deadline. Axis teh-positive or -plus took longer to search for the very reason that each Earth-analog was indeed so much like our native planet as to invoke nostalgia. In only a few cases was a planet's shortcomings so obvious that it could be dismissed in less than a day's search by perceptron.

The more nearly an Earth-analog resembled the one arbitrarily designated "Earth-Zero," the longer the search. (I say "arbitrarily designated" because *every* locus in a closed plenum of any number of dimensions from one to infinity is equally its "center"—there is no unique "zero" locus. But so strong is the egocentric instinct that even I had to keep reminding myself of this elementary geometric notion. But I knew so little about the actual potential of this apparatus I had invented that I was always afraid of getting lost—no matter how bravely I talked to the others.

For example, theory called for an angular quantum capable of holding a sheaf of universes equal to one radian divided by e raised to the sixth power twice—but I did not include this option in the controls—partly from lack of skill and tools, partly from sheer funk. Even with the help of the little computer we called Gay (and even the best computer can malfunction, as my daughter keeps reminding me). I doubted my ability to lead us back through such a maze. So all rotations by this first model were exactly ninety degrees. No matter, there were still more universes to visit than a man could touch in one lifetime, more analogs of Earth-Zero than we could see in two weeks—if we had given each one only ten minutes and never stopped to sleep, it would have taken over eleven months on teh-axis alone.)

So the best we could do was to hurry along and hope, knowing full well that our wives were forbidden to search more than eight hours per day for a maximum of two weeks. After that, the hard decision .... An uninhabited planet could be dismissed in ten minutes (other than as a possible way station). A planet too heavily populated took hardly longer. Once we popped out over our cabin-site-analog—and left at once. Not because of climate (analog worlds grew progressively warmer along Teh-Plus) but because those rugged mountains were covered with buildings as densely as in a major city; we translated at once—we did not stop to guess how badly that planet was overpopulated: we left.

A planet at too low a level of material culture took hardly longer. A hovel is a hovel no matter what its shape, and a culture that has small sailing vessels and animal-drawn carts as its major transpiration we conclusively assumed not to have advanced medicine, surgery, and obstetrics.

But most analog worlds out that axis were not so easily rejected; they had good climates, population not excessive by our standards, and high technology by the appearance of their cities, roads, harbors, aircraft, and so forth. These we approached most gingerly—that missile fired at us with no warning in the first world we visited had made both Zeb and me *very* gun-shy. We approached such planets from high up, with our radar screens at maximum—ready to bounce at the first hint of trouble.

If there was none, Captain Zeb would order me to transit down to Hilda's maximum perception range. If he still ran into no trouble, he would enter the atmosphere to let Hilda search for *Panki* at medium range under Gay's "sightseeing" voice program, while he watched radar screens, and my daughter and I watched visually to learn what we could of the material level of the culture.

I must say at once that Hilda never did spot *Panki* in any world on teh-axis—but several we left rather hurriedly because major countries were too quick on the trigger.

On one world we wasted three days—not totally wasted, as the experience was useful later. A day of "sightseeing" program showed:

a) the planet was free of *Panki* (Hilda felt certain); b) the natives were human; c) they were neither trigger-happy nor (as well as we could tell) engaged in war or any evident warlike preparations; d) the technological level was acceptable—handsome cities, good roads, mechanized farming, plentiful powered ocean travel, radio. This latter enabled us to learn that the prevailing language in North America was a dialect of English.

This latter fact seemed almost too good to be true … but consistent with the fact, already established, that Earth-analog of Prime Base shared our history up to 1965, that Earth-analog of the world Tau-Ten-Plus shared our background sufficiently that English was a prime asset to tourist couriers such as our friends Tawm Takus and Kach Kachkan. I tentatively hypothesized a very old theory: that universes branched out from a common root at critical points in history.

My dear wife told me that my hypothesis did not cover all the data—whereas the universes-of-fiction hypothesis did. I still was not quite ready to swallow "multiperson solipsism," as the idea that I myself was someone's fictional creation stuck in my craw. But I was forced in honesty to admit that Occam's Razor served her theory better than it did mine.

As may be—these people spoke a variety of English. After listening to it by radio for more than a day, we risked grounding.

How to go about making a first contact had long been a subject of debate. Our captain had cut through the fog by saying: "Look, there are only two major ways. One is to be as sneaky as *Panki*. The other is ground on the equivalent of the White House lawn and say, 'Take me to your leader!' I'm bored with this dithering. Wake me when you three have it whittled down to one opinion."

So saying, he pulled himself through the bulkhead door—we were in high orbit—and closed it, and may have napped.

An hour later, I rapped on the bulkhead; Zeb rejoined us.

"Captain," I said, "we have reached a consensus."

"Good."

"All of us are afraid of the open approach. The authorities might confiscate our vehicle; we might end up as prisoners."

"Monkeys in a cage—with our wagon taken away from us." Zeb added, "Twice we've just missed that."

"Precisely. The expression 'sneaky as Panki' is distasteful to all of us …."

"I so intended it. Wanted you all to face the realities."

I went doggedly ahead: "… but sneakiness in itself is not immoral. We have no intention to harm; we merely seek information. I am expendable; therefore I will scout on the ground."

"Wait a half! This is consensus? Unanimous?"

My daughter said, "No, Zebadiah, that's Pop's idea. He said that Aunt Hilda and I are barred from taking the risk. Pregnant, you know."

" 'Pregnant,' I certainly do know. Sharpie, how did you vote?"

My wife shrugged. "I was euchred out, same as Deety." I felt momentarily let down. But Hilda's answer was honest.

"Copilot."

"Yes, Captain?"

"I asked you all to reach consensus. You've done so, on the nature of the contact. I agree, so that's our policy. But I did not ask for volunteers. I've picked the scout I consider best qualified."

"Very well, sir. I hope you have selected me."

"I haven't, Jake. Nobody doubts your courage, you know that. But this chore is spying, not fighting. Jake, you're a genius in mathematics but you'll never be an actor. I'm doing this job myself, right after breakfast."

My daughter interrupted. "Zebadiah, where you go, I go! That's settled!"

The captain said gently, "Deety, I hope you don't stick to that … because, if you do, we won't attempt contact here. We'll go straight back to our picnic island on Teh-Five-Plus. As soon as we ground there, I'll resign as skipper and we'll elect a new one. Sharpie, you are my candidate."

"In a pig's eye, buster!"

"Nevertheless, I plan to vote for you. Deety is too sentimental, Jake is too reckless. But when it comes to a crunch, you've proved that you think fastest and most dispassionately of any of us. Oh, I'll still pilot if you tell me to … but you can command from your seat at the perceptron as well or better than I can from my seat. Deety, are you sticking to the ultimatum you handed me?"

"Yessir!"

"Even though your stubbornness could result in damage or even death for your father and Sharpie? Even in my death? I love you, dear, but on a spying mission you would simply be a drag on me—you're even less of an actor than Jake. What happened to that old 'One for all and all for one' spirit?"

"Uh ...."

"Cap'n Zebbie!"

"Yes, Sharpie?"

"I hate to interrupt a family fight ...."

"We're all one family. I hope."

"... but you said 'best qualified' and for 'spying, not fighting.'"

"Just a moment, Sharpie. Deety—do we head for Picnic Island?"

My daughter's face took on an utter lack of expression with which she has always met her deepest emotions even as a baby girl. Shortly, her eyes brimmed and two tears started down her face. "Zebadiah ... you are my captain. I will obey you without argument."

"Thank you, Deety. Go ahead, Sharpie."

"Zebbie, you've just proved that you can get tough with Deety: now let's see if you can get tough with yourself. You said 'best qualified.' You said 'spying, not fighting.' Now look me straight in the eye and tell me that you know more about obstetrics than I do and that you can be less conspicuous in a crowd than I can be and that you can sweet-talk your way out of a rumpus better than *I* can."

I interrupted. "Hilda, I absolutely forbid you to—"

"Copilot!"

"Sir?"

"Pipe down! Or set the controls and take us at once to Teh-Five-Plus and be ready to run for skipper against your wife. I've had a bellyful of crew members giving captain's orders in this bucket. I don't mean you, Sharpie; you were presenting a case. Tell me how you would swing this job and why you think you can do it better than I can. I planned to be a German tourist with a horrible accent, who can just barely understand English but reads it fairly well."

"Not bad, Zebbie, not bad at all. But I can do better. In the first place, you don't have *any* clothes that would be inconspicuous here—and Deety and I would have trouble tailoring for you; tailoring for men is very different from dressmaking. But Deety and I can whip up a street dress for me that would get by here in a couple of hours; I photographed some of the perceptron screen for that very purpose. That 'horrible accent' idea is good; I'll swipe it. But French rather than German; I can do it easier. Besides that I'll be wearing a hearing aid—

a walkie-talkie button in my ear and the walkie-talkie slung under my arm—but I'll pretend it's a hearing aid because people speak more clearly to anyone wearing a hearing aid and aren't surprised when they don't understand everything."

"How do you know what a hearing aid looks like here?"

"I don't. But neither will the Americans in the small town you're going to drop me in know what a French woman's hearing aid looks like—but they'll know that's what it is from my behavior. Now one question, Zebbie: I've seen upwards of two hundred babies born—how many have you seen?"

"Uh … none."

Twenty-four hours later I was biting my nails and sweating. Captain Zeb had a permanent scowl and spoke only in monosyllables and grunts while he held us cruising in cloud cover over a small Midwestern town. My daughter was in my wife's seat and said nothing other than brief reports.

"Captain, she's entered a large building. I can't read the sign on it. If I shift scale to read it, I may miss her as she comes out."

"Don't shift magnification. Watch the entrance."

An endless time later we heard Hilda's sweet voice: "I'm heading for rendezvous. You don't have to be cautious about being seen picking me up; we'll be leaving this world at once."

Five minutes later she was inside and we bounced, in full view of many natives—possibly causing a Fortean mystery. As soon as we shifted seats and belted down, we translated to the next analog. Zeb asked, "Any trouble, Sharpie?"

"Not a bit. People were almost too helpful. Don't you want a report?"

"You reported. Down check."

"Captain Marvel, you're going to get one whether you like it or not. Zee bewilder' French lade, she zink les American' veree gentile.' Mais les art' medical'—*poof!* More than a century out of date, for us. About 1900, at a guess. No drugs worth mentioning. No hint of knowing anything about blood types—at least the article on 'Blood' in the *Encyclopedia Britannica* in the public library did not mention them but did mention blood-letting as therapy. Infant mortality high, same for childbirth mortality. I could have left sooner but I got gruesomely fascinated."

"Hilda," I protested, "you had us all worried to death!"

"I'm sorry, Jacob—truly I am. But I did have to make certain; it's such a nice world otherwise."

Two days later our "bewildered French lady" made another first contact and I managed not to bite my nails, telling myself—correctly—that she was safer in daylight on the streets of a small town in a strange world than she would have been at night on the streets of New York in our native world.

We have been here slightly over a year now. Hilda had a rough time bearing Jacob Zebadiah—a long labor and one unit of blood needed afterward. But my daughter gave birth to Hilda Jane without anesthesia, under hypnotic suggestion (although Deety claims that she was fully conscious throughout and can't be hypnotized—I venture no opinion).

We did manage to slide in quietly, both through the efforts of our "bewildered French lady" and through Zeb's unmalicious chicanery. Sometimes he was our French lady's husband, with even poorer command of the local language than she had; other times, working alone, he spoke English slowly with a strong Bavarian accent but understood it readily. But wherever either of them stopped, they changed gold bullion into local money—as Zeb believes, and so do I, that a man with plenty of cash on hand is armed against most hazards.

The details of this are hardly worth recording. This analog of the United States (called that, although the boundaries are somewhat different from those of our native place) is not nearly as laden with laws, regulations, licensing—and taxes—as the country from which we fled. In consequence, "illegally entered aliens" (which we are) do not find it too difficult to hide, once they learn to "sling the lingo," as Zeb calls it, and understand the local customs.

Hilda and Zeb learned both rapidly during our first two weeks spent acquiring cash and knowledge in dozens of Midwest small towns, they on the ground, Deety and I "riding shotgun" in the sky. Deety and I learned more slowly, from them and from radio. But we learned. Then we moved to the Northwest, as "natives" from back east, and there coped with the only difficult problem: how to keep *Gay Deceiver* always out of sight, without hiding her, camouflaged, on some remote mountain.

Zeb and Deety did hide her in the Cascades for some three days during which Hilda and I found and leased a large warehouse on the outskirts of Tacoma. That night we moved *Gay Deceiver* into it, slapped white paint on the glass of the building's windows, and slept in Gay, with a feeling of being home again. We had a foot to the ground; the rest was mere detail.

Today we own six hectares (fifteen acres here) of much cheaper land, farther out, and Gay is housed in a windowless hangar built to fit her; and the six of us live in an old farmhouse in front of her hideaway. But even this is temporary. With plenty of land to work in, Gay will eventually be underground, surrounded by reinforced concrete; her hangar will become a machine shop. A new and better house will be built over her bunker. But there is no hurry.

One might think that a country so easy for strangers to settle in, without going through immigration, would be ripe for invasion by *Panki*. Not so. But first let me say that we could have entered legally, had we been able to claim a country of origin ... and had we not had an embarrassingly large, incredibly advanced vehicle to smuggle in. This analog United States has a low population (under a hundred million) and accepts immigrants rather freely. At one point Zeb considered buying us phony papers and using them to let us enter "legally"—but decided that it was simpler to use Gay to smuggle us while we smuggled Gay. The outcome is the same; we will never be a burden on the state—once we get that machine shop and electronics lab set up, Zeb and I will "invent" hundreds of useful gadgets this country lacks.

Panki—even if those deadly vermin find (or have found) teh-axis, the climate and the customs here give them no way to hide. We seem to be at about the warmest part of the interglaciation period. Winter wheat grows where our native world had frozen tundra; the Greenland ice cap has almost vanished; the lowlands of our world are under water and the coastlines are much changed.

Both climate and custom encourage light clothing, and the preposterous "body modesty" taboo does not exist. Clothing is worn for adornment and for protection—never through "shame." On the contrary, total nakedness is symbolic of innocence—and these people derive that symbology from the same Bible that was used (in my native culture) to justify the exact opposite. The *same* Bible—I have checked the relevant passages, word for word. (But this will be no surprise to any unbiased student; the Holy Bible is such a gargantuan collection of conflicting values that anyone can "prove" anything from it by selective quotation.)

So this is not a world where *Panki* can hide—wolves in sheep's clothing. A man who *at all times* kept his arms and legs fully covered by long sleeves and long trousers would be as conspicuous and as eccentric as one in full armor. But a *Pankera* infiltrates by being inconspicuous.

This world does have its taboos (I suppose every culture does) and one of the oddest (to me, with my background) derives directly from reversing the "modesty" taboo. The religious sects here are mostly Christian, of one flavor or another—and on a Saturday morning one may see whole families headed for church in their finest clothes. But, since nakedness is symbolic of innocence, they remove it all in an unconsecrated anteroom, then enter their temple unadorned. One need not attend their service to note this; the climate favors light, airy structures that are mostly roof and slender columns.

The Bible strongly affects their penal system, again by selective quotation: "Eye for eye, tooth for tooth—"

This results in a fluid criminal code, with no intent to rehabilitate whatsoever, but to make the punishment fit the crime as closely as possible. I saw one horrible example of this not long after we settled in the Northwest. I was driving our steam wagon south on the main highway out of Tacoma and encountered a roadblock. A policeman told me that I could take a (rather long) detour, or I could wait about twenty minutes; the highway was being used to punish a reckless driver.

I elected to pull over and wait, and then I joined a crowd of spectators, I being curious as to what was meant.

I learned too much! A man was staked out on the highway with one leg stretched out by a line at a right angle. A police wagon then drove down that cleared highway and ran over that leg, turned and drove back over it a second time.

There was an ambulance waiting at the site—but nothing was done for a timed seventeen minutes. Then surgeons got out and performed an emergency amputation right on the spot, then the ambulance took him away, and the roadblock was removed.

I went back to my steam wagon and shook for about thirty minutes. Then I returned home, driving most cautiously, my errand forgotten. At first I didn't tell our family about it, just said that I felt ill. But it was reported on radio and the evening paper had it, with picture—so I admitted that I had seen it. The paper noted that the criminal's insurance had been insufficient to cover the court's award to the victim, so the reckless driver had not only lost his left leg (as had his victim) but also had had most of his worldly goods confiscated.

There is no speed limit here and traffic regulations are advisory rather than obligatory—but there are *extremely* few traffic accidents. I have never before encountered such polite and careful drivers.

A poisoner is killed by poison; an arsonist is burned to death. I'm not going to describe what is done to a rapist. But poisoning, arson, and rape are almost unknown.

My first encounter with this brutal system of "balancing" (they don't call it "punishment") almost caused me to think that my dear wife had been mistaken in picking this world—that we should move on, or return to Prime Base. But I am no longer certain. This place has no prisons, almost no crime, and it is the safest place to raise children I've ever heard of.

But there are other things I don't understand. We are, of course, having to relearn history. "The Years of Rising Waters" explain themselves. The critical point in the change of climate came shortly after 1600; by 1620 the new shorelines had stabilized. But that had endless consequences—mass migrations, political disorder, a return of the Black Death, and a much larger immigration from the lowlands of northern Europe to the Americas while the waters rose.

One obvious result was that human slavery was never established here. Indentures, yes—many a man indentured himself and his sons to get his family away from doomed land and across the Atlantic. Indenturing is still legal, I think, but defunct in practice. But the circumstances that created "King Cotton" were destroyed by rising waters and warmer climate. There are citizens here of African Negro descent but their ancestors were never slaves. Some indentured ancestors, no doubt—but everyone claims some indentured ancestors even if they have to invent them.

But other aspects of history seem to be taboo. I've almost given up trying to find out what happened in 1965: "The Year They Hanged the Lawyers." That year is mentioned—and glossed over. When I asked a reference librarian for a more detailed account of that year and the ensuing decade, he wanted to know why I needed to refer to records in the locked vaults. I left without giving my name. There is free speech here and free press—but apparently some subjects are not discussed. Since they are not defined, we will continue to be careful while we feel them out.

But there is no category "Lawyers" in the telephone book. The legal profession, in all its many ramifications, seems not to exist. Zeb claims that this simply means that it is a Black Market—but Zeb is more cynical than I am. I simply don't know, as yet.

Taxation is low, simple—and contains a surprise that could be distressing. The federal government is supported by a head tax paid by the states and seems to be mostly for military and foreign affairs. This state (not necessarily the others) derives most of its revenue from real estate taxes. It is a uniform rate set annually, with no property exempted, not even churches, hospitals, or schools—or roads, as all the best roads are toll roads. The surprise (to me) lies in this: *the owner appraises his own property.*

But here is the sting in the tail: *anyone*, including the state, can buy that property against the owner's wishes at whatever appraisal the owner had placed on it. The owner can hang on only by raising the appraisal at once to a figure so high that no buyer wants it—and paying three years back taxes at the new appraisal.

This strikes me as being loaded with inequity. What if it's a family homestead with great sentimental value? But Zeb just laughs at me. "Jake, if anybody wants six hectares of unfarmable land and second-growth timber, we'll take his money, accept the profit, climb into Gay, bounce out of here—and buy more worthless land elsewhere. In a poker game, you always figure what's in the pot when you bet."

—— XLVI ——

Hilda

Deety got me alone while our husbands were busy in their shop. "Hillbilly, have you noticed that Pop and Zebadiah are getting fidgety?"

I went on cutting shortening into pie crust. "Men are always fidgety, Deety girl."

"Uh … you're not fidgety?"

"Meaning you are."

"I didn't say that!"

"Deety hon, don't kid your old Aunt Sharpie. When your face has no expression, something is on your mind. Are you expecting again?"

"No. You and I have each had a girl and a boy. I don't intend to raise the subject until Zebadiah does. Unless he waits too long."

"If Jacob waits too long, it may be a long wait. The years are crawling over me."

"That's just it, Aunt Hilda—the years are crawling over all of us!"

"Happens, dear. But anytime we want to stop the clock for a while, there is always Oz. Want to go stay with the Tin Woodman again?"

"No."

"Then why the fidgets, dear? We've found our Snug Harbor and fitted ourselves into it. Our men are making money; we're no longer dipping into our capital—are we?"

"No. At the close of last month, we had, net, one thousand two hundred twelve point seven more grams of gold than when we got here. Plus this place, free and clear. Plus household chattels, machinery, and *T. Kettle Bubbles the Second*—and four bicycles. Accrued taxes I've offset."

"Sounds like a good balance sheet and a solid middle-class family."

"Hilda, is that all you want? A good balance sheet?"

"Deety, while I get this pie into the oven, pour us some hard cider—there's a quart in the fridge. Then we'll sit down and find out what *you* want."

Soon we settled down. Deety approached the matter obliquely. "Hilda, can you still spot *Panki* at a distance?'

"Using the perceptron?" I closed my eyes and thought about it. "I think so. Yes, I can. Why?"

"Uh, do you remember the toast we used to have at dinner every night?"

"The one to Hilda Jane and J. Z.?"

"No, no! Earlier than that."

"Oh, the one in which Zebbie misquotes Cato."

"Yes. Zebadiah used to say, 'Panki' must be destroyed!' Pop would answer, 'We shall return!' You and I would say, 'Hear, hear!' How long's it been since they've used that toast?"

"About a year, possibly more."

"Four hundred seventy-two days. The day our tests came back positive they started toasting our new babies. We haven't drunk to killing *Panki* since that day. They don't mention the subject. Or does Pop talk about it to you?"

"No. But he thinks about it."

"I feel sure Zebadiah does, too. Hillbilly, someday soon our menfolk are going to want to leave on a *Panki* hunt."

"Deety, do you expect *me* to stop them?"

"No, no! But I'm going along, I am!"

"Are you expecting me to babysit our kids?"

"Why, Aunt Hilda! Do you think I'd do that to you? Why do you think I asked whether or not you could still spot *Panki*? But you're out of practice; I think we should go to Prime Base so that Worsel can give you a refresher. But I wouldn't put up with your being left behind! If you *really* want to go, I mean; I'm not trying to persuade you. But I'm going, I am!"

"Deety, you know what they're going to say."

"Certainly I know! Zebadiah will look solemn and Pop will shake his head sadly and Zebadiah will say sternly that you and I

463

can't go … because we have babies to take care of. Nevertheless I'm going—I'm going to kill *Panki!*"

"Deety, I'm not trying to dissuade you. But what do you plan to say when I say that I'm going, too? Who *does* take care of our kids?

"You and I."

That was the right answer but Deety girl startled me with it; I hadn't realized that she had thought it through. "Good! Hon, I said a long time ago that I am no more willing to walk the widow's walk than you are. I'm glad to learn that you see where that leads … for I am no more willing to have our kids orphaned than you are. All right, when we go—if our men agree and I expect them to be stubborn—all of us go. We live or die together. You and I can expect to change diapers every hour on the hour. But that's not hard. Just bounce high enough, or even put down on our picnic island. However—*I* think our men are going to balk. You can expect a massive case of sulks while they try to wear us down."

"Aunt Hilda, how much do DeLameters weigh?"

She had startled me again. "I don't know, I've never had one in my hand."

"I'm as big as some Galactic Patrolmen and I'm a pretty good shot. If the grip of a DeLameter is too big for my hand, I'm sure LaVerne can modify one for me. Aunt Hilda, if you'll spot *Panki*, I'll kill them. I *hate* them. They bombed our pretty mountain home, they stripped all of us of everything we owned except what we could pack into *Gay Deceiver*, and *five times* they tried to kill us—when we hadn't done *anything!* I've never forgotten it—I never shall! If I could see a way to do it, I would exterminate them, throughout the universes, to the last filthy *Pankera*. I can't … but I can kill *some* of them … if you'll help. You spot one, I'll kill it!"

I can always tell whether Deety is happy or unhappy—but I sometimes guess wrong as to why; she's a deep one. I had thought she was simply grimly determined not to be left behind. But during this fiery speech her nipples erected. Gentle Deety—possessed by blood lust … for green blood. I knew *I* felt that way—I hadn't suspected that *she* did. I had thought she simply feared them.

I answered rather inanely, "Five times: not four?"

"Perhaps you forgot Logan."

"No, I counted that. Your car—and Logan—and that 'ranger' I dissected—and bombing Snug Harbor."

"You forgot that phony extradition."

"*Oh!* So I did. They thought they had wiped us out. When they learned that Zebbie was still alive they tried to get him that way. Yes. Five separate tries."

"After you take your refresher course from Worsel, Helium should be our next stop. To find out what happened. Cart may have information we can use."

"Deety, you speak as though Jacob and Zebbie would agree to this."

"If they don't want to risk babies, let *them* stay home and babysit!"

I gasped, then chortled, and grabbed her. "Oh, Deety, you're wonderful! Yes, dear, yes! While we're away, they can join a bridge club—or roll bandages for the Red Cross. And hold a memorial service if we don't come back."

"Aunt Hilda, I'm not joking. If *we* can't go because of kids, then it follows that *they* can't go because they promised to take care of *us*. But it starts from a false premise. Back on Earth-Zero, it has been more than a century since war came packaged 'For Men Only.' Maybe there used to be a time when wars were neat and tidy, and women and children didn't get hurt. But not in my lifetime, or even Pop's. I know our husbands want to protect us and the kids at any cost, and I honor them for it. But one generation is as valuable as another, and men are as valuable as women. Oh, it's different on Barsoom where swords are still real weapons. But change the weapons, and a computer programmer is more use in a war than a sniper is. I'm a programmer. I can shoot, *too!* I won't be left out, I won't!"

"Nor will Sharpie be left out."

"You'll do it?"

"We'll *all* do it—all of us. But, Deety, let *me* do the talking. You're a number-one computer programmer ... but men aren't computers; their minds aren't logical. I'll talk. You just agree with me and be stubborn."

"I do that pretty well, too. 'I'm stubborn,' I am!"

That evening I put hard cider on the table. After coffee I raised my glass to Deety. *"Panki* must be destroyed!"

Deety stood up, clinked her glass to mine, and answered, "We *shall* return!"

Then the fight began.

— XLVII —

Zebadiah

I never will understand women.

(Bless their strange hearts and twisty minds.)

Five years ago Jake and I were discussing, at every opportunity, how—or rather "how soon"—we could get Deety and Sharpie to agree to let Jake and me take another crack at *Panki*.

They jerked the rug from under us—and I found myself trying to explain why Jake and I couldn't stay home and take care of our kids while *they* hunted *Panki*.

Before we knew it, they had us on the hip. Sharpie is the only one of us trained to sniff out *Panki*. Deety can do a far better job of teaching Gay a complex program than I can, and can set verniers as accurately as her father and faster.

Jake and I were forced to retreat to a previously *un*prepared position: all eight of us (now that more children had arrived) would go.

By now Jake and I had long since learned that their compromise with us gave the only satisfactory solution. We work best with all eggs in one basket. If all eight of us get wiped out—the human race goes on. But we are much less likely to get wiped out if we stick together.

But was it a "compromise?" Or did Sharpie hornswoggle us by setting too high an asking price? I won't pursue that question. That micro Machiavelli can out-talk me.

In our initial trouble with *Panki* we were always handicapped. Only good luck and fast footwork kept us alive. Something was trying to kill us; we didn't know what or why. All we could do was run, abandoning everything we could not carry—bank accounts, homes, machine tools, libraries, established status, incomes, identities, even our home planet; all this was jettisoned to save our necks. We were homeless orphans ... with an inflexible deadline and no way to meet it.

We didn't have *time* to fight *Panki*. (But we never forgot!)

But in our return engagement all this was reversed. On New Earth (Analog-Earth-Teh-Axis-Thirty-Nine-Plus is too big a mouthful; in public we call it "Earth" as everyone else does: in private we say "New Earth" to distinguish it from our native planet, Earth-Zero)—on our safe and lovely adopted planet we are again solid citizens, money in the bank, more capital hidden away, a machine shop and lab in which Jake and I can cope with almost anything, from designing a can opener to refitting *Gay Deceiver*.

Even were we to lose all that, we still have three places of refuge: Prime Base where we are wealthy pensioners for life and where technology about three centuries ahead of New Earth is at our disposal, Helium where we are treated as visiting royalty and where General-in-Chief Hal Halsa is eager to fight *Panki*—and the gentle Land of Oz for rest and recreation.

Best of all we have *time*.

We are no longer running under the whip, no longer under a pressing biological deadline. We have our safe home base, with excellent medical and obstetrical care.

I should explain just how *much* time we have because it is confusing—even to me, long after it has become a routine fact of my life. All analog Earths out tau-axis and teh-axis experience duration along the t-axis, i.e., for each year spent on New Earth, a year passes on Earth-Zero, and on Earth-Tau-Ten ... and on Barsoom, as it is part of Universe-Tau-Ten. These are parallel worlds, each separated from the next by one quantum along *tau* or *teh*. Like this: call the ordinates of Earth-Zero $x°$, $y°$, $z°$, and $t°$, then the coordinates of Tau-Ten (including Barsoom) are x'''''''', $y°$, $z°$, and $t°$—the same space-time framework save that one spatial coordinate has been translated ten spatial quanta in a "direction" tagged "Tau-Plus."

By the same notation, the coordinates of New Earth are $x°$, $z°$, and $t°$, but $y'''''''''''''''''''''''''''''''''''''$ —or y^{39+}.

Prime Base and the Lands of Oz are *not* parallel to Earth-Zero and New Earth; they are reached by rotation. They share the same duration coordinate, the one tagged "tau"—nevertheless they are not parallel worlds, as they share only one spatial coordinate.

This could go on through all the permutations of the Number of the Beast; I'll drop it. The important point is that time spent in Oz or at Prime Base does not show on clocks or calendars at New Earth. One evening when our first babies were small, Hilda was getting dinner while Deety was changing diapers, and Jake and I had just showered and were ready for dinner. Deety finished her chores and said, "Hillbilly, I approve of babies ... but unfinished human beings, noisy at one end and wet at the other, get tiresome. Let's go to Oz."

"All right. When?"

"Now!"

"I have a roast in the oven, Deety. Tomorrow, perhaps. If that suits our gentlemen."

"Not me," Jake answered. "I have a timed experiment running. Not sooner than next Wednesday."

"Pop! Run that through again. If we leave now and stay three weeks, *when do we get back?*"

Jake looked thoughtful and blinked. "Hilda my love, get diapers and everything else you need. We'll leave now. Zeb? Coming? Or do you prefer to stay here and batch it?"

"Do my own cooking when I can sponge on Glinda? Let's go."

"I'll turn off the roast, Jacob. Diapers and baby powder and such I stocked in the car months ago."

"Don't turn off the roast. We'll eat it when we get back."

When we got back, about a month later—I lost track of the days—the kitchen clock showed that we had been gone four minutes; we had to wait while meat finished roasting. Even that four minutes had been spent on New Earth, manning the car, strapping down—then getting out of it and back into the house on our return.

The same applies to Prime Base. We can leave with breakfast dishes on the table, be gone for months, return and find the coffee still hot. But time spent in Oz counts as duration in Prime Base, and vice versa. If we alternate (are careful to do so), we do not show up either place while goodbyes are still echoing from our last visit.

But time spent in Helium or in hunting Panki along tau-axis shows as duration on New Earth. On our first return to Helium we took everything with us that we could not afford to lose, locked up tight, and arranged for our garden to be watered. A *Panki* hunt takes no such full planning; we are rarely away more than a few hours. What does take clock and calendar time is planning and preparing for one … unless that time is spent at Prime Base.

Once we spent a long time at Prime Base. I had lost my left arm (and almost my life) in a *Panki* raid. So I spent the next several weeks in Base Hospital while "Dr. Phillips" regenerated it. I won't describe that raid; I behaved stupidly and am not proud of it. If Sharpie hadn't known the pressure points to stop hemorrhage, if Deety hadn't taken my seat at the controls while Jake handled verniers, if the Patrol had not helped, my stupidity would have cost my neck and possibly others. As it was, we were away from home less than an hour, and I had a brand-new arm.

With time to plan, we do. For three months Worsel devoted a part of his great, multiple brain to Hilda, while I discussed tactics with several Lensmen, especially "our" Lensman, Ted Smith, and discussed weapons, gadgets, and instruments with LaVerne and Jake—and Deety became a crack shot with DeLameters, which so surprised her coach (Carlos Fernandez) that he called in Port Admiral Haynes to show her off, let him see what she could do against surprise targets, some of which she was expected to hit, others of which she must instantly spot as "friendly" and not shoot. (Let me add that she surprised her husband. Will I ever really know my wife?)

Our first effort was reconnaissance. After Worsel got Hilda so sensitive that she could spot a *Pankera* in the dark at a couple of klicks, spot them by perceptron at twenty thousand klicks, search them out by spy ray even inside buildings or underground (tedious, time-consuming, and hard to keep the ray aimed at long range—but sometimes extremely worthwhile), able by direct vision to strip mentally the clothes off a crowd and point out any Panki hiding in it—after Worsel got her tuned to that sense of perception (no matter that Sharpie asserts that she doesn't have a "true" sense of perception), after LaVerne Thorndyke fitted us out with more gadgets, plus an anti-radar coating ninty-nine percent effective—after all this, we started reconnaissance.

We did not go first to Helium; I ruled against it. "Astrogator honey, we now have the advantage over *Panki* that they once had over us. They lost track of us years ago. I think we are a forgotten incident, probably one of many, scratched out of their books. They don't know we're on the prowl—and we'll keep it that way as long as possible. Even after we start hitting them, we'll still keep it that way wherever and whenever possible. Strike by surprise, just as they struck us."

"Hear, hear!"

"Yes, Sharpie, and you are a key factor. We're not an invasion force; we mustn't kid ourselves that we are. So we'll hit-and-run. When you spot *Panki* we're more likely to run without hitting—"

"I want to kill 'em!"

"Calm down, Deety. You will. But we'll hit them when and where we have the edge. I want them to think that it's bad luck, disconnected accidents, rather than a campaign. It may go on so long that Jayzee will be sitting where I am and Janie will be sitting where you are. But we aren't going to go out in a burst of glory, just for the hell of it. Instead, we'll kill *Panki* and keep on killing *Panki* and stay alive ourselves."

"Sounds good," agreed Sharpie. "I was getting mildly bored with being a middle-aged housewife, watching the mirror for gray hairs. But hunting *Panki* is far more fun than the parties I used to give. One question, Cap'n—who gets my seat?"

"Sharpie, you'll stay on the perceptron and the spy ray until you're senile. That'll give Worsel time to train Jacqueline as SuperSharpie."

"I'll raise her for it."

"Captain, who mans the verniers when I'm superannuated?"

"Your daughter, Deety. Unless she gets Gay so completely voice-programmed that verniers aren't needed. If so, Deety can raise peonies while you collect stamps and I lie in the shade."

"Don't like peonies!"

"Son, when I'm too old to fight, I'll go see what more Mobyas can teach me, then argue over it with Cardynge."

"And when Janie takes my place as astrogator, I'll become Chief Hatchet Man, who is dropped in at night to kill a key *Pankera* and make it look like an accident. 'The Shadow Strikes Again!'"

"Deety darling, by then you'll be through having babies and I will make no objection to any danger you choose to risk. But if you get yourself killed, I'll be so lonely I'll remarry at once."

"Uh … Zebadiah, maybe we could go on such strikes together?"

"Perhaps we will, dear. In the meantime, let's stop yakking and get to work."

Our first scouting trip we started with Earth-Analog-Tau-One-*Minus*, because we knew Earth-Zero was infested and Earth-Tau-Ten-Plus and therefore assumed that *Panki* were scattered thickly out Ten-Plus; I wanted a bracket on the minus side.

We popped in and bounced high, then cautiously approached the night side, by doctrine. Lighted cities, radio, television signals, and microwave—high technology. I watched the screens and listened—either they weren't using long-range radar, or LaVerne's absorption coating was better than he had promised. "Copilot, by doctrine, approach analog New York. Sharpie, it's yours, dear."

At eighteen thousand klicks Sharpie snapped, "Gay *Bounce!*" She added, "Infested."

"Execute!"

Jake flipped us to Earth-Tau-Two-Minus and bounced. Same routine, same story: heavily infested. So was Tau-Three-Minus. We flipped to Tau-Four-Minus.

Glaciation; we detected no radiation, found some dimly lighted settlements near the equator on the night side, primitive culture in the tropics on the day side. We searched at low range; Sharpie reported the planet free of *Panki*. "Cap'n Zebbie, I think they like planets where the pickings are good."

"Copilot, move on, by routine doctrine."

The ice was even farther down on Tau-Five-Minus. We placed a six-transit girdle around it by voice program in five minutes; Sharpie found nothing but grass shacks and mud hovels—no *Panki*. "Copilot, glaciations search, two hundred quanta."

"*Two* hundred, Captain?"

"Jake, we go farther. I want to be *certain* there aren't *Panki* out this way beyond the glaciations."

" 'Certain!' Could be a long, long way, Captain. You trust my theories more than I do."

"Well … reasonably certain. Please start a two-hundred quanta search."

"Aye aye, sir."

At Tau-One-Hundred-Sixty-Five, the ice was receding; we slowed down, spent a few minutes on each of the next dozen. Then we reached a high-technology culture, gave it slow and cautious treatment. No *Panki*—"Copilot, inasmuch as we *can't* search all worlds, I shall assume that the varmints never got this far. So we'll turn our attention to tau-plus axis. Comment, anyone?"

"Captain," said Deety, "can you hold long enough for me to change a diaper or two, and horsewhip all of them? They're raising a ruckus."

"Want me to ground?"

" 'Tisn't necessary, Zebadiah. But I think I'll move Zebulon and Jacqueline into the dressing room for their bottles."

"How long have we been gone?"

"Three hours twenty-four minutes."

"Why didn't you remind me?"

" '*Remind* you'—I was hoping you wouldn't notice. Zebadiah, I feel more *alive* than I have since the night I met you. At last we're doing something constructive."

"Having babies isn't 'constructive'?"

"It is, but not very—any mother can do it. Having babies is like food and sex and sleep: necessary but not enough."

"No comment. Seat belts, all. Let the kids yelp. *Gay Deceiver*, head for the stable!"

The following afternoon (Sunday) it took forty-five minutes for Sharpie to establish that Earth-analogs Tau-One-Plus through-Nine-Plus were infested (as expected), another ten minutes to prove the same for -Eleven-Plus and -Twelve-Plus. On Earth-Analog-Tau-Thirteen-Plus we again ran into glaciations and no *Panki*, and found the same thing on the next thirty-one worlds. We then checked the next four worlds, found them warming up but no infestation. "Jake, I assume that we've found a pattern. The vermin don't know about teh-axis or rotation worlds, and don't go farther once they run into ice. That gives them sixteen analog Earths—possibly all they want. Or can get."

"Cap'n Zebbie, I think it is all they can get."

"Why, Sharpie?"

"I think they're stupid."

"They damn near outsmarted us!"

"Oh, they're fast and they're crafty and mean. But not creative, not truly intelligent. Zebbie, I can feel their thoughts a little now, when I'm close to them—I haven't talked about it because they're nasty. Brutish. I think that at some time, someone like Jacob built a space shifter, one that could move on tau-axis. He tried it out and ran into them—and they enslaved him or killed him or both, then used his machine to infest other worlds. But that's all they can do; they're parasites."

"What happened to your 'multiperson solipsism' theory?"

"Your theory, yours and Jacob's—I just polished it a little. It's still there. This whole shenanigan feels like a horror adventure story by a writer in a hurry. Doesn't have to be logical, just as the Land of Oz isn't logical. This writer didn't fret about the loose ends, as long as he could peddle it."

"Hillbilly," exclaimed Deety, "that's the scoundrel I want to kill! The one who thought up *Panki!*"

"Are you sure, dear?"

"Sure I'm sure! Kill that moneygrubber and there wouldn't be any *Panki.*"

"But Deety, if there weren't any *Panki* you wouldn't have met Zebbie, I wouldn't have trapped Jacob, and we wouldn't have our mostly-sweet-but-sometimes-horrible kids. Would you rather be an old maid? I wouldn't." Hilda patted Jake's neck.

"Uh ...."

Jake said, "Thank you, my love; it's mutual. Deety, you missed an elementary fact."

"Pop, don't get logical. I'm glad I got Zebadiah but that doesn't make me like *Panki*. I hate 'em!"

"Irrelevant, and I didn't mention logic; I said 'fact.' An author's creations do not die when he does. You have observed that fact. Edgar Rice Burroughs died many years ago and L. Frank Baum even longer—but Dejah Thoris is very much alive and so is Glinda. Doctor Smith died around the time I was born, I think ...."

"Nineteen sixty-five."

"So? But we were with Worsel and Port Admiral Haynes and our other friends there only last week. So you would gain nothing by killing the writer who thought of *Panki*."

"He needs killing. For thinking of them."

"Dear, dear! He may be a she—and a widow supporting four kids as best she can. Kids like ours. The record shows clearly that many of the goriest, most terrifying characters were written by women writers; they seem to have special talent for vivid terror. *Frankenstein*. Northwest Smith. Many more who used male pseudonyms. It seems to me that the female writer feels things more deeply, creates more vividly. And remember, Deety, if she created *Panki*, she also created you and Hilda."

"*What?* Pop, I've told you again and again ... I am not a figment of somebody's imagination!"

"I don't suppose Thuvia feels that she is, either. But you can't have it both ways."

"Why can't I? Who says so?"

I said, "The meeting is adjourned. We won't try to check Tau-Ten-Plus and Earth-Zero today; we must decide whether or not to visit Helium first—Cart may have news for us. So let's get the kids out of freefall before we have used baby formula floating around aft. Deety, I couldn't love you more if you were real."

"When we get home, I'm going to bite you. You know where!"

Deety plays rough. "Honey, you're as real as I am. Maybe more so. *Gay Deceiver*, head for the stable!"

— XLVIII —

Deety

Usually all of us—Zebadiah, Pop, Aunt Hilda, and me—plan a *Panki* hunt each Friday evening and carry it out Saturday afternoon. But this war conference did not go as usual.

Pop started it by saying, "According to my records, it has been over seven months since we hit Tau-Seven-Plus; it should be ripe. Zeb, how do you feel about it? Eager? Or hoodooed by it?"

"Eager!"

Seven-Plus is where my husband lost an arm and thereby caused us to spend three months at Prime Base while he grew a new one (null time at New Earth, of course). I knew that Zebadiah's answer would be—it was mine, too! I wanted to kill at least ten *Panki*, on *that* planet, for Zebadiah's left arm (even though Dr. Phillips grew him another just like it).

"Deety?"

"Double eager, Pop! I'm going groundside this raid! I've got a score to settle."

"Your privilege, dear—if Zeb approves. Hilda my love, shall we hit target-of-opportunity? Or do you prefer full reconnaissance? Seven months is a long time."

"Neither one, Jacob."

"Eh? You have another target in mind?"

"Jacob, I have sixteen targets in mind."

"Sixteen?" asked Pop. "My dear, do you mean sixteen specific targets? Or are you speaking of the sixteen infested Earth-analogs on tau-axis? If it's the latter, I think you had better explain."

"I mean the latter. But I won't go into it, Chairman darling, unless I have unanimous consent to talk at length, without interruption, before it is thrown open to discussion."

"I'll keep quiet, Sharpie."

"Me, too," I agreed. (What was Aunt Hilda up to?)

"You have the floor, dearest. No time limit."

"Very well. But at the first interruption, I'm going to clam up ... because all of you are going to *want* to interrupt. I must ask questions—but I want answers. Not arguments. Until I'm through."

Pop glanced around, said, "The chair will suppress any interruption. Proceed."

"Thank you, Jacob. Think back to the afternoon that you and Zebbie killed our first *Pankera* by the swimming pool at Snug Harbor"—I shivered but kept my mouth shut—"you men were discussing reengineering the solar system—that solar system, I mean. Have you discussed it since?"

"But, Hilda, my love, the circumstances are entirely dif—"

"Jacob."

"Sorry! I discussed it once, simply as a theoretical possibility, with Sir Austin. But it is not appropriate to their system. No need."

"I don't think I've discussed it with anyone, Sharpie. It was just a dream ... before we learned how tough the *Panki* are."

"You've both given up a magnificent dream; that's my first point. Deety, how many *Panki* have we killed?"

"Do I count those killed at Helium, after we left?"

"Count them separately. But how many have *we* killed? We four."

"I'm glad you want a separate count. At Helium there were the twenty-three from their embassy that tried to refuse outgoing health inspection, plus an unknown number killed from later landings. Banths don't keep count and nobody knows how many the Green Hordes killed before Earth-Tau-Ten quit trying to land ships on Barsoom. We four? Starting with the fake 'ranger' and counting through last Saturday, I make it one thousand eighty-nine kills plus seventy-two probables."

"What percentage is that of the total number of *Panki* on sixteen planets?"

"Why, Aunt Hilda, how can I even guess?"

"Are there more than a dozen *Panki* left? More than a hundred? More than a thousand? A million? Ten million? Deety, *what effect are we having on their total number?*"

I tried to work an impossible problem, one in which the data were no more than samples of what Aunt Hilda had been able to sniff by perceptron from ten klicks—or higher, rarely lower. Besides that, *Panki* breed, even though we didn't know where or how.

"Aunt Hilda, I don't have solid data ... but the number has to be over ten million—and there are almost certainly more now than there were when we started killing them."

I felt suddenly depressed.

But Aunt Hilda went on calmly, "I now have a question to ask each of you, one by one. It is *not* a rhetorical question; I want a factual answer. A deep-down answer, not a superficial one. Not the answer you think I want to hear, not an answer"—she looked at Zebadiah—"that sounds amusing. I want the *truth*. Zebbie ... why do you hunt *Panki?*"

Zebadiah hesitated, then grinned. "I've never been able to work up an interest in golf and ...."

"Zebbie."

Zebadiah's face instantly became sober. Then he looked puzzled and answered slowly, "Sharpie, I'm not sure. When we started in, I think it was revenge. I never did have any notion that we could hunt them down and kill them all. Oh, I was *willing*—but I knew we couldn't do it. They are too well hidden among human beings. Even with your Worsel-trained ability to pick them out and bird-dog them for us, it isn't easy." He looked at his left hand, turned it over, and looked at it again. "Sometimes it isn't easy at all. One can get so intent on not losing the target, not killing a human by mistake, that one can wind up *being* the target. But, Sharpie, that adds zest to it. I wasn't joking when I mentioned golf; hunting *Panki* does beat the hell out of golf—or any game. I find myself living from weekend to weekend, counting the days—anxious to hunt again."

"Thank you, Zebbie. Jacob?"

"But, my dear, as I recall, you ladies announced that you two were firmly resolved to hunt *Panki* ... then agreed that we men could come along."

"Jacob, that is an argument; it is not a statement of *your* reason."

"But we could not let you go by yourselves!"

"Jacob, rather than allow this investigation to wander into by-paths, I'll withdraw my question and make a statement, one which you can deny or affirm. Before that night, some five years ago, when your daughter and I reinstituted the toast '*Panki* must be destroyed!' you and Zebbie were discussing how—or 'how soon'—you men could go hunting Panki ... while leaving us women at home. True, or false?"

Pop opened his mouth—closed it, and dropped his gaze. Aunt Hilda said gently, "Jacob, please answer me. I need to know."

(I'll never know how much hung on how Pop answered—because I will never ask Aunt Hilda; I don't want to know. But I was scared.)

My husband saved it. He growled, "Jake. Quit stalling."

Pop looked up. "My dear ... please forgive me—but Zeb and I were discussing how we could do it without endangering you two and the kids. But we never figured it out. My daughter is stubborn and—excuse me, dearest!—sometimes *you* are, too."

Aunt Hilda leaned across to Pop, kissed him, caressed his face. "My gallant knight ... there is nothing to excuse, dearest, nothing to forgive. Deety and I knew; that's why we brought it to a head. Now, sir, if it pleases you, will you tell us *why* you hunt *Panki?*"

Pop looked puzzled. "I thought I had covered that."

"Not explicitly, sir."

"Uh ... my reasons are much the same as Zeb's. This is a good world we've settled in; I like it. Couldn't ask for a better place to bring up children. But ... well, it's not enough to spend my time cobbling up 'inventions' that have already been invented—even though it pays well. Zeb and I have such a backlog of gadgets this world can use but doesn't have that I've turned out only one truly original invention this year ... and it's been even longer since I did solid work in mathematics. When Zeb and I are in the shop, we work—but most of our talk is about what tactics to use come Saturday. Sweetheart—it makes me feel *alive!* Can you understand that?"

"I certainly can, dearest man. Deety? Your turn, hon. Will you tell us why you hunt?"

"Huh? Why, you know why, Hillbilly—I hate 'em!"

"You're not afraid of them any longer?"

"Certainly I'm afraid of them! I've never gotten over being scared of them; they give me the jumping willies! I've been even more scared of them since Zebadiah lost his arm—and feeling guilty about that, too; I wasn't covering his rear properly—"

"Deety, you mustn't feel that way!" interrupted my husband.

"Order," Pop said. "Zeb, Hilda still has the floor and has yielded it for Deety to answer her question."

"Thanks, Zebadiah—but I'll never be that careless again. Aunt Hilda, of *course* I'm scared of them. I'm jumpy every time we hunt. But only 'til you spot one. Then I'm anxious to make the kill myself. If you call it off—tell us you've lost it or that it's too hard to get at, I'm disappointed. But almost always we've made at least one kill and we've averaged four point one eight eight per hunt—we're improving, especially since we started using random numbers in picking where to strike. Then there was that *wonderful* day we made eleven kills. Does that answer you, Hillbilly?"

"Yes, dear; it does. Jacob, I now have the answers I need."

"You're through?"

"No, I've just started. I want to discuss them. I think …"

"Privileged question!"

"My dear, do you yield to Zeb while he puts his question?"

"Certainly. But I still want to speak my piece."

"Go ahead, Zeb."

"Sharpie, you haven't told us why *you* hunt."

"I will—I intend to. I've been hunting for the same reason Deety hunts. It's essentially the same reason you gentlemen gave. I enjoy the hunt. I enjoy the *kill!* And that's why I'm not going to hunt again."

Pop got that frozen look they tell me I get when something startles me, so I guess I did, too.

Zebadiah's jaw dropped and he stared at Aunt Hilda. "Sharpie," he said slowly, "are you ill? In the twelve years I've known you, I've never suspected you of even a trace of masochism. But that statement sounds like it."

"No, Zebbie dear, I'm not ill. I think I've *been* ill—I think we've all been ill … and I think we've lost track of what we were supposed to be doing. We've been hunting for sport, killing for the pleasure of killing—and that's not good. It's—"

"Sharpie, you're out of your—"

"Please, I'm not through!"

"Order! Zeb, shut your face."

"I won't be long, Zebbie. I've been the worst of all. While I almost never get a shot at one, I'm in on every kill. I hunt them down and I coach you and Jacob in the stalk. Often we flash in, kill and bounce out in under five seconds—I take pride in that. Best of all, I can *feel* the vicious vermin's thoughts when it knows it's been nailed—I relish it! But that's what's wrong! It's *not* what we set out to do. We've become blinded by bloodlust. We set out to *exterminate* them, kill every one of them, rid the universes of a particularly nasty breed of vermin. Instead, we've just been having fun!"

"But, Hilda my love, we *can't* exterminate them; you know that, I don't see anything sinful in killing as many as we can—and in taking pleasure in it."

Zebadiah said, "My turn to call for order, Jake."

"You're not through, dear?"

"Not quite, Jacob. I too see nothing sinful in enjoying killing any-thing as nasty as a *Pankera*—but I do say that it's inefficient to waste time in useless sport. We don't *know* that we can't exterminate them because, so far, we haven't *tried*."

"Please elucidate, dear. I, for one, do not understand."

"The first day we arrived at Prime Base, almost eight years ago our time and about six months ago their time, my master and tutor, Wor-sel, said to me mind-to-mind in talking about how he had spanked—he didn't say 'spanked' but that was the idea—how he had spanked Sir Austin: 'I neither pleasure in it nor dislike doing it. It needed doing: I did it.' While I don't expect us to think like Velantians—"

"We can't!" I blurted out.

"No, Deety, we can't. But we can stop thinking like children; we can refuse to let ourselves be diverted by fun—even fun as exciting as risking our lives to kill vermin. Instead, we can and *should* go back to our original purpose: extermination. We can make a real effort to see whether or not it can be done."

"I don't see how."

"Zebbie, of course you don't see how ... and neither do I. Let's find out! We have the greatest mathematicians of three universes—Jacob, Mobyas Toras, and Sir Austin. We have Worsel—who could teach all of you what he's taught me, if you'll let him. We have great strategists—what would be the outcome if we asked Hal Halsa and Port Admiral Haynes to confer over our problem? There would be no language barrier; Hal Halsa is used to telepathy and the admiral has his Lens. Dear ones, we haven't even *begun* to see what resources we have. Let's find out."

"Manpower."

"But Jacob, it may not be manpower we need; it may be brain-power. Let's find out. I so move!"

"Second!" said my husband.

"Me, too!" I yelped.

"Passed by acclamation," Pop agreed. "Deety, will you take notes? Put Ted Smith's name down. And Carthoris. And LaVerne. Mmm … would Mentor advise us?"

"We can ask Worsel, Jacob. It can't hurt to ask."

—— XLIX ——

Zebadiah

Minus six hours and counting ....

I Zebadiah John Carter, quondam Captain United States Aerospace Force Reserve of Earth-Zero—definition of "Earth-Zero" to follow—quondam "research" professor and playboy, skipper of private Continua Craft *Gay Deceiver*, and temporarily commander in chief (wry laugh) of Strike Force The Number of the Beast, am making this running record for the benefit of history (histories), or so I keep telling myself—the truth being that I am making this personal record to keep from jittering in front of "my" staff officers and the crew. If I can sit here and talk into this thing, maybe they won't notice that I'm as jumpy as an ant on a hot rock.

Designations of universes and planets: the number of universes accessible via the Burroughs-Cardynge-Mobyas transformations is $1.03144247+ \times 10^{28}$ —correct to nine places, which isn't nearly enough. That sloppily inaccurate figure mislays a few billion or trillion universes. But what's a billion universes, more or less, when the total is so large that no human being, not even a Barsoomian, can possibly count it in a lifetime? Yet it is a small number compared with a googol to the googol[th] power—another finite number which does *not* approach infinity. ("Infinity" is not a number; it is a metaphysical hang-up.)

This number, 1.03+ to the 28th power of 10, is sometimes (for no good reason) called "The Number of the Beast." The expression "The Number of the Beast" is also used (for better reason) to mean the number of vermin we seek to exterminate on sixteen infested planets—once an unknown number but now closely approximated (more later). How many there may be in the totality of universes we have no way to guess—we may have to attempt to fumigate again in a century ... or a millennium ... or longer.

Earth-Zero, hereafter designated Earth^0: no universe or sheaf of universes has a unique zero point; any point may be selected. Earth^0 is so designated because Dr. Jacob Burroughs was born on that planet; the spatial axes of Universe^0 (containing Earth^0) are arbitrarily designated x°, y°, and z°—x° is Galactic North of the galaxy containing Earth^0; y° is direction from Earth^0 of Galactic Center (i.e., the direction of Sagittarius, more or less); z° is at right angles to the other two.

The duration axis of Universe^0 is t°; the B-C-M transformations include two more duration axes, *tau* and *teh*; Earth^0 does not use them but universes that *do* use them are accessible by rotation with the aid of Burroughs-Thorndyke continua devices.

We use three more relative coordinates, which refer solely to a ship or other craft (not a universe): length, width, and height—called *l*, *w*, and *h*—meaning fore-and-aft, thwartships, and up-and-down; forward, starboard, and up are arbitrarily positive.

(Confusing? Believe me, you can't get to the post office without a map—and sometimes it isn't easy *with* a map.)

In this battle, we are concerned with sixteen infested planets, each planet one spatial quantum from its two nearest neighbors, strung like beads along the hyper—or pseudodirection—*tau*. All are analogs of Earth^0 and all share duration along t-axis.

There are many, many other analogs of Earth^0, some of which use *t* for duration (e.g., the current home of the Burroughs-Carter family, Earth-Teh-Thirty-Nine-Plus = Earth-Teh-39+), and some of which do *not* use *t* for duration (e.g., the world of Prime Base and the Galactic Patrol, and the world of the Land of Oz). Nobody knows how many Earth-analogs there are, especially as *any* of the six known axes can be a duration axis ... and any one of three of the remaining five can be spatial. This could be fairly simple if all shifts were ninety degrees—but *angle* can be divided into angular quanta ... and it gets so out-of-hand that you wind up with the Number of the Beast (first meaning). Me, I have barely glanced at a few hundred of the universes and have lived for any considerable time in only five.

Minus five hours thirteen minutes and counting ....

This is being recorded in "my" flagship, *Britannia II*, on loan by the Galactic Patrol, and is simultaneously being recorded via sub-ether radio in sixteen command ships and at Prime Base, and an eighteenth copy is being flipped via Burroughs-Thorndyke message captures to a walled-off root cellar in our home on Earth-Teh-39+, or perhaps I should say that I *hope* they arrive in empty air in that root cellar. If not, there may be a crater there instead ... as we still don't know what happens when something goes wrong, and Murphy's Law never sleeps. But I have great faith in Master Technician LaVerne Thorndyke. In addition to my personal commentaries, all details of the battles on sixteen planets will be recorded automatically and flipped inside an enormous spherical net in 24-hour orbit above Prime Base.

Back to those sixteen planets: to me, an "Earth Analog" is a planet so much like the one where I was born that I can recognize its continents. The continental outlines may be changed by climate—glaciation, interglaciation, low-mean sea level, high-mean sea level; Luna and Sol are always recognizable. It would appear (not certain) that all or many of these Earth-analogs share quasi-identical histories up to some branching date or event. At our present home (E-Teh-39+) the branching point is the early 1600s, when most of the ice melted and thereby changed the history and shorelines of the entire planet. Earth of Prime Base differs from Earth^0 at a branch point in 1965; when we had Humphrey for president, they got someone named Goldwater.

Earth-Tau-Three-Plus branches about the same time but in a different way; the sequence there was Eisenhower, Kennedy, Johnson, Nixon (?), Ford (Henry Ford III?), Carter (I noticed that name as it is my own surname—but Earth^0 had no prominent politician of any name). Earth-Tau-3+ is worth noting as it is the most heavily infested of the sixteen.

1066 is a branch point; Earth-analogs in which the Norman Invasion never took place are in their history quite unlike the ones I can recognize somewhat. 1939 is another branch date; Earth-Tau-2+ is one such and worth noting because Jake, Deety, Hilda, and I spent several weeks in that universe, *not* on that Earth-analog (it's a dreary mess and will be hard to clean—badly infested) but on another planet several light years away and about two thousand years in "our" future—and all four of us are now biologically about twenty-five years old—desirable, *very* desirable, but it means that Deety and I have a daughter, Janie (Hilda Jane) who is as big as her mother; the two look more like twins than mother and daughter. The discrepancy shows even more in the Burroughs family; Jayzee (Jacob Zebadiah) is *much* bigger than Sharpie and three centimeters taller than Jake.

But anachronisms don't bother our kids. All their lives they have experienced both anachronism and switching universes. They know that they may switch relative ages, too, either through living on different time axes ... or from visiting Doc Lafe Hubert's clinic more than two thousand years up Tau-axis (as we adults did) and getting rejuvenated, then returning.

Like *Gay Deceiver*, Lafe's ship operates both in space and time, but his experience is the reverse of ours. He traveled in time along t-axis quite a bit without leaving his native universe (Tau-2+) before he discovered that he could reenter from irrelevance (null space-time) into another spatial axes ... whereas Jake and I have been aware of Gay's time-traveling potential from scratch, but have barely used it, both from lack of subjective time and from sheet funk, fear of getting hopelessly lost.

Lafe doesn't worry about that; his computer-autopilot is a couple of millennia more advanced than Gay; it (she) even has a personality *without* being in the Land of Oz. We ran across Lafe at Prime Base during the several years (Prime Base time-zero years by New Earth time) of re-education we underwent before mounting this sixteen-planet battle. Deety had her third child there (Ted, both for Ted Smith and E. E. Smith); Lafe took care of her—he was there, so he told me, studying traumatic surgery and regeneration ... but Deety took a shine to him and asked him to tend her. Lafe was well qualified—he told me one foggy night that he had delivered over twelve thousand babies, about fifty of them his own. I mentioned it to him the next day and he said 'I must have drunk too much.' No matter; Lafe is filled with stories, many of them contradictory—but he was lecturing in OB to pay for his additional training. Deety could not have had a better baby cotcher.

Anachronism *does* bother me; I'm not used to being twenty-five again after having moved more-or-less gracefully into my forties. But my background is not that of my kids. My great-grandfather crossed the plains in a covered wagon at a headlong twelve miles (19+ km) per day, the longest trip of his life. I remember him; he died when I was three—our lives overlap. I bounce around the universes via a gadget I don't understand; stay two years at Prime Base; flip home to pick up some photographs; find the pot of coffee Sharpie made two years before, still fresh and hot; stop and drink a cup while I sort out the pix I want; flip back and find I've been gone *no* time. That's not *Future Shock*, that's *everything* shock.

It was both Lafe and Mobyas Toras who caused us to back into this rejuvenation deal. One quick trip had given Mobyas a taste for space-time-universes travel; he happily accepted when invited to go to Prime Base to confer with Jake and Sir Austin—then moaned at dinner one night, in the jargon that he and Jake had worked up, that the most exciting mathematics of his life had been opened to him just as his life was closing—so much to do, so little time.

Lafe was having dinner with us; he seemed to understand the jargon (he's quick with languages). The next morning Mobyas did not show up on time for his daily wrangle with Jake and Sir Austin. Instead, about twenty minutes late, Lafe appeared with this handsome young Barsoomian warrior who insisted, in fluent English, that (all appearances to the contrary), he was Mobyas Toras—then proved it by resuming the shouting argument he had been having with Jake and Cardynge the day before—an argument that at once became four-cornered as Lafe joined in—it seemed Lafe was a field-theory mathematician as well as a physician and surgeon ... a good enough one that Sir Austin took less than two hours to accord him the same rude warmth with which he generally treated Jake.

So here we were: Deety in her thirties, me in my forties, Hilda in her fifties, Jake in his sixties—and all of us getting ready for the biggest trial of our lives. Sharpie conferred with Worsel about it, then we all went with Lafe to his home and came back the next day, having been gone two months—and we are all in our middle twenties again. I'm not going to try to tell about Lafe's household and his remarkable family; there's a battle coming on.

Minus three hours forty-seven minutes and counting ....

This fleet is assembled and now almost fully manned; the Barsoom Brigades are here; General Hal Halsa just now reported to me. But we won't rotate until minus ten seconds, whereupon all sixteen fleets will do so at once, automatically, via sub-ether radio tick—with my trembling right index finger on the manual button, just in case Murphy's Law picks that instant to sneeze—(almost) impossible; LaVerne has been outwitting Murphy all his adult life.

In the ensuing ten seconds, each ship will report (automatically via sub-ether) to its planet-force flag; those sixteen planet-force commanders will report "rotated and ready" to me via Burroughs-Thorndyke message capsules—sub-ether radio doesn't work between universes but Burroughs translation works even faster—if the messages are pre-prepared (they are) and the Burroughs-Thorndyke capsules are set to bounce to Earth^0 orbit—where I will be. But the capsules will *not* arrive *in* this ship; they will arrive in open space and at once signal arrival via sub-ether—LaVerne outwitting Murphy's Law again; no chance is being taken of a capsule 30 cm in diameter and grossing 8.91 kilos blowing the bejasus out of *Brittannia II.*

This should take seven seconds max. That gives me three seconds in which to call off the battle by punching one button that could flip forty-eight capsules to sixteen universes at sixteen Earth-analogs, with sub-ether automatic signal *not* to attack—but to rotate and go home to Prime Base.

Otherwise, on the tick of zero seconds, the attack starts, in sixteen parallel universes, tau-axis.

In front of me is an array, 4 × 4, of sixteen lights. If they all wink green, the attack goes forward. If fewer than sixteen come on, I'm supposed to make up my mind, one way or the other.

I've made up my mind. But I haven't told anyone, not even my chief of staff, Gray Lensman Ted Smith. I shan't ask his advice.

Minus two hours thirty-one minutes and counting . . . .

Why did I get kicked upstairs to this useless job? Once the fighting starts I can't affect it. Oh, theoretically I could, as there is a Velantian Lensman in each planet-force flagship, and Worsel (here beside me) should be able to reach any or all of them; the seventeen Velantians have practiced dummy runs on teh-axis from minus one to minus sixteen—the linkup worked, after Worsel restrained all but two (who got through the first time).

Ted tells me that admirals rarely can affect the outcome of a battle. They establish battle plan and doctrine—but once the shooting starts the unit commanders are on their own. I'm sure he senses my feelings (not via Lens; Ted is naturally empathic) and is trying to assure me that I am not useless. I reminded him that Kimball Kinnison had devised a way for an admiral-in-chief to handle multiple fleets during action. He agreed but pointed out that Kinnison's method did *not* apply to sixteen parallel universes—but *is* about to be used by each of sixteen planetary force commands. And so it is.

How I got here: 1) I flunked out of school. 2) Then I got drafted. Deety and Jake and I all took sensitivity training from Worsel and Dr. Phillips while Sharpie went to Arisia—no, I'm telling this in the wrong order. Hilda took a refresher with Worsel while Jake and Cardynge and (later) Mobyas discussed the mathematics of an optimum strategy for hitting sixteen planets to exterminate hidden vermin, each of the sixteen being a unique problem and rendered enormously complicated by the necessity of not hurting the legitimate population other than by mischance (and that has to be minimized), and the need not to damage property unnecessarily—but this last factor was of least importance. Sometimes the only way to kill rats is to burn the barn—but the horses *must* be taken out first.

I heard from Jake that the simplest planetary problem (Tau-8+) had seventy-three major variables, and the mathematics committee's first job was to decide which variables must be reduced to constants through reconnaissance before a strategy board could consider turning mathematics into logistics and strategy—after which weapons and tactics could be discussed sixteen *separate* ways.

All this took years.

But they were Prime Base years; time stood still on t-axis. Deety had our third child (Ted), recovered from childbirth, and was back to work—while that pot of fresh coffee never cooled off in our home on New Earth, Teh-39+.

But this trading around of time works two other ways, also. Worsel, Cardynge, LaVerne Thorndyke, and Ted Smith all were needed in the war with Boskone. But they (even Worsel) could borrow time by flipping to t-axis duration on Barsoom; LaVerne's first Burroughs-Thorndyke device had been installed as promised in a ship large enough for Worsel—and Barsoom had not only cleared out the *Panki* vermin but also Barsoom was a place used to the idea that humans need not look like *homo sapiens*. Worsel was a welcome guest in the palace, used our former giant apartment, and held honorary rank as staff colonel general. He could think undisturbed in Helium, for weeks or months at a time, on our problems or his own, and return to Prime Base at the very instant he left. So could the others.

But the third method of manipulating time could be used to "freeze" an instant both in Prime Base and on our sixteen target planets; go to Lafe Hubert's home some twenty-five hundred years up t-axis in World-Tau-2+, stay there as long as needed, then be reinserted at Prime Base or elsewhere with no elapsed clock time. I don't know how Lafe's ship works; its technology is far in advance even of that at Prime Base. It looks like a huge flying saucer and has no machinery in it that I recognize. It is usually piloted by one or the other of Lafe's sisters— although that piloting seems to consist solely in telling the autopilot in unstructured language (I *think* it is unstructured) what is needed.

Minus two hours seven minutes and holding ....

Something odd is going on with Planetary Attack Force Earth-Tau-3+—and I've had to make my first decision as commander in chief. Ships—no, *fleets*—have been showing up out of nowhere and asking to be attached to that particular planetary strike force. They are not unwelcome, as that is our most difficult target, most heavily infested (millions!), and the Posenian Lensmen who reconnoitered it reported apologetically that no accurate count could be made from space. They extrapolated that the planet would sterilize itself in ten to one hundred years, leaving nothing alive above sea level—and that might be the logical course to follow.

In this I disagreed, as did Hal Halsa, Haynes, and Kinnison speaking through Worsel. The purpose of this multiple strike was *extermination*. If we left untouched the worst-infested planet, while waiting for it to cleanse itself by suicide, we could expect the other fifteen to be reinfested before that happened—as useless as excising a skin cancer while ignoring a deeper malignancy.

Instead of letting it be, we assigned our heaviest task force to that planet—and now we have over twice that number of strangers asking to join that task force.

Gray Lensman Ted Smith sees in it a possible "Trojan Horse."

I'm *sure* that it is not, but I am not going to explain and I have not invited him to read me by Lens. Instead I have given orders that Worsel, Hilda, and all Posenian Lensmen attached to the total Strike

Force *Number of the Beast* are to search for *Panki* at safe distance in all these new volunteer ships. If a ship has *Panki* in it, blast it out of the sky at once—no quarter, no prisoners. If a ship has a dead space in it that our perceivers can't reach, bring major force to bear on it, and give it an ultimatum to open that space at once or be blasted.

Along with this I have requested Prime Base (LaVerne, via Haynes) to be prepared to attach Burroughs-Thorndyke capsules to any cleared ships, set and sealed to be triggered by the zero signal to flip to Tau-3+, then to countermarch to Prime Base on signal from the flagship of Tau-3+, then self-destruct—not a bomb, just internal self-destruction of the space-time twister. Plus the same internal self-destruction if anyone attempts to open the capsule.

Now I think I know why I'm here: to give this one order, plus orders pursuant to the same end. This will take time, so we are holding the countdown. This will not affect the timing of the strike because we are not yet in duration on t-axis. I've told Ted to advise all planetary unit commanders that they may, at their discretion, stand down from alert until notified that count is about to resume ... and asked him also to keep me and unit commanders advised as to Worsel's and LaVerne's progress, with time projections estimated in real time.

While we waited ....

Worsel tutored Jake, Deety, and me in a limited sense of perception for *Panki*—and I flunked. Not totally—with Sharpie and Worsel both working on me, I reached about the level Sharpie had reached when we first started hunting, i.e., I can spot a *Pankera* via perceptron from about twenty klicks, even in the dark. With my bare eyes I can spot one up to two kilometers by its gait or other movements; my brain unconsciously does analysis of its unhuman movements. But I *can't* strip a crowd of all clothing and pick out *Panki* by appearance. Which Hilda can do, and which Deety and Jake have learned to do.

But, hell's bells, I have always known that I was the only non-genius of us four. I'm smart, and also clever with my hands—but even my children are brainier than I am—of course; they're half Deety.

Worsel quit trying to coach me into something beyond me and shifted to sharpening my one wild talent: "hunches" that warn me of danger. I relaxed and let him fiddle with my mind. I can't be hypnotized, but I can let myself be receptive as easily as I can place a block against pain. So Worsel sniffed around inside my skull, found the area of my oddity and helped me to strengthen it, extend its range in time and space.

That's why I know today that these volunteer strangers are not "Trojan Horse" *Panki* or tools of *Panki*. But I haven't hinted this to Ted Smith and they are being inspected as carefully as if I strongly suspected that they were booby traps against us.

But aside from my minor ESP I have another reason to assume that their wish to ally with us is sincere. As these space legions have reported in, I have recognized almost all the names they call themselves—I have met them before. Where and how is mentioned elsewhere in these multiple memoirs but does not belong here.

Still holding at minus two hours seven minutes ....

Worsel offered no encouragement to Sharpie when she had asked to go to Arisia. He had thoughtcast to all four of us: *dear little No-Mustard, you have no need for a Lens.*

I neither need or want a Lens. Hilda did not speak aloud but her words echoed back to us from his mind. We needed Mentor's advice. Was our project hopeless? Were we wasting your time—and ours?

One never goes to Arisia; one is summoned. Hopelessness in a worthy cause is no excuse for abandoning it. My race fought without hope for many generations ... then hope appeared. You and yours may do the same.

Yes, my Teacher, she answered sincerely, and dropped the matter.

Four months later, Worsel stopped in the middle of a lesson, looked surprised (How? All his eye stalks stiffened at once—) and thoughtcast, *Captain Zebadiah, you, Mr. Burroughs, and Dr. Deety will go at once, capture a Pankera, and fetch it to me. I will take it and Dr. Hilda to Arisia.*

I answered, "Aye aye, sir!"—sensed that Jake was about to object, so I snapped, "Stow it, Jake. Lifeboat rules."

In the five minutes it took us three to reach *Gay Deceiver's* hangar, Jake said, "Zeb, I was not going to object to Hilda's going to see Mentor without me; that would be foolish. But they aren't leaving 'til we come back, and we need her on the hunt. Hilda is the most perceptive of any of us in spotting the beasts."

"Correct. Worsel may be sending us on a field test—find out whether or not we can work without her. Deety, you will man the perceptron; Jake and I will make the capture." (How?) "Once we are back inside with it, you will close doors and bounce about six times, without waiting for seat belts, door seal check, or anything else—just get us out of there *fast*."

"Yessir."

"Jake, this may be a field test for us three. But I think it is more likely that Worsel—or Mentor, as Worsel seemed simply to be repeating Mentor's orders—Mentor considers us three expendable, but not Hilda."

Deety looked impassive but she was not annoyed or hurt by my interpretation. Jake just blinked and said, "You may be right, Captain. I think you are ... but I'm biased."

Despite the shortness of time involved, LaVerne Thorndyke arrived before we could man the car. "Three stun guns," he said. "They'll fit your DeLameter holsters. One zap should immobilize any living mass up to three hundred pounds. Zap twice if you must. But a third zap is likely to kill your prisoner—unless they are extraordinarily tough."

"They aren't," I assured him. "We've killed enough of them to be certain of that. But what are these other gadgets? Hand cameras?"

"Tangle cord projectors. Fired like any handgun, six cords to a magazine. Accurate to fifty yards. But I suggest you get closer, because a cord around the neck will strangle—and Worsel wants it alive. Good hunting!"

It took us four days to get a prisoner. Deety spotted them again and again, and under conditions in which I would not have hesitated to kill by L-gun with Sharpie coaching—but not under conditions in which we could be sure of grounding, capturing, and getting away again. But at last Deety spotted one, on the ground, with neither human nor another *Pankera* anywhere close to it—most unusual. Jake transited almost to ground level behind it, I squatted Gay in; we came busting out both doors. By pre-plan Jake zapped it with his stunner while I fired tangle cords—and got two cords around it before it fell. I dragged it upright again; Jake put two more cords around it; we pulled it into the car—and Deety closed doors so fast that I almost caught a foot. Then we were in freefall far beyond the orbit of Luna before Deety quit telling Gay to bounce.

What we had captured looked like a sweet old lady to me—but Deety and Jake saw it for what it was, a *Pankera*—and I sensed it even though my eyes told me that it was human.

The damned thing tried to bite me while we were getting it belted down, on the deck back of the bulkhead; the stun effect hadn't lasted long. Then it argued indignantly, protesting that kidnapping "her" must be a mistake; "she" didn't have any money.

We just made sure the straps were tight while avoiding its teeth, then scrambled into our seats, belted down, and Jake flipped Gay to Prime Base.

LaVerne was still standing where we had left him, in the hangar. "Did you get it?" he asked. "Or haven't you gone yet?" To him, *no* time had passed.

I said wearily, "We got one. Strapped down in the after compartment. Somebody else can take it out; we're too beat. But warn them to be very careful; the pesky varmint bites."

The warning was unnecessary; the thing was dead. Worsel accepted the corpse without comment; he and Hilda left for Arisia.

We made five more captures, two without using stun guns—but always with the same result: dead on arrival. Captured, *Panki* always suicide once they knew they could not escape—how, we never learned.

Still holding at minus two hours seven minutes ....

All the volunteer strangers have been inspected and cleared; LaVerne's men are installing capsules. Several of their unit commanders maintain that they don't need them—but from my point of view *I* need them; I want to put every ship into position simultaneously in sixteen universes. I don't insist that they countermarch back to Prime Base—but if they don't want that option, I've told LaVerne to set the capsule for "destruct" after flipping them back to Earth-Tau-3+. Happy as I am to have their help, I will not turn over to strangers Burroughs-Thorndyke devices without retaining control of them.

But I wish I could spread these reinforcements three ways; Earth⁰, E-Tau-2+, and -3+. But they all want to hit the last one, Earth-Tau-3+. I suspect that I know what that means, but I'm not going to mention it to Deety: the idea upsets her. I shan't mention it to anyone; I find it spooky myself. That planet is going to get one hell of a shellacking. With these reinforcements we have enough troops to match the Posenian highest estimate of infestation one for one—one hunter for every *Pankera*.

What I *don't* have is perceivers to spare. We barely have enough Posenians, Velantians, and trained humans for our own ships, spreading them thin. The troops from Barsoom are going in with none, relying solely on their own telepathic talents and on the noses of hunting calots—three of those *Panki* corpses were chopped up and used to train Barsoomian hounds in the scent of *Panki*.

Each of the stranger volunteer commands has messaged me that they do not need perceivers from us; they claim that they can infallibly tell humans from vermin, and that the only human casualties, if any, will be in their own ranks.

I don't know and it is too late to test them. They want to hunt *Panki*; they are welcome. But I am not changing the order of battle. I have ordered the planetary force commander of E-Tau-3+ to assign them to sectors as mop-up forces after he withdraws his regular forces, or, at his option, to use them simultaneously. He is a Gray Lensman I have never met ... but I assume that he knows more about unorthodox fighting than I do or he would not be wearing Gray. I'll hold the countdown until he is satisfied that he has his greatly expanded force in hand.

He has just advised me that he recommends that the entire force be allowed to eat, sleep, and eat again—a full stand-down while he rearranges his plan of battle and issues operation orders.

I have signaled all fleets that "hold" will continue a minimum of ten more standard hours, with recommendation that they order eat-sleep-eat.

Ted and I are about to do the same, leaving junior flag staff on heel-and-toe in Flag Ops. I'm tired—why in hell does Deety insist on grounding? Sure, she'll be in armor while she bird-dogs, with a squad of Valerian Marines around her—but I think she's pregnant again and hasn't told me.

Why I'm here: because Mentor advised Haynes to assign me as C-in-C, that's why—and it still doesn't explain it. But Mentor's advice is why I have thousands of Galactic Patrolmen volunteers, hundreds of giant transports, and endless cooperation—and all this happened after Sharpie was summoned to Arisia. Up to then, we had received only training and advice for a hopeless venture—we had Port Admiral Haynes' sympathy and cooperation but no troops, no ships—he had his own war on his hands.

We aren't slowing up the war with Boskone; our one battle, even if it lasted for weeks—impossible—will be on t-duration, zero elapsed time at Prime Base. Only this "hold" in countdown uses up Prime Base time—and Haynes has not objected.

Still holding ....

I've just called Jake on a tight circuit—and feel better. We may continue to make E-Teh-39+ our permanent home ... but I've never felt happy about being chased off Earth[0] and becoming "unpersons." I have proposed to Jake that, after this battle and campaign is over, we go home to Earth[0], claim our rights, recover whatever has been confiscated, and *rebuild Snug Harbor on its original site*. Fill that crater. Restore the contours. Rebuild. Find the source of that spring and restore the pool. Maybe we'll use it simply for an occasional vacation—*but we shall return!*

Jake greeted the notion enthusiastically; it bucked him up. I know he's been worrying about Sharpie, because he will ground as a "birddog"—but she will ground elsewhere, as ordered by the planetary unit commander; she'll be a troubleshooter. In armor, certainly, and surrounded by Valerians commanded by our old friend Colonel van Vogt. But that doesn't keep Jake from worrying.

Sharpie apparently enjoyed every minute on Arisia.

Counting resumed; now minus two hours four minutes ....

If, at the end of this, Deety is dead or missing, I'm going to turn command over to Ted, climb into *Gay Deceiver* (here in one of *Brittannia II's* holds), and hunt *Panki*. Oh, there'll be *Panki* to hunt; this battle won't kill them all—we know that. The predicted outcome (Mobyas-Jacob-Cardynge-Haynes-Halsa-Kinnison) is a kill score of forty-six percent plus or minus eleven percent. We can't expect to find them all—too few perceivers, not enough troops. We *do* expect to break the back of their organization, put them on the run—then extermination will be up to the humans of these sixteen planets. At plus-ten hours, recall will sound in all helmets; thirty minutes later our transports will bounce. Then starts leaflet, radio, and television barrage.

This portion is complex and is tailored to each language area of each planet. I described one case; historians can look up the rest at Prime Base Library (some details require "need-to-know" clearance at top level). For South America, Earth⁰, text is in Portuguese and Spanish; pictures are in color pseudostereo, and the message amounts to: "Behold Your Enemy! These parasites are hidden among you, disguised as human—creating dissension, consuming your wealth, eating your flesh and that of your children. Find them, kill them, ROOT THEM OUT!"—and so forth, emphasizing that vermin dare not expose their bare arms or legs. Pictures show why.

This message will be believed solely because most humans of all sixteen planets will by then have seen one dead *Pankera*, or more.

Immediately after the battle (plus-eleven hours) billions of these leaflets will be loosed at ten klicks H-over-G by Burroughs-Thorndyke capsules, then our transports will flip back to Prime Base, and capsules will home automatically. But propaganda barrage will continue—leaflet, audio, stereo—as long as needed, until Posenian perceivers report each planet "clean."

If the humans on the planet fail to clean it, if *Panki* regain control despite this barrage, and their radio, television, and other media show this to be true, and spy ray and Posenians confirm it, then comes the grim decision: sterilize it.

Reduce it to slag. Remove its atmosphere. Transit it into its sun. Hit it with antimatter. Translate it to an empty universe, there to freeze. The Patrol knows a dozen ways to destroy a planet—if necessary. But it will not be allowed to live, a "Typhoid Mary" able to infect other planets, other universes. The humans of the planet will be given ample opportunity to destroy their tyrants. But they must free themselves. Freedom can never be given; it must be won.

I will have no part in a decision to sterilize (if there are any). No one has suggested it and it is beyond my competence. It will be made at high level: Haynes, or the Galactic Council, or Kinnison, or possibly (probably?) Mentor.

In a few hours I can stop being a fake admiral. If Deety is safe, we can go back to Prime Base, and our family (I have a growing hunch that

Jake and Hilda will live through it)—all nine of us will go to the Land of Oz for rest and recreation.

But if Deety does *not* come back ... I can live in *Gay Deceiver* for weeks, months, hoarding her juice for kills. Deety's gallant majesty deserves a *huge* honor guard of slain. Gay is fully juiced; if I'm careful, I should be able to offer her a full regiment.

But if they get me instead, perhaps I will go wherever Deety will have gone. That is a mystery beyond me—but I can hope.

If I live through it, I'll first provide for our kids. No problem there—Janie is already adult, studying math, and has her eye on the Council of Scientists—Cardynge says she'll make it. Zebulon doesn't know at this point whether he wants to enter Wentworth Hall or go to Barsoom and become an honorary Red man, a Helium warrior—his "Aunt" Thuvia wants to adopt him. Baby Robert calls Sharpie "Mommy" just as he does Deety, and ignores both Jake and me; he won't miss me.

So I'll enlist—apprentice spaceman. Boskone *must* be defeated; that's as important as exterminating *Panki*. (I once thought I knew how and when the Boskonian War would end, but the memory has faded—probably just a vivid dream I had at some time. I do have such dreams and sometimes have trouble distinguishing a memory of a vivid dream from something that really happened. "We are such stuff as dreams are made on, and our little lives are rounded with a sleep ...." As may be, I am a warrior, not a playboy, not a phony professor. Nor was I ever intended to "sit under my own vine and fig tree, where none can make me afraid." Earth-Teh-39+ is a fine place, just right for solid citizens and growing kids—but the quiet life is not for me. The Galactic Patrol can use professional soldiers; if Deety does not come back, that's where I'm going. After I supply her with an honor guard.)

If Deety *does* come back, I'll do what she wants to do—somehow I always have, even when I thought the decision was mine. But what Deety does and where she goes is never dull. Dangerous sometimes— but not dull.

Pvt Msg from Lafe: *After this ruckus, Maureen wants your family to visit ours.*

My reply: *Affirm if distaff confirm*—and wonder whether a way can be jury-rigged for Lafe's ship to carry Gay; she doesn't like to be left behind.

Order of Battle

E-Tau-e: sparsely settled world. Cdr Strike Force: brevet Col. K. Kachkan—mounted Green warriors.

E-Tau-3: high technology, aggressive. CdrStriFor Lensman (Velantian) Ardval, 2nd hat as chief perceiver. Velantian strike divided into 3 grps. Transports unload troops in stratosphere, then bounce, retrieve in one hour same locus, and strike elsewhere. Strike 30 major cities, starting with analogs Washington, Peiping, Moskva. 6 perceivers to each group.

E-Tau-2: 19th Cent tech, world pop ca 2 billion. CdrStriFor General Carthoris. 10 hrs low-level sweeps of population centers—1- and 2-man scouts and destroyers. Ground fighting with trained calots at Cdr's discretion.

E-Tau-1: similar to Tau-2 but larger pop. CdrStriFor Hal Halsa. Mounted Red warriors with calots. Tactics at Cdr's option.

Earth^0: high tech, aggressive, pop ca. 5 billion. CdrStriFor Lensman Admiral Trestrail. First strike by Tech ships to put out of action *all* electronic communication of all sorts, incl ComSats manned and unmanned, military Sats, 3 Lunar bases, L-5, MilitComCenters all major powers, incl Aus, Middle Kingdom, Maky, MittelEuropa, USA, Nippon. At plus-ten seconds, second strike places imperv walls around capitals and major cities. Plus-15 sec, strike teams ground, all armored. Chief Perceiver 2nd —Str Lensman Tregonsee, 1st AsstPercvr Dr. D. T. Carter. Perceivers for each strike team, each guarded by Galerian Ax Marines. Strike shifts: see Appen 3 Note: FlagComChALLPlanets above E^0, random transits Appen 1 Earth-Tau-1+ See Tau-1—StriForCdr General Roj Retnor.

E-Tau-2+: low pop, regressed tech, many vermin. Note: major areas on each cont radioactive. Anti-radiation armor and self-contained breathing units at all times. StriForCdr L. Hubert. C/S L. Monroe. Tactics: see Appen 5—subject to change by StriForCdr *all times*.

E-Tau-3+: See E^0 CdrStriFor Velantian Lensman Konvarl—see Appen 2 *Second Wave Mop-up Legions* strike at plus-10 hrs 1 min—Cdr2ndWave General-in-Chief Rufo, C/S G. Graeme. SkyCom Dr. S. Balsamo See Appen 7 for unit cdrs and sectors. Recall controlled by SkyCom, *not* FlagNmbrBst.

E-Tau-4+ ....

Minus 1 hr 14 mins and counting ....

Deety just called me via secure screen, sub-ether. Just as well that it was secure as she used "unladylike" language—seems Trestrail has forbidden perceivers to carry arms, and she had been planning to dedicate ten *Panki* to my left arm, then thirty more for our three kids. I told her that I could not give orders to a unit commander concerning a particular person under his command, but she could resign at any time up to count zero, since this entire force was totally volunteer. She stuck out her tongue at me (her helmet was pushed back).

Trestrail was right and Deety admitted it; a perceiver can't pick targets for a group while fighting herself. "How do you like my new summer clothes, Zebadiah?"

I like it just fine; that Patrol armor will stop almost anything. "But I don't see how you can stand up in it, much less walk."

"Powered, dear; I can jump over a building in it. You've been too busy to watch me practice. Besides that, this hunchbacked look covers personal Bergenholms and a Burroughs-Thorndyke twister. I can go free, bounce, or flip back to the ship, and some other options, just by voice command." She grinned. "Neat!"

I looked at her and was suddenly very grateful that Worsel had spent so much effort in extending my single ESP talent. I had a quick pre-vision of her, covered with sweat and triumphant, being helped out of her armor. Deety was going to live through it! *I know.*

But I didn't say so. Bad luck—she might take foolish risks.

"What's that big bulge in your helmet?"

"Oh. The all-inside perceptrons LaVerne has been promising. I can glance up and spot a varmint ten times as far. It has the crosshairs deal in it, too. I look directly at the target, hold down this belt switch, and every man in my strike group sees a target with crosshairs on it, by repeater. I don't tell which one to make the kill; that's handled by the group commander, any of several ways. I just pick out targets as fast as I can and that's pretty durn fast, darling."

"How do you take a pee in that thing?"

She stuck out her tongue again. "None of your business—sir. But I can. Zebadiah, have you eaten anything? You must *not* reach the end of countdown with an empty stomach. That's an order—sir."

"I've got some sandwiches here; I've been nibbling. At minus-five minutes I'm going to take a pep pill."

"Me, too. So is everybody. Aunt Hillbilly wants to say hello."

"Put her on. And behave yourself, Deety hon. Come aboard here as soon as we flash back to Prime Base, will you, please? I won't be able to leave the flagship at once."

"I will, Zebadiah. Promise. Just as soon as I finish thanking my guards and my strike group. Oh. Lafe wants us to take R-and-R with them—told him it was up to you. Here's Hilda. Bye, love!"

Sharpie's elfin face appeared. "Hi, Admiral Bligh honey!"

Again I had that sudden burst—Sharpie was going to make it! Now if Jake would call ... but suppose I failed to get that burst with Jake? Leave well enough alone, boy! "Hi, Sharpie hon. What do you wear under that?"

"Jewelry and perfume—what did you think I would wear?"

"You'll get bruised."

"No, padding is built into the armor. Has Jake called about Maureen's invitation?"

"No, but Lafe did. It suits both Deety and me."

"Then it suits everybody—I'll tell him. Now I'll get off this VIP circuit, Admiral honey."

"Wait a half. I don't have any lights blinking. Sharpie, you said that you would tell me, soon enough, why I was picked for this preposterous job."

"Sure you want to know?"

"If I could reach through this screen, I would paddle you."

"Would you kiss it afterward? All right, I'll tell you. It wasn't for your brainpower, dear, or your Napoleonic genius."

"I know that! But why was I kept out of action by kicking me upstairs to a dummy job? It's humiliating."

"Zebbie, it is *not* a dummy job. It's the *key* job."

"I know better. Everything is pre-decided for me. Everything."

"Not quite, Zebbie. Mentor said that the Patrol had all the expert strategists and operations analysts and tacticians and logistics experts that any force could possibly need. But that you had something special the others could not achieve."

"*What?* I can wiggle my ears."

"Luck, Zebbie. That uncanny ability of yours to do exactly the right thing in an emergency. That's why Worsel has been staying close to Prime Base. Not to train Deety, not to train me or Jacob. But to get you honed down to a fine point in your unique talent. So that you can use it today."

"Be damned!"

"No, you won't, Zebbie. Something will come up, something unexpected; you will make the right decision—and we will win. He—she—was sure of it."

"Mmm. Did you ever make up your mind whether Mentor is a he or a she?"

"She's both. He's a committee. When Mentor greeted me, looking like Glinda's twin sister, I told him to knock off the nonsense because hallucinations didn't fool me. So she changed into Santa Claus or everybody's favorite grandfather and I told her to change back, because I got along fine with Glinda and wasn't interested in looking at whatever life-support equipment a creature so advanced used. So he went back to being Glinda's twin and I accepted the illusion; it was nice. And we got along fine. Part of the time we talked about you. Mentor told me to tell you that if you ever want to visit Arisia, you are most welcome."

"They are *not* going to put a Lens on me!"

"You won't be offered a Lens, Zebbie. Because what you do doesn't require a Lens. You don't need one, any more than I do. It was just a friendly invitation."

"Well … Sharpie, I do have lights blinking now—see you after!"

"Kiss, Zebbie. Don't get ulcers."

Minus four minutes fifty seconds and counting ....

We're going to win! I suddenly *know* it.
    We're going to exterminate that filthy breed. Not all today. But we will. And we'll rebuild Snug Harbor.

Minus ten seconds and counting ....

Vermin, we have returned!

ZERO!

THE END